# A CASE EXA
# JOHN BROWN
# THE GOOSL

A.L. Barker left school when she was sixteen and, after
the War, joined the BBC. Her debut collection of short
stories, *Innocents*, won the first-ever Somerset
Maugham Prize in 1947, and her novel, *John Brown's
Body*, was shortlisted for the Booker Prize in 1969. She
is the author of ten novels and nine collections of stories,
the most recent being *Element of Doubt: Ghost Stories*,
a paperback original. Her most recent novel is *Zeph*.

## BY THE SAME AUTHOR

Novels

*Apology for a Hero*
*A Case Examined*
*The Middling*
*John Brown's Body*
*A Source of Embarrassment*
*A Heavy Feather*
*Relative Successes*
*The Gooseboy*
*The Woman Who Talked to Herself*
*Zeph*

Stories

*Innocents*
*Novelette*
*The Joy Ride and After*
*Lost Upon the Roundabouts*
*Femina Real*
*Life Stories*
*No Word of Love*
*Any Excuse For a Party*
*Element of Doubt: Ghost Stories*

A. L. Barker

# A CASE EXAMINED
# JOHN BROWN'S BODY
# THE GOOSEBOY

VINTAGE

VINTAGE
20 Vauxhall Bridge Road, London SW1V 2SA

London Melbourne Sydney Auckland Johannesburg
and agencies throughout the world

A CASE EXAMINED
First published by The Hogarth Press Ltd 1965
Arena edition 1989
© A.L. Barker 1965

JOHN BROWN'S BODY
First published by The Hogarth Press Ltd 1965
Arena edition 1989
© A.L. Barker 1965

THE GOOSEBOY
First published by Hutchinson 1987
Arena edition 1989
© A.L. Barker 1987

This edition first published by Vintage 1992

1 3 5 7 9 10 8 6 4 2

Printed and bound in Great Britain by
Cox & Wyman Ltd, Reading

ISBN 0 09 920181 X

# CONTENTS

# INTRODUCTION
## by A S Byatt

Writer's admire A L Barker. Rebecca West's parting shot in a ferocious *Paris Review* interview with Marina Warner was a complaint that Barker's brilliance wasn't widely appreciated. When A L Barker was a very small child God appeared to her as a pen-nib, "plain black, with a hole to regulate the flow of ink, what used to be called a 'relief' nib. It was set on shoulders and wore a shining robe and was attended by ordinary angels. The Nib was not a loving god: it was baleful and there was no pleasing it. The most I could hope was to avoid actually annoying it" Anyone who struggled to find the right word, or correct a cadence, or shape a narrative must admire Barker's passionate accuracy. She writes for the sake of the English language, though her subject is never its inadequacies and pitfalls, which is part of her distance from most major writing of our time. She has her own quiet certainties, and writes out of a primary and intense pleasure in words.

I don't know why she isn't more widely read. You mightn't put her on a reading list for The Novel Today (though you might for a course in writing) because she represents no trend, attacks no large social issues, opens no existential anxieties. You couldn't form a cult round her novels; they aren't cosy or cliquish; they are idiosyncratic and quietly estranged from the common. Because of a kind of inhuman and uncomfortable brightness in her perception I think of her in the company of Walter de la Mare, but that may be misleading.

She thinks of herself primarily as a short story writer and is a master of that form but she is also the author of novels, three of which appear in this new Vintage omnibus. *John Brown's Body* was shortlisted for the Booker Prize in 1969. It is the story of the relationship between Marise Tomelty, a child-wife who dislikes sex and is terrified of open spaces, and Ralph Shilling, who lives in the flat above the Tomelty's and is a dealer in pesticides. Marise's commerical traveller husband claims casually that he recognizes Ralph as John Brown, acquitted for lack of evidence of an atrocious double murder. Marise, living in the mind, encourages Ralph's attentions, ignoring everyone's attempts to confront her with his true identity, out of a passionate need for "idyllic fear and herself in possession of a monster". Events lead to a marvellously ambivalent climax of emotional violence and destruction, actual and imagined.

The book is a serious exploration, with a kind of metaphysical wit, of the nature of our experience of ourselves and each other – the tug between body and soul, flesh and imagination, truth and fantasy, life and death. Ralph's powerful sister-in-law, Emmeline, is obsessed by the belief that she is being weakened by invisible rays from a stream under her house, hiding from a real organic illness, the truth of death in an imaginary battle of auras and magnetic fields, which has its own meaning. Marise, who represents light and life and freedom to Ralph, is terrified of these things and wants to be annihilated. She likes the fantasy of being the beautiful body that John Brown will break up in some extremity, but dislikes intensely the actual bodily passion which Ralph and her husband feel for her.

The minor characters are all strictly necessary to the vision of our vision of ourselves. Without the few remarkably economic and solid paragraphs about Ralph's first wife, dying and deliberately conscious of it, neither Emmeline's evasive fantasy nor Marise's desire not to be would mean so much. Even people met in pubs provoke new visions of the ideas. A nervous girl in dark glasses who needs to believe that everyone is looking at her reminds Ralph that "most things only happen in the mind"; a man who can tell everyone's profession by his face creates another ironic aspect of Ralph's extended double identity as a killer, pest-controller and passionate John Brown.

But these meanings and inter-relations never become merely schematic, a writer's clever game. People and events are quite sufficiently real – Ralph's troubled humanity, his belief in truth, Marise's golden body and look of untouched newness like the baby she psychologically is, the precise *degree* of Tomelty's vulgarity and insight. It is an extraordinary novel and deserves to be read, every word, with the precise and contemplative attention with which it was written.

At first sight *A Case Examined* seems to be set in a world Jane Austen might have written about. A committee has been formed to allot a small bequest for charitable purposes. The candidates are Mrs Peachey, the feckless wife of a man who in a brainstorm assaulted an old woman, and the Church, which needs new hassocks. Sides are taken, but committee politics are treated almost perfunctorily. The central issue – presented through the consciousness of Rose Antrobus, impeccable committee chairman – is whether it is possible any longer to inhabit a world with the limitations of a Jane Austen novel. Our lives are too open to the consciousness that violence exists and impinges. Vulgarity is no longer close to sin. Those who have a concept of the "normal" are on the defensive; what was normal has become remarkable and suspect. A modern reader finds Jane Austen's world – however superficially similar to his own social surroundings – in this sense more alien than the worlds – however unexperienced – of Dostoevsky and Sartre. Because of what we know, we feel apologetic, morally, for our personal lack of acquaintance with violence. Rose becomes indeed obsessed with this problem. Her life is a struggle to preserve a meaningful image of the normal, the conventional, the tidy. Thus she supports the hassocks against Mrs Peachey.

The story is constructed around her exploration of the doubts the case arouses in her mind. As a smug Beckenham-bred child she stayed with a pen-friend, Solange Marigny, in her château.

"What my mother intended I should acquire was not so much a polish as some cracks in the glaze. She wasn't to know they would reach down to the foundations."

In Solange's company she meets violence – first, the pointless mutilation of a praying curé by a falling statue, and later, sexual violence. She begins to divide people into those who are "capacitated" for living in a world haunted by the aimless laughter she senses behind this violence and those who are not. Solange is. "I think of her, immutable and immune, as pulling violence out of the air, out of petty virtues and out of prayers."

4

Mrs Peachey is. She is indifferent – she "harboured and channelled her husband's violence by virtue of vice of simply being... She was culpable, if anyone was, for abnormality, as essential as her husband's victim and much more integral." Rose's friend and opponent on the committee, Victorine Gregory, aimlessly miserable over her climacteric, seeking suspect sexual relief from repulsive Sam Swanzy at the golf club, sympathizing with Mrs Peachey, is.

But Rose is not. She is, she considers, too vulnerable to be asked to encounter violence: it would simply destroy her.

"I am as I have been turned out with no provision for violence. With no necessity for it, either. Is it irresponsible to have had a quiet life, anti-social to want one? As to wars and acts of God, must I strip myself raw for the whole world?... It would be futile to borrow from a burden without being able to take a straw off the weight."

The vicar, by contrast persists in helplessly burdening himself. Rose reflects shrewdly:

"It isn't as if he had a choice. He would like to have – he would choose to be a victim... Suffer and you are absolved, you need not answer."

Rose is finally driven to seek a confrontation with Solange, who has, during the Occupation, met most horribly with violence and loss – comparable to Mrs Peachey's. What Rose learns – what Solange is – remains to the end ambiguous, to be pondered, satisfactorily not summed up. Although Solange sums up part of Rose's behaviour. "Once you had no doubts, now you have them, and you give no one the benefit." Mrs Peachey's "case" unsatisfactorily solves itself. Rose is not asked to suffer.

Miss Barker based an earlier novel – *Apology For a Hero* – on this conflict between the character whose identity depends on the order of home, habit, belief, and the rootless elemental character who provokes and survives violence. In that book this conflict seemed almost a private, romantic myth. But in *A Case Examined* it has made a successful and convincing novel. The book is impeccably written, the dialogue is subtle and the atmosphere of the French visits economically and brilliantly conveyed.

But the main reason for its success is the character of Rose. She is excellently drawn – with varying self-awareness, sometimes quickly prudish and censorious, sometimes metaphysically desperate. Seen through her eyes the mythical elementals take on real mystery and depth. Implacably wrong, stiff with fear, she is also worthy of respect and impossible to judge simply.

*The Gooseboy* like the other two novels, is about doubleness – flesh and spirit, innocence and malice, beauty and ugliness. Its central characters are twins, brother and sister, Doug and Dulcie Bysshe. Doug, or Bysshe, is a successful film star, Rex Snowden – now living in the South of France and contemplating a new part as a saintly doctor in an African leper colony. Dulcie, busy, energetic, is fighting to retrieve her husband, the mournful and ineffective Pike, who has absconded to Nice with the adolescent Cherrimay Pugh. At the centre of events, but not apparently part of them, is the oleboy, or Gooseboy, a creature with a double face, half a young faun and half a deformed horror. Whilst he arouses very different responses in those who see him, the boy's own attitude to his split image is unexpected and startling.

*The Gooseboy* is both elegant and grotesque, funny and appalling. Like the other novels in this collection it calls in question the relations between flesh and spirit, the ridiculous and the terrible, and gives riddling answers which irritate like sand in an oyster shell, collecting pearl. A L Barker does not agonise over the universe: she watches it shrewdly, from a distance, judges it with charity, and enjoys every aspect of its transformation into the play of language.

# A CASE EXAMINED

# PART ONE

Rose Antrobus said, "Why do you like that view?" and Eric Cade turned with his gauche, guilty start. "Whenever you come here you go and look out of that window. It's not the best view, either."

"It's the best view from where I'm standing—from the Ebone Street end."

She went to the window and looked with him.

"The potting-shed, my clothes-post, redcurrants rampant—it's only another version of somewhere back of— where was it?"

"Ebone Street, my first parish."

She nodded. "If you want contrast, why not the morning-room window? You can look across the lawn to the Weald, we had the house built so that you could. It's one of the amenities and we'd list it if we were selling."

"But you don't see what I see." He was tiresome when he would not take a teasing. Rose sometimes thought that to struggle so much was a sign of weakness. "Of course we none of us see alike, even shapes get interpreted. The shed, the clothes-post, the currant bushes—there, I suppose, you'd stop. But I go on, I see the path, how neat the path is, unbroken, and how clean. The rain has washed off even the surface dust. You could eat your dinner off that path—" he smiled wanly—"*I*'d do better, anyway, to trust it than some of the plates at some of the places—And the flower-beds are forked over, I don't see weeds, only plants thriving as the seed packets said they would. I see the shed which you use only for putting earth into pots and plants into the earth and I see it's well built and newly painted. The fruit bushes are budding, there'll be redcurrant jelly and blackcurrant pie when the time comes. It's the ideal outlook, what we'd all like to see at our backs. We'd know we were all right everywhere then." He said stiffly, "Pardoning the word, it's a sublime view."

11

"I like things to be nice. So does Ted. Do we have to answer for that?"

"Of course not." He began walking up and down, striking his heels urgently into the pile of the carpet. "We'd all like things to be nice and I think that's our salvation."

"Then why aren't we saved? All of us? Will you have more coffee?"

"Please." He stopped at the other end of the room and looked at her with guilt poking out all over him. "It really is good of you to give me lunch."

"Nonsense, it's the obvious thing to do. There's no time between the end of your Council meeting and the start of the Self-Help Committee for you to get lunch, whereas I have no one but myself to cater for at midday and I'm glad of an incentive. We'll consider it a standing arrangement before each Committee meeting."

"Rose, I wasn't criticising you; oh, Heaven knows—"

"If you had been, I would have answered your criticism."

It was a habit of his not to let well alone. "We aren't all saved because we don't know how to make things nice or we haven't the will to. But we do want to. Witness the Peacheys."

"You're going to have to make up your mind about them."

He took refuge in drinking his coffee, and Rose sighed. "I must go and set out the chairs."

"I'll help you." He drained his cup and, putting it down, was bothered by the uncleared lunch-table. "What about all this?"

"Mrs Gibb will see to it."

He knew there was Mrs Gibb, he had seen her minutes ago, did he suppose there was time, anyway, to do the washing-up before these women arrived? It was not insincerity in him, but a being slightly out of touch. He often let himself in for unnecessary trouble from people who could not or would not bridge the gap for him.

"You'll have to help me with the meeting," she said, putting her arm in his and turning him, because he was still hovering, towards the morning-room. "I think it's going to be difficult. I'm not sure now that it was a good idea to have it here."

"Why not?" He said, as he opened the door, "This is such a pleasant room, even committee work will be a pleasure in it." He was struck by another thought which arrested him on the threshold. "Are you thinking of wear and tear? Possible damage? Rose, I'm sure we'll all be very careful, oh indeed—But of course there might be marks just from the passage of six—or is it seven?—pairs of shoes across the carpet—"

"I'm not concerned about any such thing. How ridiculous." Rose drew the chairs into a semicircle. "It seemed only sensible at the time, there being so few of us. I can't see the Committee getting under way, can you, in a corner of the church hall, with no heating?"

"It really is uneconomical to start the boiler just for one hour's warmth. If we could have met on a Thursday, before the Fellowship Tea—"

"We couldn't. Only without Mrs Betts, and I do think she's important." Rose, having plumped cushions, went to the mirror and lifted her chin at her reflection. "It's a question of diplomacy. The last thing I want is to seem as if I'm trying to keep the Fund under my thumb, but as Hilda's executor my duty is to see that it's properly administered."

"You would hardly have formed a committee if you wanted complete control."

"Will that cut as much ice with the committee meeting under my own roof? You know how susceptible some of these women are." She smiled wryly into the mirror. "I must try to be discreet and not put my oar in too often. It will be up to you, Eric, to draw them off a little."

"My own attitude, or what my attitude ought to be, isn't clear to me yet."

"I intend to be practical," Rose said mildly, "but it's no use asking you to be."

The ladies all arrived within the next few minutes. There were six of them, not young, not yet beginning to be seriously old, of an age and disposition for it not to show greatly or matter much whether it was forty or fifty they were pushing. They were Rose's contemporaries and really, she thought, theirs was an excellent time of life. She could say for herself that she would never have it better, not too much, as youth had been, and not too little, as old age would be.

She wondered if they thought so too and looked, as she greeted them, for satisfaction in their faces. She could not see it, although Miss Havelock had a complacency imposed on her by her fat: there was no room, with so much flesh to accommodate, for any disruption. The others looked as if they were still on the track of something in a general way, except for little Mavis Tyndall, whose face was laced-up for something particular.

They subsided into Rose's chairs like a flock of birds into a field of corn. They wore their best hats and pearls and too much powder. Mrs Choules, the butcher's wife, was a dusky mauve under hers.

"Vicar," she said to Cade, "my husband wants me to take you to task about those flats next to us."

"Me, Mrs Choules?"

"I'm told they're church property."

"If they are, they belong to the Church Commissioners and not to St John's."

"Haven't you got any pull with the Commissioners?"

"My dear Mrs Choules, I haven't even got a string."

"I don't think it is church property," said Rose. "Ted says the block is owned by a syndicate. What's the trouble, anyway?"

"They're letting in the blacks. One of those men that wraps his head like a pudding has taken a flat there."

"That will be Dr Ahmed," said Cade. "He's a chiropodist."

"But Vicar, I call a spade a spade," said Mrs Choules, frisking the violets on her bosom, "and I call that the thin end of the tarbrush."

And charity, a kind of loving, is what we're here for, thought Rose. The idea amused her, she smiled in Mrs Choules' face.

Mrs Choules looked back blankly for a moment, then she gave one of her chesty laughs. "That's me, I have to speak out. My husband says I won't make friends that way but I'll find out who my enemies are."

There was an undue pause until Mrs Betts, enlarging her drawl, said, "Rose, how come we haven't seen Ted at the Club?"

"He's been working the last two week-ends, Sue."

"He should work at his golf, he's not the world's best player."

Rose saw that Mrs Choules was gazing about as if she were pricing the furniture and Mavis Tyndall was giving alarmed bobbing looks at everything from under her hat. Victorine Gregory put up her hand like a schoolgirl.

"May I smoke?"

"You know you can, Vee. The idea is to be comfortable. After all, it's going to be a small chore administering this Fund and I don't see why you should be troubled in the flesh as well as in the spirit."

"I need hardly tell you it's a matter of economy," said Cade, sitting down in their midst with a great rustle of practicality. "Tuesday is a blank day for the church hall, no one uses it and we should need a day's fuel to get heat up for our one hour in the afternoon. As things stand—as they've always stood, I believe, even before my time?' He waited, brows raised, placing the ball far back in their court, but the ladies sat stolidly, with bunched or spreading thighs, and let it lie. "Not a new state of affairs, at any rate, nothing individual," he looked from face to face with a confederate air, "and we must bear with it, I must ask you to bear—"

"If Mrs Antrobus hadn't suggested it, I should have," said Mrs Choules. "I'd have had you all round to our place because I couldn't sit five minutes in that cold barracks of a church hall, not with my chest."

"Why not cover the cost of the heating out of the Fund?" said Miss Havelock.

Rose nodded, to herself more than Miss Havelock whom she had invited on the Committee because she was reputed to be a sound business woman. "I suppose that would be admissible."

"Not that I've any objection to meeting here."

"It's nice of Rose to have us," said Victorine Gregory. Ash fell from her cigarette and she ground it into the carpet with her shoe. "Conscientious, too, because there's nothing to stop her doling out the money wherever she chooses. Or not doling it."

Eric Cade flung up his head. "What do you mean, Mrs Gregory?"

"If it was me, I'd take something for my trouble. A pair of gloves, a new bag, tickets for the theatre—I'd dip in now and then. Rose won't." Victorine sucked at her cigarette: the compulsive rubbing and dusting of her fingers was getting more noticeable, was, in fact, impossible to ignore. "Rose won't touch a penny of it. She's incorruptible and don't any of you think, 'Well, she can afford to be'."

"I don't like the thoughts you're putting into my head, Vee," said Sue Betts. "They're on the bitchy side."

"I don't know where this is leading us," Cade was looking round as if for a signpost. "But it's nowhere I want to go."

"Vee's teasing us," said Rose. "We'll have to get used to it."

Victorine looked at her with eyes wincing against her own cigarette-smoke. "Rose turns the other cheek and shuts me up."

Rose said, "Perhaps we ought to talk about the Fund seriously now. You've all been good enough to come here for that purpose. I've christened us the Self-Help Committee and we shall be an *ad hoc* committee, lasting as long as the Fund does. But there's no need to be rigidly official, is there? It would be nice if we kept our meetings a little more social than the Guild or the W.I. reckon to be, don't you think?"

"Social?" Miss Havelock made the word bristle.

"A relaxed atmosphere is what I'd like. It should be the most productive and it would, so to speak, be in context." Rose smiled. "Hilda was herself a thoroughly relaxed person. You all know about her Fund. She left the interest on certain of her investments until such time as her heir comes of age, when the interest will revert to him, to be used for the benefit of our church of St John's-on-the-Green

16

and its parishioners. As her executor it's my duty and intention to see that the money is used as she wished. But that's something I couldn't do alone. I'd never be sure I'd located all the deserving cases, far less examined and evaluated them fairly."

Miss Havelock's sigh gusted out of her huge body. "When does the legatee come of age?"

"Hilda's nephew is fourteen. We have seven years to benefit."

"By how much?"

"I thought of coming to that as Committee business, to keep some sort of sequence for the records. We must have records," said Rose.

Miss Havelock expended the last of her sigh with a faint whistle which was curiously flattening. "The lesser the sum the more difficult to administer. This sort of thing can be very tedious."

Rose felt chastened. The new minute book which she held on her knee, ruled and headed, "Self-Help Committee meeting (first), Tuesday, April 4th", looked naïve. The ladies, brought out in their best hats too soon after lunch she felt would consider it an imposition, the goodness of their hearts being bespoke. She said, smiling round at them, "It won't be as much fun as a bridge party."

Victorine said, "Virtue being its own reward."

"We're here to help, honey," said Sue Betts. "You go right ahead and lay it on the table."

"Is it agreed then," said Rose, "that the first thing we should do is elect a chairman?"

"Ratify, not elect," Cade called out. "The choice is surely made?"

Miss Havelock frowned. "Committee work may be tiresome, but unless it is done in open session it loses justification."

"I think Vicar should be chairman," said Mrs Choules.

"No!" Cade held up one angular hand, palm out, with a policing rather than a pious gesture. "That would be completely unethical."

"Oh why, Eric?" Rose put down her notebook as if she

did not expect to be soon convinced. "I think it's an excellent proposal."

"As a potential beneficiary perhaps I shouldn't even be on the Committee?"

"You, Vicar? A beneficiary? Well, you're certainly deserving—"

"I represent St John's, I'm answerable for the fabric of the church as well as the souls of its parishioners." He turned to Rose. "Under the terms of the Fund it's not inconceivable that St John's itself may at some time benefit?"

Rose said gravely, "It's certainly not inconceivable. Hilda did in fact put it in that sequence—'. . . the benefit of our church of St John and its parishioners'."

"You be chairman, Rose," said Sue Betts. "Look what friends you and Hilda were."

"Oh, Hilda would have wished it." Victorine Gregory butted one cigarette into the lighted end of another.

"We should put it to the vote—"

"Rose for chairman: all in favour say aye—" Victorine held up the scarlet cigarette-stub.

Sue Betts said "Aye, aye", and after a moment Mrs Choules patted her bosom and said, "Oh, pardon me—aye," on the crest of her indigestion.

Miss Havelock, looking at Rose accommodated a faint gleam on her face. That, and a grunt signified her acquiescence. Mavis Tyndall pressed her lips tight and nodded violently.

"It goes without saying that I'm for Mrs Antrobus—a vote of confidence indeed. And *ex-officio*, of course, as Mrs Loeb's executor, I think she ought to take the chair." Cade rubbed his palms thankfully over his knees. "Rose, the Committee is now yours."

"It always was," murmured Victorine.

"Do be quiet, Vee,' said Rose. "I think we should be serious."

They were looking at her and she was aware, as always when she faced a number of women, of the barrage. It was a united effort, Mavis Tyndall and the Havelock woman putting up their fire together. Once Rose would have been intimidated. She would have worried and let it dwindle her and tried to hit on some catalyst, a word or formula dear to them all which would transmute their antagonism *en masse* into warm humanity, or just a favourable disposition. But she had realised early in her committee life that the barrage was an instinctive thing, and impersonal. It got up, quite naturally, like hackles, at sight of another woman, any woman, on a platform—actual or implied—to tell them what to think or do. She noted the same reaction in herself. The defence, failing oratory which she did not have, was to isolate and crumble. There were always opponents, a hard core or a lifeless lump. They sorted themselves out and they would do that, thought Rose, even from this small chosen group.

"Thank you for your vote of confidence. I shall try to justify it." She tapped her minute book. "I propose, if you all agree, to take notes of our meetings. Mrs Loeb's executors will want to see them."

"The minutes should be circulated to the Committee first," said Miss Havelock. "We may wish to make amendments."

"Of course. I'll send copies to you all." Rose smiled at Mrs Choules, who did her husband's accounts on a comptometer. "I'm not good with machines, but if I can coax four carbons out of my typewriter it will mean typing the minutes twice only. Now the sum available—" Rose addressed herself pleasantly to Miss Havelock—"amounts this quarter to forty-eight pounds, four shillings and four pence. Next quarter we may have a little less or a little more, subject to market fluctuations. But I think we can expect the interest to remain constant in the region of fifty pounds a quarter."

"It's not going to send anyone over the rainbow, is it?" said Sue Betts.

"We haven't all got eighty-carat rainbows, honey," said Victorine.

"*I* shouldn't let it go begging," said Mrs Choules.

"Nor me." Victorine grimaced round her cigarette. "It would be something not to go cap in hand for."

"I think it's a serviceable little sum. It won't change anybody's life," said Rose, "but it could ease a burden, relieve a worry or simply help someone to keep going."

"Candidates?" asked Miss Havelock.

"There are two. First, the Peacheys."

"The what?"

"A family by the name of Peachey."

Sue Betts said, "Back home we say a thing's peachy if it's pretty nice."

"They aren't pretty or nice, poor things." In her notebook Rose had written: "Chairman—R. Antrobus elected". Under this she wrote: "Decisions—(1) The Peacheys". "It's quite a sad case. There's the mother, still just a girl, and three young children, aged six, four and a baby of six months." Rose lifted her shoulders and sighed round at them all. "The husband was committed to a criminal lunatic asylum four months ago for assaulting an elderly woman."

"Sex crime?"

"I don't think so, Vee. He didn't know her, he'd never seen her before. It happened in Wolverhampton or somewhere north—"

"Accrington," murmured Cade.

"The point being that there was no reason for what he did. He had a brainstorm, a sort of *crise de tête*."

"She was laughing at him," said Mavis Tyndall.

They raised their eyebrows, quite startled. Miss Havelock put three chins down into her neck and turned her humid moon of a face. After one wild upward glance Mavis Tyndall stared fixedly at the floor. Rose could not remember at that moment why she had invited her to join the Committee. There was no room for anyone who carried such little weight, who was quite pathologically small. Then she remembered Eric Cade's proposing her. What was it he had said? "Mrs Tyndall has energy and conscience and doesn't pride herself on anything. She could be useful to you."

She had been already, or so Rose hoped. But that aggressive humility of hers would be wearying in committee, Rose didn't want to have to be continually raising her up.

"Mrs Tyndall's been to see the Peacheys and the eldest

child is in her Sunday-school class. She knows more about them than I do."

She really had little to pride herself on. Her face drew to a point, nose, mouth and chin, like a mouse's and probably, thought Rose, she had the kind of energy for pedalling round and round on a wheel.

"Would you tell us what you know, Mavis?"

The "Mavis", perhaps, started her on the wrong foot, because she addressed herself to Rose and desperately ignored the faces left and right of her.

"They both come to Sunday school now, both the children, the little girl as well as the boy. She's only four, but she's very good, she sits so still. I don't think a child ought to sit like that for an hour at a time, she doesn't get up to sing with the others or look at the Bible pictures. The only time she moves is when she comes in and when she goes out, it isn't natural in a child that age—"

"She keeps pretty clean though, doesn't she?"

"Clean?" Mavis Tyndall went on staring, reddening and staring at Rose as if it were she who had spoken.

Rose smiled gently. "Mrs Gregory's children never stay still for a minute."

Victorine leaned into Mrs Tyndall's range. "Don't you ever wish yours would cut down on the laundry?"

Some of the fire died out of Mavis Tyndall's face. "I have no children."

"Well now," said Rose pacifically, "could we hear a report on your visit to Mrs Peachey? I don't think anyone else, except Mr Cade, knows the family. We need to be put in the picture, that's why I suggested you go and see them."

"I'd have gone anyway, about the child. I'm worried about the child—" She could see that they weren't. Why should they be? They hadn't seen what she had seen and she couldn't tell them. What words could she use? She sought, painfully and openly, for words of some acceptable sort and they came out stilted and impersonal because it was a "report" Rose had asked for and these ladies did not sit in Sunday school.

"I visited Mrs Peachey on the 25th of March. She was

unco-operative at first, she said she had nothing to add to the statement she had made about her husband. I assured her I did not represent the police nor the National Assistance Board nor any welfare organisation already known to her. She then explained that she was tired and upset because the baby had been ill all night and the milkman would not carry up the morning milk—"

"What?"

"She lives in a Council flat on the fifth floor. She claims that her neighbours are prejudiced on account of her husband and that they influence the delivery men against her."

"Do you think that's true?"

Mavis Tyndall laced her fingers in her lap. "As I left, the woman from the flat below came out and said, 'Why don't you fuss after decent people for a change? That lot up there should be smoked out'."

Decent people did not need looking after. There was something indecent about being in want, a universal prejudice. Rose could trace it back in her own mind to something from the Bible about being 'hungry and ye fed me, naked, and ye clothed me'. In the nakedness, the cold dirty skinniness, was the indecency.

"What sort of a woman is Mrs Peachey?"

"Not more than twenty-two or three. And hard—young people are."

That, Rose could appreciate, would have been Mrs Tyndall's experience, and in the fifth-floor Council flat with the baby grizzling and the indecent wants she had taken knocks which she was prepared to excuse or glorify by putting them down to youth.

"She told me her husband had been studying to take a degree—by post."

Coming from hard, young Mrs Peachey it would have been a statement of fact, respect or pity to be supplied by the hearer. From Mavis Tyndall it had a futile, catchpenny sound.

"He wanted to better himself, he wanted to better all of them, she said, and he was overworking. He felt dizzy and sometimes he fainted in the street. There was some persecution, people pointing and talking about him—"

"They talk about me," said Mrs Choules. "I don't call it persecution."

"Mrs Peachey said they're disliked by a lot of people but her husband believed they were hated by everyone."

"Why should they be disliked? Before anything had happened, I mean?" Rose was doodling, drawing bad circles in her notebook. "One can understand people turning against them afterwards, after what he did to that woman. But at first, when they were all together, don't you think that then it was just a complex? An excuse for not doing as well as they might have? There's no reason, leaving aside the other business, why they should be unpopular. Is there? Mavis?"

She must have been thinking unhappily along her own lines, well along, because she was brought back with a jerk, her long mouse's nose twitching hopelessly. "I don't think so—I don't know—"

"Eric? Do you know of any reason?"

Rose asked him as a matter of form, politeness before the others, because if he knew any reason he was in honour bound not to give it. An awkward situation—perhaps he really shouldn't be on the Committee.

Cade said, "I think their trouble has been that they've tried too hard—"

"Oh, sure!" cried Sue Betts. 'Peachey tried hard when he beat that poor woman nearly to death. If anyone ought to be helped, she did."

"Peachey's wife and children are innocent of his crime," said Cade, "but they may have to suffer for it more than he will."

"Are they starving?" said Miss Havelock briskly.

"Of course not. Mrs Peachey gets National Assistance."

"Then what will forty-eight pounds do for them?"

"In a household like that, money is always useful."

Rose said, "Mrs Tyndall has definite ideas. May we hear them, Mavis?"

"They have no proper furniture, there was never enough money to buy it with the children coming so quickly—"

"They had to get married in a hurry, of course?"

Mrs Choules, Rose noticed, had a wolfish smile for one with such a bulbous face.

Looking round at them all, Mavis Tyndall seemed to see that she needed to take up arms. She laid her words down with their edges out.

"They have one large bed, two chairs and a table. The rest is boxes and crates. The baby sleeps in a box and the two other children in the bed with their mother. When Denis Peachey was at home they were put at the bottom between their parents' feet. They have no decent crockery, everything is cracked and chipped. Mrs Peachey has one bowl for washing up and bathing the baby—"

"When Hartley and I got married," said Sue Betts, "we couldn't afford even the dime-store stuff. We used to get factory throw-outs, and we had a lot of fun matching up."

"The children haven't enough clothes, they wear the same coats winter and summer. They have no toys, the boy runs in the street and the little girl sits at home just as she does in Sunday school. She has no will, no wish, even. We can only try what we know," said Mrs Tyndall, as if she had come to the bitter heart of her matter. "When something, someone, won't go, we can only wind it up and hope the wheels will start turning. I bought her a doll. She was frightened of it, her mother said she thought it was dead."

Mavis Tyndall had not been a good person to send. She was woolly about the child, one child, and nothing else counted with her. That was a luxury which the Committee could not afford to indulge her in. Charity should be objective, should be deserved—that was to say, there should be some foreseeable return in moral fibre or regeneration. One would like, certainly Rose would like in the matter of Hilda Loeb's bequest, to prove benefit, afterwards to produce on the one hand so much money, on the other so much good.

"You can see this money being used by Mrs Peachey," Rose said, "and not just spent?"

"I can't be sure, of course, but I hope—"

She was honest: as far as she went she could be relied

upon to do her best. The question to be decided was how much her best was worth, this time and any other.

"I hope she'll buy things that National Assistance won't pay for. She's at the end of her tether, she's lost her husband, he may never come back. She doesn't know why she's trying now, or what for, and I'm afraid she'll stop soon," said Mrs Tyndall, herself stopping, with her eyes on Rose's face.

"And you believe that forty-eight pounds might restore her purpose in life?"

Rose spoke without irony, but she realised that it was an indication to the meeting that there was already a prevailing wind and which way it blew: no harm in that at this stage. Mrs Tyndall was not a powerful speaker, but she had the human case to plead, a strong one that could get half-way home on statement alone.

"No, only her husband could do that." Mavis Tyndall looked steadily, with rising colour, at all the ladies. "She's young, she wants him badly, she wants no one else—"

"Not the children?" said Victorine.

"She'd let them go, I think she'd let everything go if she stopped trying. I'm afraid for the children." She had been pushing it from the start, but this was her strongest thrust yet. " 'In care', they call it, don't they, when they have to take children from their mothers and put them in homes?"

"What sort of things," said Miss Havelock, "won't National Assistance pay for?"

"Things we take for granted. You and I use cups that are whole ard plates that aren't cracked, we have a nice set of saucepans to cook with—"

Rose smiled. Mavis Tyndall making common ground with Miss Havelock over saucepans struck her as absurd.

"Ordinary things, 'necessities' we call them, tools for the job, and we don't think what it would be like doing the job without them. Even a coat—" She touched her own lapels. "A decent coat is a necessity. The money couldn't give her a reason to live but it would give her heart."

There was a pause and Rose left it with them. To disengage from Mavis Tyndall's gaze she got up and went to the window. There had been rain before lunch, enough to rinse the air. Under the white spring sky her garden was folded and mitred and the earth drawn tidy. A 'sublime' view? How much was one entitled or common-sensibly required to take for granted?

She looked round at the ladies. "I should perhaps remind you that once the money is paid to the beneficiary we have no further say in how it is spent. We can't make conditions, let alone try to get them kept. It will be up to Mrs Peachey to do with it as we think best."

"I believe she will," said Mrs Tyndall. "She'll want to."

"We must hope so," Rose said, "for the sake of the children."

Cade joined her at the window. Seeing him fingering his empty pipe, she asked, "Would it upset any of us if Mr Cade smoked?"

He seemed not to hear. He went on rubbing his thumb round the bowl of the pipe and the words, 'Virgin briar' passed through Rose's mind and amused her in passing. Thorny he was in his way, with the barbs turned inwards so that nothing went smoothly for him. Celibacy she had settled on him long ago.

He said over his shoulder, "I think it just the kind of marginal case that Mrs Loeb meant to provide for."

Miss Havelock looked at her watch. "And the other claimant?"

" 'Candidate' is the better word," said Rose, "and I'm putting it forward myself since I couldn't get Mr Cade to. It's our own church, St John's-on-the-Green. I'll ask Mr Cade to state the case even though he feels he can't plead it."

Rose could not make up her mind whether Cade, turning from the window was shamming reluctance. She hoped so because no man in his position had any right to be self-effacing. It was going to be tedious if she had to contend with him for his own benefit.

"It won't engage your interest so much—I trust it won't engage your self-interest." He reddened, he was going to put the case badly because it embarrassed him. "We need new hassocks for the pews—" It embarrassed him because he had some notion that it was ridiculous for their knees to be comfortable and sublime for Mrs Peachey to be comforted. 'Sublime'—he had already broken in the word this afternoon. "It is a rather—frivolous need."

Rose said, "I don't agree. I think it's essential. The things we kneel on are disintegrating and dirty and there are only enough to furnish three pews."

"Hassocks?" said Victorine.

Cade put in quickly, "They're the least of our worries. I'm much more concerned about the boilers—"

"Some of the older members of the congregation actually find it painful to say their prayers."

Victorine laughed. It was possible, Rose thought, to dislike one's friends.

"The fact that we may all be poisoned by coke fumes next winter shouldn't influence us. Of course there would be no problem if we had five hundred pounds to bestow instead of fifty."

"If I took Mrs Loeb's forty-eight pounds, four shillings and four-pence," said Cade, "it would be a drop in the ocean."

"That's a little ungracious, don't you think, Eric?" said Rose, smiling.

"I didn't mean—"

"We'll discuss the pros and cons of course." Rose went to the door and called, "Mrs Gibb, I think we could do with some tea."

Mrs Choules swivelled round to Sue Betts. "I can promise those Easter lilies I spoke about. A customer of ours is getting them over from Guernsey."

"That's lovely," said Sue. "They're much more spiritual than daffs and there's nothing like being topical—if anyone notices."

"I shall," said Victorine. "Lilies make me feel fleshly."

"Could you be fleshly, honey?"

"It takes a flower to show me up, anyway."

Mavis Tyndall was listening as to a clash of giants, but Miss Havelock tapped with her finger-nail on a brass ashtray and made it ring like a bell.

"Is anyone going to plead the church's cause?"

"We're all personally acquainted with it," said Rose.

"I've stopped getting on my knees," said Mrs Choules. "I know some people feel they must, but you can be reverent if you can get your head down."

"I squat," said Victorine, "like a monkey."

"Could the money be found any other way?"

"Eventually. It would mean more jumbles and sales of work."

"We are called the 'Self-Help' Committee," said Victorine.

"It's quite shameful that in a parish such as ours any of the church furnishings should be so squalid—"

"Speaking as the church mouse," said Victorine, "we shouldn't have to go to the parish while there's such a strong smell of money in the congregation."

"Hilda would have given it. She always said she wouldn't get to Heaven if she didn't buy in. She was fixing to do something about those kneeling-pads—"

"The dead don't vote—at least, they shouldn't."

Rose was getting vexed with Victorine Gregory. She reminded herself that Victorine was going through a bad phase. A germ of something was infecting her being: she liked stroking people the wrong way, and lately it had become an ungentle rubbing. She wasn't so amusing about it either now, her nerves were frayed—and charred, thought Rose, seeing her crush out another cigarette. She was slightly over the edge, ready to be riled as well as to rile.

Rose had seen to it that tea should be aesthetically as well as physically stimulating. The china was her nice Coalport, the shallow cups so fine that a finger showed through like a bruise. Everything else was Victorian silver, teapot, cream-jug, spoons and cake-baskets. Rose had a weakness for Victoriana at its most flowery.

A rustle went over the ladies at sight of the tea-trolley. They adjusted their hats and shook out the lapels of their jackets. There was a sturdy wave of perfume and then Cade lit his pipe and the room smelt right, Rose thought, for business.

"Quite a party," said Victorine, coming to the trolley.

"Do help, not hinder me, Vee," murmured Rose.

Victorine put down a cup and saucer which she could not keep from chattering in her hand. "Since you ask," she said clearly, "mine is a floating vote at the moment."

Rose felt her temper ebb sharply. They were all looking, Cade took his pipe out of his mouth and rounded his lips like a fish. She could not keep the colour from rising to her face, knowing that she looked put out was enough to put her out.

She picked up the cup and saucer Victorine had laid down and looked into Miss Havelock's slit stare.

"Milk or lemon? Mrs Gibb is bringing China tea for anyone who prefers it."

After that the mood of the meeting sharpened and not even tea could relax it. There seemed to be an impression—which of course Victorine Gregory had given—that sides had been taken and that the situation was loaded. They sensed politics, and if to Mrs Choules it looked important to get into the right party, to a timid sort like Mavis Tyndall it would seem quite reckless to be in the wrong one.

Miss Havelock called out, "Mrs Antrobus, I have another appointment at 3.45. Do you think we could settle this matter before I go?"

"Of course. We'll put it to the vote now."

"Secret ballot?" said Victorine.

"Do you think that's necessary?"

Victorine smiled. "There may be some people here who are afraid of you, Rose."

"Afraid of me? How ridiculous!" Rose looked round for their laughter. Only Cade grinned feebly, and Rose couldn't help it, she cried, "That makes me feel utterly miserable!"

"Why, honey?" said Sue Betts kindly. "Don't you like to think you're a power?"

"Very well, we'll each take a slip of paper and write on it, 'Mrs Peachey', or 'Church'."

Rose went to her writing-table. She really was put out now, she knew whom she had to thank for it, but she blamed herself for asking Victorine Gregory on to the Committee.

She had thought she was doing a kindness. An aim, however small, it had seemed to her, might still some of that self-disruption, but now she could see that Victorine's trouble was the kind that reaches out and makes more.

"I shan't exercise my vote," said Cade. Rose turned to look at him. "It wouldn't be—just."

"You have a duty to your flock," said Victorine, "the kneelers. Surely you'd vote for them?"

"I have duties," said Cade, "and am divided between them."

"It will cost us our deciding vote," said Rose, tearing paper into strips, "but of course you must do as you think right. Now we'll write down our decisions and put the strips into this rose bowl. I take it we've all reached a decision, or been frightened into one?"

"We'll disguise our handwriting."

"This isn't a game, Vee." Rose gave each of them a slip of paper and a pencil. "Does anyone feel the need of more facts before deciding?"

Sue Betts was already scribbling. "Honey, this isn't the Rockefeller Trust."

Rose thought, they're impatient now, someone looks at her watch and they think of the time though they all have more than they know what to do with. They can't wait to make up their minds, they'll jump to conclusions.

"We might bear in mind," she said, looking round at them, "that since the sum of money involved is not great we should be the more careful to bestow it sensibly. As Miss Havelock says, the lesser the sum the more difficult it is to administer."

"No problem so far as I'm concerned." Sue Betts dropped her paper into the rose bowl. "And if anyone wants to know how I figure it I'll be glad to say."

Mrs Choules drained her tea-cup. " 'Hassocks', was it, we were to put?"

Victorine said to Rose, " 'Though I have all faith, so that I could remove mountains, and have not charity, I am nothing.' "

Rose wrote on her own paper, folded it and put it in the

bowl. She went over to Cade, who was looking out of the window.

"Will you count the votes?"

"Do you think I should?"

She said, sharply, so that they all glanced up, "Would you be tempted to swing the count?"

Cade's nose lifted with surprise. 'Yes—the other way."

"That's hypocrisy." She was vexed when he nodded. "Well, what do you want me to think? You're not a cynic— I hope you're not working up to anything, Eric, there's no virtue in being misunderstood."

She led him back to the table to count the votes. They were even: three for the church and three for Mrs Peachey.

"What now?" said Victorine. "Do we split the money or start a jackpot?"

Rose did not say she had been afraid of this. It would be like saying, 'I told you so', and they had every right to differ—in equal or unequal ratios.

"We must have a majority."

"How can we?"

"Vicar must vote," said Mrs Choules. "After all, he is on the Committee."

Cade moved his hands as if he were parting waters. "That I cannot do."

"Principles are the devil, aren't they?" said Victorine to Rose.

"I agree it would be easier if more of us had none."

"Maybe someone will change her mind," said Sue Betts. Miss Havelock stirred. Through her enormous body a tremor went, she was preparing to stand up, to depart. Rose resented the air of physical disassociation this gave to the proceedings, of brushing off something as irrelevant now as the biscuit crumbs in her lap.

"I see no reason to change my mind. The money should go to the woman."

Rose was surprised. "You think so?"

"Why do you say it like that?"

"I wouldn't have thought—Oh, it doesn't matter. Of course one can't change one's mind at this stage—"

"I put people first, Mrs Antrobus," said Miss Havelock sternly. "Especially when there is a time factor—people are at a particular disadvantage there. In this case, as I understand it, time is limited, may indeed be almost run out on the one hand, and on the other is fairly indefinite. In other words," said Miss Havelock, simplifying, "this woman should be helped now or it may be too late, whereas the hassocks have been worn out for years and we are only just complaining."

"If that were so," said Rose, "we might compliment ourselves on our patience. Mr Cade knows as well as I do that we haven't suffered in silence. We can continue to penalise the old and infirm who find it difficult even to walk to church by making them kneel down on the stones when they get there, but should we say we're doing so because they have more time?"

"Where the emotions are concerned time is not calculable," said Miss Havelock.

"How true?" cried Rose. "And I should so like her to have the money! What are a few hassocks compared with the chance of giving someone the will to—" She did not say 'live', that was overdoing it—"the will to go on? But isn't there a danger that it might do the reverse and make her thoroughly dissatisfied? People like that don't always know how to receive—"

"We're talking about one woman, Rose, about Mrs Peachey. Remember?"

"And Mrs Peachey, being human, and with a sympathetic ear to unburden herself to, might become hysterical and say things she didn't mean. It's natural, isn't it, under a strain like this must be?"

"And the chance of fifty pounds if she laid it on thick enough," put in Mrs Choules bluntly.

"I'm saying," said Rose, "that she would, understandably, have made the most of her troubles to Mrs Tyndall. Wouldn't we all, in her circumstances?"

"She wasn't hysterical, she's not the type!"

Mavis Tyndall perhaps was. She had gone scarlet and

altogether too brilliant in the face for one so mousey. "And I didn't at any time mention the money."

"How do we know she won't blow it on clothes and men?" demanded Sue Betts. "If she's young and deprived, like you say, that's what she'll do."

"Men? There are no men—she loves her husband, she wants him back. She's young, yes, she'll hope if she's allowed to. And why shouldn't she buy clothes? She needs clothes, she's only got one old raincoat to her back. A raincoat!" cried Mrs Tyndall. "All through the winter!"

"What about the children?" asked Mrs Choules.

"She wouldn't spend it all on herself—I'm sure she wouldn't. But don't you see, it would give her a lift to have a few of the things she wants for herself? It would hearten her when she needs it most. If she loses heart, if she gives up—" Mrs Tyndall looked from face to face. "It's the children I'm thinking of."

"What are you thinking of, Rose?" said Victorine.

Rose was tempted to answer, "That charity begins at home", but Mavis Tyndall would take it as heresy, and Miss Havelock who, as Rose was aware, put first whatever suited her book at the time would make a platform of it. And Victorine, from cussedness, would call it misanthropy or prejudice—or politics if she wanted a row.

"I'm thinking of what we owe to Mr Cade, to the community as a whole, and to the church itself. Because that doesn't sound so—" Rose smiled faintly—"so human as Mrs Peachey, I'm wondering if we ought not to think of it all the more."

"Rose—ladies—I'm not to be thought of at all. The community, yes, the church, yes, but there's nothing owing to me." Cade looked into each face as Mavis Tyndall had done and with something of the same appeal. "It's I who owe everything—"

"If you do," said Rose, "a disgruntled congregation won't pay for it."

She saw the unwisdom of that at once but was too irritated to be sorry for him and turned to the others. "I'm not going to swap priorities, but I think you'll agree we do owe Mr

Cade adequate conditions of worship. True, the boilers will have to be replaced, but we must hope for help from parish funds for that. What I'm asking—and believe me, I'd like the answer to be 'yes', I'm open to conviction, I'd like nothing better than for you to convince me—is, do we have the right to beg or borrow a single penny to pay for the hassocks while we have money which was intended for just such a contingency?"

Victorine said, "Was our Hilda explicit about that?"

Rose picked up her minute book. "The wording of the bequest was as follows: 'I bequeath the monies accruing, that is, the interest payable quarterly on the aforenamed stock and holdings, to be used for the help and benefit of our church of St John's-on-the-Green and for those of its parishioners who shall be considered in want and worthy and likely to profit by such benefit. . . . ' "

"Well?"

"She put the church first."

"That's just a convenient wording."

Rose dropped her book with a cards-on-the-table gesture. "Frankly, I'm not sure. I can't help thinking that in this case Hilda might have wanted the church to have priority."

"In Mrs Peachey's case," said Victorine.

It was odd that battle should come from this quarter, the last Rose would have armed against, supposing she had intended to arm. It meant that a battle was being sought with one who did not want to fight, on grounds which did not exist, by someone who didn't give a fig for them anyway.

Mavis Tyndall cried out, "Mrs Antrobus, why did you form a committee? Why did you ask us to decide when you'd already made up your mind?"

Rose leaned across and took both her hands. "My dear Mavis, didn't I just say that I'm open to conviction? That I'd be happy to be convinced? I formed a committee because I wanted advice and opinions other than my own and because this is only the first of many such sums which we shall be able to help people with. And I asked the Committee to decide because you yourself proposed Mrs Peachey as a beneficiary. You were at liberty to do so and so was any other member of the Committee who knew of a deserving case."

"But if we're to be over-ruled—"

"You can't be over-ruled," Rose pointed out, patiently, "until you're in the minority."

"We can't be blamed," said Miss Havelock, majestically rising, "for not thinking alike, but it's a pity we had no margin to differ."

"That's hardly my fault—" began Rose, but Mrs Choules was talking.

"I can't fancy that family somehow. Not after what the man did. He put one of that poor woman's eyes out, you know. He beat her breasts to pulp and cracked her ribs, then he dirtied on her—you know, relieved himself all over her while she lay on the ground. Of course you can't blame the kiddies for any of that, but I'm funny that way, over-sensitive, I suppose. I just can't fancy any of them."

There was a bad silence. Everything that the abominable Mrs Choules had said went on sinking and sinking into it. Rose wanted to talk loudly, switch on music, run water, cover it up somehow. She felt sick. Something had been started which was not as fair as a fight, and the weapon was being used by Mrs Choules—not Victorine—as if it were versatile and cunning enough to go equally well into the hands of friends. Rose panicked. Not friends! Must she own to Mrs Choules because Mrs Choules had come to her, Rose's, conclusion? The way she had come?

Cade sat among them and it would have been helpful if he had not done it so thoroughly, if he could have risen a little above them, just by virtue of being male. Instead, he used his parson's status to lower himself to their level and he sat there with this fatuity, this oppressive women's burden of thinking with their skins, carrying it to God with all the other burdens he took upon himself.

Mavis Tyndall was as pale as she had been red before and seemed, now that there was a lot she might justifiably have said, to be beyond saying it. Victorine looked peaceable, more than she had done for a long time.

Miss Havelock had that air of disembarrassing herself.

Yet why should she? She was as much to blame as any of them, if blame could get into a gathering so well-intentioned.

"I'm sorry, Mrs Antrobus, as I said, I have another appointment. If you call any further meetings no doubt you'll get into touch."

Rose went to the door with her. There *was* blame and it was Rose's only in so far as she had convened them. She had herself, in innocence, located the moment, the lapse, whatever it was, under her own roof.

"Perhaps in a fortnight's time—we must reach a decision."

"Unless there are new facts to go upon, I shall not need to reconsider mine."

Miss Havelock stepped into the afternoon. Her black moiré shoulders disclaimed the spring sunlight. It flaked off them as it might off the hide of a sea beast.

After that the meeting broke up and the other ladies went, except Victorine, who poured herself another cup of tea. The last thing Rose wanted just then was a mental game of tag.

Cade, too, was put out by Victorine's remaining. He stood banging at the side-pockets of his jacket—his way of checking that his pipe was safely stowed and of hinting that he was about to leave.

"I'm staying till four-thirty," Victorine told him. "It will save hanging about in town—I have a hairdressing appointment at five."

"It doesn't matter—I mean—" He frowned at himself. "I must be off, anyway."

"Will you come Tuesday fortnight?" asked Rose.

"I have a deacons' meeting that afternoon."

"What can you do in a fortnight that you couldn't do today?" said Victorine.

"I may think of something between now and then."

"I could postpone my deacons."

"There's no point, Eric. If you won't vote, why come to be squabbled over?"

He stopped banging his pockets and held his hands over

them like a man who realises he has lost something. "I thought you were with me over this, I thought you understood my position, Rose, you of all people."

"Why 'of all people'? I can be as unreasonable as anyone else." Rose lay back in her chair and closed her eyes. It was quite something not to see the circle of faces, such a small circle, but they had tired her out.

Victorine asked Cade, "Was it true what Mrs Choules said Peachey did to that woman?"

"Yes. I went to see her."

Rose opened her eyes. "You did what?"

"And Denis Peachey." He bowed his head. "She was paralysed from the waist down."

"You knew that? All the time?"

"I went again after she came out of hospital. There's a chance the paralysis will be cured. It was largely due to shock. She isn't a young woman and she was, of course, terribly shocked."

"You said nothing about this at the meeting!"

"Why should I?"

Rose saw him carrying this burden, a real burden this time, of human misery. Carrying it—why? It was being carried already and he couldn't take one grain off anyone else's back. She wondered, did he pick it up now and then or did he cling on to it all the time?

"Why should I?" repeated Cade. "It had no bearing on what we were discussing."

"No bearing!" She had stopped to get breath. Then she saw their surprise and in Cade's face the beginning of dismay.

Instinctively she closed her eyes again. She had shown them something personal and private, something they had no business to see. She could not deny it and she need not apologise for it any more than for the mole on her neck. What disgusted her was that these two, Victorine and Cade, would not differentiate between what they saw in Mrs Choules and what they saw in her.

"No," she said blankly, "no bearing."

She kept her eyes shut against them, knowing by their

silence that they were not convinced. They had something now to suspect her of, a bag of reasons, Mrs Choules' mixed bag.

"You look tired, Rose."

"Who would have thought there'd be so much mischief in trying to get some new hassocks?"

"Mischief—" said Cade, "if you call it that—is what I tried to prevent."

"I do call it that and you couldn't prevent it. It was an epidemic. One of them came with it and the others caught it off her. Except Mavis Tyndall—she meant well."

"Was I the one," said Victorine, "who came with mischief?"

"You were the only one who made a game of the whole thing."

"But I really want Mrs Peachey to get the money. I want her to feel that life isn't passing her by entirely and if new saucepans can do that I think she should have them." She even smiled, nowadays, with the other side of her face. "Though it's a case of the blind leading the blind—little Tyndall, who thinks she knows, leading me who hopes she does."

Cade, who had been moving about, jibbing at something, let it erupt with that naïvety which, in a man of God, was excused and indeed expected, but which Cade himself had not needed to acquire. "Rose, we must drop it—the church's claim, I mean. I should not have allowed it to go forward—"

"You could hardly have prevented it," said Rose. "And I certainly can't withdraw now."

"Not if I ask you as a personal favour?"

"You have no right to ask and I should have to refuse because, as I said before, it's culpable when a parish of this size and importance has such a poorly furnished church."

"We could raise the money—"

"There's a limit to money-raisers and I think we've reached it. We're committed to asking for money for everything from hunger in Asia to the unmarried mothers at Poll Hill. Should we ask for more? When this is just the sort of

thing Hilda intended the fund for? And what you're hoping
it will do for Mrs Peachey is so unlikely—it's unrealistic and
I'm not even sure it's just."

"Mrs Peachey's white," said Victorine, "but she's not
tidy."

Rose sat up. She had had enough, more than anyone in
her position need patiently endure. These two, Victorine
and Cade, had piled on their straws, and now she was ready,
though not to break.

"Vee, you came to make mischief and you've made it. I
don't know why. Whether you're sick in your mind or your
body, I don't think it matters. It can't excuse your attitude.
And I shan't apologise to you, Eric. You fret about keeping
in with God and the neighbours and you're not sure which
is the most important. When you've made up your mind
perhaps we'll get somewhere. Between now and Tuesday
fortnight I suggest you both re-examine your motives and
prepare to state them as frankly as Mrs Choules did."

Victorine was swallowing and relishing the smoke of her
cigarette. "Which do you think is the more important, her
frankness or her motives?"

Cade, pink and most raw where the hair backed across
his scalp, slapped at his pockets and blundered to the door.
"Excuse me, I must be off." He was gone, taking the hurt
air with him.

"He can't forgive you," said Victorine, "but he'll keep
trying."


Ted Antrobus had habits which he took care of and kept
for years. It disturbed him if any of them were broken.
Sometimes he was disturbed in anticipation. When he came
home he could not relax until a ritual was complete, it was
part of the journey and he did not arrive until then.

When he did relax he was a different person and his
fellow-commuters were struck by the discrepancy between
the man they travelled with and the man they met on the
golf-course and in the vicinity of his home. On the train he
was a loud and frequent talker. He was considered an exten-

sive man, ready to play poker or talk usefully about any of
the subjects that normally came up.

At home he was quiet, lacking conviction, his opinions
had to be pulled out of him. He had a way of gazing past
people while he spoke and it made him appear preoccupied
and distant. He wore bulky tweeds like a landowner. The
only land he had the remotest interest in had eighteen holes
and a club-house. His game was poor, but he disdained to
work at it. To Rose he said that he played because it gave
him somewhere to walk to.

Rose did not hear the sharp stories on the train, but if
she had she would have recognised that he was getting into
gear, she understood that at home he was not by any means
fully extended.

She would not have cared for him to be. When she had
occasion to be in the company of his wound-up self she
experienced a faint, persistent disquiet. Years ago she attri-
buted it to anxiety that she would not be able to keep up
with him. He was so much the centre of things, quite a
dynamo, and she still told people, 'Ted's a dynamo when
he's working'. But she knew now that her fears of not being
quite in his class were justified. His class, his working class,
was a peg lower than her own. It had been a shock finding
out and she had even thought how she might tone him
down—a little less panache, a little more reticence, not so
much club camaraderie. Thank God she had never tried it.
She soon realised that if she was slightly ashamed of her
husband there was nothing to be done except never to let
him or anyone else see it.

He had worked out for himself what he could most usefully and profitably be, and this was his interpretation of it.
For practical purposes it was successful and there was no
reason why he should be badgered to adjust it, even if he
could, by a hairsbreadth here and there. Rose did not consider her own taste sufficient reason, suspecting that it was
astringent and too particular. Easy to take was what Ted
had thought it necessary to be, and was able to be, at the
drop of a hat, for business and potentially business purposes.

His job and its milieu did advance one type of personality

which he was able to reproduce exactly. He was London and Continental Manager for a car-hire firm. He had cut himself into the job: had he decided to be a solicitor or a dentist he could as faithfully have cut himself into theirs. Rose would have preferred that. But neither profession could have paid him better than the car-hire business unless he had been exceptionally successful. Rose concluded he was wise not to attempt what he might not achieve. It was not that which she had against him. If she had anything, it was simply that between being an authentic businessman and resting from it, he had little time to be himself.

It would be ironic if anyone with two personalities should not be found in either. Rose preferred to think of them as the opposite ends of one personality, with Ted Antrobus, real, midway between. She had settled contentedly enough for the quiet end, the homecoming man who said little and whom she could therefore assume thought along her own lines.

She ministered to his habits wherever it was required of her and in the course of time they had come to formulate and fix habits of her own, so that each day, however untidily it might turn out, had a ritual to begin and end with.

Rose was glad of that on the day of the meeting. More than most people she disliked things not going to plan and she particularly disliked how they had not gone on this occasion. The ladies had proved to be a backward people, unobjective, bound up in themselves to an unhealthy degree, and Victorine Gregory, of course, was more than out of sorts.

The impression was of something residual and feminine which had no business on a committee. Rose did not like even to have it in the house. She opened windows and let in the sharp rainy air, she herself walked round the garden to freshen up. She would have liked to wipe out the afternoon and make another start. She felt that she should have handled the meeting better: she should, in fact, have handled it. It had gone agley because Mrs Peachey's was a redolent case. Rose had not known how redolent, nor reckoned how the mixture of violence, sex and Mavis Tyndall's mawkish-ness would operate. She certainly had not reckoned—how could she?—its effect on a mind as unbalanced as Victorine Gregory's. It had brought out the worst in her at a time when the worst was sillier and more contrary than usual.

Rose said something of the sort to Ted Antrobus that evening after he had changed out of his City clothes, after he had appeared to choose the sweet black sherry he invariably drank before dinner, first offering it to her and she, as always, had preferred a dry Martini, after he had closed his eyes for ten minutes, unwinding, with the empty glass held on his knee and in that spell which was reserved for broaching discussion of her affairs or a simple brief comment on her day.

Antrobus kept himself informed about Rose's activities. He knew the days of her meetings and the names of the committees she served on. He retained a potted history of the various protagonists. It was a kind of privileged after-hours extension of his methodical business mind.

"How did the Self-Help Committee meeting go?"

"It didn't," said Rose, and told him about Victorine. "I suspect she's going through a difficult time."

"Oh?"

"She's at an awkward age," Rose said delicately, "and she's always inclined to be mischievous in a silly, though harmless way. Now I'm afraid there's quite a bit of harm in it."

"To you?"

"To everyone. Of course she'll harm herself most of all."

"Of course."

"It's a period of maladjustment which certainly doesn't fit her for public life."

"Nor for private."

"I don't want to be unkind, but I think she's poisoned at the source. Physically, I mean. One shouldn't minimise the effects of the over- or under-stimulation even of glands—"

"There's no danger of that," said Antrobus, "once it's been observed by the Club."

"The Club? The Golf Club? Vee's not a member."

"Sam Swanzy is."

"Has he been talking about her?"

"I doubt it. Not if they are—" he looked absently over Rose's shoulder—"having fun together."

"Sam Swanzy? Vee?" Rose, incredulous, started to smile. "Oh, surely not!" And was at once convinced. "She couldn't!" Her disgust at its outset was less than righteous. "Sam Swanzy of all people!"

"Fun, anyway, for him."

"I really can't credit it. He's repulsive, he's—" Rose shuddered—"raw. I'm always afraid he's going to leave meaty marks wherever he touches." She got up. She could not sit there with Antrobus as a background to what she might think. She was shocked and every minute the shock deepened, she didn't know where it would end. "Of course if she's got that on her conscience it's bound to be warped. Why didn't you tell me before? You knew I was going to invite her to join the Committee."

"It was only Club gossip."

"You should have told me! She is a friend of mine—"

"I didn't believe it."

"And now you do?"

"I see no reason to. But in the circumstances you should perhaps bear it in mind."

She should of course do no more. But she did not seem to be in any mind so much as a flux. It would be a while before she could support the knowledge, suspicion, doubt, proviso—whatever it was.

"Why didn't Sue Betts tell me?"

"She may not have heard it. Gossip has to filter and there's a story to go with it that's not been made fit for ladies yet."

"Do you know, I'm inclined to believe it. It's what she would do, out of perversity. Anyone else wanting—" Rose picked it up with tongs—"anything like that, would at least choose someone presentable. Vee would go to the other extreme, the way she could do most damage to everyone, herself included."

She had done appreciable damage to Rose: not that Rose had a superfine opinion of Victorine, but she had given her credit for a reserve of decency, even at her climacteric. However, it need not have disturbed her and she was at a loss to know why it seemed to take the lid off something.

"It confirms what I was saying. She's thoroughly unbalanced."

Mentally and physically. Wanting Sam Swanzy's hands on her, wanting his meaty body, his glistening lips, his tongue—Rose felt sick. She turned her face to the wall, shamed as if she and all womankind were of the same dirty feather. "That sort of thing makes me ill."

Antrobus was looking through his empty sherry glass. "This glass isn't true at the base, it slightly distorts." When she made no comment he added, "You have no doubt what sort of thing it is?"

"Have you?"

"I?" He seemed surprised to be asked. "You know her better than I do."

"I didn't know she had it in her, but since she has it was her duty not to let it out. We do wrong to excuse so much. There used to be something else besides sickness and health, there used to be sin, and if it doesn't exist any more we don't need priests or policemen, we only need doctors."

"Surgeons," said Antrobus, examining the weave of his cuff through the glass, "to cut out the bad parts."

"Vee is as capable as I am of choosing right from wrong. The only sickness," Rose said sharply, "was in the choice she had to make."

"It wouldn't do for us all to like the same things."

"That's not funny." He was unsmiling and she said bitterly, "No doubt it was mixed up with her reason for blocking me."

It was her experience that people beyond the pale, particularly if they had put themselves there, could not forgive those inside it. They had no wish to get back, they simply wanted to deny the pale's existence and show everyone as suspect. Hence Victorine's efforts to discredit.

Antrobus said gently, "What have you got against this Mrs Peachey?"

"Nothing. Why does everyone think I have? For Heaven's sake, she's in trouble enough."

"Enough."

Antrobus had a way of picking up and dropping other people's last words and Rose, though she knew the trick, cried, "I've never even seen her!"

There was no need for his silence to pique her: she knew that it came from acceptance rather than question. He had never dug into her motives and she suspected that he scratched the surface out of politeness and a sense of duty.

"The point I make, and I think it's valid, is that given a sympathetic, not to say a sentimental hearing, she might dramatise her situation. Mavis Tyndall is a good little thing, but far from objective. Mrs Peachey would spend the money and it wouldn't change anything. How could it? Forty pounds odd," said Rose, "when what she needs is a miracle."

"Perhaps you should see her."

"What good would it do? They've made up their minds and nothing I could say would change them."

Of late Rose had caught herself in the mirror thrusting up her chin as she spoke. She was afraid it was a nervous tick, out of keeping with anything she might have to say and she was trying to break it. "I'm not the parish visitor type—" Yes, she had just done it again, an uppish jerk, defensive and clumsy. If she looked like that everyone was going to think she had something to defend. "And I doubt if I could change my mind when I don't approve the idea in principle. It's unrealistic to think that money can give her moral courage. And insulting, especially when the money's so little."

Antrobus and Rose had long ago established a method of picking out only what they wanted of each other's thoughts and emotions. Sometimes something was not soon enough refused—as now, when there were the elements of a smile on his face. Rose took it that her motives, or what he made of them, amused him. Knowing that he would not trouble to make anything upset her.

"I thought Eric Cade was common-sensible. If there is

nothing else, one may expect a pastor to have both his feet on the ground. Surely?"

"On the ground," Antrobus agreed and put the sherry glass aside to show that he was ready for supper.

Rose lifted her chin again. "I don't expect to have to chase to God after him."

# PART TWO

It's no coincidence that I think of Solange now: I don't for months at a time, then something or someone will remind me.

She's been coming on, every day a little more, and I don't need to be reminded now. Now she has so much relevance it is difficult not to think of her. I'm beginning to believe she can interpret for me. She's with me now as she was at Bonneval and Grieux, and more so because now she is in my mind and I can deny her nothing, forbid her nothing. *In absentiâ* she has the entrée of a ghost and the influence of a god, in the flesh she was most fallible.

She is a case in point. In point of this, which I can't put a name to. There may be a technical term for it, something psychological, something German, something *angst*. It's a question and not a new one. I think I've been answering it all my life.

And Solange has been my answer since the day, the communion day at Bonneval. I was twelve years old, I wouldn't be likely to have asked the question before then. Solange may have helped to pose it. She and all that she implied may be not just a case in point but a microcosm. One must particularise—I must. If I'm to answer and be done with this question which presents itself to me from all sides I must take as I find and I can only hope to find in my own past experience. It's better than any I could get now by asking other people. I must prove, or fail to, by what I know, not by what I'm told.

I am taking a case in point—I want to be secure about that from the outset. Because it is possible to look at a drop of something and assume it to be tap-water and blame the entire plumbing system on it, and then have it turn out to be a drop of lemonade or turpentine or plasma.

I know that Solange was human, a normal human being.

49

I don't go so far as to say that the other sort, if they exist, are *in*human. If they exist.

Holiness won't save anyone. I learned that early, it was perhaps the first difficult thing I did learn. Not that I was ever religious, I had just been brought up to three of everything: earth where we lived and sinned in some degree, hell where we went if the degree was excessive and heaven where there was God and unrelieved good and where we should all end up singing. To me at twelve years old that was the Establishment, I was content with it and supposed everyone was.

Remembering Bonneval is like turning back the pages of a book and re-reading, even to what was said, and how, and why. I can't guarantee the accuracy of conversations, I haven't the gift for total recall, but I do seem to have registered their impact.

Most of the time I was shocked: what happened at Bonneval unmade me, I had afterwards to do some work on myself. Then at Grieux, in Switzerland, where I was at school, the whole thing happened again, only worse because I was older and had to come down to earth and it seemed that the earth wasn't going to support me either.

I wonder how I would have turned out if there had been no Bonneval and no Grieux. Perhaps no differently to all intents and purposes other than my own. I would still have married Ted Antrobus, though for reasons which must have been the wrong ones. Because we do see what we need to in people. What I needed to see in Ted happened actually to be there.

I may have been lucky too in what I saw in Solange. If I really did see in her that special element, power, quirk, streak, quality—or lack of it—that I can see now the world over. Or did I only need to see and needing, supplied it? One can only supply what already exists and only *where* it doesn't exist. But surely if anyone ever had it, Solange Marigny did.

She was my pen-friend. Before we met I used to suppose her blonde and soft and dressed in pink. I thought her name had a squashy sound. She wrote to me in English and I had to reply in French. I still have some of her letters. They are very correct, I thought them dull.

'We go to the Bois de Boulogne which is in Paris and on Sundays full of tradesmen.' 'The weather has been bad. It has rained since Easter every day. Madame Molette, our doorkeeper, has a glass eye which presages the weather. When it will rain the eye is green, when it will be fine the eye is yellow. When we have storm she removes it because of the lightning.'

One letter, I remember, my father found illuminating. Perhaps it was one in which she wrote: 'We are not permitted to go to the Parc Parangon. My mother says we will understand presently. It is not a pretty place, there are no flowers, they have naturally been all crushed.'

He said, "That girl's a minx," and when I asked why, he said all French females were minxes, it was the national character.

He was dubious about letting me go to stay with the Marignys. But Mother was adamant, she admired all things Continental.

I was an outright English child, too keen on games, dainty as a bear, with an undiscriminating appetite for what I was sure was going to be an appetising world. I had no fear and no finesse. I had everything to learn and I was insulated against learning it. No doubt what my mother intended I should acquire in France was not so much a polish as some cracks in the glaze. She wasn't to know they would be splits, nor that they would reach down to the foundations.

The Marignys were comfortably off. Solange's father was a lawyer and was called 'Maître'. They had a flat in Paris and what Solange called a 'domaine' in the country. Bonneval was just south of Bordeaux, in the wine country, that part of France which once was Aquitaine. When the letter came from Madame Marigny to my mother inviting me to spend the summer holidays with Solange I didn't want to go. There were tennis finals in July, I was in the first eleven of the local ladies' cricket team and we had plenty of fixtures. But cricket wasn't of the slightest concern to my mother, she disapproved of my playing because it was a man's game

51

and she thought the hard balls dangerous. And so my father, when he raised objection to my going abroad, was accused of encouraging me to be a hoyden, a 'hermaphrodite' my mother called it.

"I will not have Rose becoming one of those with bosoms and no gender," I heard her say. "She needs to be taught her sex and no one can give her better grounding than the French."

My father tried to be sceptical about my having sex at twelve years old, but Mother said I'd been born with it and must learn to use it or leave it alone—but no daughter of hers was going to leave it alone.

So in the summer of 1927 I went to Bonneval. I was put in the charge of a stewardess on the boat to Calais. As it was a rough crossing she was fully occupied and I was left to myself.

I found that I was a good sailor and ate an enormous lunch. Afterwards I went up on deck where there were sick people flattened like wet flies by the roaring wind, putting their faith, I suppose, in fresh air however brutal. No one had heart or lungs enough to speak to me except a woman who strode about talking to everyone. She was not seasick and thought it proved the purity of her liver. She wasn't impressed with mine because she maintained I hadn't had time to spoil it. Whenever she passed she shouted, "Keep your liver clean!" and if I have to think of liver now I can smell wet iron and salt and feel the boat struggling in mid-air like a bird in the hand. Just before we docked, this woman slipped and cracked her skull on the deck. She was carried below on a stretcher.

I was a believer in justice, though not morbidly and as a *status quo* rather than a golden or sacred mean. Pride before a fall, good after bad, right after wrong seemed to me ordered as day after night. I had no sympathy with the liver woman, I considered she had been served right for being a fool and for boasting and I went ashore like a lion—the chosen, the fittest survivor among all the sorry voyagers.

Monsieur Marigny, who had business in Calais, was to meet me off the boat and take me to Bonneval. I had no idea what to expect, but he apparently was not in doubt about me. As soon as I stepped off the gangplank he was at my side, a small vivid man with a badly scarred and eroded face. He was pale, his hair and moustache were jetty black and I always saw him in black clothes, yet there was a reptilian brilliance about him. It could only have come from within, from something suppressed and inimical. I have not forgotten him: he was the first intimation I had that I was going somewhere completely and fundamentally foreign.

He said, "M'oiselle," bowing slightly. "Je m'appelle Quentin Marigny. Soyez la bienvenue."

I had the shell I was born with and which my slice of life had merely established. I felt no more than momentarily abashed, I was able to look away from anything that promised to be without profit and three-quarters forget it. I suppose that's what I did with Maître Marigny at our first meeting because of the long train journey to Paris and the still longer one from Paris to Bonneval he remains as a faint discomfiture, a cold-finger accompaniment. He probably wished it so, he had no interest in me except as a parcel for delivery.

There was one encounter between us just after the train left Calais. I got up from my seat to go along the corridor and Maître Marigny said, "Mademoiselle?"

That did stump me. While I was trying to formulate in French something slightly left of an unmistakable centre he leaned forward and tapped the seat beside me. "Asseyez-vous, s'il vous plaît."

"I want to go along the corridor."

"Comment?"

"To wash my hands."

He looked at me with brows raised, then he said, "Go," and sat back in his corner. He took no further notice of me until we got to Paris. It was as if I had demonstrated my normality and could be allowed the latitude of a trained dog.

I got tired travelling all day and all night and slept for most of the journey from Paris. Maître Marigny sat under his individual light reading a sheaf of papers and occasionally writing on them. He started before the train drew out of Austerlitz and he was still at it when we reached Bordeaux.

We had to change to a branch line, a little rusty train with a cow-catcher and slat seats like we had at home on the trams. It took us through miles of what I later learned were vineyards. It was very hot, the carriages and everything in them were doused with white dust, Maître Marigny was smoking terrible brown cigarettes and it felt as if every bit of France I had travelled over had been pushed down my throat. I looked longingly at the rivers we passed, lacquered black or running thin over stones the colour of pigeons. Every farm with its brown-speckled pantiles and every cow made me think of cold milk—I longed for a glass of ice-cold milk.

The train stopped every few minutes and people got in and out, women with frizzy hair and huge loaded baskets like the baker's roundsman carried at home, and men with no socks and dirty canvas shoes. Some of them wore wide straw hats and their clothes were splashed with a beautiful poignant blue. Everyone smelled terrible, I began to feel dazed. They seemed to know Maître Marigny and they all spoke to him. Sometimes he grunted, more often he briefly relaxed the scars on his face by way of acknowledgment.

It was noon when we reached Bonneval. By then I had been travelling for twenty-eight hours, I was sick and tired and hot and cross and the sweat was running down the backs of my knees. I just dropped out of the train, leaving Maître Marigny to deal with every scrap of luggage. He called a porter and the porter and people still in the carriage got my bags and parcels out between them while the train waited, sinking us in clouds of steam. I appreciated that Maître Marigny was a different proposition from my father who personally escorted every piece of luggage out of trains and always got back in at the risk of being carried on, to make sure that everything down to the last discarded paper bag stayed with us. It nettled me that anyone could be so absolutely undiminished by all that heat and noise. He was as crisp and accurate and obscurely brilliant as he had been at

Calais, the dust that was everywhere, even between my teeth, had not settled on him. I think I concluded then and there that Solange's father was mineral whereas on the whole the race of adults were vegetable.

I can remember the heat of that first day at Bonneval. When the train had gone, and the steam, it was apparent that what was the matter was the sun. It had an emulsifying effect, the metal railway lines and the bones of my body were ready to leak away together but the air had thickened, the air had to be supported.

A car waited outside the station. Beside it stood two children. Maître Marigny stooped to allow each of them to kiss him on either side of his cigarette. Then he turned to me.

"Permettez-moi de vous présenter Valentin, mon fils, et Solange, ma fille."

The girl shook me by the hand. I believe she said she was happy to make my acquaintance as if, I thought, I was going again after tea. The boy stooped and touched my knuckles with his lips. I felt ridiculous and he was obviously unaware that he looked it. He was very thin, all angle and bone, outgrowing his skin as well as his clothes. He wore a sort of Norfolk suit, I remember. It was too small and his wrists and legs sprouted, so did his neck. He was then, and always I believe, what my grandmother would have called a 'poor tool'.

Solange made little impression on me at first sight. I saw that she was dark and slender where I had anticipated someone fattish and fair, but I didn't look at her much, I was inclined to sulk because these people weren't going to understand me.

Château de Bonneval was the next disturbance. We drove through a village, just a collection of cracked and shuttered shells, and a church, then along an unmade road that climbed through fields of vines to a bleached common ringed with mauve flowers. Solange, who was sitting opposite, said politely, "Voici le château". I looked, and there it was, on a terraced hill with a sort of tumult of green woods at its feet. Ordinarily I would have been enchanted and later on

I was, but that first glimpse upset me. I got angry with Solange for not preparing me. She had written of 'our house in the country' and my father had maintained that French people called anything a 'château'.

"We're the same" he'd said, "putting 'Ivanhoe' and 'Windsor' and 'Harlech' on every front-yard gate." The obvious interpretation, that it really was a château with candle-snuffer towers and arched windows and a front door that a coach could drive through, had never occurred to us. I came to it unapprised from the mustard villas of South London.

Buckingham and the Crystal Palaces were monuments, cathedrals were religion: I discounted them, and Paddington Station, as geographical rather than designed and had supposed that our new baroque cinema, the Otranto, was the most I could except to take architecturally.

From the vision floating in that hot nacreous light out of the pages of Hans Andersen and the Rose Fairy Book, I looked at the Marignys. I had grown out of this sort of thing and so, I considered, should they have done. They had no right to live in such a place, but it was the sort of far-fetched foreign thing they would do and might have been excused— like the Japanese fancy for living in paper houses—so long as they hadn't brought me into it. A fine fool I should look, and feel, in a place like that, a fish out of water, a bird out of air.

My tennis-racquet was on the floor of the car at my feet. I have large feet and Mother used to make me wear broad shoes to give me room to grow. Beside my tongued leather brogues which looked pretty stylish at home, I saw Solange's bare foot in the same sort of canvas slipper that the men on the train were wearing. The same sort of dirt was on it too, a patina of dust grained into the cloth and into her brown ankle. The bone was polished and slaty with it. How foreign, I wondered in disgust, was it allowable for these people to be?

As the car choked up the hill to the Château, Maître Marigny spoke to me for about the third time since we had left Calais. It was quite an 'histoire' for him. He told me, I think, because I never could follow his French very well, that in the seventeenth century Château de Bonneval was the home of the poet and essayist, Edouard Brindille, famous for his intrigues as well as his writings. He was murdered at the Château by a lady of quality whom he had betrayed. She pushed a hat-pin into his ear.

"Vous voyez donc que Bonneval est un château très intéressant, très historique et très romantique," concluded Maître Marigny.

I said, "Evidemment," and he looked at me as if I'd made a rude noise.


I expected the Marignys to put on airs at living in a place like that, but I soon found that their airs had nothing to do with the Château. They took that for granted.

There was none the less a sort of collective air which, although they had quite different personalities, was peculiar to all of them and to the place. It was indigenous perhaps, bred up out of that country of vines and dust, parrot-green forests and bath-tub heat. An unsettling air—it unsettled me, I didn't feel safe, in a daily sense, with any of them. They were incalculable, and although I was too brash to calculate anyone, I wanted people to abide by my rough and ready reckoning of them. The Marignys were slippery but not deceitful. They did not hide what they were, it was up to the beholder to make it out. I never could, I beheld it in all of them, at times as uncalled for and disquieting as the lightning that always seemed to be blinking like a white eyelid at the back of the sky.

The Château didn't impress me so much on the inside. The entrance hall was grand enough in a medieval way: it had a stone floor and rather chewed wooden roof-beams and a great cowled fireplace with one of Edouard Brindille's *bon mots* carved above it. There were swords and daggers on the walls but not the hat-pin that had killed him. The rooms downstairs were darkened by the Spanish chestnut trees outside the windows and by the panelling which sometimes continued over the ceiling like a box. There was a library, that was enormous too, with a ladder to get to the top-most shelves, and as I dislike the smell of old books it was noisome. The family camped out in a corner for after-dinner coffee.

From upstairs there was a view across miles of vines, meadows and forest. The walls of the principal rooms were covered with patterned fabrics. Solange told me that her great-grandmother had done it when material was cheaper than wallpaper. There were three storeys to the Château. I liked the rooms inside the towers, they were circular and too small to lie down in and their slit windows were the only ones without shutters.

Apart from the addition of basket chairs, stuffed stools and woollen rugs, the Marignys didn't appear to have changed the furniture much since Solange's great-grand-mother's time. I thought it all ugly and shabby, though now I appreciate that they must have had a lot of good things, real antiques—chiffoniers and escritoires and those slender bow-fronted chairs, massive beds and court cupboards that you could get into, marquetry tables, buhl clocks—that sort of thing. There were even some tapestries which could have been Gobelin. None of it was looked after, whatever pride the Marignys had, it wasn't pride of possession.

Solange told me, that first day, that the Château belonged to her mother. It had been in that side of the family for over a hundred years but wasn't likely to remain so much longer. I gathered it was something of a white elephant, a white mammoth, costly to run and much in need of repair. The vines had been sold and the farms. There was only the forest now, and what little money could be made out of the timber went to pay the bailiff who was unscrupulous and lazy. Solange told me this politely since I had asked questions, but indifferently. She was with me in my room while I unpacked and was more interested in my clothes than any-thing else. I began to feel scandalised, from being angry with her because I expected her to put on airs I switched to being indignant because she didn't. Anyone who had a place like this, I reasoned, ought to regard it as their duty to keep it for their children and their children's children. English people did, I said, they starved in drawing-rooms rather than let their ancestral homes out of the family. I was mixed up there, but from the beginning Solange had a knack of making me righteous, however misinformed. She just shrugged and smiled, I remember, and tried on my dressing-gown.

I didn't reach her then, or ever, but it was a long time before I gave up trying. I couldn't get used to living on anyone's periphery although that was as far as I got with any of the Marignys. For such a discrepant group they were strangely united. It was as if their differences kept them together. They relied on each other for the essential grit in their lives: it was the only thing, I sometimes thought, that was essential to them. They loved to differ and they aired their differences without acrimony, a point of interest more than honour. They didn't seem to go in for deep committed things like honour, they had plenty of opinions, but I never was sure what they believed in.

Madame Marigny was the most unaccountable. Her husband I placed, or rather wrote off, under his profession: I allowed only for law in a lawyer, medicine in a doctor and teeth in a dentist. Madame Marigny, although French, was a mother and should have known her place. Had she stayed in it I could have allowed and appreciated a few foreign quirks.

Madame Marigny didn't stay anywhere, even while we were at meals she would get up and wander round the table. This I considered inexcusable since she had the gall to supervise her children's manners. One moment she was all she ought to be, she was 'Maman' and the household goddess: the next she was chattering and gesturing and grimacing like mad—literally like, no-one sane could have swallowed so much air. Or she would move away, stiffly, and because she had blue bulbous eyes and pink bulbous cheeks and puffs of flaxen hair she looked like a badly-jointed doll. Sometimes she ran. If, for reasons known only to herself, she needed to get away quicker, she picked up her skirts and flashed out of the room. Once I saw her, while they were having an evening party, run like that across the moonlit terrace and into the garden and come back a minute later looking as if she'd caught and eaten something. Sometimes she just beat the air with her hands. Sometimes she laughed, quietly and glitteringly—she had gold fillings in her teeth—and that was the only time I really minded her.

Valentin favoured his mother in looks. He had the same overshot eyes and boiled yellow hair. He was growing too fast and the sun which darkened other boys fetched him up a raw, painful red. He was said to be lazy, the family said so without condemnation, as they would say that the soil was chalk, but later on Maître Marigny, looking for something specific to say of his son, could find only that and made it a crime.

I didn't understand Valentin any better than the others, but I liked him better. I thought him preoccupied rather than lazy, he was trying to use his mind. The time he spent lying on the grass and dribbling a ball about the garden was devoted to questions which most people didn't ask. He asked them of me, he probably hoped that a foreigner could give him a new slant. I couldn't, of course. He either put his questions badly in English or too well in French and I wouldn't even try to get the substance. They were, I thought, the sort of presumptuous nonsense God might answer with a thunderbolt.

Céline, the youngest, was called Chelle. She was nine years old and she was the practical one. She was plain in a monkeyish way, dark and small like her father but without his suppressed brilliance. She sometimes twinkled with private glee and darted out her tongue when she laughed. I felt uncomfortable in her presence. She was so quick and I mistrusted speed in people, but I couldn't snub her as I might an English child of her age because she pretended not to understand either my French or my English.

Finally there was Solange, and I have left her until last in the hope, even now, that she might clarify against my impressions of her family. I want to be fair, to see her in the round. It will be difficult because in remembering what she was I can't put out of my mind what she became. What we both became. Impartial, perhaps I can be in one sense, since I was never sure what I felt for Solange. I am still not sure: for anything that I liked about her I can remember something that I disliked. There's no bias but there may be some myopia—she's so much a part of the furniture of my mind I shan't see for looking.

She was pretty, and being at that time part child, part woman gave to her looks an ideal quality. We'd all like to be fixed about then, with a foot in both worlds. She had fine dark hair and a strong luminous pallor. She was very slender, almost spun. I felt like a rough pony beside her. She weighed about two stone less than I did, yet I have seen her carrying Chelle with ease under one arm. She took everything easily, win or lose, good or bad. Hers was a protective polish and nothing could get a grip on her.

I resented that. Life hadn't gripped on me either, but I often had to try for what I wanted. Figuratively speaking, Solange didn't lift a finger.

She acted as a catalyst on me, inducing emotions I didn't recognise as my own. There was a lot of prejudice and prissiness—I was trying to supply what was lacking in Solange. I began as soon as we met, when I had no more than got wind of it. I went on prickling and puffing up until the last.

During those first days at Bonneval the physical and mental climate was as remote as darkest Africa from anything I had known. The heat confused me, I have always preferred to be temperate, and I got into a waiting frame of mind, waiting for the pressure to lift, to stop, to go back to normal. Tomorrow, I used to think, when it's cooler. . . It never was cooler, not that summer. In the mornings, early, there would be a semblance of it, patches under the chestnut trees that might be damp, the forest tented and dark, and a thin green sky without a sun. I was seldom awake so soon.

, We children had breakfast—coffee and unbuttered bread—at nine o'clock in the kitchen. My father had told me that French bread was good but this was dark and slightly sour.

Breakfast was prepared by Madame Dubosque. She was a distant elderly relation of Maître Marigny, she and her husband stayed the year round at the Château. Everyone called her Tin-Tin, but I didn't care. She was a formidable old woman, dressed all in black, with nicotine coloured hair and negroid lips that looked horribly as if they were puckered for a kiss. She had a clownish sense of humour. On my first morning I asked if I might have a boiled egg for breakfast. She flew at me, flapping her skirts and clucking like a hen and chased me round the kitchen. I was very much put out, but Solange and Valentin rocked with laughter.

"You might have warned me she was touched," I said bitterly afterwards.

"Comment?"

"Mad." I tapped my forehead. "Folle."

Solange said Madame Dubosque was not mad, she was very 'sage' but she liked to amuse herself. I thought, she shan't do it at my expense and thereafter dipped my bread in my coffee as the others did and ate it soggy. It seemed revolting, but I had to eat something, I was always hungry.

Maître and Madame Marigny seldom appeared before lunch, and Chelle breakfasted earlier than we did. She was 'affairé', they said. It puzzled me what affairs a child of nine could have. Perhaps she was studying for something. But I found out what Chelle's standing was with the family when an American student who was writing his thesis on Edouard Brindille was shown round the Château. Chelle kept running from room to room so that she was always there before him with a big edition of Brindille's works held prominently before her. That time I felt it was my turn to laugh.

But Valentin said seriously, "Chelle thinks it is good for business."

The staff at the Château was made up of old women with faces like brown crusts. I couldn't tell them apart, nor could I understand their accent. With Monsieur Dubosque I had some intelligible conversations because he insisted on talking to me in dumb show as if I was a deaf mute. He worked in the garden, sorting over bits of gravel or picking off leaves, and whenever I appeared he seemed to be seized with intense pity for me. He went to a lot of trouble to communicate: there we would be, I talking primer French very slowly, he gesturing, capering, stretching and bunching his empty rubber jaws. I finally had to accept the fact that he thought I was mentally deficient, a cave-dweller and a heathen, doomed to extinction in the rush of progress. He worked hard to make me laugh. I can see him now, putting his hat on back to front and doing a soft-shoe shuffle in the gravel. He was the only person at the Château who was *concerned* with me, who put himself out for me and I appreciated it, whatever his reasons.

We children were left to ourselves, no one entertained or instructed us. I was glad, I didn't want to go looking at graves and old buildings. At the same time my conscience or conceit took exception to the fact that no one tried to show me anything.

"My parents will want to know what I've seen," I said to Solange. "I'll have to tell them I didn't."

"Didn't?"

"See cathedrals and tombs."

"You wish to?"

"Of course not. The point is, my parents expect me to see the historical stuff while I'm here and I'll have to write an essay for school."

"There are books."

"It's not the same thing. I'm supposed to see the places myself—"

"Who shall say you have not seen?"

"That would be lying—cheating."

Her trick of smiling things off was still new to me. She was twelve years old and so was I, yet she could smile and put into my head the notion that I had a long way to go to catch up with her. It was only a notion, but it was insufferable because I didn't realise then that the way she was going I neither wanted to nor could catch up with her.

"I'm not a liar," I said. "Even if you are."

She went on smiling. "Like George Washington?" and I thought, you see what it's worth, she has no respect for anyone and that's not advanced, that's retarded.

Solange may have mentioned this conversation to her mother because a few days afterwards she and I were sent into Bordeaux with Madame Dubosque who was going to

63

buy herself some new corsets, and that was the farthest we went from the Château.

Solange and I spent the days together, in the forest, in the garden or sometimes we lay like dogs on the cool marble floor in the library. Occasionally Valentin was with us, more often he mooched about by himself.

Chelle had no time for us. She was forever scurrying about being busy. Or a busybody—I couldn't take her seriously. Everyone else did. It was she who kept Madame Marigny's accounts for the timber transactions. In an old scullery they called the 'office' were parcels of yellow papers and bills on hooks and old calendars. The calendars hung all over the walls, the earliest one being for 1905. Chelle had found them in a cupboard and put them up, perhaps to give her some of the time she was so short of. Also on the wall was a map she had drawn of the land the family still owned. Even to me it looked a most competent affair, contour lines, buildings, tracks, streams were all drawn in—how accurately I don't know—and the varieties of trees were shaded in different colours. It was possible to see at once where fir predominated, or chestnut, oak, pine and beech. Felling in progress was shown by black markers on pins. Chelle sat at a roll-topped desk with a huge horn-backed ledger before her. In this she wrote spidery French figures, the sevens all crossed like fives and the ones tabbed like sevens, credit and debit columns fenced off in red and violet inks.

Chelle was so sure of herself and everyone else was so sure that I refused to be. I asked Solange, "Why does your mother let Chelle play about like that?" Solange said Chelle wasn't playing, she was working and Madame Marigny was glad to have someone to do her additions.

"She ought to be pushing her dolls' pram!"

"Pourquoi tu te mets en colère?"

"I'm not angry! I just think it's mad to trust a kid her age—"

Solange went behind me and wrapped both my plaits round my neck. I thought she said in French something about me never being as old as Chelle, it was the sort of thing she would say.

Discovering a tennis-court in the Château grounds was a great thrill to me, although I was horrified at the state it was in. Weeds had cracked it, the net had never been wound in and fell apart like a cobweb, the posts were rotten and there weren't even vestigial markings left.

"How on earth could you let it get like this?"

Solange didn't see why not. She began to pull the remains of the net to bits.

"Don't! We may have to make do with that." I was beginning to realise that I wouldn't ever know the Marignys. "Will you ask your mother to get someone to see to it?"

"To see?"

"Clean it up, put it in order." I seized a head of the yellow daisies that were growing all over the place and swung them like a racquet. "Not that I'll put up much of a game in this heat."

"Maman will not permit."

"You mean she won't let us play?"

"She will not think it necessary to clean the tennis." Solange put a finger on one of the posts and rocked it in its socket. "There is no one to do it, everybody is working."

"Then we'll have to do it ourselves. We'll get Valentin to help."

"I do not think it necessary either," said Solange.

I ignored that. I worked on that court, day after day, and got Solange and Valentin to work too whenever I could, which wasn't often. It took days of weeding, raking, making do, mending and marking before we could play.

Solange wasn't keen even then, though I found that she played well enough while she kept her attention on the game. Every so often she would drop her racquet and walk away smiling and shaking her head just as I was about to serve.

"J'en ai assez—tu as l'air si drôle!"

"What do you mean—funny?" I said furiously the first time it happened.

"You are so feroce—" Solange giggled. "Like a man killing a pig."

"There's no such word as 'feroce' in English and you've never seen a man kill a pig."

"I have seen Uncle Dubosque do it."

"I don't look like Uncle Dubosque—how dare you!"

"Dare? Qu'est-ce-que c'est?"

It was not a word she needed, as I was to find out. She was neither bold nor rebellious, she had no principles of her own or anyone else's to rebel against. I wonder what she thought of principles and what people had them for. Mine always amused her.

We took lunch and dinner with Maître and Madame Marigny. At table I heard the family talking together. I marvelled how they talked: not sporadically, turning up subjects as we might stones and dropping them, but bringing out opinions, airing, flashing, fooling with them and never for a moment getting saddled.

Sometimes the subjects were ones on which I considered I was more of an authority than they could ever be—when the conversation turned to London, for instance, or tennis. They heard my solid facts politely, then they were off again at their own pace and I couldn't compete with Madame Marigny chasing, and being chased, by some windy notion; with Maître Marigny, acid and sibilant; with Solange, making an extreme stand for the fun of it; with Valentin, pushing his abstractions, or even with Chelle, just laughing and darting out her tongue. They didn't want information, they wanted entertainment. They didn't want truth, I thought angrily, they wanted to hear themselves.

It was no better if visitors were present. The pace might be faster or they might range farther, depending on the company, but so far as I could see, French people were all the same, they didn't want nor could they give a straight answer.

When the priest came to lunch I knew he was there before I saw or heard anything of him. He had a strong sweetish smell—of Catholic holiness, I supposed. By all accounts Father Benedict was an especially holy man, the Marignys conceded that without argument, they listened with even a touch of deference when he talked, and he talked as much, if not about as much, as they did.

He was youngish, cream-faced, with a lavendar jaw. I stood a little in awe of him, but pleasantly, because he was spruce and kind. That sexless garment, the soutane, and that sort of carnival hat with a pom-pom on top, became him. I liked the look of him and I think he liked the look of himself—which gave a touch of cruelty and wantonness to what happened.

One day at lunch they talked of the years he had spent working in a leper colony. Madame Marigny said something about physical decay and disgust killing pity and I remember he said one got into the habit of looking at without seeing the faces of one's friends. I thought of that afterwards and hoped it was some help to him.

I couldn't make up my mind that I liked Solange. It seemed to hinge on whether I could approve of her, but of course it was the other way about—my principles weren't all that developed. Sometimes I liked her very much: sometimes she let me in, or went where I could follow. Skins were down between us, we had the run of each other and I didn't question anything she did. At other times there was no knowing and I told myself there was nothing I cared to know. Solange always gave me an excuse for an attitude. The day we went to Bordeaux I took up an attitude that was too big for me in the end.

We went on the bus. It was an hour's tedious journey over bad roads with the heat blowing back from the open windows like the blast from an oven. Madame Dubosque knew everybody, she went between the seats talking to each person for the benefit of the whole bus, getting tossed about like a bag of beans. Her hat slipped to the back of her head and she steamed under the armpits, but she talked and clowned in her loud urchin way even, I think, about her new corsets. She tried to bring Solange, who was her favourite, into the fun, but Solange turned her face away.

"I wish she'd shut up," I said irritably. "She makes it hotter."

Solange said that Tin-Tin was making show of herself, to which I agreed and we looked along our noses at the old woman. It didn't stop us from eating the ice-cream and cakes she bought for us in Bordeaux.

Being my first experience of French pastries I ate too many of the richest and rarest. I felt sick, too sick to go to the corsetière with Madame Dubosque. So she took us into a church near the pastry-cook's for safety as well as coolness, and told us to wait for her there.

It was a nice church and I would have been content to sit quietly in the semi-dark, but Solange started pacing about as soon as Madame Dubosque had gone. I said could I help it if I felt sick and she said yes, I'd made a pig of myself. It looked bad, she said, particularly as Tin-Tin had to pay for our refreshments out of her own pocket. I had thought that Madame Marigny was standing treat, but Solange said her mother did not think of that sort of thing, and I could well believe it. When I proposed to reimburse Madame Dubosque, Solange said I'd get my ears boxed if I tried, and that I could believe too.

Solange wouldn't stay in the church. She was going to see the 'momies', she said, and I followed her though I dreaded the heat that was rammed down into the streets.

Close by was a tower. Solange paid some money to the man who sat at the door. I asked her what 'momies' were, but all she would say was that they were 'très historique' and I could write about them in my school essay.

We went down steps into a round stone room. I had only begun to suspect Solange and to be ready for her. After that day I realised that she had means and a mind that were beyond me. She would always go one or two better, and if I couldn't foresee what she would do I should, for my own sake, foresee that she would always do something.

The room was lit, not brightly, by an oil lantern standing on the floor, It was, in fact, only a few degrees less than pitch dark down there, probably with some idea of heightening the effect. A blaze of electricity would have left nothing to the imagination and in this case imagination was more merciful.

The figures were propped round the walls. They were as Solange had said, 'mummies', flesh harder than wood, drier than leather, and about as human as a meteorite. I couldn't reason it out then, but I believe that's what upset me most, that's what made it such a laugh. I don't know who for—not for me, not for anyone who looked at them. There were about thirty and every one was fixed in some horror, or oddity or agony. Some were arched, the head forced back and out of joint, their jaws hung down their necks—they were the idiot dead. A child had the skirt of her dress and a hole where her chest should be; a priest had part of his cassock and his hands out, like claws, in a parody of blessing; a woman carried the cadaver of her baby, sliced like a specimen, in her dried-up womb.

The lantern made liquid shadows, they all seemed to be flowing upwards and never getting away. I looked into their faces, the holes and sockets, the congealed eyeballs, the red and black hair stuck to the bone, and I felt that a nightmare was coming true.

Solange said they had come from a common grave, preserved by the nature of the soil they were buried in eight hundred years ago. She touched them, rapped with her knuckles on their heads and chests and they gave out a solid sound like hide. She picked up a woman's breasts and flapped them, cracked her fingernail against the vitrified child in the womb, without disgust or much interest.

People turn old clothes over like that and thumb second-hand books. I couldn't stand it and I thought then that it was the irreverence of what she was doing to dead people that I couldn't stand. But now I think it was because she couldn't see the laugh, that the laugh was on her, on us all, and I couldn't bear for her not to see it.

I asked her to stop, but of course she wouldn't, not while she thought she was shocking me.

"Voici un sale type," she said, smiling and tapping one of the mummies on its thighs. So I went away up the steps and left her there and as I came out into the heat of the sun it no longer made me feel sick, it made me feel full of juice.

Looking back now, the summer at Bonneval is less like a succession of days than one long day and a sample night.

After dark the Château closed up and withdrew, it became a bubble place holding above miles of woods and plain. The heat of the day relaxed, but only to blood temperature, there was no real sense of release, and moving about under the dim lights indoors or the darkness outside I always felt that we were inside our selves.

The bats flew about at night, very fast and vivid, a pelting of blackness that made it unnerving to walk out of doors. I remember the monstrous beetles that bumbled round the lights and fell, buzzing and dying, into my hair, and I remember that the towers turned pewter colour after dark and the fairy-tale effect was laid on with a trowel, but there was a goblin side too, because by the same process the crimson hangings in my bedroom took on the colour of viscera round about dawn.

I remember footsteps gritting on the terrace and smelling Maître Marigny's brown cigarettes, and when there was a wedding party at a farm miles away I heard the singing and dancing. It was so still I heard it all, down to the clatter of their knives and forks and the scrape of their chairs on the stone.

In that summer in a day events seem to me now to have had a morning or an evening feel. Chelle's battle with the bailiff, for instance, is all noon. We used to hear about it at lunch. Chelle brought her business worries to the family for sympathy and, I suspected, some practical advice. She got neither from Maître Marigny. Solange told me that he refused to have anything to do with his wife's property. He was a lawyer, but so far as he was concerned Bonneval was outside the law. It was well known that anyone might poach and pilfer, cheat and fiddle with impunity. The Maître would not trouble himself this side of Bordeaux and Madame

Marigny was no business woman. That left only Chelle, who was certainly a business child.

Whenever possible what was produced on the estate in the way of wood and fruit—even the sweet chestnuts were harvested by the indefatigable Chelle—provided on a barter system for something that was not produced: for butter, coal, bacon. A man called Pochart looked after the timber. There was a considerable acreage. Pochart had a cottage in the woods and a small cutting-plant and was recognised as a scoundrel. No one thought of sacking him, an honest bailiff was apparently as easy to find as an apple without a core.

Villainy Chelle must expect to cope with if she coped at all. Pochart was also known to have an illicit still in the woods, to manufacture his own spirits and to drink them. Everyone called him 'Pochard', which means 'boozer'—Chelle was also expected to cope with that. Madame Marigny didn't give it a thought anyway, and Maître Marigny had washed his hands of the property and everything pertaining to it, his daughter's safety included. I wondered what my parents would have made of that.

Chelle coped, I believe, as well as anyone could. She lacked years and experience, but she had the power to frighten Pochart out of his wits. When roused she was less than human, and anything to do with money could rouse her. Pochart had been known to swear that she wasn't a child, she was a devil.

Chelle haunted him. She believed he was selling timber behind her back, and all that summer, if she wasn't poring over her ledger in the office, she was in the woods trying to catch Pochart. She crept about like an Indian, Solange said she could move through brushwood without cracking a twig. Sometimes we would be lazing in the shade, not talking, the air still enough to hear the creak of the oxen's harness a mile away as they went round the vines, and we would look up and she'd be beside us, thin as a twig, with her old faded frock shrunk up to her knees and one of Monsieur Dubosque's split straw-hats weighing down on her ears.

I saw her in one of her rages once. It was unnerving, I wouldn't have thought there was room in her for so much passion. We were half-way through lunch when she came in, slipping silently as ever into her chair. Her hands were unwashed and there was sawdust in the roots of her hair. Madame Marigny reprimanded her, she apologised and poured herself a finger of red wine which she diluted with water. Solange asked her what she'd been doing. Chelle said she had been occupied with a serpent, a 'serpente à sonnettes'—a rattlesnake.

"Dans notre forêt?" asked Madame Marigny, taken with the idea, and Chelle said yes, in their forest. Valentin wanted to know if she had killed it and Chelle said she intended to next time she saw it. She took up a knife to show us—first she would dig out its eyes, then she would cut off its hands, then its feet—

"Feet? Hands?" said Valentin. "On a snake?"

"It was Pochard, wasn't it?" said Solange.

Chelle cried out that Pochart was a beast, a drunken pig, she would crush him like a cockroach.

"Tu as un ménagerie, ma petite," said Maître Marigny, relaxing his scars.

Chelle rose to her feet. Her face darkened horribly, it wasn't blood under her skin but some bitter gall. She spoke so fast, spitting out the words, that I couldn't follow the sense. Solange told me afterwards that Chelle had discovered that Pochart was allowing someone to cut wood in the forest and pocketing the money.

Chelle's anger was fantastic. She was consumed with it and it wasn't righteous, it was evil. I couldn't take my eyes off her. The child had become a monster, brilliant with venom. Her bones, arms, hands, even her spine, were hooked out of all humanity, and as she crouched over the table I thought that if Pochart was a cockroach she was a spider.

Maître Marigny went on eating his lunch, so did Valentin. Solange, smiling, crumbled bread. Madame Marigny murmured, "Chérie, chérie—"

Chelle did not hear. She was spitting Pochart's name and out of her mouth it came as an obscenity. I kept wondering what my parents would have thought or what anyone at home would have made of her. She was nine years old and she froze my blood.

Maître Marigny said, without looking up, "Assieds-toi," and Chelle obeyed. She sat down as if a switch had been thrown and a current stopped.

Madame Marigny appealed to her husband. "Qu'est-ce nous allons faire, alors?"

He shrugged. Chelle, a grubby child again, picked the sawdust out of her hair.

"Pochard!" Her tongue flickered out with the name on it.

Valentin's trouble with his father was no doubt a trouble for years, but to me it was all at tea-time because it came to one of its heads then.

Madame Marigny had what she called 'English tea' out of a silver pot, with hot milk and biscottes, at half-past four, on the terrace under the trees. One afternoon a business acquaintance of Maître Marigny's arrived. He was motoring through to Spain and professed great interest in seeing where Edouard Brindille had lived and died. Maître Marigny showed him round and brought him on to the terrace for tea.

I don't think the Maître was pleased to see this man. He was very courteous to him, but towards everyone else he was more than usually acid.

Solange and I had been knocking up on the tennis-court, we were hot and untidy, though I don't think we deserved his comment, as he presented us, about dirt being the privilege of the very young and the very old and only those of the years between must wash. We took our biscottes and sat at a distance on the stone balustrade where Solange amused herself trying to catch lizards.

Valentin had been lying on his back in the shade since lunch, only a yard or so from the tea-table. Maître Marigny ignored him, it was Madame who called him to be presented to the visitor.

Valentin was less presentable than we were. He wore a singlet and dirty shorts, his chest and arms were tripper's pink and peeling from the sun. He got up, blinking. Gravel was stuck all over his bare shoulders and Solange said, "Qu'il est paresseux!" with amusement.

I wasn't sure. If Valentin's questions were so unnecessary that only a lazy person would ask them, on the other hand a lazy person wouldn't seek so diligently for an answer. That afternoon he had told me that he proposed to examine the subject of death because at his age he could look at it academically and he had asked, politely, if I had yet considered the question. I said what question? Everyone died and there was the end of it. Of course Valentin wanted to know if it might not be the beginning or at least the middle of something else.

"You mean Heaven and all that?" I wasn't scornful, I had been brought up to take it for the top end of my scale of values.

But Valentin said death was nothing to do with religion, which startled me because I had always thought that dying was a Biblical thing.

I was sorry for Valentin, being called away from his meditations to face a complete and critical stranger. Watching him shamble over to the tea-table, I wondered if he might even question his father's visitor on the subject of death. I wouldn't have put it past him, he was eager, he seemed to hunger for other people's slants.

Madame Marigny, who had stayed seated only long enough to pour tea for the guest, went behind her son and presented him with a flourish, hands on his head, framing him as if he were a delectable picture. She saw nothing to be ashamed of, she never did see anything in front of her nose, she had to look over her shoulder.

The visitor's name was Latour. He wore a cream flannel suit striped with grey and smoked cigarettes through a silver holder. Solange and I had already entertained him, his smile as we were introduced was entirely to himself. Confronted with Valentin, he looked from him to Maître Marigny and back again with barely concealed surprise.

Of course they were chalk and cheese, or rather jet and cheese, a pop-eyed dreamy boy with his skin in shreds and his bare toes fishing in the dirt, and a senior lawyer dressed for the law in his sombre suit and his pure lawful linen, his burned-out face and his fingers tented together.

Solange said softly, "For papa it is—what do you call 'ennuyer'?"

"Boring?"

"It is boring that this man comes and sees us like this. He is a great talker, he will tell everyone."

Madame Marigny suddenly went off on one of her forays to the far end of the terrace, leaving Valentin facing the two men. Monsieur Latour asked him if he liked games. Valentin said no. Monsieur Latour suggested, with an eye to his grubbiness, that he was perhaps of a mechanical bent. Was it engines that interested him? Valentin shook his head. What then did interest him? Valentin smiled and shrugged. There was an awkward pause, the visitor toyed with his cigarette-holder.

Valentin, ducking his head politely, turned to go, but Maître Marigny, who had so far not said a word, called out sharply, "Attendez!"

Valentin waited. He looked at his father and Maître Marigny looked at him with the corrosive stare he used on his foes and friends alike. There was another pause, it was loaded and as it went on it became quite suffocating. Monsieur Latour said something graceful about the view—he might have been a cicada chirping for all the notice Maître Marigny took.

Solange nudged me. "You are going to see a little comedy."

She might laugh, I didn't think I'd be able to. Valentin pushed his toes into the grit and waited. He wouldn't look up, he was feeling his dirt, I don't think he'd been aware of it until then, no more than an animal is of the dirt on its fur.

Madame Marigny suddenly came hurrying back along the terrace. I thought she'd break things up because she certainly wouldn't notice the atmosphere, but she passed us without a glance and disappeared round the corner of the house.

Maître Marigny looked as if he were preparing a case. It

turned out that he was, against his son. He picked up a spoon and rang it against the side of a cup.

"A quoi est-ce que tu t'intéresses?"

Poor Valentin. No wonder he went a sort of scalded mauve over his sunburn. How could he tell his father what interested him, the 'questions' that he worried at as he mooched and lay about? 'Death,' could he say, "I've been interested in death this afternoon, whether it's a graduation or an end", and trust Maître Marigny to take it as gospel and not as impudence? He did the only thing he could, he shrugged.

Monsieur Latour suggested that it was also the privilege of the young to do nothing. Maître Marigny began interrogating Valentin. It was really a cross-examination conducted, I'm sure, as Maître Marigny would have conducted it in court. Sometimes Valentin got no time to reply, one question was overshot by the next, answered by it, re-formed and presented as a statement of fact that damned or denigrated or poked mild fun with all the wisdom and tolerance on Maître Marigny's side and all the stupidity on Valentin's. Sometimes Valentin was left high and dry, his tongue in his open mouth visibly searching for an answer. Then Maître Marigny would tell him to take time, to think back and not be too modest. One minute he was calling him 'mon fils', 'mon vieux', the next he was firing words, rattling them off the side of the cup with the spoon and laughing—if you could call it laughter, a quacking sound with his mouth going down instead of up.

It was like bringing out a sawmill to cut up a seedling and everybody was embarrassed while it lasted—not for Valentin, for Maître Marigny. He, of all people, was showing off. I'd seen him as a mostly malignant superman who could, if he wished, bring off things that my own father would have blenched at and it was a shock to me to find him out in such a childish failing. Valentin looked sick, even his shame was for his father, not for himself.

Madame Marigny ended the scene. She came running out of the library with Brindille's book and oblivious of anything but her duty as hostess, began to pour tea and read poetry for Monsieur Latour.

Solange got the giggles as Madame Marigny's high murmurous voice took over from her husband's, and the visitor, dazed by the switch, had to ease a finger under his collar. Valentin remained where he was, head bent, until a click of his father's fingers released him.

Shortly after, Chelle raced by in her shrunken dress, shrieking and battering after an escaping hen. Maître Marigny waved a hand at her and told Monsieur Latour that this also was his child. He probably felt that his debasement should be complete.

I expected that that would be the end of it and a good thing too, but next day Solange told me that Valentin was to go to St Cyr.

"A school for soldiers," she said.

"Does he want to be a soldier?"

"Idiot! It is my father who thinks it will be good for him."

"Good?"

"Teach him to march and shoot and stick his neck up."

"But he'll hate it—"

"Of course. Or my father would not do it."

"But why?"

"To pay him. My father always pays people."

That I could believe. "But Valentin isn't people, he's his son."

"You are a fool, Rose."

I sought out Valentin. "Is it true you have to go to military school?"

"My father has said so."

"That's awful! You won't like it at all!"

"Don't disturb yourself," Valentin said kindly. "I shall not be a soldier."

I didn't see how he could get out of it and I was relieved when Madame Marigny asked the Curé to speak to her husband.

Solange, Valentin and I were setting off for a walk one afternoon and we met Father Benedict on his way up to the Château.

He greeted us gaily. "I am glad to have seen you, Valentin, because I am about to talk to your father on the subject of your—" he winked—"military training."

Valentin murmured something about its not being necessary.

"Then you wish to go to St Cyr?"

"I do not," said Valentin definitely.

"Perhaps you think I have no influence with Monsieur le Maître?"

"It isn't that. I beg your pardon, Father, I'm very grateful to you for taking the trouble."

"Ah well," said the Curé briskly, "we shall soon see what is necessary."

"I'm glad you're going to try, anyway," I said in English. "It's awful to think of Valentin stabbing sandbags and all that."

The Curé raised his eyebrows, but when Solange had translated he burst out laughing. "My child," he said kindly, 'ma petite' I think he called me, which sounds much nicer— "St Cyr is not like that, never fear. It is a complete education, a very fine one." He turned to Valentin. "What do you wish to do?"

"Do?"

"In life you will wish to do something, to be something."

"I don't wish to be," Valentin said calmly. 'I *am*.'

"That is enough?"

Solange laughed. "It is enough that he is lazy."

The Curé shook his head. "Valentin is not lazy. When his mind enquires he cannot choose but try to answer it."

He smelt holy even in the sunshine. It was a pity his faith was misdirected: being Roman Catholic was not as bad as being an unbeliever, but I did wonder what the position was with regard to godliness that did not come from the right God.

He was saying to Valentin, without irony or fun, "How have you answered?"

"I haven't, but I will."

"You believe there is an answer to everything?"

78

"Of course." Valentin added cryptically, "We are complete."

"Only in God," said the Curé.

It occurred to me that his God could be the right one approached through the wrong channels. It occurred to me also that I knew little about Roman Catholicism. What did they believe? Something to do with the Virgin Mary. I supposed God wouldn't be too hard on them for worshipping his own mother.

"Is it wrong to ask?" said Valentin.

"A question is not wrong. The answer may be."

"Sans doute," Solange said unkindly, "when he takes his bachot."

"Do you always ask yourself, my son?" said the Curé. "Do you never ask God?"

"I've been given a brain and I intend to use it." Valentin said roughly, "I don't expect God to tell me everything. Do you?"

"I have no other expectations."

There was a special intimacy in his voice, at once humble and proud. We all felt a bit put out and wouldn't look at him, though he was looking at us and out of the corner of my eye I saw that he was bringing us into his smile.

He left us to go on to the Château. We watched him stride away, ornate and black, his cassock swinging gracefully. At the bend of the path he turned to wave.

"Perhaps he is stupid," said Valentin.

"He's good," said Solange. "That makes him very happy."

I said to Valentin, "It's jolly nice of him to go and talk to your father. If anyone can make him change his mind, the Curé will."

"My father won't send me to St Cyr."

"How do you know?" He shrugged, but I insisted. "Why won't he?" and I remember that Valentin, who was polite and always talked to me in English, lapsed into French.

"Il s'en fiche."

"What?"

"He doesn't care enough to do it." He went to where the

dust was thickest and hottest and pushed his bare feet into it, one at a time. "I would prefer if he did."

Solange said scornfully, "You would prefer he should take you up like his little dog and keep you in his lap. You would prefer he should not let you out of his sight so there should be nothing for you to do, nowhere for you to go."

Valentin went on slowly and pleasurably running the hot dust into his toes.

"Well that is not what I want," said Solange. "No one shall tell me what to do. I shall do always as I wish." She had her hands on her hips, teasing us. "I wish already there was no papa, no maman, no Valentin, no Chelle, no Rose to tell me what to do—"

"I don't tell you what to do!"

She picked up my plait of hair and danced round me with it as if I were a maypole. "You tell me, but I don't do it."


I expect I did try to tell her. It was inconceivable to me how everything slipped away in that household. At home when we talked we planned, even if it was just how to remake the garden, or a day's outing, and we carried through our plans. The Marignys talked of 'l'année dernière', but never of the future and not of the present with any decision. Chelle was the only one who did anything. They really were 'en vacance' at Bonneval: if not content with, they were acquiescent in its timelessness. At home every day had its character whether it was a holiday or not. I could have been dropped out of the blue into Beckenham and I'd have known at once that it was Monday or Friday. And imagine not being able to tell Sunday!

At Bonneval there was no use for the days of the week or the time of the day. You could walk through the village and it would be shuttered against the heat, there might be a chicken scratching about and an old woman emptying a pail—there was always an old woman doing something. They opened the shutters and sat outside their houses and played boules in the road when it got a little cooler, which was when the sun went down, which was as near as they came to clock time. I suppose they had no business with it, only needs—theirs and the land they worked. They got hungry so they had a meal, they got tired so they went to bed: the seasons came round, they might be soon or they might be late, but that had nothing to do with the calendar. On Sundays everyone went to Mass, I daresay only because the church bell reminded them.

The weather did have something to do with it. In a colder or a wetter climate they'd have hustled about. Here, where the same prodigal heat was spent on the green grapes and the dust in the ditches there was no incentive, the air would have blunted anything like a qualm or a worry.

The Marignys probably gave themselves up to it the moment they got off the train. I used to wonder what they were like in Paris. I couldn't imagine them anywhere but here, what they were here I took to be their basic selves, stripped of business and social etceteras.

But perhaps they weren't complete and that would explain why they seemed to be lacking, why they didn't take anything seriously—because they didn't take Bonneval seriously.

I didn't think of it then, to me they were irresponsible people, especially Maître Marigny who held himself in abeyance. Still wearing his dark formal clothes he appeared at intervals for meals or a constitutional on the terrace. He was so acid and dry that even the heat couldn't involve him. I don't remember ever seeing him put out a hand to anyone, and when he interrogated Valentin in front of Monseiur Latour he used a probe, not his finger.

Solange said it was because he disliked Bonneval. He went there on sufferance, not by so much as one word of advice would he help his wife manage her property. He wanted it ruined or shut up, most of all he wanted it sold.

"Then we could have a villa at Arcachon," said Solange. "A cake house, you know?"

"A what?"

She squared her hands. "Like this, very à la mode, and white like an iced cake. We would have a roof garden and sun umbrellas and you, my poor Rose, would swim all day in the sea and make your chests big."

"Chest," I told her sharply. "It's singular unless you're talking about several people. And I'm not keen on swimming."

Actually I was with Maître Marigny about the villa, it would be more fun than Bonneval. I also felt that Madame Marigny was right to keep the Château in the family.

Even in those days when everything was cheaper it must have cost a lot to maintain. She tried to make it self-supporting, but she was no manager and there was only Chelle to watch her interests.

Chelle cared, Chelle was serious, Chelle had made herself responsible and that was the last straw, the final affront to common sense and normality. A nine-year-old child running a business, juggling with the accounts, haggling, cheating and being cheated, her father not bothering to look on and her mother not knowing what she was looking on. If I told them that at home they wouldn't believe me, they'd think it was only how it seemed.

One day we took a barrowload of small plums—'mirabelles', they were called—to one of the farms to be exchanged for butter. We were all going because the barrow was heavy and Chelle couldn't manage it by herself. At the last moment Madame Marigny said she would come too. Chelle pulled a face. Solange told me that Chelle liked everything on a business footing whereas her mother was apt to play the 'grande dame'.

We set off, Valentin and Chelle trundling the barrow, Solange and I on either side to keep the plums from toppling, and Madame Marigny strolling in the rear. It was a long walk to the farm. We had to wait while Madame Marigny made sorties to pick wild flowers and examine the butterflies and other insects. We were more like four adults and she the child. She kept exclaiming and running after us with this and that and once we lost sight of her completely. The only clue was some gigantic yellow cow parsley threshing about as she moved among it.

"Quelle idiote!" raged Chelle.

When we drew near the farm two huge, gaunt dogs rushed at us, barking savagely. Chelle screamed at them and they slunk round behind us, growling. Madame Marigny, harassed by the dogs, dropped her flowers. I was going back to pick them up for her but Solange said, "Leave them, they are rubbish," and called sharply, "Dépêche-toi, maman!"

I was sorry for Madame Marigny, but I need not have been. She hadn't noticed that her flowers were gone. As we reached the house two women ran out, one hastily pinning up her hair and the other pulling at her apron. Madame Marigny greeted them serenely and they chased the chickens out of her path and ushered her in with as much bowing and hand spreading as if it were a golden coach instead of a broken-down farmhouse.

Chelle shovelled some plums into the skirt of her dress and went off with it held up above her skinny thighs.

Solange said, "Maman is a fool, Chelle is a peasant."

Valentin took my arm. "Come, Rose, you shall see this farm."

It was a surprising place. First we looked into the room where Madame Marigny was being entertained. The women had brought out a bottle of wine and Madame Marigny was sitting at one end of a huge settle. The other end was piled with blankets and a quilt as if it were used for a bed. The room was very big but crowded, besides the furniture there were barrels and baskets and logs and sacks and half-plucked chickens and more blankets heaped on the floor.

"They cannot sleep upstairs," said Valentin. "The roof is fallen."

The ceiling of this room didn't look very safe. It was cracked from end to end, black with smoke and cobwebs and hung with skeleton bunches of herbs, sides of bacon and the bodies of hares with bloody bags over their noses.

Madame Marigny sipped her wine. The women were talking to her both at once, pouring out troubles long bottled up or glorying in something—I couldn't tell which. They had urchin voices and a strange accent.

Valentin said they were Normans. They worked well but were bad-tempered.

I said they weren't very clean either and he smiled. "You will see."

I certainly had a surprise when I saw the animals' quarters. They were a miracle of cleanliness and modernity, tiled in white and equipped with running water and electric light. The stove where the pig-swill was cooking would have put many a kitchen range to shame for the depth of its polish. I think the pigs themselves had been scrubbed, their trotters were like newly shone shoes.

One of the sons was a hunchback. He wore a torn singlet, the lump on his spine stretching it taut like a fist in a glove. He followed us round, bursting with pride and talking incomprehensible Norman French. We had to see everything, the cows—curry-combed and immaculate; the young bull with a hide like velvet and a gold ring through his nose; the horses, bright as chestnuts, their manes and tails hanging smoother than my own hair. One slender mare with a wild white eye was kept to pull the black-and-silver gig: the man fetched an egg and cracked it for her and she ate it and delicately dropped the shell into his hand.

"You see, Rose," said Valentin, "the beasts live like people and the people live like beasts." The hunchback nodded and grinned at us, showing his black teeth.

Chelle came back to the barrow of plums followed by the farmer. He was saturnine and unshaven, black beard guttered down his jaw, he had the pink-rimmed angry eyes of a pig. But Chelle looked a match for him, she was sharpened up for business, talking as fast, and to me as incomprehensibly, as the hunchback.

She was picking up plums and displaying them in her palm, she broke one open and thrust it at the farmer, thrust it right into his mouth. He spat it out immediately. Thereupon Chelle worked her arms in deep and brought up plums from the bottom of the barrow to prove that they were as good as the top ones. This man was not talkative, he walked round the barrow, estimating its capacity, and then he said something which caused Chelle to throw up her hands and try to wheel the barrow away. She couldn't, the load was too heavy. Shoving, scarlet in the face, she shouted over her shoulder. Whatever it was seemed to anger the farmer. He spat in her direction, kicked at a chicken that came near his boot and went into the house. Chelle followed him, so did Valentin and I, as far as the doorway.

I found it embarrassing, this palaver to get a pound or two of butter on the cheap. Madame Marigny had money to buy it at the shop, she did anyway when there were no mirabelles. I would have preferred to do without butter altogether than tangle with these people.

Madame Marigny wasn't tangling. She was in the farmhouse kitchen sipping wine and the two women were with her. They were still talking, with battering tongues and hedgerow-gipsy faces turning and swooping. The farmer was in the doorway and the hunchback had come in from the yard. Solange leaned against the wall. Everyone was there, everyone standing except Madame Marigny, who sat smiling through a cloud of grace.

The younger woman suddenly crouched down and pulled her dress off her shoulders and showed her back covered with liver-blue bruises. Madame Marigny looked serenely— they might have been marks on the floor—the other woman threw out a spitting of words. Then the farmer said something and whatever it was got through Madame Marigny's cloud. She went pink, china pink spread from her cheeks down to her neck and up under her hair. The hunchback burst out laughing; his jaws working with joy set the women laughing too.

I asked Valentin what it was about and he said that the men beat their wives and the wives liked it. I was hurt, there was no need for a snub, if he didn't want to answer he only had to say so.

The farmer grinned across the room to Madame Marigny. She smiled, tightly at first, then she put up her hand and covered her mouth—she was laughing. Everyone was, except Chelle, gnawing at a plum. The woman with the bruises spun round and round like a top, slapping laughter out of herself.

\*

I badly wanted the Marignys to commit themselves. If I could have found them out in one thing which they had to stand by, couldn't drift away from, leave high and dry—or low and dirty as they had left the people at the farm—I could have excused them and been comfortable. A proselytising itch wouldn't let me be. I wasn't a crusader, it was just that I had no doubts, I could have put the world right— I didn't need to, of course, because there had never been much wrong with it. That there could be attitudes to life hadn't dawned on me, there was life and there were rules which the Marignys, allowing for foreignness, heat and Catholicism, ought to have kept as everyone else did, except lunatics and criminals. I was lucky I could still believe that at twelve years old: the Marignys, had I known it, were a first gentle intimation that I shouldn't.

All that summer I tried to see where they were pinned down and Solange I tried to pin down where I thought she ought to be. My interrogations of her had a way of coming back to myself. It was difficult to get a straight or satisfactory answer out of her and she invariably turned the tables and heckled me. I entertained rather than puzzled her. She wasn't involved enough to more than wonder, momentarily, about anyone, and I expect she found me a bit of a freak. My interests were games and film stars, and I was a voracious reader of schoolgirl fiction. My world was in Beckenham with outer planets such as Bexhill and Dymchurch where we went for holidays. As soon as I left it Bonneval became a planet too, a lunar and, my tastes being what they were, not such an attractive one.

Solange was a great gossip. She gossipped at me rather than with me. I suspect she was also a fancifier, mystification being her amusement that summer. She wouldn't accept my small talk in kindred spirit, she picked it up for puncturing and twisting and open scorn. I had to take some sweeping if not crashing statements from her, and if I jibbed she would either be French and shrug, or Marigny and bubble.

When I knew that she and Chelle went to a convent school in Paris I imagined them learning only sewing and enough Latin to read their missals. I was surprised, and chagrined, to find that Solange took the same subjects as I did and her class at school was farther advanced in all of them. By her account that was, and she wasn't likely to dream up American history which we hadn't begun, and trigonometry which was still a threat. On the other hand, did nuns know about such things? Weren't they limited to holy ritual, lives of the saints and Hail Mary's?

It was the sort of discrepancy I encountered with all the Marignys: there was Chelle, touting plums and haggling over a pound of butter they could well afford to buy: Valentin, asking himself questions that weren't intended for answering: Maître Marigny, a legal eminence letting his wife be rooked by peasants; and Bonneval, which was historic because of Brindille and slightly comic because of the hatpin and which none of them wanted. Even Chelle who fought to keep it wanted the fight, not Bonneval.

I thought I had a logical sticking point in Solange's attitude to religion and I could have been satisfied with just that. After all, she was a foreigner, her religion was not right nor proper nor even clean—witness, thought I, their saints and martyrs, the awful and dirty lengths they went to get sanctified—but better for Solange to believe even that sort of thing because I could at least relinquish her. If she believed nothing at all I couldn't see how to accept her in the first place.

We talked about Catholicism. I asked and she answered and on the whole she was ready to answer, she was explicit. She must have been irritated by my crassitude, and she had reason. I shudder now to think of the things I said: why did Catholics worship the mother of God instead of God Himself? Did their priests wear skirts because their God was a woman? Was it true that they could sin all day provided they confessed in the evening? Or that they could pray first and sin after—the bigger the sin the longer the prayer, and for robbery to murder they could pray on the instalment system? Did Solange think she was married to Christ? What did she actually say as she told her beads?

Solange, who was ready enough in other respects to mock and mystify, showed herself patient and sincere when it came to answering my stupid questions about her faith. She really seemed to want to make me understand, ignorance such as mine was an offence.

"We cannot lose our sin unless we resolve also to be better. And this we must do from the heart. Nous devons promettre de tout coeur de ne jamais commetre ces mêmes péchés."

"Anyone can promise anything, and mean it at the time. If you eat too much chocolate you can promise never to touch it again and that's not being saved, that's being sick."

"I think anyway it is the same thing for the stomach and for the heart."

I wasn't interested in the Catholic faith so much as in Solange's. I got the impression that neither could be lightly put aside. I was a bit disappointed to find that Catholicism wasn't so lurid and fetishtistic as I'd thought, and this brought Solange a peg or two nearer my estimation of normal.

I was easier with her while I could believe in her belief, and I was ready to take the rest of the family on the same terms, which shows how hard put I was to find others. Though I wasn't devout, I could no more visualise the Establishment without a Heaven than a room without a ceiling. God went without saying, so did the fact that one cleaned one's teeth before going to bed. It was on fundamentals rather than terms that I was taking the Marignys and stretching the point because to my mind their fundamentals were sadly misplaced. For the first time since coming to Bonneval I was, if not reassured, at least resigned to these people. I could let them alone. Latched on to heresy, I could feel pity for their delusion.

It was Solange's idea to go to a confirmation service in the local church. She may have meant it to enlighten me but more likely she hoped it would be entertaining for us all.

There weren't many occasions made for us at the Château. As I've said, we were left to our own devices. For one reason and another Solange never did come to stay with me, but if she had, my parents would have taken us about and shown her everything of interest and I dare say we'd even have hankered after some time to ourselves.

Anything we did that was rounded and eventful, like the visit to Bordeaux, as distinct from the long blanket-day at the Château, has a place in my mind like furniture in a room, and what happened in the church at Bonneval is furniture that I cannot shift or do away with.

Details persist, irrelevancies have combined over the years to give the event its special inhumanity and horror. I remember Solange's dress, which was bright yellow, the colour of cheap lemonade and I thought wrong for going to church in. And my hat, a white straw trimmed with cornflowers, had simply been my best until then. Thereafter it acquired a significance, a dedication to the day. Solange twisted a chiffon scarf round her hair and looked ten years older. She probably wanted to, it was only a little while since she had been confirmed, but I was very conscious of her seeming sophistication.

Valentin came to the service though he chose not to walk with us. He followed about a hundred yards behind and when we stopped he stopped too and stood with his head down like a waiting horse. Solange said he was 'affairé' and when I said that he didn't look busy she said that I didn't look anything although I was, she supposed, some classifiable lump of something.

It was uncalled-for, I wasn't criticising Valentin, but she would have said it anyway, out of the blue if necessary. I think she had been waiting to deliver it as a pronouncement rather than a gibe because it was her concluded and irrevocable opinion of me.

I wasn't used to being misjudged. People tended to trust me and take my word on the very face value that Solange denied. That she, slippery and equivocal, should be the one to deny it proved her own insufficiency. So I managed to think, and was ready to tell her, but I didn't get the chance. The bell rang for the service and she started to run and Valentin came up and put his fists in our backs, hustling us. I remember the dirt smoking up as we ran and it seemed to me to epitomise the moral and spiritual poverties of the place. This Catholic place. What else could I blame, apart from its not being English?

That smell which the Curé had about him, of hot pencils and wax, was a power inside the small church. To me it was like a great aromatic sleeve that would wrap round and stifle those who clung to it. It is, now, the sweet holy smell of what happened.

There were six children being confirmed, three girls and three boys. Confirmed in what? They came, two by two, down the aisle, the girls in white dresses and veils like brides and the boys in their best suits with white sashes on their left arms. Each carried a small wreath of white flowers. I looked at them with curiosity as if they were going to damnation: to my way of thinking, they were.

The church was filled with women in black and some younger children wearing clean pinafores. They had dressed up, put on something special and the Curé was there with a sort of embroidered bookmarker round his neck, all bloomy in the light of the candles. That's the colour of it, that pinky gold, tender and grand—I've hated it ever since.

There was an enormous figure of St Thérèse of Lisieux haloed with roses. Behind every rose blazed an electric light bulb. It all looked as if the paint was still wet, the Saint's apple cheeks and yellow sausage curls glistened with newness. I thought of our chemist's shop at home where they had something very similar, except for the roses—an eight-foot model of Hygeia to advertise health salts.

I sat down, I was present as an observer and had no intention of taking part in the service. Someone would see that, I thought, and nudge someone else and that would go on until they all knew that there was an unbeliever in their midst and then they would murmur and the murmur would grow to a clamour, drowning the singing and the organ music and they would turn on me and buffet me with their hands and throw me out because I wasn't one of them. It didn't frighten me, I folded my arms across my chest and frowned at the altar. I felt absolutely right, a bulwark of truth in the midst of heresy.

No one took any notice of me, except Father Benedict

who smiled and lifted his hand, almost waving, over the heads of the children. They sang, standing shoulder to shoulder. Everybody sang, the organist loudest of all. She was a young, fat woman in a fruit hat and she had the lungs of a London coster. I didn't sing though I'd have liked to, it was as rousing, whatever they were singing, as 'We plough the fields and scatter', which is my favourite hymn. I looked up at the roof to show disapproval and disassociation, then I worried lest they might think I was praying. I couldn't look down at the floor for the same reason, so I stared in front of me at a swarthy boy in a frilled shirt and long white socks. He is the only one of the children I remember individually and his the only reactions. The rest massed together like the general hubbub of a storm.

The children being confirmed had to walk in procession round the church and they formed up, two by two, with robed boys carrying a golden cross and censer in front and the priest following behind them. But they had gone only a few steps when the boy with the frilled shirt ducked out of line and ran back to the congregation. He had forgotten his wreath of flowers—nor could he find it at once because it had dropped under his chair.

The procession came to a bewildered stop, the boys and girls looking back over their shoulders and the last pair, trying to keep going, blundered into the ones in front. Father Benedict was taken aback, he stood with brows raised and hands on his hips, and the organist, craning to see what was happening, played a jumble of wrong chords. Solange, of course, was laughing, and just as the swarthy boy groped under his chair she nudged the wreath out of his reach with her foot.

But he found it. He said, "Le voilà!" and showed it to everyone before he carried it back to his place in the procession hanging from his hand like a spare tyre. The procession shuffled on again with the organ music battering after. Father Benedict followed. He held his hands palm to palm and smiled up as he walked, sharing the joke, I expect, with the angels.

Finally they lined up before the altar and were pledged

to renounce their sins and accept God all their days. By God, of course, I reminded myself, they meant the Virgin. They simply weren't looking high enough, their concepts must be profane or mean if they couldn't grasp the facts of sublime Genesis. Or were they all being kept in the dark for some creaming-off purpose, to afford special privilege and entitlement to the chosen? I found it hard to believe that Father Benedict, for instance, had a mean or profane mind.

I had to admit that wherever his prayers were going they went well. He had a nice tenor voice, every prayer was an aria and I liked the way he used his hands to offer, shape and present what he said. It was so courteous, a change from the apocryphal delivery of our vicar at home; his was a take-it-or-leave-it attitude, even to God.

Listening to Father Benedict I wondered if, after all, the thing, the important thing, might be to pray, the act of faith, to ask of and confide in an almightiness, whatever the name, provided it was an almighty goodness.

This thought, which had never occurred to me before, seemed at once blasphemous and sound. I didn't know what to do with it, but as I sat there it began to settle into a conviction. Perhaps I'd got an answer—though I wasn't the one who made a purpose of asking. The nature of goodness would have seemed to me academic if ever I'd thought about it. Now that I came to think, I saw that it needn't be national or sectarian. It could be, it ought to be, universal. So there wouldn't be quibbles from above at the purely regional labels that were put on it at this end.

It might have been a nice idea to have had at twelve years old if I could have held on to it. I still remember what a spacious feeling it was and I realised even then that there would be more to it than the immediate relief of not being in the company of souls already lost. I was happy, selflessly and spiritually happy for two or three minutes.

Most people have had experiences like that, once or twice in their lifetimes. I read somewhere that such sensations are quite physical in origin, something like the feeling of well-being you can have when you're about to catch a cold, a sort of screwing and priming of all the natural defences of the body. Anyway, it didn't last, I might have become a crank or a missionary if it had.

The Curé had blessed the children and was turned away, praying for them and, I think, for all of us, when the thing happened. There was first a soft stirring sound like a small creature moving about overhead. I looked up but I couldn't see anything.

Father Benedict went on praying. When he stopped it was too late. The rustling was followed by a sharp cracking like a burst of fireworks, then a dragging, tearing noise, and then silence, which was like nothing and kept on and on for days.

It was the figure, the eight-foot-high figure of St Thérèse of Lisieux which had been dedicated only a few months ago and now was breaking from its supports. I have as perfect a picture of that pink vacuous face descending—roses, wiring, plaster-dust and all—as if it had happened in the slowest of slow motion. It seems to me now that there was ample time, there must have been, for Father Benedict to get clear. Someone shouted to him, but he didn't move. He stood there, stopped in his prayer, hands clasped, looking up. He could have saved himself, there was no question of saving anyone else, the children and all of us in the front rows of the congregation had crowded back into the aisles.

Perhaps he was still miles away in his prayer, or perhaps he was paralysed with fright, or it was like a nightmare and he couldn't move. Perhaps he was stupid, as Valentin had said. Anyway, he just waited, not lifting a finger to shield his face, for St Thérèse to hit him.

The statue was of wood and heavy, though I don't think the body of it touched him. The damage was done by an electric light bulb in the halo. The plaster roses came down sideways, with the most momentum, and the bulb, already broken, sheared into his upturned cheek. Then the statue, crashing to the floor, seemed to rebound and twist until it lay with its sausage curls on the altar steps and its big dimpled feet on the altar-cloth. Father Benedict spun round, showing us the terrible havoc of his face, then sank submissively to his knees. There he stayed until the organist ran to him and touched his shoulder. He keeled over then. He had fainted.

As I said, I don't remember anyone's reactions in detail, except the swarthy boy's. There was a lot of noise, screaming women, crying children, someone hysterical, but the silence was where they could not break it. They all crowded round the high altar, it was impossible to see the Curé and I was glad. I stayed where I was, so did the swarthy boy. He sat down and pulled his white wreath to pieces.

After a while Valentin came and took my arm. He said they had sent for the doctor, there was nothing we could do and we had better go.

I was still raw with shock when supper-time came that evening. I'd been close enough to see clearly what the electric light bulb had done to Father Benedict's face. There was something else that was going to worry me if I looked at it, another answer, a likely one, to my question. I was trying not to look at that, but the Marignys picked it up and brandished it at me.

Maître Marigny was thinking of the legal side. He talked about something called the Curia, and compensation from the ecclesiastical furnishers at Angoulême who had made and erected the St Thérèse. I don't know if he was talking seriously or frivolously or to himself. I never could tell with him but I didn't expect him to be human.

I see now that he was the only one who looked at the matter from Father Benedict's standpoint. Perhaps it wasn't Father Benedict's only standpoint, perhaps not the right or final one—I hope it wasn't—but either from kindness or force of professional habit Maître Marigny did give thought to a problem that was not his own.

Madame Dubosque, when she carried in the soup, said that the Father had been taken to hospital in Bordeaux. The local doctor's opinion was that he would lose the sight of one eye and be badly disfigured on the left side of his face. Madame Dubosque blamed the statue itself. It was damned. She had it on good authority—did not her belle-soeur have a cousin in Angoulême?—that it was modelled after the likeness of a local woman of bad repute.

I doubted the likeness, not the reputation—that statue had a face as blank as a button mould.

Solange and Valentin were amused about the model. They teased Madame Dubosque with a knowingness that puzzled and discomforted me. I neither knew what was making them laugh or how they were able to.

Maître Marigny grimaced because the soup was too salty. Madame was lost to some prospect of her own. I didn't have anything to occupy my hands because I wasn't hungry. I stared in front of me until old Tin-Tin leaned across the table and pulled faces at me.

When she had gone to fetch the next course Solange said that perhaps it was fortunate that Monsieur le Curé had had experience among the lepers. I remember how she spoke, politely and formally as she might start a conversation with strangers and I looked for a loophole, a word I had missed. I thought not even Solange would say that, and then Maître Marigny remarked that of course one could see one's own mutilation in every unmarked face.

I looked at Valentin. Had he no questions? Or wasn't this useless enough to ask? I thought, of course not, because it is answerable and they all have the answer. They didn't know that I needed to be told. I should have to make them know. At the risk of ridicule, and of Maître Marigny's sarcasm I must make them see that I badly needed to be told. I had one question to put, it had already made a hundred others, but they could give me their one almighty reason to satisfy the lot.

Maître Marigny began to serve our plates from the main dishes. I always watched him do that, he had such a delicate derogatory method of dissecting the food. He said—and the euphemism bothered me afterwards—that it might be a little difficult for Father Benedict to continue with his chosen career.

"He'll have the other eye," said Solange.

Maître Marigny spoke directly to his wife—something he seldom did—first tapping on her glass to bring her back from wherever she was. Monsieur le Curé, he said, was a vain man in that he had a private mind and a closed religion. He was therefore ambitious, said Maître Marigny, believing that his capacity for good should be given preference. Bonneval was but a phase, he had a goal set. Maître Marigny suspected, wryly, that it entailed a cardinal's hat.

Madame Marigny was attending. She fanned herself with the scarf bit of her dress, she was hot, perhaps, because she was angry.

Her husband went on, as he rolled little round roast potatoes on to our plates, that if Father Benedict's appearance was greatly spoiled he might find himself unacceptable in the sphere of his choice. A lawyer could be disfigured without prejudice to his professional chances—here Maître Marigny tightened his own seamed cheeks—and a priest of character might overcome it. But not Father Benedict.

He meant, I suppose, that what other people saw in him had been Father Benedict's best chance. He may have been right, I hardly knew the Curé, but I thought I knew enough of Maître Marigny to see that he would twist the best of everyone.

Madame Marigny cried, "How ridiculous!" and we waited for her to go on from there. She looked at everyone, except her husband, with her normally protuberant eyes straining out of their sockets, but she spoke not another word.

Solange said, "I shan't mind looking at him."

"Will you mind, Maman?" asked Valentin.

"Of course not."

"When he blesses you?"

"Why should I?"

"When he says Mass will you look at him?"

"Naturally!"

"Won't that be like offering the Host on a broken Paten?" said Solange.

They were teasing her as I would never presume to tease either of my parents, but what sickened me was their teasing on *this* point. I blamed their father for starting it, for acidifying their minds.

I asked my question, I asked why it had happened. I

couldn't see why, I couldn't really, unless I'd been right in the first place and God was a strict God and jealous, and Hell was every other denomination. If that was the case I'd have to ask what was there to choose between earth and a heaven governed with that blend of spite and officialdom. "Why did it happen?" I asked Maître Marigny, but I looked round at them all, I was ready to take the answer from anyone.

"Because the rivets pulled out of the wall," said Valentin.

"Because St Thérèse didn't like the statue," said Solange.

I meant why had it happened to Father Benedict, I said, while he was in church and while he was praying. Solange pretended to take my hand to coax my wits. Where was the statue? The statue was in the church above the altar. And where did the priest most often pray? He prayed at the altar. So where else could it happen?

That was how it happened, I said, but I wanted to know *why*.

For once nobody spoke. Maître Marigny laid down his fork and they all looked at me. I was determined. They knew the reason why, they only had to open a mouth to tell me. I was worried, though, that if Maître Marigny opened his mouth a flow of words would come out which I might not understand. It would be best if Madame answered.

I asked her: "Why did it happen to the Curé, he's a good man, isn't he? And he was praying!"

Although she was looking, it wasn't where one usually does look at other people, but right through my forehead to a spot at the back of my skull. I don't believe she ever looked at anyone, I don't think she would have recognised me if we'd met in the street a week after I left Bonneval.

It was Maître Marigny who answered and he merely said, "God knows."

"But don't you?"

"There would be no need for God if I did." And I remember his pouring and drinking a glass of wine with a briskness that made it plain that he thought me a fool.

Solange often told me that I was 'simpliste'. I was indeed over-simple for my age, but by the time I left Bonneval I began to appreciate that rich and poor, good and bad were only subdivisions because there was, primarily, another sort.

# PART THREE

"You must do as you wish."

"I hoped you'd see my reason."

"Believe me, I do."

There was satisfaction in seeing it so clearly, a relief in being able to despise someone so completely. But Rose was angry, too, with an anger which she drew upon. No one had inspired it, not even Cade. The offence was rooted and pertained to the whole business of Hilda Loeb's bequest. Perhaps to more. Rose only knew that she had a fund of rage for moments such as this.

"I was at fault in the first place. If I'd thought twice before agreeing to serve on the Committee I'd have seen how liable I must be to the fear of appropriation—my own fear, of course. It won't help me to do justice either way. Falling over backwards to be fair," said Cade wryly.

"In the very first place I was at fault for asking you. Or should we go back to the place before that and blame Hilda for leaving the money?"

"We were friends, Rose—a good deed can't spoil that."

"One wouldn't think so, but there's the naughty world to complicate matters."

Cade got up with a helpless dusting of his hands and went to the window. He stood looking at his 'sublime' view of potting-shed, clothes-post, currant bushes. He was an ordinary man and it had recommended him to Rose in the past, she had sympathised with his efforts to make himself extraordinary, a man of God. He would never be that, not in a thousand years. It was not that he didn't amount, he wasn't even in the same column as, for instance, Father Benedict.

If any man had the right to assign himself to God, Father Benedict had. He was chosen, marked down, one might say. Apart from his personal disaster and what he had made of it there was a quality about him which she only remembered because it had grown up, later. In conclusion, she might say, and for good and all, he had singularity—which was the first essential for a leader, especially of souls, whereas Eric Cade was not one but a personification of the many.

"If you're not going to serve on the Committee who will look out for the church's needs?"

Cade turned, straight-faced. "I'm sure I can rely on you to do that."

"Can you? I'm not an officer of the church, not even a deaconness. But I'll do my temporal best."

"It's a wonderful thing to know where one's duty is."

He spoke without irony or malice. Rose could detect a hint of wistfulness. She said, "I find no difficulty in this instance."

Cade had nothing to say to that. He relapsed into his thoughts, unhappy ones, which did not appear to include Rose or his present whereabouts.

"Will you stay to tea?"

Previously she would have brought it for them both without asking. Rousing himself, he recognised the distinction.

"Thank you, better not." But he made no move to go.

Rose picked up and folded a newspaper. "Everyone's most concerned about Mrs Peachey, but, relatively speaking, she's comfortable."

"Comfortable?" He, anyway, couldn't have looked bleaker. "Relative to what?"

Rose smoothed the newspaper. "A thousand dead and five thousand homeless in Indo-China. I suppose some of them might envy her."

"She doesn't want much to make her happy."

"That's enviable if through no fault of your own you're left wanting pretty nearly everything."

"Can we refuse her on the grounds that there are others, too many others, we can't help?"

"Of course there are others," Rose said irritably, "there always will be. It's a matter of perspective."

"How you look at it," he said obediently and drifted towards the door. It was valedictory, the way he paused as if to peel off the room. "How do you look at it, Rose?"

102

"With pity. I do believe, though, that such things are allowed for."

"A pattern?"

He was giving her half his attention, the rest was for the room which he now looked at, round her, so that she was piqued into saying, "Whether it's an earthquake or a rush of blood to the head, violence has to go somewhere that can take it. They don't explode rockets, do they, without fortifying the ground under them?"

He was not sure, she could see, what he had heard, let alone what she meant. She said, sharply, "People are equipped for it—the people that suffer it."

"Equipped? Old people—children?"

"How much do they feel? Actually feel? As much as some of us thinking—*trying* to think—of it? I often try, often enough to know I'm not cut out for the real thing. I shouldn't last," said Rose, "longer than a snowball on a hot griddle."

"So you expect not to suffer the real thing?"

"I trust not to be called upon to."

"I shall pray to God you're not." He opened the door and, turning back, tapped at his pockets. "But He may, in His wisdom, will otherwise."


Hilda Loeb had been capricious in her lifetime, apt to cancel out what she did. If she bought at the wrong moment, she sold at the right one; if she helped a man she would at the same time broadcast her bad opinion of him. She could afford to and on the whole she finished even because people liked her for herself. This bequest of hers showed the familiar contradictions. It was a nice thought, a good intention that had done harm already. Rose had lost two friends over it and feared she might get too close a look into the natures of some others.

Victorine Gregory was capable of keeping up a pretence of friendship and that would be irritating, possibly disagreeable in view of Sam Swanzy. Cade was another matter, and really regrettable. He was entitled to principles and to distorted ones—provided he didn't exalt them. Now Rose could not overlook them because he would not allow her to. He was pigheaded, which with him passed for strength. Their relationship which had been pleasant and productive would become a rubbing along, with the Self-Help Committee always there to grit up even that.

Rose did not feel she need blame herself. The present deadlock was about as foreseeable as a fall of soot and as tedious to clear up. She might, in the beginning, have chosen the members of the Committee differently and they might have voted differently and the net result might have been the same. She could have chosen better-known quantities but she, too, was entitled to her principles. Once the thing had started to go wrong there was little chance for management, except by preventing a brawl—no one knew better than Rose how overheating committee work could be.

She took a cup of bad coffee which she did not want in order to talk to Miss Havelock whom she saw sitting in a coffee-bar at nearly lunch-time. But that was in obedience to an old-fashioned sense of duty: one should not shirk the unpleasant, however unprofitable it might appear to be.

"May I join you?" said Rose. "Do you mind?"

Miss Havelock minded so little that it was slightly offensive. She said, "I have a train to catch in ten minutes—to a stockholders' meeting in the City."

"I know how busy you are. It seemed sensible," said Rose, "to find out your free dates before trying to fix another meeting of the Self-Help Committee."

"Have there been any developments?"

"In what way?"

"Unless someone has changed her mind we shall waste another afternoon. I can always employ my time."

Rose wondered how. With money? She was not known to be especially avaricious. With getting it, a game for all seasons?

"Mr Cade has withdrawn from the Committee."

"Why?"

"He's sensitive about his church being a beneficiary. It doesn't help us, of course."

Miss Havelock grunted.

"I feel we should discuss it and vote again," said Rose. "Someone may have second thoughts."

"Shall you?"

Rose smiled. "My decision is unchanged, but my mind is still open."

Miss Havelock took a mirror from her handbag and adjusted her hat.

"The Choules woman will do as you do and I doubt if Mrs Betts has had first thoughts, let alone second ones."

"Surely that's a little unfair—"

"Mrs Tyndall has obviously set her heart, so that leaves Mrs Gregory. She's unstable, you might get at her."

"Get at her?"

"To change her mind."

"But she's on your side."

"Mrs Antrobus, I have no side. It is immaterial to me where the money goes. My vote was the expression of an opinion, not a declaration of war." Miss Havelock snapped shut her handbag. She would have done well, Rose thought, to powder her nose which was caking. "I too may resign at the next meeting. The Committee made a bad start. Not surprisingly," said Miss Havelock, "since it's so illogically composed. Mrs Choules is not a committee woman, she'll be a passenger every time a decision is wanted. Mrs Betts plays golf and I've never heard of her doing anything else."

This was not criticism, Rose reminded herself. From whence it came it was betrayal of Miss Havelock's own deficiency. Grotesque, really, that a woman of her size should be so petty—a sport, or economy, of nature to put a small mind in a body as big as an ox's.

"I chose the Committee very carefully, I'm sorry you think it illogical," Rose said mildly. "There were good and sufficient reasons for everyone; I still think they're sufficient, with perhaps one exception. That's what comes of trying to be kind, it really is rather a bad reason for anything."

Miss Havelock raised her eyebrows, refusing to be drawn. Rose said, "Well, never mind, we're often mistaken in each other. It *was* a bad start, but it need be no more than that.

We must learn to work together. We can, we're responsible people."

"Opinions vary as to which of us is," said Miss Havelock. Her face then struggled, with diligently curling lip and arching brows, to accommodate an expression which Rose supposed was sarcasm. "It wasn't by any chance me you were trying to be kind to?"

Rose laughed. "Good heavens, no!" She hesitated. "As a matter of fact, strictly between you and me, it was Vee Gregory. I thought she needed taking out of herself."

"Committee work is not a therapy."

"I see that now!" cried Rose. "And I'm afraid it may even be bad for her from a practical point of view. Of course, if I'd known how she was involved I would never have invited her."

"Mrs Gregory is difficult and somewhat affected but presumably she voted according to her convictions. Yes, I would grant her that," said Miss Havelock generously.

"Would you? I wonder. And how much respect should we give the convictions of a woman in her situation?"

"What is her situation?"

"Oh!" Rose subsided, troubled, and began fiddling with her coffee-spoon. "Please don't ask me that."

"I have asked."

"I can't tell you."

"Then you shouldn't hint," said Miss Havelock. "And if it affects the Committee I have a right to know."

"It doesn't really. Oh, I don't know!" Rose was distressed. "The thing is, how much should we expect from her while her standards are so low?"

Miss Havelock looked at her watch. "In two minutes I must leave to catch my train. Either you do me the courtesy of telling me what you're talking about or I shall waste no more of my time on your Committee."

"You're forcing my hand," said Rose, and told her about Victorine and Sam Swanzy.

"Gossip," said Miss Havelock.

"Oh, I know! And were it only that, do you think I'd have repeated it, however you insisted? But my husband is not in the habit of gossiping. His word," Rose said gently, "I do respect."

Miss Havelock picked up her gloves and her nice fox fur. "It doesn't change anything so far as I'm concerned."

"Why should it? If you share her opinions you don't necessarily approve her morals."

Miss Havelock's face mottled to the blemished pink of blotting paper.

Rose sighed. "I have a casting vote, but I would so much rather not use it."

Although Sunday morning church could not have seemed a business potential to Ted Antrobus, he always went with Rose and sat attentively through the sermons, hands in his lap, ankles crossed. He knelt assiduously, stood up promptly, and sang the hymns in a loud voice, but Rose did not know what he thought about religion. She had certainly tried to find out in their beginning. He had given stock answers, dryly, as if to a forward child. She was later convinced that going to church was one of his habits. She noticed his fretfulness if for any reason he was prevented from going: it was the same, exactly, as when he was prevented from changing out of his City clothes and taking his sweet sherry before dinner. Who was to say—of him or of anyone—where habit left off and faith began? An amalgam of the two was the acceptable, the expected, compromise. Religion should be a habit, and so far as Rose was concerned habit might be a religion since it had made Ted Antrobus what he was and since she was satisfied with that.

She said as they walked home on Sunday morning, "I have a feeling Eric meant the text of that sermon for me."

"The poor chap may have meant it for himself."

"In his own mind he's blameless."

"But he can't accuse you of faith without works."

"He disapproves of my works."

"I wonder," said Antrobus, "if you really approve of this one yourself."

"What do you mean?"

"It's a prickly business."

"That's not my fault," Rose said sharply. "I only wish I was always as certain of the right thing to do."

"And you're sure about the wrong thing? You're sure that it's all wrong?"

"I've heard as much as I need or want to about Mrs Peachey."

"Shouldn't you see something too?"

"The idea was that Mavis Tyndall should do that."

"Should do that." Antrobus nodded and dropped her last words over a garden wall.

Rose understood that that would be the end of it for this morning and for as long as she took to raise it again, or for it to come up in the course of anything else.

"You might as well say we ought all to go, all of us who voted against her, and have the poor woman recite her troubles."

"I might." She could tell that he disliked being detained on it. "You've all seen the hassocks."

There was in this absurdity a grain of justice. She picked it out because it contributed to a decision already reached. If she went to Mrs Peachey she might see for herself facts which Mavis Tyndall had not seen or hadn't mentioned, facts which might confirm her own opinion and justify her casting vote. Or she might see something to change that opinion. There was, as she had said, her mind to be kept open.

"Very well, I'll go. No one shall say I did less than I should."

She did more by taking sweets for the children. Now that she had decided, it was obvious: going in itself was the solution. It had been a small matter, she thought, feeling able already to regard it as closed, though full of unpleasantness—the implication being that there was plenty more where that came from. A pity that Hilda's bequest should have provoked it, Hilda had meant so well. So had they all. It was discouraging, to say the least, to get this sort of petty bad where only good was intended.

Mrs Peachey had a flat in a Council block on the wet side

of the town, the side the rain came in across the Weald. The new slums, Rose thought, climbing concrete stairs, ten flights between concrete walls, cream-painted and lavatorial. On every landing aprons of damp were driven in through the balcony openings. The building was cold and without being particularly clean smelt disinfected. She met no one, heard nothing except a high Arctic whistling of the wind in the stair-well.

Mrs Peachey's door stood ajar with a broom in the crack. Rose knocked and a tiny girl came out and held on to the broom as if Rose was threatening to take it. It was, Rose, noticed afterwards, her practice to attach herself to something.

"Hallo, dear, is your mummy in?"

The child had lint-white hair and the tender poverty that goes with it. Almost repulsive, Rose thought such thin blue pallor, and surely it was pipe-clay, not ivory her bones were made of?

Something moved on the other side of the door. Rose said, "Won't you tell Mummy I'm here?"

This was the child that Mavis Tyndall was concerned about, the little girl who kept so still. Well she might. Four years of life and she had a look of utter exhaustion, like a delicate weed swamped with rain.

Rose knocked briskly at the door and it swung open, showing her the room beyond, all window and cold stuffy white clouds. Of course it was absurdly high up, at the mercy of the sky. And there was nothing much else to fill it, no curtains, no carpet, just a table, a chair and a drugget over the floorboards and a wooden crate upended to hold books.

"Is anybody at home?"

"No," said a voice.

Rose looked round the door. Behind it crouched a boy, a little older than the girl, with the same lint-coloured hair and the same pallor under a tidal grubbiness.

There seemed not to be anyone else about, but Rose called, "Mrs Peachey?" towards an inner door.

The boy called back, "Nobody at home."

"Where's your mother?"

109

"Gone to the corner."

"I'll come in and wait for her."

She welcomed the chance of seeing without being seen and she could, she thought, also look at these children and they would probably answer questions in their own funny way without her asking them.

But when she got inside her instinct was to walk straight out again. It was the most comfortless place she had ever been in, not so much squalid as uncommitted, the furniture and what served as furniture scattered about, left standing rather than placed. It was bleakly clean and tidy because the signs of living were so few—a folding pram and a cigarette packet seemed to be all.

Rose walked about and the boy followed her.

"I'm Arnold. Who are you?"

"That's a nice name." Rose picked up the cigarette packet. It was empty. So she could afford to smoke—

"Who are you?"

Rose stepped round him to look at the books in the crate: 'The Jury System', 'Litigation and Tenure', 'Governing Slander'. The titles puzzled her, the books themselves were the most solid things in the room and they looked crated up ready to leave it.

"Who reads these?"

"I've seen you before," said the boy. "Oh, my lord!"

Rose looked at him. He affronted her. Children always did, she found their conversation tedious and their hands dirty. This one had a crust round his mouth.

"I've seen you at the church," said the boy. "With Mrs Tinribs, you're thick with her."

"Is that what you call Mrs Tyndall?"

The little girl came and pressed against Rose's side. She wore a pink cardigan shrunk to her elbows, a stale sweetish smell came off her skin.

"What's your name, dear?" Rose touched the child with her fingertip.

"Hers is Flossie." The boy choked with laughter. "Flossie's her name!"

Rose thought she heard a noise from the inner room.

"Who's in there?"

"I don't like you," said the boy.

She pushed the door wide and looked in. On the double bed lay a baby, wide awake, staring at her. Rose withdrew at once.

In the outer room the other children stood silent, watching, and then the girl, drawing close again, took up the corner of Rose's coat, fondled it and made as if she would carry it to her mouth.

"Don't!" Rose brushed off the child's hold. She said to the boy, "Does your mother often leave you alone like this?"

"My name's Arnold. What's yours?"

Rose reminded herself that children need handling and was relieved it was in a figurative sense. She found the scant bird bodies of these two repulsive, the girl particularly. There was something parasitical and sick about her.

"I've brought you some sweets." Rose sat in the chair and opened her handbag. Then she snapped it shut again. "I expect your mother buys you sweets when she goes for her cigarettes, doesn't she?"

"What sort of sweets?"

"Chocolates and jellies."

"Oh, my lord." Grinning, he put his back against the wall and slid down on to his heels. The girl crept to Rose's side, her breath rustling in her chest.

"Wouldn't you like some chocolate?" When Rose held it up and the child stretched out her hand, Rose said, "What's Mummy gone to the corner for?"

Her reactions to stimulus were entirely mechanical. If something was held out to her she lifted her hand, if it was withdrawn she let her hand drop. She showed no disappointment or impatience, she simply sank to the floor beside Rose's chair and Rose was left with the chocolate upraised as if she were making the children sit up and beg for it.

If it looked like that to the woman who came in the door just then it was not the sort of thing she would resent. She wouldn't extend it any farther than the children themselves and they might indeed be performing dogs for all the identifying she did with them. Rose was soon easy on that score but at first she felt at a disadvantage, she even felt guilty.

"Mrs Peachey, isn't it? I do beg your pardon for installing myself, but I wanted to wait and see you and the little boy let me in—" Rose smiled, holding out her hand—"in the sense of allowing me in. The door was open."

Mrs Peachey had the long hair, loosely wound and pinned on top of her head, the provoked and disenchanted mouth, the uniform face of her kind. Hers was the young kind and she was, thought Rose, going to put off being any other kind as long as she could. There was nothing of Denis Peachey in her face, nothing of the children, nothing of anything. Either she had schooled it out or it had never got through.

She took Rose's hand without enthusiasm.

"I'm Rose Antrobus, from St John's Church."

"I don't know anyone from any church."

"You know Mrs Tyndall?"

"Oh, she's from Sunday school." She didn't seem to think it had any connection.

"And our Minister, Mr Cade, has been to see you."

She sat on the edge of the table, still in her raincoat, looking mildly at Rose. "So many people come."

"We like to keep in touch with our parishioners in case there's any way we can help."

"That's what they all come for, to help," Mrs Peachey said softly. "Have you got a cigarette?"

"I don't smoke."

"I'm taking it up. I don't really care for the actual taste, but it's nice when you first light one." She took a packet from her raincoat pocket, broke the cellophane and shook out a cigarette. "This is the part I like." Bending to the flame in her cupped hand she drew with puckered lips and then rounded them to let out a wisp of smoke. "It's like starting a conversation. I suppose I'll get addicted and won't be able to do without. I don't care, it's a private conversation." She gestured without rancour towards the children. "Private from them. I get pretty tired not having anything they don't have."

"Still,' said Rose, "smoking is a costly habit to get into

and unfortunately that's the least harmful thing one can say about it. And there's such a lot to be done with your money, isn't there?"

Mrs Peachey did not concur. She went on puffing and blowing at her cigarette in a diligent mechanical way as if it were something she had to keep going.

"You must find it hard to make ends meet."

"I don't try. What I can't pay this week I'll pay next. People know that, they let me carry over because they know the money comes regular. You might say we're better off."

It would be tiresome if she was going to try to score points. Rose, looking sharply at her, could see no signs of cleverness or aim, except at keeping the cigarette alight.

"No one gave us credit when Denis was here."

"But aren't there things you could do with?"

"What things?"

"You can specify them better than I can."

"For this place? Furniture you mean? What could I do with furniture that I can't do now? I can sit down now and eat my dinner and go to bed—there'd be nothing else to do with it except dust it. I can't draw the curtains and I don't want to, if that's what you're thinking. I want the daylight in and at night I want to look out at the lights—there are a lot of lights from here—and I want to be seen, I want people to see me."

How old was she? Twenty-two or -three she must be to have a child of six, though she looked in her late teens. She gave Rose the impression, even Rose did not think it was arranged, of a premature ending, something started for a sufficient reason and now barely existing because reason and means had gone. Rose was reminded, and it seemed appropriate, of the acute personal poverty of the child, the little girl.

"Nothing for the children?"

"We're all fed and clothed," said Mrs Peachey. "They don't want anything else at their age."

Was it, Rose wondered, only an assumption of negation and only Mrs Peachey's, or did they really have no use for the things that other people lived by and often lived for?

"It won't be long, will it," she said smiling, "before Flossie grows out of that cardigan?"

"Who?"

Rose wagged a finger at the child. "You'd like a new coat, wouldn't you, Flossie?"

"For Christ's sake get your facts right," said Mrs Peachey. "Her name's Arlette."

"I beg your pardon—Oh!" cried Rose. "I'm so sorry, really I am—it was the little boy said her name was Flossie—"

"He'll say anything for a giggle." Mrs Peachey bore no resentment, she sat on the table swinging her legs, the cigarette in the middle of her mouth like a whistle. "Nut case, aren't you?" she called to the boy. "Dead or dead-funny?" To Rose's surprise and annoyance they both laughed and Mrs Peachey's was the same laughter, bubbling and noisy as the child's.

She stopped as abruptly as she had begun. "You have to laugh," she said aimlessly and again it was the absence of reason that chilled.

"You don't want anything?" Rose avoided irony, but her eyebrows went up because from where she sat it was a manifestly absurd thing to say. Moreover she suspected that Mrs Peachey did not show herself in the round, she had sides and turned them according to whoever she was with. Whether that was instinctive or expedient Rose had yet to decide.

"Letty's taken a fancy for you." The little girl, crouched beside Rose's chair, put up a hand like a crab. "If people ignore her she creeps after them."

Rose stood up and went to the window. "So money wouldn't help?"

"How much money?"

"I haven't said there'll be any yet."

"Where would it come from?"

"I'm not at liberty to tell you."

"It doesn't matter." Her interest flickered out. The cigarette, too, was finished and she plucked at the buttons on her raincoat. "There wouldn't be enough to buy Denis back."

From this height the new estate showed its small beginnings: unimaginatively small they had been and the plan, the tidy garden city plan, had got lost. Rings of red brick houses snaked round it, shoebox flats overhung it. Looking down at naked roads, bald playing fields and an agglomerate of factories, Rose could see neither shape, colour nor co-existence to make it memorable. At night perhaps darkness gave it unity.

"Does anyone have that kind of money?" said Mrs Peachey. "To buy them off?"

"To buy who off?"

"The people who've got Denis. They say he's sick, well how am I to know when he's better? And if I know, who's going to listen? They can say it's for the common good and they could keep him for ever for that."

Queer how it was the inflection of the voice that counted with Rose. Children whined, complained, excused—'I couldn't help it, it wasn't me, they made me do it—' and yet there was no question of sincerity. They felt all that they were able, and if they pitied themselves they had their reasons. So had Mrs Peachey. She was no less miserable, Rose told herself, because she did not keep her dignity.

"I'm sure that when he's better—"

"They'll let him out?" Mrs Peachey uttered a sound from the back of her throat, but it wasn't laughter. "If you think that you're simpler than I am. 'Mrs P., we've cured your husband, he's now a responsible citizen ready to take his place in the world—' Oh yes, I can hear it, the bells ringing, the people cheering and the neighbours putting out flags."

"I know it's hard, but you must try—"

"Try what? That's what he did, he tried. He was studying, see, to be a lawyer and better us. What he really wanted, if you ask me, was just to be better." She had asked herself and come up with this answer, and if it hadn't embittered her it had taken the last grain of sense. "Have you tried studying at night, Rose Thingummy? Night after night after night with three kids in the room? We had to keep quiet, I can tell you—we've gone quiet now—and so did he. He had

115

to stick his fingers in his ears when the baby cried, I couldn't always stop the baby."

It was irony or justice, whichever way you looked at it, that trying too hard to be better should cause a man to get so much worse. And better than what? Agreed that there was room for improvement, but how much better did Denis Peachey want to be without the natural equipment, poor wretch, to accomplish it?

"He learned that legal stuff by heart." Mrs Peachey gestured with her foot towards the crate of books. "He could say pages off, word perfect, and all they needed when it came to it was one little word to put him away for good."

Rose had an uneasy feeling that Mrs Peachey was goading herself.

"He used to walk about reciting, memorising it, all the way to the bus, in the queue, on the bus and any minute of the day he could get to himself. When people laughed he didn't like it. He was better than them, why should he stand for them laughing?"

"They were showing their ignorance—"

"He hit that bloody old tramp for her ignorance, that bloody, dirty, pissed old whore."

"Please!" But she had not goaded herself to more than the form of words, she was calm, even contemplative and Rose could only say, "The children are listening—"

"They'd tell you the same." Sighing, she stretched and relaxed without refreshment. "Sometimes I think I'll go and start something else."

"Start something?"

"Who would, with me now? I'm past it."

Mentally she was about seventeen, which would be the age when she had her first child and, thought Rose, stopped growing as compensation. Couldn't she see how futile and silly these attempts to shock were for one in her position? If she didn't grow up soon she ran the risk of being permanently retarded.

"Denis took everything. Anyone else would have left me something to pick up and go on with. I'm not specially faithful, it's just that I had it all with him. I'm glad to God I did."

Rose said, using the formula—it wasn't her place to give moral correction, "You have the children, that must mean a great deal."

Mrs Peachey put both arms round herself. "It means that we wanted each other and we got married because he wouldn't have me without. He was as full of principles as a bird is feathers. The kids came, you've got to pay for principles."

"I asked if there was anything you needed—"

"Be a right church that could give me *that*." Mrs Peachey laughed her bubbling child's laugh and the boy joined in.


The question was, just how irresponsible was she? Rose thought she overplayed it, only a crank or an imbecile could be so imprudent. On the other hand she obviously gave no thought to practicalities. Even taking into account the chronic shortage of money, the Peacheys lived bleaker from indifference than from poverty. Of course, some women had no idea how to make a home, with money or without, and some could manage it with a rag rug and a geranium.

The sweets for the children were still in her handbag. She dropped them in the ashcan. Then she made tea for herself and held the cup between her palms to warm them. She felt chilled, which was understandable, the day being cold and the Peacheys' flat so dreary. What was not understandable was the sense of disruption she had, confusion and doubt in excess of anything she needed to feel about the Peacheys.

She was not disposed to look for causes, not this afternoon. There could be several, tiresome and ephemeral. This afternoon she still thought that Hilda's money should go to the church. The fact that the Peacheys needed money was never in doubt; so did a lot of people, more or less desperately, and there was no sign of desperation about Mrs Peachey. She could as well benefit next quarter as this, if indeed whatever she chose to do with the money could be called benefiting. It was inane of Mavis Tyndall to be so sentimental, a childless woman with a fixation about some-one else's children. For that she would hamstring the Committee and sabotage Hilda Loeb's goodwill and testament.

This afternoon, thought Rose, she had confirmed that the Peachey problem was beyond the scope of the Self-Help Committee and should never have been raised in the first place. The interview had shown her a line of argument.

"I put it to you," she said, rehearsing, "should this—or any committee—meddle with emotional problems? We can't help Mrs Peachey until she helps herself. Her problem is her own—" Rose had her eye on Mavis Tyndall—"peculiarly and personally in her situation. She shouldn't be incapable of tackling it, and until she does I don't see her using Hilda Loeb's money the way Hilda or any of us intend. I see her letting it slip away without herself or the children being a penny the better. If we give her the money we must be prepared to forget it, and her. We can look for no positive good and we may do her a disservice." Rose paused for someone—Victorine probably—to ask how she worked that one out. "Having seen Mrs Peachey and talked to her, I'm the last to deny that she has difficulties. The sooner she faces up to them the better. It may be that by the time we allocate the next benefaction she will have made a start and then I should myself move that we give her any practical help we can."

It was a reasonable argument, not that it would convert Mavis Tyndall or Victorine, they were beyond reason. All Rose asked was that Miss Havelock should be swayed.

She thought there was a good chance. She ought to have been satisfied enough to leave the subject alone. But she couldn't get Mrs Peachey out of her mind, there was something ominous about that kind of indifference. She could never have been normal, that was a state of mind, manners and body which she came as fatally short of as Peachey himself. She had harboured and channelled his violence by virtue or vice of simply being, of bringing children into the world, of requiring to eat, breathe and exist. She was culpable, if anyone was for abnormality, as essential as her husband's victim, and much more integral.

The last person Rose wanted to see that afternoon was Victorine Gregory. She arrived just as Rose was trying to contain herself. Rose had discovered a tendency to go to pieces, to turn around to find not only opinions and concepts but the standards of a lifetime quietly leaking. It was frightening. Rose would have panicked if she hadn't held onto the knowledge that it was a temporary reaction: tiredness, due largely to recent frustrations and disappointments. To revive she had only to put right out of her mind this question of poor Hilda's money and everything connected with it: a change of mind, thought Rose, not of heart. She knew she had no hope of achieving it when Victorine turned up.

"I've had the kids and the flower-pot men all day," said Victorine. She came sauntering in, her casualness looked too pronounced. "When I stay alone in that house I start to lose my identity."

"It's your home, it should reflect your identity."

Victorine threw herself into a chair. She looked at Rose as if expecting no great entertainment from that quarter either. "It's all right for you with your blasted committees."

"Yes," said Rose, "one makes friends that way."

"Have you got friends?"

"I think so."

"I haven't, thank God—only you."

"How am I meant to take that?"

"Sue rich-bitch Betts and Mrs Butcher Choules are your friends."

"You're a snob, Vee."

"I've met all the friendly ladies with their claws in each other's backs."

Rose guessed that something particular was provoking this. She guessed what the something was and felt mollified. If the rewards of virtue had to be winkled out it was right that the punishment for vice should be insidious.

"Your back too," said Victorine. "I tell you, it's a closed circle."

Rose recognised a red herring.

"They can't find anything to dig into. They hate that, naturally."

You had always to read into her, Rose thought. If her own conscience troubled her, she maligned everyone else; if she wanted information she sought it by discrediting the source.

"Don't you know yourself, Rose?"

Rose said coldly, "The question seems to be do I know other people."

"The principle's the same, the working one, I mean. Prick us and we bleed." Victorine smiled. "That woman's name in *The Water Babies*—Mrs Do-as-you-would-be-done-by—that's sound primitive ethics, but they're no easier to stick to than the complicated ones."

"Would you like tea?"

"Be clean, be tidy," said Victorine, "where it shows, and that's the best anyone can do if the principle's a dirty mess."

Rose was surprised. This had every appearance of leading to a confession, and Victorine must be hard pushed from some more than moral direction if she thought of making one. Rose was also annoyed. She had no wish to hear details of the affair with Swanzy and no intention of taking any of the burden of it.

"Vee, there are people coming to supper and I've things to do—"

"It's the same for all of us—that's sanity. Mine, anyway." She lay in the chair, holding up a lazy hand to Rose who was about to go out of the door. "I like looking at you, Rose, you've got such a lovely crust."

"Don't talk nonsense."

"I long to crack it. So do Betts and Choules. Little Tyndall's the only one who thinks you're solid."

"I'm obliged to her."

"Certainly that's the impression one gets over the Peachey business. There but for the grace of God you never would go."

"No," said Rose, "I never would. And I say so not because of what happened to Mrs Peachey but because of what she is."

"What is she?"

"She's a trollop."

Rose had surprised herself. The word tasted of dirt and was not all, not half to do with Mrs Peachey. It had been declared, smacked down between Victorine and herself, there was no need even to stoop to pick it up.

"Why should I try to identify myself with a woman like that?" Rose said deliberately, "Could you?"

Victorine did not pick up. On the contrary she seemed to let go of something and what was left was not in the least remarkable, in a crowd would hardly serve to identify her. But what was left was Victorine Gregory, the essential. Rose thought, essential to whom?

"I wonder if you and I can work together on the same committee," she said without wonder, and Victorine put her head back against the chair and shut her eyes. She was tired of something, had no hope of it and Rose knew it was neither the money nor the Committee nor Mrs Peachey.

She nodded with approval at Victorine's blank eyelids and went out to the kitchen.


Solange taught me about that sort of thing. Not in words, she wouldn't have thought words necessary. By the time I went to Grieux I was sixteen, I knew about what was crisply called at school 'the reproductive system'. Privately I considered it unnecessarily nasty even for animals. I thought that Nature, said to be so ingenious, could have found some nicer way of propagation, but if we understood aright, the same grotesque and chronically unhygienic method had to be employed between men and women.

I didn't believe we had understood. How could we, confused as we were with Latinised words and textbook diagrams of pollination and genes and the structure of eggs? I didn't believe that the actual mechanics of it were as crude as between ourselves we made them out to be. There was surely a qualifying factor, a saving grace which we overlooked or couldn't know about. I was not romantic, but I liked things to be nice.

I had the sense to keep that to myself. I put up with the whispering and rumouring that went on among the other girls. When they nudged each other about the Song of Solomon I nudged too. I was more irritated than titillated when I read it. The saving grace wasn't there and in the Bible it surely should have been. When they passed round forbidden books what was in them seemed as apposite as the personal habits of the aborigines, of another country and another climate.

My father would have preferred me to go straight from school to commercial college, and I would have liked that. Mother wanted me to finish at a school abroad. She settled on Winterthur House because Solange Marigny was going there.

I still corresponded with Solange, it had become a chore for us both. At sixteen we had less in common than we had at twelve, and although it was still more than we were likely to have in later life it wasn't much and wasn't communicable in letters. I wrote in poor French about tennis clubs and hockey matches and Senior Guiding, and Solange wrote in correct English about clothes and someone called Joanno, a friend of Valentin's.

My mother thought it would be nice for Solange and me to be together again. She had great unfounded faith in the Marignys' shrewdness. Any school they chose was bound to be the best of its kind for its price.

"The French know about establishments, it's the same with restaurants and hotels—go where they go and you can be sure of value for money."

I couldn't see Monsieur le Maître bothering with prospectuses and I did not believe that Madame Marigny, who never finished anything, should be so trusted when it came to finishing her daughter's education. Solange told me later that she herself chose Winterthur House because it was near Basle and Joanno.

I was afraid that being 'finished' with Solange might entail finishing like her. From what I remembered she was more likely to impose her pattern than have any imposed on her. This was not communicable either, not to my mother. She had her way. Father and I crossed a week after my sixteenth birthday to Boulogne and from there went by the Simplon Orient to Basle and from Basle by road to Grieux.

Grieux just missed being a place for tourists. It was over a thousand feet above the sea with a drop to the Belfort Gap on one side and a step up to the Jura on the other. The town itself was level, the buildings old but not especially fantastic. There were some carved eaves and a cobbled square with a stone bear in the middle and two stout grey churches. It was sober and tidy rather than contorted and cute.

My father liked it. I remember his saying it was a gentle place, perhaps he thought it would do something for me. I was a big noisy girl, a problem just then. My mother was constantly trying to get me to walk on the balls of my feet, to laugh with my teeth together and to cherish myself a little.

We stayed a night at an hotel with feather bags on the beds and at breakfast the bread came still smoking from the oven. I told my father, not for the first time, of my doubts about this school. It would be too late to complain, I pointed out, when in a year's time I finished up like Solange Marigny, and then I tried to tell him what was lacking in her. He didn't take me seriously when I put all my faith in the force of her character and none in the combined powers of those who were to teach us.

As we drove out of Grieux next morning I felt feminine and defenceless. That was new to me. So was the glassy cold air, so were the mountains and the goat-bells and the people with apple faces and woollen stockings, talking their clackety gibberish. It was packed with foreign potential which at best was not the slightest use to me and might be downright dangerous. What were my parents thinking of to send me to this half-baked place? What did they expect to be done for me here that couldn't be done in Beckenham?

Winterthur House, named after the town near Zurich, was nothing special to look at. The special in architecture and landscape never has impressed me anyway. I don't like to be bounced into admiration. This was a brown stone house, dignified in a functional way, with plain shutters and wide eaves to take the weight of the winter snows. I was comforted to see a hard tennis-court, marked out and tidy. It could nearly have been English.

We were taken to the Principal's study. We saw no pupils, nor signs of them. This part of the house was all black panelling and bearskin rugs. There were stuffed stag and wolf heads with papier maché snouts and banks of muscular plants in copper troughs and something which I can never disassociate from Winterthur—a copy of the Laöcoon. I think of it now as indigenous to the place, all that yellow plaster contortion signified.

I don't forget the smell peculiar to the house. It was at once aromatic and bitter, muffling and sharp: the sweetness, I suppose, from the old wood and the polish used on it, the bitterness from the damp soil and the strong dust held in the hairs of the living plants and the dead animals. I am not likely to encounter just that blend anywhere else and it wasn't to be met with in the pupils' quarters. For me it is the smell of Winterthur, of the fields, trees and mountains, the people and everything that happened.

The Principals were the Merkur Kulms. He was Austrian and she German. They were called Dr and Mrs Kulm by staff and pupils. When they received us that first day I saw that he was unimpeachably handsome and that she smiled too strenuously, but as foreigners they were acceptable. That first day it was all aggressively strange and Merkur Kulm made no demands. I was aware of him, as of a vein of richness. I looked at him with some of the dread I had of being left in this place, but I did look. Perhaps I wasn't to see afterwards what I saw then because that was the first time and the only time I was not committed.

He had the luxurious good looks of a cherished creature. He was both solid and graceful, he had a bright academic beard and curling chestnut hair that grew over his collar. My father looked faded and abused beside him.

Mrs Kulm had a broad slab face and black swimming eyes. She spoke English with such care and conviction that her lips were constantly flecked with spittle.

I don't remember what was said. They wanted to show

my father the school, but for some reason he was against seeing it. He and I sat moping while they talked and then he suddenly said he was returning to Basle immediately and might I be allowed to walk with him as far as the gate.

He seemed satisfied that the Kulms were qualified to have charge of me. I asked him as we went along the drive and he said yes, absently yet definitely, so there was no hope of getting away. I felt fatalistic after that and my father who was worrying about something quite irrelevant—like how long the parcel post took from England—didn't get any great show of emotion when he kissed me goodbye. He was relieved, I dare say. We always preferred to keep command of ourselves in our family.

I was ready to put up resistance to Solange, but at first I did not need to. She was genuinely glad to see me and she didn't tease, not at first. Winterthur House was new to her also and she had other things on her mind.

I hadn't anticipated so much change in her appearance. There was little enough in mine. I was taller and what my mother called 'filling out'. I rarely bothered to examine my face in the mirror, it wasn't beautiful and it wasn't hideous, so what was there to look at?

"Your nose," said Solange, "still looks damp."

She was a different person. 'Quite the young lady', Mother would have said, and indeed Solange was working at it. Her hair was permed and the perm in those days was inclined to be rigid. Crisp little gables ran levelly and punctually every two inches all round her head. I coveted those waves, my hair was in the mutable state, like two dropped wings either side of my face.

And that strong pallor of hers held good. She did not suffer from colour in the wrong places, greasy sallows or acne. Her skin was dry and white, like a good wine I remember her saying matter-of-factly. She chose her own clothes, they did not do for her what the big-girl dresses our parents put us in did for the rest of us. She looked neither like a full sack tied in the middle nor like a maypole with ribbons.

In style her clothes were ten years too old, yet she never looked ridiculous, she managed to look unique.

I was jealous. I thought I didn't want to look as she did because it was questionable and too fast by the calendar reckoning. I told myself that I wasn't going to be her sort of woman, I already had an inkling what sort of woman that was.

I wasn't the only one to be jealous of her. She did not become popular. She had a small following of people like me whom she called upon whenever she wanted, for whatever she wanted. It wasn't much, it certainly wasn't friendship and we, her cronies, were always ready to ally against her.

There were forty girls at Winterthur, several youngest at fifteen and the eldest, Dutch twin sisters, were eighteen. They and the seventeen-year-olds were known as 'jeunes dames', the rest of us were 'les filles'.

I've since wondered who was responsible for setting the curriculum and conclude that the practicalities were Laura Kulm's and the niceties were her husband's. She would insist on languages, she herself taught us French and German and the literature readings were hers. We had much to assimilate if we were to give the impression of a University education and that, I think, was her ideal.

She was dedicated to the present as a means of bringing about what struck me as a drab, free-for-all future. We were hustled through the classics to ground us for the moderns. There was only a year or two to accomplish it all.

Current affairs was her forte. She told us things that would have constituted an intelligent woman's guide, had we been intelligent women. I forgot, even as I heard, how the Bourse worked and the Stock Exchange and the Reichsbank and I don't know the first thing now about the politics of industry. She was a Socialist, she thought everyone could and should have everything. The first time she outlined for us the theory and practice of her brand of Socialism I had a quite adult feeling that she was only seeing what she wanted to. When her eyes blazed and her bosom actually heaved I decided she was capable of suborning her brain to suit her blood.

She was younger than her husband and we wondered what he had seen in her. We couldn't see anything for him in her teased-up negroid hair and coarse skin. She had been a pupil at Cologne University, he an extra-mural Professor of Greek and Latin, subjects unlikely ever to have been of use to her. She was restless and eruptive, she had a powerful crudity. Solange said she was an 'educated peasant'.

Inevitably, so many adolescent girls penned up together carried a torch for the only personable male penned up with them. Some claimed to dislike him because he was pleased with himself, but they were trying to be different. He had reason to be pleased with himself, we made no secret of how pleased *we* were.

Being Viennese provided the operetta streak which charmed and bemused us; being older, but not too old, made him discriminating and worldly-wise. We believed it did, just as we believed he had depths. I think he was an unhappy man and we took his occasional sombre moods for their face value, we were glad of them. Knowing he had depths made us feel cosy, and if we thought of sounding them it was for the sake of what we might do in them and not what we would find.

I suppose when he visualised the girls who came to Winterthur House as future women of the world it was his world he saw them in, hence the emphasis on the fine arts which we had to learn to appreciate by practising them. With many of us it was a waste of time. With me it certainly was. I couldn't tell one note of music from another nor move to it without mixing my feet. As to drawing, it was pitiable the messes I made. He used to say, puzzled and pleading, "But that is not what you see—it cannot—it must not be!"

Even so, he achieved a greater degree of success than anyone else could have done because so many of us impure little virgins were competing for his favour.

Also resident at the school were Signorina Piotta, who taught Italian and tried, in the open discussion sessions, to involve us in astrology; and Miss Gurney, young and shy, who had joined the staff direct from college to take English classes and games. She was a rabbit at games. I remember her as perpetually running to and fro, bleating on her whistle.

There were some itinerant lecturers and some regularly visiting professors, none of them memorable apart from Polichen, the dwarf.

Our quarters at Winterthur were Spartan. Furniture in the dormitories, cubicles and classrooms was minimal. We were not encouraged to spread ourselves—Mrs Kulm's influence again. In the common-room we had some armchairs, hand-woven rugs, a radio and an ugly epergne which we were required to keep supplied with flowers or decorative leaves.

We slept in dormitories of six to eight, with one of the 'jeunes dames' to keep an eye on us. I have always disliked sleeping in the company of other people. At Winterthur I got into a habit, which I afterwards found hard to break, of never quite losing consciousness as I slept. Some of the girls talked and cried out in their sleep. Carème Rossli, the senior of our dormitory, snored like a hunting pig.

Solange had the bed next to mine. She had engineered that: I supposed because she was glad to be with me again. Later I found that she had a better reason.

The proximity of others did not trouble Solange. If she chose, she did not acknowledge them, and until she chose they existed only as a shuffle of air she might feel on her skin. She was naturally lazy. Often in our free periods she would lie fully dressed on her bed, eyes and face wide open, blank to the point of unconsciousness.

I supposed I was seeing her kinship with Valentin, I thought she too was arguing things out in her head. I asked her, curious to know the problems which absorbed her.

"What are you thinking?"

She moved her lips, they were dry from stillness, they had to unseal.

"I am not thinking."

She was bored. There was nothing at Winterthur House that she cared or needed to take trouble to do. The lessons were too easy, the routine too rigid, the company insipid.

Not to me. It suited my temperament and capabilities. I have always preferred order.

"I came to fetch you. Dr Kulm is going to play us some records."

"Amusez-vous." She sealed up her lips again.

I made friends. Four of us came together and kept together during the year I was at Winterthur. They were ordinary peaceable girls—Lisl Norderney, Connie Dace and Mary Sawdell. The odd thing was that being friends of mine seemed automatically to commit them to Solange. Whether we wanted it or not, we four constituted her circle, when she wanted a circle.

None of us knew what to make of her. I found it tiresome being appealed to as an authority. The others would ask, "What does she mean?" as if she spoke a language only I could understand.

"Well, you're her friend," they said.

Was I? Was anyone? I had started to think that there were no friends of Solange, only people who knew her from Adam. But someone, apparently, she took trouble to be with. We had been scarcely a fortnight at Winterthur when she began.

We were getting ready for bed, at nine o'clock as usual. Lights had to be out by nine-thirty. We thought it a childish time. Some dormitories contrived, by a system of sentry-go and water-pipe rappings, to support life for another hour after the Dutch twins, as the supreme seniors, had been round to check on the dark. In some dormitories they read, played cards, ran clubs, ate chocolate, washed their hair and smoked until midnight. Connie Dace liked a good story and maintained that they also drank Fraise des Bois and gagged and bound the girls who got noisy on it.

Nothing happened in our dormitory because Carème, our senior-in-charge, needed her sleep. She was capable of putting the lights out before nine-thirty if we seemed anything like ready, so of course we dawdled. Solange dawdled longer than anyone. It was not unusual for her still be to fully dressed when Carème put the lights out. She was that evening, curled up on her bed, buffing her nails.

Carème called to her, "In one moment I am putting you in the dark."

Solange took her purse bag out of her locker and her gloves and laid them on her pillow.

I said, "Are you going somewhere?"

To my amazement, she nodded. "I'm going out to supper."

"What?"

"Listen, I want you to open the front door and leave it open—at about one o'clock. Yes, I shall not return before then."

"Open the front door? Are you mad? I can't possibly."

"Why not?"

"It's against the rules as you well know. We'd be expelled."

She said something under her breath. I was terrified, I felt as if a pit of iniquity had opened before me.

"At one o'clock." She was polishing her nails again.

"No! I should be seen—"

"You must take care that you are not."

"The door—they'll see it's open!"

"Not at one o'clock." She smiled. "They will be in their beds."

At that moment Carème put out the lights. I was left crouching in the blackness at Solange's bedside.

"I won't do it!"

She did not answer. She knew I would do it, and I knew too. Already the ordeal was weighing me down. I would never, I thought, survive the night.

I whispered, trembling with anger and panic, "Where are you going?"

"That's my business."

"I won't do it unless you tell me!"

She leaned down and spoke close to my ear. "Joanno is coming to take me to supper and to dance—" perfunctory and calm as if she were telling a pestering younger sister.

"You said he was in Basle—"

"Tonight he is in Grieux."

I didn't ask any more. I didn't want to know. Despairing,

I crept into my bed. I hated Solange that night. I prayed for her to be caught as she went out, struck down, destroyed. If there was any justice, any defence of the innocent, she would be.

The dormitory was by no means quiet. People were muttering and laughing and settling in their beds. I heard Solange, her breathing and the rustle of her clothes, as loud and clear as the crack of a whip.

I lay on my back. When it began to ache I realised I was hooked stiff with anger and dread. Presently Dutch Rena came in. She woke Carème, who was starting to snore, to say something to her. Rena was laughing. Carème hated being roused, she whimpered and grunted in reply.

After that, the dormitory settled down. I knew when they were all asleep, it was like a tide running out, leaving only me and Solange whom I hated—and was afraid of. Yes, being careful of her turned out, after all, to be fear. I blamed myself. What advantage had she, except my chicken-heartedness? And I had made her a present of that. I had crouched down so that she could stand higher, now I was going to lie flat so that she could walk over me. I would do as she wanted, this time and other times, with everything to lose, because I had put myself into the way. A slow conditioning it must have been. What else? What was there to be afraid of? She was a schoolgirl like myself—like, anyway, in her capacity. There was no more nor less to fear from that.

I was claiming the initiative for my own defeat and managed to keep it a litle while without self-analysis or the fret of redemption. I did not understand then that this was Solange's own game, she would always beat me at it and I was neither equipped nor required to play.

She waited a long time on her bed, perhaps one hour, perhaps two. It was the longest wait I had ever had for anything. I lived it over and over again in discovery and disgrace. I was naïve even for my age. What she planned and my part of it was shocking and iniquitous because it went against my every grain.

I didn't hear her move off her bed, perhaps I'd only

imagined I could hear her lying there. She stooped over me and from so much staring the darkness had become semi-dusk and I was able to see that she was smiling. I thought that she used this particular smile a lot on me. It was more than a smile, it was a deepening, as if I brought out her self in her. But there was nothing to be gathered from it, except that she knew all about me.

"Don't go to sleep, Rose." She moved away between the beds and I pushed myself up on my elbow to watch her. She had a scarf over her hair and she wore a dark coat which she must have smuggled into the dormitory. At the door she waved without looking back.

I still hoped. Between Carême's snores I listened for some other sound, some sound of commotion that would mean she was caught. Nothing happened. I pictured her having to hide, making a dash for it, being seen, being chased, being brought back.

Then a car started not far away and roared off in low gear up the road to the Col.

She was gone. A man said, "I'll take you to supper," and she went, though it was an experience we were not considered ready for, not yet. It was forbidden, a progressive culpability starting with the offence of being fully dressed after lights-out and culminating in the crime of keeping company unapproved and unknown to authority in a place unapproved and unknown, for reasons unapproved but soon surmised. And surely culpability ended there and liability began—the innocent's, the green girl's, the virgin's liability to the lust and infamy of men?

It horrified me. I thought how could Solange expose herself to such dangers? She was no fool, she knew what it entailed when a man took an unchaperoned girl to supper.

She knew. I realised that I should never understand her. She was of another race, another creed, another sort.

She hadn't troubled to arrange the pillows to look as if she were still in her bed. It was I who did that, and when the clock chimed one I crept down and unbolted the front door.

I don't know what time she came back. She was just a

thickening of the dark beside my bed. I had been dozing and dreaming but I knew she was using the smile when she said, "I would do the same for you, Rose."

That was the first time. She went again. And again, and each time I swore I would not help her, and she went just the same. Once it was past two o'clock before I unbolted the door. I knew I was going to do it but I hoped she would come back and find herself locked out and have to wait, and I hoped it might scare her, alone in the cold and dark. It was only me who waited and was frightened enough for both of us.

I reasoned that if she were caught she would inculpate me, not from spite—it took trouble to be spiteful—but because she had no conscience.

Towards the end of term they found the door open one morning. I had opened it. Solange was unconcerned. Hadn't I said I would not let her in—wasn't I too nervous, or too tired? Naturally she hadn't relied on me, she had made her own arrangement. It had been complicated, but it had worked and she had not needed to go to the main door. How could she dream I would change my mind? As she understood me, it was a matter of principle, she did not expect me to change that.

When we were interrogated I had to lie. Solange could speak the truth and listen to me lying. She was the only one who knew, but I heard through my own voice and thought everyone else heard through it too.

One of the kitchen staff was already suspected of staying out at night. Nothing could be proved, but fault was found with her work and she was dismissed.

Solange did not go out at night again that term. She resigned herself to Christmas at Winterthur—the holiday was too brief to allow us to go home. It was not the exhaustive festival we made in England and I was thankful. I hadn't much peace and I didn't feel entitled to get or give goodwill.

Merkur Kulm was a failure manqué. I think he would have

had a more compatible brand of unhappiness if he'd been left with his own might-have-been's, if he hadn't been mercilessly fixed in a candle-glow at Winterthur. I know it's easy at this distance of time to add people up, but it's not within my power to be particular. There's no necessity. Everyone must amount to so much, more or less, in a final analysis. This one of mine cannot be checked, let alone corrected: I must take what I can find.

I find that Kulm was a man who would be private and she, Laura Kulm, was a king-maker. That would be enough, neither criminal nor very comic, and I would not have looked further, I would not be looking at all if Solange hadn't shown me.

The school was the Kulms' kingdom, his to reign over, hers to police. She had a precise idea of what she wanted for him and she prevailed because he had no idea what he wanted for himself. It was his undoing that we all had our own ideas of him. Ours were mawkish, yet I fancy Laura Kulm's provided for and to some extent depended on them. It must have suited her down to the ground to keep him hobbled among schoolgirls who could not come near him intellectually or emotionally. That way she secured for him both the prerogative and limitation of royalty. No doubt the balance was painfully kept: to us in our ignorance it appeared to be tipped. We wanted more than a monarchy for Kulm, we wanted a beloved despotism.

There were two seasons that winter. Outside was the feral cold and a grandiose backdrop of mountain and forest. You could sooner walk unawares amongst a brass band than amongst that. After the raw bloomy winters of home it was meretricious. Within doors was the private season which was more than a season, it was an expectation of life. We did not doubt who gave it to us.

I see now how insufficient Kulm would have been alone. He could never have established himself against the ructions and disruptions of forty adolescent girls. He would have gently proffered what he had to give and we were at the stage when it needed to be imposed.

As I knew him he was a mixture of men, incomplete and

biddable most of them. I say as I knew him because I think that without Laura Kulm he would have been faithful to his shortcomings. I can imagine him being content with them. What he gave Winterthur, what she obliged him to give, was essentially his own. I put it as a private resource which would have kept him comfortable and comforting at whatever level he chose to drift to. The struggle was to stretch the private resource to a public fund. They both had to work to do it.

It was Laura Kulm who made the laws and punished us when we broke them; it was she who watched us, her black eyes swam everywhere. They couldn't see into our souls, but they looked into places which we considered private. The state of our finger-nails and the backs of our stockings were near personal; as near, we thought, as hare-lip or acne. Such things ought not to be remarked on in public.

If we laughed we were empty vessels, if we ran we were tomboys, if we gathered more than two together we were geese.

"She thinks she owns us," we said. "She wants a box of tin soldiers."

"Shooting us down is more fun."

"What's it to do with her if our suspenders are twisted and our face-flannels smell? She's no right to go sniffing them."

We tried to mimic her—"You may be sisters under the skin, but you have a choice of company this side of it."

"It's no use, you can't spit as far as she can—"

"What's it to do with her if I fix my hair with a rubber ring? It's more hygienic than hair-ribbon."

We were women enough to resent a woman's thumb over us, but what really disturbed us was the thought that Kulm was under it too.

"Why doesn't he put her in her place?"

"He's too kind."

"It's not kind to let her get above herself. He should exert his authority, after all, he is the Principal."

"So is she."

"He's a man. She's forgotten that."

We decided that he was himself to blame.

"I'd surely like to remind her."

Solange said, "Children, how do you remind a woman that her husband is a man?"

We said coldly that we could show our own regard for him. But of course we already did that, it was expected of us.

We thought that if she could see Miss Gurney or Signorina Piotta acknowledging his superiority she might remember it herself.

Solange said, "Any man can be a man among women."

We left it there because we couldn't see how he was ever to be a man among men at Winterthur.

Is studied kindness less kind? At the time I wasn't to know that Merkur Kulm was keeping to pattern. I would have been humiliated if I'd thought he was doing what was required of him. Although he was a warm-hearted man can I be sure—could he, even?—that he actually wanted to do what he did for me? That he would have done it without Laura Kulm's blueprint? I can't be sure. The sweetness has dried out, I see myself as another score to be made. The truth, I suppose, being six of one, half a dozen of the other. There's no place for that in a final analysis.

Kulm had an uncritical affection for music. He delighted in everything from hill-billies to Bach. Nose-flutes, Welsh choirs and symphony orchestras—he tried to show us the best in each of them, equipping us for a world where we would cultivate our pleasures. I don't think he visualised our needing to cultivate much else. Yet he could never have known the world he was at such pains to make us ready for and I doubt if anyone had—it did away with such a lot that has always been with us.

Not with dancing: we were expected to dance as an obligation of citizenship. Only physical deformity could exempt us. As I have said, I was big and maladroit, the dancing lessons were a trial to me and I considered them a waste of time.

"I shan't do this sort of thing after I leave here," I told Kulm.

"Do not pump your arm so—You mean never to dance? That's entirely absurd."

I said, "Obviously it would be better if I stood still."

"Why? You are not a tree."

"Only the Rose," someone said.

I despised dancing and I wouldn't have cared about looking a fool at it, but suddenly I felt written off. I felt I would never make a woman, not Merkur Kulm's sort of woman, and suddenly I didn't want to make any other sort.

It was a shattering discovery. I was shattered. I stood staring, probably I had my mouth open—it was dry because my heart was beating in my throat.

He said, "Miss Rose, it is just a little turn with the feet—so," and I tried but of course I couldn't do it, certainly not at that moment. My turn went into a spin and they all laughed. Kulm called out sharply, "Take partners for a waltz," and turning to me asked with ceremony and no mockery for the pleasure of this dance.

It was only what was required of him. To me it was a beautiful nightmare. I trod all over his feet while he smiled and supported me as if I were a vine. What with the clumsiness of my feet and the giddiness of my heart I expected to fall right over. I had to cling although his touch shrivelled me. Once his smile froze and he murmured into my ear, "Please do not *shove*, Miss Rose."

When the class was over I tried to get away by myself. The others wouldn't allow it, they came round like cats circling another with a strange smell on its fur. They made me out to be a bit of a clown.

"Why Rose? He was asking for the pleasure, wasn't he?"

"She's nearer his build than anyone else."

"Do you think he likes big women?"

"They made a handsome couple," said Solange.

I was afraid that they would see how wide open I was. I thought I had as much chance of hiding it as of hiding chicken-pox. This was the first time I had been delivered over to someone else and as it turned out the experience did approximate to a chronic and febrile sickness. It shook me out of a quite sturdy optimism and for a long time after I left Winterthur I could not trust myself because there had been intimations, to say the least, that there was more to me than I needed or cared to have. It was an awkward age and of course it passed, but there were times when I not only felt diseased, I felt disfigured.

Love, in this crude form, I had to try to keep whence it came—underground. There was no room for it at Winterthur. I hadn't known there was room in me for such splendours and miseries. Thank heavens I can't remember them in detail, they would be painfully absurd.

I dreamed, not always unashamedly, and shuddered to think what the others would have said if they knew. I suffered from the contrast between their idolatry and mine. My wants were imprecise and Kulm was the source of them all. I doubt if he could have supplied them all because sometimes I was one negative ache for everything under the sun—the state, I suppose, of just being in want. I had to listen to the gossip of those who manoeuvred to touch him and bribed Carême, a flagrantly bad artist, to paint miniatures of him which they put in lockets and albums. He was common property, in the exchange I saw him lose a little every day and every day I recouped the loss. His was an acutely physical presence that had commandeered me during the moments we danced together. I remembered him somewhere deeper than my heart and with parts of myself that until now had served mundane purposes. My skin was still apt to fire all over as it did when he had touched me, and either my blood ran too fast or stopped altogether—anyway I felt dizzy. Then there was my nose, shamelessly recreating, so that I was aware of him as one animal is of another. I was hungry to smell his clothes, his soap, his cigarettes.

I worried about that. It was different from anything the others felt and I didn't think it could be nice. Coming from me it might indicate something I should have to suppress in later life.

I was apprehensive of Solange more than anyone. Her

own affairs never completely absorbed her, she had a knack of seeing the germ of other people's at a glance.

It wasn't easy to dissemble because the joke now was to pretend that I was his favourite. I dared not let them suspect that I pretended it too in secret and dreamed abysmally stupid dreams in which he took me away and held me, not dancing, just holding me and kissing the palms of my hands.

Solange said it was unhealthy the way we all fastened on Kulm, it was bad for women to be without men and for me particularly bad. When I asked why she said because I was 'très sensuelle' and might become perverted. I knew she was just passing the time, she often did at my expense, but of course I got frightened and when she said I should meet more men I overdid it and cried out, "How can I—here?" as if we were in a nunnery. She told me, though not conclusively, that I was a fool. She was dangling a line, I think she had a whim to involve me with herself.

That was the last thing I wanted, so I left my foolishness for granted. I was reminded soon after of what I would have been involved in.

Less than a month after the new term started the six of us from our dormitory, excepting Carème who, as the senior, was interviewed alone, were summoned to the Principals' office.

Mrs Kulm was waiting for us. She was angry. As we went in she looked searchingly at each of us, not to find so much as to confirm what she already knew. I suddenly felt sick with dread. Surely I was the only person who could make her so angry? Somehow she had guessed how I was thinking and what I was thinking about her husband. She was going to denounce me to those I might have contaminated with my sinful thoughts. She was going to rub me out like a dirty mark.

Of course I looked guilty. As a girl when I blushed I swelled, the skin of my face felt ready to burst with blood. She said to me, "Which of you has left the school by night?"

I grunted as if the wind had been knocked out of me.

"Miss Rose Tedder, was it you?"

I don't know why—hearing my name brought out like that

perhaps, at any rate it was purely mechanical—I said, "No, Mrs Laura Kulm," before I could stop myself.

She gave me a blazing stare. It killed my upsurge of relief and rekindled another anxiety.

"Then who was it?"

I dared not look at anyone. We all kept still and Mrs Kulm's mouth, never pretty, broadened without humour like a monkey's.

"I need not remind you that leaving the school thus is violation of the rules, in my opinion to the extreme, and punishable with expulsion. This I promise you, mesdemoiselles, I will discover—" she spat the words with care, "I will break this practice!"

Solange asked, "Why must it be us?"

"I am reasonably assured," Laura Kulm said bitterly. "Which one, or ones, I shall wait to discover."

"Wait?"

Solange might not be that sure of her ground, but she knew she could always walk somewhere else.

"I shall lie in wait," said Mrs Kulm and it seemed so simple that the moment collapsed. She could never do enough, I thought, to harm Solange, but it could poetically or scientifically or wantonly turn back on herself. I didn't at any time fancy her chances.

"Make no mistake, I shall watch, I shall not ask someone else to do it. One night, ten nights, a hundred." She stared at me, I think she had decided that I was the one. "I never sleep until two in the morning. It will be enough."

Solange would be smiling. I knew the sort of thing that amused her without always knowing why. I was afraid of her smile, it wasn't broad and grinning, but sometimes I saw it like the Cheshire cat's, without her, without her face or her lips, just the air smiling.

No one else spoke. There was obviously a great deal that Mrs Kulm could have said. She must have thought we were not the people to say it to. She warned us again. She was determined, she said, to end this situation, and looked as if she wished it was a matter of ending us too. Then she dismissed us. As we turned to go she cried, "I will lie in the door!"

We looked back to see her standing, drawn up to her full height—she was short and dumpy—her head thrown back with an assumption of dignity. She only managed to look defiant and I suspected that if browbeating wouldn't do it she simply did not know how to put the fear of God or herself into us.

When we got away, the others asked what it had been about and they asked us if I was the one who could tell them.

"It's not me," I said, "whatever she thinks."

"Then who is it?"

"What did she mean about lying in the door?"

Mary Sawdell turned to Solange. "It's you, isn't it? You're the one who goes out at night."

Solange smiled. "Where would I go to?"

"I can see how bad it would look for the school," said Mary gravely. "Of course you wouldn't think about that."

"I'm always thinking about the school. What else, when I am always here?"

Someone said cautiously, "Whoever it is won't be able to again because Mrs Kulm's going to be on the watch."

"Lying in the door!"

"That's a figure of speech—"

"Don't be sure," said Connie Dace. "She worked day and night to get this place started—I don't know about him but I guess he worked days anyway—and she won't let anything happen to discredit the school's good name. Rena told me they have a whacking great bank loan. I guess Mrs Kulm will lie down any place to keep that paid up."

"Naturellement," said Solange. "She is a peasant."


I used to wonder how I could ever be finished when I left Winterthur. Half the time I didn't know myself and for the other half I didn't like what I was getting to know.

The curriculum, too, confused me. Whose world was it? To my way of thinking there were only two possibilities, though even at sixteen I didn't expect it to be all music and picture galleries or all money and politics. There was bound to be something of everything and a finishing school should surely help us get our proportions right.

We weren't being helped at Winterthur, we were being loaded with irrelevancies in the hope that enough of them would stick to give us sense or sensibility. To me, the worlds were quite personal and wildly different and there was no question which I wanted to live in, music, picture-galleries and all. Laura Kulm's wasn't spread for us like her husband's, she kept it to her classes and it was about as rich and heady as a glass of liver salts.

I wrote to my father telling him that I was more unfinished now than when I came, that it was a waste of money to keep me at Winterthur, that I was unhappy and wanted to come home. When I read the letter through it sounded querulous. He would wonder between the lines, he knew me better than to believe that waste of money and lack of finish would make me unhappy. I carried the letter about for a week. Nine times out of ten I could not bring myself to post it. At the tenth, unnerved and homesick, I dropped it in the box.

I felt no better and no less about Merkur Kulm. The feeling was in my heart and my head and in places I hardly reckoned to exist, except in a medical sense. And whatever it was—'love' I still called it—was alienating as well as corrosive. I felt transparent, it isn't too much to say that I felt unclean.

Everyone knows the formula, if not from direct experience, from fiction—the fact that one can find it in magazines evidences how commonplace it is. I've seen it in print, with and without pictures, for the world and his wife to read about, the same tragi-comic and, as I thought then, unique affair. I suppose I'm lucky I can say it's been unique within my own experience. Outside adolescence it might be less painful but a great deal more shaming.

Being the magnetic centre at Winterthur, Kulm made the place electric for miles around for me. He had his own problems and as a kindly man would have been disturbed to know how much depended on the crooking of his finger.

Luckily for him, he was completely unaware—with me taking fire in front of him, burning up yet unconsumed like the bush for Moses.

Speculation as to who could be breaking school was never rife. The suspects were Solange and myself. We were uncommunicative, nothing further happened and no one knew for certain if Mrs Kulm was actually keeping watch. The subject turned into a joke. Only Carème respected it, out of officialdom. Every night as she switched off the lights she said, "No one is to leave the dormitory except for natural causes," and five minutes later we could all have stamped out and slammed the door without waking her.

Not long after Mrs Kulm's interview I awoke one morning and saw how restless Solange was, turning on her pillow and murmuring. She seemed distressed and I had never known Solange distressed, even in her sleep. I leaned across to look.

She had make-up on. It was smudged into the pillow, lipstick that made her mouth purple in the clinical daylight, and crusted powder, and her lashes sticking black on her cheeks.

I guessed at once what it meant. She was mad or doomed or invulnerable but I had to try. I shook her.

"Wake up!"

She looked at me from the bottom of somewhere. I got out of bed and bent over her and I could smell where she had been. A bitter-sweet hard smell it was, foreign in an inimical way.

"Take that stuff off your face!"

Her eyes were glassy and almost foolish. She wouldn't see, she rolled away from me with a groan.

I wiped her face as best I could with a damp flannel.

She was the last to get up that morning. She had no breakfast, I think she was sick.

We had a free period from seven till nine in the evening. We were expected to make up discussion groups, listen to intelligent radio programmes and read the classics. It was

Mrs Kulm's method to cram us with culture at every point of entry hoping that we would retain the quintessential. What we mostly did was gossip and play dance music.

I waited until evening before I spoke to Solange again, and then I walked her up and down the corridor so that we could be private. I said I knew she'd been out again the previous night, she was a fool, she'd be caught, I said, sooner or later and it wasn't going to be my business but this once I was warning her. She asked why, what did it pay for, and I must have said something about owing it to myself because she pretended not to know what that was about and said surely no one would think I'd been letting her in all the time? She would explain that it had happened infrequently— Once! it had happened once! I cried—but she pointed out that we might not be believed because Mrs Kulm would naturally not care to think that her rules could be so easily broken by a girl, one girl, going in and out as she chose.

I knew I had to draw the line then, she would panic me just as far as I let her. We were in the passage giving on to the hall. At that time of day the hall was regarded as part of the Kulm's private residence, pupils were not expected to intrude there. I walked away into it without another word, intending to get out through the conservatory door.

I should have known Kulm would be there at that time of the evening, but for once I hadn't been thinking of him. Seeing him—he had something pretty, a pot of camellias, in his hands—caused me the shock of glory I always had at sight of him. I was dismayed too, because I had no business there. But he smiled as if I had been invited.

In my exaltation I felt the world dropping away from me and when he looked past me at Solange who had followed me in I did not grudge her anything. It was intoxication to be so suddenly in his sight, his private sight, without twenty others diffusing it.

He did not reprimand us, it seemed to me he was glad we were there. He talked about the flowers in the conservatory: 'beautiful freaks' he called them, and he said we would see true flowers, gentians and hyacinths growing wild in the mountains. I knew it was right to prefer simple things and it showed how right he was, but I thought the hothouse blooms were prettier.

Of course I didn't say so, I didn't say anything, I just hung on his words. Solange said she liked to have things when other people didn't. She picked the head of a camellia and threaded it into his buttonhole.

I couldn't have done that, not as she did, as if she were both saying and bestowing something. I wouldn't have dared even to pick a flower and I was jealous of everyone and everything with the privilege of not caring.

Kulm looked thoughtful and talked about the best things in life being for everyone. He's Socialist too, I thought. I disliked the idea that any of Laura Kulm should rub off on him.

Solange was bored. She walked away, fingering the plants and when her back was towards us he took the camellia out of his buttonhole. With the point of his gold propelling pencil he dug a hole at the base of the camellia plant and buried the flower.

"Miss Rose," he said, tamping down the soil with the flat top of the pencil, "I have this morning had a letter from your father."

I was watching him. I could appreciate the significance of the ritual, I wished Solange had seen it.

"Yes, I had one too."

There was a middle door in the conservatory. He closed it and we were cut off from Solange. She turned round, I think she watched us, stroking her own cheek with the tip of a great fern.

"Do you know what he has written to me?"

"No."

The last thing I wanted was for the Kulms to suspect that I had asked to be taken away. I had made that very clear but I didn't know whether my father had respected my confidence.

"He asks for a report on your progress." Kulm put the pencil in his waistcoat pocket and looked at me. "I am not sure what I shall say. You have been with us only a little while."

I can still remember corners of his face, the triangle between the cut of his beard and his lower lip and the perfect nib of bone at the end of his nose.

"I sometimes think you are not happy, Miss Rose."

"That's not the point, is it?"

"Not?"

I expect I sighed. I was living, had lived—at that moment I felt immeasurably older than him. "One can't expect to be happy."

"Of course not. One cannot expect, one must *be*." He seized my hands, I thought he was going to make me dance. "It is a duty, Miss Rose, a sacred duty. All else is stupid sin."

I said, "I don't believe we are meant to engage in the pursuit of happiness."

He burst out laughing and pushed my hands back at me.

"What do you know of it? Or of anything that is not written on the blackboard?"

It occurred to me, without titillation this time, that I didn't altogether know him. Experience was allowed for, was in fact required, but not jealousy of it. And here he was, shutting me out before I had got a foot in the door, using his remembrance of things past as unfairly as if he had used his man's strength against me.

"There is nothing to pursue, nothing to run like a mouse. We are not meant to chase, we are meant to achieve. What else is perfection for us but happiness for a minute of time? We cannot be long perfect and we cannot choose when the minute shall come."

I hadn't known him harass a backward pupil, but he was practically stoning me with words. I suppose I went wooden because he sighed with patience regained.

"Why aren't you happy?"

"I didn't say I wasn't. According to you," I said miserably, "I wouldn't even know."

"That was not consistent, I was being resentful of what you have not. Forgive me, forgive all of us who think that to be young is to be happy."

He was inviting, coaxing me to mock him, doing what he

was required to do. This was the old mixture, Laura Kulm had mixed it herself and she knew it would work.

He asked again why wasn't I happy and I mumbled that perhaps this was not the right school. That was stupid because of course he wanted reasons, specific ones. Why wasn't Winterthur right? What was wrong? He was thoroughly alerted. I was sure that if he kept looking at me so piercingly he must see the reason staring him in the face.

"Not right for me, I said. And I only said perhaps."

Nevertheless, he insisted, obviously some aspect of Winterthur did not come up to my expectations. Which was it, the standard of education, the system, the régime or the accommodation and what, precisely, were my expectations? I must appreciate that for him as Principal it was essential to know.

"It's nothing really, just a feeling—" I blushed and tried to slip past him. He put his hands on the bench behind me so that I was restrained without being touched.

"Is it a question of personality? Someone you are not in sympathy with? Miss Rose, is this so important? Is it not bound to happen throughout your life that you cannot love your neighbour as yourself?"

He was so close I felt I was getting drunk on him and I must have looked like a fish, a mullet, open-mouthed and scarlet.

"But perhaps you are worried because it is one of your professors? Is it someone you cannot wish should instruct you?"

I cried out truthfully that it wasn't that sort of feeling and untruthfully that it wasn't really any sort, just a feeling, and then I knocked his arm aside and ran to the door.

"Miss Rose!"

He spoke softly, though as I remember it there was an edge in what he said.

"If the school does not appear right for you could it be that there is something to be learned? Could it be that you will not be happy until you have learned it?"

I did not leave Winterthur House before my course was finished. I had a further letter from my father saying that he was satisfied I was in good hands and should give the school a fair trial—his idea of a fair trial being another six months. If at the end of that time I still wanted to leave he would be prepared to reconsider. That had to suffice for me, though I speculated what his reaction would have been had he known my reasons for wanting to get away.

The strong and lavish winter has taken over in memory. I can't always separate it from the spring and summer that followed. I remember the heat of the sun and a vulgar profusion of wild flowers, but I am more likely to coincide everything that happened at Winterthur with the snow. The snow seemed eternal, and looked it. Only the black ribs of the trees demonstrated how pure and nearly almighty it was. When it went it uncovered a secular world of forests, fields, villages and roads, identifiable and human. The sound of melting snow, the shrillness, was never out of the air and still when I think of Winterthur there is this sibilance as of something extra and private going on.

The seasons decided to some extent what games we played and how we spent our leisure hours, but Winterthur was our kingdom and its frontiers were never really crossed. Not for me. In the holidays home was narrow as a dream and I waited to get back to reality.

That rarefied existence was real. I think most of us were satisfied with little, provided it was a little of the right thing and provided we could believe there was any amount more to come. There were a few for whom Winterthur was like living in a paper bag, but for me everything outside, my own life included, was incidental, and after that one attempt I gave up all thought of going back to it. Having made my gesture I accepted defeat: I welcomed it.

I gave myself up to my emotions. Being denied other outlet they tended to heighten and romanticise my consciousness all round. Kulm was the sum of existence, everyone and everything at Winterthur had a smattering of his glory—Miss Gurney and Polichen and Signorina Piotta. Even Signorina Piotta's stars. They were an establishment superstition. We blamed or consulted them in the same spirit as we threw salt over our shoulders, there was nothing to lose and there might be something to gain. On the occasions when one needed to enlist all the powers it was better to invoke some that weren't than leave out any that might be.

There was more to it so far as I was concerned. I like to think—I still do—that not everything is left to chance. I would sooner suppose that the scope of my life was delimited aeons ago by the solar system than that it is a matter of luck or just my own uninspired doing. Hearing Signorina Piotta talk about ascendancies and conjunctions, crediting one man's misery to Saturn and another man's joy to Jupiter comforted me like a spoonful of syrup comforts a sore throat.

It is difficult now to define that place and how it could contain us. At the time we weren't even aware that we had needs, though from Merkur Kulm we certainly had the impression that they were being met and that they always would be.

I cannot define, either, what he did for us. He wasn't a particularly good teacher of music or dancing—why had he given up Greek and Latin to teach us these pastimes? What mattered to him? The school? Laura Kulm? I suspect he had lost sight of whatever it was and had to concentrate on what mattered to everyone else. Had we all been collectively unhappy and the gift of himself not enough, I don't think he would have known what else to do. His was a lateral talent for heartening the timid and promising the bold. One can have a talent for being or for seeming to be. Where others were adequate at best his talent was to seem so much more. Since Laura Kulm exalted and exploited it probably it was the only one he had.

At Winterthur we were a mixed crowd and might have been expected to be constantly living down each others' foreignness. We lived with it instead, we were cosmopolitan to a skin-depth, a matter—no more, of admitting and celebrating each others' holidays, saints, talismen and attitudes. Co-existence did not much increase our understanding but

149

it created the blithe and mildly scatty atmosphere which we believed to be worldly.

And the Kulms did their best to bring us out into their approximation of the world. Between them they reckoned to provide the essentials for the sort of people we were likely to become. It was as important to be able to amuse ourselves as it was to label our governments and identify our classics. We had 'evenings' once a fortnight when we danced to an energetic little orchestra borrowed from the town band. Connie Dace said she could hear the 'oompha, oompha' in every waltz, tango and foxtrot they played. I couldn't, I have never had any ear for music.

One afternoon the substance of Winterthur leaked out during, of all things, a history lesson. We were in high summer then, pink dust crept across the tennis-courts and to hear waterfalls we needed to go high up into the mountains. We didn't, we were too lazy, the heat exhausted us, we fanned ourselves with our books, we dabbed on Eau de Cologne and Witch Hazel.

It was the end for us all, though to Solange it was probably no more than the end of another day or night, circumstance or habit. And why should I suppose it was the first time for Kulm? Or that there wouldn't be another? Laura Kulm was invincible, she wouldn't admit a defeat in the family.

I can see a funny side to it now—stuffed as I was with novelettish nonsense and urgent and ugly longings. I hadn't been warned about the pangs of growing up and I refused to accept that we shared the principles of the farmyard. I was forever putting those longings behind me. Every time was the last time I would feel like that. I was always newly converted, but I managed to keep private the vision I had of myself calcined and matured by suffering and it was snuffed out that afternoon.

I suppose there's some recognised specification for a dwarf, some minimum height a normal man must grow to and perhaps Polichen wasn't a dwarf. People and places get glorified at a distance of time. If I were to see him now as he was then I might see just a man of under average height, shortsighted and none too clean.

He lived in Basle and came to Winterthur House every week to lecture us in history. The lecture was, in fact, his sole method of instruction so far as we were concerned. We were not expected to interrupt him with questions, and if he questioned us it was to illustrate his conviction that we did not know what he was talking about. He had a poor opinion of our mental capacities, he told us frankly that we were being required to use what we hadn't got. Women, he maintained, had other talents, and although he did not leer there was no doubt about the *double-entendre*. It disgusted us, coming from him.

All the same, his lessons were interesting. History came to us tuppence coloured, his colour. He had a monopoly of the past and he made it live on his terms. Perhaps it was a way of compensating himself for his size.

We tolerated him, as I daresay he knew. We were big even about his penchant for touching us. He was restless and wound-up, he always had to be moving as he talked. In humour, mock anger or sheer necessity he would every now and then put his hand on one of us. He had no preference, it depended who was near at the time and we accepted it as some sort of compulsion, like a nervous tick. Although we didn't care to have his tobacco-brown fingers pressing into our arms and his big head nodding at our shoulders we thought, 'Poor Polly, it's as far as he can ever hope to get.'

It was unusually humid that afternoon. There was a storm coming, it arrived the same night and the thunder and the rose-red lightning seemed fitting after what happened earlier. We were all feeling the weather, Polichen had been prowling since before classes began. When we arrived one of the shutters was flung back and he was padding in and out of a slab of sunlight. He wore the same suit winter and summer, we excused it because of the trouble he must surely have getting anything to fit. He hadn't even left off his waistcoat and his face shone like lard.

We flopped at our desks. We were at a low ebb, I felt it was the lowest ebb possible to sustain life. The sun forged in at the open shutter, putting a finger of heat on us all. The cicadas chirped endlessly and made me homesick for the sparrows chirping through the rain. I longed for some English rain.

We waited without enthusiasm for the lesson to begin. When Solange went and pulled the shutter to it was a relief. Although the air still packed us in it was under wool, not brass.

But Polichen said, "Why did you do that?"

"To make the room cooler."

"I did not hear you ask my permission."

"It's for the general comfort."

"I am in charge of the general comfort, mademoiselle."

Solange inclined her head politely. "Your pardon, Herr Professor, I thought perhaps you could not reach the latch."

There was a rustle. No one laughed. Polichen hooked his thumbs into his waistcoat pockets. There was time for what Solange had said to be said again. And again. And no doubt it was, in his mind. Then he twitched his elbows and began to talk about the First French Republic.

His method was to split open major historical events and shell out the facts for us like peas from a pod. Whenever we laughed about him, we qualified it by adding that he had a brilliant mind.

The heat did not make him lethargic. He never seemed able to relax. If he sat at his table he immediately got up again. The chair was too high for him, it amused us to see him fish about with his toes when he lost contact with the floor.

He trotted to and fro, talking all the while, touching our desks, picking up our pencils, leafing through books. He licked his thumb and rubbed at a mark on the wall. In his way he was bursting with something and we rated his pride or his entitlement to it so low that we did not think of anger.

"The queen—" he was talking of Marie Antoinette— "was enceinte at the time. Enceinte—" he turned on Mary Sawdell. "What is that?"

Mary wasn't terribly bright and she had been half asleep.

"Enceinte—from the French," said Polichen. "There are

152

two meanings, one for a castle, one for a woman. What would it mean, miss, if I should say you were enceinte?"

Mary only suspected the word. She blushed when somebody giggled.

Polichen pulled her hair none too gently. "If I should say that, it would mean a miracle. For you a miracle, an immaculate conception—" Laughing, crouching, holding on to his knees, he turned to Solange. "But not for you, eh, mademoiselle?"

Solange was as surprised as the rest of us. I could see her trying to put two and two together. Polichen set his hand on the back of her neck and brought his face close to hers. "It would not be such a miracle if you were enceinte. Au contraire, it would be something of a miracle if you were not."

"Please." Solange made a frank gesture of distaste and tried to push his hand away.

"Please? Indeed you have pleased certain people if I am not mistaken."

"You are mistaken."

Of us all she could least endure being touched. As she moved her shoulders, Polichen tightened his grip. She tried to stand: he held her, smiling with clenched teeth.

We didn't know what we were seeing, the others knew less perhaps than I, and I felt as if a very wrong record had been put on the gramophone. In the hot vacuous afternoon a little bit of private history was being made.

"Why do you fidget, mademoiselle? You cannot pretend you have not been held by a man before."

"A man, yes—but not by a petit monstre."

She had gone white about the lips, there was no blood in them and they quivered—not, I thought, with anger, but from necessity. She felt sick.

And Polichen was not what we had been used to, bulking no bigger than an undersized child, indifferent to us except for those moments of touching, without pride and with only his one conceit of shelling out the past. He was undersized still, but all there was of him was overcharged with a very present, personal fury.

153

He had this raw spot about his size and we were seeing it pressed upon. He lived in Basle, he could have come across Solange and her friends and been scandalised. Whatever she went to Basle for it wasn't to behave herself, and for all we knew the immoralities of history had made Polichen a phrenetic prude. And he was, as we all were, under the weather that afternoon. But I don't think that was enough, I think something else had already happened, or Polichen thought it had.

He held Solange by the neck and the more she objected the more violently he held her. He was not a powerful man, he did not scruple to use both hands and to brace his knee against the desk.

She too was a bit beside herself, she tried to beat him off like a swarm of flies. He kept reminding her, panting with courtesy, that we were in the middle of a lesson, that he would be obliged if she would stay, that he would say something to interest and enlighten her.

The rest of us just sat there, the record on the gramophone was the wrong record for us all. We listened because we didn't know how to stop it and because we suspected— anyway I did—that it would get worse.

Then Solange broke free. It was an ungraceful movement for her and we rose to our feet. Someone cried to her to run, we wanted it to finish. But Polichen ran too. As she snatched open the door he pulled her back. I cried out and so did others; some of us were frightened, even those who were enjoying it felt that any moment they might not be.

Left to Polichen it might have left off there. Solange, feeling herself caught, became quite frantic and instead of turning to fight his hold fought round her, fought the air. She was so much taller than him, it looked as if he were trying to pin down an overlarge butterfly.

He was only trying to stop her leaving the classroom. Her frenzy had abated his, he must have realised that it ought to be kept to ourselves. If Kulm had not come neither would the moments which none of us enjoyed. Except perhaps Solange because I never understood how or where she found enjoyment.

Our relief was almost corporeal, it fixed Kulm at the other end of the pole from Polichen, the wholly fine and large end. Kulm looked startled, as well he might at finding one of his professors struggling with a pupil and the class bunched round, watching.

He asked if anything was wrong. Polichen said no and Solange said except that the Herr Professor had gone out of his mind.

Kulm considered the rest of us, scared but eager as a crowd witnessing a brawl.

"Should we discuss this in private?"

Polichen said there was nothing to discuss. He had always understood that how he conducted his classes was a matter for his discretion.

"Tell him to let me go." Solange plucked at her fingers as if they were sticky.

Kulm said that Mademoiselle Marigny might safely be released and Polichen replied that it wasn't a question of safety, even for him. He would be obliged if Dr Kulm would not think it necessary to intervene. Dr Kulm would surely agree that to be taught history, to be taught anything, a pupil should remain in class, subject to the teacher. Dr Kulm would surely appreciate that if authority was a nice balance how much nicer it had to be in his, Polichen's case—

"I can't stand any more of this," said Solange.

She looked quite desperate, trembling, her lips pale and her fingers dusting themselves in panic.

"Release her," Kulm said sharply.

"She has made a name for herself—did you know?"

"I order you to release her."

"A bad name for this school—"

Kulm knocked off Polichen's hold. It was a sudden movement and Polichen's hand, flying up, struck off his own glasses.

There was a hush, we were shocked and glad. Everyone looked at the glasses lying on the floor. Polichen was so short-sighted he wasn't sure where they were. He stooped and groped for them.

Kulm himself bent and picked them up. "I'm afraid they're broken."

Polichen fumbled with the spectacles, trying to join the broken halves.

"I'm sorry, Herr Polichen, I apologise. Of course I shall pay for the repair—"

"It's of no consequence. I have others. We will resume the lesson." Turning, Polichen stumbled into the wastepaper basket.

There was a murmur and a laugh.

Kulm said, "If you wish to fetch your other spectacles I will take charge of the class."

Polichen stood behind the table, there was something chilling about his stillness, he who was forever fidgeting about.

"Go to your places," he told us. "Everything is history but everything is not memorable."

Solange turned to Kulm. "I must speak to you—" but Polichen said that she was wasting time, time he was contracted to teach in. If she was not contracted to learn he asked her to do him the courtesy of sitting down while he went through the motions.

"I can't stay here!"

"In the circumstances, Herr Polichen, I think she might be excused."

"In the circumstances?" It was apparently an insult, the last required straw to break his self-control, although I fancied he was himself snatching at and throwing on the straws. "What circumstances? The ones you have engineered, the ones God inflicted on me or those which this girl has brought on you?"

Kulm frowned. "Whatever this is, I think it is not history."

"Permit me to judge that!"

"I insist we adjourn the class before discussing it."

"Permit me to decide that." Polichen's voice, always high-pitched, turned shrill. "I do not require anyone to carry the spoon to my mouth—contrary to appearances!"

"Herr Polichen, remember yourself—"

"I do, though not so highly as you remember yourself, Herr Doktor. Which is strange, when one thinks of it!"

Solange appealed to Kulm. "Can we forget he is small if he himself cannot forget it?"

Polichen tried, with his wet eyes, to focus her. "I have a good memory and I have good sight with my glasses. Yes, at two in the morning I see like a fox. Like a mouse if you wish, like a flea! I have seen your name in the dirt, Herr Doktor Kulm and the name of this school. I have heard you remembered without charity—"

Kulm turned his back. "Please go with me to my office," and I think Polichen might have gone if Solange hadn't said, "Don't leave us, Dr Kulm, we're afraid, we're all afraid when he's like this."

Kulm looked round. "It has happened before?"

To our knowledge it hadn't, but we felt that we had never trusted Polichen and the point, surely, was that it had happened. I felt no great scruple about giving a wrong impression, though I was uncomfortable about the way Solange bowed her head without replying.

Polichen swore that she was a liar, we all were. He swore that he had seen Solange in Basle at a time when she was supposed to be in her bed. There were places where a woman of discrimination would not go, he had seen this young girl in them, this 'fille-de-joie' he called her, and in his towering rage gestured, dazzled, at the rest of us. For all he knew we were in the habit of creeping out to men at night. If the eye had not seen the brain could surmise.

Solange said he was mad. By then Kulm was himself having misgivings. I remember how he touched the dew of heat off his upper lip with his silk handkerchief, his face openly trying to make itself up one way or another, whichever way was best suited to the situation.

There was us, of course, we did complicate things, but at the time I assumed we *were* the situation and was confident that Kulm would handle it.

Polichen demanded an apology from Solange for saying he was mad.

157

Kulm said patiently, "We will consider the matter closed until classes are over."

"Closed? Is it nothing for a teacher to be insulted by a pupil during the conduct of his class? By such a pupil?"

Solange appealed to Kulm. "I was held by the neck like a dog. It's kindness to say he is mad, so why should I apologise?"

"Will you not tell her?" cried Polichen.

"This is neither the time nor place—"

"What other time, what other place? Are you indifferent to a gross dereliction of discipline?" Polichen was fond of tall words. "Is it your intention they should all take a leaf and spit upon me at will? Oh indeed—" he dashed the water from his eyes—"anything is permitted here." He went close to Kulm, plucked at his lapel, raged with his finger-tips over Kulm's waistcoat. "I have seen such things here as only a flea should, a flea between husband and wife, Herr Doktor. But this flea was under a stone—" blindly he pushed his chin into Kulm's chest—"in the garden—this flea has a voice and can speak—"

"Restrain yourself!" Kulm's face was scarcely his own. It was blunted and moist as if the stifling air of the classroom was melting him.

Polichen crouched, bending his knees, twisting his neck, squinting up, pretending to look at a giant.

"God made you big and your wife has made you bigger. Bigger with what? Greek? Latin? I have some Sanskrit in my little finger—enough for a doctorate—" Polichen hissed up at him—"*in nubibus*, Herr Doktor, for here we shall surely not be asked for more."

"You are not yourself, Herr Polichen—"

"Am I not? Yet I am more than you. More than a little music, a little dancing, a little whoring." Polichen, on tiptoe, seemed to be trying to spit the words into his face.

Kulm said nothing. To us it looked as if he was not even parrying, just bending his neck.

"Herr *Doktor*—" it blistered on Polichen's tongue—"if I am to be insulted and my word despised it shall not be here.

I shall choose who looks down, I am not to be ridiculed by women or by a woman's doll."

We waited. There was so much for Kulm to do. Probably most of us favoured violence—I wanted Polichen destroyed with a word, a single withering word, not a blow. Whichever way it was done we were eager for it, none of us doubted that this was Polichen's zenith, that he had been allowed to go so far in order to fall the harder.

Kulm said nothing, did nothing except look over our heads at a piece of vine caught in the top of the shutters.

We were all naïve, and I was naïve enough to wonder why Solange should smile at Polichen and why he should appear to crumple before it. He had been given the last word, it still rang round the room. It was unnecessary and defensive of him to cry as he blundered to the door, "I have better to do than teach history to strumpets!"

# PART FOUR

"You're going to tell her," said Sue Betts, "in so many words?"

"I've already said I didn't think we could work on the same committee."

"What did she say?"

"Nothing."

"She'll keep stalling if she thinks it bothers you."

They were in the church, doing the flowers for the week. Rose had brought Baronne Tonnaye tulips, white narcissi and branches of double cherry from her garden. The blossom was in balls which would open by Sunday but were still fragile. It irked her when Sue too briskly disentangled the sprays.

"That's Vee, permanently off-centre."

"She's aiming for the soft private centre," said Rose bitterly, "and she thinks she's located mine."

"There's nothing personal in it. She's made so she can't go straight."

"Straight?" Rose looked up from bruising the stems of the cherry.

"Well, direct. With her it's method and no matter."

Were the stupid, Rose thought, like the pure in heart, to them all things stupid, all things pure?

"I don't like the method, but make no mistake, there's matter too. Vee's an intelligent woman." Rose propped the blossom in an altar vase and stood back to judge the effect. "She'll make a show but she won't obstruct me." Rose was ready for her to try: the Committee meetings gave scope and audience for Victorine's witticisms, she might be as unwilling to part with them as a comedian with a good stooge. Rose was quite ready. If a request for resignation went unheeded there was a consideration—Rose would not say 'pressure'—which could be drawn upon and which even Victorine Gregory, intelligent or stupid, impersonal or

163

malicious, could not afford to ignore. Rose had only to say, naming no names—certainly not Swanzy's—that there was a rumour among the Committee members which she had been obliged to hear, a feeling which she, Rose, did not share, that Vee should be kept out of public life. Especially when it was associated with the church and reflected morals. Hypocrisy, Rose had only to say, was what the Committee feared to be accused of. "Who to invite in her place is what's bothering me."

"There's no problem, surely? I could name half a dozen right off."

"Name them."

"Jane Frossart and Beryl Kinnear for a start—"Rose had known that she would start with her golfing cronies—"and Peggy Vine and Kate Putnam. They're all sensible."

"You mean they'd think as we do." Rose began to settle the narcissi as a background for the tulips. "They would, wouldn't they? It would be said I'd picked myself a quorum. I want to be fair, Sue, and I want to look as if I'm being fair. In any event, Jane and Beryl are too new to the parish and Peggy Vine's abroad half the time."

"What's wrong with Kate?"

Rose said patiently, "Kate's too right. She's Secretary of the W.I. and we both belong to the Townswomen's Guild." Sue was now absently picking buds off the cherry. Rose twitched it away. "And don't propose Mrs Parradine. Her husband and George Choules are at daggers drawn."

"I wasn't going to. What have you against the Colebrook sisters?"

"Nothing, except that there are two of them."

"Honey, I declare you're being obstructive."

"I'm being careful. I'll think of someone, but it won't solve the immediate problem. Vee's vote on the Peachey question will have to stand."

Sue Betts groaned. "That name again! My stomach grabs every time I remember what Mrs Choules told us."

"There was no need," Rose said sharply. "It was irrelevant and sadistic."

"What made you pick her for the Committee?"

"She'll be useful. It's as well to include someone in the trade on a welfare committee."

"I wouldn't like to have her take up golf."

"She's not the type."

"We're not getting the type any more." Sue took out a pink face tissue. "They all come."

"So Ted was saying. People like Sam Swanzy."

Sue raised her eyebrows. "I wonder he told you that one."

"What do you mean?"

"Did you cotton on? That was clever of you. I had to have it spelled out and then I didn't laugh enough." She swept up the stubs of cut stalks with her tissue. "Those jokes are too technical for me."

"What jokes?"

"I must say I didn't think Ted would repeat that sort of thing to you. Hartley says I'm broad-minded if you take 'broad' as a female noun. I shouldn't talk this way in church—"

"Why shouldn't he tell me? Vee's a friend of mine." Rose said tartly, "I'm one of the few people with a right to know and if I'd been told sooner we might have avoided this impasse."

Sue Betts had scarcely any eyebrows of her own, but she pushed high her two pencilled arches and in an oddly guarded way opened her eyes wide. "How and all, honey?"

"I wouldn't have invited her on to the Committee. Personally it doesn't matter to me one iota." Rose carried flowers in a white plinth vase to set on the altar. "Vee has the right to manage or mismanage her private life without me sitting in moral judgment. But if indeed she is so mismanaging her private life I have to question whether she's likely to lead a responsible public one."

Rose, before the altar, twitching the tulips to rights, felt she had put that quite well. She was vexed when Sue Betts said, "You surely aren't thinking that old thing about Vee and Sam Swanzy?"

"Old?" Rose swivelled round. "How long has everyone known?"

"What's there to know?"

"Unlike Mrs Choules," said Rose, "I've no intention of filling in the details."

"Could you?"

"What do you mean, Sue?"

"In my opinion it's just bad-natured gossip and I give Vee the benefit of the doubt." Sue Betts spoke carelessly but with a pin-pointing stare. "So do you, don't you?"

Rose recognised that this was an engagement, if not a prepared pitfall. Vee herself had said, "There are claws in your back too—"

"Privately I do. Publicly I can't."

"Honey, people are such worms."

She had gone and Rose was picking up her things to leave when Cade came in from the vestry.

He said, "I thought I'd find you here." It seemed to afford him discomfiture more than pleasure. He stood looking at her with something so patently on the tip of his tongue that Rose disposed herself for one of his appeals, irrelative and usually unanswerable.

He waved at the flowers. "They're nice."

"Yes, I like the Baronne Tonnaye. Tulips are such a hard flower, they do best in these soft colours." She waited, so did Cade—for impetus, apparently. He still had his hand extended and his mouth ajar.

The opportunity given, Rose pulled on her gloves. "I must see about lunch."

Cade shut his mouth and swallowed whatever he had been going to say. It went down lumpily and the voice he was reduced to was his pulpit—announcements and church business—one.

"We're starting a fund—" he corrected himself—"an *emergency* fund for the hassocks. It will have to run concurrently with our standing appeals—Famine Relief, Pensioners, and the therapy garden at Overcourt. Oh, and there'll be John Dance to pay for the yews, he's too poor to do it for nothing. But people can be made aware and we shall press ahead as from now. We wondered if something might be arranged in conjunction with the voluntary societies—"

"Who wondered?"

"Mrs Tyndall and I." Warned, but unprepared, he held tighter to his ceremony. "She has been good enough to go into this with me. She herself is organising a bring-and-buy sale and undertaking to contact people who will set up the usual money-raisers. She is also investigating the possibility of a new plastic manufactured, I believe, by a cousin of hers—"

"*Plastic* hassocks?"

"They would be cheaper and well-nigh indestructible. I suggested we enlist the women's guilds through you. The church has been so much your concern—"

"Has been?"

"Is," said Cade quickly. "Of course it still is."

Rose smiled hard. "How nice to know that Mrs Tyndall is such a comfort."

"She has been most practical."

"Don't be misled. Fundamentally she's not a practical woman. Her heart rules her head—she has such a full heart."

"This is our church, we all kneel in it to pray. I don't see the necessity—I never have—" he hesitated: there, at last, was his appeal—"for a clash of personalities. We must supplement each other's efforts—"

"And the fund may even grow if there's no prior claim on it."

"Once donated, the money could not be diverted."

"Not to some vital human need?" It did her injustice, but she could not stop herself. "A retarded child without toys, perhaps, or a criminal lunatic's wife without saucepans?" His face goaded her, it was the stricken standard face, not venturing more than standard dismay. "We all kneel down, all of us who take time from our own affairs to come and pray. The unbelievers can stay standing. They've chosen to."

Outside the sun was shining. A shaft of tumultuous dust was launched between them through the Baptistry window. Cade looked across it as from some high, dry, privileged

place. Was he going to tell her—it would still be standard—
that prayer was acceptable however it was offered, provided
it came from the heart, knees could be straight, hands could
be working, eyes wide open to temptation?

"Are you a believer, Rose?"

Ready for the banalities, she answered sharply, "I try not
to confuse sentimentality with faith or carry those who are
able to walk."

He smiled as if he too had been ready. Rose felt her anger
rising to its true, its native occasion. Sue Betts had only
disturbed it, the origin was earlier and now was here, the
origin was Cade.

"I also try," she said, "not to mistake conceit for conscience. I never have thought it within my power to put the
world to rights."

"Fear is the worst part, fear always is so much worse than
the realisation."

"Fear?"

"Would it be so terrible," said Cade, "if you were to feel
something?"

I am in church, thought Rose, I must remember that. She
looked at Cade; she thought, despise him—you must—he is
not worth more. He has merited nothing but vexation, I see
now that he is not the origin.

"What are you saving yourself for? Rose, can you be so
prudent—" he was frankly mystified—"so rash?"

It was a gap which she had no intention of bridging for
him. Only he would be stupid and presumptuous enough to
ask her. She picked up her basket.

"If you are going to preach, Eric, I suggest you wait for
Sunday."

"I do remember—" he was, as usual, unable to leave well,
or ill, alone—"that you believe some are chosen, to be
suffered but never to suffer because they have too great a
capacity for it, not being—" he was getting it down, in
all earnestness, to layman's level—"what you might call
reinforced, like the many of us. It was your contention,
wasn't it, that such people are sacrosanct, never to be plun-

dered or in any way destroyed, except peacefully, by the grave?"

"Is it a sin," said Rose, "to be peaceful?"

"Immune from wars, pestilence, earthquakes, all acts of God?"

"It might be one of His more logical acts."

"Liable neither to sickness, sorrow, nor bereavement? Apartheid," said Cade, "by special dispensation, from the ills that flesh is heir to?"

"There's no one here to appreciate that kind of humour."

"I'm not being humorous. I can't condemn what I can't altogether see." The golden dust broke over his head as he poked urgently through it. "I want to see, I'm trying to—"

Rose was walking away down the nave. "It doesn't matter whether you do or not."


If Ted Antrobus brought home a business worry he did not air it until it was a *fait accompli* and occasion for worry was past. His method of induction, of acquainting one world with another in so far as was necessary to balance them, was to disallow all immediacy. By the same token, when he brought home a business pleasure, he hitched it on to anything but business.

Now that he had carried through a long-negotiated link with the French Balto Company he was pinning his pleasure to the trip to Paris which the deal necessitated.

"I've a fancy to see that old witch at Croix-Rouge with daffodils in her baskets. Drenched, of course, she keeps a Flit spray full of water."

He sipped his sherry. For him the moment was complete, he would be lucky if any on the trip amounted to as much. "All the times I've been to Paris, but never in the spring. Isn't there a grain of truth in every cliché?"

It was to be a social event, cocktails at the Balto office followed by dinner at the Tour d'Argent. Antrobus was pleased that Rose had been invited.

"It will be a refreshing change from routine for you."

"From parochialism."

"Balto have their executive hive in one of those bankers' streets off the Rond Point, behind the Théâtre Marigny. Very dignified and solid, one would think they'd started hiring cars when Haussmann was building. Their money is all over France, they don't tie themselves to passenger vehicles as we do. They hire out heavy-duty equipment, trucks, tractors, diggers, cranes, drilling-rigs—they have roots. I think we can look forward to a nice little celebration."

"Marigny?" said Rose.

"The theatre. You remember it, a pretty little place on the grass. Played and owned by the Jean-Louis Barrault Company."

"It would be nice if we could have some time to ourselves."

"We might go the day before the party or stay over a day afterwards. Which would you rather?"

"It doesn't matter."

"If you're thinking of shopping, the party is on Tuesday but the big stores close on Monday. It would be no use going a day early."

"No."

"Are you thinking of shopping?"

"Perhaps."

"What else?"

"Nothing else."

Antrobus shook his head. His smile irritated her. It was indulgent and she was not used to being indulged.

"We had better go on Tuesday morning. The notice is short enough as it is."

Naturally whatever was nearest looked largest, but he was seeing it as a question of scale—sometimes ants were almost human too. He tilted his glass to watch the sherry slip in sweet curves down the side.

"Should I make an anonymous gift to the church for favours received—the Balto agreement is quite a favour— and asked—we want a safe journey, don't we? It would be an appropriate gesture, though barbaric. Just a modest sum, say fifty pounds?"

And what was this, thought Rose, this refusal to appoint values except on his own scale, but a kind of parochialism? If his skin was his parish, could there be any getting away?

"The occasion has been priced." Antrobus smiled. "Why pay more?"

"You needn't pay as much. I understand the church is being provided for."

"It is? By whom?"

"By Mrs Tyndall," Rose said bitterly.

He would not wonder how, he did not wish for details. He said, "So it's settled?" and added to her resentment by being frankly prepared to drop the subject for good.

"Nothing's settled until the Committee meets again."

"But there is no deadlock?"

She might have told him that the deadlock had ceased to be important and then he would have asked what was worrying her and she was unable and certainly unwilling to tell him.

"I haven't changed my opinion about where the money should go. I still maintain it would be doing the woman a disservice to give it to her at this stage. Even though that makes me a monster."

When he raised his eyebrows she cried, "To Eric Cade it does."

"You all appear to have lost your sense of proportion over this business. It has brought out—" he paused—to modify his words, she thought—"a new side of you."

"Perhaps you too think I'm a monster."

"Don't be ridiculous."

"There's nothing new, I hope, in my refusing to go along with sloppy thinking and mawkish sentiment. Of course this thing has been exaggerated, it's been laboured. I'm surprised," said Rose. "I wouldn't have believed intelligent people could be so petty. I've tried to be sensible, but when everyone else is making mountains it's hard to remember we're dealing in molehills."

"Not molehills." Antrobus closed his eyes. "Hassocks."

For him, that epitomised it all, her part as well as the rest. He needed neither to deny nor ignore, he was simply

171

unaware of any further dimension in her, though she was beside him, within touching distance, though they spent some third of their lives together. She knew, moreover, that he would wish to be unaware: he would, with relief, have chosen to be.

"I could give chapter and verse for all of them. The person who surprises me most disagreeably," said Rose, "is Eric Cade."

There was a faint recession, a withdrawal, from under Antrobus's closed lids which she recognised as his preparation for tedium. She had seen it before when people did not realise that he had finished with a subject. She herself was usually ready to finish or relinquish it at his moment. Now she felt a disproportionate dismay.

"I thought he was a sensible man, I reckoned on it."

Sensible was the word if one gave it its due, full measure. 'The same', she could have said, 'I thought he was the same'—because ultimately there was only one way to be. "He's not even adequate. Surely we're entitled to expect something slightly above average from a man in his position?"

Antrobus had not expected anything. If he had claims they were not laid in that quarter.

She said furiously, "Sanctimony and a sheep's heart is all he can bring us."

"But he's by way of being a shepherd. His flock expect a certain affinity with themselves."


It is a convention still to look for more. Convention is a kind of order too and if I go to church out of tidiness that's as good a reason as habit and a better one than caution.

What did I look for? From the man of God a little godliness, I suppose, though I learned as long ago as Bonneval that the Infinite does not rub off, even on those nearest.

He should at least know where he stands. It isn't as if he has a choice. He would like to have—he would choose to be a victim. It would be his surety. Suffer and you are

absolved, you need not answer. He would like to be cruci-
fied, then he would know he was right.

I don't know if I am right. I know I could not bear to be
wrong. I shouldn't survive, I should simply cease, have to
turn my back. Events have shaped and not rough-hewn me
and I must take it to mean that I amount to more or less
than the other sort. Or to something different.

I am as I have been turned out, with no provision for
violence. With no necessity for it, either.

Is it irresponsible to have had a quiet life, anti-social to
want one? As to wars and acts of God, must I strip myself
raw for the whole world?

The other sort does not require anything of me. Certainly
not my vicarious participation in their affairs. It would be
futile to borrow from a burden without being able to take a
straw off the weight. Besides, they are self-sufficing, capacitated one way or another.

Solange was not just capacitated. I think of her, herself
immutable and immune, as pulling violence out of the air,
out of petty virtues and out of prayers. Perhaps she enjoyed
it. Perhaps it was the only way for her to live.

She was young, she might have changed. She will be a
woman of my age now, surely she won't want to start anything? Did she ever want to? Perhaps she was the catalyst
that brought it on, perhaps she still does and it breaks over
her like a dry wave.


"Is that what you want to do?"

"Yes," said Rose, "that's what I want to do."

"You won't have much time."

"It shouldn't be too difficult. Her father was a well-known
lawyer and they had a flat at Neuilly."

"Why haven't you tried to find her before?"

If she said because it hadn't mattered before he would
feel obliged to ask why it mattered now.

"It's a whim."

"You don't have whims."

"I have this one."

"An old school friend?"

"I want to *know*—" Meeting his gaze, she amended quickly, "I'd like to know what happened to her, that's all."

"Too much, probably, to track down in one afternoon. How long since you heard of her?"

"It must be thirty years."

Rose understood that he did not wish the day in Paris to be pre-disposed, he wanted it left to turn out as it might— at this moment of euphoria he could see it turning out very pleasantly—"She may be dead—" but he was unlikely to make any positive fight to retain it. "If she is, of course there's an end."

"What's the connection?"

Rose was surprised that he should ask, although she appreciated that the last thing he wanted was to be told.

"Connection with what?"

"It has the smell of principle." He drained his glass. This was the moment, precisely by the clock, when they reckoned to finish their drinks and go into supper. "If a few preliminary enquiries could be made we might discover whether the person you're looking for is in Paris."

"Now you think I'm being sentimental—"

"The Balto people might investigate so far as the present where-abouts are concerned."

"How could they? Why should they?"

"Because they are in Paris and because I should ask them. They have a man, Bonnetante, for the public relations side. This should be within his scope."

"Bonnetante? Good Aunt? What a funny name," said Rose. "Would he mind, do you think? This is a personal matter, nothing at all to do with your business."

"I shall say it has charitable connections."

The affair was well organised. They were met at Orly by Bonnetante in one of the Balto cars and driven to the Place Vendôme. Their hotel was Balto policy too, Antrobus said. He defined it as the art of giving always a little more than was expected, even though it might mean supplying a little less than was needed.

There was certainly a little more at every turn in the hotel. White gloves and a coachman's cockade for the commissionaire, gold fretwork cages for the telephone booths, a kiosk selling chocolate and tiaras and in the lifts inlaid wood panels of Eastern scenes. And, as Antrobus pointed out, the telephone booths were less than soundproof, the kiosk was locked and there were no floor indicators inside the lifts.

It worked another way: the place was baroque, tarnish and a little dust would have made it blowsy, but there was instead a sense of a great deal being done, devotedly, out of sight, to be served up with a flourish, with ice, or the manager's compliments. A sense, in fact, of an expensive hotel. More expensive, Rose decided, than they would have chosen for themselves.

"You will not lack comfort here," said Bonnetante, and his tone inferred, "whatever else."

He was a young man with a vast body, a behemoth in a hopsack suit. One leg of his trousers would have clothed Antrobus. He appealed to Rose, "Comfort is the important thing?"

"On a short visit," agreed Antrobus. "I should think they do you pretty well here."

"Indeed it is much in favour with visiting firemen." Bonnetante beamed, inviting them to share his pleasure at the phrase. He ushered them into the lift. "If you will permit I shall see if they have forgotten anything."

At the doorway of their room Rose exclaimed, "Why, it's a suite—"

"I thought yes, a sitting-room. Mr Antrobus will have business papers to read." To Rose he politely drew down his chin into the solid folds of his neck. "And ladies like to retire."

The sitting-room was a study in tapestry and fumed oak. "It is the Windsor Suite," Bonnetante said proudly. "Do you feel yourselves at home?"

"My dear fellow," said Antrobus, "it will be difficult to remember we're in Paris."

Rose hardly had time to put down her handbag and take off her gloves before a waiter arrived with tea.

"I thought yes, the four o'clock." Bonnetante detained the man while he checked the tray. "With cold milk and arrowroot biscuits. It is all here."

"How very thoughtful of you," said Rose.

"It is my pleasure. Should there be anything lacking, but anything, acquaint me, please, immediately." He backed to the door, his suit ebbing and rucking on him like the hide of an elephant. "I will leave you to take tea. A car will be here at seven. Until then, au revoir."

At the door he lifted his hand and seriously twinkled two fingers at them.

"He reminds me of Oliver Hardy," said Rose when they were alone.

"Do you begin to see what I mean?"

"It seems ungracious when he's so painstaking."

"The point is, we could have done without this—" Antrobus gestured at the room and the tea-tray—"whereas what I do need is an hour's hard talk, figures supplied, with one of their people, one intelligent, unequivocating man off the road."

"You could ask for it?"

"I could, but I wouldn't get it." Antrobus lifted the lid of the teapot. "Mystique you're bound to encounter in any business and with Balto we're not even consanguineous. Blood will be thicker than oil."

"Teabags," said Rose, "with a label to hang outside the pot. The milk may be cold but it's been boiled. I think I remember where we are."

"The smell's no different. Less acrid, perhaps, than in winter. I wouldn't say it was loaded with anything indefinable—anything I wanted to define, that is."

"I didn't like to disillusion you," said Rose, spooning a flake of fat off the milk, "but whenever I've been to Paris in the spring there's been a gritty wind."

Oddly enough, Rose herself supplied a little more than was

expected—more, anyway, than she had expected of the Balto premises. As Antrobus had described, they were in one of the seemly boulevards having neither cause nor incentive to move with any time other than their own structural depreciation, and that would be leisurely, judging by their ample set on the ground, their slabbed and stone-faced walls and the ecclesiastical spread of their doorways. Outside, the chestnut trees too had stood a long time and the pink blossom looked ill-advised, already it was browning and being surreptitiously dropped.

Inside, Rose was at once aware of a familiarity with the place without the slightest practical knowledge to justify it. In some purely atmospherical way she had been there before. The curious appeasement, the sense of arrival, had always come to her inside that door.

She indulged it at first, luxuriated while the introductions were made: here, she was moved to think, she would meet no enemy. That was feasible, of course, since she was unlikely to get to know any of these people well enough to make friends or enemies.

As it happened she had no opportunity even to find out how much of Cavour, Balto's managing director, was face value. At first sight he impressed, a mighty, angular old man, impeccably turned out, with the curling beard of an Assyrian. His looks did not reflect his capabilities, whatever they were.

In shape his wife was a reversed 'S', carrying her breast and buttocks like offensive weapons. She was vividly powdered and pegged out with jewellery. She spoke no English, to Rose's careful French she adapted her face like someone listening to a badly-tuned radio.

There were a dozen guests, regional agents and their wives, the Company's lawyer and a silent boy in a rusty tuxedo who was thrust forward as Cavour's grandson.

Rose could have picked Bonnetante's wife out of any group. She was a saffron blonde with his same soft debility. She was pretty in an unhealthy way and already getting on for drunk.

There was pressure on people to drink. Wedged behind

the bar, Bonnetante was filling glasses, young Cavour was plucking them empty out of hands and off the tooled-leather top of his grandfather's desk. Rose held on to hers, she had taken only a sip. It was not her wish to cloud or colour her own sensibilities. They were rosy enough, at this stage she needed to clarify them. And as she looked about she had to credit them to something altogether physical, irregularity of glands or corpuscles or gastric juices. Because what comfort would there be for her in this French business-house? Assuming she needed comfort. She had not come away for it, she had simply come away, and if she were to look back now it would be too soon for anything to be resolved. Time, a distance of time, was the essential factor. The most she could hope for was that when she went back she would have no more questions to ask.

But where was the promise—here? The air of permanence was Balto's business climate, it could have no significance for her. The rest was walls and windows, nice, serene old walls, and a group of people to whom she owed nothing and with whom she had nothing in common beyond this place and time. She was, she concluded, herself putting out the promise, hope, comfort, whatever it was, and getting it back like a full echo—the only known stimulus, she thought with amusement, being a teaspoonful of gin.

"You smile, madame" said old Cavour. "What amuses you?"

"Not amuses—pleases," she said tactfully. "I was admiring your offices."

Cavour opened his hands as if the place had blossomed out of them. "Ah, indeed, this is a beautiful building. It was occupied for many years by Henri Pecuchet. Here he made two fortunes, two great fortunes, and spent them." Cavour sighed. "I should be so happy to make one little one."

"You can count on that, surely?" said Antrobus, smiling.

Cavour's cheeks hollowed like a lantern. "In France, today? Today only the Government makes a fortune. The big flea is on the little fleas' backs."

"I should feel worried if I thought you couldn't handle that."

"But what has become of us? Pecuchet would not be possible today, if he were to make such money he would see it only on paper. No aeroplanes, no racehorses, no yachts, no safaris—"

"It is becoming true," said Bonnetante, "that to earn a hundred francs you must first spend a thousand."

"Who will work for paper?" cried Cavour. "Even I, an old man without pleasures, must work for something—a little money to keep body and soul together and to bury me when they come apart."

Madame Cavour remarked that Rose looked German.

It was an odd moment, they all turned and considered Rose. She was abstracted, cut out from their dubious kinship. In that moment she felt they had settled something on her.

"Actually my wife comes from Beckenham," said Antrobus.

"Beckenheim? It is a German name," said Madame Cavour. No one corrected her.

Cavour raised his glass to Rose. "I have remembered something to tell you, madame, of the history of this place. During the Occupation a man was hiding a long time, perhaps a year, in the wash-cupboard—the lavabo. At the top is the basin and taps, so: underneath is the pipe in a little cabinet. In this cabinet he hid. The building was full with rubbish, no one living here save this one. He was Polish, Dutch, Russian, perhaps a lunatic. Some say he was only frightened. In this cabinet he curled like a serpent—"

"Round the waste-pipe?" said Antrobus.

"Like a dog," said Bonnetante. "He was called Bijou like a dog."

"In this cabinet he slept all day. At night he went across the roofs, he found some bread, he was not ambitious. Who was, in those days?" Cavour's beard arched to a winning smile. "It is true I was never in Paris then. I was in Switzerland, with good friends. I had food, clothes, daylight. I had only to please myself. But I was not pleased, I could not be happy. My heart bled for my country, every mouthful choked me because there were people in France eating dirt.

Every kind word was a blow because in France women and children were punished with death. Every hour of freedom was a mockery because I was confined—here." He tapped his forehead. "I was Occupied."

"En effet," said Madame Cavour, "il était désolé."

"This one, this Bijou, he too had only to please himself and he was pleased. In his cupboard no one could come behind him, he was content. Imagine, it was his shell, he did not wish to stand upright. Ah, the happiness of being able to turn one's back! Then at last Paris was liberated, Paris was free and there was no longer need to hide. But he would not come out. Why should he? Out of his wash-basin he was homeless—naked, madame," said Cavour delicately, "if you will think of a hermit crab."

"What happened?" asked Antrobus.

"They had to smoke him out. Then it was his turn to choke. There was always this one," Cavour said to Rose, "who was sorry to be free."

Bonnetante sighed, first gathering the air into his huge skin and then letting it rustle out with a noise like a tree turning its leaves. "Crossing the Champ de Mars he died of exposure."

They all laughed. Except Rose. She supposed that the story had all along been funny and laughter was now in order, was due.

"I'm sorry," she said to Cavour, as one who cannot pay a small fee.

"You don't like stories?"

"I thought this one rather cruel."

"Cruel? To myself?"

"To Bijou it was rather kind," said Antrobus. "He had the best days of his life in that wash-cupboard, it was a return to the womb, the only place one can be completely happy."

Rose turned her back. "I have a mundane sense of humour."

Cavour flung his arms wide as if to embrace her. "Madame, you should never ask pardon for a kind heart."

When the party broke up to go to the restaurant for

dinner, Antrobus said she had been too sharp with the old man.

"I don't like him. He's insincere."

"Well?"

"All that talk about suffering for his country. He was still having the cake that he'd eaten in Switzerland."

"I've no business with his morals, and neither have you. Will you come off those hassocks!"

"Must I laugh when he crooks his finger?"

"My dear girl, it was only a story and palpably untrue."

"If it wasn't true, or funny, or interesting, why tell it?"

Bonnetante had arranged that after dinner they should go to a night club. Cavour and his wife dropped out of the party, taking their grandson with them. The old man pleaded weariness, but he looked as curling and lustrous as ever.

Rose was glad to see him go. For him Antrobus brought out his business side plus a tongue-in-the-cheekness to accommodate the snide in Cavour. She heard all through dinner the bogus bonhomie put up between them. It occasioned her certain qualms which she had had before and could expect to have again, but now she wondered whether they were symptomatic of more, between her husband and herself, than two ways about the same thing. Was a man who could enjoy Cavour's sickish humour and cap it, being expedient only? Was it an eye to another kind of business that he turned on Bonnetante's wife? Was it six of one and half a dozen of the rest with him? Could it be, with any man? He had to have a larger half and perhaps she should be prepared to find that this was it.

The club was somewhere in the Bois. Rose had never seen a more curious place. The motif appeared to be frustrated endeavour and misplaced strength. It reminded her of a nightmare in which one tried to run and was fixed to the spot. Untrimmed beams clambered up the walls, the black glass bar was supported on coiled iron like massive bed-springs and the light fittings were in sockets that would have carried railway sleepers.

"Why do they try so hard?" she murmured to Antrobus as they were taken to their table.

"I imagine it's not easy to be different and right too."

Bonnetante seated them at a floorside table with himself and his wife. "One is not annoyed here. The cabaret is often clever—and nice." He looked pressingly at Rose. "One cannot say this of everywhere in Paris. The décor is nice also. Distingué." He picked up a match-stand that appeared to be rivetted with coach-bolts. "Do you agree?"

"My wife is single-minded," said Antrobus, "but not necessarily a prude."

"Pardon?"

"And even that's a phase. It will pass. I've always found her ready to live and let me live with my inabilities intact. She's not really intolerant, you know."

"But I am not complaining!"

Antrobus smiled. "In England we say, 'Ah, but you should have seen my garden yesterday'."

If Rose had come in now and seen him suddenly without the time to grow on her it would have taken a moment to recognise him. He had his same tidy shape, adequate for all his reasonable purposes, not to be picked, for good reasons or bad, out of a thousand others, but there was a different man inside. He managed to change everything. The usually pale, rather flaccid face was brickish, packed for action. The dark chin had a business bloom and nothing was withheld in this man's eyes. He was ready to spill himself and her too if it would carry a moment.

She said, "Am I being difficult, Monsieur Bonnetante?"

He looked shocked. "Chère madame!" and Antrobus gave him a mock salute.

Rose felt uneasy. She understood that so far as she was concerned something was going awry. At this stage she had not expected to be much concerned. This stage was still essentially a business function and she was present as a social accessory. Her social duty apart, she had expected to be with Antrobus—that only, and certainly no less. When champagne was put before her she picked up the glass and drank, seriously and privately.

Antrobus was drinking whisky, not privately, leaning across to the next table to the rest of the party. They responded, smiling, toasting him, tossing up and defining words with their hands. Rose could not hear above the throbbing of the small orchestra. She told herself that the sense of what was being said would bear out the suspect look of it.

"I don't cry easily, either," she said to Bonnetante.

"Madame?"

"Humour's so personal." She was thinking that some people would find him comic, poor man, he had such a crumpet face—all those big pores and baked freckles and the buttery shine. "I don't like extremes, they're vulgar. I don't like vulgarity, do you?"

Poor man, he probably did, he probably wasn't equipped to like anything finer. She took another serious drink from the glass he had just refilled for her.

"You mustn't believe what my husband said about me. I may have disappointed him this evening and he would be chagrined, naturally. But it was unkind to call me single-minded when he meant that I had a one-track mind. It goes to show what a very, very little way he sees into it." She rolled the stem of the champagne glass between her finger and thumb. "It's terrifying—" here was what this evening had surely been designed to prove—"how little we want to know about each other."

Bonnetante had only just settled the bottle back in the ice-bucket but he took it out again without so much as the twitch of an eyebrow.

"I have made enquiries, madame, and am happy to be able to tell you—"

"Really, Monsieur Bonnetante," said Rose, "what about?" She heard herself laughing for the first time that evening. She thought, this really is funny. "I thought you were engaged on public, not private, relations."

"About the matter you are interested in." Bonnetante filled her glass and wiped the mouth of the bottle with the table napkin as tenderly as if it were a child's. "The famille Marigny."

Antrobus had asked Madame Bonnetante to dance. He called her 'Yvette'. Was that her name—like a French maid in a British farce?

"Maître Quentin Marigny is dead," said Bonnetante. "Of the family there remains his wife, Madame Marigny, living at Neuilly, and a daughter, a Madame Danièle. She has a boutique, a nice small business in rue Lapalisse near the Bourse. It is called 'Céline'."

"Chelle?" Chelle was the business woman. "Is she dark and small and quick like a monkey?"

"I have not seen these ladies, madame."

"There was another daughter—"

"There is no one else."

Antrobus danced badly, jigging against the rhythm and hustling his partner into other people's backs. He and Madame Bonnetante could be identified as a travelling eruption on the crowded floor.

"And Bonneval? They had a château at Bonneval, it would belong to Valentin now—"

"There is no one else now."


Chelle in rue Lapalisse, black little Chelle with no time for anyone or anything except money and the people she was getting it from, had the Bonneval noonday with her, she had those hours when the leaves took the weight of the sky and one blade of grass wagging was a signal in the stillness and the towers shone like tin and at table the family watered their wine. Chelle had the forest, she *was* the forest. Thirty years after I can't remember all those canyons, galleries and torrents of trees except as Chelle. It's not surprising that she should emerge as the spirit of the place. She imposed herself on it because she was strong enough and the only one who cared enough to do so.

I found I could visualise Chelle as a woman. She would have grown up smart, her hair that used to have sawdust in it would be tinted an unsuitable colour. She would pretend not to know me, perhaps she really wouldn't remember. It would make no difference. She was always so taken up with her own affairs she would in any case be unaware of any but the barest facts even about her own sister.

Solange I couldn't imagine as other than she had been. I certainly couldn't see her at my age—not that there was anything Peter Pannish to go on—I simply didn't see her getting to it. She would have died first. And it would be beyond Chelle or anyone to tell me how she died. All I could hope to hear now was what terminated her life and I could draw my own conclusions, which I would have had to do anyway. Alive and talking Solange would never have told me what I needed to know.

As Bonnetante had said, 'Céline' was a good business. I wouldn't have bought anything there without first fixing a reserve price in my mind and it would need to be steeper than I normally pay. Not that I'd be tempted, I don't know who would—rich women perhaps, for their trousseaux, actresses, what used to be called the demi-monde. The things were exquisite, made with artistry and of the finest materials. With a woman inside them they would be obscene, she would be better covered by a spider's web.

I tried to decide what to say to Chelle. She had never been easy to talk to, as a child she was already older than everyone else. She could brush me aside, she had been good at that and would be better still now. Although she could hardly refuse to answer my questions she might answer them so that I was left with new ones. I didn't want to go to Madame Marigny, her cloud of unknowing would surely have become a fog.

I walked past the shop and looked into a confectioner's window. Facing Chelle didn't worry me so much as facing what she stood for. I've always regarded Bonneval and the Bonneval summer as the making of me.

I decided that attack was my best method of preservation. I decided to tell Chelle right away that she would not recognise me and that I didn't require her to. I would tell her that it would be enough if she would cast her mind back to recall that there had been such a person as Rose Tedder and would accept me as that person and indulge my legitimate curiosity for five minutes.

I went into the shop and a man, tall and languid, drifted to me, smiling. He took one look at my feet and asked in English if he could be of service.

"I'd like to see Madame Danièle."

He was sorry, Madame Danièle was just then otherwise engaged. Was there something he could show me?

"I'll wait. It's a personal matter."

He had beautiful eyebrows which he used to identify his reactions. His smiling jaws, like his black coat and striped trousers, were de rigueur. The rest of his face did not move.

He bowed me to a gilt chair. I should take a seat—it might be one moment, it might be ten before Madame Danièle was available. Certainly he would acquaint her, but with what name?

"She doesn't know my name. I'm a friend of her sister's."

His eyebrows crept a shade higher. "A friend from America?"

"From England."

Why America? What was he thinking? Was it native caution or something specific that made him hesitate? Or was he registering details to pass on?

He went away smiling his dress smile and I looked at the shop. It was all dove-grey and gold, a small place, 'intimate' I suppose it would be called, lined with tinted mirrors. I could see my head and shoulders in them. My hat, which had looked smart when I put it on, was now entirely me, the emphasis misplaced on aspects which did not bear on the matter in hand. For instance, a tendency to what, in a younger woman would be fluffiness, in me was a smudging of outline. I've always wanted to be clear-cut. At my age it would even be preferable to be a little haggard. People have said that my name suits me, and what can be worse than a middle-aged rose?

My hat was wrong that day, so was my oatmeal-coloured suit—there was surely never such a colour for spreading. And my amber necklace, perfect with the suit, was perfect for any number of occasions excepting this one. I nearly went away, I felt at such a disadvantage. Then I comforted

186

myself that I wasn't seeing a true image because the mirrors were tinted and I turned to the showcases.

In one of them a night-dress was trailed from the beak of a crystal bird. It gave me a curious feeling as if I, not the garment, was being offered for sale. It was scarcely a garment, it was designed to accentuate a woman's nakedness and I would cheerfully have paid for the satisfaction of stuffing it into the fire.

A woman appeared at the back of the shop. I saw at once that it was not Chelle. She was tall and moved deliberately—painfully, I dare say. She had the sort of figure which at her age can only be achieved by corsetting. Her hair was dyed the colour of peach dust and wound round her head like a turban. She carried one hand within the other, which most women do out of awkwardness. She did it out of self-possession. She was a complete stranger.

"Madame Danièle?"

When she nodded I said, "Née Mademoiselle Marigny?" and she did not bother to nod. I had to face the fact that Bonnetante's enquiries had gone wide. It was the last thing I had allowed for. I wanted to find out where the mistake was, but in my embarrassment it did not occur to me that this woman might understand English. I felt myself colouring up, swelling with colour as I used to when a girl. My French sounded pidgin and vulgar.

"Mais vous n'êtes pas, je suis sure, la fille du Quentin Marigny, le Maître Marigny de Bonneval?"

"La même."

I don't think I've seen anyone else off the stage or screen wearing such a zealous make-up. It was a dense mask, almost a fabric, with the skin pores showing through like the weave. Shadows were feathered in under the cheekbones and laid greenish and moist on her eyelids. Her mouth was boldly shaped, impossible to see how much of it was her own. Her lashes were stubbed with mascara, the shape of her eyes lengthened and changed with it, all I could see of them was a glimmer, a sign, no more, of occupancy.

It must have taken hours to put that face on, it was

grotesque and misleading as a clown's. How should I know that it misled when I'd never seen her before?

"Rose-red," she said, "comme d'habitude."

I couldn't believe it, I couldn't believe anyone could hide so completely. I kept trying to place something of hers, but only the way she looked at me was unmistakable.

"You have improved, Rose, but you still have too much blood in your neck."

I touched the beads at my throat, lifted them and felt myself as absurd as an immensely fat woman whom I once saw perspiring and slapping her chest with a rope of pearls. It convinced me that this was Solange.

"What ashames you?" She widened her eyes, the glimmer became a glint of laughter. "There was always something, so what is it now?"

"I'm sorry." It was ridiculous that I should have to stop myself straightening and twitching and trying to divert her attention from my face when God knew it was my own and I had nothing to be ashamed of. "I didn't expect to find you here, I expected to find Chelle—"

"The shop is named for her."

"I didn't expect to find a man here—"

"Lutèce, my partner."

"It was a shock seeing you—I mean," I said hopelessly, "when I'd thought—Solange, I'm so glad, so very glad."

I would rather it had been Chelle, anyone—not even a Marigny. Solange had never let me be, I had always to watch with her and suffer, by myself, my own normal legitimate actions turned antic. I did not like her, but it had taken thirty-five years to assemble discomfitures, mischiefs, reservations and inadequacies into that plain fact which wasn't going to help me now.

"Chelle is in America, Valentin is dead and my father also. There is still Maman and myself to be glad for."

"Did Valentin—was it in the war?"

"He did not need the war, he did it himself."

"You don't mean he committed suicide?"

"He died with food poison." She took one hand out of

the other and spread it with a touch of the old impatience. "If you wish to talk we can go to the office."

The man, Lutèce, was in the room behind the showcases. I fancied he had just moved from the door. If so, he had been listening. He and Solange did not speak, he passed us, smiling, and swayed away into the shop.

The room contained a desk, armchairs, and in an alcove a divan bed. Solange watched me look at it.

"You know what you must think, Rose?"

"I beg your pardon?"

"You were always so pure in the heart, since then you have been given to think." She turned her back to take a bottle and glasses from a cupboard. "Even if I tell you that sometimes I sleep here, sometimes I do not go home, you won't believe me. Once you had no doubts, now you have them and you give no one the benefit."

"I really don't know what you mean."

She poured a cognac and pushed it across the desk to me. She did not smile as she used to—I think the glaze would have cracked on her face—but it was still my drawback to be aware that she was getting the same sort of entertainment out of me.

"I can't believe you've changed sufficiently to care what other people think."

She drank her cognac and poured another. "Do you never exercise your own thoughts?"

"I didn't come here to quarrel—" But it was needless to say because she never quarrelled. "Or to argue the point."

"What point?"

"I came out of friendship."

She sat down in the chair opposite and with the toe of each foot prised off her shoes. They had heels like pencils.

"I wanted to know what happened to you all. Is that suspect?"

Of course it was. Everything I said and did was for re-examination to make holes where she could not find any. But suddenly, as of old, she had had enough. She turned her mask towards me.

"This is what happened. My father died, Valentin also.

My father was already old. Chelle married a life-saver and lives in Florida."

"A life-saver?"

"They have a house on the beach. Tin-Tin is dead many years, so is Uncle Dubosque. What else? Maman and I live at Neuilly."

"With your family?"

"I have no family."

She was pouring her third brandy. I hadn't touched my first.

"You married—you're Madame Danièle?"

"Je suis veuve."

Yes, she had had enough. She was ready to drop everything outside herself. If I had stood up and said goodbye I believe she would have let me go without another word. And she would drink the brandy I had left. It should be possible to detect at least some tremor in the movements of her hands.

"And you had no children? Neither did I, though I'm lucky—I still have my husband."

"I'm glad."

She hadn't lost the old trick of cutting the ground from under me by suddenly taking her tongue out of her cheek.

"He's here in Paris. I'd like you to meet him."

The mask had tilted as if it was heavy on her neck. I remembered her saying once that no one should tell her what to do, she would always do as she wished. Presumably this was it, a part if not the sum of what she really wanted— to paint her face and drink alone.

"Why not come with me to the hotel for tea?"

She drained her glass and let her wrist drop with it on to the desk. Her fingers, uncurling, rubbed around in the direction of the bottle. She did not look at them but I don't think their deviousness was for my benefit.

"Are you writing a book, Rose?"

"Heavens no. Why?"

"Then you want us all in parcels with the string tied and labels—'This one is dead, this one will be dead soon, this one would be better dead.' "

"Why must you question everything I do? Do you serve everyone the same or am I the only one who isn't an ordinary human being? Is it so improbable that I should have ordinary human feeling? Some interest in my friends? Just enough to care what happens to them?"

"Poor Rose." A spasm passed over the mask. She must have been smiling, really smiling, under it. "I'll tell you what happened."

"Don't if you feel it's none of my business."

"It's as much yours as anyone's now." She picked up the bottle. "If you will permit me?"

"Who am I to stop you?"

"You are my old friend, Rose Tedder. But you have another name. What is it?"

"Antrobus."

"That is a sea bird?"

"You're thinking of albatross."

"Rose Antrobus. It becomes you." She pushed her glass aside as if she meant to take no more. "I had three children, two daughters and a son."

"Had?"

"They are dead in the war. They and their father."

"Solange, how terrible!"

"Yes, what happens is terrible. My husband was rich, a very quiet, good man who expected himself in everyone. He was a Jew, he did not practise his religion but he had a nose—so—" She sketched it on the air—"and everyone could see that Danièle was a Jew."

She had not cared for him. She was always an island and the sea round her had grown cold.

"You have friends, Rose? Are there ladies who call on you and ask, 'What shoould we do today? What should we play at—tennis, golf, cards?' At school you had so many friends."

"You had yours outside school."

She went and lay down on the divan, clasping her hands under her head. "We lived in Toulon and in Paris. Danièle was buying and selling, what you call real estate. Some of it was nice property, nice villas, hotels, shops. Some was not nice, that was not his fault. He did not build it nor make slums or bordels of it. He was a quiet, good man," she said again. It sounded more like an excuse than a commendation. "Details are not necessary. In any case they are mine—yes, the details are my business."

I would have liked them just the same. I wanted to know what sort of house she had lived in, what she had done with her days, how often her husband was home. Did she think about those things? If not, what did she think about? What other details?

"When the war came Danièle would not leave, not even when the Germans came to Paris. He did not believe those stories about the Jews, he said there were always such stories in wartime, he said he had nothing the Germans wanted, they could take anything of his without taking his life."

I couldn't decide what impression she meant to give me. He might have been a fool, a hero or an abysmal coward. But one thing I was sure about: from this distance of time she was mocking whatever he had been.

"He was right. They took everything, all that was left was his life, and this they destroyed because they did not want it. A Jew's life," she said softly. "They came and fetched us, even the children, even the little boy, a year old, in a big white car, an American car. Danièle put such hope into it, he thought no harm could come to us in an American car." Underneath the mask she was smiling, really smiling. "They said he was a member of the Resistance, they said he was using his hotels and villas for small-arms factories."

"Was he?"

"It was a game. First they pretended not to notice that he was a Jew, then they pretended that they had nothing against Jews. And Danièle believed it. I don't know for how long—perhaps only until he came to Dachau."

She looked relaxed and peaceful lying with her hands under her head. I remembered how she used to lie on her bed at Winterthur because anything that we might do was not enough for her.

"And the children? What happened to them?"

"What happens to the children of a Jew?"

192

She propped herself on her elbow. It was horribly inadequate, all of it. I couldn't take her word, I wasn't sure that those children had even existed, or the man, or any such quiet, stupid man. I was being all I could be—polite. It was her own fault: the way she lolled there with her cardboard face tilted on her hand and her skirt rucked above her knees did not bear her out, it didn't relate. It was the wrong picture for the sound-track.

"Now we all know. We have read that what happens to children happens to men and women also. What else? There is only the worst and that is not for wood and stone, it is for flesh and blood."

"But they didn't—They let *you* go?"

"For me it was worse to let me go, and of course they wanted that each of us should have the worst."

She swung her legs off the divan, with moistened finger smoothed her stockings over her ankles.

She herself had said that the worst was for flesh and blood. Even at Winterthur, even at Bonneval there had never been more than a pretence of being that.

"Oh God," I said.

"God, I think, is satisfied."

"Satisfied?" I was spilling my untouched brandy. I put the glass from me.

She said, "Why don't you drink?"

I'm not good at consoling people. Naturally they want to be concentrated on and I don't seem able to get beyond saying how *I* feel, how sorry *I* am. She gave me no scope for the stock phrases even if I could have found them.

"Perhaps you prefer something else? English women like to drink gin and tonic. Or the Four o'Clock?" She peered at a watch lying on the desk. "But it is only half-past three."

"The Devil might be satisfied," I said, "if he existed."

"Que tu es encore enfant!"

It was also fairly childish to blame God, but she was entitled if not justified in putting the blame where she wanted. It would be presumptuous of me, thank Heaven, to try to chat her out of it.

"I've been—lucky." I couldn't say 'normal', and anyway

193

it wasn't quite the word. There had always been an element of performance for me in talking to her—now there was restriction too. There was so much I shouldn't ask, or answer, for fear of hurting someone badly hurt already. Although that's a conventional fear, people want to talk about their pains. In Solange's case it was hypothetical too.

"Was there no chance? One hears such extraordinary things—children saved and finding their families after years—I'd never give up hope."

She said, as if it was I who had to be handled, "That is the first thing you must do. If for this you cannot do penance, how should you escape a moment of it?"

"Penance?"

But she had dropped me and that was something else I remembered, wondering, furiously, if she had the choice, what piece of the world she would pick up to entertain her. She was palming both hands down her tight thighs, straightening her dress. She went to a mirror and leaned close into it. She seemed to be checking on the condition of every inch of the mask. What she could do with her fingertips, rubbing, lifting, stirring, she did, and I could see that they were so customary as to be automatic, almost reflex actions. I believe she would have had to do them in the dark.

I had no intention of being dropped.

"What did you mean, you can't do penance?"

"It was the wrong word. My English is not good."

"Your English is excellent."

"Then let us say I wish to spare you details."

"A penance satisfies the sinner, not God. Why should you want that sort of satisfaction?"

She was touching, with her curious blind precision, the pink turban of hair. If she didn't tell me I should think what I could. If 'penance' was the wrong word—and it always would have been wrong for her—what was the right one?

"I shall give you a present, Rose." She went to a shelf and took down a flat cardboard box. "Because you are always the same it shall be something that is not like you."

I had no opportunity of seeing what it was just then. She

194

took it out of the box and bunched it in her fist. When she opened her fingers it was to show me how the natural verve of the material caused it to spring from her palm. Other people might have jingled or tapped or played with something as they talked. She kept bunching and releasing the scrap of silk. As a matter of fact it was ridiculous the way it leaped like a live thing in her hand and it made what she was telling me peculiarly shocking.

"We all had to stand while they questioned Danièle, even the children—especially the children. That was part of the game. I had the baby to hold, he was unwell and the weather was hot, the sun was hot enough for me to smell the wood of the chairs and tables as if it had just been cut. For two hours, perhaps three, we were standing, they only had to take a drink of water for the children to suffer. Danièle kept asking if the children could sit on the floor, just five minutes, and he was told if he would show he was not of the Resistance we could all go home to bed. Danièle thought he had only to speak the truth. They pretended to be not quite convinced. He tried to prove how little he knew and then he tried to prove that he knew nothing, that he was an idiot."

She was smiling openly, stretching her mouth, and I suppose she usually avoided that because it must have been uncomfortable, the mask wasn't big enough.

"I knew that none of this mattered, it was a game until they were tired of playing. But I could not wait for that, my children were tired already, we had to hold them up or they must have fallen. What I did was the only thing to be done. Then, now, and in a hundred years I shall never know better."

"What did you do? What could you do that was so terrible?"

"You must understand there was also the heat of the moment. Such heat," she said smiling, "of the weather and the heart. There was nothing I would not do then to spare my children. So I cried out that I was not a Jew and neither were they."

"It was the truth—"

"And Danièle—what do you think Danièle said to me?"

It struck me that I had hardly ever heard her laugh, and Heaven knows she must have had a pretty private sense of humour to be able to laugh just then.

"He said, 'We are not on trial for our race'."

"How could he be so blind?"

She shook out the piece of silk she had been bunching in her hand and I saw what it was.

"I denied my husband to save my children and I saved only myself."

I can honestly say I shall never wear such a thing, I shan't even try it on.


The ladies were not disposed to be constructive. Their moods combined to a tacit though ragged opposition. Victorine and Mrs Choules were gossipy, Sue Betts was being Middle West, Mavis Tyndall did not open her mouth and Miss Havelock was grim. Watching them settle, Rose was disposed to be analytical.

It was no sudden affinity between Victorine and Mrs Choules causing them to put their heads together. Victorine was putting up a front—aware that she needed one, afraid of being pinned down and someone getting a long enough look to see what Victorine Gregory was made of. Sue Betts was proclaiming her difference, locating herself somewhere wide and handsome away from them all. The Havelock woman was waiting to refuse to be coaxed, and Mavis Tyndall was saving herself up. Some women found it impossible to be objective, it would be bad luck if Rose had a majority of them on her committee.

"Isn't the Reverend coming?" asked Mrs Choules.

"He has a deacons' meeting."

Rose had already decided that Cade's withdrawal from the Committee should come up when the business of the meeting was done. She had his formal letter setting out his reasons and intended to read it to them.

"I seem to remember he had scruples, too," said Victorine.

"I hope we all have," said Miss Havelock.

"That's a point." Victorine looked brightly. "One woman's scruples are another woman's headache."

"Hartley says we could invest Hilda's money while we're figuring what to do with it," said Sue Betts. "He says why don't we make up a syndicate and try the market."

"With forty-eight pounds?"

It was remarkable how a woman as fat as Miss Havelock could smile so thinly.

"That would be the basic, the pork strip sort of. We'd each put in something of our own, like we used to put flour, lentils, apple-rings, whatever we could afford, to our neighbourhood suppers."

"As the lowest common contributor I'm in favour, provided we each qualify for an equal share of the pot," said Victorine.

"We'd have systematical gains, of course."

"Meaning if I only bring lentils I only get lentils?"

"Honey, it wouldn't be all the same as a cook-up, but it would be a lot of fun."

"The money or the goods, that's my maxim," said Mrs Choules. "Nice it would look, wouldn't it, gambling with church money?"

"It's not church money yet. Remember?"

"Hilda would have been tickled pink to know we were playing the market."

Miss Havelock's distaste disassociated her. "What grounds have you for thinking so, Mrs Betts?"

"The grounds that I was a good friend of hers."

"Then I trust I shall have no good friends to read my mind after my death."

"I should think you're safe enough there—"

"We could make the profits, when there were any, over to the fund and stand the loss of our own stakes." Victorine said, "No one would object to our doing a wrong thing for a right reason—"

"We've unfinished business to attend to," Rose broke in. "Shall we begin?"

Miss Havelock held up a large palm. "May I say that if

this business is not finished this afternoon I shall attend no further meetings on the subject. I am a busy woman, I can't afford time for idle bickering."

"I'm sorry if we've bickered," said Rose. "Though I don't think it should be called 'idle'. We're conscientiously trying to settle a question and I have every hope that we shall settle it now."

"Then," said Victorine, "Mrs Choules must be joining the humanitarians."

"I can't join anything, dear, just now. I'm fully taken up at the end of the financial year."

"Didn't you say it would be cheaper to build a new church than keep furbishing the old one?" Victorine looked disappointed. "We already know there'll be boilers to replace, you said, and hadn't I noticed how the ridge tiles are cocked and the vestry floor is tenting like a piecrust—I took it to mean you intended to switch your vote. You're not one to throw good money after bad, you said, and I thought well, we haven't thrown any money, good or bad, at Mrs Peachey yet."

Mrs Choules turned mauve. "I never said nothing of the sort—"

"No one need back down," said Sue Betts. "As chairman Rose has a casting vote."

"Ah well, we know where that will go."

"As chairman," said Rose, "I am required to regard the casting vote as held in trust for the general opinion and not for a section."

Victorine smiled. "Here have we been, Miss Havelock, Mrs Tyndall and me, waving our little flags at the great stone faces. Wouldn't you know we'd be outnumbered by a technicality? Someone should tell the Peacheys we tried."

"It won't be necessary."

Mavis Tyndall was wound up and ready, now that she had been touched, to run on. And on, Rose thought. She had more than something to say, she had something to unload.

"None of it's necessary now."

"Why?"

"Mrs Peachey's gone."

"Gone where?"

"No one knows. She's left the district."

This was what she had been saving up for, believing she had blame to lay, believing they would feel the weight of it, as she did. Now she would go on, brooding and fretting and chalking up a cross for herself and for them—and bitterly having to bear it alone.

"We might have stopped it if we'd lifted a finger. We can't be sure of that, can we? We can never sit back and say there was nothing we could have done. I don't mean just *her*—if she'd only got herself to harm I'd say good riddance. I might say good luck because she'd need it and I'd sooner—we all would—not have to see her about. But there are the children. Their home's broken—what there was of it was theirs, they belonged. Oh yes," cried Mavis Tyndall, "children can belong with orange boxes and cracked china."

Rose had no intention of resigning them to the longueurs of this sort of thing. She said crisply, "What exactly has happened, Mavis?"

Mavis Tyndall wore a hat with a half veil, and it was this veil, trembling delicately with strain, that chiefly vexed Rose. Mavis Tyndall was a small woman who would impose her high soul on them all if she weren't prevented.

"Exactly? Mrs Antrobus, I can't tell you exactly what happened, I wasn't there. I wasn't told, I had to get to know."

Rose could appreciate how that would rankle—finding out, when all was done and done with, and not even a sixth sense to warn her.

"Through the police, the police if you please, coming across my name and address in the flat—because I'd told her to turn to me with anything that troubled her. Did I know, they said, where she'd gone? She'd have told me, they said, she'd be bound to because I was her friend—*her* friend!—and I could see they thought I was shielding her. They wouldn't tell me what had happened to the children. I had to go and ask the neighbours—"

Rose stood up. She disliked coincidence. There was no

need for Fate to tap her on the arm nor for history to echo itself inside a week.

"Nothing so terrible, surely, could happen to the children?"

"I would have thought," said Mrs Tyndall, standing up too and levelling her chin at Rose's top dress button, "that losing their mother was terrible."

"She didn't take them with her?"

"That would be no part of the plan," said Victorine.

"What plan?" cried Mavis Tyndall. "What plan could she have that didn't include them?"

Victorine blew cigarette smoke down her nose. "The plan any woman has when she wants to kick over the traces. It doesn't stretch to having the kids along."

Rose was beginning to understand that Victorine's vulgar streak had not needed to be acquired. It would account for Sam Swanzy.

"Where are they now?" asked Sue Betts.

"They've been taken into care—a Council home. You know what that means!"

"That's hardly fair," said Rose. "I'm sure they'll be well looked after. There are some very worthy people on the Children's Board—the Reverend Cade is one."

"Boards!" cried Mavis Tyndall as if it were an expletive. "Committees!"

Mrs Choules patted her hand. "I know what you mean, dear, children need their mothers. But some mothers don't deserve the name."

"So if we'd given her the money," said Sue Betts, "she'd have blown it on this spree."

"With some man—or men."

"When I talked to Mrs Peachey—Oh yes, I've been to see her," said Rose, "I reminded her that she had the children to live for. It wouldn't have been necessary with any other woman, but I got the impression that Mrs Peachey intended to live for herself."

"We don't know, we're not sure we couldn't have prevented it—"

"Obviously we couldn't when she was so ready to go," said Miss Havelock.

Victorine said idly, "What did she do about the kids? Leave them to fend for themselves?"

"She telephoned the police station—on her way she must have been then—and said there were three young children left unattended. Why didn't she ring me—I told her to—Anything she needed, I said. Why didn't she?" Mavis Tyndall, looking from face to face, was searching for Mrs Peachey's reason. She couldn't accept that she, who had involved herself, should have counted for nothing. And Mrs Peachey had neither known nor cared that she had a hold.

"It was the little girl—" She was childish herself, the way she looked up, even at Rose—"she needed—" She couldn't bring herself to say what the child needed, not to them. "She *needed*," she said hopelessly and went back to her chair.

"Of course we're all sorry about the children," Rose said. "They at least are innocent. But it does transform the situation we're immediately concerned with."

"People should not need paying to shoulder their responsibilities," said Miss Havelock.

"I don't understand women who abandon their children. I can make allowances for a lot of things—we don't know the half, I always say—but there's no two ways about being a mother. We learn that from the brutes," said Mrs Choules.

"What sort of home was it, anyway? They're better off with the Board than with a psycho father and a maverick for a mother."

"Mrs Antrobus was right—"

"Mrs Antrobus is always right," said Victorine.

Miss Havelock drew on her gloves. "I shall wish you ladies a good afternoon."

"You're going? Before we've settled anything?"

"It has settled itself. The bequest now goes to the church. There remains only the formal closure of the meeting. I am sure," said Miss Havelock without humility, "that it can be managed without me."

"Hilda would have been pleased," said Sue Betts. "She

always said her kneecaps wouldn't let her concentrate on her prayers."

"I don't agree." Rose picked up her minute-book and wrote 'Proposal' and ringed it heavily. "I think the money should go to the children."

"What?"

"You're not serious?"

"Is this your idea of irony?" said Miss Havelock.

Rose lifted her chin at them, but spoke mildly. "I know I'm generally supposed to be heartless, but I'm as concerned for these children as any of you. As I said, they're blameless. Giving them this money seems to me the least we can do."

"You're right," said Victorine, "about it being the least."

"What good would it do them?"

"It could be put into a fund until they are old enough to use it."

Miss Havelock lifted her lip. "Sixteen pounds, one shilling and fivepence each."

Rose looked at her directly. "It's a nucleus. Charitably disposed people can always add to it. I am formally proposing that Mrs Loeb's bequest for this quarter be donated to open a fund for the three Peachey children. Will anyone second that?"

"I will," said Mrs Choules.

Victorine groaned. "The needle's in the groove."

"Frankly I don't see how anyone can object," said Rose. "It's a Christian act."

Sue Betts shrugged. "I'm no Bible-pusher, but I'll go along with you."

"Mavis? What do you think?"

"Does it matter?"

"It would if you were against it." Rose said gently, "You, of all people."

"I'm not against it."

She had her chin buried in the dreadful little squirrel collar of her coat. She didn't realise how alienating sulks could be.

"If you're not against it you must be for it."

"No one can be against the motion, Mrs Antrobus, as you are well aware." Miss Havelock was really going. She paused at the door. "But between now and the next meeting I think you must decide whether this is to be a committee or a conversazione."

"Oh dear," Rose said when she had gone, "I thought everyone would be glad to be informal."

"She goes to Share meetings to relax herself," said Sue Betts, "and it's the ones with the smallest holdings that have to have the t's all crossed and the i's all dotted."

"I don't think I've had it all my own way, have I?" Rose smiled wryly. "It wasn't the general idea. I picked everyone for their capacity to see two sides of a question."

"It's nice we could agree in the end," said Mrs Choules. "Everyone's happy."

Rose glanced down at the crown of Mavis Tyndall's hat. "We shouldn't expect that even if it's passed nem. com. Now I think we'll break for tea. Will you excuse me while I fetch the trolley—Mrs Gibb isn't here today."

Victorine followed her. "I'll help you cut the cake."

"There's only the tea to make. Everything else is ready."

She didn't want help, Victorine's least of all. Not that she was going to get any—when they reached the kitchen Victorine went straight to the trolley and helped herself to a sandwich. She ate it while Rose switched on the kettle.

"You didn't ask me how I'd vote. You'd got your majority, of course."

"I intended to ask you. I don't take anyone for granted." Rose was annoyed to hear herself add, "Whatever Miss Havelock thinks."

"Bother you, does it?"

"Bother—no. What interests me," Rose was rearranging the sandwiches, "is how this suggestion of collusion could come up. Collusion I neither need nor want. If I did it would be spiking my own guns to form a committee. After all, I might have allocated Hilda's money without let or hindrance from anyone."

"It wouldn't have been such fun for you though." Victorine took another sandwich. "I didn't have time for lunch."

"I'm asking you," said Rose, "because you know as well as anyone—how I got this reputation for power politics."

"You like it, don't you? It's quite flattering and someone has to be the *force majeure*—you or Havelock. I'd rather be coerced by you than pulped by her."

"For Heavens' sake," said Rose, "all I wanted was an honest opinion out of any of you."

"Why did you change your mind about the money?"

She was perched on a stool, an éclair in her hand and her mouth full of sandwich. This was cosy chat, women's gossip, or something to do while she ate.

"Let's say my mind is flexible enough to appreciate a more pressing claim."

"It's not though, is it? Not more pressing, I mean. The kids will have to wait ten years for the money and according to you the hassocks couldn't wait ten weeks."

"Are we still arguing about it?"

"Of course you didn't so much want the church to have the money as for the Peachey woman not to." Victorine prised the top off the éclair. "I understand that. But I wonder why."

"It's become obvious, I thought, to the most gullible of us—which you are not."

"Giving the Peachey children the money would certainly seem a way of paying off my conscience." She put the éclair back on the trolley and took a strawberry tart. "Only they're not really on it."

"How nice for you."

"Should they be? I didn't break up their home and if she couldn't cope it was the best thing the poor bitch could do."

"Of course you'd think so. The best for her—and for who else?"

Rose was ready, at a look, to tell her, but Victorine chose not to put a personal interpretation on it. She said, twitching her sticky fingers, "And for the kids. That's why I'm surprised they're on your conscience. Give them the money? But there's nothing to pay. You know that as well as I do."

Rose poured an arc of boiling water into the teapot.

"I don't know what you know, Vee, and I'm glad. It seems unwomanly to be so hard-headed. Will you bring in the trolley? And for Heaven's sake let me close the case. Please! That's all we have to do now."

To the
ANONYMOUS DONOR
of the Cheltenham Award

Seventy per cent of writers never earn more than
£500 a year from their writing, and many always
earn less. They must work to live to write. If working
and living use a minimum of twelve hours a day,
that leaves them eight to sleep and four to write—
or four to sleep and eight to write—in theory, and
if no-one calls, no-one is ill, nothing burns or peters
out, it is not Christmas, nor holidays, they are not
tired and nothing stops them. They may try to write
on buses and in trains, standing, sitting, while the
dinner cooks, before the shopbell rings, in any and
every moment which can be got. It will depend on
the individual conscience whether the moment is
redeemed or filched. Time to write in peace is what
seventy per cent of writers want and do not get.

I should like to think that this book is the better
for being the product of time neither redeemed nor
filched, but generously bestowed.

# JOHN BROWN'S BODY

# 1

Marise saw at once that this place was far behind Plummer Court. It had had years of people living over it and their rubbing and breathing had turned it grey. The carpet and the curtains and even the bunch of lilac she had brought in with her were grey, the colour of other people's air was bathwater.

Her habit was to case anywhere new for the harm or benefit she could expect and she saw that she would be the loser here. She could not open her mouth without tasting the tall rooms and the plaster cornices and the swaybacked couch which smelt like a lion.

She saw herself running beautifully away under flamboyant trees, her hair jumping on her shoulders, silkily springing and falling. People turning to look drank her up with their eyes, she was an arrow flying from the fire to the sun.

At Plummer's everything had been new and the little gilt lift came whining down with the company director who lived in the pent-house flat. Plummer's was a good address, she had lived there for six months, all of her married life. One of the small mercies of being married was living at Plummer's and the other mercy was not having to provide for herself. By keeping these in mind she had kept herself from running beautifully away.

Now one mercy was gone, never to be replaced, not here, anyway. Here was practically a drawback of being married, as if she needed more drawbacks. These windows looked on to a drive made of black stones rammed into the ground, nor was it possible to see the road because the drive was pincer-shaped round laburnum trees and a dry basin full of laburnum pods. From Plummer's, eight floors up, she had a view of Lords and the river at Putney Bridge. "You take Jack Tomelty," her mother had said, "he's not much but he'll do for a start." "What of?" "Don't try to tell me you don't need a start, girl."

209

One of the first words she had learned was "lounge" and it still amused her. "This is the lounge" she said aloud, passing with her lips very rosebud into what was undoubtedly the bedroom.

This struck her as disagreeable. She saw that it never would agree with her, she wouldn't enjoy looking out from under a stuffy tree and twittering leaves, she was particular about what she wakened to, she needed to open her eyes to happy promising things. Hardier people could wake and wolf the day pushed into their faces but she needed to be coaxed and gentled.

At Plummer's there had been uncluttered sky through the window, and twin divans. She poked the swollen pillows of the double-bed, what gentling would she get from Tomelty in that?

The wardrobe exploded when she opened it. Inside was a full-length mirror so blotched that it required contortion to find one clear place to look into. On the shelf was a coil of fine wire. She picked it up and was ready to be sick when she realised that it was not wire but hair, a ringlet of dead hair. What she could smell here was the hereafter.

Quick as she thought she stepped into the wardrobe and pulled the door behind her. She often did the last thing she was expecting. Now it was pitch dark, around her the old wood ticked, protesting, and dust was shocked out of crannies. Her fingers touched the walls and the scabby mirror. The door had clicked in the lock, it could not be opened by her – of course not, what provision need there be for opening a cupboard from inside? She was shut in, in a mahogany coffin. She had only the air she stood up in, not grey air this but black from the black clothes that had been hoarded here. It was air not fit for human consumption and it hung in stiff folds and was balled-up into the toes of shoes. When it was all breathed, which would be soon because it was such poor stuff, she would suffocate, unless someone came, which no-one could because she had the only key to the flat. She would soon begin to choke and by tomorrow or next week or whenever someone had occasion to look into the wardrobe she would be found to be purple and puffy as a plum.

"No! No!" She hammered with her fists. Her heart raced, tears sprang to her eyes. "Let me out!" Already the air was cloying in her throat. Weeping and clawing she sank to her knees, pumped the screams out, bringing on an ecstasy of fear. "Let me out! I don't want to die!" It really did send her right out of herself, she was like a rocket rushing away in a shower of sparks. When it subsided she felt very frail and pulped. Moaning a little she opened the door and stepped out.

The sun had come through, the pebbles in the drive were polished iron and a man's check shirt jazzed as he came to the house carrying a basket of bread.

Marise made signs from the window. She could not find her purse. But I live here now, she thought, he knows where to find me, and she said to him on the front step, "A white loaf, please, and we shall be having one every day."

"I've only got brown left."

"Brown bread is peasants' food."

"Whose?"

"Bring me a Coburg tomorrow. We're living at No. 1 flat. I'm Mrs Jack Tomelty."

"Well, I'd like to be Mr Jack. He's alright, eh?" He smiled at her and she recognised his sort. With his sort it was never an encounter, it was a barrage, requiring her to be constantly on her guard. She was tired already of his tight trousers and his fringe down to his eyebrows. "Just moved in, have you?"

"I shan't stay if I don't like it."

"You're a nice change from the rest. The only one under forty is Shilling's cat."

"Shilling?"

"Old Ralphie. He's got the top flat. You watch out for him, he's dynamite."

She said coldly, "I don't discuss the neighbours with tradesmen."

He rolled up his eyes and wickedly pinched one of the fat loaves in his basket. Marise went back up the steps. In the porch name-cards beside each bell-push read: "Madame Silva Belmondo" and "Mr Ralph Shilling." There was not yet a card for the Tomeltys.

The baker called out, "Let me know when you're going and I'll come too."

She shut the door on him. Anyone listening would suppose she was the same sort. Was anyone listening? At Plummer's everything came through the walls, the walls identified but did not contain. Marise could lie in bed and not be lonely because she was surrounded by meaningful sounds, from the vacuum cleaner in the next flat to the shuffle of traffic in Goldwater Road.

She now listened for someone listening to her. There were rubbings and creakings and the tinkle of a spoonful of dust. She had the impression that she wasn't being listened to so much as recorded. Very well, there would be something to record.

The suitcases were on the floor where the taxi-driver had dumped them. She supposed she should unpack and put their clothes away, it would be a wifely thing to do. She had never had any difficulty knowing what was wifely and surely the thought should be taken some way towards the deed? It wasn't her fault if she was made of other stuff than wives.

She did open one of the cases to see what would turn up and on top was Barbra-Bear. Tomelty had pushed it in at the last moment. Marise remembered him half-angry, half-laughing at the spectacle of himself packing, "We'd owe another month's rent before you got round to it." The Barbra-Bear was made of honey-coloured plush filled with foam rubber. Marise took it out of the suitcase and coaxed back the rubber pieces that were leaking from a split in its side. She held the seam together, if she had had a safety-pin she could have mended it, but where to find a safety-pin in this new, strange place?

She said to the bear, "I'm new to it but it isn't at all

strange to me, it's a most *usual* place," and walked about with the bear in her arms saying, "Usual doors, usual windows, usual floor, usual offices, there's nothing you could call strange. Here's a kitchen and a sink and a larder and a gas-stove, is that staggering?"

It did not need the stone sink and the brass taps to recreate her childhood because she had felt the point of similarity as soon as she set foot in the place. It was on the way to being the same – it was not there yet, but it was of that order, farther up the scale of that same order – as her parents' home. Our new flat is old, she thought, and had not the courage to voice it because she had married away from oldness.

She went to the window hoping to see birds fly. At Plummer's she spent hours watching the sky; but apart from the starlings which were no better than animated tea-leaves there were few fliers. Pigeons floundered and sparrows peddled from chimney to chimney. She longed for birds shearing into the clouds, once she saw swans on the wing but they had their necks out and their feet dangling and looked silly.

"See, Barbra," she tilted the bear's snout, "there's room only to paddle in the sky."

Someone turned into the drive and trod confidently over the black pebbles. His hat was pushed back on the rims of his ears and his overcoat hung open. He carried a small suitcase in one hand and a bottle by the neck in the other. This was Jack Tomelty and now everything would be different though not necessarily better.

It was like him to leave her to move in by herself. "I've business to attend to, this shag's off to Brussels in the morning, I've got to get his order. You'll be all right, Gipsy, if I give the cabbie the address." He could always have business when he didn't want to be bothered, but of course Marise was alright. With the bags packed and the taxi-driver informed where to take her she could not be so terribly wrong.

She watched him bounce up the steps. It was he who was wrong and it could be terrible for him. Soon after they were married he had suddenly jumped out of bed and stood with his back to her hitting his temples with his knuckles. She recognised a strong emotion and was humbled and touched that she could so deeply move anyone.

"I love you too, Jack," she said timidly. He turned round, his face broke and his stomach heaved. He had doubled up, laughing like a maniac.

He sent the door of the flat wide to the wall, his first action was to knock down a piece of plaster.

"What a time I had getting away. Come and have dinner, they said, we've plenty to talk about. That's certainly true, said I, but I've got a wife waiting to be carried across the threshold. What do you think? Do you like it?"

"It's old. You didn't tell me."

"Not run down, though, not yet. And we shan't be here long."

"Why must we be here at all? We were all right where we were."

"I'm slightly in the red, not much, more in the pink really. We'll be out of here before you know. If you don't like it – don't you like it?"

"Where will we go? Will it be nicer?"

"You can bet your life it will. Are there any glasses?"

"How long shall we be here? A week?"

He said loudly, "Come off it, the place isn't that bad," and unwrapped a bottle of whisky. "Give me time."

"The bedroom's full of white hairs."

He noticed the suitcases and his nose blanched, it did when he was annoyed. "You haven't even unpacked!"

"Even? What else haven't I done?"

Tomelty threw his hat into a chair. He had a counter-jumper's skull someone had remarked, so neat and narrow, and Marise had overheard just at the moment when she was, or supposed she was, indissolubly bound to him. At her wedding breakfast, in fact. So that from then on she had the thought to carry with her that she had thrown herself away.

Later she realised that death was only one of many things that could part them.

"Glasses." He turned his blanched nose to the kitchen. She heard him opening cupboards, running water. He came back shaking dry two cups he had rinsed. "There aren't any glasses."

"There's no bread either."

He didn't upset her when he was angry. She didn't always notice. Now she did, she noticed that he slopped the whisky into the cups and some of it splashed out and he planked the bottle down in the wet. Ordinarily he was a fastidious man, even fussy, and vain in his movements. He liked to watch his small, sinewy, spry hands and complete their actions with a flourish, an arabesque for five fingers and a wrist-bone.

"Here – " He picked the cup up by the rim and pushed it at her, and when she protested that she did not like whisky because it hurt her throat he drained both cups one after the other. "Here's to Lilliput."

"To what?"

"They call this place Lilliput Lodge. Don't ask me why."

"Because Lilly put it here."

He glared at her. "Silly bitch," and then he laughed. They both laughed, they had always been able to do that together. "How's the bedroom? How's the bed? Now that matters," he put out his hand to her, "we should look at the bed."

"Not now."

"Why not now? What else is there to do now?"

Marise picked up Barbra-Bear and twisted her shoulders away from him. "I don't like that thing in the daytime."

'You don't like it any time." He poured a cup of whisky and sipped it as he wandered round the room. He had a wellnigh indestructible sunniness which perhaps, since it did not warm but only sparked, came from somewhere colder than the sun. "Look at this clock, it's a German line from Westphalia. I carried it for years and this is the first time I've seen one that wasn't in going order. You know," he

215

took a sip of whisky, drawing it piercingly through his teeth, "this place will be good for you. You'll be on the ground here."

"I liked it at Plummer's, I didn't want to change."

"Eight floors up had a bad psychological effect." In the bay window he twitched up the curtain and wound it like a coif round his face. "You were getting above yourself. Not holy – rarefied I should say, but not rare." He winked. "You'll be able to see everyone coming in and out."

"What everyone?"

"The neighbours all have to come through that door."

"Why should I want to see them?"

"To remind you that someone else is alive. Gyp, I think you sometimes forget."

"What do I forget? I didn't forget to unpack, the minute I got here I thought I'll get my own things round me and it'll seem more like home. And I didn't forget bread, the baker came and he hadn't any white, I didn't forget that you like white bread."

"You'll see every move everyone makes." He clowned to himself with the curtain across his nose. "Little Sister is watching."

"I shall be too busy washing and cooking and cleaning." Under this banner she bustled across the room and took a shoe-tree out of the suitcase. "A woman's work is never done. *You* forget that."

Tomelty had taken nearly half a pint of whisky, but alcohol did not go to his counter-jumper's head, he soaked up and held it without evidence and neither pressure nor twisting could wring any of it out. It firmed his rather trumpery good humour into joy, as if he had at last found reason to be joyful.

"Here's one you'll see, one of our neighbours. No butcher, baker or ten per-cent census taker: age forty to forty-five, presses his pants under his mattress and dreams about Ernie."

216

"It'll be Mr Shilling." Marise sat on the couch and pulled rubber cubes out of Barbra-Bear's side.

"Another form of life for you. What a whirl."

"I know lots of people, I don't have to chase after anyone."

"We must get you something finer than these curtains. It's like looking out of a meat safe." He pulled the curtains back, leaving the window bare, and Marise caught a glimpse of a man who seemed to be staring into her. It went a long way in his favour, the first plunge of the eye, for a moment the three of them were fixed – Marise, Tomelty and the man outside. It was as soundless as lightning and, to Marise, as electric. Then the curtain fell back into place and of their own volition her hands began pressing back the pieces into Barbra-Bear's side.

Tomelty said, "I've seen him before."

"You've seen everyone before."

"And I remember everyone, that's the secret of my success. I tell you, I know this hom." Tomelty came away from the window to the whisky bottle. "He polishes his boot-soles."

"I know a lot of people to." Marise went to the door of the flat and opened it. The man who was stepping into the entrance hall looked round. He was tall and solid and she saw at once that he would be remembered. He had a packed face with uncompromisingly functional features, a big nose with a spade-shaped end and a wide mouth with strong red lips. Only his chin looked as if it might let him down, it folded too suddenly into his hard collar.

"Excuse me, I thought you were the postman," said Marise. He transferred his briefcase and newspaper to his left hand and lifted his bowler an inch off his forehead. "Are you Mr Shilling?"

"Yes."

Marise nodded and closed the door. To Tomelty, standing with the cup halfway to his lips, she said, "He lives on the top floor, he's got a cat."

"Why did you do that, for God's sake? Now he knows."

"Knows what?"

"I'm trying to remember. The thing is, I may not care for him to remember me."

Marise was slightly impressed, partly because of Tomelty who was a bouncer and had put bouncing into the technical class. Bouncing was more than his nature, it was his diploma, his college education. It had maintained her in a style to which she had soon grown accustomed. But her impression was partly, and more, to do with this place in which she now found herself. It was unagreeable insofar as it did not agree with what she regarded as her expectation of life. If these rooms were going to pull their grey woolly old air over her eyes and tell her that everything had been used up, what was there to expect, except to sit where other people had sat – in their laps almost – and put her fingers into their finger-holes and rub where they had rubbed? Except to leave a hair, except to be here long enough to be able to leave a white hair.

"Shilling you say his name is? I knew a Bob Penny. This one looks a cold fish, cold fish wear bowler hats."

Had she been able to put her hand into Tomelty's side and pull out the rubber stuffing, she would sometimes have pulled it all out from his feet to his head and left him as an empty skin.

"It pays to remember," he said. "Sometimes it pays more than others."

"What good can it do us to be in this awful place?"

"I don't see anything awful. I see a nice high airy room with gracious furniture and gracious trees outside. This place has graciousness, Gyp. Naturally, you wouldn't recognise that. Plummer's was too new, graciousness is never less than fifty years old."

"There was an old woman here who hadn't opened the windows for fifty years. The wardrobe's full of her hair."

"This place will save us a pony a month in rent, that's the good it'll do."

218

"How long shall we be poor?"

Tomelty burst out laughing. "We're not poor, we're careful. I'm a careful man."

He had to be. A careless technician is still a technician, but a careless bouncer is a common enemy.

"Not with my life," said Marise. "I can look after that."

Tomelty had foxy white teeth when he grinned. "You don't have a life, you have me."

He liked to think that she was an extravagance which he could afford and other men couldn't. She was pretty and he wanted her silly: whatever she said or did he made it to seem silly. Having a silly, pretty wife cut a bigger dash than having an expensive car, it was likely to go on longer and cost more than money. Marise knew this because she wasn't silly.

"Full of hair?" He took the whisky bottle delicately by the neck. "Let's see."

Marise recalled that Ralph Shilling had the cat. She hoped it would be ginger with white feet and that it would play with her. Perhaps Ralph Shilling would give her his key so that she could make friends with the cat. It was easy to be friends with a cat because there was no personality involved, the trouble with friendships was that people made up their minds that she was this person or that and blamed her when she was herself.

"So this is where we cooshay," said Tomelty from the bedroom. "Did you ever see such a gracious bed? It's matriarchal, solid Empire this bed is. Did you say it had a horsehair mattress?"

"The wardrobe smells."

"Because it's air-tight I expect and it's been shut up. We'll keep the door open for a bit, that'll freshen it." He poured a drink and toasted himself in the spotted mirror. "I want you to be happy."

"How can I be when you take me away from my friends?"

"I want you to make friends."

"I was well liked. And understood. I didn't have to explain

myself – 'I get up late because I don't like to get up early'
– 'I have no shoes on so that I can find my way in the dark'
– 'My husband is in Manchester, this is only his coat, I am
trying to think that this is not only his coat' – "

He shouted, "I want you to make friends!" In the hush
the old grey dust puffed up in shock. Tomelty dropped on
to the bed. "You know I can't help being away, Gyp, it's
my job. You've got to stop shutting yourself up and talking
to the walls."

"I talked to the baker, he asked me to go away with him."

"I want you to get out of the house every day. You're not
to have things sent, go and buy them at the shops."

Marise said with dignity, "I am hardly ever in. If you only
knew, it's difficult to get everything done in the time."

He looked at her sombrely. "This bed's comfortable.
Come and cooshay with me."

"I wish you wouldn't use those words."

"What words?"

"I know they're vulgar. Keep them for your drinking
companions."

He rolled on the mattress, his sleeked hair split into tufts.
"You're a marvel you are – " suddenly snatching at her he
pulled her to the bed. They fought bitterly, she buffeted his
face with her hands. There came a twangling from the bed-
springs, and hearing it she wondered why there should be
music, why deep old organ music should be glorying over
them. Then she was on her back on the bed, his chest on
hers and his breath, very fiery, in her nostrils.

He had his eyes closed, he always did when he kissed.
Raptly dreaming he looked, like a tombstone face with white
eyeballs. Marise, who kept hers open, was furious with
everything – especially with herself for bringing on this kind
of thing. She groped around, found Barbra-Bear, and
rammed its woolly snout into Tomelty's mouth.

There was an explosion. For a slight man he made a lot
of noise. Marise, tossed bodily aside, felt a correspondingly
strong satisfaction.

"You bitch!"

"We have unpacking to do," Marise said primly.

"Women have been murdered for less." He stared at her, his hair shocked over his eyes. "I could kill you, Gipsy! I'd like to."

"With a knife? We don't know where the knives are – in the dresser drawer, I expect. Would you bury me under the floor? Then you could lock up and go away, no-one would think anything of that because it's your job to go away. You could say I was staying with my mother and people would believe it. They always think they know what I'd do – "

"You think you know what *I'd* do – and what I wouldn't do.'

"I'm next to your skin, I ought to know."

"You're under my skin, you're a tick and I should tear your head off!"

Marise had to laugh. She had just seen the Barbra-Bear on its back, its grubby skirt round its neck and paws up as if someone was pointing a gun at it.

"Did you ever see such a fool?" she said. "We had a dog that used to roll on its back. My father said it was asking to be forgiven its sins. Do you think animals can be? Do you think they count as heathen? Is hell-fire stoked up with them?"

Tomelty sat on the bed, staring, but she could see that the brunt had moved off her.

"It's like a club. You've got to belong to God, but not everyone can join. There should be somewhere for those who can't, not so pearly and without music. I'd rather have dogs than angels – "

"Will you shut up?" said Tomelty. "I've just remembered. My God!"

"What?"

"It's come to me from a long way back. I never forget a face." He lay down and clasped his hands under his head. "If I gave my mind to it I could recall the doctor who delivered me."

221

"What face?"

"Shilling you say he calls himself? He gave me a shock because I remembered the face but not whose face. I knew it was nothing much good."

"I think he has a kind face."

"When I knew that I was remembering – " he yawned – "it's what they call a stimulus. The poor old brain got a message it hadn't had for a dozen years and being without new instructions did what it used to do."

"What did it used to do?"

"Prickled up, boggled a bit. I was a skinny kid at the time and though you may not believe it I was pure in heart. Mind you, I'd begun to think along my own lines, but I must have been pure because I thought I was the only one with such thoughts. This fellow with his insurance book came every week to collect half a crown from my mother. She had us paid up for burying, you see. Well, I was used to him, we all were, he was one of the family. He always came at Saturday dinner time and stayed to eat with us. It was a shock, not to say an earth-tremor, when he was taken up for murder."

Marise sat on the bed with Barbra-Bear in her arms. "Did he murder anyone you knew?"

"He did a very fancy job, it made breakfast reading for several Sundays."

"What happened?"

"He was acquitted. Insufficient evidence."

"Did he do it?"

"Oh, he did it, he did it all. No doubt about that. What shook me was how he did it. I wasn't short on imagination and I thought I was original – nasty, you know, but different."

"What did he do?"

"Never mind."

Marise pouted. "What's it to do with Mr Shilling?"

"Only that he's the dead ringer of this character, face, walk, bowler hat and all. John Brown his name was. What a name! I can tell you, I got quite a turn just now and I couldn't think why. Defence mechanism that was, perish the thought of John Brown. I had to dig up the memory."

Marise poked into Barbra-Bear's side and brought out a cube of rubber. "Here's an early memory of hers, of when they sewed on her eyeballs. All her early memories are painful."

"If you must keep that thing why don't you mend it?"

"You like to think I'm a child, don't you, so that you can shut me up while you're away? You don't want me to live when you're not here. You're the one that wants a toy." She went to the mirror to exchange looks with herself. "Perhaps Mr Shilling *is* the murderer." There was one particular black spot on the mirror the size of a sixpence. She stood so as to get it in the middle of her forehead.

# 2

Twice Krassner had picked up the tossing-stone which Ralph Shilling kept on his desk and twice put it down again – out of respect, one would hope, for the occasion. If so, it was the only respect he did show and was short-lived because finally he took the pebble and rolled it from hand to hand while he explained.

Reviewing the conversation afterwards Ralph realised that Krassner had not actually explained anything. Ralph had postulated and Krassner had accepted.

"I needed money, I had to have it and I took it from whence it would least be missed."

"You borrowed it?"

"What?"

"You were going to pay it back?"

"Oh Lord yes," he said very quickly and easily. As he would if it were true. It must be true, thought Ralph, because other considerations apart, how could he expect to survive if it wasn't? "The Sweetland account gave me the maximum time, you know how Sweetland sometimes settles in January, sometimes in June. Well, he settled in January this year, in dirty fivers."

"Which you didn't pay in?"

"Oh I paid it in – into another part of the forest."

"You knew it would be found out."

"It was a risk I had to take."

"Mr Pecry's probably spoken to Sweetland already," said Ralph, "about the new consultant fees."

Krassner shrugged. "If the matter of the account had come up he'd have been after our blood by now."

"*Our* blood?"

"Well, Sweetland's on your patch and Pecry believes in the chain of command. He'd never approach me without approaching you first."

Ralph had sometimes wondered at Krassner, more with

224

curiosity than envy, though he would have liked to possess some of what he called Krassner's "aplomb". But apparently it was not worth possessing – Ralph would have expected something-carat from it, or at least a guarantee.

"What are you going to do?"

"I?" said Ralph.

Riding smooth-shod over everything had not smoothed everything for Krassner. He was in a hole, his easy manner was not easiness, he couldn't raise two hundred pounds of his own and Ralph was saddened as he always was by all that glittered and turned out not to be gold. "Why didn't you ask me in the first place?"

"Would you have lent me the money?"

"I think so."

"I had to be sure, old boy. You might have refused and then you'd know I wanted it and you'd have been on the look out."

"What did you want it for?"

"That's my business."

"Women, I suppose." Ralph could not keep a tremor from his voice.

"Is that the worst you can think of?" Krassner was a good-looking man and his face broke into laughter like a flag. "What can you think of it, anyway?"

"What do you mean?"

"You're not a flesh and the devil merchant, I'd say you catch life on television."

Ralph said mildly, "Living isn't only what *you* do, Krassner, there are other ways."

"Yes, but let's be honest – " he could still bandy the word, it was Ralph who stiffened – "your way is the straight and narrow. You're lucky, to you doing what's right is doing what comes naturally."

"Is there something comic about having principles?"

"It's not such a battle for you, old boy. You don't know what I'm up against."

"How can I if you don't tell me?"

"It's no use telling you. You'd have to be born again – a sinner."

He took out his cigarettes – they were, Ralph observed, still in the packet – and lit one with a match. So he had sold his case and lighter. This seemed to make matters worse, it verified them and so far nothing had done that, not even the blank space on the Sweetland sheet – which simply looked innocent. Ralph had found himself having to refer back to an anomaly, almost an abstraction, certainly to a strain on his credulity because without being the soul of honesty or the soul of anything, Krassner had made it seem inconceivable that he could cheat the firm of two hundred pounds. Two thousand perhaps. Was that the shame, that such a man should have to steal two hundred pounds?

Something landed on Ralph's blotter and rebounded against his hand. It was the tossing-stone. He looked up and saw that Krassner had thrown it.

"Why so glum, old boy? You're not the felon."

He was impatient, a little annoyed. Ralph felt foolish, there was a joke somewhere which was going against himself. He put the stone into a drawer.

"Don't call me 'old boy'."

Krassner said again, "What are you going to do?"

It had been on Ralph's conscience that he would have to do something. He resented his part in the matter. He would have to have a part, in fact he already had it. It began at the moment he picked up the receipt book, or at least at the moment when the adding-machine in his brain registered that there was a gap in the sequence of stubs.

Krassner sucked at his cigarette. "The first – and last – thing you need to do is tell Pecry. That takes it right off your hands."

"You must pay the money back. At once."

"Certainly. Will you take a cheque?"

"You've got a bonus due in a couple of months. I'll bring it forward and make it payable now."

"On grounds of merit?"

"We must do something about that stub." Ralph fretted around his desk searching for the receipt book.

"Why?" said Krassner. "It's evidence. You'll need it in Court."

Ralph looked at him. He was smoking peaceably. "Don't you care about being found out?"

"If I told you that being found out was the least of my worries you wouldn't know what to say, would you, old chap?" He was bitter-pleased. At the moment this was as high as his credit went, but it was high enough for him and he was assured, perhaps, that it could never go lower.

"I'd say you were a fool."

"Would you? Would you, by God. Well, I wasn't born a whole man like you."

"Me?"

"Sufficient unto yourself. In the round." Krassner voluptuously shaped the air with his hands. "That's you, old chap. Damn me if I wouldn't rather be lacking and have something to go after. That's life in my opinion."

His opinion had never weighed much with Ralph, but life – yes, Krassner must know all about life. It was the knowledge Ralph would have wished to have, as he would once have wished to be a lion-tamer or a fireman.

"Is this what you're looking for?" Krassner pushed the receipt-book across the desk. "Pecry will be able to tell you there's a stub short just by looking at the thickness. Do you remember when poor old Jeffney defied security and took the overseas ledger home? Pecry bowled him out because he had spilt a drop of gravy on it."

Ralph put the receipt-book in the desk drawer with the tossing-stone and locked it.

"Aren't you going to take it to Pecry?"

"No."

Krassner raised his eyebrows. "Just going to put the money back and say nothing?"

Ralph had seen the joke against himself. It was an old one. A long time ago, at school, he suffered agonies of guilt when other boys cheated. It was so burdensome that he even thought of turning Catholic so that he could go to confession and get absolution.

"Puts me in a bit of a spot," said Krassner. "You see, that bonus was keeping a tiger at bay."

Ralph looked up fiercely. "Get out!"

Krassner nodded and stretched himself. His chest arched splendidly, his nylon shirt snapped hard against the square of each breast. He stood up, and he had the playtime air that he used to adopt after their monthly "progress" meetings.

"I daresay you're wise, old boy, not to tell Pecry. He'd be bound to ask why you didn't spot it before."

That was Ralph Shilling's day, that and the encounter with the new little creature. Seeing her suddenly, out of the brown so to speak, made him wonder if she had just been born. She was so absolutely unmarked. He could not recall such newness even in a baby. Of course a baby was not completed as she was, she was a completed woman. And little she could be without diminution. Ralph then forgot her. She provided bright though not comic relief to the day and he had other things to think about.

He liked an even tenor. He liked the way the cat greeted him when he went into the flat. He always arrived home at the same time and the cat, waiting on the other side of the door, rose to its feet with a mutter. They did not touch each other, each ventured a little way towards a common ground where for a moment they communicated as equals. Thereafter each resumed his place, the animal's undefined, the man's mapped and bounded with his every breath.

The cat knew what time Ralph came home just as it knew that he shut up the flat and went away on Friday nights for the week-end. The cat absented itself and then Ralph supposed it went hunting, two days and nights red in tooth and claw. He worried about it when the weather was bad but it was always there to greet him on Sunday nights.

228

They did not require each other, that was the crux of their association. Anything Ralph did for the animal was permitted, even his own permission for it to sit on his chairs and come in through his window, even this was permitted him. Skirting the animal now as it crouched in the middle of his floor, it was in fact Ralph who felt gratitude for the continuum.

As Ralph saw him, Krassner was not so much a criminal, was not good or bad, except in his function as a disruptive agent. There Ralph saw him as being very good indeed. Whichever way things went, Ralph would be disrupted.

Disruption had already begun. His head was buzzing with voices – Pecry's voice saying, "I regard it as a serious reflection on your handling of the department," and the Chairman's voice picking up words – "Shilling states that he was unaware" – and stripping them – "Unaware?" How shameful, how naked a word! And Bertha's voice, "But dear, that's not bad judgment, that's trust. You have to trust people."

I shan't think about it, thought Ralph, until I have eaten. I cannot be objective on an empty stomach.

He prepared his meal of a lamb chop and frozen peas. For the cat he had bought its favourite, tinned pilchards. These he cut up and set the dish on a sheet of newspaper because the cat was a messy eater. It had a bit of beard to which particles of food clung, and a habit of chewing with its head in the air, at once ruminant and wary.

Ralph thought again of the new little creature downstairs. How she had surprised everything: she set the old place quite aback, they were not used to strangers here. Old Miss Hanrahan who had died in the downstairs flat had lived there for thirty years. Ralph himself was the latest comer and he had been at Lilliput Lodge for six years. For eighteen months after he came Madame Belmondo, in the rooms below his, would scarcely say "good morning" or "good evening" when they passed in the hall. Ralph found out afterwards that she thought he worked for the Inland Revenue.

"Off to inspect more taxes?" she said viciously one day as he raised his hat.

"I beg your pardon?"

"Of course taxes are the last thing you'd inspect, Government departments don't put their house in order."

When she knew that he worked for a firm of pesticide manufacturers she became friendly and even arch. Ralph was puzzled by her archness which was like the approach of men in bars offering what they called "connoisseurs' lines". Not that she said anything out of place, it was her beckoning and nudging looks that signified.

Ralph speared his chop and a little pink blood came through. It was not inconceivable that he would one day accept what Madame Belmondo was offering in order to find out exactly what it was.

The cat had finished its meal and looked at Ralph with an unanalysable stare, baleful and triumphant. He sometimes thought that it exulted in its power to make him provide food. It would feel powerful, coming in and dropping its flank down and getting its stomach filled without hunting, without effort. Perhaps it despised him for not providing the taste of blood. "Git!" Ralph said to it and the creature switched its tail and leaped on the window-sill.

As Ralph ate, his mind went back to the affair of Jeffney and the gravy. What a scene that had been. Jeffney had cried and actually wrung his hands and Pecry – Pecry should have paid for the performance because he enjoyed it so much. It was a rare opportunity for him to use his wit in full company. The investigation had not excluded even those who had no access and no reason for access to the ledgers, they were all present in Pecry's office to identify the gravy stain.

Whose gravy? That was the question. "It looks like steak and kidney," said Krassner, "with mushroom. Too dark for curry – can you rule out mulligatawny?"

Pecry sat at his desk and waited like a maestro for silence before the overture.

"I am not satisfied that everyone here has a proper conception of loyalty. Or of honesty. We must first examine what is in shortest supply – your honesty to your employers and to each other."

Krassner always said that Pecry's function was to louse up life but Ralph sometimes thought that Pecry was a missing link between present and far future man and was glad that he himself had already been born.

"It would seem," Pecry had said later when the net was drawn tight, "that the working day is not long enough for you, Mr Jeffney."

"I didn't mind putting in some extra time, I didn't mind at all – "

"That is, not long enough for you to do your work here in the office where you are contracted to do it."

"This is the first time, I swear it!" Jeffney clasped his hands beseechingly and they all looked away. "I swear I have never before removed a ledger!"

"Since you had to continue to work throughout the evening I can only conclude that the work here is too much for you. Altogether too much," said Pecry. "You could not stop for a meal, you had to go on working even while you were eating."

"No! It was an accident, the ledger was on the table and my wife must have – as she passed – a drop of gravy – "

"You should have told me you were behind schedule. It was not your secret, Mr Jeffney, inefficiency is not anybody's secret." Pecry, looking round, drew them all into the net. "That's what I mean by honesty to your employers. The principle should be paramount. Evidently it is not."

Ralph chewed steadily at his chop. If a spot of gravy on a ledger was lack of principle, what was a deficit of two hundred pounds? It was dishonesty, he had to admit, to the most impartial assessor: to Pecry, the fanatic, it would be a capital crime. Pecry could invoke the law and for two hundred pounds he would invoke the Public Prosecutor and the Lord Chief Justice and probably M.I.5 as well.

Ralph had no fear for Krassner, whatever happened Krassner would end on top, certainly on top of the Board. He was made to best everyone without being definably better himself. Krassner would not suffer more than a temporary inconvenience, but Ralph would. He pushed his plate away and fetched a sheet of paper from the bureau. This he ruled into two columns. On the left he wrote 'Telling': on the right, 'Not Telling', and underneath each he put a sub-heading: 'Losses'.

At that point it occurred to him to wonder what it was all about. Was Krassner involved with a woman? How could she cost him two hundred pounds? What was he getting for that? Ralph decided that he had a right to know, he had every right to know since he would be the loser. He wrote "reputation" on the left and then scored it through and wrote 'standing'.

But men like Krassner did not need to pay for their women. Ralph had seen him in action. Charm was an extra dimension which took the woman right out of herself and made her at once mistress and slave and adept at a game they two would each win. On that occasion Krassner hadn't even paid for her drinks.

Ralph wrote 'catalogue' in the 'Telling' column. He was responsible for compiling the yearly brochure of the firm's products for circulation at home and overseas. The job carried a certain cachet and was coveted by senior members of the staff. But after one of Pecry's showdowns there was invariably a stripping of marks of distinction or favour. It was three years since the gravy incident and Jeffney had still not been reissued with his rubber name stamp which Pecry had withdrawn at the time. The catalogue would certainly be taken from Ralph.

Krassner made no secret of the fact that he lost, and won, on the horses. But never large sums – "No four-legged brute's going to skin me." Ralph couldn't picture him playing cards, he had too restless an eye, nor roulette – he couldn't endure to stand and wait while fate was settled for him, certainly not by a ball and a wheel. There were other forms of gambling which required active participation – legitimate business, for instance. Krassner's debts could be honest though his method of meeting them wasn't.

'Peace of mind', wrote Ralph, large across both columns because he had already lost it and wouldn't get it back for a long long time. The necessity of deciding was what Krassner had put on him, the necessity of choosing from two unpleasant sequences of events. Were they equally unpleasant? And, if they were equal now, might they not become wildly unequal later on? For instance, if he did not tell, if he covered up for Krassner and the whole thing came out, he would stand convicted of aiding and abetting.

If he told Pecry, if tomorrow he went to Pecry's office: "I have just discovered, it has come to my notice, I was checking the receipt stubs, I check them regularly, yes, I'm responsible for the accounts, personally responsible, yes, no I have never delegated nor trusted – a deficit of two hundred pounds has existed for three months – yes, three months – I didn't notice, I must have overlooked, I'm unable to account for it – " that would be item one. Pecry would sack Krassner and probably prosecute him but Krassner would amount to little more than nine days' wonder. For Ralph there would be a process of attrition, an infinitely graduated disciplinary action.

Under 'Telling' Ralph wrote 'job'. He would certainly be demoted, publicly or circuitously, whichever gave Pecry most scope. It turned him cold to think what a razor edge he was on, had unknowingly been on ever since the money became missing. Krassner's bonus would take time to put through and there was a further hazard which money ran with Krassner: it never kept its shape. Ralph had noticed that although Krassner rarely had money in his pocket he always had much more than the market value of it in himself. Thirty pounds a week couldn't have bought him ambience

– five thousand a year couldn't buy it for Pecry – but Krassner had it. What a pity ambience wasn't negotiable, could put people in its debt but couldn't repay.

Ralph wrote 'two hundred pounds' in the 'Not Telling' column. It was a solid figure and helpful among so many abstractions, though it had to be written as a solid loss. He saw small chance of intercepting Krassner's bonus cheque before it was folded irretrievably into Krassner's hand. Yet if he, Ralph, was to get off the razor's edge the money must be paid in at once. He, Ralph, must pay it, but not out of his own banking account because it was his and Bertha's jointly.

Thus was Bertha brought into both columns. If 'Telling' meant telling her as well as Pecry, 'Not Telling' would mean not telling her the truth. Obviously she would have to be told something, most of the money in their account was hers, residue of a legacy from her father, and Ralph would require a valid excuse for withdrawing two hundred pounds. Bertha wasn't mean, she was analytical – it came of having so much time on her hands.

"I'm not mad," Ralph told the cat, "but the circumstances are. The circumstances are mad as March hares."

He decided to go out for a while, he needed to hear voices outside his head. Already Bertha's voice was saying, "You know best, dear, but is it an act of friendship to lend anyone that amount of money? And who is there to lend it to?" She knew that there was no-one, he was not involved in friendship to that degree. His own voice said, "You'll have to trust me." Why should she? She wouldn't benefit. The best that could happen to her, the very best, would be that she would be no worse off – if Krassner repaid the money and Pecry did not find out and Ralph was not demoted. She would have to subsidise her husband because if she didn't he was liable to a cut in salary and that would be the worse for both of them.

As he went downstairs Ralph realised, too late, that

Madame Belmondo was on the watch. She came clattering out in her wooden exercise sandals. "Mr Shilling."

"Good evening, Madame." Hers was not a voice he wanted to hear. He tried to raise his hat which he was not wearing and the gesture became a fumble.

"Mr Shilling, I must talk to you about that cat."

"The cat's fine, it's had its supper."

"I know you look after it, you're kindness itself. But the creature's savage, it's savaged me." She held out her grubby little white hand. Across the fingers was a long coral coloured scratch.

"I'm sorry."

"You're not to blame. Neither am I. It was looking in at my window and I didn't like the way it was looking. I tapped on the glass and it wouldn't go so I pulled down the upper half and told it 'Shoo!' and waved my hand out and that's when it scratched me."

"It knows some words," said Ralph. "It's pretty intelligent."

"My dear, I wouldn't hurt it! I know how you value it. But this isn't the first time it's stared in at me in that malevolent way."

"It springs from sill to sill. Quite a feat when you think of the overhang."

"You're so trusting. Windows open night and day. Of course it's company for you." There was a tiny wickerwork sound, Madame Belmondo was dimpling. "A man needs more than a cat."

"I'm sorry it scratched you," said Ralph. "What can I do about it? Shall I pull its claws out?"

She shuddered. "I think you should be very careful," and suddenly coming close and reaching up on her toes said in a great whisper, "Have you seen the new people?"

"I saw the girl." Ralph's nostrils twitched. If anyone smelt professional, this woman did, with an almost plangent perfume.

235

"A girl is it?" She found and lightly squeezed his wrist. "And her husband, what is he?"

"I don't know, I didn't see him. She's pretty," said Ralph. It was not the word he wanted, although of course she was. She was pretty as well as, but whatever else she was was the more important. The impressions she had left were oddly assorted. Pooled, he thought they might add up to someone outside his range and was surprised at the degree of thought he had given such a brief encounter. "She's very pretty," he said.

"I expect her husband's a strong young boy."

Ralph couldn't be sure whether Madame Belmondo's evident satisfaction in that was on his account or because of something she saw in it for herself.

In the bar of the Pilot a few people looked round and one man nodded to him. The walls were lined with mirrors, man after man lifted his chin and nodded. Ralph sometimes amused himself trying to calculate the maximum and absolute number of times any reflection could recur. There were eight mirrors in all, of varying sizes, so it was a nice exercise, though not as alarming as it might have been because the root equations had to be hypothetical, he couldn't very well ask to measure the actual areas of glass. He would have liked a hard answer which he might have flashed around – 'There's a mathematical limit to the number of times one object can be reflected. I calculate it – ' if someone had brought up the subject. And why shouldn't someone? Everything was talked about here sooner or later. "You don't say! Is that a fact? This is something we all should know." But a hypothesis wasn't enough, men in bars were not dazzled by mathematical hypotheses. 'If' would stick in their throats, 'assuming that' would be cold gristle.

The barmaid wished him good evening as she served him but when he remarked that it had been a nice day she smiled with personal bitterness and did not reply. In the mirror

Ralph saw that among all the moving mouths his own grinned in isolation.

The Pilot was a noisy place. It was patronised by a restless crowd – though not restless enough to get up and go. The crowd did no more, on the face of it, than raise its voices and shuffle its feet. An impression of vigour and alertness could be given by controlled fidgetting. Ralph had observed, not without envy, that the right degree of dash and disregard could carry off foot-wagging and hand-flapping, tic, lip-licking and open scratching of the crotch. Add a loud voice and a willing laugh and the general impression was of a live-wire, a comer. There were a great many comers at the Pilot in the evenings, which was what drew Ralph to it. He liked life – as a spectator, Bertha said. Bertha had given it thought.

He sat down and crossed his legs, carefully avoiding the hem of a coat which a woman had slung over the back of her chair. On the table his glass stood in a slop of someone's beer. He shifted it to a beer-mat, rubbed it gently back and forth to dry the bottom. The barmaid was watching him. She had a moment to spare, incredibly no-one wanted serving, she leaned her elbows on the bar and watched Ralph.

It would be pleasant if he could think that she was interested. He did not think so, he thought that she was tired and that as she leaned on the bar he happened to be in her line of vision. If the old woman in the flower hat had been sitting where he was, the barmaid would have looked at her.

Ralph shifted his chair to one side to prove it and at that moment someone called the girl away to serve. He was a bit mad to be thinking like this at this juncture. Was he seeking a diversion or another complication? Hoping, perhaps, that two wrongs would make a right?

He raised his glass. It might profit him to reflect how much he would have to give up. He was a prudent man, but a prudent man still finds it expensive to run two homes, especially when one is not wholly his. Any question of reversal and his flat would be the first to go. It would be cheaper

237

to pay the inflated fares from and to Thorne each day than to keep a separate establishment. That meant, literally, no place of his own. Thorne Farm was Emmeline's – how it was Emmeline's!

"I want you to look on it as your home," her voice said in his head. She wanted to have her cake and eat it, he and Bertha paid for their share of everything, they paid for more than their share because the only privacy they had was their bedroom. So far as he was concerned Emmeline ate her cake but did not have it. He went to Thorne on visiting terms.

There were useful voices at the Pilot, they scrambled the voices in his head – he had a dutiful head, bent on giving others their say.

"The Colonel left Thorne to me, but he wished Bertha to share it." The Colonel had not known Ralph. The late Colonel was fond of Bertha. And the Colonel's lady was no fool. Thorne took some keeping up and although she had plenty of money Emmeline was not averse to saving it. Expenses shared were expenses halved, last year it had cost Ralph two hundred pounds towards a new roof.

Two hundred, the sum exactly. "These things happen", he might say to Bertha, "like the roof – you can't budget for them'. But there could not be another roof.

He went to the bar with his glass. "Make it a double."

"Aren't you devoted to this stuff," said the barmaid unquestioningly.

"It's an old Navy habit."

Had she really been interested she would have asked was he in the Royal or Merchant. She looked beyond him, called along the bar, "I've only got one pair of hands."

There was a group which Ralph saw stationed always at the same end. The group fluctuated in size but the composition was stable: the members of it were steak-eaters who knew their way about, had beaten out their ways whenever the line of least resistance was not also the most profitable. They could be thought of as a crux, the Pilot's tone – perhaps it amounted only to timbre – came not from the brewers or the publican or the neighbourhood, but from these men at the bar. Ralph had watched them putting up topics and shooting them down, putting each other up and blowing each other to blazes. They were privileged people, for them wheels turned and switches were thrown.

When one of them finished a joke they roared all together and fell ritually apart with laughter. The place brimmed with noise, it was a change from the voices in Ralph's head.

From the far side of the room someone appeared to be contemplating him. A stranger with his overcoat hung open, his hat pushed back and bending the fleshy rims of his ears, raised his thumb in greeting. Or had Ralph imagined it?

"You're sitting on my gloves," said a girl.

Ralph stood up, there was nothing on his chair.

"You don't mind me asking? I was keeping that seat for a friend."

"I beg your pardon – "

"Sit down till he comes, *if* he comes. I don't feel comfortable with an empty place beside me."

Ralph sat down reluctantly. The girl wore dark glasses which he found intimidating.

"You have to be careful who you speak to. I wouldn't have come if I'd known I'd be sitting here alone. I'm hypersensitive and it's an ordeal. 'Half-past eight in the Pilot, I'm dying to see you,' he said. I think he's died and been buried." She covered Ralph with her shiny round knees like a couple of guns. "It cost me something to go and ask for this little gin for myself. People make it very clear what they think of a woman on her own in a bar. As soon as you step over the threshold of a licensed premises they let their thoughts go. I feel like asking is the licence to slander as well as to drink."

Ralph was surprised. Didn't the modern girl like to be thought liberal?

"This place is a jungle. Do you see that tiger over there? He's been eating me up with his eyes ever since I came in."

239

Of course the man with bent ears was looking at her, Ralph could see that now. The gesture with the thumb had been invitation, not greeting.

"He thinks I'm with you, he'd try to make a kill if he knew I wasn't."

I'm not being watched, thought Ralph, I just get in the way every time anyone looks at anyone else. That's Krassner's doing.

"Have you a cigarette?"

Ralph hadn't. He preferred to smoke a pipe when at leisure.

"Isn't it silly? Even that barmaid scares me. I see what she's thinking, honestly, it flays me when people think like that."

"I haven't any cigarettes – "

"God, how that man stares! Hasn't he seen a woman before?" She pushed her dark glasses up on her forehead. "There, he'll know me next time."

It seemed imprudent for one with such a terribly thin skin – and such a bare face.

"I don't think he means any harm," said Ralph.

"That depends what you call harm. The barmaid gave me a dirty deep look and not because I'm ambidextrous. She thinks I'm here with my flag up."

Ralph felt that he was being taught, it was being demonstrated to him that the most things only happen in the mind. He should remember, it should always be a consideration with him.

"I can't go and ask her for another drink. You know that? I just can't!"

"Inez is a very nice girl." Ralph said earnestly, "She wouldn't harbour such thoughts. I've heard her rebuke people for loose talk."

"Then there's that tiger waiting for me to go and get myself a drink. When I do – crung!" She pounced with her hand. "He'll be on to me."

"As a matter of fact, I thought it was me he was watching.

240

It shows how wrong you can be about where people are looking and what they're looking at. Resting your eye is another thing. We all do occasionally when we're thinking about something entirely different – "

"Oh stuff it!" the girl said loudly. She got up on her fierce black Dr Zhivago boots and went to the ladies' room.

Ralph gazed into the bowl of his pipe. He wondered why she had ended up like that. After all, she had begun it, so why the rage? Why with him?

She wouldn't have told Krassner to stuff it. Krassner would have handled her as he handled all women – successfully. But when did handling begin? How soon? Or was it a built-in mechanism that worked on sight?

Krassner would have brought her a drink as if he were bringing light into darkness. Ralph had been about to do that, to get her a drink, but she hadn't given him the chance.

He *was* being watched. The man across the bar propped his neck on his hand and lazily considered him.

# 3

Marise had a visitor while Tomelty was away – her Uncle Fred Macey. He was not actually her uncle but her mother's cousin and unattached, except loosely to Marise. He did not like Tomelty and Tomelty had no time for him, but on Marise's side of the family it was agreed that Uncle Fred was attached to her. They said, according to their natures, that he had a soft spot for her, that he had his eye on her, that he made a fool of himself.

They were wrong. One of his life's preoccupations had been taking care that he was not made a fool of, he certainly wouldn't allow it to happen by his own doing. Uncle Fred knew just how far he could safely go with Marise. It was really no distance and he had gone all of it. From time to time he dropped in on her to check the limits he had set and establish his position within them.

He was not communicative and ordinarily Marise hardly noticed, she had enough to say for them both. Nor did it bother her what he might be thinking, she thought for both of them. But when she wanted information, as she did now, and came slap against his rooted objection to words, she could have screamed. She did in fact go and scream at half-cock in the kitchen and Uncle Fred remarked that the water pipes were noisy.

"I know I shan't like it here," Marise had said, "it's all so used. We had everything new at Plummer's, we were the first to live there. We're about the hundred and first here, I should think the thousand and first. It's Georgian, Jack says."

"Never. It's Victorian."

Marise was perching on the edge of the couch. She didn't like its grubby patina nor its jungle smell. It disgusted her to see Tomelty spread out on it, and now Uncle Fred.

"This place has graciousness, that's what you can smell. Jack says it takes fifty years to come. I haven't felt clean

242

since I got here." Her skin twitched delicately like a cat's fur. "There are some queer people here. The woman upstairs wears two hats, one on top of the other." It was a new experience for Marise to see challenge in Uncle Fred, she found it tiresome more than exhilarating. "And there's someone who calls himself Shilling – there's nothing to stop him doing that, I suppose. I should think anyone with his name, his real name, and there must have been a lot of them, got rid of it quick."

"What name?"

"John Brown."

Uncle Fred didn't so much sigh as refute. Dissidence erupted from under his waistcoat and the band of his trousers, dissidence and disassociation. He got everything off his chest in one gust.

"You should know," said Marise, "being a policeman. Don't pretend you've forgotten, you never forget anything. You could go on the stage with your memory, Jack says with your memory and his nerve he'd be rich." Actually Uncle Fred's memory was not special, except after a few brown ales when he could be relied on to tell about his days in the B.E.F. But Marise still had to find out how far flattery would get her with him.

"I was a special constable."

"That's what I mean, you know all about it. All the things we couldn't know. They don't let everything out at trials, they keep it on the police records. But you don't need to look at records – " Marise drew her finger across the crown of his balding head – "everything's in here. Jack wouldn't tell me, he pretended it was too awful. The truth is, he doesn't really know."

"I did patrol duty."

"That's not all you did. You had to go to court, you had to guard prisoners – did you guard *him*?"

"Knowing's one thing, telling's another."

"But you ought to tell me! I might be in danger. How would you feel if it all happened again – to me?"

Uncle Fred took a biscuit and crunched on it.

"I'm so alone in this great empty house. At night when Jack's away I feel frightened, I die of fright, not knowing for sure. He looks like a murderer, he's got a murderer's face."

"Where is he?"

"Upstairs. What he did, it was awful, wasn't it?"

Uncle Fred stood up, ham-fisted. "Show him to me."

"I can't, he's not here now, he's out at this minute."

Uncle Fred sat down again. He picked up his empty plate and turned it over and looked at the underneath. He had his code of manners, he never asked for more and he always indicated that he had finished by shoving his plate into the middle of the table.

Marise cut him a slice of raspberry tart. "You've seen so much blood I suppose it wouldn't worry you to see mine."

Uncle Fred bit the slice of tart and red jam leaked over his chin. "I haven't set eyes on this geezer."

"He comes in at half-past six. Always the same time, you'll be able to see him from this window."

So it was that Ralph, coming home with conscience well saddled, was unaware of eyes watching from behind the curtains. The thought did occur as he went towards the house that he had compounded a felony and was now on the wrong side of the law. He felt a sense of insecurity, as if he had forfeited all civic and moral rights. He was ready to find that he not only had to empty his own dustbin but that it would not be an offence to run him over, there being no more legal objection to it than to running over a cat. Being a criminal made everyone else law-abiding and he was ready to find that he looked as different as chalk from cheese and that everyone could see why. He did not allow for the extenuating circumstance, the best he had acted for – not, anyway, at the moment of going into the house where was all the best for him.

Being here and not at Thorne Farm was sustained rebellion, a mighty piece of self-indulgence. He could have lived at the Farm, as Bertha wanted him to, and worked in Chelmsford, if not equally well, well enough. But he had insisted on living here from Monday to Friday, it was essential to him, he was like a man with an air-hole, he had to have it and he hadn't really tried to justify it. Now he had compounded a felony to keep things the way they were. This way, he thought as he stood at the door of his flat, this admirable way.

People like Krassner would ask what was admirable about it. He heard Krassner say, "Is this what you want, old boy? Is this what you call living?"

The cat was crouched on the window-sill, elbows out, a lozenge of black in each golden eye. Ralph dropped his hat and briefcase and lit a cigarette. So far as he was concerned this was living and perhaps was comic. Perhaps because he needed to do less than most people and not nearly as much as Krassner to live, it was pathetic. It was nonetheless a precious state of affairs.

He kicked on the gas-fire, lit it, and in his overcoat sat down. It would be hard to justify his liking for this – all right then – this existence. He had few material comforts here and no company. At Thorne he could have both, and more money left in his pocket. But there had never been a question in his mind as to what he wanted, he knew before he knew what he was missing that he could not let himself miss it.

Bertha asked, "What do you do with yourself?" She sounded wistful and he had to be careful what he said. They all lived on the edge if not of a volcano, of a trapdoor. He invariably answered, "I read, listen to the News, take a walk to the local, go to bed early". Which was true as far as it went, but Bertha used to look at him – and so did Emmeline – as if to say, "Is there nothing else?"

He drew hard on his cigarette and in the dark the lighted end pulsed, the cigarette grew visibly shorter and he took it from between his lips and held it in his fingers. Bertha and Emmeline would never appreciate that what he did only carried what he did not do – expediently, as a cable carries a current. Yes, there was something else which had to be nameless and which he admitted might be the reason for what he had just done. He had just withdrawn two hundred pounds, his wife's two hundred, and paid it into the firm's account. And he had about two hours, the time it would take him to get to Thorne, to think of a reason to give her.

She was going to ask questions, one or two a day, for the rest of their lives. She simply did not have enough to think about. He would do better to have an attitude rather than answers. But what attitude?

She would have to trust him – poor woman, she would have to. He could guess how difficult that would be made for her in his absence. She might promise him not to tell Emmeline and might not want to tell her, but she would have to tell someone. There was only Emmeline, there was always Emmeline, he was as good as married to the two of them.

Bertha would maintain, "Ralph has made the decision, it was right that he should" and Emmeline would say, "He is stubborn, that's not the same thing as strength of character," and each time he went to Thorne he would have to repair the erosions. He would have to do that for Bertha's sake, because doubt in any form made her unhappy. Luckily it was easy to reassure her, it only required his presence. She subsided into that sometimes as if it were a warm bath, at other times she stood up in it as if it were a tin suit and no-one could harm her through it. To make her really happy, to implement her against Emmeline and other sources of misgiving, he should stay with her. Those were the two sides of the coin, her happiness and his.

Ralph washed up his tea-things and the cat's dish. He had a small 'fridge and looked inside to check his needs. It did not escape him that he was already looking forward to Monday evening when Thorne would be miles away: it did not escape him, it annoyed him. Was there no justice in him?

No humanity? It surely was inhuman to want to discount all the caring shown him at Thorne.

Into his briefcase he put the day's *Telegraph* and his rolled mackintosh. He put on a corduroy cap which he wore at weekends at Thorne. "Shoo!" he said to the cat in farewell.

In the hall he met Marise who had been to the gate to wave goodbye to Uncle Fred. It was a surprise to both of them, although she had had Ralph in mind. In fact, coming face to face with him on this particular evening was little short of a bombshell. Uncle Fred had disappointed and aggravated her by his attitude. After one glance at Mr Shilling through the window he had stated positively that he was not John Brown.

"I do know your name," she said, "I haven't really forgotten. It's a short one, like Smith or Jones or Green. Isn't it a colour, isn't it White?"

She was wishing that Jack and Uncle Fred could see his face. He was thunderstruck, she told Tomelty later.

She didn't exaggerate, she did have a striking effect on Ralph. She had been far from his thoughts and suddenly seeing her was like having a light brandished in his face. There was more to her than light, there was a flesh-and-bloodedness of purity, such purity, he thought, that it could come second only to cellulose.

Yes, he thought, she had the total absence of congenital harm that fresh flowers had. When he looked at fresh flowers and now that he looked at her he saw no badness to break out or soak through or twist awry.

"My name is Shilling."

"I ought to remember because your other name's the same as my husband's but everyone calls him 'Jack'."

"My name's Ralph."

Uncle Fred had told Marise, "That's not him," and when she asked why not, he got angry, and so did she. Knowing how long it normally took him to make up his mind about anything she was sure he had made it up in advance so as to know better than Jack.

"I suppose I didn't recognise you because I haven't seen you wearing a cap before."

Ralph would have liked to touch her, he often touched flowers, trying to identify their purity and he had a strong temptation to follow the curve of her neck with his finger.

"I've only spoken to you once," she said, "but I watch you coming and going."

Uncle Fred had shouted – when he was angry he said nothing at the top of his voice – "He didn't wear a bowler!" So now she was sure and she felt reckless and dangerous to herself.

"I watch you every day."

"Do you?" Ralph said wonderingly. He was full of amazement. The encounter seemed no less than a miracle and could not last at the present pace. It was gathering momentum all the time. Already he had gone too far ever to get back to the same place. "Do you? Why?"

"My husband makes me. He makes me watch everybody, he says I think I'm the only one alive."

"Do you?"

"Yes," said Marise. "Except for you, I think you're alive."

"Indeed I am. It must be the first time," said Ralph, and Marise, who had been going to remark, "But you shouldn't be, should you?" gave him a stare of appraisal instead.

Ralph flushed. He hardly knew what he was saying, and yet it mattered acutely. "There *is* only the one time, isn't there?" He added, with pleading out of all context, "As far as we know?"

The situation had moved a little out of Marise's hands but she saw the lovely way it could go. She saw idyllic fear and herself in possession of a monster and was ready at once – she always presumed on the moment, and seeing what might be as good as being, she was often right ahead of time and it was one of the things that upset Tomelty.

"Come in and have a cup of tea," she said to Ralph.

248

He looked at her in anguish. "I can't, I have to catch a train."


He got out of the train still smarting at his inadequacy. How long was it since a miracle had happened to him? And he had said, "I can't". Was ever a man so dead? He felt deprived and by his own act and when he saw Bertha waiting in the car he heard the old cogs turning. He knew their creaks, he had let himself be lulled by their creaks, he passed his week-ends in a lull.

Not this week-end, he thought, and remembered that he hadn't decided what to say to Bertha. Instead of using the journey to reach an attitude, he had sat in a daze. The new little creature had gone to his head. Only his feet remained resolute. They had carted him to the station and hoisted him aboard the train, they were the reason, the sole reason, he thought without humour, why he was here.

"There you are, dear," said Bertha. She always said it with a hint of shyness. She could still be shy with him. "I'm so thankful you've arrived safely." She had a debt of gratitude and paid it. Each time Ralph came she did not thank God or Fate for his arrival, she thanked him for coming – to be sheltered and served and surrendered to. "I fancy the train's a little late?"

What would she have done if he hadn't come, would she sit all night waiting, and rejoice in the morning when he did?

Bertha took off the handbrake and put the car into gear as it rolled downhill. She was a bad driver though enormously careful. Emmeline said that a car needed a lot of tractor in it to survive Bertha's care. As the gears engaged they were both thrown forward and Ralph's nose stubbed the windscreen.

Bertha said, "I must ask Emmeline to have that looked at."

The car was Emmeline's. Very little in Bertha's world was

not directly or indirectly Emmeline's. Except Ralph, and for him there were incumbent benefits.

"How have you been, dear? You're always so busy, we can't help wondering if you make time to eat properly. You looked tired last week and you didn't want to walk the long way home from church. We noticed. Oh dear, have you a cold?"

Ralph shook his head as he wiped his eyes which were watering from the blow on his nose.

"You don't really take care of yourself," Bertha said wistfully. She braked hard at an empty pedestrian crossing. "Emmeline says you're not sustaining your frame. You have a big frame, Ralph."

It was possible to get glimpses of the estuary across the fields. Bertha and Ralph, before they married, used to walk to the estuary to watch the ships pass. Neither of them hankered to sail away, they left that to people who had business away or could not settle at home. When the salt wind blew inland Bertha remembered a Cornish town where she stayed as a child – not the sea nor the sands, just the grey street with aprons of spray between the houses. Ralph only remembered when he was off guard.

He wound down the car window and watched the coasters and liners each reduced to a pip of light bowling in and out of Emmeline's hedges.

"Dr and Mrs Chinn are coming to dinner tomorrow."

Ralph made an acceptance noise and Bertha said, "We thought you'd be pleased."

Normally he took his cue, Bertha always gave him one – to be glad, to be sorry, to be indignant, to be amused – and it all went smoothly. Now he saw no just cause for Dr and Mrs Chinn, no reason, not even an excuse.

"It's for your sake, dear." Bertha could not make up her mind to emerge at the T-junction. "We thought they'd be company for you." She waved on the car which waited behind them. "You are pleased, aren't you?"

Why didn't he take the cue? Why did he shrug and con-

250

tinue to look out of the window? He knew what his silence
would do to Bertha. Her dismay was tangible as she ground
the car in bottom gear along the dark lane to Thorne. She
signalled desperately with her headlamps at every bend.
When at last they stopped outside the house he was about
to put his arm round her and tell her that he'd been looking
forward to just the three of them together this week-end but
he was of course pleased at the prospect of Dr and Mrs
Chinn, but before he could move, the door opened wide,
golden light trumpeted out and there was Emmeline crying,
"Ralph, darling!"

He was never sure which there was in her cry – pleasure,
pain, or blame.

When people remarked on how the sisters complemented
each other, they meant that there would never be room for
two Emmelines. Not in the same family nor, thought Ralph,
in the same cognisance. It was not likely that he would ever
know another Emmeline: if he were obliged to, within the
same lifespan, he would be crowded out of himself.

The late Colonel Openshaw had been too late for Ralph,
Emmeline was already a widow when he met Bertha. By
Emmeline's account – Bertha said little more than that he
was kind – the Colonel was out of Ralph's class. He had to
be, to take Emmeline. She was a challenge which Ralph had
never accepted, in fact they all lived together at Thorne on
the understanding that he did not.

"Ralph has something on his mind," she said as they sat
at supper. She was finishing the last of three gins with which
she had prefaced the meal. Beside her plate was a lighted
cigarette.

"We shouldn't expect him to slip into our life at a
moment's notice," said Bertha. "It's a far cry from his."

At week-ends they often discussed him in his presence as
they did out of it for the rest of the week.

"If he feels disjointed it could be the beginning of the end

251

of something," said Emmeline. "Personally I'll be glad if it's the end of his commuting."

"He knows how we feel about that." Bertha put the plate of bread at Ralph's elbow. "The soft pieces are towards you, dear."

"I have nothing on my mind," said Ralph, "except the joy of being with you both."

"His mind is putting out some interesting rays, mostly emotional, though there's a hard streak too. Our darling's twisted his envelope out of shape."

"Don't tease," pleaded Bertha. "He must be so tired after his journey."

"I hardly noticed the journey."

"No, that's not a suffering streak," said Emmeline, "it's too solid. And I'm not sure about the joy, he has such soft pink joy, has Ralph."

He smiled. "I think the boot's on the other foot. You have something on your mind, Emmy."

She dropped her knife and fork and picked up the cigarette.

"Isn't the beef to your liking?" Bertha asked anxiously.

Emmeline turned to Ralph. "Do you know of a good water-diviner?"

"What?"

"Divining's in your line of country – weed-killers and pest control – surely there's a file on Dowsers in your office?"

"No."

"Don't you look for the springs of life as well as the springs of death?"

"What do you want a water-diviner for?"

"Darling, to divine water."

"It's no joke," Bertha warned in a stage whisper to Ralph and sounded sorry that it wasn't.

"Hurry up and finish eating and let's get away from the table."

Emmeline was not interested in food. She regarded it as fuel and to her a meal was a stoking operation: Ralph, eating

Bertha's excellent Yorkshire pudding amid Emmeline's fuss and fume, wondered not for the first time if the sisters complemented each other to the extent of each offsetting the other's qualities with her own defects.

"I want a diviner for this room," said Emmeline. "And for the room above it, my bedroom. Bertha and I find the atmosphere oppressive in them both. There's a sense of effort. Don't you feel it? But you wouldn't, you're not here all the time."

"What effort?" Ralph smiled. "In your bedroom?"

"If there's a stream immediately under this room we shall know why it's twice as much effort to lift a finger in here as it is anywhere else in the house."

Ralph looked at Bertha. She sighed ambiguously and he chose a slice of bread from which the crusts had been trimmed.

"I have no difficulty lifting my fingers."

"You wouldn't, over a week-end. It's a cumulative effect."

"Of what?"

"If there's a stream under the house we're being bombarded with ionising rays. I feel a tug," said Emmeline, "when I do the smallest thing I feel a tug the other way."

"Dusting this room makes me hot," said Bertha.

"Water is a conductor. Living over it is equivalent to continuous treatment with weak radium. We've lived here for fifteen years – how much radium can the system take?"

"I should think you're super-charged," said Ralph.

Emmeline twisted out her cigarette among the food on her plate.

"It could ultimately be lethal." Flakes of ash settled on Ralph's last piece of potato. "I'm not going to die that way."

The secret of living, or partly-living with her was to be passive. If she was left to her devices they petered out.

"What worries me," said Bertha, "is what do we do – what can we do – if there *is* water under the house?"

Ralph smiled. Here was Bertha's quality offsetting this

253

defect of Emmeline's, Bertha took Emmeline's theories and held them up like knitting to see what the final measurements would be.

"We could move."

"Don't be absurd, Ralph. This is my home."

And the final measurements were shown to be nothing.

"Thorne is well-built and structurally sound, Arnold would never have taken it otherwise. Where he came from they didn't merely pinch the fruit before they bought, they ate it to see if it was worth paying for. He checked everything, he sent men up the chimneys and down the drains, he even had the brick content analysed. But he overlooked something that mattered more than any of that."

"Not to him," said Bertha. "I really don't think it would ever have mattered to him, except insofar as it mattered to you – "

"Of course it wouldn't. He was desensitised by his years in the East, he had reached maximum absorption and saturation point. He felt nothing."

"He wasn't *bothered*," Bertha explained. "By it, I mean." She had a way of tidying up after people, interpreting and representing them when they were dead or absent, in the kindest light.

"To my mind the terrestrial rays are more important than bricks and mortar. If they're bad, a dry roof and good plumbing can't compensate."

Bertha put her hand on Ralph's. "I've made you baked jam roll. Emmy and I are ending with fresh fruit. We sleep better without pudding."

"I've never known you sleep badly."

"Emmy has very disturbed nights."

"Is it to be wondered at if I'm subjected to electromagnetic radiation all the time I'm in bed?"

Ralph knew better than to ask how it had started. How did it ever start? Not with a bang but a whimper, as someone once said.

"If there is a stream under the house it is here," she said.

"That I know, I feel." She tapped a cigarette smartly on the table before putting it between her lips. Ralph observed that she tapped the wrong end. "I shall close this room and move my bed to the other side of the house."

Things being as they were it would be better if he did not observe so much, he had no intention of changing anything at this end, he accepted what had emerged at Thorne. Indeed, almost any other combination of the ingredients would have been the worse for him – and he was obliged to take whatever shaped up. Things being as they were, he had run a considerable risk.

"What do you think, dear?" said Bertha.

"Does it matter?"

"Of course it matters! We're waiting for your opinion, aren't we, Emmy?"

"I think Emmy should get married again," he said, and filled his mouth with pudding.

"What's that got to do with anything?"

Bertha went turkey-red with alarm, Emmeline's powder turned mauve.

Ralph said thickly, with pastry loading his tongue, "It would solve all your problems."

Emmeline got up and left the room. Her chair, pushed back too violently, fell on its side. Bertha hurried to pick it up. "You shouldn't have said that."

"I suppose not. It would be a poor lookout for us if she did marry again."

"Why did you say it?"

"I wanted to rough her up for talking such nonsense. This is excellent pastry, Bert."

"It was unkind. Sometimes you can be unkind, dear."

But he knew that she did not think seriously of it, only as seriously as if she had been obliged to say that his hands were sometimes dirty. To her, unkindness and dirt were skin deep.

He licked in some sweet flakes and tidied his lip from

corner to corner with a sweep of his tongue. "It's true. She needs a husband."

"Marriage is the answer to a lot of things," agreed Bertha. She sat beside him and kissed his ear and he chose that moment, or was it chosen for him, to think again of the new little creature.

After leaving the train he had put her firmly from his mind, intending to regard the journey down as being a journey away from her, with Thorne as its farthest point. When he got into the train to go back to London, when the first bend of the track hid Bertha from sight, that was to be the time to re-start thinking. But here he was, remembering the miracle with shocking clarity. Shocking because the locale was wrong, the time was wrong and the physical circumstance – Bertha nibbling his ear – was ludicrously wrong.

"I've got something to tell you." He jerked his head away. "I've cashed a cheque for two hundred pounds on our account."

It wasn't doubt that made Bertha ask questions. Of Ralph she had no doubt and she was quite easy about the money. She simply wanted to be easier still. She was like that in bed, stirring gently round and round before she went to sleep, making sure that everything was in the best possible place.

"Shall we make a lot of money?"

"No-one makes a lot nowadays with capital gains tax."

Perhaps it hadn't been a good idea to tell her that he had invested the money.

"Stock market dealings are like this, you get a tip and you have to be ready to take a chance. I took this one for both of us."

"I think it's exciting. When shall we know how we've done?"

He wanted the thought to occur that she might not see

the money again, she need not retain the suspicion, but it ought to cross her mind.

She asked if the investment was anything to do with kaffirs. Emmeline had told her that kaffirs could be gold shares.

"I don't want Emmy to know about it. What we do with our money is our business."

The plural was justified because he had done it for her too. It *was* a kind of investment.

Later she asked who had given him the tip. Was it someone he could trust?

"You must trust me," he said. "Do you trust me?"

"Of course, dear. And it's your money too."

She wanted to know what it was they had bought. Shares in what? "Perhaps I shall see something about them in the paper. Emmy reads the financial page, so shall I now."

"If she sees you, she'll cotton on. You know how quickly she can."

"The gardening notes are on the same page and I always read them. She won't see anything different."

On the Saturday evening, just before the Chinns arrived, she asked what would affect the price of their shares. What caused them to go up or down.

"A lot of things that we can't control," said Ralph, "at home and abroad – trade, strikes, politics, takeovers. Shares are vulnerable."

"I hope they won't be affected by the Vietnam war – I shouldn't like to profit from that."

The answers seemed to be lying about in his head, any number of lies lay about ready to be told. And it was easy to deceive Bertha, she didn't ask for the fiction whole and tongued and grooved and caulked to hold water, she was satisfied with snippets of lies and took each one away and stored it in her mind and came back for another.

But he heard her voice bringing them all out again one by one, and if from him they had sounded like truth, coming from her they sounded like lies. He had to rely on her not telling them to anyone, he had asked her not to, but he was going to get his own back for years because she would not forget it. He cursed Krassner, Krassner need never lift another finger, he was already built into their lives.

"Do they give you certificates like they do when you buy premium bonds?"

"Why?"

"It's nice to have something to show even if you're not sure how much it's going to be worth."

"I can't show you, I haven't got them with me."

"They wouldn't mean anything to me, dear." They were changing for dinner and she was putting powder into her neck, excitement had made her neck pink. "I can't read small print. Oh, is that a car in the lane? I must put some Parmesan on the table in case they take it with soup."

The Chinns were important people, they moved in unmysterious ways through local politics. They had unshakeable faith: if it did not move mountains it shifted many molehills.

"What's the matter, Shilling? You look as if you've lost a fiver and found yourself."

Dr Chinn did not smile at his own jokes but he expected others to, and faced with his strong wolfish stare they usually did. At public meetings he could stare titters out of an audience of several hundred. Ralph had himself tried the stare before a mirror but he had not enough white to his eyes to make it daunting.

"Ralph's in a mood," said Emmeline, "we're hoping you'll shake him out of it."

"He's a little tired," said Bertha. "He has such a busy week, so much to think about and do, it can't be any wonder if he likes to be quiet."

"I daresay I can match him," said Dr Chinn. "I've seen a hundred or more patients this week, delivered a baby, driven to Colchester for a consultation, written an article on Zygotes and Eggs, inspected the effluents at Bull Marsh and Neap and lime-washed a hen house."

"The pace is so different in London," said Bertha. "It's

so wearing with everyone rushing about. I always start to trot as soon as I get out at Liverpool Street."

"We're all rather tired," said Emmeline, "and I have my own idea why."

"Indeed?" Mrs Chinn raised her eyebrows. "What is your idea?"

"If I were to state it in present company I should be laughed to scorn. It isn't nice to be mocked for having the courage of one's convictions, especially by those one has been obliged to regard as one's nearest and dearest. But of course I am the only one under that obligation. Shall I pour you a whisky, Dr Chinn?"

"Dear lady, please." The doctor turned to Ralph. "What have you been up to, Shilling?"

Ralph felt Bertha's hand touch him for comfort or warning or both.

"Scorn? Mockery? I wouldn't have thought it commensurate with your nature." He stared round, hunting up smiles. "What's that thing of Burns's about giving us the giftie of seeing ourselves as others see us?"

"We had a slight difference of opinion," said Bertha. "It happens in the happiest of families and my sister has been under considerable pressure lately. There was no mockery, no-one scorned anyone."

"A little leg-pulling?" The doctor stooped solicitously to Emmeline. "One cannot always take it from whence it comes. Or if one can, the source may make it harder to take at all."

"It was a serious discussion," Bertha said firmly.

Mrs Chinn drained her glass. "What pressure has Mrs Openshaw been under?"

"I may tell you later. It would be a relief. Ralph, do give Mrs Chinn another sherry."

Ralph hoped she would tell them, he looked forward to hearing the doctor on terrestrial rays and ionization by secret streams. He wanted to ask if anyone had noticed pressure at Bull Marsh, walking about over the effluent. Shouldn't that sort of stream be twice as lethal?

During dinner the Chinns talked about themselves. The subject should have been a varied one since their activities were, but they seemed always to follow the formula which brought them out one hundred per cent right. Ralph couldn't blame them. Had he been able to find such a formula he would have kept on it too. He listened without rancour through the soup, with Parmesan, through the stuffed roast pork and the green salad, the apple and lemon pie, the Bath Olivers and cheese, and blew a silent fanfare right into their faces.

He tried the Krassner incident their way, by their formula. How would it have come out for Dr Chinn? Krassner had said, "I'm glad you're human, old boy, it's a weight off my mind. If people are born putty saints how are the rest of us poor bastards going to feel, having to fight temptation all the time? Yes, I'm glad you're going to put up the money, it shows that temptation's where you find it." Krassner had said, "You've been tempted to save your office skin, old boy."

Ralph heard Dr Chinn reply, "You've just made your second big mistake, Krassner. The first was to steal, the second is to suppose I would compound a felony."

Dr Chinn wouldn't have replaced the money, the formula would have seen him right, the formula would have taken care of everything and taken the blame to the top. To Pecry? That would have made history.

"Ralph! What are you dreaming about?" Emmeline called down the table. "Ralph! Dr Chinn is speaking to you."

The doctor disliked not being attended to. He leaned across and tapped Ralph's plate with the side of his knife. "I said it's not smart to work in London. You should consider your arteries."

"Ralph takes exercise," said Bertha. "He walks everywhere."

"He doesn't have an expense account," said Emmeline.

"What could be wrong with his arteries?"

"Nothing, dear lady, provided he remembers that he has them."

"I think we should look beyond flesh and blood for the causes of our illnesses," said Emmeline.

"We should, we should!" cried the doctor. "Of all creation our flesh and blood is most qualified to be perfect. Only yesterday, as I held a newly-born child by the heels I said to Nurse, 'Here's a brand new creature, a perfect being. What will we make of him? What will he make of himself?' "

Ralph stared. Here was his miracle stated, here was medical authority for it.

"We should look at the infected universe, everything in it is pathogenetic," said the doctor, fixing them for the joke, and Ralph was wondering with alarm and despondency how many men had seen the perfectability of the flesh as he, Ralph, had seen it. How many had already discovered her in her flower of life?

"We should look at Shilling's pesticides which preserve the crop and poison the eater," said Dr Chinn.

"What happens to arteries," Bertha wanted to know, "to make them harden?"

"They fur up like a kettle," said Emmeline.

"Dear lady, that's a whimsical thought. But I'm sure we don't want to discuss the degenerative changes of animal tissues."

"I do," said Bertha. "Will anyone try a pear?"

Ralph felt sad. It was true that in the new-born child Dr Chinn had observed only the theory while Ralph himself had been privileged to see it in its beautiful practice. But the miracle now seemed less of a miracle. I'm being absurd, thought Ralph, if I expect to have a monopoly of truth.

Mrs Chinn turned to Emmeline. "There was something you were going to tell us. About pressure."

"It's a family matter." Bertha stood up. "Shall we go into the garden-room for coffee?"

261

"It helps to talk about family matters outside the family," said Mrs Chinn. "Disinvolvement is an asset."

Ralph stood up beside Bertha. Dr Chinn began to pick up and sniff the pears. He selected two and put one on his wife's plate. Ralph and Bertha sat down again.

"I'm seriously wondering whether this is a good place to live" said Emmeline.

"Good? In what sense?"

"Whether it's good for our health."

"Salubrious? From that point of view I consider it one of the best sites in the district."

"On the face of it, yes. I'm considering what's underneath."

"Dear lady, what is underneath?"

"I mean to find out."

"How will you do that?"

"I shall employ a water-diviner."

There was a pause during which Dr Chinn quartered his pear and peeled each piece as if he were removing a membrane.

"I shouldn't have thought this house was damp," said Mrs Chinn.

"It isn't. There's something much more potent about water than its wetness." Emmeline crushed her cigarette into the crumbled pastry on her plate. "There are radiations. They operate with or against, and here at Thorne they are against us."

"But only in this part of the house. And of course Emmy feels it," said Bertha, "because she sleeps in the room over this one."

"Feels what?"

"I can only describe it as a pull in the wrong direction." Emmeline signalled to Ralph and he fetched the cigarette box from a side table. "It's tiring to have to fight little fights all the while."

"Would it be correct to say that you are having trouble with the plumbing?"

"No." Emmeline got up and began to stir around the room. Her dress was unfashionably long and of some noisy material which cracked across her knees at every step. "Do you know anything about radiesthesia?"

"I'm familiar with the principle of the copper bracelet."

"Are you familiar with the principle that everyone, every living creature, every *thing*, has an electro-magnetic field? An area of influence, of radiation? I don't end here – " Emmeline slapped her cheek and spread her arms wide – "this is also me. And this – " she embraced the air above Dr Chinn's head – "this is also you. This room is full of radiation, our magnetic fields are here, Mrs Chinn's and Bertha's, Ralph's and this auricula's – yes, this plant has a magnetic field, so have these chairs and this carpet and curtains and that bit of iron in the chimney-breast."

It was necessary for Emmeline to be seen doing whatever she was doing. She always pushed herself to an extreme in public, though never to an extremity. "Who shall say where we finish?" She whirled, with crackling skirts, around Dr and Mrs Chinn. "Can you be sure of a place, any place, where there's none of me, nothing of you?"

Dr Chinn dissected a brown speck from his pear. "There's nothing of any of us out at Bull Marsh."

"Time and distance don't finish us!" cried Emmeline. "Nor does death."

"We are not in that effluent area," said Dr Chinn.

"You don't believe me?"

"Dear lady, I never disbelieve anyone as sincere as you are. Occasionally a doctor has to suspend his critical faculties and recognise the power of unreason."

"I'm simply looking beyond my nose. Moonshots and space probes are done by mathematics – I shan't say 'simple' mathematics although comparatively speaking they are, because the equations are on the blackboard waiting to be worked out. But there are some things that cannot be written down. Sometimes I think that chimney-breast is to blame."

"To blame for what?"

"For the way we feel, my sister and I."

"It looks like an old oven door. An admirable piece of casting." Mrs Chinn said briskly, "if you're thinking of removing it I should like to buy it."

"I've not yet discovered what it is you feel." The doctor looked at Ralph. "We might start from there."

"Oppressed," said Emmeline. "We feel oppressed and tired in this room. If I stay here all day, by evening I can scarcely lift a finger." It was hard to believe. She had flesh as strong and sappy as celery, a limp Emmeline was a contradiction in terms.

"Iron has such polarity with the earth's core – oh even Ralph would feel iron! But I think these emanations come from water. I feel water under this house."

"Dear lady, I think indeed you may. Since almost three-quarters of the earth's surface is covered by water there's bound to be plenty of it running about underneath. Carrying your principle to its broadest conclusion, what about the British Navy? If radiations from water have a depressive effect, how do our sailors stay on their feet?"

Bertha said, "Oh dear," under her breath and Mrs Chinn smiled. Ralph thought it was not a fair smile, not fair to Emmeline whose house this was and whose dinner they had eaten.

"Any principle can be reduced to absurdity." The Chinns were now her enemy. "There's all the difference between radiations from a concentrated spring and from a body of water like the sea."

"I'm relieved to hear it." The doctor fixed them, face by face. "Or how have we contrived to rule the waves?"

"Ralph's going to bring a water-diviner," said Bertha, and the doctor's white eyes rolled round to Ralph. "He has business connections everywhere. Most people wouldn't know where to look for a water-diviner, would they?"

"Do you feel oppressed, Shilling?"

"He feels as we do," said Emmeline. "More so."

"Why more so?"

"It comes harder on him, when he's been working he needs rest and relaxation here. He's the breadwinner."

Dr and Mrs Chinn raised their eyebrows together, though without apparent collusion.

"You mentioned a difference of opinion," said Mrs Chinn.

"Not between ourselves."

"And no mockery, dear lady, from your nearest and dearest?"

It was Emmeline's turn to fix the doctor's eye. "We feel the same about everything."

"Why is London bad for Ralph's arteries?" asked Bertha.

# 4

Marise had been doing some history. She did not actually write it down, though one day she would. It was of course her own personal history and was called "Everything being I am" and included times before she was born as times in preparation for her being. The current section began: "This was the darkest hour. She had been torn from the lap of luxury and imprisoned where harlots and murderers lived. It was his plan to crush her spirit, she who had a spirit like a thousand birds."

Marise had spoken to the harlot and it had been a very significant conversation.

"I knew at once," she told Tomelty. "She was an open box."

"You mean book."

"Why should I mean book?"

Tomelty yawned. He had just come back from Newcastle, sitting in on a poker game. The rattle of the train was still in his head and the warm beer he had drunk all night had given him heartburn.

The flat showed signs of Marise as a picnic spot shows signs of a picnic. When Tomelty walked in he saw a record of what she had been doing. She had knelt on the chairs, pulled the curtains back and leaned her cheek against the window and rubbed a clean patch on the glass, she had eaten a cake and an orange as she wandered about the room and left crumbs on the mantelshelf and peel on the piano. She had tried to play the piano, looking under the lid at the hammers while she struck the keys, the silk runner hung askew and she had taken a glass out of the china cabinet and put a feather in it. A broken string of beads lay on the table, some of the beads on the floor – he trod on one and crushed it. The toy bear was pushed snout down between the cushions of an armchair.

"Is there any bacon, Gyp?"

"It's only ten o'clock. I haven't been shopping yet."

She wore his dressing-gown. She often spent half the day in it, her hands hidden in the sleeves and the skirt like a bell-tent round her. She said once that it comforted her in his absence and once he had believed her. It was soon after they were married, while there were some lies he still wanted to hear and he wasn't above making some up for her to tell him.

"You could have got it yesterday."

"Yesterday was Sunday. You could have got breakfast on the train."

"Couldn't run to it." Also in his head was the rattle of the five pounds he had lost at poker to complete strangers. "Take that thing off!" He tore at the scruff of the dressing-gown as she passed him.

It dropped over her shoulders to her waist and slid from there to the floor. She stood naked and for a moment they were utterly surprised. Then they laughed, Tomelty slapped his knee and Marise, looking down at her stomach, laughed the more to see it quake.

"You're a marvel," said Tomelty fervently and so she was, standing unashamed, the colour of wheat straw and with the same patina of pale gold where the light touched her. Tomelty felt plain covetousness and put out his hand to take her as he would any rarity.

Marise dodged and still laughing ran into the bathroom. She took the precaution of locking the door while she dressed. When she came out he was making tea.

"Did you have a good trip?"

He grunted, he was sulking and Marise thought how ridiculous he was. If it had been anything else he wanted, was always wanting, she could have taken it seriously. She didn't wish to be unkind because it was how he had been born, but she could see the funny side, only the funny side.

"Newcastle's a dirty place." She had been no farther north than Barnet but she knew what coal sacks smelled like. "Somebody has to do the dirty work and it's a good thing they do it up there. Coal sacks smell like kippers." She poured tea into the cup he had set for himself and sipped from it. "Shall I get you a kipper for your breakfast?"

"One day, Gyp, I'll do for you. Other women can be left, I can get up and leave them. But not you, you'll have to be finished. I'll finish you and the harder you push me the sooner I shall do it."

She pouted. "I've been all by myself all the week-end, no-one to talk to, nothing to do. You know I don't like being alone on Sundays."

"I'm not going over that again. This Newcastle client was a hard sell and if I hadn't been prepared to soften him up, plenty of others would. You may not realise it, but the ones that pay the money call the tune." He poured himself tea and liberally splashed in whisky. He was lucky, for all the whisky he drank the first mouthful still had power to fire the roof of his head. "That's better. Who cares about food anyway?"

"I stayed in bed." It wasn't true, she disliked the bedroom and had slept all night curled up in a chair. She said it because bed was part of his ridiculousness, and showed him her pointed pink tongue. "I stayed in bed all by myself."

Tomelty took a mouthful of whisky and hot tea. He grimaced and took another mouthful and grimaced again, but pleasurably. "You're a bloody marvel." He was comforted, the whisky, the hot tea, comforted him.

"You know they are harlots and murderers in this house?"

"That's right."

"I didn't speak first, this woman came over to me at the window. 'You must be our new neighbours,' she said. 'And you must be a harlot,' I thought to myself. I knew by the way she walked."

"What about her tail? You can always tell them by their tails."

"She had green powder in her nostrils and nothing on under her dress. I could see everything."

"Pretty?"

"No, she's old and fat." Marise blew out her cheeks and mimicked, 'My name is Sophie Belmondo and I live in the first floor flat. I know you'll be happy, we have such nice people here.' "

"This is a nice place."

"I shan't be happy. I was happy at Plummer's, that was the happiest time of my life."

He looked at her gloomily. "I brought you a present."

"Oh, what is it?"

He threw her a package. "Put it on, let's see you."

It was a mini-skirt apparently made of sharkskin. Marise held it against her, it was scarcely eighteen inches long. "I can't wear that!"

"Of course you can. You've got a nice pair of jinoos so why not show them."

"You're trying to corrupt me. And that's not all. If you get me to expose myself to evil eyes there'll be evil done and that would save you the trouble, wouldn't it? You'd like to see me murdered."

"That's right," Tomelty said calmly, "but I shall want the satisfaction of doing it myself."

Marise was going to try on the mini-skirt. She could have become a model, a man she met on a train had once offered to make her one, 'a pocket Venus' he called her. But she did not care for the modern styles, they were too jokey.

She straightened up with the skirt tight across her thighs. "It doesn't even come to my knees."

"It's not meant to. They've got kind faces, your knees, kinder than your face. I like to see them smiling."

"I couldn't wear it, I'd be frightened."

"What of?"

"The man upstairs." She bent her knees and tried to pull the skirt down over them. "If he's done it twice he can do it three times."

"Who's done what?"

"Murder."

"What murder, for God's sake?"

269

"You said he was John Brown, didn't you? You said John Brown was a murderer."

"I said he looked like him. John Brown's pushing up daisies by now."

"How do you know?"

Tomelty's nose began to blanch. "He's dead and buried. I'm telling you – that's how *you* know."

Marise stooped to look at her knees. "They don't smile. But I'm looking at them upside down so I suppose I wouldn't see it. Uncle Fred said it wasn't him."

"Fred Macey? Has he been here?"

"He came to tea. He saw him through the window." Tomelty was looking at her in the mini-skirt. She recognised how he was looking – he could shout and bully but in the end he could only look. He could only stand a mile off and look. "Shall I draw your eyes on them?" She flexed and relaxed her kneecaps. "And put a moustache on this one and lipstick on the other?"

"I said I didn't want Fred Macey coming here, I said don't ask him and don't let him in if he comes."

"I didn't ask him, he came. He likes me."

"I know what he likes, dirty old goat."

"He's not old, only older. I like older people."

"Don't think I haven't noticed the way you rub round him."

"He's my uncle. I was brought up to be fond of my relations."

"You're fond of dirt but you don't want to get yourself dirty." Tomelty's nose turned the colour of a newly-peeled stick, greenish against his unshaven cheeks. "I won't have him letching after you and I won't have you playing kitten. If I catch you at it I'll make you both sorry but I'll make you sorriest of all."

"That would be incest." Marise took Barbra-Bear from the chair. "I never think about that sort of thing but if I did I wouldn't talk about it. I shouldn't care for anyone to think I had such thoughts."

She sat cross-legged on the floor, cradling the toy between her knees. Tomelty looked at her and his face fell as if he were about to cry.

"You don't have thoughts, Gyp, only spasms."

Whatever he chose to believe suited Marise. She had taken him partly for his beliefs because they were convenient. So long as he believed that there was nothing for him to share she was saved the trouble of keeping herself to herself.

"Uncle Fred said he isn't even like John Brown."

"What does Uncle Fred know about it?"

"He was a special constable." Marise pulled Barbra-Bear's skirt up to its armpits and dandled its limp legs at Tomelty. "He could always go to the Rogues' Gallery and see their photographs."

"That old goat knows nothing about it. I knew John Brown, I talked to him and I say this one's the dead ringer of him." Tomelty took off his jacket and dragged at his tie. "Run away, Gyp, I'm going to get some sleep."

Marise said, "He's the live ringer," as Tomelty was going into the bedroom. She took his ballpoint pen from his jacket pocket and settled down to draw faces on her knees.

Ralph had not been having a good week: or, rather, he was not having a standard one. That was to be expected since things had moved out of true.

In the first place he was unable to get Pecry to advance Krassner's bonus – it was not standard for him to get Pecry to do anything and usually he did not try.

"Service bonuses are calculated on a percentage over a period, between two calendar dates, and fall due and are paid on or after the calendar date of expiry. You know the procedure, Shilling."

Ralph did know. He knew that if a man had worked for twenty-five years, starting in the afternoon as a teaboy, he would not receive his bonus until twenty-five years to the calendar day p.m.

"I should like to request that in the circumstances the procedure be waived."

"What circumstances?"

"He has done good work and I think he should be encouraged."

"He is paid to do good work." When Pecry looked at Ralph or when Ralph looked at Pecry, it was possible to believe that Nature had progressed beyond the human condition. "Is he living on his expectations?"

"He doesn't expect anything," said Ralph.

"But he has asked for realisation of a sum of money which is not payment but recognition. I should not need to remind you that recognition must have its full term. If Krassner was given his bonus a day in advance he might, between that day and the next, cease to merit it."

Nature had bypassed the wasteful old method of growth and decay and created Pecry *in situ*, as he was now and always had been, an archetypal fifty, of something harder than bone and drier than blood.

"A bonus is the price of virtue received, not a bribe for virtue to come. I should like to know where *your* interests lie."

An infant Pecry could only be possible as a miniature Pecry, believed Ralph, just as the early medieval Christ child was portrayed as a miniature man – it made Pecry not divine so much as daemonic.

"I draw my own conclusions about that, Shilling. Why have you been such a fool?"

Ralph wondered also. If he didn't actually credit Pecry with second sight, he had to allow that he had a nose for trouble. It had been foolish to raise the subject of Krassner's bonus.

"I'm thinking of good staff relations."

"Words, Shilling, words. The jargon of our time. There's no such thing as staff relations. A man contracts to do a fair

272

day's work – in the equitable and worthy sense, not the merely passable sense – for a fair day's pay. If he does not give satisfaction he gets the sack, if he does not get satisfaction he is free to go elsewhere. That's all there is to it." Pecry's gesture of impatience released a whiff of rubber. "When everyone gets something for nothing the something becomes valueless."

Ralph had had some foolish idea about asking to be allowed to hand Krassner his cheque privately and without ceremony. "He would prefer it that way," he had been going to say, and had hoped that Pecry wouldn't notice that it was right out of Krassner's character. Now he saw that if he wanted to confirm Pecry's suspicions he should go ahead and make that request. It would in any case be refused. He could hear Pecry saying, "There will be a formal presentation by the Chairman in the usual way. You need not be present if you think it would fuss you, Shilling."

He looked Pecry in the eye, trying to look sincere, eager, a little fat-headed, "I'm sorry, but I do believe in staff relations. I've watched Krassner and I think the money would mean something really great to him now, whereas in two months' time it will just be routine. Not that he's in actual financial need, it's nothing to do with that."

"I don't believe in the bonus system," said Pecry. "It operates on the assumption that a man is not being paid enough. The Board knows my views."

"I always thought the bonus was a practical appreciation of good work."

"Does he owe you money?"

Ralph tried to keep his eyes still by focussing them on a rosy pimple, a delicate fleshy bubble on Pecry's forehead.

"Certainly not." But Pecry with his second sight was looking directly at the receipt-stubs and at the gap in sequence which Ralph had by heart and which came back to him like heart-burn. "Why should I lend Krassner money? I don't know anything about him, he doesn't confide his personal affairs in me, we're not on intimate terms." That was wide of the point, suspiciously wide to someone like Pecry who did not know what intimate terms were. Ralph smiled with his jaws. "I couldn't lend Krassner money, I couldn't lend anyone money. I'd like to see myself lending two hundred pounds, I'd like to see myself able to." He was careful not to sound wry lest he be suspected of hinting about his own salary. "I mean I certainly should relish being in that situation."

"Who said anything about two hundred pounds?"

Ralph shut his mouth. His jaws were stiff with careful smiling but he hadn't been so careful with his tongue. He reminded himself that Pecry did not actually know, had only as near as dammit been told.

"What's the matter with you, Shilling?"

"I beg your pardon, I was thinking of the bonus money – isn't it two hundred pounds Krassner gets?"

Ralph lost sight of the rose-coloured pimple, in its place was Pecry's fish-shaped eye.

"There will be a change of policy at the end of this year. It might help Krassner to endure the strain of waiting two more months if you tell him that he is unlikely to have to do so again."

In the second place there was the absence of the cat. It was not waiting for him when he returned to the flat on Sunday night and did not appear on Monday or Tuesday. He missed it, as much as he would have missed any part of his routine. Routine had crystallised round him. When he realised that not only could he tell what was going to happen, he could ensure that it did happen, it seemed to him next to godliness.

But he had always had an ungodly dread that it couldn't last. A slight deviation in the Monday to Friday chain was insidious. The slighter it was, the more insidious, and the more dangerous. In a chaotic world any semblance of order was suspect and people would like to dissolve his – Bertha and Emmeline for the best possible reasons, others, like

Krassner, because they were simply doing what came naturally.

He couldn't blame Bertha and Emmeline for the defection of the cat but he saw it as a move against him, another move, for Krassner was already doing his part. Perhaps it was a move by the cat itself. He had never actually liked the animal.

On Wednesday evening he went looking for it. The back garden, which none of the tenants used or tended, was a mash of long grass and laburnum pods. Ralph poked about half-heartedly, resentful more than anxious. He got his feet wet and rubbed off some green slime from the wall with his sleeve. He found a mattress and a cache of empty bottles, but not the cat.

He called, "Put, put, put," and looked at the house, conjecturing which sills the cat came up by. There was none within cat-jumping distance from ground level, so it must jump from the dividing fence between the gardens on to Madame Belmondo's sill on the first floor. Not a straight leap, it would require concentration with the bay to negotiate and not much purchase on the top of the fence.

Ralph went to the fence and tried to look through. From his window he had seen a grating in the next-door yard: it gave into the cellar and was broken. Old Miss Hanrahan used to say that she watched the rats going in and out of the grating like Christians. Why Christians? Going in and out of church could be the ultimate in decorum, decorous rats would be sinister. While he was beating the elder bushes to get to the fence Marise opened her window and called to him.

He looked up and there she was, shining out of the bricks and he knew that he had been waiting all the time – all his time – for this. Perhaps he had actually been cut out for it, it was perhaps the only situation he hadn't drifted into. There could be just so many gratuitous events in a life and one that was essential, just one, whatever form it took.

Some people's essentials never came about, their throws in the dark went unredeemed. He was lucky.

He let the tough twigs of the elder slap back on the fence. "I'm looking for the cat."

"Your cat?"

"It's not mine, it isn't anyone's." He had to be absolutely truthful. Afterwards, he remembered that strange necessity.

"What colour is it?"

"Tabby. It comes every night for food but it hasn't been since Friday. It may have fallen down the grating in the next door garden."

"What are you going to do?"

He had thought that something might already have been done and that he need not expect to see the cat again. The event of Marise, of seeing her and realising that he had come into the garden for that purpose and in that hope, flustered him profoundly. In order to acclimatise a little, he put the event off, put it back, and concentrated on the cat.

There would be no need to buy any more food for it. He had gone on, the last two days, buying tins as if he expected it to come back and demand to eat all the meals it had missed.

He knew himself, he couldn't be trusted, he would ruin everything. If he didn't have a moment to fear he would trample in ahead of the angels.

"I must keep looking." He stared down as if he meant to go over the ground with a microscope.

"I can see into the next-door garden if I stand on the chest of drawers," said Marise. "But you're tall, you wouldn't have to stand on anything."

Ralph held his tongue, lesser events than this had fallen apart at a word, at one of his words.

"You'd better come in," said Marise sharply. She was thinking that he ought to frighten her. He ought not to be standing there with his head down and the seams of his suit shining, as if he had never done anything. Perhaps he was hiding – of course he was hiding. He had given himself another name and another manner, a quiet manner to fool everybody but it didn't fool Marise. She had to smile at herself for expecting to be frightened, waiting for a bogey-man. Naturally he wouldn't let her see what he was. Not yet. Pretending to look for his cat.

"I'll open the door," she called and watched him slowly cross the garden, pausing to prise open the tussocks of grass with his foot. What was he looking for? She felt a thrill of conviction and she too moved slowly to the door, savouring the consequences of opening it to him.

She was excited. But she could stand back and marvel at herself. She had on her red dress, the one which Tomelty said made her look like a glass of blood, and a pearl necklace was twined round her elbow.

"Come in," she said, "I'm all alone."

No-one would understand how she could do such a thing. She did not fully understand herself, it was simply one of the things she could do and it was going to be the biggest and possibly the last.

Looking into the mirror after she had let John Brown in, she knew that she would never see her face grow old. This was July, she might not see her face in August, she certainly wouldn't see it at Christmas. She touched her cheek and turned to him.

No-one could understand. She was a mystery, no-one ever knew what she would do next. There were people who thought they could tell her, people who wanted her to stop living while they weren't looking at her.

John Brown was two-faced and now that they were so close she could see the two sides of his face. Turn over any feature and there was the converse, there was John Brown.

"I wish you'd keep your hat on," she said. "Your bowler hat."

He put a hand to his head and blushed.

"You don't look anything without it." What would Uncle Fred say if he could see John Brown now? Uncle Fred would say no because Jack had said yes. Which meant that they

277

had both said yes. It was as simple as that. Marise did not mind being thought a fool when she was actually cleverer than any of them. "Why did you say the cat isn't yours?"

"It's a stray."

"Would you like a cup of tea?"

"Thank you."

She observed him while she lit the gas under the kettle. He stood waiting, a big neat man in a respectable and respecting City suit. He had everything packed away, he was a quiet one, the quiet ones were the worst. Thinking of Tomelty who was a riot and was merely not good, she could see that a murderer would be very, very quiet.

"Aren't you going to look out of the window? Isn't that what you came for?"

He started to move, cautiously, like a giant in a doll's house, but nothing here was as small as that. Marise laughed: embarrassed, he put his hand to his head and smoothed his hair.

"What's the matter? You look all right, you look very nice." She was feeling great pleasure. The situation was perilous and she would be taking her life in her hands, taking and throwing it away in style. She had felt this undercurrent of passion coming to her from other people and now it was coming to her from a murderer. There couldn't be anyone more passionate than this murderer. "Go and look out of the bedroom window, it will set your mind at rest."

He went quickly into the bedroom, glanced through the window and came back.

"Well?"

He shook his head.

"I don't think you care about the cat. I wanted to be friends with it. Where we lived before there was nothing to be friends with except the birds. I used to feed them on the window-sill. They ate out of my fingers." It was a picture she had seen, of herself covered with loving birds. Once in Victoria Station a pigeon blundered on to her bare arm but

she had hated the sight of its dirty old mauve feet on her
skin.

"We can be friends," he said, "you and I."

She frowned. "I don't know."

"But surely, surely – "

She did not miss the pleading in his voice. "Friends have
to trust each other."

Then he gave her what she described to Tomelty as a
funny look. Oh, he knew what she meant, John Brown knew
that she knew and that was how she could suddenly see what
he saw – no Marise, no charmer, just a tender pink parcel
for tearing open. Suddenly she was frightened in a plain,
cold way. "I don't like his eyes," she told Tomelty, "I look
at the holes in his chin while he talks." She added, "He
doesn't talk much."

Not that he was another Uncle Fred. This man would tell
her anything she asked, he *wanted* to, she could see that,
but he did not know where to begin. She tried to help him.
She explained about herself and the life she lived. It was
necessary to go into a few details about Jack Tomelty.

"He'd like to stop me living when he's not here. He'd like
to switch me off until he comes back so that he needn't
bother about what I was doing. Of course I don't do anything, I'm very happy."

She took a cup from the china cabinet. It had a pattern
of green peacocks and would still have been pretty if the
glaze had not cracked. Inside the rim was dust which she
forgot to wipe off.

"I love this cup, I don't know what I see in it – just about
everything. I bought it the last time Jack took me out. That
would be last Christmas, he took me to see the Christmas
tree. A shilling was all I had, and that's what the cup cost."

Tomelty had picked it out of the china cabinet the day
they moved in and told her it was genuine Spode. It was
when he was talking to her about graciousness and Marise
had asked if Spode meant a cracked old cup and Tomelty

said she had to learn that things need not be new to be good.

Tea ran out of the crack and made a pool on the table. "It's very old, old things are best. Except me, I don't want to be more than twenty, ever." She watched him take up the cup, trying to catch the drips in his hand and putting his lips to the rim to drink the dusty tea. "Are you married?"

He nodded.

"Why haven't I seen your wife?"

"She lives with her sister."

"Why not with you?"

"Her sister's a widow. They lived together since before Emmeline married."

"Emmeline Shilling? Is that what she calls herself?" Somewhere at the end of the newspapers, not on the front pages, would be a mention of Mrs Emmeline Brown, alias Shilling, the murderer's wife.

"Her name's Openshaw, Emmeline Openshaw."

"But she's married to you?"

"Bertha's married to me, not Emmeline. Bertha's name's the same as mine, but Emmeline is my wife's sister and her name is Openshaw."

"Do make up your mind!" Marise picked up Barbra-Bear. "Emmeline Bertha, Bertha Emmeline – I don't like either." She was bouncing the toy on her knee and his eyes followed it as if mesmerised. "Marise Tomelty is my married name. I'm not really used to it. When people say 'Good morning, Mrs Tomelty,' I look to see who is behind me."

He gathered up the cubes of rubber that were falling out of Barbra-Bear and gave them to her. Marise shut her hand and suddenly opening it let them jump out and spill to his feet.

"Jack threw her out of the window and she burst open. He's so jealous, he hates me having anything of my own." How about John Brown's wife? she was thinking, how stupid the woman must be to be married to him. "I suppose she's pretty – " she did suppose that because he had the pick of

women and would choose the best looking one to keep –
"Bertha's pretty, isn't she?"

"No, she's not pretty."

"Why did you marry her then?"

"I needed her."

"I can see you'd need someone, but why her especially?"

"It's a long story."

"We have plenty of time." She stuffed Barbra-Bear
behind the cushions. Then she knelt up in the chair, smoothing her dress under her thighs. "Tell me."

He stood up violently, like a man coming up for air rather
than leaving a tea-table. "I'll go next door and ask to look
in their cellar. The cat may have gone in after rats and not
be able to get out."

"It's gone courting," said Marise. "It's waiting for the
she-cat, it will wait for weeks."

"Weeks?"

"It will sit in one place waiting and waiting. The grass will
grow up into its fur." She laughed and he had to smile, but
then she said, "You'd think they'd get past it, a man couldn't
wait so long, could he?" and he looked away.

Marise never considered that she might have gone too far,
she simply grew tired of going in the same direction. She
plumped herself deep into the chair. "You were going to tell
me a long story. About Bertha, Bertha-who-isn't-pretty."

"She's kind," he said hurriedly, "the kindest person I
know."

"Not now, I'm the kindest person you know now. Do you
think I'm pretty?"

"Yes!"

The ferocity of his answer amused her, as did the way he
avoided looking at her while she was looking at him. He
wouldn't meet her eye because of what she knew. She hoped
he wasn't ashamed, an ashamed murderer.

"Very well, I am pretty and kind. Now tell me about
Bertha."

"What do you want to know?"

281

"If she's big and fat or small and thin. Where you met her, when you married her." Whenever she took her eyes off him he looked at her. She gazed down into her lap to give him time to get a good look. "What was it like before – " she started to say "before anything happened," but it struck her that things had happened to this man all his life and she wanted to know about all of them – "before you were married?"

"Like? It wasn't much different. I tended to do certain things over and over again. Now I do other things over and over again."

"So do I," said Marise, "shut up here and virtually a prisoner."

He had a changeable face, she was able to change it with whatever she said. When he smiled, as he did now, Jack wouldn't have recognised John Brown.

"Bertha's short and plump, Emmeline's big but not fat. You couldn't call her fat."

"I couldn't call her anything, could I, I haven't seen her. You're not married to her too, are you?"

"Sometimes I think so."

"Are you a bigamist as well?"

"As well as what?"

"Where did you find them and when did you marry them?"

"We met on a boat, crossing from the Isle of Wight. There was a storm and they thought the boat would sink. I found them on deck, waiting beside the life-boats."

"What did you think about them?"

"It was pouring with rain. I made them go down into the saloon – "

Still more she wanted to know, "What do you think about me?"

She was watching him closely for his unspeakable thoughts, but after one glare of dismay his face turned wooden.

"I think you're very kind."

282

"You're a nice one to keep talking about kindness," she said crossly. "I don't call that a long story. What were you doing on the Isle of Wight."

"I went for a day trip. I like the sea, I wanted to go to sea as a boy, in the Merchant Navy. But things turned out otherwise – and I think for the best. The last five years have been the best for me."

"Not before? Ten, eleven, twelve, fifteen years ago, wasn't it nice for you then?" Fifteen years ago he should have been dead.

"I've only known Bertha about five years. It was Bertha you wanted to hear about."

"Five years?" So that was it, and if the woman had married him and stayed married without knowing what he was she must be even stupider than Marise had supposed. Perhaps she had found out too late, perhaps he wouldn't let her go. What kind of private fun had he had in the last five years, the best years for him?

"So it all happened before Bertha. And this is the best you can expect now." Marise nodded, any time was better than none, any living was better than hanging. "You can tell me if you like. And if you like I'll promise not to tell anyone else. If," she added scrupulously, "there's anything you don't want anyone else to know. I would never break my promise without your permission. Yóu'd have to come to me and say, 'Marise Tomelty, I release you from your vow, you may talk without fear or favour about me and anything I told you'."

"I didn't come here to talk about myself."

"You came to talk to me and what I want to hear about is yourself."

He sighed, the sigh provoked her, she hated people standing away and sighing at her. "I have been the receiver of confidences from very important people. Like my uncle. If I mentioned his name you'd get a shock."

"I've nothing to confide."

"I could surprise you."

283

"You do surprise me," he said.

"But while I'm under a vow of silence wild horses can't drag anything out of me. I shan't tell you what I know about my uncle."

"I wouldn't want you to break a promise – to me or to anyone."

"My Uncle Fred Macey – " Marise threw at him and waited.

"I ought to be going." He lifted the cracked cup from its pool of tea. "I'm afraid I've made a mess."

"He was at Scotland Yard until he retired. Detective-Inspector Macey. He was constantly in the Sunday papers."

Wiping his fingers with his handkerchief he seemed about to wipe the table with it as well. The tea was seeping steadily out of the cup, overwhelming a grain in the wood it rolled to the edge of the table, caramel-coloured. "Hadn't we better mop it up?"

"It's shaped like a camel," said Marise.

He dropped his handkerchief into the puddle. The initials in one corner stood out white a moment longer, then 'R.S.' turned fawn with the rest. "The tea will take the polish off."

"My uncle was at Scotland Yard," Marise said again, not so much a reminder for him as a launching point for herself.

"That must have been interesting." He was mopping and fussing with the handkerchief. "If we had a saucer it would save further leakage."

"There isn't a saucer." The veins on the backs of his hands intrigued her. Why were they green? In butchers' shops the meat was red, purple and yellow, not green. Was he different from other living or recently living creatures, did he have something stronger than blood under his skin? Was that what made him go farther than anyone else? If the green were drained out would it make him safe, ordinary and safe? "My uncle was in the Murder Squad."

He looked up. "I hope he didn't tell you anything unpleasant."

She declared to Tomelty that her uncle's name had struck

terror into him. "Uncle Macey was the scourge of the under-
world" – and Tomelty's laughter did not dismay her because
she had seen this man's look, she had seen all his capability
in his face. "His face split", she told Tomelty, "like a
banana", and Tomelty told her she was lunatic.

But she had been frightened and it was not the same, not
anything like the same as when she frightened herself. With
this man from upstairs she was cold and burning and quick
and numb and meek and frantic all at once.

Taking her life in her hands she threw it in his face. "He
told me all about you, John Brown."

## 5

Ralph had escaped from the house, he knew that he wouldn't be able to subdue his thoughts under the same roof. He took his thoughts into the park and walked about. It was a long time since he had felt so confused, probably he never had been so confused. He saw everything getting complicated – though delightful. From such a source of delight everything must benefit, already the thoughts he had brought with him to this municipal place were making the grass greener and the geraniums redder.

A silly illusion in anyone, and dangerous at his age: she must be only a reference, he thought, walking fast, a reference of potential joy. Though not for him, he had not the capacity in his life for her – always supposing there was capacity in her life for him.

The proviso depressed and alarmed him, and then he felt further alarmed by his alarm. He would have to be very careful, could he be careful enough?

He paced on slowly, knowing that already it was too late, it had never been soon enough to take care, taking care couldn't modify anything.

He worried about what she thought of him. He would have worried less if he could believe that she simply found him wanting because he was quite used to people wanting what he did not have. But she had an idea, she seemed to have a wrong idea of him altogether and he would have to demolish it to offer her the truth. He wished to offer her nothing but the truth.

He had been angry when she said that someone had told her all about him, shocked that she couldn't recognise lies, lies should fall apart when she looked at them. But her uncle had told her lies about him. Why? There had to be a grain of truth somewhere, where had this man got his grain? What lies? He did not know any Fred Macey. Or any John Brown.

Some of the geraniums in this park were a crude pink, an

286

inorganic colour. "John Brown?" he said aloud, hoping to drop the name into context, but all that occurred to him was that John Brown had a shipyard on Clydebank. And his soul went marching on.

He turned his steps towards the Pilot and conscience, or sense, or straitlacing subsided as he crossed the thresh-hold: sinking his principles in the smell of beer, he thought.

The steak-eaters were at their end of the bar. He glanced at them and turned away, the vision he carried would be as safe with them as a lamb with tigers. Inez, the barmaid, raised her eyebrows as he mouthed his order. The bar was as noisy as ever, but the voices would be no use to him tonight, tonight he wanted to listen to the voice in his head.

He was suddenly shattered by the thought of her. In the act of reaching in his pocket to pay for his rum everything went to pieces, himself and the bar and everyone in it flew like sparks off a wheel. He felt giddy and shut his eyes. What he was experiencing – it was not cerebral enough for thought – were some of her possibilities. He remembered them in detail which he had not yet had time to discover.

A woman asked if he was all right and took his arm. In pulling away he dropped a handful of loose change and had to get down on the floor to retrieve it. He groped among legs and cigarette-butts and tried to pick up a florin of spittle. Finally he got to his feet chastened, and sixpences the poorer.

In the lavatory he stood washing his hands. But first he washed the coins he had picked up. He was soaping half a crown and some coppers when someone came to the basin beside him. In the mirror he encountered a narrow face, hard black eyes and soft-topped ears bent under the rim of a corduroy hat. He recognised the man who had watched him the last time he was in the Pilot. Ralph tore off a paper towel and went out with his wet money in his hand.

Inez made a face when he gave her the coins. He said, "They're quite clean now," and she dropped them from her finger-tips into the till.

Why had he come to the Pilot? He didn't want company and he didn't want a drink, a drink couldn't help him. He emptied the glass with one swallow, impatient to get away. There was only one place he wanted to be and it was unnerving how much he wanted to be there – only a little while ago he had run from it like a scalded cat. I am certainly frightened, he thought, frightened in every direction except the moral one. Morals don't come into miracles.

If he could have gone back to her and done what he wanted to do – Was it possible for anyone to do what he wanted to do? Only, he thought, if it were the last thing, the very last thing, because afterwards would be a life-long anticlimax. He had a strong inkling, practically a memory, of the smell of her skin, it smelled like children's sweets.

There were names for what he was experiencing, and for the condition he was in there were neurotic, technical, bathetic, biblical names. Each was applicable to a part, none could identify the whole. Once upon a time he had cherished illusions and he had lusted after individual women, but nothing of this whole kind had happened to him before.

What was he to do? More accurately, what was he to expect?

"She's not grateful," said a voice and he found the man in the corduroy hat beside him. "After you washing your money for her she talks about how wet you made her small change."

He was a dapper young man, busily turned out in a pin-flecked suit and a gold chain on his tie. He had come across the bar looking for Ralph, seeking him. He had brought his drink and he tipped the glass to Ralph before he drank.

"Women enjoy a little bit of dirt," he said cheerfully, "and there's nothing pure about the one behind the beer-engine."

What did he want? Not company, not Ralph's, not to track him across a crowded bar for the pleasure of it. Why didn't he join the steak-eaters? They had company and to spare, he would be sure of pleasure with them.

"I'm new to this district," said the young man, "but I know a feel de joy when I see one."

Ralph held up his empty glass intending to wave it and go to the bar and not come back. He had nothing to say to anyone, he wanted to get away and hear again what had been said, what she had said half an hour and half a lifetime ago.

"Refills," said the young man. "What'll yours be?"

"Excuse me, I'd rather get my own."

"Suit yourself."

Ralph decided that he wouldn't buy another drink, he would just leave and walk about, no-one would talk to him if he walked about.

"I keep thinking you know me because you look like someone I used to know." The young man smiled. "I could swear you've got a green Singer sports outside and tally books on the seat."

"I haven't got a car."

"And you don't remember the Tomelty kids who used to ride on the bumper when they got a chance?"

"Remember who?" The name was surprising, as an invocation of her it was utterly inapt but he was unlikely to forget it. "Tomelty?"

"Jack Tomelty, that's me. Your new neighbour at Lilliput Lodge."

The idea of her marriage was a confrontation which Ralph had not yet faced. He certainly wasn't ready to face the substance of it, the husband.

"Your name's Shilling and you've got the top flat. Will you have that drink with me? Rum, isn't it?" He had been watching. Now that Ralph came to think of it, someone had been watching him all the time and it could only have been this man. Tomelty nodded towards the bar. "The poolette says rum's your drink."

Why was he interested in Ralph? Interested enough to ask the barmaid about him, enough to watch and follow and try to buy his company?

Ralph watched him carve his way to the bar, shouldering people aside, but lightly, so that they could not object, holding his glasses over their heads. He was smiling, people looked round and smiled at him. He was the man who had discovered her, she was his wife and he was entitled to her perfections, they carried his name. She was stamped 'Tomelty' all through.

Ralph had a pang of impure anguish. His feelings were getting increasingly complicated and he had no right to them, he had no right to object to Tomelty, to the physical unnecessity of the man, to resent his claims on his wife and to claim her himself – dreaming of bestowal, never of theft. No right, but would legitimate feelings have been easier to bear?

"Are you married?" said Tomelty, coming back. "Then you know what it's like."

Ralph gazed at him with incredulity. What kind of man was he? Didn't he know that his marriage was made in Heaven – or did he suppose every marriage was?

"Women," said Tomelty with satisfaction, "here's to them," and tossed his whisky into his throat.

He must be a fool, thought Ralph, he had to be, because there was no sufficient reason why a man like him should get her, she must have fallen into his lap, he didn't merit her and he couldn't have won her. Look at him, thought Ralph, looking with anger, he didn't even know what it was that he had.

"I'm just back from Liverpool, Sefton Park," said Tomelty, "just touched down in fact, haven't been home yet. I'm putting it off. I like the idea of being neither here nor there, not still in Sefton, not yet in Lilliput. What's your line?"

"Line?"

"Business. I'm in brushes, household and industrial – bristling with possibilities – don't say it. I'm a traveller. You're truly hobbled, aren't you?"

Ralph didn't care for him saying it, he didn't care for Tomelty, he cordially despised him.

"You can tell a traveller by the way he wears his watch." Tomelty showed his, strapped inside his wrist. "On his pulse, to keep it synchronised."

Ralph had been ready to respect him and to find himself put in his place and having to fight out of it. He was ready to fight, was even ready to lose. But this young man was not only inadequate, he measured up to something entirely alien from her.

"Not in insurance are you? That would be a turn-up for the leevre."

He should have been enviable, after all he did possess her, but how much was he capable of possessing? Ralph set himself to think about that, it promised to be painful thinking and the sooner he faced it the better.

Tomelty tucked his whisky glass into his breast pocket and took out his cigarettes. The flame of his lighter cast shadows like tear channels down his narrow cheeks.

"I said to her, 'If Shilling's in insurance, it proves something.' "

"Proves what?"

"About the job making the man or the man making the job."

Ralph was facing the prospect of Tomelty in bed with his wife – could just about face it. There was a callowness about him, he was physically unfinished, like a fourteen-year-old boy, and the sexual demands of a fourteen-year-old wouldn't be extensive. It was still an ugly thought but not beyond endurance.

"Why does she call me John Brown?"

"She's out of this world is Marise, never got properly into it. You have to make allowances. If I listened to everything she said!"

Ralph realised that although he hadn't mentioned her name Tomelty had known at once whom he was talking about. Ralph had the feeling that Tomelty had been waiting to talk about her.

"She's buttoned up right, make no mistake but she's fanciful. You can say something to me, it may be stupid, it may be libel, but that's as far as it'll go. Say the same thing to her and she'll blow it up in your face."

"But why John Brown?"

"I'm telling you. It was a chance remark I happened to make – stupid if you like, and I could have said you look like Johnson or Nasser and she wouldn't have given it another thought." Tomelty was smiling, insisting on the funny side, that there was only a funny side. "And if I'd said to anyone else that you look like John Brown, they wouldn't have given it another thought."

"*You* said?"

"Happened to mention, that's all, I happened to mention. If you happened to mention that you dislike somebody's guts, would you have to stop and worry that your wife might go and wave a knife at them?"

Tomelty's smile lengthened, uncovering two childish fangs at either end of his mouth. 'That's how it is with her. Not that she'd do violence but she lays herself open to it. By God, she does."

"John Brown – he's not a politician, is he?"

"Drink up and I'll get you another."

"Who is he?"

Tomelty paused with his glass half-way to his lips. "You don't know?"

"I know that Queen Victoria had a gillie of that name and there's a song about his body mouldering in the grave."

"Don't you remember Johnny Brown and the Whybrow women?"

Ralph shook his head.

"Then there's no harm done. Let's forget it."

"I want to know, I've a right to."

Tomelty shrugged. "If you see it like that. I seem to be the only one who remembers anyway. I knew him when he

292

had this insurance book and collected half a dollar every week from my mother. Fran and Elvie Whybrow lived in Casimir Terrace, the next street to ours. He used to visit them twice a week, once on business, once on pleasure. They were saving up to get buried – as well they might." Tomelty threw the last of his whisky down his throat. "Fran was a singing teacher, Brown killed her and got Elvie to help him carve her very small – women would do anything for him and Elvie must have thought she was getting him all to herself. They planted Fran in flower-pots, a hundred and fifty geraniums blooming like mad."

"Geraniums?"

"They would, wouldn't they, on the fat of the land? Well, that left Elvie – coerced, bloody Elvie, and what did he do with her? He strangled her and split her down the middle and hung her up by the heels like a pig. Sharcootry, that's what he thought of Elvie."

"You don't mean that *she* thinks – that she associates me – "

"He got away with it, that's the point. They knew he'd done it but couldn't get a shred of proof. No blood, no knives – no flies on him. 'John Brown's body was the one they couldn't hang, but his soul goes mouldering on.' " Tomelty tapped Ralph on the chest. "You see, it could be you."

"I don't see."

"Look at yourself." Tomelty pointed to the mirrors. "You're the dead ringer of John Brown – the living ringer, Marise says."

"*She* says? She thinks I'm a murderer?" One or two things dropped into place, others dropped out.

"Let's say she likes the idea."

"That's a lie!" It burst from Ralph, wrapping up his dislike of Tomelty. He could even have come to blows, for one of the few times in his life he wanted violence.

"Oh, it's a fact," said Tomelty. "Nothing personal, you've

293

just got to appreciate Marise. You'll be John Brown as long as it amuses her."

"Amuses?"

"She doesn't get out enough. It doesn't take much to amuse her, except in one way, of course, it takes too bloody much. She never sees anyone except that daft old uncle of hers." Tomelty's smile faded. He stubbed out his cigarette on his own reflection in the mirror. "What do you make of a woman who shuts herself up with only a teddy-bear to talk to?"

"I don't ever want to be twenty," she had said.

Tomelty said soberly, "We're going to be neighbours and I'm telling you what my wife thinks for your own sake. I'm telling you what her thoughts are worth for my sake. Funny thing, though, the more I look at you, the more I see John Brown. He used to ride me round the block on the fender of his old Singer – when he didn't know I was there. He'd remember me. 'How did you manage to get a Turk like him?' he used to say to my mother."

Ralph was finding Tomelty hard to take but he had to take him because of his connection with her. He needed to know how Tomelty had perverted that.

"If you're John Brown back from wherever he went, you're laughing. And if you're not John Brown, if it's only wishful thinking, you're in luck. She'll cherish you."

"Wishful thinking?"

Tomelty smiled. "By her, not by me. To my way of thinking Brown should have hanged, though I don't say I wished it – he was good to us kids. I shan't forget him. I'd have thought the case was something to remember but of course there've been Haigh and Christy and the Moors since. You remember them, I suppose?"

"What are you trying to do? Keep her?" Ralph said with anger and disgust, "Is it the only way you can?"

Marise saw them coming back, John Brown in front, swinging his arms. He had a large white jug face, a murderer's face. No other shape would do, not the cottage loaf of Uncle Fred Macey's, certainly not Tomelty's black muzzle. And those were murderer's arms, they did not end in pity or in shopping baskets.

Tomelty sprang as he walked on the balls of his feet, it was one of his ways of signifying his mood. Marise did not bother to identify it nor to look at him beyond noting that he was there. She had eyes only for John Brown, held back the curtain to watch him, and he saw her.

Telling Tomelty what happened when she met John Brown's eyes Marise said that he looked through her. But it was really something of a devastation because there was not one fibre left of Marise as Marise. She was emptied out of herself and refilled with his presence. The refilling was not an experience she enjoyed. It was the first time it had happened to her and she made up her mind that it would be the last. An excursion was one thing, dispossession was another.

"If he'd looked through you," said Tomelty, "he'd have seen what a little sham you are."

"At least he's a gentleman, I think that's important. Not knowing how to treat people is the root of all evil. Of course it won't be *his* least, he has to be something much, much less. Is being a murderer less than being a gentleman? I should think it's more."

"You should think," said Tomelty, "but you don't. I pulled his leg, made out I wasn't sure about him."

Marise clasped herself in her arms. "He makes my blood run cold."

"I warned him about you. I don't know if he took it in or not. He's a bit bazaar. I caught him washing his money."

"Did you warn him about *you*?"

"He thinks I'm lying about you to keep him away."

"You hate me having anyone else, don't you? Look how you hate Uncle Fred. And you'd even try to stop me speaking to a murderer – even though he might murder me and save you the trouble."

Tomelty pulled two tins of rice pudding out of his pocket and tossed one to her. "Have fun, but not at my expense. I don't want the poor sod stepping up his adrenalin every time he sees me. He's never experienced anything like you, he'll believe whatever you like to tell him."

Marise snuggled into the crook of her elbow. "Are you afraid of him?"

"Leave him alone."

"Because he's dangerous?"

"Because we've got to live here. Because you're a kindle and he's a married old man with grown children."

Marise lay down on the couch. It had become a favourite place of hers now that Tomelty and Uncle Fred had rubbed the unknown people off. She could smell Uncle Fred's tobacco crumbs and Tomelty's hair-gum among the dust. "He's not so old. And he's got two women. Did he tell you about them? He keeps them in the country, two sisters, just like the last time."

Tomelty put down his tin of rice. His nose blanched from the nostrils, whitened and swelled, like an onion Marise thought, his angry nose was the shape of an onion.

She got up to look in the mirror – seeing other people's faces as things made her wonder how her own might be seen. But there was no part of it that looked like something else, not as else as a jug or a loaf or an onion.

"Listen to me, this is what John Brown did and you're going to think about it. He chopped Miss Fran Whybrow into pieces. She was a big woman, she weighed twelve stone and he cut her into little bits as big as your pinkie. He made Miss Elvie help him and she was the one who cried over flies on fly-paper, she was so sensitive she couldn't bear to see them kick. He made her chop up her own sister. Do me a favour, think about that, remember there was more to it than fingers and toes, there was the head and he wouldn't get that off in a hurry – ask any butcher – and he scraped

up the brains, they're slippery, brains are – can you see
Ralph Shilling doing that?"

Marise picked up his tin and the spoon. "I think I like
this better than real rice pudding."

# 6

The cat came back. One evening it was waiting for him as though nothing had happened. Perhaps nothing had happened to the cat, it had all been happening to Ralph.

He was neither glad nor sorry to see it, merely surprised that the routine should persist, or try to, because there was no longer any routine, only recurring gestures. The cat rose to greet him, ironic as ever, but he was not sure whether it could still serve his purpose. He wasn't sure what his purpose now was. Why should he take it back anyway? It would go off again at any time, without warning, and come back or not come back. What sort of man let himself be picked up and dropped at the whim of a cat?

He sat down and lit a cigarette. He was beginning to need cigarettes, positively to grope for them whenever he paused. In the night he paused in his sleep and smoked two or three. What Bertha would say if he did that at Thorne – she was a light sleeper, she heard the dew drop – he could guess. He was bound to wake in the night, he probably wouldn't sleep at all, would lie thinking with Bertha beside him. With Bertha beside him, what could he think?

The cat sank on its forepaws, elbows up. It looked away, not soliciting. Sometimes he stopped fretting and drifted between fact and fancy, one nugget of fact to a welter of fancies. No use questioning the fancies, they were laughable at best, and at worst they tickled a sense that was not of fun. Tomorrow he would go to Thorne, for no reason except that he went on Fridays. It was the only reason he needed – everything had to look the same. He had the ridiculous feeling that the cat knew all that had happened, like God it turned and gazed at him over its elbows. It knew, but it was outside moral judgment.

When she knocked at his door and he opened it and saw her standing there he could not believe his eyes, no matter

298

how often he saw her he would never be prepared for the revelation.

"Has the cat come back?" She was panting slightly and the soft sound of her breath was as private as a whisper between them. "I was worried, I had to come and see."

Her two hands were spread on her chest and it occurred to him, with joy and dismay, that she was a little frightened. He wanted to take her hands and bring her gently against his shoulder.

"I was worried," she said again. "I think of animals like I think of people. Suppose the cat is lost, I thought, lying hurt in some horrible place, I'd die if it was me. Jack says I have no stamina. Are you going to ask me in?"

"Of course – "

He had thought of her here, sometimes he thought that it would be in this room that he would first touch her.

"It's bigger." She looked about. "It's not what I expected. There's nothing of you in it. You don't want to be remembered, do you?"

"I don't mind."

He minded the way the cat was watching, confederating with them both and he furiously lifted his hand to it.

"Don't." She took his hand in hers. He had been waiting for her touch, it shocked down his arm and flustered him, his blood thumped and his heart ran cold and only the soles of his feet remained personal. "I want to be friends with it. What is its name?"

"I don't know."

"What do you call? You have to call something."

"Put. Put, put, put."

She gave him back his hand and said gravely, "You like to hurt. Of course you're cruel." She wasn't accusing or condemning, he thought he observed a certain satisfaction.

"I'd never hurt you."

"Yes you would. I'd be the one to hurt." She stooped to flick her fingers at the cat. "What does it play with?"

"Be careful, it scratches."

299

"Be careful, be careful," she mimicked. "What good will that do? It won't stop what has to happen." She turned to look at him. "You're careful but you're not careful *of* anything, like Jack – Jack's careful of me. He won't let me out, he's afraid of people looking at me."

"Afraid?"

"They might see something he can't."

Ralph understood that. Tomelty saw so little that almost anyone else would be able to see more. It was criminal to keep her a prisoner but Ralph understood that too. If she were legally his as she was Tomelty's, he would go to lengths, perhaps criminal lengths, to keep other men's eyes off her. Yes, he thought, letting his own dwell, he would want to hoard her.

"Have you a photograph of your wife?" Nothing on the mantelpiece was his, except the clock. "Jack carries a picture of me in his wallet."

"There's something I must tell you."

She sat down and folded her hands and when she looked up at him his heart ached. Like a drowning man he saw a series of pictures and his were of trampled snow, broken flowers, slaughtered lambs.

"I'm not a murderer," he said, "I've never killed anyone."

"Jack's written 'Gipsy Moth' on the back of my picture. He calls me 'Gipsy'. I expect you've killed moths, haven't you?"

He couldn't tell what she was asking. Of course it was inconceivable that he should know anything about the working of her mind but he must try to show her the working of his.

"I'm not John Brown."

"No." There was no meaning in it, she was not saying no and meaning yes, she certainly was not meaning no, she was just saying the word – "I should like to see a picture of your wife and her sister – " and having said it, she put the subject aside. Well, he knew what that meant, it meant that she could not agree and was reserving her opinion. What opinion did she have? "I want to see if they look like I expect."

He took a step towards her. "Don't expect anything. I'm Ralph Shilling, I've never done anything."

Her eyes moved sideways and upwards in her serious face and she chanted, "Ralph Shilling, there's no Ralph Shilling – " putting her hand out to him to bring him into the joke. "I like looking at pictures but you haven't any, so you must tell me everything. About Emmy first."

"I know what you think of me. Your husband told me."

"Jack doesn't know what I think. Nobody does." She had eyes of a beautiful wetness, with the limpidity of tears but no brine. When he looked into them he felt himself swimming. "Is Emmy kind too?"

He turned away. "I must feed the cat."

She followed him into the kitchen, it amused her to see his cupboard stocked with tins. She picked them up and read the labels. "They're all spaghetti and pilchards."

"I like spaghetti and the cat likes pilchards."

"You go to the shop and buy them – " She watched him empty the contents of a tin – "and you cut up the cat's dinner and you wash its plate – "

She spoke as if that were only the half of it. Knife and fork in hand he said stubbornly, "I'm not John Brown."

"I don't care who you are. You seem to think it matters, but you only live upstairs and anyone will do for that." Her scorn lacerated him, he bent over his plate of fish, chopping. "What a fuss! Who is John Brown? Why shouldn't you be him? John Brown Shilling, the man who feeds cats." This time she was not offering to share the joke.

Ralph put down the cat's food. It rose and came to the dish.

"Oh look, it trusts you. I wish I had a friend like that. I had to leave all my friends behind. I only have Barbra now."

"Barbra?"

"You remember her, the one with her insides out. She was all I had time to snatch up when we ran away. We had

301

to leave in a hurry, there was a man concentrating on me and Jack was afraid."

"Concentrating?"

"Like you are." She spoke without coquetry and he was grateful, gratitude swallowed up all the other feelings he had been having and left him hopelessly indebted. "He was only a boy, there was no need to run away. I was just being kind, but Jack doesn't understand kindness, he thinks there's only one thing between men and women."

"Suppose," Ralph said fearfully, "suppose he takes you away from here?"

"You'd follow, wouldn't you?"

It struck Ralph first that that might be true, then came to him forcibly that it *was* true. He wondered was she condoning or asking – might she actually be asking him to follow her?

"I expect he knew you were here and that's why he brought me."

"Why?" echoed Ralph. It was dizzying, finding himself home and dry at one minute and at sea the next. He struggled to keep afloat. "You're frightened of him, but you needn't be, he's only human – " "inferior human" he did not add, for her sake – "he doesn't own you." But if she thought he did, by God, he did.

"He's jealous of you."

"Jealous of me?"

"Well whoever heard of Jack Tomelty? Or Ralph Shilling?"


Ralph had never before looked at himself with passionate detachment, nor had he looked so often out of the corner of his eye. He found that he could occasionally surprise an absolutely unfathomable expression on his face and stared at it, trying to read a meaning. He realised that whereas other people knew his face, he was merely used to it.

Bertha certainly knew it. He recalled the day after they

had first met, just the day after, he caught a cold from the drenching on the ferry and she had said, "It's made your lips all puffy." How was she able to tell, on so short an acquaintance, if his lips were puffy or normal?

Emmy had said, "I don't know what you must think of us, acting so stupidly." Emmy had been so sure what he thought of her. But Bertha knew his face, she watched it with constancy and he had grown used to finding her turned to him. She was watching for confirmation, of course, but was she ever surprised?

He found that he had written down an equation:

$$R.S. = a\ Shilling$$
$$J.B. = ?$$
$$R.S. + J.B. = M.$$

It wasn't much of an equation but it gave an unequivocal answer. Not that he accepted it, he was merely enquiring about the general principle.

Krassner was the only person he could enquire of, Krassner was an authority. How to bring up the question was the problem – without bringing out the smuttier-than-thou in Krassner.

He called him into his office and asked him about an invoice, choosing the first name that came into his head.

"It's settled," said Krassner. "You put the cheque through yourself." He sat on the edge of Ralph's desk. "Worrying, are you? What a pity you can't bug me, plant a little radio button somewhere – in my navel, perhaps, so that you could listen in to everything, including my stomach rumbles."

"It's time we were thinking about the catalogue."

"I don't have to think about it until you've got out a dummy."

"I think we should try to keep the costs down."

"That's up to you." There was a silence while Krassner shot back his cuff and looked at his wrist. He smiled at Ralph. "I keep forgetting my watch has gone."

"You're lucky not to have a wife – it's the first thing she'd notice."

303

"Sensible, not lucky."

"You think you know a lot about women, don't you? Tell me," said Ralph, "would they rather a man was bad than ordinary?"

Krassner raised his eyebrows. "If you mean do they prefer villains – yes, they do."

"Really bad, I mean – a murderer, say. Would they prefer a man to be a murderer than a nobody?"

Krassner said good-naturedly, "Do you really need to know?"

"I want to know what you think. I have my own ideas."

"Who is she?" Who are you going to do murder for?"

"It isn't meant to be funny."

"Funny? It's elementary. Where have you been all your life that you have to ask a question like that?"

"I said I have my own ideas. But you think – even a pure woman?"

"The pure ones are the worst."

Ralph now saw what a fool he was to seek an answer merely because it could be given, and without taking into account from whence it would be coming.

"Tell you what, old boy, if you're going to do murder for her, kill two birds with one stone and murder Pecry."

Ralph recalled Tomelty saying, "Women enjoy a bit of dirt". Krassner and Tomelty were pot and kettle, he saw that what they both had was indiscrimination, not authority.

Questions got the answers they deserved, but there could be no harm, surely, in wanting to know what sort of man this John Brown was. Conjecture would not do.

"Murder trials?" said the young woman at the library. "We have hundreds."

"A man – " he found himself reluctant to speak the name – "was tried for murder and acquitted. If you'll tell me where that kind of thing is on the shelves I'll look myself."

"What kind of thing? We don't index murder *qua* murder. Was it political or psychotic? Crime passionel? Who did he murder?"

"Two women, but it wasn't proved – "

"Sexual. Has the case been written up? Not all of them are. There has to be something to peg it on, it's the peg that matters in these fictionalised accounts."

"I don't want fiction, I want facts."

"Then you'd better look at the newspaper reports."

"Yes, of course, the newspapers."

"Although it's arguable – " the young woman seemed ready to argue – "whether facts alone bring you nearer the truth. There's a lot in how they are presented, they can be misrepresented in newspapers. Leaving aside incompetence and human frailty, journalists make up their minds too, you know, without being qualified to – in fact being well qualified *not* to. Which is why some people prefer digests. What was the name?"

"I'll try the newspapers. Shall I find them in the Reading Room?"

"In our Reading Room you'll find the current week's papers on the desks and last week's on battens."

"This would have been about fifteen years ago."

"The London Library," said the young woman, "if you're a member."

"I'm not – "

"Newspaper offices keep files of their back issues."

Looking for John Brown he realised that world events had to be geared down to the personal to be felt, and to be felt at this distance of time they had to be geared to personal history.

1953 was Coronation year, the year Scobie died. That cold, wet second day of June the excitement and ceremony had gone over his head, he hadn't seen any of it, not one Duchess, not one ermine. The day stuck out, disjointed, belonging neither to the ceremony nor to the wet, and fifteen years after it fitted where it touched. And touched on a sore point still.

There had been a discussion, as usual. Scobie discussed everything with herself, something which she had perfected after she began to be ill. It helped her, she knew she could say to her own face what was in her mind. "I'm sick in body," she said, "and sorry in mind, and what comes out is regretful."

She had tried to decide whether to listen to the ceremonies on the radio. She didn't really want to but was afraid of missing something.

"What use is it going to be to us? We should ask that, don't you think, if we're to sit listening to gestures all day?"

When she had first started to leave Ralph out, still saying 'we' and 'us' when she meant 'I' and 'me', was when she finally accepted the truth about herself. She was a reasonable woman and had not found it easy to accept that truth could be unreasonable.

"Of course there'll be music but the whole thing is simply a mammoth sequence of gestures."

When Ralph pitied her pain she said that it wasn't pain which made a coward of her.

"Well, what else shall we do? What magnificent thing shall we do if we don't listen? Is there anything we *could* do, for God's sake, more important than listening?"

Ralph had waited, looking out over the wet roofs, to be told whether to switch on the radio or not. It made no difference to him, he would be staying all day in this room with her, going across the passage to prepare their meals, to the corner shop for a paper.

"It would be wonderful, it would be healthy if we ever did anything without holding an inquest first. We kill everything with talk, we've killed the Coronation. Oh, what nonsense! It's history in the making, who are we to turn a deaf ear? Who are we to be dozing or reading or cutting our nails while history is being made? But will any of it feed a single soul?"

Ralph turned to the beginning of the file of newspapers, to January, 1953. It could be a tedious job. Here were the year's events cut and dried and trussed, and the Whybrow murders and John Brown's trial were but a few straws. Hard news – the death of Stalin, for instance – would push them off the front page. He skimmed through the inside pages for more local events.

There seemed to have been murders almost every day. He was surprised at the number of people who met violent ends at the hands of other people. From the newspaper reports, anyway, it was murder *qua* murder.

He could appreciate that why one man killed another could be too complex to go into a ten inch column. So he must expect to read about John Brown the murderer, not John Brown the man – what Scobie might have called reading about a gesture.

In July the Korean armistice was signed and on the 31st Senator Taft died – the same day as Scobie.

Coming away from the hospital – she had died at three o'clock in the afternoon – his concern was how to get through the rest of the day. How to pass the hours decently and fittingly until her death was no longer that same afternoon. There were people to notify, he might go back to the flat and start writing: 'I am sorry to have to tell you that my wife died today – '

That would be a lie and he had an almost hysterical determination not to tell it. In fact he had already refuted it. As the nurse drew the sheet over Scobie's face he said, "She won't be sorry that's over, neither am I." For the first time since her illness Scobie had not left him out.

He thought of putting an announcement in the paper: 'On 31st July, after a long illness bravely borne, Scobie, dearly loved wife of Ralph Shilling – ' But he would have to give her other name – Flora. She had disliked it so much that she would not let it be used. She was 'Scobie' to her friends and 'Miss Scobie', before her marriage, to everyone else. 'Flora, dearly loved wife of Ralph Shilling.' That also would be a lie, he had never loved a Flora.

Reading accounts of murder trials he encountered a cursoriness, as of a tall story baldly told. None of them rang true unless he chanced upon an odd statement which jolted

307

and threw light. Then he could not be sure if it was the right light, or the right subject, or if the subject was part of the case or just part of his own mind.

It wasn't until October and another atomic bang at Woomera that Elvie Whybrow's body was found, *in puris naturalibus*, and almost bifurcated, in the cellar of No. 14, Casimir Terrace.

Two days later, echoes of Woomera fading, Casimir Terrace was front page news when the remains of a second woman, believed to be Miss Francis Whybrow, were found buried – in flower-pots.

Neighbours could recall nothing unusual, except that Mr Brown, from the Insurance, who was by way of being a friend of the Whybrows, had got no reply when he called and was worried about them. The police were requesting him to come forward to help with their enquiries. It was courteous, but the net was out.

A sliding window shot back and a man in a leather apron asked Ralph if he knew what he was looking for.

"I've found it, thank you." Ralph put his head down behind a page of the newspaper.

"Found what?" The man leaned on his elbows. "Have to know for the records, have to keep records."

Ralph didn't believe him. He was surprised that anyone in a busy newspaper office had time for idle curiosity.

"The Whybrow murders."

"Ah, that was nice, a very nice story."

"You remember it?"

"I never forget a lead. We had some nice pictures, some real interesting pictures."

Ralph looked through the pages. "Of the murderer?"

"They didn't leave much to the imagination. I remember the trial, those women would have torn him limb from limb if they could have got to him."

"What women?"

"I remember the business with Madame Tussaud's afterwards. They wanted him for the Chamber of Horrors, it would have made a nice little scene."

"But they couldn't," said Ralph. "It would be libel, he had to be presumed innocent. He never was proved guilty."

"I'll tell you something else. If he walked in here now I'd know him, same as I'd know Evans and Christie."

Ralph looked him in the eye. "Would you?"

"He strung himself in Broadmoor so I shan't get the chance."

"Who did? Who are you talking about?"

"The one you're talking about, the Brighton Baby Butcher."

Someone should remember John Brown, thought Ralph, someone besides Jack Tomelty. The front pages had broken out banners for him – 'BROWN HELD, FACES MURDER CHARGE' – and carried his photograph. Ralph found that he was instinctively shielding the page with his hand and was vexed to think how much faith he put in Jack Tomelty's theory of his physical similarity.

"Is that him?" He deliberately tilted the heavy volume so that the man in the leather apron could see the photograph.

"Didn't I say he was a funny looking bastard? I said he had murder written on him, didn't I? I don't need the type-setter to tell me where a face like that goes. It goes to the top of the spread."

"It does?" Ralph peered closely at John Brown's picture.

"Bent as a hairpin he was. You're looking at something special."

"I don't think he looks special."

John Brown looked ordinary. So far as could be seen from the newspaper print he had an unremarkable face, well-shaved, well-composed, and nothing, one would say, had discomposed it for a long time.

Was there a likeness? Was it possible to tell, when Ralph didn't know how his own face looked to other people? Should he try to compare flesh and blood and printer's ink, or take the representation of one thing and try to see it as the representation of another? Perhaps if he could visualise a newspaper photograph of himself –

Bertha would have known: any angle, any mood, if there was a similarity she would have seen it. If he could hide the context – he would have to do that or she would cry indignantly, "It's not a bit like you! How can you think so?"

Perhaps there was a resemblance. Perhaps in the mirrors at the Pilot he had seen himself like that, much like that. Perhaps if he thought as much of himself as this man obviously had, he would look prized, there was a prized air about John Brown which even the newsprint could not suppress.

"If you're writing a book," said the man in the leather apron, "I can give you inside stories about all of them."

"I'm not."

"You couldn't print it, mind, unless it was privately, for limited circulation. Collectors' pieces mine are, not common currency."

"Does this look like me?" The bound volume was bulky and Ralph propped it against his chest. "Would you say I was – " what had she said, what had Tomelty said she had said? – "the live ringer of him?"

"Arthur Rosenberg, that's who he's like. Rosenberg had a lot of trouble from women thinking he was hanging around their prams. He nearly got lynched. Besides, he was red-haired."

"Who was?"

"Red as a fox. If you're not a writer, what are you?"

"I'm just looking. If there's a charge of course I'll pay – "

"I'm looking through this window," said the man in the leather apron, "to see you don't mutilate, destroy or deface the files."

He slid the pane to between them and Ralph laid down the volume and turned the sheets. The account of the trial would be the nearest he would ever get to John Brown and to hearing, out of his mouth, testimony for or against him.

What he got when he had read through the report of the trial was an overwhelming impression of mystification. Most people had been unable to make up their minds and those who did had obviously done so in defiance. There was a small core of decision against John Brown, but it was too small to convict him.

Ralph was discouraged by the verbatim reporting. There was a ludicrous baldness about the questions and answers. If he must learn about John Brown from what was not said, how many minuses would it take to make one plus?

The trial lasted two days, hit and miss. The Prosecution frequently missed and its few hits were not consolidated, they were unrelated facts which did not jell.

The Defence had called some unimpeachable witnesses and produced their evidence with a flourish, so much so that the Judge was obliged to rebuke Counsel for his bravura.

So far as Ralph could make out, Brown's neck was never in danger. The Crown had not even established that it was a practical possibility for him to have murdered Miss Elvie at the material time. Or at any time – except future time, said Counsel for the Defence. It was some of his bravura.

Brown had witnesses to swear to his movements and to his character, that he was balanced, likeable, good-tempered, popular, not the man to murder women and butcher them. He owed no money, he had some detractors, but no enemies. True, he was one for the ladies: he came, saw and acquired, but not, to do him justice, other men's preserves. The Whybrow sisters were acquisitions, unmarried ladies living in their own house on a small income which died with them.

"You were a regular visitor. How often did you go?"

"Twice a week."

"On business or pleasure?"

"Both."

"The business was to collect their insurance premiums. What was the pleasure?"

"We played cards."

The Prosecution suggested that the ladies had played for his favours. Brown denied it though he admitted to favouring

311

them both. Whereupon the Prosecution wondered how impartially and hinted at jealousy, at degrading and depraving quarrels between Miss Fran and the gentle Miss Elvie.

That Brown had been the lover of them both was an integral part of the case against him. Sex, of a rustic sort, the corsets and braces, featherbed and velvet stout sort, was back of everything at Casimir Terrace. Not so surprising: the ladies, though virginal, were approaching middle age when John Brown appeared and they entered into Sex with the gusto of women who had had time to know what they were missing. Anyone else would have found them a handful. John Brown had come to an arrangement, vulgar and opportunist, but very cosy, very satisfying. It satisfied him, did it do less for the Whybrows? The Judge, in his summing-up, asked who could say what had gone on in the minds of those two ladies. It was still relevant to ask the question because nobody knew, not their neighbours, not their friends, and whatever the supercharged atmosphere of Casimir Terrace had been charged with had died with them. Only John Brown, the charger, remained.

"Did you speak of marriage to them? To either of them?"

"No."

"Did they speak of it to you?"

"No."

"Which one did you like best?"

"I liked them both."

"You slept with them both?"

"No."

"Ah, you only slept with one. Which one?"

"I didn't sleep with either."

"You have admitted that sexual relations took place."

"Yes, but I always went home afterwards."

It was preposterous. How could anyone say such a thing? How had John Brown said it? Ralph winced, hearing the titter go through the courtroom.

There was some fundamental absurdity about the case. Proof was not being sought, proof either way would make no scrap of difference to what everyone knew – that Brown had killed these women. In fact he had produced all the proof that anyone could want to show that he had *not* killed them and what breathed through the newspaper reports was a general scepticism as to the value of proof. Which meant that the grain of salt was being taken with everything that Brown established in his defence, and was also being weighed against him in lieu of evidence.

Of that there was no shred and witnesses swore to his physical presence elsewhere, miles from Casimir Terrace, at the time of Miss Elvie's death.

On the face of it, the Whybrows were no trouble to him. He kept them happy and he was not the sort of man to find it an intolerable burden. They were not rich, under the terms of their father's will whatever they left when they died went to specified charities. Yet who else under the sun knew them well enough to kill one with the connivance of the other? And if Miss Elvie had stabbed Miss Fran, who but John Brown could have strangled Miss Elvie? What other seducer could seduce a tender and fastidious woman to the act of dismembering and disembowelling her own sister? Elvie had obviously helped with that grisly business: there were stains on her clothes, some of them half washed, others half burnt in the kitchen boiler.

No very great fist had been made of any of it. And one of John Brown's suits was incomplete, the trousers were missing, and the waistcoat. And people remembered seeing him in a pair of bottle-green suede shoes. And none of these was found, even half burned or half washed. How did anyone get rid of suede shoes heavily stained with something that could hang him?

As the Judge pointed out, the fact of the vanished clothes was not a palpable fact. They might have been destroyed because they were incriminating or they might have been worn out and discarded. They were gone but that was not evidence. Only inferences could be drawn and inferences were of no help to a jury.

Again, the fact that John Brown had a key to 14 Casimir Terrace, a key which Miss Fran had had cut for him, was a negligible fact. To do the deed for which he was on trial John Brown did not require a key. He was well known to the sisters, an intimate in every sense, and they would admit him at any time. On the other hand, the Judge reminded the jury, the affidavits sworn by unimpeachable witnesses as to the accused's presence at the material time, these were facts of the matter and could not be discounted.

Which sounded, thought Ralph, as if he meant to say that he knew and they knew, and wasn't he glad that he wouldn't have to subscribe to the verdict of them all.

John Brown hadn't said anything when it was over, or if he had, the reporter hadn't reported it. There was a picture, very fuzzy, as if it had been taken through cheesecloth, of him waving as he left the court. Rather a seaside gesture, Ralph thought it.

# 7

"I don't think that these things are less important because they're imaginary," said Bertha, swerving violently as she leaned forward to dip her headlights at a road junction. "I mean, if they're only in her mind they're absolutely real to her and we've still got to cope and it won't be as easy as if there really was something we could do something about."

"I'd like to know where she got it from," said Ralph. "One of the Sunday supplements, I suppose."

"I'm not even sure that it is imaginary. Not absolutely. There have been scientific and medical tests and it was definitely proved, Emmy says, that everything, every single thing, has its own emanations and they need not be harmless, they can clash with one person and not with another."

Ralph braced himself for her last-minute dead stop at the empty zebra crossing.

"It isn't as if she's gullible," said Bertha, going down through the gears. "She never believed in the stars. When we were girls it was all the rage to get your horoscope done but Emmy wouldn't. 'I'll paddle my own canoe,' she used to say."

"I shall look a fool, asking about water-diviners."

"Oh I don't think so, dear. Emmy says they're used in industry nowadays."

"Emmy says! Haven't you got a mind of your own?"

There was a hurt silence and when, in her unhappiness, she forgot the handbrake and the car began to run backwards he said sourly, "You'll kill us one of these days."

They roared up the hill from the estuary in bottom gear. Conversation was impossible but she looked round at him and he thought she said that she was sorry. So was he, but he did not admit it.

As they swung into the Thorne Farm track she said humbly, "I have to tell you what Emmy says because I no longer know what she thinks," and Ralph almost asked did

315

she really expect to? Didn't she know that the most that could be done was to think thoughts for other people? Even sisters, even blood sisters' thoughts were not the same. Certainly one of those women at Casimir Terrace had not dreamed what the other was thinking.

"She's going to be ill and we must do something. *She* can't. She won't change her room, she says what would be the use. I don't even know if she really believes in the rays."

"I thought you said it didn't matter."

Bertha stopped the car outside the house and turned to him. "Oh my dear, if we don't care, who will?"

She was not rebuking, only asking if he could care, really asking what would become of Emmy if he couldn't.

He saw a change in her. She had puffed up like a sick fowl. She made a business of moving around and sat down as if she should not have been expected to get up, her rather splendid discontent tending to fretfulness. It could be self-induced, it could be one of her extremes which she was pushing herself to. Anyone could act tired.

He sighed as he dropped heavily into a chair and there was Bertha crying, "Ralph's worn out!"

Why should Emmy want to be seen to be ill? She had always queened it, she had the material advantages – money and the house – and had made it appear a little ludicrous that he and Bertha only had each other.

"Has it been a busy week?" Bertha would have brought him his slippers but Emmy did not like people wearing slippers except in their bedrooms.

"Eventful more than busy."

Emmy herself wore high heeled court shoes and each instep stood up like a ball. Did her feet usually swell towards the end of the day?

"What events, dear? What's been happening?"

"Nothing really, at least nothing that would mean any-

316

thing to you." He was struck by the enormousness of the lie and stared at Bertha in dismay.

Emmy was the one who would not accept it. "Why shouldn't it mean anything to us?"

"It was business."

"Was there a take-over bid? For Picker, Gill?"

He wondered, if he were to tell them – "I met a rare creature, her name is Marise and she believes I am a murderer. She believes I murdered two women, two doting sisters like you – "

"Was there a merger? Why not a consortium of weed killers? To make them more lethal?"

If he told them, "She *wants* to believe that," they would have the bare bones of the truth –

"Why stop at weeds?" said Emmy. "Or pests? Who's to say who isn't, definitely isn't, a pest?"

– bare enough to be a distortion of it. And this they would accept, Emmy would insist on it. First and last Emmy would insist on a lie.

"You'll never be out of business. 'Killing Unlimited' – hasn't anyone realised the possibilities?"

"No take-over bids, just development. In business nothing happens for months, then everything happens in a week." In life too, and he had cherished its uneventfulness, one day following another had been his method of happiness. Happiness was the desired norm then. Not any more, not for him, because a norm had to be shared – if only with his own past. "I don't want to go into business history."

"Why not? We have the time."

"Supper will be ready in five minutes," said Bertha.

"Let's go into the history of one of your deterrents, from when it was a little noxious grain blowing about on the wind to now when it has a helicopter to drop it on the fields."

Bertha leaned over and touched him in a rallying way. "I should go and wash your hands, dear."

"What are we having?"

"Chicken. A little white meat will be good for Emmy."

"I don't want anything."

"Emmy, you must – "

"Except perhaps a brandy."

"You must eat – Ralph, she hasn't had a thing all day."

"Why not?"

"Because I'm not hungry. Don't worry, it's not serious. You needn't ask me how I am."

"I told him," Bertha said quickly. "We talked about you all the way from the station."

"How fascinating." Emmy lay back in her chair and closed her eyes. "Is he going to get me a brandy?"

"Ralph will look after you," said Bertha, "while I see to the supper."

Neither of them knew that Marise was standing at his elbow. He had been keeping her for his own use, so to speak, but Bertha and Emmy had conjured her up and her presence filled the room. He might believe in ghosts, but she was much more than spirit. If Emmy had not had her eyes shut he believed she must have seen Marise standing out all over him.

"You don't care what happens to me," she said when he took the brandy to her. He remembered Scobie saying that in much the same tone: it was a help to her, a luxury almost, to have an imaginary pain after so much of the real thing. He remembered what sickness was like, watching Scobie die had made him an expert. He had come to know the testimony of every pore and every hair. "You don't care so long as it doesn't happen to the side your bread's buttered." Emmy was not really ill, she was slightly distempered as a matter of policy. Under her puffiness was a robust constitution, she couldn't hide the small signs of health.

"Of course you'd like me to die. It would be a really useful thing for me to do, and leave everything to Bertha, to you and Bertha."

She was wide of the truth but it struck him that she wouldn't like the truth any better.

"Nothing's going to happen to you," he said.

"Go away." Her hand, lifted to wave him away, struck his chest and she let it lie, palm down, against his waistcoat. "You're such a terribly small man."

"But I think you're trying to make something happen and we ought to care about why."

Her eyes blinked open as suddenly as one of those china dolls with their eyeballs on lead weights. "Bravo, darling!"

"If you'd ever been really ill you wouldn't try to make it happen again."

"Is that what I'm doing? I'm making quite a good job of it then." Taking the brandy from him she threw up her chin and drained the glass. "There's something wrong with this place. There has to be."

Afterwards he told Bertha that Emmy was persuading herself that she was ill but would soon tire of the pretence.

"She can't endure restriction, she won't be able to keep the act going."

"She's never been ill in her life," said Bertha. "It doesn't make sense for her to pretend to be now."

"Depends what you call sense."

"There's something wrong somewhere. She won't let me send for the doctor. She says here – " Bertha pointed to the floor – "down here is what's wrong. Won't you do as she asks, dear? If someone came and divined, or whatever they call it, it would set her mind at rest. After all, she *believes* and it's what we believe that matters, isn't it?"

"She's jealous, that's what's wrong."

"Jealous?"

"Of anyone who's got anything she hasn't."

"But she has everything she wants, within reason, and she's not unreasonable. She wouldn't waste time wanting anything she knew she couldn't have."

"She might if it was anything that had to be given, and wasn't."

Bertha said reprovingly, "She's not alone, she's got us."

She hadn't got him. Nor had Bertha now.

319

Tomelty told Marise to get dressed.

"Put on everything you've got, that pink suit and some sparklers and a face. I've forgotten what you look like in a face."

"Have I got to go out?"

"That's right. I have to see a couple of homs and I want them to see you."

"Why?"

"Never mind, do as I say."

She knew why, she had been exhibited before. Tomelty liked to show her to his business acquaintances. She was well aware that her effect was of several double whiskies – which Tomelty had not had to pay for. And she enjoyed leading them all on, really it was a continuation, an amplification of the leading-on of Tomelty which was one of the mercies of being married.

But she no longer needed to count mercies. Something had happened, an important development. Tomelty did not realise: Tomelty, as usual, was in black ignorance.

"I don't want to go out."

"You've got ten minutes to fix yourself."

She laid her hands on her stomach. "It's like a saw-edged bread knife turning in a wound."

"What is?"

"The pain."

"You haven't got a pain!"

"Barbra has, she's got stomach-ache."

Tomelty seized her by the chin. "But I can give you a pain, I can really give you something to think about, ma cherry."

She shook her head and he gripped her chin. "Do you think I couldn't?"

His capacity no longer interested her, she no longer wondered how far he would go. She had, she now realised, always known that he would go no distance at all.

"You'd just do it if you were going to, you wouldn't talk about it. He never says a word about what he did."

"Who?"

"He never once said to them that he would kill them."

Tomelty gave her a shove and she fell on to a folding stool which folded under her, so she sat on the floor laughing, the white stripes of his fingers still showed where he had gripped her cheek. As she laughed the stripes were flushed out, her skin turned pink, silver pink.

"You're talking rubbish," said Tomelty, "you always talk rubbish and that's how you've lived this long. I spare you because you're not responsible."

"You've never had your picture in the papers, have you?"

"Not for murder, no."

"Nor anything else. Not even in an advertisement. Even Barbra's been in an advertisement for stockings."

"Don't push me, Gyp. Try shutting your mouth."

Marise lay flat on the floor and clasped her hands under her head. "You're jealous, I can see that. He says there's a lot of jealousy, people getting jealous of what he did."

"He says? Bobsworth upstairs? What does he know about it?"

"He says people are jealous because they'd like to have done it themselves. You wouldn't like to mess about with those women, would you? You wouldn't like to touch them? He'd have to, wouldn't he, he'd have to touch them everywhere for what he did?" She shone up at him from the grubby floor, fresh as a daisy among the old brown sticks of furniture. "I'd die if he was to touch me."

Tomelty, who had been losing his temper, suddenly got it back, better than ever. He went on his knees beside her.

"I'll prove to you he isn't Johnny Brown."

Frowning, she pushed her chin down into her neck. "My bosom's not big enough, I can see my feet over it."

"It's big enough for me." He put out his hand and she rolled away from him on to her side. "I'm going to stop you talking rubbish. There's someone who knew him better than I did – she'll tell you. Whatever she tells you stays told." He said softly, "And she knows you, Gyp."

321

"You can't stop me talking. Unless you kill me. Do you think he'll do it for you?"

"She never liked him, not really. They used to be very thick and she used to pack us out of the way when he came. That was some friendly society! And she often gave him a meal, I daresay she'd have given him anything else he fancied if he'd fancied it. But when she heard he'd been arrested she said, 'I never trusted him'." Tomelty smiled. "She didn't want to."

"She can't stop me talking."

"We'll have her over and show her that wuzzo upstairs. She'll tell you who he is."

"I shall keep talking about Mr Shilling. I like him."

Tomelty stood up, dusting his knees. "Talk about him, like him if you like, but don't call him John Brown."


Towards the end of her life Scobie had felt extraordinary – after all, it was extraordinary to be dying and to know it – and when Ralph saw that she excluded him along with the rest of the world, he was hurt. Then he came to understand why she was excluding him and that cruelty was bigger than both of them.

"You're the same as everyone else," she told him and it still hurt although he knew that she was loving and envying that sameness. She meant him to rejoice in it and cruellest of all was having to think himself lucky. He had tried to tell her that he was not one of a gay mob, but he could see that it only complicated things for her. She had reached a stage when she could not differentiate, indeed she had no time to.

Of course he was the same as everyone else – conformity was what civilisation was about – and throughout Scobie's dying it was not the fact of being the same as other people which bothered him but the fact of not being with her, being cut out, surgically excised.

Now Marise told him, "You're different. Jack thinks so."

322

"I don't care what he thinks, what anyone thinks – except you."

"He's going to bring his mother to look at you."

"His mother?" When he was with her Ralph often thought he must be dreaming because there was a kind of dream-like logic, a private sequitur between the two of them. What she said made crazy good sense just for him. "And will you think what she tells you to?"

"Of course not. I make up my own mind. If I did what I was told to do I'd be dead by now. Jack tells me to do killing things – 'Get into the cupboard,' he says, 'and shut the door and let's see how long before you suffocate.' He says he'll know where he is with me when I'm dead."

That also made sense and for Tomelty it was terribly sensible. Legally she was his for his lawful enjoyment but he could not even enjoy breathing her air for fear someone else had breathed it too. He was justified, thought Ralph, exultantly breathing it.

"You mustn't let her see you," said Marise urgently. "You must go away when she comes. We'll arrange a signal, I'll put something in the window to warn you. I'll put Barbra. Like this." The thing had lost more of its stuffing and when she propped it on the sill it melted into a crouch. "Don't come in if you see Barbra. When the coast is clear I'll take her out of the window."

"I don't know his mother, why should I mind her seeing me?"

"She knew John Brown." She was constantly leaving him with nothing he could profitably or safely do. He wanted to damn John Brown to hell and make her hear and understand. This was what he ought to do and now was the time. "Do you think she wouldn't talk? Wouldn't she just! She's not like me, you don't think she's like me, do you?"

"No-one's like you."

"If she saw you she'd tell everyone, she'd tell the whole street."

"Tell them what?"

323

"Madame Belmondo would have forty fits. Jack would shout murder and you'd have to go."

She didn't want him to go. He moved towards her, moving suddenly in his joy, suddenly feeling free to touch her, and she moved too, seeming to melt down and crouch, permissive, like the broken teddy bear. He stood with his hand outstretched and she waited, her skin tensed – he could see it tensing – for him to touch her.

"You mustn't let her see you."

There it was again, their private sequitur, she was mortally afraid of John Brown who was not here and had never been here.

"You don't want me to go, do you?" He touched his chest, Ralph Shilling and blazingly glad of it. "They can't do anything to me, I'll be here when you want me."

"Suppose she lies in wait for you? She's cunning, suppose she hides – "

"Suppose I'm not John Brown."

She stamped her foot. "Oh, good *heavens*!"

Scobie used to say that there was too much truth, that really there was nothing but truth. She challenged him to produce a hundred per cent lie and he said black was white and she said yes it was and he hadn't produced even a half-truth. When he tried to argue, she said that anything could be true but nothing in this world could ever be false. He had supposed that she was grieving: after all, the truth she faced was grievous. But now he thought if there was so much truth about, why try to escape it, the goldfish might as well try to get out of the bowl.

"Good heavens," Marise said again, "I should worry who you are, who anyone is in this place! Can't you take a joke? You should see your face! You look like that old cat of yours. Jack says people do get to look like the things they like, he says I look like Barbra – "

"That's ridiculous."

"You think I'm pretty? Am I the prettiest girl you've ever seen?"

"Yes."

"I don't know what girls look like now, I don't see any."

"Why not?"

"He won't take me out. He doesn't want people looking at me."

"I'll take you."

"Will you? Where?"

To the end of the earth, he thought, remembering a place from far away and long ago, a beach of sand as fine as pepper with a quiet sea punctiliously rolling in, a private place without the ever present threat of Tomelty returning, where she would have no fear.

"Somewhere we can be alone." He went close and she did not move away. She touched his hand, following with interest a big green vein with the tip of her fingers.

"Can it be anywhere I like?"

"Anywhere."

"Then," she said joyfully, "I'd like to go to your house."

"My house?"

"Where you go at week-ends, where the women are, in the country."

"To Thorne?" He was shocked. "Oh no!"

"Why not?"

"It's out of the question, I can't take you there."

"It's where I want to go."

"But why?"

"I like the country. We went to Epsom once, to the races, and I ran away, I wanted to go where it was quiet but Jack was so angry he put me on a string like a dog. He missed the races, you see, looking for me."

"I'll take you to the country, it'll be quiet, I promise."

She curled into a corner of the couch, turning her back and hiding her face from him. Her voice came muffled and fretful. "You promised I could go wherever I wanted."

"It wouldn't be suitable for you to go to Thorne, it wouldn't be the thing. You must see that." He looked at the arch of her back, he had no experience of children but wasn't she acting like a child, too young a child to follow an appeal to reason? "Thorne's not pretty. When the tide's out the estuary is all mud, miles of grey mud. We'll go to the sea, to Hastings or Folkestone or Leigh."

Suppose he treated her as a child, picked her up and slapped her hands and made her listen to him?

He couldn't, of course, no child had a line like that from ankle to thigh. "My wife would wonder, she always does." He could hear Bertha asking, saving her questions from one week to the next, slowly getting through them if they both lived long enough.

"And there's Emmy, her sister, she has imagination and she tends to think the worst. She'd have plenty to say."

What might be said or asked did not shake him as much as the notion of Emmy and Bertha and Marise all together in the same place.

"It isn't pretty," he said again. "At this time of year the mud dries fast, it's very pervasive, the smell of drying mud."

"It doesn't matter," she said into the bowels of the couch.

"It can be unpleasant. People say it's healthy but people often believe that unpleasant things must be good for you – "

"Jack doesn't like me going out, anyway."

"There are plenty of places, nice places we could go. Epping or Kew – but it's not so quiet there, of course. We could take a boat from Hampton Court – would you like that?"

"I don't like listening to you. You talk like everyone else."

He was not coming up to her expectations. If only he knew what they were he could try to act the superman. Better still if he knew what they weren't. She seemed to expect a kind of devil. He felt helpless, more so than at any other time of his life. When Scobie was dying he had desperately wanted to do something, but now he *had* to, it was a crying need – what else could he call the clamour inside him?

The teddy bear was doubled up, so was she, with her face on her knees, her cheek scarlet.

"You'll make yourself sick."

Through the window he saw Tomelty and a woman approaching the house. Tomelty was panning wide his feet as he walked, he had turned up the brim of his hat and crammed it over his ears. The woman struck him amicably on the chest.

Ralph watched them through the curtain and as they reached the porch he said, "I'll take you to Thorne."

Marise looked out of her fingers. "When?"

There was a day in each week when Bertha and Emmy went to Chelmsford shopping. He thought that if it were possible for her to see Thorne without seeing them, there would be no harm done – and perhaps some inconceivable good. He couldn't conceive it but his cause certainly needed it.

The door opened and Tomelty came in. He still had his hat crushed over his ears and he was laughing, bringing the joke with him.

Marise uncurled herself. She looked at Ralph, sharing her fright, and he thought that if it was fright on his account it was another inconceivable thing.

"Well now, my wife's entertaining," said Tomelty.

"The postman left a parcel here for me," said Ralph. "Mrs Tomelty kindly took it in."

"That's neighbourly. Don't let her take *you* in, though." Tomelty blinked, but there was nothing blurred about the look he gave Ralph.

"What have you done with your hat?" said Marise. "It does look funny."

"I was demonstrating." Tomelty turned to the woman who stood in the doorway. "Mamie, I want you to meet Mr Shilling, the gentleman from upstairs."

She had clear, canine eyes and Ralph felt them go through to the back of his skull, look round, and withdraw.

"You wouldn't think she was my mother, would you?"

327

Tomelty put his arm round her shoulders, Ralph saw that he was proud of her. "All women should raise a family while they're young, then the children have something to look at."

"Listen to him." Mrs Tomelty looked at Marise.

"People take her for my pettit ammy. Did you ever see such a girl of fifty? She still gets whistled at, that's some sort of record. But you'd be surprised what a long memory she's got."

"I shan't surprise this gentleman," said Mrs Tomelty.

"What are you demonstrating with your hat turned up?" Marise asked Tomelty.

"That a bowler doesn't suit me." He nudged his mother. "Go on, Mamie, surprise Mr Shilling."

"She doesn't remember the same things as he does," declared Marise. "How can he be surprised if he's never heard of them?"

"I can remember quite a lot myself," said Ralph. "We should probably cover much the same ground."

"I fancy not." Mrs Tomelty folded her arms. "If I have some nasty things to remember it's through no fault of mine."

"But Mr Shilling's not one of them?"

Marise cried, "How could he be? He's been a sailor, he's been to sea, he hardly ever came to England."

Tomelty rounded on her. "What's this?"

"He was captain of a ship and he gave it up to be near his invalid wife. He started as a cabin boy, he's been to America and India and China and round the world a hundred times."

"He is not John Brown!" shouted Tomelty.

"Of course he's not."

Ralph, looking from one to the other in his own surprise saw that they each had a different expression. Marise's was all joy, Tomelty's nose was white and his mother was stoking her disapproval by staring round the room.

Ralph himself was concerned about Marise's lying for him, and charmed by the transparency of it and happy that she had done it. Her wrong reasons didn't matter, she had done it for the right one – that she wanted him to stay.

"I see she's still got that thing." Mrs Tomelty pointed to the teddy bear. "It should have gone on the fire long ago, twenty years ago. You know that, don't you?" she said to Tomelty. "You're in a fix, boy, and you'll have to get yourself out."

"I shall." Tomelty pulled the hat off his head. "So help me God – " the hat shook in his hands as he forced it back into shape – "I don't care if He bloody hinders me, I'll get out of it."

"Tea for everyone, even for Barbra." Marise picked up the toy and swung it by one leg. "And especially for Mr Shilling."

"Thank you, I must be going upstairs."

"That's right," said Mrs Tomelty, "and don't come down here again unless you want to play dolls."

# 8

Ralph did not choose the moment to ask for Tuesday, with Pecry no moment was better than another.

"Tuesday off?" To serve his purpose Pecry would pretend not to understand a colloquialism.

"Not come into the office," Ralph said patiently.

"I believe you have exhausted your leave entitlement for the year."

"This is a special case." Certainly it was. Ralph looked down, squirming on his feet. Pecry had put his cold finger on lesser secrets than this one which stood out all over him. But he heard himself say flatly, "I'm afraid I can't come in on Tuesday."

"Can't, Shilling? What impediment can you foresee to doing the work for which you are paid? Am I to understand – " Pecry lifted Ralph's gaze with the force of his own – "that you are refusing to work on Tuesday?"

"I'm asking to absent myself. It's family business, something I must attend to."

"Family business? What family?"

"I have a wife and sister-in-law."

"You have no progeny." Pecry sighed.

"Two women are trouble enough," said Ralph cautiously. Habitually Pecry did not express regret or relief or impatience, habitually he did not express himself at all.

"I have a son – "

That was unwonted too, the way he stopped short, the way he looked at Ralph. Everyone knew that he had a son – by asexual reproduction, Krassner said. Anyone else might have chosen that way to begin a confidence.

"Is it all right about Tuesday?" said Ralph.

Pecry did not seem to hear, he who heard and weighed everything. He asked Ralph a question – and not one of his probes either – on an entirely different subject. He asked what sort of man Ralph thought he was. Ralph kept silent

330

because he had not got beyond the question whether Pecry was a man at all.

"Am I the sort to father a mental and moral shipwreck?"

"Of course not."

"I gave him fibre, integrity, principle – " The words were pushed out, perhaps he had rehearsed them to himself, over and over, examining and assessing and cataloguing, but they came battering out now – "and I gave him shelter, a boy needs to be sheltered until he learns how not to make a fool of himself. Now – " a bead appeared, a clear bead of moisture on Pecry's dry lip – "now he makes fools of all of us."

No-one had been able to make a fool of Pecry, not even Krassner to whom it had been worth the sack to try.

"I can't walk down the street in his company. People laugh at us. Shilling, he's a – " the bead broke as Pecry's lip curled – "a Flower Person."

Ralph wanted to smile at the notion of a weedy young edition of Pecry in a carpet coat and daisy-chain but the old edition's humiliation was not funny. It was disturbing: having always known where Pecry stood, Ralph preferred him to stay there, he certainly didn't relish the prospect of his coming nearer.

"He'll grow out of it."

"I shall never trust him again."

What was Ralph to make of that? It was a gratuitous piece of information, a confidence, a declaration of despair from Pecry who never confided and had never been known to despair. But Ralph supposed that no-one could stay in character all the time and confidences weren't so much reposed in other people as thrust upon them.

"At sixteen I held a position of trust."

Pecry talked a lot about trust, about expressing and main-taining it and Krassner had done a sketch of him as Dog Tray with a nude girl balanced on his nose.

"It's a phase, he'll laugh at himself in six months' time," said Ralph. Being allowed to see under Pecry's skin was a privilege he had not sought. "There's nothing unusual about it, it's part of growing up."

"But what into? What is he growing up into?" Pecry seemed to be appealing, asking for a right answer, one which would be right for him. "His clothes are fit only for scarecrows, renegades, apes!"

"It's a kind of uniform. All kids like to dress up. With me it was the Boy Scouts, I wasn't content until I had a bushwhacker's hat."

"Depravity I could root out, but if I extirpate this rottenness, what remains? Not a man – " Pecry's scalp blazed through his thin hair, "nor a woman, either."

"There's nothing sinister about it and it's better than the Hitler Youth."

"The only uniform I ever wore was the King's and I put that on when I was ordered to."

"For which? Hitler's or the Kaiser's?"

"What?"

"Which war did you wear it for?"

"Does it matter? I'm asking you, Shilling, is it possible for a properly functioning brain, however immature, to conceive that the world's problems can be resolved by sentiment?"

"Make love, not war?"

Pecry fixed Ralph with his fish's eye. He was trying, pressing – pressing Ralph, of all people, for an answer which he could accept. "According to your theory is it part of a child's development to lack moral and common sense? To believe that wrong-doing should be licensed and crime go unpunished?"

"You may not like the idea and it's definitely anti-social – " Ralph found himself wishing that Pecry, even Pecry, could see the joke, but of course it was private, wonderfully private – "but some people do get away with murder."

"What do you know about it? Or the issues involved? Issues? They're root and branch!"

"I could give you a case in point. You may remember it.

A man named John Brown murdered two women and it was generally known that he had. Why did he do it? was one question. When? was another. If one answer could have been found, just one, they'd have hanged him. Think of it, all the forces of criminal justice couldn't pin anything on him. There's a song about John Brown's body mouldering in the grave – but his goes marching on." Ralph rocked up on his toes.

Pecry frowned. "I'm talking about my son."

"It's lunch-time, come and have a drink." Ralph startled himself, asking Pecry to drink with him.

"I never take alcohol in the middle of the day."

Yet when Ralph turned to the door Pecry stood up. Somewhere along the line a break had been made and he needed to show it to someone. He was not entirely the man people thought he was and he was showing Ralph because castewise there was no-one else. Pecry came first and Ralph came next – a long way after, but in lieu of family, friend or lover Pecry turned to the order of seniority.

"This is to go no further." He settled his Homburg levelly above both eyes. "This is in strict confidence, Shilling, it must not go beyond these walls."

Ralph left him to follow if he chose. He expected that Pecry would not choose because habitually he didn't drink. He hoped that he wouldn't because if he, Ralph, accepted – was obliged to accept – Pecry's confidences now, he would also have to accept the blame for them later.

But of course Pecry wasn't acting habitually and in the bar across the road Ralph found him at his elbow.

"This will help me to listen," Ralph picked up his glass, "though that – " he nodded at Pecry's lemonade shandy – "won't much help you to talk."

"I talk? I came to hear you develop your theory that immorality and imbecility are part of normal mental growth." Pecry spat out the words with passionate disgust. "I could have sent him to a school where they undertake to eradicate that kind of thing, stamp it out. I'd have given them *carte blanche* to discipline him physically as well as mentally. *'Mens sana in corpore sano'* is a fact and the regime is fully comprehensive. You understand? Punishment is designed to remould not merely to chastise. But the boy has a heart condition."

"You were afraid they'd go too far?"

"They refused to accept him."

Ralph felt slightly sick. Pecry really wasn't human, but was he above or beneath humanity?

"You're too hard on him. Leave him alone, he'll be all right."

"By whose standards?"

"By yours. They're the ones he's grown up with, aren't they? He's your son and heredity counts for something."

"I have nothing to reproach myself with."

There was no feeling sorry for anyone who could say that. He was rather to be envied. Ralph himself sensed reproach wherever he looked. It seemed to him that even living and breathing was done on someone else's neck.

"My father brought me up to cherish the thought that one day I should be like him. He set me an example and I did the same for my son. Whatever good I have done has been for him to emulate, the bad I have not done has been for him to avoid."

So he was a blueprint. It was one thing they hadn't suspected. From Ralph down to the woman who came in to make the office tea, Pecry gave them all cause for surmise but no-one had thought of the obvious – that he was a pattern for a Pecry.

"My father swore that if he saw any of himself in me he'd thrash it out." Ralph took a mouthful of rum and rolled his tongue in it. "It boils down to the same thing. He couldn't set me a good example but he could knock the bad one out of me."

Pecry put his shandy aside with lips hard primmed. "I believe that a man's best memorial is his son and I gave him a first-class education. I paid for private coaching, for extra-mural subjects, for encyclopedias and reference books, I paid for vacations abroad, study tours, season tickets and subscriptions. I paid doctors and dentists – my son often needs the doctor. I paid for his clothes, more clothes in one year than I could have use for in ten."

"You've spared no expense to make him a fitting memorial," Ralph said warmly. "There's nothing wrong with that, everyone wants to be remembered and we'd all like to choose how and for what. I don't think I'd choose your way even if I had a son. I'd prefer something strictly personal, more relevant, if you know what I mean. It might not last so long or it might outlive people and pass into legend – or into the records, anyway."

Pecry frowned, but Ralph felt they were getting on to something interesting. "Which lasts longer, fame or infamy? That's a knotty question. Of course Shakespeare said that the evil men do lives after them and the good gets buried with their bones. Let's hope he was wrong."

Ralph went to the bar and brought back another rum for himself. "Would you remember a murderer more than a saint?" he asked Pecry.

"I don't anticipate my son being either."

"He's more likely to be a saint, the way he's going, the first of the Flower Saints."

Pecry stood up. "You haven't been any help, Shilling."

"I'm sorry – "

Pecry turned his back and Ralph raised his glass and murmured, "Marching on!" A girl in a group raised her glass and drank with him.

When Pecry had gone Ralph went across to her. "That was a private toast."

"Did I intrude?"

"I shouldn't mind fifty like you intruding."

She smiled. "Quite the man, aren't you?"

"Let me get you another drink."

"Better not. I'm with my friend and he wouldn't like it."

She was passably pretty although she couldn't hold a candle

335

to Marise, she was only flesh and blood, no miracle. "Some other time, shall we?"

No, no other time he thought, remembering how Marise had leaned out to him that morning from her window. She was in her nightdress, the chiffon or nylon or whatever it was kept slipping off the round bone of her shoulder, off her breast and just catching, clinging on the tip so that he could see where the pink began and that it was pink and not brown or red, it was the same colour as her lips.

He had stood there bemused by the wonderful pink triangle they made, her lips and her breasts. And as if that wasn't enough to happen to a man on his way to work, she had leaned out and said, "Come in for a minute, it's all right, Jack's asleep like the dead."

"I can't, I have to go."

Her face clouded, it really could lose heart as if an outside sun had been covered up.

"You're always going somewhere, you're never here when I want you."

"When do you want me?"

"If I start to think about you I can't stop. But I suppose there'll be an end sometime," she said sadly.

He had wanted to ask what she thought, but outside her window at eight-thirty a.m. was not the place nor time.

"I don't believe it will be long now." She had lifted her nightdress over her shoulder and it immediately slid off and down again to her elbow. Riveted, he watched it catch on the same pink point of the same imagined triangle. "Soon I'll have thought of everything you can do."

"You won't," he said fervently, "I promise you you won't," and it seemed to bring out the sun again. She laughed, putting her head back and he had marvelled – as he was continually marvelling at something about her – how the scrap of nylon or chiffon or whatever it was clung to the point which wasn't so much a point as a bud.

"Wasn't it funny last night – Jack introducing you to his mother?"

"Very funny."

"You knowing her all the time and she knew you, I could see." If she wanted to think so and it made her happy, he wouldn't ask why at the moment. "I put her off though, didn't I? She doesn't know what to think now. But be careful, she'll be watching you. She'll catch your breath for you. When I was first married she used to spy on me. She doesn't trust me, she thinks I'm not true to Jack. You don't know what she's like."

"I'm supposed to though, aren't I?" he had gently reminded her.

What did she expect to find at Thorne? He looked for it himself that week-end, he was ready to put it there, whatever it might be.

But Thorne was Emmy's, there was scarcely a trace of Bertha, let alone himself. The way the chairs stood and the grass grew was Emmy's. There were some stuffed ibex heads and Gurkha knives. Would Marise be satisfied with those?

"Why does Emmy keep them?" he suddenly said to Bertha.

"Keep what?"

"These severed heads."

Bertha looked at them in surprise. "They were the Colonel's trophies. Of course she keeps them."

"Would you keep my trophies?"

Her surprise turned on him. "You don't have any."

"No severed heads."

"You aren't the sort of man who likes to kill things."

"If I were, I wouldn't make it so obvious.'

Marise had said. "You don't want to be remembered," and if she was talking about Ralph Shilling she was right. He had no children, no talent, no trophies, he made no marks. But was she talking about him?

"Of course I should do the same, I should keep your things," said Bertha, "if I lost you."

337

"My razor and my umbrella, there's nothing else."

Yes, Thorne was Emmy's and although Marise had imagination he couldn't see her making Thorne into John Brown's. The idea made him smile.

'I expect I should keep your umbrella, you so often carry it, it would seem like a link with you." Bertha looked anxious. "Is anything the matter?"

"I daresay you're right, an umbrella's more my symbol than severed heads and knives."

"Why are we talking like this? I didn't know they upset you, you've never said so before." Bertha took his hand. "You see, the Colonel was such an outdoor man, he didn't have time to think much. And he had no head for business, he was only trained for the Army. Hunting was his hobby, it's only the same as if he'd collected stamps, you might say he had nothing to leave but his dead animals." She pressed his hand to her cheek. "An umbrella gives shelter."

Ralph watched her turn her lips into his palm. Her skin was soft, dry soft and rather thin and sometimes he felt in danger of breaking through Bertha's skin. He withdrew his hand.

"Do you still go to Chelmsford on Tuesdays?"

"Yes. Why?"

"Just changing the subject." He could feel her waiting, beginning to be prey to thoughts and fears that had their turn all the week and came round, like dragons on a roundabout, when he was not there.

"We haven't planned anything for this weekend, with Emmy not feeling well, but of course if you mind, if you find it too quiet we can go out, we could have the car or we could ask someone to make up a bridge four – "

"I was merely wondering if Emmy is up to going to Chelmsford."

"She wants to get some darker curtains for her room. It faces east and she can't sleep after daybreak, just when she feels like sleeping, she says."

Emmy had changed her bedroom to one on the other side

of the house. There had been some improvement in her health, but not enough Bertha thought.

"I've asked Dr Chinn to call. I'm worried about her, she's not herself. I've never known her this way before."

"You've known her other ways and they've all of them been Emmy. Remember when she took up charity committee work? We couldn't speak without an agenda. Then it was local politics, she and Chinn playing the power game. There's a ton of campaign paper still in the garage."

"She's not taking up anything, Ralph, she's ill, and I don't need the fingers of one hand to count the number of times she's been ill in her life. She had measles and she had her tonsils out. Nothing else. She's never had any time for sickness – her own or anyone's."

"She won't thank you for calling in Chinn."

"He's going to let it seem as if he was just dropping by."

"People don't just drop by at Thorne you know that. It's geographically impossible, they have to set out to arrive."

"He's promised to be tactful."

"And Chinn doesn't drop by anywhere, he's called to a place or he descends upon it."

"Help me, please dear," pleaded Bertha.

So Ralph tried. They were finishing their coffee that evening when the doctor's car drew up.

"Are we expecting anyone?" said Emmy. She had eaten a lightly boiled egg, or rather she had eaten the yolk and with a sharp gesture had crushed the shell and the white between her fingers. Ralph had reflected that she destroyed what she did not want as a matter of principle, some principle which didn't do her much credit.

"I believe it's Dr Chinn's car," said Bertha from the window.

"What does he want?"

"Hadn't we better put the whisky away?"

"Why?"

"I don't think it does you any good, dear."

"What's that to do with Chinn?"

"Oh, I don't know," Bertha said miserably.

Ralph picked up the decanter. "Bert's thinking about the look of the thing."

"Put it down. I can look as I like in my own house."

She moved the decanter to the middle of the table, grumbling at him, "You're a fine one to talk about the look of the thing," and he nearly said, One of the finest.

Bertha, opening the door, overdid her cry of, "It *is* Dr Chinn!" as if they hadn't dared hope for so much.

"Good evening." He creased his smooth equine face at them. "Dear ladies."

"Nice of you to drop in," said Ralph.

"Shilling?" The doctor always seemed to feel that there was some question about Ralph.

"Come and sit down," Emmy invited him. "We've just finished supper. Will you have a whisky?"

"A taste, thank you. I cannot stay, Mrs Chinn and I are to be the guests of the Young Conservatives tonight."

Emmeline poured a whisky for him and another for herself. "Then is there something we can do?"

The doctor glanced at Bertha, raising his brows.

"You're a busy man," said Emmy, "too busy to drive a mile up our track just for a drink. Though don't think you aren't welcome at any time."

"I was passing and it seemed neighbourly to call."

"Bringing your black bag?"

"It's only the same as the elephant bringing his trunk," said Ralph.

"We think it's very kind of the doctor to come," said Bertha. "Don't we?"

Dr Chinn put down his bag and took up the whisky. "Do I see you well, Shilling?"

"Ralph has rude health," said Emmeline.

"Health is never rude, it is a gift of God." The doctor looked at her and Emmy lowered her head and looked at him over her pink rims like a bloodhound. "You were feeling a little below par when last we met."

"I'm as well as can be expected."

"Which is not well at all!" cried Bertha.

"Expectation, the lack of it, is a symptom. As your friend and medical man I would recommend you to optimism, dear lady."

"She doesn't eat properly and she can't sleep. I found her walking in the garden at two o'clock this morning. – "

"I was testing a theory. My brother-in-law knows all about it."

Dr Chinn turned to stare at Ralph.

"As an expert he's ready to learn. He should be, shouldn't he?" said Emmy.

"Ralph's not sure yet," Bertha hurried to explain. "He does like to be sure."

"Deterrents have come into our lives," Emmy went on. "From now on we shall have to be deterred from pretty nearly everything."

"Nonsense!" declared Dr Chinn vigorously. "Life is as full of possibilities as an egg is of meat."

Emmy nodded. "Egg production is an example, but the battery system can only be the thin end of the wedge for us. To debeak and immobilise us won't solve the problem of space. We shall have to be stopped. Slowed down – " she pushed her glass across the table until it crashed against the whisky decanter – "and stopped."

Dr Chinn looked again at Bertha and Bertha looked at Ralph who wondered how many drinks Emmy had had. There were scarcely two fingers left in the decanter.

"But I don't intend to be slowed down or stopped fortuit-ously because Arnold chose the wrong place to live."

Dr Chinn fixed her with a strongly twinkling eye. "If you will allow me to examine you, dear lady, I may save you the expense of moving house."

"Have you something in your bag to measure ionisation?"

"Something like a voltameter," suggested Ralph, "for the terrestrial rays?"

Dr Chinn did not smile at other people's jokes though he

sometimes bared his teeth. "I should be the last to put a brake on progress, Shilling, and I am well aware of the paramount need for increased food production. As a medical man I am also aware of the dangers. We are tampering with the delicate balance of Nature."

"I believe Emmy thinks that Nature is tampering with *her* balance."

"Why examine the tree?" said Emmy. "The lightning comes from another place."

Bertha said, "Oh dear, I'm so sorry, doctor." and Emmy asked, "Why be sorry? Dr Chinn is here socially, he's not disappointed because there hasn't been a chance for him to use his stethoscope."

"But he could prescribe something to help you sleep – "

"I am suffering – and so are you – from over exposure to a magnetic field. Pills won't remedy that."

"Are you feeling unwell, dear lady?" Dr Chinn asked Bertha.

"I sometimes get a little tired – "

"She also gets tingling sensations in her finger-tips, like a mild electric shock. There is a force striking from under the ground and up through the walls. Imagine it," Emmy urged them, "a hostile current, a kind of undomesticated circuit through the house."

"We should call in an electrician," said Ralph and they all looked at him as if he were a long way off. "I'm a non-conductor, I don't feel anything here." They didn't know how true that was.

Dr Chinn picked up his bag. "If you change your mind, Mrs Openshaw, you know where I am."

While Bertha was showing him out Ralph told Emmy, "This visit will cost you double."

"Why should it cost me anything?"

"He'll fine you for contempt of his professional services."

Emmy's brows moved out of their pencilled line. "You're in a mood, what's happened to you?"

He didn't say that he was being taken for a murderer, nor

that the taker was so rare that he would rather she took him
for a murderer than not at all.

"You were on Chinn's side," said Emmy, "but he
wouldn't have you."

"I'm not on any side."

"I know you're not on mine." She splashed the last of the
whisky into her glass.

"I agree with Bert, that doesn't do you any good."

"It does me the only good. Look upon it as a placebo to
comfort something between a canker and a technical hitch."

"Look here, Emmy, there's nothing wrong with you or
with the house."

"There's nothing right with me, either, is there?" She
stood up, confronting him in a rage of appeal. It was a knack
she had, quite a knack, of putting an answered question and
brandishing her defeat.

But the blaze of honesty surprised him. She wouldn't
forgive him for it, he knew. She had never forgiven him
since the Isle of Wight ferry.

"Don't be a fool, Emmy." He didn't say, "I chose Bertha
because I didn't feel up to you." He said, "If anything
happened to you, I'd be done – " which was true, and "We
cherish you," which he could afford to say.

She steadied herself with fingers braced on the table. "I'm
sorry."

"You don't need to say that to me."

She put her face into her hands. "I should say it to
Bertha."

Bertha came back looking troubled. "I'm afraid he was
put out."

"He'll get over it when he sends his bill," said Ralph.

"I do wish you'd take advice, dear." Bertha touched
Emmy's hair, her fingers hesitating over the alert waves.

"I have," said Emmy, and turning bulkily went out of the
room.

"What does she mean?"

"I hope she's starting to believe what I keep telling her – that there's nothing the matter with her or with Thorne."

"You haven't seen her as I have. She's better when you're here. I've tried to get her to bed for a few days, at least it would give her somewhere to *be*. She seems so out of place."

"She can't stay in bed."

"Why not?"

Not if it meant that she would be there on Tuesday. She mustn't – they mustn't either of them be at Thorne on Tuesday.

"It's the wrong thing for her. She shouldn't be encouraged to sit around or lie around, brooding. She needs a change of scene, she needs people."

"People?"

"Take her shopping. Women love shopping, don't they? Take her to Chelmsford."

"Do you think so?" Bertha sounded wistful more than hopeful. "You may be right, dear."

"It's what Chinn would prescribe, it's only common sense but he'd wrap it up – 'Dear lady, life is an egg full of meat'."

"There *is* a sale next week. Emmy might like to go on Monday."

"Go on Tuesday, don't you always go shopping on Tuesday?"

"The sale starts on Monday – "

"It's too soon." Her bewilderment oiled his tongue, "I think she should rest a day or two, try to get her strength. Tuesday will be fine, not too soon, not too late."

"If she's well enough, we'll go."

"She's got to be well enough!"

Bertha's jaw dropped a little and her mouth opened. She did not understand but she wished to.

He put his arm round her. "I mean she's got nothing wrong with her physically."

"I wish I was as sure."

"Well, why aren't you? If I say so?" He shook her gently.

344

"Now go and make us some more coffee, there's a good girl. Mine's gone cold."

She said wonderingly, "You *are* sure."

When he was alone he returned to the question that was on his mind. What was Marise going to see at Thorne? What did he want her to see? A place fit for John Brown to live in? What did the house of an unconvicted murderer with a knack with women look like? He couldn't for the life of him think what she would make of it.

Then all at once he realised that he could safely leave it to her. She'd make something, she always did, she made something of everything. Including himself, especially himself – on the face of it no more promising than this place.

The relief was wonderful. He might even look forward to seeing what she made of Thorne, he knew he would prefer it to Emmy's version. But perhaps he was wrong about the face of it because on his face, anyway, she had seen plenty of promise.

To Bertha, coming in with coffee, he said, "Would you say I look like John Brown?"

"Who, dear?"

"You remember John Brown, he got away with murder."

She answered indignantly, as he had known she would, "Of course you don't."

"How do you know? Have you ever seen him?"

"What a thing to say!" It was no less an offence because he had said it of himself.

"I'm told I'm his double."

"Who told you?"

"Someone who actually knew him. I'm surprised you don't remember the case, it was memorable."

"I do remember." She filled his cup and dashed the spoon into the saucer. "I remember it very well. He was vile and I can't think why you want to look like him."

"Who said anything about wanting? Everyone has a double, it's a freak of Nature."

345

y

"I think it was a horribly unkind and unnecessary thing to say."

"Some people think he was clever to get away with it. I suppose he was."

"Unkind of you, I mean."

Ralph smiled. "Of course you wouldn't fancy being married to the twin of a murderer."

"Please don't mention it to Emmy, it would upset her."

"Being sister by marriage to a murderer's twin? Oh come, it would amuse her."

"She knew Elvie Whybrow. They were at school together."

It was the last thing he expected. "Well, that's a coincidence."

"Elvie was older, already a young lady. The senior girls used to take Bible Groups for the first year children and Emmy was in her Group."

"So she'd know what John Brown looked like? She'd have been interested in the case?"

"I don't think she knew anything about him. We were still in India when it happened and we didn't see all the English papers. She's never said you look like him – " Bertha was struck with alarm. "She hasn't, has she? It wasn't Emmy who said that?"

"No, it was someone who actually knew Brown in the flesh."

"He had a dirty mind – oh, not just for nasty jokes – really dirty. He thought of certain things and made them possible – " she was thermal pink, poor Bertha, with shyness – "and between women like that. They were devoted to each other. And Elvie was sweet and gentle, she'd have made a beautiful nun. What he did, what he made her do to her sister – she couldn't have done that to an animal."

"She was the one," said Ralph, "who couldn't bear to see flies on flypapers. It must have been some brain-washing."

"Washing? In vileness? In corruption? He *blacked* her."

"Don't fret, it was all a long time ago."

346

"It's the worst thing I ever heard. I thought, I still do, if that could happen, there can't be any hope for any of us."

Her eyes brimmed and Ralph put his arms round her. "It couldn't, of course, not just like that. Depend on it, the newspapers left something out or put something in, a bit of embroidery here and there."

"Embroidery? I can't bear it when you talk like this!"

"When I talk like what?"

"No-one's ever mentioned it before." She held away and looked at him through tears. "I couldn't bear it if you were like that man."

"Nor could anyone else, they'd have me in a criminal asylum."

He had asked himself what became of John Brown, where did he go after the acquittal and after that holiday wave? Where did he take his memories and what did they afford him – pleasure, pride, remorse? Not remorse, not likely. He had got something out of his system at Casimir Terrace and probably he didn't need to think about it again. Some purge, thought Ralph, some system.

"Who would say such a wicked cruel thing? No-one *I* know!" cried Bertha.

It seemed logical to suppose he was dead. Logical? Tidier, anyway, not to have two of them around.

"What is it, dear? What's the matter?"

Mouldering in the grave, that was logic. "I'm a fool, Bert – " he couldn't keep an exultant note out of his voice. "But that's all I am."

"Something's the matter, I knew it as soon as I saw you. Please tell me!"

"There's nothing to tell."

"Is it the money?"

"What money?"

"I don't want you to pretend to me about money – or about anything."

"Don't worry." He almost added, "You must take me as I am," but he wasn't on offer to her.

347

"Whatever happens to the money can't make any difference to us, it's not *capable* of making a difference. And you aren't a fool," she said strongly, "no-one can tell what stocks and shares are going to do."

"The money's all right, it'll come back to us like a homing pigeon."

He hadn't thought about it for days. He recalled it now – the writing of a cheque on their joint account and paying the cash into the firm's account – as the action of another person.

"Why did you start talking about that creature? Of all creatures? Dogs, rats, jackals are cleaner and sweeter than him – "

"Forget it. It was a joke, some fellow in a bar thought it was funny."

"How can I forget it? You – and John Brown – "

"You want to know what I did with that two hundred? I'll tell you – I invested it in the firm."

"In the firm?"

Perhaps she really preferred to save up her questions and put them one at a time, perhaps she liked to be ready for the answers, perhaps voluntary answers, out of context, baffled and did not enlighten her.

"In Picker, Gill, yes. You see it's a private transaction, nothing to interest the brokers. You'll just have to wait for me to tell you what there is to tell. And that will be nothing for a long time. It isn't the open market, dividends won't go up and down like a yo-yo."

"I thought you said that strikes and politics and wars would affect the price."

"I was generalising." He could see that she was hurt. When she felt hurt she crumpled as if slack had suddenly been let into her skin. "Well, what did you want, a game of snakes and ladders?"

"I wanted to share something with you. That would have been real shares. Of course it was silly of me."

How much more self-condemnation would she take? If he

let her, surely she would take it all? If he waited, would he hear her blame herself for everything, thus complementing Emmy who did not blame herself at all?

"It was a nice thought," he said, "about the real shares."

"Does it make you a Director?"

"Why should it?"

"Why else would you do it?"

Why indeed? Ralph was tempted to tell her, "You have to be full of yourself and of no-one else, and you have to be frightened, frightened of Dog Tray with his Flower Boy balanced on his nose."

"Let's just say it was a declaration of faith."

# 9

The weekend over, he needed to go straight back to Marise. "Be as the well, bottomless, not as the pump that needs priming." But he was the pump and the priming he needed was sight of her.

He had to wait through eight and a half hours of gestures of work and then when he got home to Lilliput Lodge, Tomelty was there. She had arranged to let Ralph know – "I don't like him," he had said, "I don't want to see him" – by putting Barbra-Bear in the window when Tomelty was at home. And there was the thing, lolling against the pane. "Why don't you like Jack?" Ralph had told her, "Because he's your husband."

He went up to his flat. When he opened the door the cat was already watching his face with its split eyes. God knew for how long and from how many miles away it had watched him.

He had asked her what Tomelty said about him. Tomelty could say whatever suited his purpose and Ralph felt desperate at the idea of such opportunity. "Don't you see?" he had said to Marise. "He's made you believe I'm some sort of maniac. That's how it all started."

The cat winked at him, a double wink with both eyes. He went down to the hall and looked at their nameplate.

She was locked up inside 'Mr and Mrs Tomelty', the door was shut as if never to open. Perhaps it was bolted? Everything was so quiet, if they weren't talking – and he was sure they weren't – if they weren't eating or sleeping, what were they doing? Tomelty, shut in with his lawful wedded wife, could be doing any lawful wedded thing.

Ralph blundered out of the front door of the house into Madame Belmondo who was coming up the steps.

"Mr Shilling, you're the one I want to see. I must speak to you about the cat – "

350

"Damn the cat." He went on down the steps, lifting his hat to her.

The shade of Tomelty was at the Pilot but it was small use going elsewhere because Marise would go too, and Tomelty by association, the association of the worm and the bud.

Ralph stood at the bar and swallowed his first drink as if it were bitter medicine "Your friend is here," said Inez, and he would have been glad to see Tomelty since it would have meant that he was not with Marise. "Over there." She pointed to the young woman in dark glasses. "She says you're acquainted."

"I hope she'll be happy ever after."

"After what?"

"After she gets out of her bad patch."

The steak-eaters had spread along the bar, Ralph was on the fringe of them. They were noisier and there seemed to be more of them and they looked individually larger.

"Give me a double before you go," he said as she turned to their end of the bar.

"Are you in a bad patch too?"

"I'm in the best patch I was ever in."

Was that all he would receive, a patch of time, a patch of Marise? It was humanly impossible: he had to accept that there had been a beginning – but once begun there could be no end.

"What about this one? Here's a suitable case for surmise."

A pair of spectacles appeared beside him, two mighty black 'O's' riding a nose.

"Cashier in a bank, local branch."

"Real estate. I see him sticking his penknife into windowsills."

"What about a doctor?"

"He'd be taking surgery right now."

"Excuse us, old dear." With the spectacles went sandy pink hair and freckles. "Tony Ginsberg swears he can tell a

351

man's job by looking at him. You won't mind if he has a crack at yours?"

All the steak-eating faces were turned on Ralph. He was part of their evening, along with their gin and tonics, their whisky and water, their Manikins and Patellas.

"It's only for a giggle."

"And it's clean."

"Let's buy you a drink. Fair's fair, if we're going to have your hair down. Whisky?"

"Rum," said Ralph. "Thank you."

"It's scientific, you know. Two-fifths science, two-fifths common and five-fifths luck. Well, you want more than one whole for this game."

"Hendon's my name," said the man with the mighty O's. "Of Style and Hendon, the car people." He pointed to a man who kept flicking his nose with his thumb and fore-finger. "This is Tony." Now that Ralph was in the thick of them he saw that the whole group was alive with such inconclusive gestures, like a bush full of sparrows.

"How is it done? What are the two-fifths science?"

Ginsberg smiled. "I only do what any charlatan with a glass ball does."

"I don't think there's anything to show what I am." Ralph turned over his hands. "No corns or callouses, no sawdust, no soot, not even a Union button."

"You're not a doctor or a dentist, and you're not in real estate or cars. Your hands aren't right and, if you'll pardon my saying so, you haven't the image for big spending. It's all pretty obvious, you see."

"What's wrong with my image?"

"Old dear, this is the truth game," said Hendon.

Ralph sipped his rum and a wave of laughter rolled around inside him. They little knew that they were trying to read two faces.

"There's more than one version of the truth," he said. "I can see more than one in these mirrors and they're all true likenesses." Steak eating had given them similarity and no finesse, he could see now that it was bunch-strength he had coveted across the bar. "Exactly how many is a mathematical calculation based on the area of glass – "

"No," said Ginsberg.

"Assuming that the mirror area on one wall is eighty by forty square feet, from where I'm standing I see myself fifty-eight-thousand times. Of course after the first few times the image is blurred and reduces out of recognition – "

"From where you stand you see three images of yourself."

"Three?"

"An image of an image plus one reversal."

Hendon pushed another rum into Ralph's hand. "Tony's by way of a Brain."

"Alright, but there are more than three versions of the truth and a reversal of truth is a lie."

Someone was getting impatient. "Come on, Tony, what's his line?"

Ginsberg flicked his nose. "He's something to do with death."

"An undertaker?"

"That's it, I recognise him, he packed my auntie up last week."

"Is it right, old dear?"

Ralph asked Ginsberg, "What made you say that?"

"Call it intuition."

"Killing unlimited," Emmy had said. Looking round, he was surprised to see that steak didn't keep them altogether confident. One or two were eyeing him as if they feared they might get their trousers splashed.

"You could say I'm something to do with death. But I'm not an undertaker."

"A butcher?" suggested Hendon.

Ralph shook his head. "You could say my business is selling death, equally you could say it's selling life. Everything's bought and sold – " but even to them, especially to them, because they would never hear it otherwise, he had to speak the truth. "Almost everything – " Though they

353

weren't capable of knowing what the exception was, they were a pack and had no use for exceptions. "Sometimes death is a benefit. We benefit the community, we sell death to further life. How many of you can say as much?" He said to Hendon, "People don't need cars to live."

"They do, by God. What other reason is there?"

"You're in insurance," said Ginsberg.

"Why do you say that?" Ralph asked again and Ginsberg shrugged. He reminded Ralph of Emmy, Emmy and Ginsberg had something in common. And the others reminded him of tail-waving dogs waiting for a game.

"Suppose two men have the same face and the same body? Look the same exactly, I mean. What happens then?" He said to Ginsberg, "I've seen what happens. Do you do water-divining too?"

"What are you talking about?" said Hendon. "Just tell us, yes or no, is Tony right?"

Ralph thought that he should throw a ball for them and whistle and slap his knee to encourage them. He wished that Marise were with him to share the joke, their John Brown joke. No-one else could share it, being so private made it so rich.

"It's not mouldering in the grave," he said, "it's marching on and this is the body that's in insurance."

"What the hell's he talking about?"

"Tony's right."

"Glory, glory allelujah," said Ralph.

"He's high."

"On two rums?"

"And the rest. He's been drinking here all evening."

"You're not driving, old dear, are you?"

Ralph slapped his chest. "*He* drives, I don't. I've been drinking but *he* shouldn't be drunk." He felt he should try with them, they should be given a chance. "There's no copyright in faces, d'you see? They're not like fingerprints, people have doubles, they really do, and the differences

354

aren't visible to the naked eye. You don't look at faces with microscopes and callipers."

"The one time Tony boobed was when the girl turned out to be a bricklayer's mate."

"If there was a face for the job," explained Ralph, "fishmongers would all look like him." He pointed to a man wearing a brown raincoat and carefully fitting his pint tankard between the loose ends of his moustache.

"They do, old dear," said Hendon. "And car salesmen all look like me."

"Someone looks like me exactly," said Ralph. "Microscope, callipers, you wouldn't find a millimetre of difference between us. And he sells ant-powders."

"Where?"

"Anywhere."

"Where is this man who looks like you?"

"Nearer than you think. The point is, would you be right – you ought to be – if you said *I* sold ant powders and that man, the fishmonger, is a ladies' hairdresser because somewhere is a man who looks like him who *is* a ladies' hairdresser?"

"He's not a fishmonger," said Ginsberg, "or a hairdresser. He's a policeman."

They all looked at the man and no-one smiled when Ralph suggested, "A Keystone Cop?" It reminded him of something, a tune or a game or a ritual of his childhood, the old ring-o'-roses ritual.

"Go on, Tony, tell us his force, and his number."

"I don't believe it," said Ralph, "I don't believe that's a policeman."

"So find out."

"Find out?"

"Go and ask him."

The children used to stand round and the ritual was to load the boy in the middle and the purpose was to leave only a crowning absurdity for the victim to break out by.

"I couldn't do that."

"It's your place to, you're the unbeliever."

"He wouldn't tell me. I mean, perhaps he's disguised – he won't want to be known."

"Then watch for his reaction. You can do that, can't you?"

A crowning absurdity. Ralph turned away.

"Afraid he'll book you, old dear?"

"Inez! Bring him a whisky to get his nerve up."

"Make it a double."

"If Mr Brown wants another drink he'll ask for it."

"Challenge him so that we can all hear."

"We don't care how you do it, twist his arm, threaten his wife, but make him tell you the truth."

"What did you call me?" Ralph asked Inez.

"Brown's your name, isn't it?"

"Who said so?"

"I don't remember."

"But you must remember!"

Inez shrugged. "I hear a lot when I'm not listening."

"You're trying to back out, old Brown dear."

"It was Jack Tomelty, it must have, been." Ralph had a clear vision of Tomelty's string-tight grin. "It's his idea of a joke."

"Is it funny to be called Brown?"

"He should have been called yellow."

"Turd and turd alike," said someone.

"My name isn't Brown!"

"It's Zunt."

"Look here, I'll do as you say, I'll try – "

"It's not what we say, old Brown Zunt, it's you who said he's not a policeman."

"All right, I'll ask him – "

"You can't," said Ginsberg. "He went when he saw you looking at him."

Ralph knew that if he went back to Lilliput Lodge he would knock and go on knocking at their door until he saw

Marise. He had such a need to see her, unreasoning, like a thirst, and what excuse could he give for knocking?

He remembered a performance of *'La Bohème'* and the girl knocking on her neighbour's door because her candle had gone out. Suppose he said to Tomelty, "Will you light my little candle?" It fitted into the John Brown joke, but he couldn't laugh alone.

The steak-eaters had broken their ranks round him, casually dispersed into knots of two and three. Now there was no pack, just people in private groups which he could not join. Inez, who had called him "Mr Brown", was talking elbow to elbow with one of them. Ralph and the girl in dark glasses were the only two not deeply engaged in conversation.

He went out to the car park and leaned against someone's big car, a steak-eater's probably, and looked at the black sky. It was a fine night, tomorrow would be a fine day. Tomorrow he would take Marise to Thorne. That was another absurdity.

Scobie would have seen the joke. She had assumed the status of the dead before she actually died. The dead know everything, are mixed up with everything. It seemed so to Ralph. Since Scobie died he had never had a mind entirely his own. If there was any wrong in what he did, it was done to Scobie who could not be harmed but who always knew. That was why he thought of her, because she was the only one who knew. Bertha, in ignorance, was – or ought to be – in bliss.

He began to walk, conscious that he was wambling, treading on mattresses. The rum lodged inhospitably in his stomach and he remembered that he had not eaten. Bertha would have worried, what a lot of worry she was saved by being so unknowing.

Tomorrow he would see Marise, hear her speak, touch her, he might even – he paused and tenderly explored the contours of a wrought iron gate post. Miracles were right and there was no wrong in this one. He fondled the gatepost and wondered if Scobie, now on the side of the angels, had worked it for him. It was her style, she had always sought to disturb him for his good. He was too tidy, she said. But not any more, he thought, he could never again be tidy. He wasn't disturbed, he was split.

He sat down on a garden wall. Trehearne Park was the name of this quiet residential area and there was no-one about, no movement except for a breeze rustling a bush. Just that one bush.

There was the question which he had already asked – why should she want to think that he was a murderer? and accepted the answer – because it amused her – and then been ridden by some God- or man-forsaken curiosity which wanted to know if by "amuse" was meant "entertain". It was fun? Comic? What sort of fun? What kind of comedy? And was she laughing with him? And with someone else too? Last and longest with someone else? And what could be genuinely laughable, even after fifteen healing years, about John Brown? Which was the funny side of murder and mutilation?

He spread his knees along the wall and took out his pipe. He was not bothered tonight. Tonight he believed that these questions had answers which would be entirey acceptable when he knew them. After tomorrow, perhaps: he would know much more after tomorrow.

As he lit his pipe he saw the lilac bush on the grass verge opposite wag in the wind. Just enough wind for that one bush, not enough, on his side of the street, to bend the flame of his match.

Perhaps he should be prepared never to know the actual answers. He might have to be content with the feeling of content, he might have to hold on to that long after tonight. There must have been faith for the miracle to happen and there would certainly have to be faith for it to continue. Before he asked questions, he told himself, he should be sure that he had the right to. He should also be sure that he had the wit to understand the answers.

He held the matchbox over the bowl of his pipe. When he let the smoke out of his mouth there was enough light from the street lamp to see it slowly shred away. He found a loose stone on the top of the wall and threw it at the lilac bush.

What happened next was confused by the headlights of a car which swung round the corner. Something came out of the bush and went away down the shadowy street. It was brown in colour and big enough to be a man. The car stopped in front of Ralph and he got off the wall and walked away too.

He was sorry about throwing the stone and startling some poor devil probably trying to attend to the wants of nature. The thought made him smile, it *amused* him. Wasn't it unkindly fun – and the difference between her amusement and his only in the degree?

Life, now that he was coming to think of it, supplied the answers. They were all ready, the whys and wherefores – no ball without a socket, no put without take – the only need being to recognise them, as he had this little demonstration of what made people laugh. If he kept his eyes open he ought to be able to pick out the truth, bit by bit, in all its shapes and forms. He wasn't worried about the shapes and forms, nor about the truth itself, the truth of a miracle had to be good.

Pausing to attend to his pipe which was burning too hotly, he had the feeling that he had suddenly been challenged. He looked up. The street stood empty, the lilacs and Scotch pines were still as paint and if he heard anything it was the gritting of someone else's shoe – that poor devil, perhaps, still trying to meet the needs of nature. Ralph gently knocked out his pipe and walked on.

He was strolling along the Causeway, a locality lively with people and traffic, when he knew without doubt that he had company and was being accompanied as well. This time, when he turned, there were people behind him, and one of them wore a brown raincoat. Ralph saw long loose moustaches and recognised the fishmonger whom Ginsberg had said was a policeman, the brown shape which ran out of the bush, the scrape of the shoe, the poor devil not attending to the wants of nature in Trehearne Park. He was following Ralph.

Thereafter the evening progressed to its logical inconclusion and later Ralph realised that there had been another little demonstration, another answer supplied. He had not recognised it at the time. Indeed he chose not to recognise it, and the moment he started to run from the man in the raincoat he had chosen to play games.

At first there was nowhere for them to hide and seek. The Causeway was a well-lit thoroughfare, and wide. They dodged among the passers-by, at least Ralph dodged. He infiltrated into a group leaving a bar and crossed the road in their midst. When he looked back from behind a stationary car the fishmonger was barely two yards away.

Ralph walked on, catching reflections in the glass of the shopfronts. He was able to watch the fishmonger's tactics: they were not subtle, they were dogged. The fishmonger was determined to keep an eye on Ralph, irrespective of what that eye might not see.

Ralph was unnerved, prepared to dodge and duck and ignominiously hide to get the fishmonger's eye off himself. At a road junction he darted across as the lights changed from amber to green. The roar of burked engines warned him that the eye had not waited for the red and he ran into an Underground station.

It was easy buying a ticket, but he couldn't decide whether to go east or west. It seemed important, but finally he ran down the stairs towards the rumble of an incoming train. The fishmonger ran too and they got into the same coach.

They looked at each other, Ralph to see what he was running away from, the man for reasons known to himself, strong ones seemingly. He put his hands on his knees and blew out his moustaches like some outdated animal working up to a charge.

Ralph thought that he wouldn't be able to appreciate the joke much longer. He considered asking the fellow why he was following. But he might not be following, it might be coincidence that he had left the same bar and run for the same train and got into the same coach. The thing to do was put him to a test.

Ralph sat back and closed his eyes and after the train had stopped four times, he got out. The station was Drayton Park. He walked in the direction of Holloway Road. He was as certain as he could be without actually turning to look that the fishmonger was behind him.

Traffic was heavy, he had a lively time – and so, no doubt, did the fishmonger – dodging back and forth. Ralph's idea was not to shake off pursuit but to establish it and he waited occasionally to give the follower a chance. He was following all right, as surely as if Ralph had him on a string.

Ralph found an alleyway running between the shops. It skirted a builder's yard and he stepped into the shadow of a stack of timber.

Someone came stamping along the alley and it annoyed Ralph that he made no attempt to muffle his footsteps. As he drew level, Ralph came out and barred his way. They stood chest to chest, the other man's breath gusting out, smelling of beer.

"Why are you following me?"

The man wiped his face with his hands, snorted into them as if they held water.

"You must think I'm a fool not to see what you're up to."

He was in his late fifties, with no claim to distinction save inverted oxbrow moustaches which gave him an embattled look.

"I don't like people following me – especially fishmongers."

He stared at Ralph, still breathless and pushed from the chase and not yet adjusted to the end of it.

"If you wanted to speak to me why didn't you stop me?

361

I've been having you along for the sole purpose of finding out what you're up to."

Was he up to anything? Anything acceptable or translatable? He might be a poor devil with a fixed idea that had chanced to fix on Ralph. He looked as if the idea had got lost and only the fixity remained.

"Do you want to speak to me?"

He opened his shoulders and made a violent sound, a kind of explosion of breath. His moustaches shot out with the force of it. Ralph got a clear impression of complete repudiation.

"And I don't want to speak to you, so there's an end of it. If you keep tailing me I'll turn you over to the police."

Ralph walked away, the man watching him. Could he be a deaf-mute? It would be a funny thing, but funnier things were happening. Ralph swung round, shouting, "Look out behind you!" and the man immediately looked behind him.

At the other end of the alley was a street of small houses. As he passed under a railway arch Ralph heard the rails whine with the vibration of a train. Beyond the arch was a football field. It was very quiet, the few sodium lights planted in the dark showed him that he was no longer being followed. He didn't know where he was nor why he should have come. The incident with the fishmonger rankled. It had no relevance, he had tried to give it some by running like a rabbit at the pop of a paper-bag.

He found his way back to the Causeway and traced a smell of coffee to an espresso machine in an Italianate restaurant. At least nine hours had passed since he had eaten anything. Bertha would worry – and why not? What else had she to worry about?

People were still eating at the red and white check tables. Ralph asked for steak and a cup of coffee.

"There's no steak," said the waitress. "Not this time of night. There's cold beef and pork pie and fishcake."

"I don't want fishcake. I'll have poached eggs and I'd like coffee right away."

"Now?"

"Yes, now."

A man and a girl were sitting at the next table, the girl was younger than Marise – she had puppy creases in her neck – and the man was older than Ralph. He took her hand and she took it away to draw salt rings on the tablecloth.

Ralph reflected that he and Marise were not like that, he and Marise would never be like anyone. Marise was unprecedented and she had made him exceptional. Like it or not, John Brown was exceptional. Bertha was not, neither was Emmy. Bertha was Ralph Shilling's wife. There was the sameness, there was his sense of guilt. That was why he had run away, like a guilty man. He looked up in anger and at the table on his other hand sat the fishmonger.

It was the last straw. Ralph got to his feet and stood over him. "I told you not to follow me."

"I've as much right here as you."

He was going to talk, but that changed nothing. Ralph picked up the lapel of his raincoat. "I'm going to give you in charge."

People were watching them, the fishmonger looked round to make sure of that before he said, "Why shouldn't I come in for a cup of tea and a sit down?"

"Who are you?"

"It's who you are that matters." He nodded round at them all. "By God."

Ralph was aware of some eyes and mouths open and an appetite for trouble. He released the man's coat. "You don't know me and I don't wish to know you," and sat down at his table.

"I know you, " said the fishmonger. He looked round again, took off his hat as if acknowledging applause and then placed it under his chair.

The waitress brought Ralph's coffee. "We don't want any trouble."

"I shan't make any. I'm waiting for my supper."

363

"I've only got one pair of hands." She asked the fish-monger, "What's for you?"

"Tea."

Without his hat he looked more like a butcher. Or a bricklayer, or a plumber. Or just a character part, a cue for a titter from an audience. Hair grew boisterously out of his ears and nostrils, the few strands left on top of his head were combed across and stuck down.

Or was Tony Ginsberg right? Ralph turned his shoulder and sipped his coffee. If this man was a policeman in disguise there was still no cause to be uneasy. He had done nothing, proposed nothing against the law.

"I've got a message for you." The man was staring at Ralph with lowered head and moustaches like tusks. "Leave my niece alone."

"I beg your pardon?"

"End of message."

It would make a humorous story, but who could Ralph tell it to? Bertha would be alarmed and Emmy suspicious.

"The message is – leave her alone!"

The girl and her elderly escort listened openly, so did the waitress. They weren't smiling, it wasn't funny to them.

"And next time I'll give it you another way."

Ralph supposed that the steak-eaters would appreciate the story, but it would have to have a snappy ending.

"I don't even know your niece."

"She told me all about you."

"Told you what?"

"You didn't know she had me, did you? And I've got something too." He sat back in his chair and told the room, "I've got something you won't like."

"Look, just who do you suppose I am?"

"She hasn't only got that teddy bear, you know."

Even as it was explained, Ralph understood why it had not been genuinely funny. He had been afraid of something like this, he had been afraid of exactly this.

"She's got her Uncle Fred Macey," said the man.

The waitress brought him his tea. She had spilled it into the saucer and he took up the cup and poured the tea back and briskly stirred in sugar, so briskly that the tea slopped out again.

Ralph's eggs arrived. He prodded them with his fork. What was 'all' to Marise? What had she told?

"You thought there was no-one to stop you. Thought you were going to have your way."

Ralph got up and went to his table again. "Did she tell you who I am – who she thinks I am?"

"I know who you are."

"But you see, I'm not who she says, it's just a joke between us."

"Ho, ho, some joke."

"It is rather macabre," agreed Ralph, "and I'm never sure how far she'll carry it. People might think she meant it. I suppose if you saw a likeness to someone you knew years ago you might be inclined to believe her."

"I never forget a face."

It was to have been private, for just the two of them to laugh at. If she had spread it to Fred Macey it wouldn't be the same joke.

"I was trained to use my eyes." Fred Macey's eyes were cut-away sections of foggy blue. "The Government paid for that."

"I'd expect a Government department – yes, even a Government department," Ralph said bitterly, "to require more than a chance resemblance to identify a man."

"I can identify you."

"My name is Shilling. It would be ridiculous if a private joke were taken seriously."

"I was a Special, they trained the Specials better than they did the Regulars. I know what you're after." There was a hint of collusion in his leer and Ralph's skin prickled. "You can't fool me."

"I tell you I'm not John Brown. Ask Tomelty if you don't believe me."

365

"Ask Jack Tomelty?" The foggy blue focussed on Ralph's face, yet Ralph had the impression that Fred Macey was looking furiously somewhere else.

"He knew John Brown, if anyone could identify him, Tomelty could."

"Ask *him*?" Ralph had shown the red rag to the bull, Macey saw only the red rag of Tomelty. "Ask that counter-jumper to tell me what to think?"

"His mother too. She knew John Brown, she'll confirm what I say."

"That to Tomelty!" Macey pushed up his first two fingers. "And his mother!" He reached for his hat and beat his way through chairs and tables.

From the door he shouted "Murderer!" and left Ralph to pay for his tea.

# 10

Marise was disappointed when she found they were not driving to Thorne. She had fancied going in that car, the one that Tomelty had ridden perched on the bumper. While it was annoying to be told that John Brown had no car, it was a lie to say that he could not drive.

"You mean you've forgotten."

"I never learned," said Ralph.

She was accustomed to conceding advantages, people did better than she did because they wanted to. She did as she wanted without considering the relative quality of what she did. But she didn't like liars, not even one whose interests wouldn't be served by truth.

"*He* had a car, Jack used to have rides."

"We could go somewhere by motor-coach if you prefer. There are excursions to all sorts of places. The Isle of Wight's very pleasant at this time of year."

"I don't prefer motor-coaches, I prefer cars because they're smaller."

Ralph had an idea. "We could go on a Mystery Tour. Would you like that?"

"I'd like to go to your house."

"Why?"

Marise thought that a tiresome question. To be asked showed his tiresomeness to the full – he was often not like what he ought to be – and to have to answer would be the most tiresome of all.

"I shan't tell you. It would be pandering to your bad side."

"My bad side? If I could be sure it was mine, I wouldn't mind. But I never know if you're mixing me up."

"You're mixed up already. Yes, no, right, left, that's you." He was obliged to turn away, realising that if he had thirsted for sight of her, looking at her was going to make him hunger. "Saying you can't just because *he* could. Jack

367

says the trouble with liars is they don't know where to stop."
Jack said that it was the trouble with her and he would be
glad to know where she began. He didn't understand that
she told the real truth. That was beyond him, sometimes
she had to pinch herself to try to see what he saw. "Are you
going to say you're alive because he's dead?"

"I'm not going to say anything about him. Shall we go?
There's a train at nine forty-five." He had a primitive feeling
that even this – especially this – bad start could be wiped
out if the actual name was not spoken.

"If he's alive you'll have to be dead. I can see through
you." Marise went to take Barbra out of the window. "She
shouldn't be there, Jack's gone away."

"Where to?"

"Ireland. He won't be back for a week. We needn't go to
your house today, we can go tomorrow, or the next day."

Ralph said quickly, "We must go today, it's all arranged."

"Arranged with who?"

When she looked at him like that, yes, he believed she
saw through him. His deceits couldn't stand up, she had the
innocence that swamped them and washed them away.

"I've taken time off from the office."

"You can take time off tomorrow, can't you?"

Ralph flinched, thinking of Pecry. "If you don't want to
go out we could stay here." He went close but did not touch
her. He touched the teddy bear which she had put on the
couch. "That would be nice."

"I want to go out. You must understand," Marise said
firmly, "I don't often get the chance. Jack won't let me, he
wants me to think I'm the only one alive. And when I'm
alone in this room I am the only one alive. I haven't got
used to it."

"To being alone?"

"No, to being alive." She went into the bedroom and
came out carrying a brown and white pony-skin coat.

"Shall I wear this? Jack brought it from Liverpool, he
says it's trendy, but I don't want to embarrass you."

Touching her under the soft hairs of the coat made him dumb. She said, as he helped her on with it, "Are you angry?"

He nodded. It was a kind of rage, one unknown to him, he trembled with the effort to suppress it.

"Then let's go!" She took his hand and pulled him to the door, she was suddenly completely happy with him. He wondered at the reason for it, which might be wrong, which in the context could only be wrong.

They walked hand in hand, it was the supreme moment of his life. He did not ask for better or more to date – the best was still to come.

"Do you see who that is?" Marise waved her free hand to someone on the other side of the street. "It's the old Madam from upstairs. Why does she wear two hats?"

"It looks like two but it's only one very elaborate one."

"She looks like two the way she's staring at us."

Ralph didn't care that Madame Belmondo was staring, he wouldn't have cared had Bertha and Emmy been staring too. They came into another story altogether and he wouldn't be at the ending of that one.

"I feel like running!"

Marise pulled at his hand but she soon had to give up. There could be no running beautifully with him, he was so clumsy and his money rattled in his pockets. People turned to laugh and no wonder, he was running with his knees pump, pump, pumping like pistons.

Marise laughed too and he asked her, "Are you happy?"

"Happy! You kill me!"

"Don't say that."

"You kill everyone when you look so funny."

He wanted to talk to her, he had a lot to say to himself as well as to her. Perhaps it was all to say to himself: he was the one in the net, she was poles apart, she was more than free. Tomelty couldn't come near her.

"Let's run somewhere we'll never be found."

It was what he might have said, would have started out

to say and after thousands of words might have bungled through to it.

"Do you mean that?"

There he went, fogging the issue, throwing up a defence against heaven. Why not take her at her words, why not *take* her? "I want you to be sure."

"Jack would never stop looking for us, he'd give up his life to it. So would Uncle Fred. But we'd vanish into thin air."

"I'm sure, I haven't a grain of doubt. We've both got the world to gain, I promise you that."

"Would your Bertha and Emmy go into mourning? Would you leave two widows?"

"I couldn't assume you felt the same, you see, I had to give you the benefit of the doubt. I'm careful by nature and with something as important as this – the most important thing, I may say, that has happened to me – I expect I shall be ultra-careful. If I didn't come forward quickly enough it wasn't because I don't feel – it was because I couldn't believe that you could think that much of me – "

"Let's run," said Marise. "There's a bus."

All the way to Thorne he was tormented by that conversation. He began to doubt whether it had taken place, and if it had, whether it meant what he thought it meant. Marise sat opposite him in the train, what was she thinking so calmly while he was trying to handle the bare bones of the idea of that conversation? Was she thinking about it? Or was she fifty-thousand thoughts ahead, was that how everything came to her, without question or surprise, just the doing?

He leaned across and asked, "Did you mean what you said about running away?"

"Of course. Aren't we?"

"Yes – but not now. Not today."

"Why not today?"

She was fifty-thousand thoughts and the deed ahead. She was already away, this railway carriage the start of her new

world. He felt both envy and compassion for the courage of
youth.

"For one thing, I haven't any money."

"You have in your pockets, I heard it."

He pulled out a handful of coins. "How long would we
last on that?"

Marise saw that it was going to be left to her, as usual.
People had absolutely no idea. Ralph Shilling was as bad as
Jack Tomelty for making the worst of himself and if she
didn't stop him she was going to be bored, he would stamp
her right into the ground with boredom.

"We should need money," said Ralph and noticed the
implied condition – *if* they went away, *if* he took her, *if* he
allowed miracles to happen. "Don't worry, I can get it."
Where and how were some of the fifty-thousand thoughts,
but the deed was at the end of them and he would get it.

"Which is Mrs Brown? Bertha or Emmy?"

She watched him put the coins back in his pocket, he
was not like Jack who started something else when he was
stopped. Nor like Uncle Fred who had to be turned out.

"Oh look!" A flock of birds wheeled across the sky. That
was what she looked for, that cutting and driving and smoothing away was the finish of something she herself had
begun, something that forever needed finishing. The day
would have been worth it, even if there was no more to
come.

"They're gulls from the estuary. We get out at the next
station."

There were no taxis in the yard and he said they would
have to wait for one to come back. He hoped it wouldn't
be long but there was no telling at this time of day.

"Don't let's wait," she said, "let's walk."

"It's a long way."

"I don't want to wait any more." She had been maintain-
ing her interest since they left Lilliput Lodge. It wasn't easy
because her instinct was not to be here at all. "Where's all
the light coming from?"

371

"The estuary. When the tide's out it reflects like a mirror."

"What is this estuary?"

"You'll see in a moment."

As they walked down the road the enormity of it overcame him. What on earth was he doing, bringing her here to Bertha and Emmy? Emmy had not been well, it was ten to one they hadn't gone to Chelmsford. The prospect of bringing Marise face to face with them turned his inside over.

"Let's go back." He pulled her round. "The up-train's signalled, we haven't long to wait."

She shook off his hand and ran and he watched her. He had not had an opportunity of seeing her from a distance before. He saw that she took it all with her, everything moved down hill into category. For a moment there was just a girl, some girl in a pony-skin coat, just an earthquake, just a world-shaker. He thought never mind, she doesn't know which way to go.

But she stopped to ask some men working on the railway bank. "Where's Thorne Farm?"

"Thorne Farm?"

"Over there. Maybe three miles."

"Mrs Openshaw's? More like four."

"How do I get there?"

"You've got a long walk. Why don't you wait for the bus? It'll take you best part of the way."

"There won't be one for half an hour."

"More like three-quarters."

She cried, "I don't want to wait!"

They began to direct her but she heard Ralph's footsteps and turned. "I know what it is, you don't want me to see where you live."

"There's nothing to see."

"There's a farm, isn't there?"

"It's pointless. A waste of time."

"Why? What else would we have done?"

He drew her out of earshot of the workmen who had downed tools to listen. "What do you expect to see?"

"Cows, pigs, ducks."

"Please be serious."

She looked puzzled. "It's called Thorne Farm, isn't it?"

"It isn't a farm and I'm afraid you'll be disappoined."

Afraid, yes, because her disappointment would be the death of him, and in taking her to Thorne he was sabotaging his chances. What interest or kinship or illusion remotely helpful, even remotely kin to himself could she find there?

"We could have gone anywhere you liked, we could have gone to the sea."

She pointed to beyond the next curve of the road. "We are at the sea."

"That's the estuary. The open sea is miles away."

"I hate the sea." She turned her shoulder to the empty sky, the hairs of the pony coat split softly against his hand as they walked. "Why did those men say it was Mrs Openshaw's?"

"It is Emmy's home. I'm only the weekend guest."

Marise sighed. She was finding it a strain to keep interested with so much bright air chilling and belittling her. It was a relief when he helped, she was sure now that he had something to hide.

At the turn of the road they came into full sight of the estuary, cubic miles of sky and inch-high land. The mud gave back the light, and more. On a bright day it was like looking across the flashing blade of a knife.

"I suppose the truth isn't enough for you," said Ralph. "I see why, of course, but I can't help wishing and hoping you'll make do. It's so hard to live up to anything else, good or bad." He hesitated, then tried it with a smile, "I do find it terribly hard to live up to someone as bad as John Brown – in the way he was bad."

"It's so bright – I can't see." Marise hid her face in his shoulder.

"There doesn't seem to have been any reason for him to

do what he did. It wasn't for money or revenge or to get out of trouble. You know, I have to have a reason, I have to have something to go on."

"What reason?"

"The trouble is, I can't think of any."

They stood in the road, he was stiffly holding her and a strand of her hair blew against his mouth.

"I don't like it here, all this light makes me cold."

He held her closer. "We could go into the field where it's sheltered and the sun is warm."

"There's too much of it. I don't like a lot of anything. You should have told me it was like this."

"It's only air." The strong scrupulous light always bucked and excited him. "Air and mud."

"I shan't look again." She moved resolutely forward, head up, eyes tightly closed.

"Why not? The estuary isn't so beautiful but it's not ugly."

"It makes me feel sick to death." She opened her eyes to accuse him. "Is that why you brought me here?"

"Why do you say such things?"

"Let's get away!"

She pulled at his hand and absurdly they ran to get away from the estuary and the estuary followed them, the fields like moss and the houses like dice – and farther than the eye could see, round corners, behind backs, the strong shine of the mud.

"Wait – please – " he was soon out of breath – "presently you won't see it, we'll be in the village."

"You can't run," she scolded him, "because your pockets are full of money."

"I wish they were, we'd run far enough then."

"Would we?"

"If my pockets were weighted down with money we'd run like the wind."

She couldn't follow that sequence. In her thought she often ran away, simply opened the door and went. Why shouldn't she do the same in reality? The running was important, she ran through places she knew and did not know, past people she knew and did not know, ran beautifully for their sakes. She took them out of themselves, they would always remember seeing her run.

"I want to get away from here. There's too much of it!"

"I'm sorry you don't like the estuary. I'm rather fond of it. When the tide's in it doesn't look so big. And although all that mud looks empty it isn't, it's full of life. Crowded, in fact."

"There's too much life!"

"You can't have too much life – " only a dealer in pesticides could – "or too much air or too much breath."

"I can," said Marise, "and there's too much time to wait before it's over."

"All things bright and beautiful" were words that came into his head as he looked at her. She shone, but not like the estuary. She was probably the sum of bright things, of all beautiful creatures great and small. It must be the balance of Nature which caused her to talk like that, every bright and beautiful creature had to have its imperfections. But if she could only be faulted by her own unhappiness it was Tomelty, not Nature, who was making her unhappy.

"You've got to get away – " he held her bare wrists, the sleeves of the pony coat were too short, Tomelty couldn't even get her size right – "you've got to leave him."

"Leave who?"

"It won't be wrong, it will be no crime, he's not your husband in the true sense of the word." The small cold bones of her wrists made him wild. "He's only your keeper – "

"Leave Jack?"

"And come to me." As he said it he saw pictures of his future, he saw the scene with Bertha, he was leaving her and she was crying: he saw the encounter with Pecry, he was leaving Pecry too, and he saw the confrontation with Tomelty who snarled like a dog. He saw Marise and himself indissolubly together at last.

With the power of the moment he bent to kiss her but she broke away.

"I can't leave him."

"You can, you must."

"I can't stay here, I'll die!"

To his consternation she began to cry "I can't bear it!" and to cover her ears with her hands and to sink to the ground. The tears came through her skin, her face was slippery with them but her eyes were dry. She was crying and fighting to get down to his feet and he believed she would have lain with her face in the earth if he hadn't held her up by force. "I can't, I can't, I can't!"

"We'll get away, right away," he said, not really knowing what it was all about. In desperation he half-carried her, shielding her face, holding down her fists. "Just a little farther and you won't see it. It's almost gone, we're coming to houses, look – a street and houses – "

It was the middle of the morning and there were people about who turned and stared. They could hardly do otherwise, Marise was raging like a small storm and Ralph was at the centre of it. An unimportant part of his mind hoped that nobody knew him.

She calmed down when she felt the houses round her, she could only have felt them because she was past seeing and identifying. He judged her well advanced into hysteria and as she returned to normal he felt the full shock of it.

Guiding her into the lounge of a small hotel, a place he had not been into before, he said violently, "We'll stay here and rest. We must rest – "

He was the one in need. Now that it was over, she looked almost unblemished. He saw that she was drying out like a plant in the sun, retaining only a slight extra tenderness after a storm.

Marise looked about. The brown Windsor dusk and the thick carpet solaced her.

"It's nice here."

Ralph felt shaken, extremes always did shake him. So far

as he was concerned both ends of the scale were unhappy, he trusted only in the medium. But this extreme of hers committed him even more deeply to her, and committed her to him. And he was glad, he was indebted to anything that did that.

"What frightened you?"

"That place. I shall die in a big empty place."

"You don't go out enough. You're like a plant – " he was going to say "pot bound", but it didn't sound nice. "He's done this to you," he couldn't bring himself to utter Tomelty's name either. "You're deprived of life."

He had no key to Thorne. As Emmy said, it was unnecessary because she or Bertha would always be there to let him in. So he had been obliged to borrow Bertha's key, without mentioning it, of course. He planned that when he and Marise left the house he would drop the key into some corner where Bertha would find it sooner or later. She often mislaid it so it wouldn't seem curious.

But the nearer they drew to the house the uneasier he felt. At best the episode could only be a waste of the scant precious time they had together, at worst it would damage him, and if it didn't go according to plan would lay him in ruins.

There wasn't even a plan in the proper sense, simply an assumption that Bertha and Emmy would be out of the house. If they weren't, if for any of fifty reasons they had stayed at home. . . It didn't bear thinking about and thinking certainly didn't help.

"It's big." When they came to the beginning of the track and Thorne was in sight Marise was surprised. "I didn't think it was a big house."

"There used to be a dairy and a farm kitchen. The dairy's been made into a garage and the kitchen is used for storage. There's not really all that much living space." Emmy took the living space for her private battle, the estuary would not have been too big for Emmy. He knew that he would know if she was in the house as soon as he opened the door.

"Why don't you stay here? It's nicer than Lilliput, that place is fit to drop."

The car was missing from the garage and he saw grounds for optimism. Of course Bertha might have gone to Chelmsford leaving Emmy at home and it would be neither materially worse for Bertha's not being here.

"Are we expected?" wondered Marise.

It was so quiet, as they walked across the grass she heard the stalks brushing her shoes. Naturally he would choose a lonely place.

"What a lot of flowers," she said disapprovingly, looking at Emmy's garden.

When Ralph opened the front door he confronted the very material difference of Emmy's not being at Thorne. The place hung together, exhausted.

Now that Marise found herself where she had wanted to be she saw at once that the house was not as she had wanted. Things rarely came up to her expectation: she was happiest with expectations, could have a wonderful time, any time, expecting. She might, she supposed, come to want what this house was – if she could make up her mind what it was.

Ralph closed the door, resisting the impulse to carry in a parcel which the postman had left in the porch. A little thing like that could give them away.

"There's no-one at home. Come and sit down, you must be tired."

Marise hadn't expected that they would be alone at Thorne. She had expected to see the women and talk to them. She expected them to tell her illuminating things.

"They've gone to Chelmsford shopping."

She had expected to pity them. They were to be pitied, she thought, looking at Emmy's Benares brass.

"Did you know they wouldn't be here?"

"It makes matters easier anyway."

What matters? It might become utterly illuminating being

here alone with him, miles from anywhere, beyond help. With a prickling of her shoulders and thighs she watched him opening doors and looking into rooms. He was making absolutely sure that they were alone.

"What are you going to do?"

He turned and looked at her for a long moment, he was thinking what he could do, she supposed, thinking what he had done last time.

"We'll have a drink."

From the window she saw that the trees and hedges stood closely round the house and the sky was slotted between, not enough sky to have any colour, less sky, even, than she could see from her window at Lilliput Lodge.

"Is there anyone next door?"

"Next door's a mile or more away."

No-one would hear her scream, if she screamed. That would depend on him, perhaps he had brought her here to scream, perhaps he fancied a little screaming.

"I didn't think it would be like this."

Indeed she did not, thought Ralph, she couldn't imagine anything so alien as Thorne, the living couldn't imagine partly-living.

"I come at week-ends and keep a razor and pyjamas here – and slippers, we don't wear our slippers downstairs. You see, it isn't my house to do as I like in."

"In hotels you put on your shoes to have breakfast."

"In hotels you pay to do as you like."

"What are these?" She had seen the array of elephant whips and Khyber knives and Caucasian daggers. They were arranged in a circle on the wall above a stuffed oryx head.

"They're relics of a fondness for killing."

"There you are!"

"No, you are not. It wasn't my fondness and they aren't my relics."

She stroked the oryx, pushing her fingers into the dead fur of its nose. Her back expressed non-hearing, it was the duck's back and he was water running off it. She did not hear Ralph Shilling, she heard John Brown, she saw John Brown in the Colonel's hunting trophies, she would see him all over the house, she would have seen him in Emmy, she would even have seen him in Bertha.

"Did you expect to find Miss Fran's head stuffed and hanging on the wall?"

"That's not nice."

"It's nonsense. All of it's nonsense." He poured a shot of Emmy's whisky. When he turned round Marise was taking off her coat.

"I want to see everything."

"A guided tour of John Brown's body's place? Would you like a drink first?"

"Don't you think about anything but heads and bodies?"

She said she wanted to see upstairs, where he slept with Bertha. She didn't put it like that but he did: thinking of the double bed there was no other way of putting it. He couldn't look anywhere in that room without seeing it. The bed – not putting too fine a point on – was the big white sign of his one and only fusion with Thorne.

Unwillingly, he took her upstairs. He didn't wish to see her in his and Bertha's room, it would be all wrong. And then, even as they went in, he was struck by the notion that if it became even more wrong, if he were to see her actually in that bed, in Bertha's bed, it could tip over into being absolutely right.

"It's small for two people."

"Is it?"

"Isn't there a bigger room?"

"On the other side of the house. That's where Emmy sleeps."

"She must be mean."

"She isn't. She thinks if there's a stream this side it might be bad for her health."

"Why?"

"Well, if she thinks so, I suppose it is. There's power in thought." He looked at her steadily. "Isn't there?"

"If she thinks there's a stream and there isn't really – there's isn't really." Marise went to the bed and prodded the pillow. "Hasn't she ever looked?"

"She's thinking of underground streams. There might be, I suppose, running into the estuary."

"She'll have to dig to find out, won't she?"

"She wants me to get a water-diviner."

"With a twig? To walk round with a twig? Can I come and watch?" She sat down on the bed. "It's comfortable, I think I'll lie here and rest."

She did, she lay back on the pillow, the scanty skirt of her dress peeling up round her thighs, and she looked at him gravely.

"Tell me about your Emmy."

He could hardly believe his eyes. Seeing her there was so wrong and so right, in Bertha's place in Bertha's bed was wrong. Then he forgot Bertha, for the rightness of Marise was supreme. He knelt beside the bed and reached out for her.

Marise knew the gesture. She took a practical interest in sex as the means of getting her softer options and she kept a temperate eye on the reactions she aroused – the eye any mechanic with pressure to maintain might keep on a gauge. She had learned how to take evasive action and when it didn't succeed in evading, how to keep herself for herself.

She rolled away across the bed and stood up on the other side. The eiderdown filled out as her body left it, Ralph was left with his arms in the pink satin billows.

Marise picked up a framed photograph of Ralph and Bertha on their wedding-day. "Is Emmy in love with you?"

"Emmy wouldn't let herself get into love with anyone. She likes to keep tidy."

He got up off his knees and brushed his trousers and Marise said, "So do you."

He wondered if he should tell her that he was in love with her. But he didn't think she knew the meaning of the words if she could use them in connection with Emmy. Although she didn't, of course, know Emmy.

Marise put down the photograph. "Why didn't Bertha carry a bouquet for her wedding?"

"She carried a prayer book."

Marise sat at the dressing-table. She took the lid off Bertha's powder-bowl and smelt the powder and tried some on her face. It was too tawny and looked like mustard on her. She examined each item in turn with an interest that vexed him. Picking up Bertha's hair-brush she gazed into the bristles. "I hope she's not grey."

He ought to get the situation in hand, he was allowing things to happen, prejudicial things, and since when had he been able to risk prejudice?

Marise imagined herself sitting at this mirror every day. It would be an enormous relief, like the cessation of life-long tooth-ache.

"I wish I could stay here," she said, meaning from the moment on, so that her hairs were in the hair-brush and the furniture was hers in all the rooms and had never been anyone else's and no-one had sat on the chairs and slept in the beds before her, nor would after her, so long as she lived.

"You can't."

"Why not?"

The absurdity of what was happening, the sheer nonsense of it, made him hot. "For two good reasons – Emmy and Bertha."

"Get rid of them."

"What?"

"There must be a kind way, you like to be kind, don't you?"

He watched her curl a strand of her hair in one of Bertha's curlers. "That won't be necessary. I'll simply go away and take you with me."

"I want to stay here."

"We'll find somewhere by the sea, the real sea – or in the

country if you don't like the open space. I promise I won't put you through that again. We'll go as soon as I can make arrangements – it will only take me a day or two – "

"Talk, talk, talk!" She cried into the mirror, "Nothing happens any more. It's all happened to other people!"

"No!" He put his hands on her shoulder blades and struck her rather than pulled her into his arms. She turned her face aside and stood, dangling stiffly, her chin in her shoulder, and between his fury and tenderness and fear of doing the wrong thing or not doing anything at all he was ready to break her neck to get to her lips. "This must happen – "

"I don't believe you're John Brown." She spoke out of his fingers. "Nobody does. You're as like him as a tenpenny rabbit."

He had believed that he would brush the dew off for a moment, an exclusive, recurring moment, recurring only to him, and had bitterly longed to do it.

"Then why did you pretend – " the less to accuse her he amended that to – "Why did you let me think it was important to you to believe it?"

"I tried to help you." His hand felt like the flat of a knife pressing between her shoulders. "Jack did it for a laugh, but I did it to help."

She was so close that her neck curved out of his own chest. With his finger tips he stroked the moist skin of her cheek and pressed the flesh into the bone.

"You wouldn't help yourself," she said, "you left everything to me. I've had enough, I shan't try any more." She wanted to move away because she had had enough of that too. He was pulling at her as if he meant to pull her to pieces. She put her hands on his chest. "You're hurting – " He was worse than Jack, she saw that he wouldn't laugh or cry and it caused her a stab of uncalled-for alarm.

She began to fight him. They struggled in desperation, he was unaware of the damage she did to him but she was mutilated by every hurt and plundered by the restraint of his hands. She tried to slip through them like a child in a tantrum. Her head fell back and her dress rode up. He dropped with her to the floor, chest to chest, and pinned her down with his weight.

It was a shock to him afterwards to realise how he had refused to hear the roar of the car along the track. He wondered what sort of madness it was, fallen angel's or risen beast's, that could ignore Bertha's first gear like a tractor going up a mountain. Some saving instinct brought him to earth when the engine stopped. He got to his feet and stood over Marise, straddled her as she lay.

"Help me." There was her torn and twisted dress – put that right, he meant, but didn't think it could be. If she was willing and able to hide what had been done to her, she couldn't hide what had been done to her clothes. He raised her and pushed her into a chair. "Do something, please – "

But going down the stairs he wondered what he was worrying about. It must be force of habit because what Bertha and Emmy thought was of no consequence now and never would be again. Damn them, he thought without rancour, agreeably even, it was such a free feeling.

Then something, the good-plus atmosphere of the place, extinguished it. He had better be prudent, not over-concerned nor throwing anything away, not yet.

He brushed himself down and paused to check in the mirror. What they might notice about him was his freedom, that was glaringly obvious. He stood smoothing his hair as Bertha opened the door. He had the brave feeling of being about to upset his own applecart.

They exclaimed at sight of him. Bertha was startled and said "Oh!" and Emmy uttered her cry which could be of pleasure or pain. They were both so familiar – like the start of the National Anthem. They could never surprise him again.

Bertha put down her shopping-bag and came to him. "Is something wrong? Ralph dear, whatever's the matter?"

"What are you doing here?"

He did not miss the suspicion in Emmy's voice.

384

"Aren't you well, dear?"

Bertha was eager, always looking for trouble to take on.

"How did you get in?"

He smiled. So Emmy suspected him of forcing a lock. "With Bertha's key."

"You had it? I thought I'd lost it."

"*Why* did you get in?"

"Oh Ralph, you didn't come all this way just to bring back my key?"

"No."

"Then why?" said Emmy. "On a Tuesday?"

"Why not? On Tuesday or any other day?"

"One would expect you to be working in your office on Tuesday."

"I took time off." They were mystified: Bertha preparing reasons for him, Emmy preparing to explode them. "You're back early from Chelmsford," he said.

"Emmy was tired, she couldn't even stop to have lunch. Now we can all have it together." Bertha told Emmy, "That will be nice," and it irritated Ralph, it always did, having her try to make a treat of him.

He said coolly, "I don't imagine you can cater for two extra, we'll get something at the Plough."

"*Two* extra?"

"I have someone with me."

Emmy glanced towards the stairs and there was Marise coming down. Emmy's face seemed to collapse, the carefully erected eyebrows and the powder put on like fur and her boldly painted mouth suddenly lost coherence, as if something essential had been whipped away.

Marise had combed her hair and put on the pony-coat. She was solemn and looked at Emmy.

"Ralph, you didn't tell us we had company!"

"Who is this?" said Emmy.

"This young lady is a professional diviner," said Ralph. "Isn't that what you wanted?"

"I'm sure there'll be enough for four – "

385

Emmy caught at Bertha's arm. "A water-diviner? Is that what she is?"

"My name is Marise Tomelty," Marise said firmly. "How do you do?" She held out her hand. Bertha took it, Emmy did not move.

"You must excuse us, we had no idea my husband was bringing you, and my sister has been unwell, we had to come back from town because the shops tired her, and it's a good thing we did. They serve such stodgy food at the Plough and when you've come all this way you must have a nice lunch."

"We can't stay," said Ralph. "We're catching the two-fifteen back. I'll ring for a taxi."

"She's got a headache," Marise said of Emmy, and drew her finger across her own forehead at the hair line. "From outside in."

"How do you know?"

"She looks as if she's trying to see through eggwhite. I take two aspirins and lie down when I have a head like that."

Emmy was holding on to Bertha, leaning on her, Ralph noticed, and she was no light weight, Emmy was considerable in every way.

"Dear, you should be resting." Bertha tried to lead her to a chair but it was Emmy who obliged Bertha, as her prop, to move with her towards Marise.

"What did you find?"

"She found nothing," said Ralph.

Emmy ignored him. "Where did you try? Which part of the house? What happened?"

"She tried everywhere and nothing happened. There's no water under this house."

"There," said Bertha, with loving comfort, "isn't that what I've said all along? Perhaps now that Ralph's set your mind at rest we'll ask Dr Chinn to look at you – "

"Is it true?" Emmy said to Marise.

"Would you like a dowser's deposition?" said Ralph. "A signed guarantee that she found no water?"

"But I did."

Marise's coat had fallen open and as she pulled it round her Ralph saw the tear down the front of her dress, he hoped he was the only one who saw it.

"You told me to," Marise said to him, "and I did."

"I didn't tell you to do anything – except try for it."

"Well, I found it."

"Where?"

"Under the stairs."

Absurdly, they turned and looked at the staircase. Emmy left Bertha's side and started up it, she stood at the pedestal of the banisters, leaning on it and looked down at them as if she were in a pulpit.

"It's here in the middle of the house, where there's no getting away from it. I knew, I feel it taking my strength, bleeding me." She stooped towards Ralph, "You feel nothing, you believe nothing, care nothing. You were going to deceive me."

"He wasn't there," said Marise, "I was by myself when I found it."

"How did you find it?" asked Bertha.

"She can't tell you that," said Ralph, "it's a professional secret."

"Did you carry a hazel twig?"

"It's not essential. She could carry a rod, or a ball and chain or a penny marble on a string. She need not carry anything at all."

"My twig broke to smithereens," Marise told Emmy. "I expect you'll come across the bits."

"We must be going. I'll ring for the taxi," said Ralph.

"That won't be necessary," Emmy said sharply, "Bertha will drive you to the station."

"Bertha's tired – "

"We're both tired and I'm tired to death." Emmy turned to Marise with an eagerness which Ralph found alarming. "There's war in this house, in the air, in the timbers, in the

387

bricks." She made one of her old violent gestures. "And I'm the only one who will fight."

Marise nodded, glancing at Bertha. "She's the quiet one, isn't she?"

"She doesn't fight, she endures. Oh, don't make any mistake, she's stronger than me, she'll endure for ever, she'll never lose and never win."

"You'll never win either," said Marise.

Bertha began to say, "Of course I'll take you to the station, but what about lunch? You mustn't miss your lunch, it's so bad for you to miss your lunch, Ralph – "

"We'll get a sandwich." He took Marise by the elbow. "We must go now."

"You understand what I'm going through," Emmy said to her. "Lassitude, headaches, sleeplessness, that's the lesser part. I have pain, that's a protest from my body at having to put up such a resistance. Or is it a warning? Of what? What breaks down first under constant stress – heart, lungs, liver, bowels?"

"She isn't a doctor," said Ralph.

"My identity went first. I don't have my own thoughts now and I cannot manage my own body. I don't have my own nightmares either, God knows whose bogeys those are."

Marise looked at Ralph. "*He* knows."

"My brother-in-law has no imagination, he knows only what he sees." Emmy slid down and sat on the stairs. She looked unutterably tired and Ralph thought she could have her reasons for acting the fool – as Scobie had had hers for cutting him out. "I've always been physically strong, I've fought this for years without knowing it. Now that it's beginning to undermine my health and pull me into the ground, now I know what I'm up against."

"Ralph, talk to her," begged Bertha.

Emmy closed her eyes. "Yes, talk to me."

"You need Chinn to talk to you, not me."

"You're a man of few words and you mince even those. Why don't you say I'm mad?"

"You're frightened."

"I'd be a fool if I wasn't. Life's all I've got to lose, it's really all any of us has. You too, Ralph, for all the life you've taken, every little hour of every little bug must make quite an aggregate, but it hasn't put a minute on yours. Doesn't that frighten you, darling?"

It was Marise who answered "No."

Bertha blinked at her, Emmy seemed to accept that she spoke for Ralph. "He's only a killer by trade," she said, "he couldn't harm a fly if he had to watch himself doing it. It's so clean and tidy with sprays and aeroplanes. I think I should like him better if he did it for love."

"Love?" said Bertha.

"Enjoying it."

"I make my living," said Ralph.

"And was there no other way?" Emmy opened her eyes. "To do the worst for no reason is to be damned to hell."

"You've torn your dress." Bertha was gazing at Marise whose coat hung wide open. "How did that happen?"

"I think there's a waterfall under your stairs," said Marise.

# 11

That was on Tuesday. By Wednesday Ralph had reached some conclusions. One, he was finished with Thorne: whatever had been there for him had run out or ceased to matter: two, he was going to take Marise away: three, he needed money to do that: four, he could get his two hundred back, he now had nothing to lose from that quarter or from any of the old quarters. He recognised that the money was not absolutely his, but it was unquestionably more his than Picker, Gill's, or Krassner's. Two hundred pounds was the right shape and it was the only money in sight.

Throughout Wednesday morning he sat at his desk and thought. He scribbled on his noteblock, he saw that he was scribbling pound and dollar signs, and rows of boxes. It was inconceivable that he could have had that much money actually in his hand, the essential sum, and let it go again. He couldn't accept that it was gone, at this very late moment he experienced the sheer disbelief that would have followed had he just dropped it down a drain.

By lunch-time he was so occupied with the problem of the money that it went without thinking that everyone else was too. Pecry certainly must be, Pecry had the devil's own job of making the problem insoluble.

When Pecry asked, as they stood side by side washing their hands, "Did you settle that matter to your satisfaction?" Ralph did not reply immediately. He had no intention of telling Pecry everything, even though Pecry needed no telling. He pretended to be absorbed in soaping his hands.

"The family matter," Pecry said sharply, "which you had time off to attend to."

"Oh, that. Yes."

"No problems?"

"No."

"You're lucky."

"I had nothing to lose. That's freedom, when you realise it."

"Freedom?"

With Pecry's stiff collar choking the knot of his tie, the word came from his throat frivolous and brilliant, exploding over the washbasins and changing everything. One thing, one relatively small thing changed was Ralph's attitude. He was no longer afraid of Pecry, Pecry was invoices made flesh, a money sign, in himself worthless.

"It's an attitude of mind, ultimately it's just mind – " in his own case, Ralph remembered, there was body too – "you've only to change it."

"Change what?"

"Your problem's reputation, face is what you're afraid of losing, isn't it? So either settle on something lesser to lose, like your sleep or your money's worth or, better still, on something to gain – " but that was what Pecry was really afraid of, of gaining something lively and bloody which would disarrange his frozen grey muzzle – "and you too can be a free man."

Pecry tore off a paper towel and dabbed his hands. "I trust you're not trying to be offensive as well as nonsensical. I'm entitled to ask the nature of your family business since you were given the firm's time to conduct it in. Incidentally, it is not to be regarded as establishing a precedent."

"I promise not to have any more family business." Ralph said, eyeing himself in the mirror, "I think I can promise not to have any more family."

Pecry also looked at him in the mirror. "Questions of immorality are referred to the Board." He touched his dry mouth from corner to corner with his tongue. "You know the Chairman's views."

Ralph knew. Marriage was the bridge by which the Chairman of the Board spanned the gulf between himself and members of Picker, Gill's staff. They were all married, he told them, from the office cleaners through to himself, and those who weren't had soon better be. The advantages of marriage – material benefits and spiritual blessings – and, roguishly, the teeny drawbacks, came into his speeches and directives. He sent a personal gift when a member of staff married, as yet no-one had had the courage to get divorced.

"Tell him I intend to commit adultery as soon as I can afford it," said Ralph after the door had closed on Pecry.

He thought of borrowing money but knew no-one with that much to lend, except Emmy. He liked the idea of Emmy financing his escape with Marise, he would like to be the kind of man who could bring it off. Why not? He had only to think up a reason for the loan, a reason that would seem reasonable to Emmy. Like what? Like if he was unable to take Marise away from Tomelty he would soon be crazy. Yes, he thought soberly, I'll go out of my mind.

She was in his blood, sometimes a rage, always an ache. Everything tended to go into her as into a chasm – Bertha, Emmy and Picker, Gill, everything and everyone was swallowed up. Except Krassner: Krassner remained just outside, a finger-hold.

There was one other course open to him. He could cash a cheque on their joint account. The money was really Bertha's. Surprisingly, there was enough left of him for scruples, he would much rather not do it. He would do it, though, he would have to if he could get nothing out of Krassner.

He returned to the office after lunch, perhaps for the last time. He had been bound to the place, cherished his goings and comings at the same times with the same thoughts, and dreaded deviation. He had been content. Or dead. It didn't matter, he was alive now and fully operative, all his components working, the greater parts of him which had been sealed up and idle were working strongly and fluently, he was unafraid. He had the answer to everything. He had, he was going to have, Marise.

Krassner and a girl were cheek to cheek in Krassner's

office, her elbows on his desk, her rump elevated and swaying. Whatever they were doing they weren't working.
Krassner took a coin from his pocket and dropped it into
the neck of the girl's blouse. She shook herself lingeringly
– shoulders, breasts, hips and thighs – and the coin fell at
her feet.

"Tea money," Krassner told Ralph.

Ralph had given this girl dictation, she was self-possessed
in a narcissistic way, constantly stretching out a leg to look
at her ankle, lifting her lashes on her finger and checking
over her hair. None of that had been directed at him, she
was merely working at herself, she had found time to correct
Ralph's grammar.

He picked up the coin, as he handed it to her he wondered
what her melting point was. Krassner knew it, of course.

"I want to talk to you." He told himself that Krassner's
was not so much a golden as a buttery touch.

"Talk away."

"In my office," said Ralph.

As he sat at his desk to wait for Krassner the touch looked
more like a dirty thumbprint. It must make for sameness:
even success, he thought, even sexual success would pall if
it was a built-in feature.

"Shut the door," he said when Krassner came lounging
in.

"Secrets?"

"Yours."

Krassner back-kicked the door. It slammed and in the
draught the leaves of Ralph's noteblock stood up covered
with pound and dollar signs.

"I only have one," said Krassner, "and that really is
secret."

"Two hundred pounds is what I want to talk about."

"Whose?"

"It was Sweetland's, it became Picker, Gill's."

"Oh that two hundred." Krassner sat down and crossed
his knees. He wore yellow suede boots.

393

Ralph said sharply, "It was never at any time yours but it was, and still is, mine."

Krassner nodded. "Somewhere among Picker, Gill's bloated profit margin are those crisp clean Shilling pound-notes, back in the dirty waters of commerce where they originally came from."

"No!"

Ralph stopped himself, he couldn't say that the money was Bertha's and there was no point in saying anything else. "I want that money, Krassner."

"I understand your feelings, you're talking to one who loves money, though not as platonically as you."

"You're going to give me back my two hundred pounds."

"I am?" Krassner smiled. "Old chap, I'm so much in the red it shows through if I scratch myself."

"I'm not joking, I paid that money to cover your debt, your *crime*. You'll go to jail for defalcation, Krassner."

"Maybe I shall. You'll have a case to answer too. To Pecry. We know Pecry, he'll make two cases out of it, concealment of fraud and breach of trust. Oh boy!" Krassner shook his head and whistled through pursed lips. "The bigger they come, the harder they fall. I'm only fodder, but you're senior staff and Pecry will have his foot on your neck for life."

"I don't give a damn about Pecry – "

"He'll have you up before the Board, court-martial you and publicly unbutton you."

"Or about the Board, or about Picker, Gill. This is your debt, I met it to save your skin."

Krassner reached for Ralph's tossing-stone. "You met it to save your own. A stiff price for an office skin, but you knew what it was worth to you. Or did you?"

Ralph felt a rocket blast off inside him, illuminating Krassner, his mischief and his faculty for spreading it.

"You can't threaten me, not any more. I've nothing to lose. And I warn you – I warn you – " the blast reached

Ralph's fists, he was no fighting man but he had an urge to use them now.

Krassner smiled. "You've changed your tune. All right, you need two hundred pounds, a nice familiar figure and I can understand it, but I can't give it to you. Even if I had it. There are some prior claims, very prior. You're not even the left hind leg."

He was voluptuously slipping the polished stone from one palm to the other. Ralph leaned across and knocked it out of his hands.

"I don't care what else you owe or where you owe it."

"Why not ask Pecry? Legally it's your money, surely even Pecry wouldn't expect you to suffer *and* pay?"

"I don't care how you get it, just get it!"

Krassner good-humouredly picked up the stone and replaced it on the desk. "I'm truly sorry, old chap. Wish I could help. If it's so important why don't you do what I did?" Ralph had seen him smiling like that at women, handing them drinks that he hadn't paid for, touching them, stripping them with his smile. "You've got the motive and the opportunity – help yourself."

"I could kill you, Krassner!"

Indeed he could. The essential thing was to wipe out the smile and at the moment he could have killed to do it. But the desk was between them and the desk saved Krassner.


Marise had spent the day in bed. It was her practice to do so when too much had been happening. She curled herself up like a French roll, a 'cross aunt', as Jack said. She did not like to be taken far in any one direction unless she herself had chosen where it led.

Under the blankets, in darkness and privacy, she remembered the happening of yesterday. It made her tremble, it was almost the worst ever. The first time had been the worst because she had been totally unprepared and had almost died and had known that she could die, cut out of her bones while people looked on and held her down. She knew what it meant to be the butterfly on the pin when someone set fire to its wings.

She moaned, curling deeper into the dark. Nothing was finished or forgettable, Jack said that everyone went off balance sometime – at spiders or red rags or, in his case, temperance hotels. But this thing of hers was so almighty that she would have prayed to it if it would have done any good, asked to be let off a little, excused just enough to make it endurable. Painlessness she did not expect, not without she died and was born another person, but a little less cruelty, a grain of consciousness – the final humiliation was in not knowing herself – this she would have begged and prayed for if she thought anyone or anything was listening.

But she knew without being told that this was beyond human relations, that was what made it so terrible. It wasn't natural, either, it did not strike like lightning or swallow like an earthquake, it was all over the place and going on all the time.

Presently she was able to lie quietly, the dried salt on her cheeks, and think about the other. And she could smile, wondering how kings and policemen expected to be taken seriously if they all did this monkey thing. She had yet to meet with any style in it, let alone any mystery. And she had met it often enough, often and often. Propping her elbows, she lifted the bedclothes on her knees glimmering like eggs. Did style and mystery hide only a multitude of monkeys?

People who supposed Marise a fool believed themselves to be clever: 'fly' was the word Tomelty used, with him it was a matter of shadow-boxing so that no-one should go behind his back. Marise had noticed that people had to have other people to achieve cleverness, they couldn't achieve it on their own. She couldn't achieve it anyway, nor did she wish to. All she need do was wait for the monkey.

In the afternoon Uncle Fred Macey arrived. When she did not answer his knock he went to the window and beat

on it. She was afraid he would break the glass, she had to
get out of bed and let him in.

"What's up?" he said.

"Nothing."

"I thought you'd got trouble." He pressed down his chin
and looked at her as if she were a needle he was trying to
thread. "Thought I should have to force an entry."

"I was in bed."

"Are you ill?"

"Of course not." Marise walked about squeamishly in
bare feet, experiencing gritty dust and the cold pang of lino.
"I was still in bed from last night."

"You shouldn't go about like that."

"I like my feet bare." At Plummer Court she often didn't
wear shoes, walking on the wall to wall carpet was like
walking on birds. Jack had called her feet "P.A.New".

"In that shift thing you're damn near bare all over. Suppose someone was to see you?"

"You're seeing me."

"I'm family." Uncle Fred rubbed his mouth with the back
of his hand and left one bar of his moustaches cocked.

Marise had come across a packet of cornflakes and realised
that she had eaten nothing since yesterday. She took the
box to the window and ate the flakes from her fingers. It
was a grey day, the pebbles in the drive were the colour of
iron but a woman walking towards the house wore a hat
which Marise envied, butter-yellow and bristling. Marise
might have eaten it or warmed herself at it or just sat in its
glory. She recognised the woman without interest. Bertha
Shilling was a dull person and Marise did not care what she
might have come here for.

The cornflakes tasted of cardboard. Had Jack been at
home they would have had a meal and perhaps some of the
pink wine called 'Rosie'. She wanted him to be home
because the dread of yesterday was still with her. He always
understood and held her, gripped into a merciful little blackness. He wouldn't be home for four more days.

"What if that geezer upstairs was to see you?"

"Well?"

"It's incitement, that's what." Uncle Fred's clothes creaked with strain and all but broke down. In a moment he would come near enough to press his knee against hers and to breathe down her neck. Jack said he was a flesh engine: feed him food and combustion started, feed him sex and his cogs engaged. "You're asking for it, my girl. I've seen some that asked for it and I've seen what they got."

Marise watched Bertha climbing the steps to the front door. "He has a house with knives and whips all over the walls."

"Whips?" Uncle Fred, negotiating his bulk between the furniture, paused to stare.

"He has two women there and they do whatever he wants. They wouldn't tell me anything, they were too afraid. What does he want to do in all that space?"

"Space?"

She had not asked for it but the reminder came and she flung herself on Uncle Fred and screwed her face into his chest. The rank flavour of his old jacket was in her mouth and nostrils, her eyes were squeezed shut and still she was blindingly, hideously lost in white bottomless light.

"Here, here," said Uncle Fred, touching her with alarm.

"He took me to that place – horrible, horrible – "

"What place? Who took you?" Uncle Fred cottoned slowly. "Whips? Women?" and then, more rapidly, "You mean it was one of *those* places?"

"I can't bear it, I can't, I can't!"

"Here, here," he held her as if she were a damp baby. "You don't have to bear anything. Tell me what happened, tell me about this place."

"I'll never tell anyone."

"Did he force you to go? Against your free will, was it?"

She pulled away, his waistcoat buttons made weals on her cheeks. "I won't think about it any more."

"Listen, my girl, if he forced you to do what you didn't

want to, that's criminal assault. I know his sort – " Uncle
Fred's breath grew steamy – "rape, with specialities, three
in the bed and whips all round. Did he make you whip
him?"

"Of course not." She noticed that her arms were prickling
with cold and found Tomelty's dressing-gown. "He's a tenpenny rabbit." She put the robe over her shoulders and
crossed the sleeves under her throat.

"Tell me what he did."

"He did nothing."

"You'd better tell me or I shall make you." Uncle Fred
opened wide the tea-brown whites of his eyes, "Don't think
I couldn't."

Marise did not think so. She hadn't seen him violent
because the direct object of his violence had never been
present at the same time as herself, but if she were to be
the direct object she knew that he would not only be capable
of violence, he would enjoy it.

"Oh he tried, he tore my dress but he couldn't make
me." She said scornfully, "He couldn't make water run
downstairs."

"He tried, did he? He did try?"

Marise had just thought of the business of the water under
the house. She wanted to know more about that, though not
from Ralph Shilling, she preferred to be independent of
him, he was such a liar, look how he had lied about her
being a water-diviner. She wanted the truth about the water
– she could get the truth from Bertha Shilling.

"I'll make him pay for your dress – " Uncle Fred spat on
his knuckles – "I'll make him pay for trying. I'll be waiting
here for him when he comes in."

Marise had opened the door a crack. There was Mrs
Shilling in her splendid hat sitting in the hall. But Marise
couldn't question her and Mrs Shilling wouldn't answer with
Uncle Fred on hand.

"It's no use you waiting tonight," she told him. "He's
gone away."

"Gone away? Where? I'll find him – "

"He's gone to that place."

"Ah!" From under his waistcoat Uncle Fred erupted satisfaction and appetite together. "That place now, where is it?"

"I don't know. We went into the country where there were no streets and no names. We walked and walked, it was at the sea – "

"At the sea?"

"A horrible place." Marise shuddered. "I feel bad thinking of it."

"That bastard will feel bad when I get to him."

"You'd better go. I'm ill, I'm going back to bed."

"You said you weren't ill – "

"I am now!" cried Marise. "And I'm going to be sick!"

Uncle Fred had no ministering instincts, he left hurriedly. But when Marise looked out again, Mrs Shilling and her hat had gone.

# 12

Ralph admitted that Krassner had a point in suggesting that he ask for his money back from Picker, Gill. But Pecry wouldn't give it to him at once, Pecry would make him wait, would hold up repayment by putting it through all the hoops – Board meetings, Committees, agendas, staff policy – and on the question of precedence could examine and re-examine his conscience until the furthest of further notice.

It seemed to Ralph that he had been waiting through all his lifetime and through all women, through Scobie and Bertha anyway, without knowing what he was waiting for. Now that he knew, he ought not to wait any longer. Miracles could get cold.

He was living by degrees: the first to see her, the second to touch and apprehend her, the third had already begun, on the floor of Bertha's bedroom.

He obliged himself to go back over the fight, sitting woodenly at his desk while his inside flesh burned and froze at the memory. The fight had been shameful and had started something which, he knew, would give him no peace or other satisfaction on earth until it was finished.

Before time – he was no longer keeping to time – he left the office and hurried back to Lilliput Lodge. He could feel her, wave after wave coming out of the bricks of the house in deadly assault on his senses. But his senses didn't die, they awoke: many more than five of them flinched wide, wide awake.

His hand was out to knock at her door and then as he stepped into the porch he saw Bertha. She was sitting on a chair in the hall, her bag and gloves in her lap and her hands clasped on top. She wore her best suit and her important hat. But only the hat looked important, it bore no relation to her face.

Ralph's hand fell to his side, he only just stood still. His impatience carried him to the brink and something over. He looked at Bertha from the other side.

She stood up, dropping her gloves and bobbing to retrieve them. The sight of Ralph disrupted her though she must have been prepared for it. A strong pink flush ran up under her hat, totally unsuited to the yellow silk arabesques at the brim.

She said, "There you are, dear," and Ralph said, "What do you want?" and having said it was himself confused. But why should he be? After all, he had reason to ask and no time to ask any way but outright.

"I wanted to see you. I hope it's not inconvenient, dear."

"You saw me yesterday."

"That's why I want to see you today." She blushed deeper as at an improper witticism, and busied herself putting her gloves into her bag, snapping it shut with a beaky sound. "You're nice and early, I thought I'd have to sit here a long time yet." She managed to smile, apologetically, apologising for what she meant to do but meaning, he could see, to do it. Under the soft rind was the essential Bertha.

"We'd better go upstairs," he said.

She meant to ask questions. He could have asked them for her in one: "Why must it be different?" and answered: "Because I am different." And since it could not help her to know how different, or why, that should have been that, she should have said goodbye and gone straight back to Thorne.

"I'm so glad to see you," she said. He could have told her that that part was over, they had moved on and were past gladness in connection with each other.

"You saw me yesterday," he said again, impatiently.

"I don't get tired of it." She put her hand into the small of his back as she followed him upstairs and he sprang up the steps out of her reach.

The cat was waiting on the other side of the door, watching them both as they came in. Bertha took one quick, panicking look round the room and held out her fingers.

"It still comes – "

"Do you want anything?"

She looked up humbly from the unresponsive cat. "Only to see you."

"I meant any refreshment," he said irritably. "A cup of tea?"

"That would be nice, if it's not too much trouble."

He could feel Marise reaching up to him undiminished through two floors. Through Madame Belmondo's flat she drew on him like one of Emmy's underground streams. But she didn't make his head ache – he grimaced and smiled – not his head.

"Is anything wrong, dear?" said Bertha.

"I'm waiting for you to tell me." He filled the kettle and set out cups, thinking if it's going to be a tragedy it'll be an English one, with tea. "Emmy's not worse, is she?"

"She's no better." She exclaimed with sudden artificial gaiety, "Pussy wants its din-din – aren't you going to give it anything?"

"Why should I?"

"I thought you were fond of it. Emmy said it showed how kind-hearted you are – "

"Emmy said I was like a spinster with a neutered tom."

He turned to find her gazing at him with her shyness amplified into fear. She was on thorns and wouldn't get herself off them. She had come to ask questions and she wasn't asking. If she was so scared why didn't she simply wait and let things happen? She might have had another week or two's peace of mind, he might have thought up a story, he just might have left her something to keep her going a little longer.

"Ralph, I'm so worried, I had to come. Emmeline only has you and me and she trusts us and she's in our hands – "

"In our hands? You know better than that."

"She believes what we tell her." Bertha looked unhappy, "I think she would believe anything *you* told her."

"Emmy thinks what she likes." He turned up the gas

flame until it roared under the kettle. "You haven't come here to talk about her, have you?"

"I had to. You must know how things stand before ever you see her again."

"Why do you say that?"

"It's a matter of life and death."

It was the way she had said it that momentarily roused his curiosity, as if she already suspected that he wouldn't be seeing Emmy again, it was the "ever" that made him ask – not that it influenced anything in the long run.

"Every day counts. I can see the difference, what you'd call a difference in degree but every day it's a degree less of Emmy and a degree more of – something else." Bertha was trembling, the arabesques on her hat snapped and twinkled independently.

"What can I do? She won't listen to reason – from me or anyone."

"She listened to unreason from you."

"What do you mean?"

"That girl was not a water-diviner."

Here they were, here they went, Bertha and Emmy, hand in hand, with a whimper. He was glad and relieved that they were going together.

"She lives here," said Bertha. "I saw her name on the door of the downstairs flat."

He got on with the business of making tea. Let her ask, it was her chance to get an answer from him. When she brought the questions out again later on, one at a time, one a day, she would have to answer them herself.

"You lied to us."

"It wasn't the moment for truth."

"Truth?" She spoke fearfully, then, because this wasn't the moment either, put it aside, to come back to. "Emmy thinks it was the truth."

"Well, she'd want to."

"She's going to leave Thorne, she says she'll sell it and get away, she says before it – kills her."

"Emmy has these fads, they're the aim of an aimless woman. If it wasn't electro-magnetic radiation it would be food reform or anti-vivisection. She'll con herself out of a perfectly sound property and that will be a pity. But she's a business woman, she won't lose on the deal, not financially."

He set the tea tray on the table thinking how this would have disturbed him once: any threat of any change in the pattern of their lives had disturbed him. He used to cherish his routine and his habits, aware that they would seem pitiful small pleasures to most people and hoping thereby to rouse no envy and be allowed to keep them.

"Ralph, she's ill, organically ill – she can't run away from it." Bertha's eyes filled with tears. "That's the truth and that's what she can't accept."

Bertha was going to find it hard to accept too; he wished again that she had waited for the truth to come to her instead of chasing after it.

"Dr Chinn wants her to have an X-ray but she won't. She won't talk to him about herself, she says it would be like trying to treat sunstroke while sitting in the sun."

"Don't worry too much, she'll treat herself. If she does sell up the change will do her good, she needs something to keep her busy."

"Change? Busy?" Bertha was not afraid of these words as she had been of the word "truth", these she scorned and rejected. "Have you *seen* her lately? Really looked at her? Have you caught sight of her when she didn't know you were looking and wouldn't have cared if she had known? Of course not! When you're there she always knows and she always cares."

"You're wrong. Emmy despises me."

"Oh Ralph, Ralph – "

"There's nothing I can do."

"You can tell her the truth about that girl."

"Tell Emmy? Why?"

"Because I can't. You must see that I can't."

Neither could he, she must see that too. It was one thing

to tell her about Marise, one imponderable thing which he wanted over and done, and another to tell Emmy. The idea made him squirm.

"This is entirely your business and mine, not hers. I'll tell you what you should know and that's enough."

Bertha clasped her hands as if she were praying. She said her prayers each night kneeling by her bed and she might feel that an extra prayer might save her, she would know that she was the one who needed saving.

"Please, say that it was a misunderstanding, the girl misled you, you didn't know – "

"I'll say nothing of the sort. I don't care what Emmy thinks."

"I'm so afraid she may die because of what she thinks. She shouldn't be running to property agents, to lawyers, making out inventories, packing up furniture, she should be resting and having treatment. Ralph, I beg you, if not for her sake, for mine!"

He cut the air between them with a furious gesture. "Tell her yourself, tell her anything!"

Her skin darkened and thickened, this time with dismay: again, under the important hat, it was the wrong colour. She put down her clasped hands, prayer-time was over. She began to understand that she wasn't going to be saved.

"She'll be so angry, she'll never forgive you. Don't you see, if you don't tell her, she can't forgive you. She'll want to, later – " she looked up at him, "that will be the worst of it."

"I don't care if she forgives me or not."

"If I tell her she'll stop you coming to Thorne."

"If you don't tell her, there'll be no Thorne to come to."

"I could come to you. I should, shouldn't I?" Her gladness suddenly shone out, transforming her. "I'm your wife, my place is with you."

He picked up the teapot and put it down again. This was the moment, whether she was ready or not, but it wouldn't be appropriate to be pouring tea.

"The question won't arise. I'm going away."

"Away?" The gladness was still there, it had been so real and could not fade so swiftly, but it was losing depth. "Going away?"

"With Marise." The name was spoken between them for the first time, it broke out like a banner. He had to say it again, brandish and fly it. "Marise!"

Suddenly he wanted her so blazingly that to stay where he was was an injury. He got up and paced about, passing and re-passing Bertha who suddenly hadn't even an identity. The cat sprang from under his foot, the cat was nothing too – and knew it.

"This is the truth?" She had no doubt, she was formally acknowledging the enemy.

The truth was always hurtful to someone. Today it hurt her, tomorrow might be his turn. He would take the hurt as he meant to take everything, he was wide open, no reservations, scruples, conscience, manners.

"Yes, it's the truth."

Bertha had ceased flushing an unsuitable colour, she looked normal, a normal woman in a super-normal hat.

"You're going away. With her." Now that she was bringing out the questions she did not ask them, she used them – "You're leaving me" – tapped each one home like a nail.

"You can tell Emmy what you like. Tell her I'm a liar, pink Ralph's as black as hell. She'll believe you, she'll believe anything bad about me." He felt drunk with freedom. "Tell her I'm a murderer!"

Bertha did not smile, she couldn't see the joke, of course. Her normal face was setting into normality and he thought that if it set much harder she'd be able to take it off at night and it would stand up until morning. Perhaps that's what she wanted.

"It was a miracle," he said sharply. "None of us has a defence against that."

"It can't have been long – "

"No."

"I think I knew yesterday. So did Emmy."

"I'm not married to Emmy!"

"Ralph, Ralph – " She put her face into her hands.

"I lied to Emmy. She wouldn't understand and it's none of her business. I would always have told you the truth – "

"Make me understand. Please," she said into her hands, praying again.

He looked down at the hat, wondering why she had put it on. Intimidation? Moral support? Armament? Didn't she know – or did she – how that hat was going to look on her today? She was clever, in her way she was cleverer than Emmy, she could twist his arm with things like this sharp hat. He turned away and there was the cat watching with slit eyes from the sill. In a rage he snatched up a tea-cup, the cat moved, but not fast enough, and earned every dinner he had given it. The cup rebounded from its flank and smashed completely on the floor. Ralph took a deep breath of relief.

"You used to be so fond of it." Bertha lifted her face and looked at him fixedly. "I think I understand. Yes, I do."

"I was never fond of the creature, it was a habit."

"About the girl, I mean. I understand that. What a fool you must think me – how thick!"

There was almost gaiety in her manner, she would not meet his eye except briefly sideways. Perhaps he should be frank and tell her how little he had thought about her side of it.

"I was selfish enough to think, to hope, anyway, that we had enough, you and I. It was – oh more than enough, it was everything for me and I thanked God for it. Yes, I did." She touched each of her cheeks, aware of their sudden heat. "I saw no harm in thanking the Author of our being, it was what you might call – I *did* call it – the Act of our being. And it never occurred to me that you might want, might need more. Oh, it should have done!" She forced a smile, "That's 'I'm alright, Jack,' I suppose. Even though I understood – I was given to understand – that other men – I've

408

thought of you – but I haven't really thought of you at all, have I?"

"Other men?"

"Of your age."

"What are you talking about?"

He knew, but what he didn't know was what to do first, laugh at her or strike her. Not as he had struck the cat, not by shying a teacup – to satisfy the feeling he had now he would have to strike her down.

And then she said, "You'll come back, that's all that matters."

"Come back?"

"When you're ready." She looked steadily up at him, her cheeks pink but no longer painful. "I can wait if I have to."

What he should do was laugh, probably it was all he should do. But not yet. She had just done him a service, she had relieved him of the duty of pitying her.

"Come back? To Thorne? To Emmy?"

"To me." With her old shyness she touched his hand, her smile was a grimace before tears.

She thought he would return. Let her think so then, if it saved her anything. Let hope die a natural death a long time from now. But he wouldn't forgive her for it. He turned away, treading the fragments of broken china. She had insulted him with her hope. It was based on the premise that he was a middle-aged man among middle-aged men, needing to relieve himself with a girl, any girl. She had made him out a goat and she was sending him to rut.

"I shall want some money," he said.

# 13

She was scarcely out of the house before he was on his way downstairs. He had such a sensation of light and freedom, there had been a wonderful clarifying of the air. He tasted it, got a little drunk.

He flung the front door wide to the hinges at the risk of causing Bertha to look back at him from the drive. He didn't care, she was not even part of the landscape now. Behind him his life lay flat, collapsed as neat and paltry as a pack of cards. He knew now how Marise felt about running.

At first there was no answer when he knocked at her door. He seized the knocker and pressed the bell and knocked and rang together. The bell made no audible sound on his side of the door although he knew by the vibration under his finger that it was working. His knocking filled the hall and the well of the staircase.

Why didn't she answer? Had she gone? Where could she go? Where couldn't she go, a creature like her, a miracle, a mirage? Had she ever really been here? He called her name, he was making an appreciable din and would make more; would waken the dead if necessary.

She opened the door and he almost fell in. Joy was as shocking as pain.

"Thank you," he said, "oh, thank you – " He wasn't in the habit of calling on God in extremity and didn't have to thank Him either.

"You were trying to frighten me," said Marise.

"I was frightening myself."

He had never realised before how ruthless perfection could be, thrusting out of a dingy room. It was his own fault for not being ready, he never would be ready for her. To be ready would be to be untouched.

"When you didn't open the door I thought something was wrong."

"Why does everyone think that?"

410

She still wore Tomelty's dressing-gown and her perfections
– neck, shoulders, thighs – thrust out of the stuff like flowers
out of an old brown calyx he thought.

"Everyone?"

"Uncle Fred Macey nearly broke the window. I didn't
want to let him in. I was in bed."

"You're not ill, are you?"

"Yes. You know why."

He would have wiped out that struggle on the floor and
started from now if he could, he would be strong and reverent now, now that he knew how to begin.

But when he moved to touch her she twisted her shoulders
sharply out of his reach.

"Marise, I'd give anything for that not to have happened.
I've no excuse, none that you'd understand. You're not a
man – " he smiled – "first and foremost you're not that."

"I used to think you were so clever, you used to frighten
me."

"And now?"

"Oh good heavens, I should say not!" She let Tomelty's
dressing-gown glide off her shoulders, watching her reflection in the mirror.

"I'm glad I don't frighten you."

She was absorbed in her peacocking and it caused him
acute physical distress to see her draw the sleeves of Tomelty's robe tightly under her breasts.

"You're just like everyone else. Why didn't you keep your
bowler on?"

"Marise, listen to me – "

"I don't want to listen." She turned on him, "I'm ill, you
made me ill, you took me to that great empty place – "

"The estuary? Oh my darling, I didn't know – tell me
what's wrong – what is it? What's the matter with you?"

"I don't want to talk about it. I want Jack, he knows, he
helps me."

"I'll help you – "

"You can't." She huddled into Tomelty's robe, held it

411

tight under her chin. She looked forlorn, incongruous and untouchable by him. He longed to touch her, his longing was so strong it was a bodily deficiency.

"Where's Bertha? She was here, I saw her."

"She's gone. All that's finished – Bertha, Emmy, Thorne. I shall never go there again."

"Did they find out about me?"

"I'm going to take you away." He dared to touch her – but Tomelty's garment came first to his hands – "I'm taking you away from him."

"Why did you tell them I was a water-diviner?"

"I've got the money, I've got two hundred pounds, there's nothing to stop us – "

"That's a lot of money."

"It's enough to get us away and keep us until – " Until what? He knew the why of it and he had solved the how, but there remained imponderables. Beyond the fact of having her with him it was all imponderable. Until he could get more money? Until he could get another job? Until they settled what to do? Who would settle that – he, or Marise? Would he be able to go off and do whatever he had to and leave her to wait for him? Could he risk that? Where could he leave her where she would be happy waiting?

"The important thing is to get you away from here and then – " Then at least he could stop thinking of Tomelty with her.

She allowed him to hold her and he did so almost gingerly because he was beginning again and dared not begin wrongly. She wanted to know where they would go.

"Far away, wherever you like – but no sea, no estuary, no wide open space."

"Now?"

"Not actually now, not today, but we might get away Friday." Folded into his arms she smelt of sweets, the small perfumed sweets he remembered from childhood.

"I want to go now."

"There are just one or two matters I have to see to."

"Can I take Barbra?"

"You can take anything you like."

She rolled round and broke out of his hold. The teddy bear was face down on the couch, Marise picked it up, buttoned its woollen jacket and straightened its tattered dress.

"We're ready." She went to the door, in her nightdress, with Tomelty's dressing-gown over her shoulders, her feet bare, the ragged toy held to her breast.

"I mean what I say. I'm not playing, Marise, we're going away for good."

"Yes, for good."

"We'll go on Friday. I should be able to settle everything by then. It can be no later than Saturday morning anyway because Tomelty comes back Saturday night – "

"I don't want to go on Saturday."

"If I could tie everything up by Friday we could go Friday night – "

"I want to go now."

She stamped the ball bone of her bare foot on the floor and he cried, "If you knew what hell it's been for me! So do I want to go now, I want to take you out of here, I want you to myself!"

"We know what you want. Barbra knows, she's seen it often, at least she did when she had her eyes. Now she just listens – " she put her lips to the teddy bear's muzzle – " 'Air on a Bed Spring' Jack calls it."

"For God's sake, Marise!" – there had never been an extremity like this.

"Then there's Uncle Fred Macey, he's family, but he wants the same. So do you. So does the Pope, so do monkeys. Did you think you'd surprise me?"

"It isn't like that, I love you – I shall surprise you."

She was surprised already. "Love me?" and opened her eyes wide and parted her lips as if to have it overwhelm her. Then she shook her head. "If you loved me you wouldn't be ashamed of me."

"I am not ashamed of you!"

"You are. You're ashamed of being seen with me like this, you think tomorrow or the next day I may have my clothes on. Well, I may, I may not."

He caught the lapels of Tomelty's robe and pulled her to him. "I'd take you wearing a sack, I'd rather you wore a sack than anything of his."

"I'm not going with you anyway."

"You don't mean that – "

"Tomorrow or the next day – I mean it!" She began to cry, with anger or despair he couldn't tell which.

"Listen, there's nothing to be afraid of. I'm taking you away from here and no-one can stop us." Holding and rocking her he heard himself say, "I'll take you anyhow and any time, now if you like – yes, tonight if you like – "

I can write, he was thinking, there's no umbilical cord tying me to Picker, Gill, I can do it all by letter – "circumstances beyond my control oblige me to tender my resignation" –

"We'll go where Tomelty and Macey will never find us, they shan't touch you again."

"But you will." She stilled herself in his rocking arms. "You'll touch me."

He wasn't sure if she was asking, or how she was asking. He couldn't identify the look she turned on him.

"You'll touch me everywhere, won't you?"

"Marise, I love you, I reverence you – " It would not be too much to say he worshipped her and later on he would say it, he would go down on his knees and worship. "When we're together I'll show you – "

He was to think afterwards that that was where he had gone wrong. It was so easy, she was sensitive, she had been badly used. But what could he have said with truth, with more truth, when he was in such a rage of longing?

Anyway, it was the beginning of the end: he began it, he practically ordained it, from that moment the sequence was set. Perhaps he had known all along that it wouldn't get any farther than this room and that was why he couldn't plan. Making arrangements was like trying to put the miracle on tap.

He had confused memories of what happened between them then. One thing led to another, that was all he could be sure of, each word and action made the next inevitable. He marvelled at the cunning of the escalation – God's was it, or Fate's, or the nature he was born with?

Marise merely obstructed him at first, twisting and stiffening, making herself awkward in his arms. He wouldn't let her go, he was having the same feeling, the over-toppling rage for her that he had had at Thorne. But this time he knew that he could lose.

He circled his arms and locked his hands to contain her – it reminded him of a children's game, children chanting "Chop, chop, here comes a chopper to chop off your head."

It was all wrong, Tomelty's dressing-gown, the teddy bear and the way she whined and twisted in his arms. She was only petulant then, not bothered enough to make a real effort to get away. If she had, if she had seemed to mean it, to mean something, he would have let her go. Holding her was a rage and a torment and there was the dressing-gown and the teddy and "Chop, chop, here comes a chopper" to burke him.

She kept saying she wouldn't go, she didn't want to, turning her head like a fretful child and he tried to stop her and make her listen.

"It's the only thing we can do, we can't go on like this, we can't stay here. I can't be apart from you any longer – don't you understand? I can't stay up there knowing he's down here with you. We must get away!"

"I won't go with a murderer!"

She shouldn't have said that, it shouldn't have come into her head to be said.

"I can't bear you touching me, I keep thinking what you touched last time."

"Last time?"

She lay quite still in his arms. "You cut her up, didn't you? You cut all of her up."

Why did it happen? Why did she turn their private joke against him? Why didn't she smile when she said it, or look scared? Fear wouldn't have cut him off, it would have bound them together as it had at the estuary.

"How do I know you won't do the same to me?"

What was she feeling then, limp in his arms, with the teddy bear's muzzle in her neck and her chin on its balding head?

"Here comes a chopper, last, last, last!" He snatched the bear from her. He tore off the clothes, split the arms and legs, wrenched off the head and burst it in his hands like a loaf of bread. He crumbled the body and foam rubber chips rained around him. "Last, last, last!"

It was an explosion and an implosion. After such an all-round detonation he scarcely registered what they did. Events were like the topside of an iceberg and his own actions were superfluous. Marise might have screamed but he thought she only whimpered. He had a last glimpse of her face and remembered that her eyes seemed to have opened inwards into the back of her head. She was probably frightened then – probably. He wasn't even sure of that. It no longer mattered to him.

He reached out for her, it was a reflex and not a hopeful gesture – after all, he was in the habit of reaching out for her, trying to touch her. And she must have run away from him because she was there and then she wasn't and for one minute or five, until – for no purpose at all – he went up to his own rooms, he stood alone in a welter of rubber chips and torn velvet.

He didn't go in search of her or question whether she was within hearing. From the doorway he made one more observation but it was no parting-shot at her, just a rubbing-in to himself.

"It's Ralph Shilling you're afraid of, not John Brown!"

416

and went upstairs without noticing Madame Belmondo listening in the hall.

Marise heard him go. She tried to keep quiet until she was sure, but she had never been able to cry quietly. Also she would be sick at any moment.

Ralph Shilling was sickening, over and over again she saw his green-backed hands, murderer's hands, murdering over and over again. In the dark where she had taken refuge the atrocity went on and on. The body was plundered and spilled before an eye which she could not shut. She heard the stitches unripping and smelled Barbra's private dust. She pressed her fingers into her eyeballs until they flashed blue lights and blood-red skeins. Still the foam rubber chips ran down over her feet. She bit Tomelty's sleeve, there was comfort in the taste of it – taste was the one sense that wasn't given over to Barbra.

The walls of the wardrobe were solid but if he was in the flat he would hear. She had to cry out loud to relieve herself, she wouldn't, she couldn't care any more if he found her.

He was wrong anyway, he hadn't frightened her, only disgusted her. He hadn't frightened Barbra either, Barbra was lying out there disgusted beyond words.

Of course things had always happened to Barbra, it wasn't to be supposed that she would have an easy life. Jack understood that, he tossed her around, kicked her and, to punish Marise, had once put her down the lavatory.

They had laughed because she blocked the pipe and had to be fished out and Jack said she looked like a dose of salts in a petticoat.

But it wasn't to be supposed, either, that she would be torn to pieces.

Marise had no secrets from Barbra so she had been surprised to see that Barbra had had one from her. A cardboard disc with a metal plate attached had fallen out of Barbra's stomach. She had been a squeaking or growling bear but she had not squeaked or growled for Marise. The disc lay out there on the floor, Marise wanted to go and examine it.

Everything was quiet, she couldn't hear even the bedroom clock.

She yawned, beginning to be drowsy, safe in the wardrobe. Wardrobes were safe, especially this one. Jack said that the name meant "ward" – to keep. This one still kept its old clothes smell. She had sprinkled Tomelty's aftershave lotion about but the old clothes won, their smell was in her nostrils now.

She used to wonder so much what John Brown Shilling could do and had set herself to find out. Well, now she knew and it didn't matter whether he was waiting out there or not because all he could do was the old monkey thing they all did. There was nothing to be afraid of.

Was this achieving ambition, this flat skint feeling?

Around her the wood ticked, protesting. Her fingers touched the walls and the scabby mirror. The wardrobe door had clicked in the lock and could not be opened by her. Of course not, what provision need there be for opening a cupboard from inside?

She had only the air she stood up in, black air that hung in stiff folds and was balled up into the toes of shoes. When it was all breathed she would suffocate, unless someone came, which no-one could because she had the only key to the flat.

She hammered with her fists, already the air was cloying in her throat. She dropped to her knees, pumping the screams out, bringing on the ecstasy of fear.

"I don't want to die!"

It really did send her out of herself, she was like a firework rushing away in a shower of sparks.

# THE GOOSEBOY

# 1

Bysshe could be seen, not so old nor so young, walking in
his garden, a dusty lusty place of greed and rapine. The
fig assaulted the cypress, the bamboo contended with
the agave, mats of Bermuda grass smothered the
flagstones and the Jerusalem thorn forced up tiles said to
be Roman. It was a wilderness which he would one day
have to hack his way through, breaching his own
solitude. The plants would be at each other's throats as
soon as he had passed.

Someone, it turned out, was watching him. He had
supposed himself visible only to his private audience,
that reliable claque located between his inner ear and
eye. Nothing had warned him that he was under
observation; the extra senses which he had acquired in
his profession were not functioning. The standard five
made him supremely conscious of himself, a supremacy
which in his youth he had taken as his due, the fact of
living. Nowadays he was aware of the brevity of prime
and mindful that his might be already past.

This morning, snuffing up every sight and sound, he
tasted the green stink of ivy and spread himself in the sun
like the basking lizards. He was glad that he could still
experience simple appetites and impure joys, it was an
assurance that he was human and had not been pushed
by circumstance into the upper echelons. But as a public
performer he was obliged in his private and even
prurient moments to keep up an appearance and would

421

have preferred not to appear as he must have done before this audience of one.

The man had got in the day after his agent had telephoned. Carver came through at 11 p.m., as the day in the Midi was folding. Where Carver was it was early evening; Carver never related to other people's convenience.

'Rexie?'

'Ici le préposé.'

'Rexie, where are you?'

'Ne quittez pas, s'il vous plaît.'

'Get me Eel Murry.'

'Attendez un peu.'

'I want to talk to Lord Snowdon.'

'Quoi?'

'This is the United States of America calling the subcontinent of Europe.'

'J'ai bien compris l'origine de votre appel, monsieur. Patientez un petit peu, nous devons contacter L'Ile Marie.'

Carver had discovered Bysshe playing whodunnits in Bournemouth. He came backstage where Bysshe was trying to unblock the ladies' toilet, having just been carried off as the first murder victim and prior to his next walk-on as a vicar. 'Are you taking this up as a career?'

Carver wore an actual bootlace as a tie. 'Ever thought of going into pictures? What's your name, kid?' he asked.

'Douglas Bysshe.'

'Like in fish?'

'No, it's spelt with two esses and a y, as in Shelley.'

Carver, who was crude, said, 'I don't care if it's spelt with two tits as in Nelly, I don't see Bacall teaming with a name like that. We'll call you Rex, it's dignified and manly. And – I've got it – Snowdon. Rex Snowdon. So people think you're related.'

'Qui est ce Milord, monsieur?'

'You've got Alps over there, haven't you? You've seen the white stuff on top – that's him. Snowdon, the earl of.'

'Don't call me that.'

'Rexie, that you? They talk Chinook where you are. When are you coming back?'

'I'm on holiday.' He might have said 'recovering', but Carver would have jumped to the wrong conclusion.

'You've been away too long. Blood and traffic aren't the only things that circulate. People say to me "*Rex* Snowdon? His name's Tony." I couldn't get you a dandruff commercial.'

He was not here to recoup or reinstate, but to thicken his hide, and there were ways of doing it which he did not understand. It was something to do with the sun. It was all to do with the sun. But not just that: here, of all the places he knew, were assembled the factors for his rearmament.

'Erckmann's going to do a biopic about Zwemmer.'

'Who?'

'Anatole Zwemmer, the leper doctor. They want you.'

'They *want* me?'

'Get the next plane back.'

'Why?'

'Are you asking me? What are you asking me? Can you afford to pass up the chance of a lifetime? Who gets a lifetime? I've talked my ass off and I'm still talking but I can't do it all.'

'You said they wanted me.'

'You're not in the picture yet. You've got competition. Brando for one. He's too old for the young Zwemmer but Erckmann's getting Clint Rose for that. Lancaster's spoken of. Erckmann says it's a deep part. I told him you're the one who can get to the bottom of it. Christ, what's that?'

'Thunder. It's been threatening all day. I can see lightning. We get every kind here, tiny and twitchy like nerve ends, sheet, forked, zigzag, ball –'

'Whassat?'

'We're in for a storm.'

'I didn't call to talk about weather. Why are you hiding? Are you doing a Garbo? Think you've reached the top? Let me tell you, there's a hill of dirt for you to climb yet.'

'Could I do Zwemmer?'

'How do I know? I tell them what's good about you; you're not just a pretty face. You use everything you've

got. I tell them if they pick someone who can only lead
with his jaw they won't see him act for hair because
Zwemmer never shaved. He was homely. Does that
bother you?'

'He was a latter-day saint.'

'They're taking the story from his dissolute childhood.'

'Dissolute?'

'He was on the streets by the time he was six.'

'Aren't *I* too old?'

'I don't get you, I don't get anything. This could do
for you what *Calcutta* did for Kingsley.'

'*Gandhi*.'

'Gandhi was only in newsreels.'

'I just don't know if I can do Zwemmer.'

'My Gud –' Bysshe had often wondered if Carver
benefited by having a personal deity – 'for years you
complained about being typecast, said you were sick of
romantic roles. At your age your worries on that score
are over. But here's a second chance. They're taking the
film on location and it'll be one hundred per cent real –
cultural elevation with guts. Zwemmer was a fashion-
able surgeon in his day, he made more with his knife
than Ford with his motors.'

Rex/Douglas – which did he dislike most? Snowdon,
without doubt. The press had fun with it and the
daughters of America claimed to see a likeness. One
woman had asked was it on his father's or his mother's
side, whereupon her friend had shrieked with shame
that everyone knew the mother's name was Armstrong-
Jones. 'Bysshe' was rightfully his, and there were the
other matters of 'Music, when soft voices die', 'My name
is Ozymandias, king of kings: Look on my works, ye
Mighty, and despair!'

He wanted the part: he who had been the object, or
more truthfully the objective, of the simulated passion of
nymphets, mouth to mouth – more murder than
resuscitation – and the pressure of countless scene-
stealing busts on his rib-cage. He wanted to do
Zwemmer, of whom he knew only that he had gone to
Africa and lived among lepers at a time when the

civilized, and uncivilized, world banished them to hives in the jungle.

'What happened to him?'

'He went to the river and didn't come back. The crocs ate him.'

'He could still be alive.'

'He'd be one hundred and thirty-five years old. The final scene will be unfocused fade-out, the sun coming through the jungle, lighting up his halo or was it his hat. Quality movie.'

'Did they actually ask for me?'

'Why would they ask for you? They think you've only done skinflicks. It was me said you could act. I made myself believe it.'

'Thanks.'

'You've got the chance and that's all you've got. Erckmann's toying with the idea of Charlie Palk.'

'Palk does Westerns.'

'Did that stop Cooper? Or Grant? Or Newman? If Larry Oliver could do a dance routine and *King Lear*, why should you fret?'

'I'll call you tomorrow.'

'Call from the airport or don't bother.'

Tomorrow and tomorrow and tomorrow, but what Bysshe by-rights meant was the hypothetical time when he might be ready. And who would wait for that? Not Carver, not the world, not anyone. Erckmann wouldn't even look round.

After Carver hung up, he heard the frogs. Carver's voice had drowned theirs. Carver's voice, over the wire, was the essence of the man as distinct from his assemblage. One could do equally well without his factors: it wasn't necessary to see his blue mountainous face and smell fifty glorious years of Bourbon on his breath to be caught up in his indecent haste. Carver seemed to be tearing through life to get to the best bit. Tomorrow and tomorrow: Bysshe was waiting, and Carver running, and they would both end up with only their yesterdays. Like everyone else.

The frogs by night, the cigalles by day, and the clicking, ticking, rustling, bustling of his anarchic garden was what sustained Bysshe; the knowledge that the garden was in the recycling business and that hell and high water, when they came, would only accelerate the cycle. Carver would have said, 'Tape the frogs and bugs if they mean so much and bring the tape to L A and play it for vibes.' What Carver didn't know was that in his contemplative moments Bysshe would lie with his face to the ground, appreciating every skeletal leaf and cannibal ant and willing the detritus to crumble or pupate or jell or in some way evolve before his eyes. He had resigned himself to wait and was hoping to use this summer to acquire a scarfskin.

He slept badly that night. Thinking of Zwemmer and knowing so little about him, Zwemmer got grafted on to Carver and appeared in his dreams as a blue-bearded hustler in a pith helmet, sweating whisky and jeering at Rex Snowdon for being unable to portray an odour of sanctity.

Soon after dawn he rolled off his bed and went naked into the garden, thrusting his feet through the St Barnaby thistles. He felt the need of a positive spite after the cloudy malice of the dream. He cracked his ankle on the roots of an olive. The wood was cool; it first chilled, then burned him to the bone.

The grains of darkness were running out of the sky, and from the point where it was possible to see the sea – though not to desire it, for the shores were polluted and degraded – the light magnified his nerve endings. He took refuge under the dark leaves of a carob tree in this, his favourite hour, when he was sure of being alone.

The garden itself was walled. Under the walls were ditches, into the top of the walls were cemented fragments of wine bottles; real glass, green and yellow and barbarous. The padlocked gate was knitted up with barbed wire. The house itself was hidden from the road by olives and gorse and tamarisk. There would appear little incentive to break through to it.

Years ago it would have been a lustrous folly, all-white, with balconies, fretted shutters, curly eaves and domed roof: a Taj Mahal from the chines of

Bournemouth. It was chalky now, and cracked like a
clown's face. The woodwork was gently discharging
itself: Bysshe had been greatly heartened when he first
witnessed the operation, slivers drifting to the ground as
they might be moths or stale snowflakes, being seized
and carried off by ants. Not a grain, not a particle
ignored. It cheered him to know that his house was
contributing to the recycling business.

But there had been interlopers, despite the decay.
Walls, padlocks and the general air of grot didn't deter
the most persistent. The Rex Snowdon fan club in
Danceville/Deever/Tarkoe or somewhere, arrived and
battered at his gate. When admittance was denied them,
the maturer members tried to climb over. Two had
spiked themselves on the wire: another, even more
mature, fell and fractured her coccyx. Rex Snowdon
was obliged to come out of hiding and organize first aid,
whereupon the uninjured mobbed him. Heedless of
their wounded, they reached for him with the lust of
predators.

Once he had found a girl under his bed. She refused to
come out. She had seen him in *The Consul's Lady* eight
times in Pittsburgh and five in Tusa and in other places,
she said. She was a travelling beautician and moved
around. It was dusty under his bed and she had
scrambled through the gorse and over the wire and a
beautician need not be beautiful any more than a doctor
need be healthy. Kneeling, with her elbows on the floor,
she had glared at Bysshe from between the bedsprings.
She was wearing giant horn-rimmed spectacles and
reminded him of the dog with eyes like saucers in the
fairy tale.

Sighing, he had locked the door on her and passed the
night in one of the guest rooms. The girl in possession of
his bed and the irrelevance of her being there only
seemed like one of a string of irrelevancies which had
started in his pram.

In the morning, inspired by an uncharitable notion,
he had taken the oieboy upstairs. The girl was resting
peacefully on his bed. He pushed the boy into the room
and awakened her by kicking the leg of the bed.

Opening her eyes, she got the full shock view of the boy's face – the wrong or, in this case, the right side. One look was enough. She screamed, sprang off the bed and ran as if a devil of hell was after her.

Bysshe thought of privacy as a prisoner thinks of freedom, as the state of being, and all else mere existence. Achieve privacy and be assured. As an actor, it was virtually impossible for him to be sure of anything. Carver had threatened to make him the World's Lover. 'Why not? Pickford was the World's Sweetheart. Times change, people don't. They want someone to sweep them off their feet. Look at history: Joan of Arc and Joe Louis, Adolf Hitler – he was German and he didn't happen here, but the Kennedys did. It could be you next, Rexie. The lover with the fully comprehensive range.'

Bysshe might hazard a guess, but Rexie knew what was meant by that. Rexie had done some blue-black films to make ends meet, and the memory of them enlivened his nightmares. Repugnance was legitimate but he feared that in making those films he had utilized feelings which were genuinely his own.

The watcher was in the strawberry patch, eating strawberries and making no attempt to hide. He squatted, groping the plants, pulling off the fruit and watching Bysshe. Well he might. Bysshe had been enjoying himself. A sense of absolute uniqueness had set him leaping, singing and clapping out a rhythm on his buttocks in the purity and privacy of his morning garden. Like Adam before Eve.

He saw the man and stopped in mid-caper. The song died in his throat, he teetered on one leg. In his rush of anger he could have killed the fellow, but wiping him out would not wipe out the vision he had of himself. It had passed from the man's eye to his, a camera-shot which he wouldn't be able to forget. He lowered his leg, let his hands drop to his sides and stood naked, trying to look unashamed.

'Surprise, eh?' prompted the man.

'What the hell are you doing here?'

'Surprise all round – as the dog said to the lamp post.'

'This is private property.'

'No kidding.' The man laughed with a forced conviviality which Bysshe found infuriating.

'I can charge you with breaking and entering.'

'I haven't broken anything. I used an old commando trick; I'm pleased I can still do it.'

'Then get out the same way you got in.'

'I can't. There aren't any ditches this side and the way it's done –'

'I don't give a sod how it's done.'

'You never used to cuss.'

'Just get out.'

'Dulcie didn't approve of cussing. Whenever I catch myself doing it, I say that's a sin according to Dulcie. But it doesn't stop me. Some of us are born to blaspheme. I used to say to her, "I could do worse", and she used to say, "What could be worse than offering a direct insult to the Almighty?"'

'I don't know what you're talking about.'

'I mean to say, if sin's original –' Bysshe did not miss the direction of the man's grin, pink-stained teeth chumbling strawberry pulp – 'we can't be held accountable. Dulcie maintained it was our duty to better ourselves.' Bysshe covered his privates with his hand, a reflex activated by mention of the name more than any impulse of modesty. 'She was a god-fearing girl. I'd go further and say she was an angel.'

'You can go to hell.'

The man rose up from the strawberry bed. 'You don't remember me.'

'No.'

'Tom Ewing.' He came across, sticking out his hand as if they were meeting at a party.

Bysshe turned his back and went into the house. In an hour, or less, there would be scarcely a cool place in the garden, but he had been standing in a bar of shadow and was shivering. He put on a bathrobe.

The man calling himself Tom Ewing came up the steps to what Gluvas, the gardener, called the 'terrasse'. The paving stones had tipped, each to a different depth, a different angle, like a scattered pack of cards. They looked as if a touch would straighten them. Ewing appeared to consider it. He toed a slab, then stooped and seized it with both hands. His shoulders could be seen bunching with effort, his knees stood up atavistically beside his ears. He was not a man who would care how he looked and he was right not to. Bysshe classified people by their looks, but realized that those without any had the ultimate advantage over him because they had nothing to lose.

He stood beside Ewing, noting and half envying his bald patch and the comedores on his nose. 'Leave it.'

Ewing tried to prise up the slab. His neck turned puce with tension. 'It wants re-settling. I had the same trouble with my patio at home.'

The word 'patio' identified him, and thus was he rendered harmless. Bysshe had a vision of the same rump suspended to the sound of mowing machines and the smell of Sunday roasts. 'I don't know you from Adam.'

A retort could be made to that, with the laugh on him, but Ewing was too disappointed at not shifting the stone to take the opportunity. 'Can't you get someone to do it for you?'

'I don't want it done. I prefer it as it is, I prefer everything as it is. Saving your presence, which I can do without.'

'They told me you don't encourage visitors. I was in the fish market and they slit up a fish to show me the sort of welcome I could expect.'

'The fish market?'

'In the town. The cabbie who brought me said it was a publicity gimmick.'

'I don't give interviews or charity chats or autographs, and I'm giving you one minute to get out.'

'If you don't remember me, what about this?' Ewing pulled something out of his pocket and thrust it at Bysshe.

It was the figure of an animal of some sort, crudely stamped out of metal and painted municipal green. As Bysshe turned it over, his memory unwillingly, resentfully, stirred.

'Tearing through the countryside, up and down the

roads, in and out of people's gardens, round and round the war memorial. We were tearaways,' Ewing said proudly, 'and we each had one of these on the handlebars of our bikes. We called ourselves the Green Dragons.'

It was not a time Bysshe wanted to recapture. Pubescence had been a pain. He had ridden his old Ariel in rages of frustration and disgust, and a form of joy which he had believed to be special until he understood that it was surrogate sex. And he had suffered with acne. The thing in his hand was chipped and shabby, barely recognizable as a rampant beast. All it did now was evoke a shabby time.

'Those were the days,' said Ewing, 'free as birds and larger than life.'

'We were a bunch of skinny kids on clapped-out motorbikes.'

'Mine was new. I forged my father's signature as guarantor and got it on the never-never.'

'I don't remember you.'

'After I crashed it and lost my licence I rode pillion. I rode to Glasgow with you to your cousin's wedding.'

'My cousin lived in Edinburgh.'

'Where I first saw your sister.'

'Which sister?'

'You only had one.'

Bysshe tossed him the metal dragon. 'I'm going to make coffee.'

'*You* were skinny. Who'd have thought you'd be a film star.'

'Why have you come?'

'To see you.' That was what they came for, the travelling beautician, the Danceville crowd, the snoopers on the hill with picnics and telephoto lenses. Out of some sort of priapic curiosity. Ewing grinned mateily. 'I've seen all of you.'

'How did you know where I live?'

'The cabbie knew.' Ewing followed him into the house. 'You never were friendly. We called you "Jeeper's Creeper".'

'Did you?' Bysshe was pleased. So he might indeed be

the right one to play Zwemmer, the private man forced into a public situation.

'You're comfortable.' Ewing was looking round the kitchen.

Dishes waited to be washed. A cat slept in a basket with peaches. The windowsill was crowded with petrified cactus plants. 'I expected something a bit different.'

'I came here to forget things like emptying the teapot.'

'And putting on your clothes.'

'I remember to take them off.'

'You married?'

'No.'

Ewing made a grimace of pure misery. 'I am. An air hostess. She brought me down to earth.'

Bysshe turned from putting on the coffee to scrutinize his visitor. Ewing wouldn't be able to lose or control the solid fat which was accumulating over his hips, not converting its sugar, not doing its chemistry, putting him at risk. His shoulders were hooped with the premonition of it.

It struck Bysshe as significant that a gangling youth – although he could not recall Ewing in any detail, they had all been gangling – should carry within him the shape and substance of his self to come, like a woman with child. But a man was committed, without the hope of an abortion, to producing himself.

There were times, looking in his mirror, when he saw what he himself was bringing forth: a man who could be credited with integrity and a lot of living. His features were still well-defined, his waist and hips still localized, his hair still plentiful with as yet only a few white cottons in it. Only his eyes singled him out from other well-structured men, possessing as they did a deep and irrevocable hurt. It was always there, he had checked on it at mundane moments. While he was shaving or tying his tie or licking a postage stamp his eyes looked hurt, though it was a poignant awareness that he could locate nowhere else in himself. 'If you didn't have eyes like an organ-grinder's monkey you'd still be playing stiffs in Bournemouth,' Carver had told him. But his face was changing, sharpening, awakening. Hawks' eyes were cold, inimical, and the valuable hurt would soon be lost.

'If I had your chances,' said Ewing, 'I know what I'd do. It's not your looks or your success I envy, it's your freedom.'

Bysshe's snort woke the cat. Freedom – when it was a question now of what he could do, what he was capable of, and would be allowed to try. Carver was right. Nobody was going to look for his potential any more, he would have to put himself over. And his potential could be nullified by commercial considerations. 'Show business is the biggest bondage there is.'

'I wouldn't mind being bonded.'

'Do you like your coffee black?'

'Who's that?'

The oieboy had come into the yard, his arms full of brown roses. He carried them carefully, his head bowed, solicitous, even tender. The dead petals were falling in showers and he kept stopping to lift each foot and shake it, like a cat on hot bricks in slow motion.

'He lives here.'

'He's pretty.'

'It depends how you look at him.'

'How *I* look at him?' Ewing was a bad winker, had trouble uncoordinating his eyes.

Bysshe went to the window and whistled. The boy put up his face to the sky. Bysshe whistled again, a short blast such as he might use to alert an accomplice or summon an animal. The boy threw down the roses and came to the window. His jeans were soiled and too big for him, so that his body could be seen moving with grace inside the bloated cotton. For grace of movement he could be relied upon, and the sun, doing its bit, shot to blazes every wire-gold hair on his head.

Ewing said, 'Are you going to introduce me?'

The boy was a few feet away, his head turned to one side. He tended to look sideways, probably because he could see more clearly with one eye than with the other. Bysshe pointed along the terrasse. The boy followed the direction of his finger and the sun which had irradiated his hair did the same to the left side of his face.

Ewing gasped. 'Christ almighty!'

Bysshe smiled the smile which complemented the hurt in his eyes and had persuaded so many women that he was looking only to them for comfort. 'I fancy the damage is secular.'

'What?'

Bysshe whistled again and made a dismissive gesture. The boy, turning to look, presented the perfect right side of his face, with a scarlet geranium looped over one ear.

'How did he get like that?'

'Nobody knows.'

'Bloody hell,' said Ewing. 'It gave me a turn.'

'The first time's the worst.' Considerately, Bysshe poured him a tot of marc.

'It's obscene. How can you stand having him around?'

'I don't see him often. He keeps to the orchard and the hillside. He sleeps in the gardener's shed and looks after the geese.'

'Geese?'

'Toulouse geese. They're excellent watchdogs and they live off the land. He's probably taken them to the orchard, otherwise they'd have raised the alarm when you came.' After the Danceville invasion Bysshe had introduced the geese, reasoning that they were more alarmist than dogs, cheaper, and less corruptible. And natural enemies of women.

'So if they don't keep people out, his Sunday face will.' Ewing drained his brandy. 'Suppose I'd had a dicky heart.'

'Then you wouldn't have been jumping over my wall.'

'What does he say? About the way he looks?'

'He doesn't say anything about anything. I've never heard him speak.'

'You mean he's dumb?'

'And deaf to all but high-pitched sounds.'

'Poor little bastard. Where did he come from?'

'Over the wall. Like you.'

One day Bysshe had gone to the slopes of La Roquette and found the boy escorting the geese with a forked stick.

They appeared to have no objection, though Bysshe had. While they waited amicably, he questioned the boy. Getting no response he had tried to hustle him off. The birds at once advanced, clanging, their round inimical eyes fixed on Bysshe, and snapped at his legs. 'The geese can take care of themselves. He gets his food and a shakedown and something for helping Gluvas about the place. He's settled here.'

Ewing sighed. 'I stick my neck out, I tend to nowadays. My wife says I'm getting stupid. She comes from a different world.'

'You mean she's extraterrestrial?'

'What I mean,' said Ewing, without dignity, 'is we're not in the same class. My father was a potato merchant and hers managed a shoe shop. I went to the comprehensive, she went to a secondary modern. She makes it matter.'

'You married a high flier.' Bysshe did not stifle his yawn. 'Did you bring her with you?'

Ewing shook his head, peered uneasily through the window. 'Has the kid gone?'

'He'll be in the orchard.'

'What I mean to say, if I'd been to grammar school and my old man worked in an office, she'd take me for what I am. Whatever that is.'

His lips pushed out like a hurt child's. Bysshe, who was wondering how soon he could be rid of him, asked where he was staying.

'I haven't booked in. I got off the train and came straight here.'

'I'm flying to New York today.' Bysshe was surprised and not displeased to hear himself say it. The matter seemed to have been resolved and his objections blown wide open. They were prompted merely by natural disinclination and contrary to his interests.

The whole man should refuse nothing, his duty was to experience. 'I expect to start on a major new film.' Ewing sat staring as if he had all the time in the world and didn't want it. 'I shall be leaving almost at once.'

'What happened to Dulcie?'

'What should happen to Dulcie?'

435

'Is she married?'

'The last time I heard, she was.'

The last time was when Dulcie Pike, née Bysshe, had explained to him the condition of wedlock. He ran into her on the occasion of a family funeral. Ran into, when his intention had been to run out. He had taken a wrong turning among the graves and come face to face with his sister as she picked her way reverently past the floral tributes. 'Bingo!' she had cried, and snatched at him – she probably did indulge in that deadly game – 'you're not going to sneak away, I want to talk to you.' Talk she did, about her husband, whom she referred to in Dickensian style only as 'Pike'.

Bysshe believed that the fact that he and she had shared their mother's womb was the origin of the contention between them. It was in the womb that she had acquired her resentment. To Bysshe, with full partiality and no justice, had been given the favour of the gods. It had been a matter of common consent, people looked into their double pram and said how funny it was – 'funny' was the word their mother, a guileless woman, used – that the prettiest of the twins wasn't the girl.

'What's he like, Dulcie's husband?'

'Not a man I want to remember.'

'She was pure in heart.' Something had got into Ewing, or it had been there all the time and was finally getting out. 'I knew as soon as I saw her.'

'How soon was that?'

'At your cousin's wedding. In Glasgow.'

'Edinburgh.'

'She sang "Love's Old Sweet Song". I'll never forget it.'

Nor would Bysshe. Dulcie he remembered as a source of embarrassment: she had too much femininity. Her disposition, and her figure, had been aggressively female since she had risen five. There was nothing she could have done about it, but she kept on with little-girl and kitten play until her developed and developing bust was forcing up the hem of her gymslip. Bysshe often had to look away. It used to worry him to think that his flesh was the same mix as hers, and he was afraid of it getting the better of him, as it had of her. Then, when she was thirteen and Bysshe still struggling with acne and hot flushes, she suddenly became a woman, missing puberty altogether. Dulcie became in some contentious but undeniable way, mature. She had enjoyed watching his emergent manhood emerging in the wrong places, she who might then have looked away. It was a happy time for her; even her voice, which had been a whine, strengthened to a rich contralto.

'It was a revelation,' said Ewing.

'I thought so.' Bysshe had seen the women dabbing their eyes and the men looking into their beer and the newlyweds locked in a death-defying kiss. 'I wonder if what was revealed to you was the same as was revealed to me.'

'I was a roughneck, a yob. Dulcie made me realize there's more to life than taking what you want.'

'Indeed?'

'What I mean to say, I was out for all I could get, I didn't know how to give.'

'And my sister showed you?'

Darker blood coloured Ewing's jaw. 'She wasn't that sort.'

'Indeed,' Bysshe said again, without question.

'I didn't know I had anything to give. She made me realize I had to give myself.' Ewing, who had given to his air hostess, stared at Bysshe with dismay.

'Oughtn't you to have married Dulcie?'

'I wasn't good enough, quality-wise. But you see, with her it was *me* that was under par, not where I came from.' Ewing, whom Bysshe would have supposed an immodest man, seemed to think he had made an essential point. 'I've always remembered her, she's always at the back of my mind, if not right in front. I mean to say, a girl like her was special.' The confession excited Ewing, he leaned over and punched Bysshe lightly on the shoulder. 'When they open me up they'll find "Dulcie" stamped through me like Brighton through a stick of rock.'

Credulity was not one of Bysshe's failings. In his

profession he was obliged to turn everything inside out
and examine it. He did so now, and concluded that
Ewing had come, not to eulogize Dulcie but to extort
money. It would have to be a lot of money to make the
trip worthwhile.

'Tell me where she is. I don't even know if she's –'
Ewing licked his lips without pleasure – 'alive. I mean to
say.'

'Oh, she's around.'

'The day before yesterday it was, I was getting the car
out and I pressed the starter like I've done a million
times and I thought it's no good, I've got to know. You'd
think I'd been working up to it, but I swear to God I
hadn't. Not knowingly. It just came over me. I dropped
everything and I'm here because you're the only one
who can tell me.'

Bysshe, doing a thorough job, turning out the seams,
thought that Ewing could be cherishing some idea of
blackmailing him. About what? For whose protection?
Dulcie's?

'Don't get me wrong. Keeping her in my thoughts has
been enough. Till now. The day before yesterday my
wife said something, and after that it wasn't enough.'

'What did she say?'

'She said I had no background.'

The unknown quantity of Ewing's wife, all unknown
to Bysshe and probably not much known to Ewing,
dwindled between them. Dulcie remained, a sacred
relic, if you please. Ewing, dewy-eyed, was obviously
pleasing, and it was no occasion for pity. His delusion
might serve him better than his common sense, as
delusions often did.

'You don't mean to say –' it was catching but things
could be too simple – 'you came here looking for a
background?'

'Twenty years ago I fell for your sister. The moment I
saw her I knew what she was.'

'What was she?'

'A pure woman, and I'm proud I had the wit to see it.
Sometimes I think it says more for me than anything else
I've done.'

'You could be right. Did the taxi driver have a ponytail?'

'What?'

'The one I'm thinking of wears his hair long and tied back with an elastic band. He charges double to bring people here; he tells them they'll be asked in to see the live show.'

'I don't know what he charged, I gave him a note and he kept it.'

'We aren't identical twins, Dulcie and me. Not from the same egg.' He had had to fight for his life from the beginning and the idea was repugnant: two specks jockeying for position in the amniotic fluid. 'We're as different as chalk and cheese.'

'Chalk and gold.'

Bysshe felt the wry satisfaction which a flagrant miscasting always afforded him. 'We were never close.' As a child he had been crowded out. Her presence filled the house, filled everywhere. So did her absence. As a child he went in mortal awareness of her, she blew him apart like a dandelion clock. Only in clandestine moments was he able to get himself together and be what he was entitled and intended to be. 'Being twins, they tried to make us a pigeon pair. They had us photographed sitting side by side, but my grandmother cut Dulcie out of the picture and had me enlarged and put in a silver frame.'

'Why?'

Bysshe shrugged. 'People judge by appearances, Dulcie's qualities weren't immediately apparent.' They had never resolved the problem of twinship. It had been a problem, despite their separate eggs; God knew what a kerfuffle it would have been had they split one egg between them. The battle had been for life, and every particular of it. Having appropriated the female gender as the most likely to succeed, Dulcie had coveted the best of the male attributes as well, and had overcompensated with feminine ones. Overdoing it had become a habit. Bobbishness was the armour wherein she trusted. She bobbed everywhere, up and down, in and out, and bobbing, could not be held accountable.

'Where is she?' Ewing was looking at Bysshe as if Bysshe were a packet which contained something he badly wanted.

Bysshe, when bored, was wont to provide himself with a scenario. He decided to encourage Ewing. It would be doing him a kindness and Dulcie something less than harm. He sighed. 'I don't suppose I shall see her again.'

'Why not?'

'It's a long story.'

'I want to hear it.'

'I haven't time, I've got to pack.'

'I'm not going till you tell me.'

Bysshe, hastily assembling a few facts, hoped that others would present themselves in the telling. 'You could come with me on the plane and I'd fill you in on the way to New York.'

'You're not going anywhere.' Ewing stood up, stood in the doorway, legs apart, arms folded. It was wonderfully hopeless, the wonder evidenced by how a man could carry a straw in the belief that it was carrying him. Saints and martyrs did, but had there ever been a straw like Dulcie?

'I don't know that I ought to tell you. She wouldn't care to have her private life discussed with a stranger.'

'I'm not a stranger.'

Dulcie of course would have preferred to do the talking: she was about as private as a highway hoarding. 'Sit down, you're making me jumpy.'

Ewing was without grace, and suspicious. He hooked a chair with his foot, positioned it between Bysshe and the door, sat astride and ordered, 'Get on with it.'

Dulcie had come once to Ile-Marie, just after Bysshe had acquired the place. Nothing had been done, the shutter bolts were rusted solid and no window could be opened, there was a pool on the floor of the kitchen with some curious creatures knotted on the bottom, and the salle-à-manger smelt of what he suspected was pot.

He was camping out in the garden at the time and had feared that she would spoil everything and he would have to leave. Then he realized that the place was on his side. No power on earth, she said, and meant it, would get her here again. She was sorry she had come. She had wanted to see how her famous brother lived; and now she could go back to Sidcup and tell them he lived in a stinking ruin.

'Does the name Genghis Pike mean anything to you?'

'What?'

'It's not a name you'd soon forget –' Bysshe loved the 'Genghis' – 'it was front-page news in the *Nursing Mirror*.'

'What are you talking about?'

'The man Dulcie married. Pike by name, Pike by nature. I don't know what she saw in him.' (What Pike had seen in her was womanhood, superabundance: it must have seemed limitless.) 'I think she married him on the rebound.' That much was irrefutable, her being a bouncer. 'There was someone she really cared about in a big way, the once-in-a-lifetime way, and it hadn't worked out. I don't know why. Perhaps,' Bysshe gazed steadily and innocently at Ewing, 'he didn't declare himself. Perhaps he didn't realize how she felt about him. She never spoke of it. My guess is that she fought back by taking Pike, although crève cœur is not a sound basis for marriage.'

'What's not?'

'Heartbreak.'

'She would never do anything that wasn't right.'

'All I know is it wasn't right for her to marry Pike. He was in pharmaceuticals, ran a small business making vapour rub and fruit salts. The firm's trademark was a picture of the founder with walrus moustache and choke collar. That sort of thing inspires confidence. A lot of people swear by the old remedies. Have you heard of Pike's Patent Painkiller?' Ewing shook his head. 'Well, it was a respectable family firm and they did nicely. Then they brought out a new product. It was supposed to be a blood purifier. They called it Pike's Perfecta, and the inference was that whatever you had, or didn't have, would be taken care of. A dose a day to give you germ-free blood, a strong ticker, and the do-it-yourself of a stud bull. Pike himself – I have to say it – was a good advertisement for his medicine. He looked a world-beater. Of course the stuff sold like hot cakes or, I should say, like a panpharmacon.'

'A what?'

'A universal remedy.' Bysshe saw a glint in Ewing's eye which might be suspicion. 'It's funny how people think their blood's to blame for everything. But that medicine made some pretty bad blood. People lost their teeth and their hair. Genghis was raking in the money and he didn't care.'

'Who?'

'Genghis Pike, Dulcie's husband. The BMA stepped in and he was struck off, or whatever they do. He was ordered to pay compensation, but the business finances couldn't sustain it. Genghis was discredited and absconded with what cash and valuables he could lay his hands on.'

'Swine!'

'Oh now,' Bysshe said reasonably, 'he couldn't be blamed for wanting to stay out of jail.'

'Did they catch him?'

'He's not been seen from that day to this.'

'And Dulcie? What happened to Dulcie?'

It was what Ewing wanted to hear, knowledge he had come over land and sea for, powered by some mysterious urge which you could call love – you had to, there was nothing else to call it. Curiosity wasn't enough, passion too much. Love was what Rex Snowdon was known for and could, by means of tried and trusted stimuli which he had learned to administer to himself, enact as promptly as Pavlov's dogs. He could put on a demonstration not to be distinguished from real, whereas Tom Ewing, who knew real, couldn't demonstrate it. He leaned forward, fixing Bysshe with a furious eye. 'What happened to her?'

Ewing as lover, even with lower-case letter, was unlikely, to say the least. And Dulcie as the beloved was sheer pantomime. But it had to be possible that there was more than one love style.

'Genghis Pike and his Perfecta happened. You'd think she'd have had enough. Any other woman would have disassociated herself, gone where she wasn't known, changed her name, made a big mystery and enjoyed it.'

'Enjoyed it?' For Ewing, of course, there wasn't any other woman, there was only Dulcie, his Perfecta. He wouldn't see that there might be too much woman, or that merciful Nature would have made up Dulcie's quota with man and beast if Dulcie hadn't forestalled her. He rose from his chair. 'Where is she?'

'Looking after the sick.'

'Sick?'

'The people who swallowed Pike's medicine. If you were bald and toothless you'd feel sick.' Rage or determination – or was it desire? – had suddenly increased Ewing's girth. He stood, his shirt drum-tight over his chest, his neck as square as a newel-post. Bysshe spoke gently, 'It wouldn't help to know where she is. You couldn't see her, except through a grille.'

'A what?'

'Like they have in prison doors. And travelling cages. A convent is virtually a prison, but it was of her own choosing.'

'You mean she's become a nun?' Ewing's complexion, naturally unrefined, turned meaty.

'Joined a silent order.' For Dulcie that would be fate worse than death. Bysshe did not envisage actual bodily harm for her, only a lifelong martyrdom. And incarceration in a nunnery, especially a speechless one, would ensure that. 'You could talk to her, but she's not allowed to answer.' Dulcie wouldn't thank him for fixing her up with such an image, but he hoped it contented Ewing.

Of course Ewing owed it to himself to demolish the nonsense, but to do so he would have to question Dulcie's sanctity. Bysshe saw the difficulty. What was instructive was the way his own subconscious had evolved the nonsense. It was a cartoon version of the Zwemmer story, the instruction plainly being that he was already committed. He was being worked on. It had to happen with any role but was usually a conscious and unseemly process. The memory of getting himself ready for his scenes in *The Consul's Lady* still revolted his stomach.

'I don't want to talk to her.'

'What *do* you want?'

'Something to go on.'

'Haven't I given you that?' If Ewing asked for more it would be tiresome. 'I've given you background.' The scene should finish with a shot of Ewing's emotively twitching jaw as he turned away. 'Tell your wife that before you met her you were in love with a latter-day saint.'

'When's the next bus to the station?'

'There isn't, and there's no station till Antibes. I'll call you a car and take you to the gate.'

'I can find my own way out.'

'The gate's locked, barred and bolted.'

'What are you afraid of?'

'I'm protecting my seclusion. There have been interlopers less disinterested, or should I say more interested, than you.'

Ewing gave a dry spit of disgust. Bysshe picked up the kitchen extension and phoned Gluvas's grandson who drove an old Maigret saloon. When he put down the receiver Ewing said, 'Were you codding me?'

'Certainly not. Technically the unconsenting male is not as vulnerable as the female, but there are more ways than one of rape.'

'About Dulcie I mean.'

'Why should I?'

Ewing did not know. He would carry the doubt with him, forever unable to resolve it.

'Have you got a bit of paper?'

'What for?'

'For you to write your name on. Rex Snowdon. That's the sort of background my wife likes.'

With Ewing gone, everything started up again. It always did after people had been: business was resumed with joyful frenzy. The business of detrition and metamorphosis. Visitors were an interruption. When

Dulcie came there had been a virtual freeze.

Bysshe felt the resumption within himself. His need of privacy and the need of the place coincided. The discipline was transmutation which, after all, was his chosen profession, chosen before he had had time to put two and two together, when he had known in his bones that the answer would come out wrong. He might say that every part he had played, every simulated passion, every embrace, every rubberoid kiss, was a step in the same direction.

He found the idea both comic and comforting. Here he was taken care of, along with the frass and the peace-loving olives. At Ile-Marie he could at last evolve.

The hard shoulder of sky under the carob tree had turned cobalt blue. Mornings were the worst, but not here; here mornings were best, although the nights weren't so good. Sometimes, bedtimes, he needed somebody. Some other body, because that was one thing he didn't do alone. Of course he could supply himself: occasionally he invited someone to stay, or went purposely to Nice or Antibes, but purpose in that connection was aborting. He preferred to take his pleasure randomly, allow himself to be tempted.

The geese were honking on the hillside. They did not discriminate between living and inanimate objects. He had known them be provoked by a burst mattress in a ditch. The gaggle instinct moved them as one, and they stretched their necks, splayed their clowns' feet and gave the alarm. As they had done for the Romans, probably in this same place. In two thousand years they had found nothing better to be than geese.

He couldn't afford to wait a thousand days nor a thousand hours. If he went to New York and played Zwemmer he might break the time barrier and become different overnight: if he went to New York and did not play Zwemmer he could become a turd.

At the back of his mind was the memory of some bloomy old frames of Anatole Zwemmer sitting with a group of his lepers like a captain with his football team. They had no eyes, no hands, and lion faces.

Carver was promising real jungle and real animals

and would have promised real leprosy if he had thought of it. That was the sort of job Make-Up would revel in. Bysshe had watched the transformation of Billy Muir for his part as a thing from the grave. They gave him a rubber skull with tufts of yak hair punched in, the skin of an egg over one eyeball, fully credible maggot holes, and a jaw of plastic teeth like a cowcatcher. A peruke, a tricorn hat and latex cobwebs completed the vision. It wasn't Make-Up's fault, or Billy's, that when he stepped out of his coffin on the set he resembled an Edwardian lady motorist in travelling veil stepping out of her tourer. On screen the effect was chilling enough.

Fake leprosy would whet the public's morbid appetite, Bysshe's job would be to interpret what the real thing might have done to Zwemmer. There was something he had to do before that, something more important and much more difficult. He had to act the man who could act Zwemmer.

Perhaps he should read up on him, obit notices and whatever biographies there were. Except that Erckmann would have discarded all there was to know and would have put together, or be keeping on the boil, a lot of irrelevant facts and fantasies of his own.

Erckmann was known as a spellbinder. Certainly he worked like a charm – entirely without reason. Carver maintained that the Erckmann Experience was something no actor or technician could afford to miss. The bugs and demons could never get the better of anyone who had lived through it. Bysshe doubted if *he* could live through it. He needed toughening, not degutting.

At this point the prospect was of the remains of old vine terraces dropping to the service road among broom and bramble, and rocks like mammoth turtles slumbering in the grass. On a clear day the clobbered coast from Nice to Cannes could be seen. This morning nothing was visible beyond the slope of La Roquette. Bysshe came to a standstill.

It was feasible that Zwemmer had not allowed himself to be emotionally involved. Clinical detachment was essential to a doctor, and to live with lepers he would have to be a very cold fish. Otherwise he could drown in pity and rot in the sights and smells. There was a difference between corruption and decay, between sweet drying and dying, and chemical regression to a basic mess.

The role of Zwemmer, whether as a feeling man or not, would require a very different performance from the kind Bysshe had brought to an art. He was not a deadpan actor; he used his face and had amassed a reliable stock of delusions, perversities and night thoughts with which to start the action. He had learned finesse. What he had in his eyes was an invaluable asset which could compound emotion with effect. Only at rare and culminating moments did he permit the hurt to be picked up by the rest of his face. One could overdo it. Carver's crack about the organ-grinder's monkey was relevant.

In any case, sensibility, which Zwemmer must have had, could hardly get past the facial hair which Zwemmer was known to have had. Only his eyes would be free to play their part. A lot would have to be conveyed by movement and arrested movement, by stillness, by stance. It would be a matter of timing and, of course, voice – inflection and accent. What sort of accent did Zwemmer have? There was so much Bysshe didn't know about him, he wasn't even sure if ignorance would help or hinder. A working knowledge could rate as preconceived notions. Erckmann would be looking at him, if he looked at all, to see if he would make up to his, Erckmann's, idea of Anatole Zwemmer. And what that was, precisely, God alone knew.

Bysshe could see the roof of Gluvas's shed through the olives. It was what was left of a vigneron's cabin, holed and greened by an ancient vine which still produced grapes of singular bitterness. 'Mon fort' Gluvas called the place. He seldom put in an appearance before noon, and frequently later.

Bysshe wondered if he should leave a note saying that he was going to the States. It would be months before he could come back to Ile-Marie, whether he got the part or whether he didn't. Having made the trip he would have to stay and take what was offered or what Carver could snatch: commercials, soap opera, porno flicks. Carver was of a desperate disposition where money was involved.

In the 'fort' Gluvas's machete, his gun and saw hung on the wall. His strength was here, the congenitally indolent man's cherished show of action. Round the string bed were assembled cider casks, above it hung bunches of onions.

The floor had not been swept for years. Whatever had been dropped, provided it was not wanted or to be used again, had been allowed to stay and congeal or petrify or wither. Bysshe stirred about with his foot. In a corner a hip bath was half full of sacks and goose feathers. A necklace hung on a nail, it was not a rosary, just the sort of thing, crudely carved and painted, on sale to tourists as 'fabriqué dans la région'. That was no lie, except that the region happened to be Korea – or Hong Kong.

Lacking pencil and paper, Bysshe considered tracing a message on the floor. But Gluvas would never notice changes in the grit. He went to the door of the cabin, put a hand on the lintel.

*Framed in that rough entry he looks out at the native compound, the mud huts, pot-bellied children, the green maw of the jungle. Seeing – what?*

The milk of human kindness? In Zwemmer's case it was surely cream. He would be seeing death, his own included, his past life and what he was missing in the way of career, women, games. Turning with a suddenness both warding and passionate, Bysshe addressed the string bed, the hip bath, 'You are my children' – it was the sort of thing a monolithic old man with a touch of God would say.

Erckmann would want music. He always wanted music. One of his spells relied on upsetting the applecart, especially the applecart of a storyline. There would be shots of unrelated but arguably metaphysical significance to break the continuity: a man dying, a woman undressing, a child skipping. Then the camera would switch to surf riders or an air balloon over English meadows, or a lion at its kill. With sound, he would employ snatches of flagrantly inappropriate music to sharpen the moment on the screen, juxtaposing, and overlays of pop and classical. For Zwemmer it could be a Bach chorale and The Animals.

The orchard trees were covered with a painstaking scab, silver-grey, the same colour as the olives. Easy on the eye and mind, a non-grab colour. Restful. You could rest in it and dry in it and break, if you had to, like the twigs and seed-pods. Bysshe hoped not to break, but to harden and get himself a tegument for all seasons, all eventualities.

One might have supposed that at his time of life his psychic skin would have thickened along with his corporeal one. In fact it had thinned, which if he thought about it – as he did – was also supposable since he had less to commend him now.

The trees ended on the bleached slope of the Roquette. Walking down the hill he felt the metallic grasses clicking his bare ankles. On the lower slope, watered by hidden streams, there was green pasture, periwinkle, rockrose, mallow and wild orchids. It was where the geese liked to forage.

They were there now, they had heard him and were standing stock-still, looking up the hill. That they made no sound might mean that they recognized him. Or were holding their fire. They did that, they waited, not a feather stirring, even on the downy young ones, and then all together, stretched their necks and gave tongue.

*He is a gaunt old man smelling of sickness, following the path beaten by the bare feet of the women who go down to wash in the river. He is deaf to the scream of parrots and the chattering of monkeys, he thinks not of his children, the lepers, but of the woman he has loved and left, the beautiful Viennese. She is married to an Austrian count, an important government official. They are Catholics, divorce is out of the question and she had noble, not to say high-stomached moral principles which even their passion could not overrule. Also there is her husband's career. They were forced to renounce their love and he had come to Africa to forget, and to atone for crimes which no moral principle had kept him from committing. But he cannot forget her and he knows that he smells not only of his children's sickness but of his own mortal sin. He is never alone at the hospital, but he is the loneliest man in Africa. He is going to the river to find solitude, to be free, at one remove, of the unending demands on him. The jungle waits, pandanus leaves as big as umbrellas, and giant lianas hanging in ropes.*

Bysshe fingered the hair he might expect to have on lip and chin and over the disciplined nerves of his cheek.

*On the bank of the river, the same river that he had travelled years ago on a little steamer which shrieked at every bend in the hundreds of miles of bends, the old man stands looking into the brown water. Something moves, slips away. A crocodile. He sees its unwinking malevolent eye going down into the smoking mud.*

The geese, with an internal chuckle, moved away and began to clip the grass round the oieboy who was lying on his back among the periwinkle and mallow, as he often did. Bysshe had accepted that he must support layabouts – workers would not have suited him or his garden – but he wondered at the boy's indolence. It was not, as in Gluvas's case, sheer bloody disinclination. The reverse: there was expectancy in it, the boy was waiting. His body was spilled on the grass, prodigal – even profligate – of its youth which could only be spent and might with greater profit be squandered. He still had everything to lose. Bysshe felt a pang of resentment which only deepened when he asked himself what it was the boy waited for. What could he expect?

Through the overlarge jeans, split by someone else's patellas, shone the bones of his knees. His feet were planted soles down as if in a moment he would leap up on them. His chest rose and fell, softly, scrupulously expelling each breath. His fingers, curled into his palms, were the fingers of a child, cushion-tipped and tender, for all their scabbing and bruising. He appeared to be sleeping soundly. One eye was closed, the other showed its habitual glaucous streak beneath what was left of the lid. Bysshe had never been able to decide how much, if at all, he could see with it.

He sat on his heels beside him. He still felt a shock of disbelief whenever he looked into that face. Zwemmer could not have looked at anything much worse. Disbelief demanded that he look away, preferring not to believe what he saw.

One side of the face had been denaturized. What served as flesh was the colour of raw meat, an old rawness in which the blood had darkened and the living tissue had dried hard and rigid as wood. It was covered by a membrane of terrible flimsiness, thinner and more brittle than a beetle's wing, yet stretched mercilessly taut from brow to chin without a wrinkle or any provision for movement or variation of texture.

The mouth was badly scarred and healed short, catching up the corner into a permanent joyless rictus. The left eyelid, overburdened with scar tissue, hung low and half concealed the glimmer of something like a clouded jelly. In sleep, or the heat of the day, the boy had pushed back the hair from the fruitful side of his head, leaving an area of stitched-up skull. If he was aware of the state of his face as compared with other faces, he did not try to conceal it.

As Ewing had said, it was obscene. But the obscenity lay in the contrast between the halves: the pure half was mocked and forgotten. The crippled half mocked and was remembered.

Bysshe, when he remembered it, did so not in entirety nor as a worsening sequence. He had glimpses like flashes from a nerve end. As if he was being warned about something that was going to happen, or had happened, or ought to be stopped. He might have been alarmed, but recognized these glimpses as one of his ploys. His practice was to summon visions to help get an action going for the camera, and naturally – his nature being as loosely organized as anyone else's – visions could come unsummoned. And unproductive.

But this was his chance. He should touch the membrane which served as skin to cover what served as flesh. He should know the actual texture of mutilation. He needed to know it as a physical fact for himself. And for Zwemmer. And if he said for Zwemmer, he must say for Erckmann too.

He had a longing to break and relieve the stricture of the boy's cheek. But when he approached a finger to it, the geese advanced on him, hissing like a hostile audience.

451

# 2

'You know where they've gone.'

'I didn't say so.'

'You saw an address.'

'It wasn't an address.'

'So what was it?'

'Why?'

She tries to stop things happening by asking why. When we were in infants' school if she didn't know how many beans made five or if someone was going to sit her in a puddle she'd cry 'Why?' and open her eyes so wide it was hurtful. She had round Muppet eyes then; now she wears glasses and her eyes look poached.

'They're our responsibility,' I said. 'Yours and mine. We must go after them.'

'I can't go and leave everything!'

Everything being pension Thursday, Tesco Friday, *Coronation Street* Monday and Wednesday.

'Tell me what it was you saw.'

'It was what she'd written: "Hotel, grand place, nice." "Where's this then", I said, "what's nice about it?" and she ate the paper.'

'She what?'

'Oh, I don't know!'

To Darlene, ignorance is a commodity and she's careful with it. Incomplete information tempts people to put two and two together and do the work for her. Most of the time she keeps herself in an adjustable twilight.

When things get too near the bone – her bone – she chooses total darkness and opts out.

I said, 'She watches too much television. She wouldn't have gone with him otherwise. He's not televisual, but the situation is.'

'It's been going on for months. I've seen her get droopier and droopier, weeping over the phone. She wets the receiver. I knew it was a man. I said to her ask him round, why don't you?'

'You must have known there was something wrong.' With a girl like Cherrimay everything could be wrong. I've known her weep because her half-moons weren't showing. 'Of course it was right for him. He's become a new man. There's only one Pike, so that just means a lot more of the old one. It was obvious to me what was going on. He's tried before, but he always comes back for his morals and I don't interfere unless my plans are upset. Of course I would have if I'd known it was your Cherrimay.'

'I keep asking myself why. Why couldn't it be some nice boy? She's seventeen years old and he's fifty if he's a day.'

'Forty-eight.'

'He's abducted her.'

'More likely she's abducted him.'

'You think it's funny. You don't give a damn how I feel!'

'Of course I do. But she's taking my place and I feel bound to ask what she's putting into it. The difference between her age and mine is a minus quantity so far as I'm concerned. There has to be something else, something more.'

'Anything I could do you could always do better!'

Darlene's let herself go. I'm big, but built to scale. Darlene's bones are lost in flab. Only her feet have stayed dainty – like pig's trotters. I said, 'You were better than any of us at ballet.'

'I had it in me to be a dancer. That wasn't enough for you, now it's my daughter who's not enough.' I hoped her heart was sound, it was jumping about in her throat. She cried, 'Not enough for what?' and I could see that

she was drawing on something from way back. She can't
help it, she hasn't advanced. Cherrimay, her daughter,
has picked up the short change. They both open their
eyes wide and see their own noses. I used to try to help
Darlene with the school exams; I worked out a system of
signals for her but she couldn't even remember what
we'd arranged.

'You know,' I said, 'your French wasn't so hot, was
it?'

'What's that got to do with it?'

'Are you sure the word was "nice" and not "Nice"?
Could it have been the place, not the taste?'

'What word?'

'The word you saw on the paper, before Cherrimay
ate it. Have you thought it could have been Nice,
France?'

'Why should I?'

'It could be where they've gone.'

'Why would they go to France?'

'I wonder. Pike doesn't like Abroad. Perhaps it was
her idea.'

'You think she started it? A girl just out of school
chasing a man old enough to be her father? Or her
grandfather!'

'Not grandfather. Pike didn't make an early enough
start for that. I expect he got round her and she was
flattered.' I had to work at my expectations, but they
are, have been, maximum and private, whereas
Darlene's are merely those of an outsider. 'He's still
presentable when he's shaved and tidy. That's how I
knew he was meeting someone. Not only did he have a
bubble bath, he left off his thermal underpants and he
wouldn't do that for snooker evenings.' I said, seeing
Darlene's face, 'Don't worry, it would be for the purest
possible motive. He'd want to be young all through for
her.'

'It's disgusting!'

'It's human. Predictable. He's taken the car and his
nylon shirts. If he's taken his passport I'll know where
they've gone.'

'Where?'

'To Nice. Like in nephew.'

I know my way around Pike, where everything is in him and how it works, up to the point at which it works. He was given to me to know. I started studying him before we were married. I could write a book about him and it would make interesting reading if you like horrors.

I admit to being totally surprised by this affair, I could have been knocked down by a feather at there actually being an affair. For Pike to have a girl is contrary to all expectation – an expectation I've learned to live with. The refrain: blessed are they who expect nothing because they won't be disappointed, has also become my policy.

It's not true that there have been other women. He's picked up the general idea because it would be hard not to, but he can't put it into practice. I cover for us both: whatever may be seen to be wrong with my marriage it's not going to be that.

If he could run away with a girl, if he could believe there was a future in it, Cherrimay Pugh would do as well as any. In fact she would do better, being the daughter of my old schoolfriend, Darlene Lufkin that was, our near neighbour, and a source of information. Darlene leaks information droplet by droplet and you pool it to suit yourself. You have fun at someone's expense, only this time it would be at mine. Up to the point. Because in the circumstances no one was likely to question Pike's manhood. He had done me a part favour by taking Cherrimay Pugh.

If the words on that piece of paper which she ate had been in a different order – 'Nice hotel, grand place' for instance – I shouldn't have given it another thought. But 'Hotel, grand place, nice' didn't add up. You don't call a place nice if you've just called it grand. Besides, I remembered how Darlene used to entertain us in school when she conjugated French verbs with a Merseyside accent. So I took a chance on the address, that it *was* an address – like 'Hôtel du Grand Place, Nice'. I had nothing else to go on.

On the plane I had time to think. The hotel might

have another name, it might just have been described to
Cherrimay as 'grand' and there might be more than one
Grand Place, and hotels in all of them. Those two would
hardly sign in as Mr and Mrs Pike. And they might
already have left for somewhere else.

Where would Pike take a girl? Being scarcely able to
believe he would take a girl anywhere, both widened
and narrowed the field. They could be making for Spain
or sitting on Southend pier.

By the time I was breaking the clingfoil off my lunch
tray I couldn't believe any of it was happening to me. I
suffered complete loss of credibility. Something to do
with the altitude I suppose. I looked down at the sea and
thought now that's not necessary, I could drown in one
of Darlene's droplets.

Then after all, it was easy. I found a taxi at the airport
and told the driver 'Grand Place'. He shrugged. I tried
'Hôtel du Grand Place', and off we went.

I'd been to Nice before. It's Abroad, banana trees and
sunbrellas and wedding-cake buildings. I can take it or
leave it. The cab pulled up in a narrow street alongside a
huge new smoked-glass and steel block. The lower floor
was full of agricultural machinery arranged on grass
mats.

'Where are we?' There was no square and I couldn't
see any hotel. The driver pointed. 'Chambres, douches,
confort' was daubed on a wall. 'This is the Hôtel du
Grand Place?' He nodded and put up the fingers of one
hand, so I gave him five francs. He put them up again.
He kept putting them up, and each time I gave him
another five francs. Then he put up the fingers of both
hands. I said, 'I don't know what you charge for a ride
but I think you've been paid,' and picked up my bag and
walked away. He shouted after me. I turned and looked
at him. He exploded ten fingers, shut them into fists,
beat on the steering wheel and drove off.

The street was one-way; it was too small to be
anything else. The top storeys of the new block flamed in
the sun, while the other buildings lurked at the bottom
of a cut-glass canyon. They were old places with shutters
and balconies, and I noticed shops selling wine, bread

and video tapes. People were eating at tables on the
pavement. Cemented into the walls were stone basins
planted with geraniums. I didn't like the look of the
hotel. It was tall and skinny and pocked, as if someone
had dug pennies into the brickwork.

Inside I was met by the smell of garlic and French
fries. That's all. There was nobody at the desk, and what
I took to be damp on the walls turned out on closer
inspection to be tapestries, old snail-coloured pictures of
women in steeple hats draped over stags. The plumbing
was hammering away in the depths, the place had seen
its best days. Pike, I thought, is this your love nest?

I went to the desk, and prodded a cat sleeping on
something which could be the hotel register. I needed to
look at that, so I felt no qualms. The cat leapt up and
arched its back. I got the book, turned it towards me, but
couldn't read the writing which was mauve, spidery,
and sloped backwards.

'Madame?'

She must have come from under the tapestry, a small
blonde, heavily made-up. I'm blonde – I chose to be
when my hair started to go streaky – but at least I don't
paint. I've a nice skin, nothing to hide. Women who
paint themselves are putting on a disguise and must
have cause.

I said, 'This the Hôtel du Grand Place?' She nodded.
'Have you got someone here by the name of Pike?' She
picked up the cat and cuddled it round her neck. 'Pike,'
I said, tapping the register. The cat clawed its way over
her shoulder. She took up the book and ran a blood-red
nail down the page. 'English. Like me.'

She made her lips into a pink bud. 'Pew?'

The French language has to be mouthed, made a
meal of, and I don't speak it unless I have to. 'P-I-K-E,' I
spelled it for her.

'Non. Mais Monsieur et Madame Pew sont anglais.'

The penny dropped. Mr and Mrs Cherrimay Pugh.
So she *had* brought him here to the 'grand place'. How
had she managed it, what had she used? It could only be
hope, which he has never lost. I tell him miracles don't
happen, you are as you are.

'Have you got a room?'

'Une chambre?'

'Single.'

'Pour combien de personnes?' I held up one finger.
'Pour combien de temps?'

It was going to be a battle. She didn't care if I took a
room or not. One of us had to be at a disadvantage,
linguistically speaking, and it wasn't going to be me.
'For one night. Or longer. I don't know.'

'Voulez-vous voir la chambre?'

I knew I wouldn't like it, but there wasn't much
choice. 'Which room are Mr and Mrs Pugh in?'

She took down a key. 'Par ici, s'il vous plaît,
madame.' I thought she was going to take me to them.

She unlocked a door on the first landing. It was pitch
dark inside the room. She went in and threw open the
shutters. I saw a bed, a wardrobe and a washbasin with
enough pipes for a church organ. So this was the
accommodation being offered to me. 'Haven't you
anything better?'

'Madame?'

I dropped my bag and went to the window. The view
was into a sump full of barrels and fruit boxes. Looking
up, I saw the blue old Riviera sky as if through the wrong
end of a telescope. I suddenly felt sorry – and mad – for
my poor Pike. It wasn't his fault, it was in his stars that
not even this once could he get something right.

'Celle-ci est propre, tranquille, et très confortable.
Peut-être madame désiré-t'elle quelque chose à un autre
étage?'

She had got something wrong too: the measurements
of the face she had painted over her own. The effect was
too big and bright. I said, 'I'm here to get my husband.'

She didn't bat her false eyelashes but she knew what
I'd said, she could speak our language. The idea was to
make me speak hers.

'Je suis Madame Rosier,' she said.

'Mrs Pike.'

'Je vous assure qu'il n'y a personne ici de ce nom.'

'There is now,' I said.

\*

My glance out of the window hadn't been inspiriting, but it had been informative. As I looked up between the walls to the sky I caught sight of a familiar and very personalized object. Seeing it in that foreign place brought the situation home to me. For the first time I saw what I was getting into – what I was being done out of. Pike's stars could queer things for me too.

Someone had told him once that germs generate on a wet face flannel, so he always dries his after use. At home he puts it in the airing cupboard. Here it was now, draped over the shutters of a room above. Not the sort of object to turn anyone on. It turned me into a fighting force. When Madame Rosier had gone, I checked the location on the floor above, left my bag and went up the stairs.

History was on every tread: spillages, cigarette burns, stiletto-heel holes. I took note of all of them because this was Pike's love nest. I knocked on a door, it was room 32, and had it turned out not to be theirs I would have tried the next one. And the next. But Cherrimay herself opened it to me. She took one look and her jaw dropped so low that I could have posted a small parcel in her mouth. 'So here you are,' I said. She made as if to close the door but I had taken the precaution of getting my foot in. 'Mr and Mrs Pugh.' What happened next was typical. It was the sort of thing Cherrimay did, and the sort of thing that happens to Pike. In that respect they were suited.

She flung wide her arms and started dodging in front of me as if keeping goal. I saw the goal over her shoulder – my husband, Pike, lying on the bed.

'You shan't!' she kept saying. 'You shan't!'

'Shan't what?'

She meant it as a general veto: she didn't want me to exist. But Dulcie Pike was here, and all Cherrimay Pugh could do about it was dissolve into tears. I said, 'Stop prancing about and stop crying. Nothing puts a man off like a messy weeper.' It was sound advice, but what I intended was to advise him about her and her wet nature. 'Pike, what's going on? What are you up to?'

'Nothing!' cried Cherrimay. I could believe that,

certainly, but I couldn't understand why they should come all this way to get up to it. It didn't make sense. 'He's ill!'

'Ill?'

'He's hurt his back. Can't you see?'

I took her by the shoulders and put her aside, though I would like to have put her out of the window. My husband, a roaring boy when in form, lay whimpering among the sheets. I asked him what it was all about.

'I've pulled a ligament.'

'The same one?' He got his back years ago and it's been a boon to him ever since.

'I think I've torn it.' That figured. Given the situation, he had to increase the odds; a mere strain wouldn't be enough to release him from his current obligations. I plumped myself down on the end of the bed. 'For Christ's sake, I'm in agony!'

'Don't swear.'

'That wasn't swearing, it was praying.'

'How did it happen?'

'The way these things do.'

'What way's that?'

'Does it matter?'

'There's one way that would matter a lot to me.'

I looked him in the eye and he had the grace to colour up. 'How the hell did you find us?'

'*That* doesn't matter.' I got up to take a look round the room. I was interested to see what he had brought with him, the only time in his life when he had had to pack for himself. For his second honeymoon. Perhaps he would call it his first. He is still capable of blaming me for the botch-up at Tossa de Mar, Spain.

His pyjamas were brand new, crisp blue poplin with a motif on the breast pocket. He had bought himself a dressing gown: at home he wears a cast-off of mine, when he wears anything. Pike in his striped pyjamas is a familiar sight to our neighbours on Sundays; he dresses when it's time to go to the local, and given a warm summer morning he washes the car in his night attire. He had brought the flight-bag, though they hadn't flown. This was the one we took to Majorca, stained by a bottle of duty-free which had been smashed inside it. His brushes, which I hadn't missed so much as I missed their smell, strong and hairy – subconsciously I prepare to smell it as I approach our dressing table at home; the cuff links I gave him for Christmas, and of course that face flannel outside on the shutter. He had also brought his grandfather's watch with the bullet on the chain. Pike has a fixation about that watch, it's his link with the past. For him it *is* the past; he doesn't believe in the Wars of the Roses, Julius Caesar, or Henry the Eighth because he has nothing to show for them.

Her things were there too, her make-up stuff: lipstick, foundation, eyeliner, nail varnish and a little brush for her lashes. It really got to me, seeing them lying with his things on the dressing table.

The room was frowsty. They might not notice the stain on the carpet where the radiator leaked, and the veneer peeling off the wardrobe, but bliss would wear thin, I knew. If it hadn't already. 'What made you come here?'

'My pen friend recommended it,' declared Cherrimay.

'The French Riviera?' I looked at Pike.

'My pen friend used to work here in her school-holidays. Doing the bedrooms. She got us fixed up and the lady downstairs has been ever so kind. She fetched a doctor.'

'And what did he say?'

'We don't know,' said Pike. 'He stuck a needle in my backside and charged two hundred francs.'

I had to smile. No doctor can take Pike's back away from him.

Cherrimay knelt beside the bed and laid her head on his arm. 'He's coming again tomorrow.'

'A few more visits,' said Pike, 'and we'll have to go home.'

'Fine,' I said.

He looked at me, greenish round the gills. 'I'm not coming back to you.'

Cherrimay, Darlene's daughter, whom I had known as a baby wet at both ends – and so had he – put her arms round my husband with a protective gesture and looked at me, the brave little doe defying the wolf.

That did it. I took off my coat. I've said I'm big, I can loom, and I loomed over that bed. Their bed. Cherrimay shrank from me, tried to shrink into Pike, which caused him more pain than pleasure judging by the way he winced.

I rolled up my sleeves. 'Move over,' I said to Cherrimay.

'What are you going to do?'

'What I always do when he gets a bad back, gentle massage and manipulation.'

'Leave us alone,' said Pike.

'Anything that French doctor can do I can do better. For significantly fewer francs. Now move over!'

'You and me are finished, Dulcie. Have been for a long time.'

'What you mean is you never got started.' To Cherrimay I said, 'But that's my business. I contracted to cope, one way or another. Marriage is using what you're given, making the best of it. Sometimes making the best of the worst.'

She gazed up at me out of his arms. 'We love each other.'

For her that solved everything. I don't call it innocence, or ignorance, I call it dimness, under-endowment, and it's dangerous. Not to her, to everyone else. Especially to Pike. 'He's old enough to be your grand-daddy.'

'There's no telling you anything,' said Pike.

'There's no telling me *that*.' I plucked Cherrimay off the bed. She was pluckable, she came away in my hands. I rolled Pike over and he yelled like a baby. I stuck my thumbs into the small of his back.

'You're hurting him!'

'Did you bring a hot-water bottle?'

'Of course not.'

'Go and buy one. Buy two. Your love may keep him warm but his back needs toasting.' She stood there blinking. 'Go on,' I said, 'or would you rather spend your money on French doctors?'

She went reluctantly. Pike and I settled to our routine, me easing and coaxing his muscles, he whickering and burying his face in the pillow.

'You're making a mistake,' I said. 'Cherrimay Pugh's no good to you. I'd like to know why you thought she was.' He mumbled something. I pulled his pyjama trousers down to his knees and he begged for mercy. 'While we're on the subject, why did you come to Nice of all places? It's not your scene.'

'She had this address. And Webb-Ellis is buried here.'

'Who?'

'The man who invented rugger. He was the first to run with the ball.'

Everyone has something sacred. With Pike it's rugby football. He likes to believe he got his back playing scrum-half in his work's semi-final. I happen to know he did it slipping on something nasty outside Woolworth's.

Now Pike's back is an understood thing between us. It allows him to lead a free and active life when he wants to. For reasons best known to himself it 'flares up' from time to time. That's how he puts it: 'My back's flared up again.' There's nothing fiery about it though, it's a steady progression, from bad to worse, as required. It can be trusted to restrict and hamper and put him out of action if there's anything he can't or doesn't want to do. Obviously a godsend like that shouldn't start from a mess on the pavement, so it's been what you might call canonized.

That poor child, Cherrimay, hadn't a clue about any of this. She thought fate was against them. Perhaps she felt guilty and that she was being punished, and Pike's pain was part of her punishment. I wouldn't be surprised. But sooner or later it must become obvious, even to her, that there would be no idyll. She would realize that the most she could hope for was to be allowed to lie beside him on the bed and wipe his forehead and slip out occasionally to Uniprix to fetch him beer and pizzas.

I didn't sleep that night. There were people coming and going on the stairs, flushing the toilets, having

baths, conversations, quarrels, nightmares and telephone calls. It all seemed to be happening outside my
door. I got up once and looked out. A man and girl were
right outside. He was kneeling down fixing her girdle. It
shouldn't have been difficult because it was all she had
on. 'Stay calm,' he said to me – or something like it – in
French. I slammed the door and turned the key. I was
probably the only one alone in that place. Keeping
myself to myself. What for? *Who* for? I often used to ask
that question. Knowing the answer doesn't help me
now.

When I went up to their room next morning,
Cherrimay had locked me out. I waited a while, then
knocked. She called, 'Who's that?' I replied, 'La femme
de chambre, madame,' and she opened the door. 'Don't
do that again,' I said, 'or I'll have to ask for the master
key.'

'They won't give it to you!'

'If I tell them the facts they will.'

'What facts?'

'That my husband is ill and I have to attend to him.'

'He doesn't want you. He never has!'

'You're taking too much on yourself. Pike's my old
married man and what I don't know about him isn't
worth knowing.' Though it might be to her, because odd
scraps were all she was ever likely to know.

'You never even call him by his name!'

'Pike's his name. He's a big eater, like the fish.'

'You've never understood him.'

'Listen, childie –'

'I'm not a child, I'm a grown woman! And I'll tell you
what else I am –'

'Tell her nothing!' Pike had heaved himself on his
elbow. 'I'm sick of this!'

'I know what you are,' I said to Cherrimay. 'I've
watched you hold your breath with temper because
your mother wouldn't buy you jellybeans. And that was
only yesterday.'

'I'm not ashamed of being young, I'm glad, and
proud!' Cherrimay Pugh could be seen stretching up to
meet the occasion. 'I've got something you never had.

You're not his wife, there's a whole lot more to marriage than you've given him –'

'You surprise me.' I tapped Pike between his shoulder blades. 'Does she surprise you?'

'Go away and leave us alone.'

But by evening I had him out of his bed and sitting in a chair, though not without protest. There's no one like Pike for making himself heard. The day we married, my brother called him the 'loud baboon'. Of course I asked Doug what he was getting at. He said, 'The wedding-guest here beat his breast for he heard the loud baboon.' He'd been drinking and anyway he has a minimal alcohol threshold. But he was right.

I was well aware that Cherrimay was getting restive. The signs were unmistakable. My own feeling was that the ceiling had come down a few inches every time I went into that room. She roamed around it, twitching things, poking her finger through holes in the curtains, leaning out of the window to see the sky. I guessed she was trying to stop herself from wondering. By the afternoon I knew that I only had to wait for things to take their course – and there was only one course.

I even rang Darlene and told her I'd caught up with them. 'You needn't worry,' I said, 'she'll soon be home.' 'How do you know?' 'She's fed up with him. I can tell.'

I could have felt sorry for them individually, but those two together, those particular two, cancelled out my finer feelings. Cherrimay on her own was a chip off the old Darlene Lufkin block, no smarter, no prettier, and really no different from her mother, except that she had it all still to do. But with Pike, tied to him with a love knot, she had become the last person in the world. There was no pitying *that* combination. They were simply ludicrous.

However, there was no need to be bored whilst waiting. I went out, walked around the town, looked at shops, sat in the gardens where there were fountains and palm-trees and statues of Liberty, Equality and Fraternity. I avoided the usual Côte d'Azur attractions. I'm not a beach person, I don't take my clothes off and lie on the sand with the Kentucky fried chicken boxes. I didn't even go to look at the sea.

One thing I did find that cheered me: our old Escort parked near the hotel. It was thick with dust and scrawled with French words, no doubt insulting. But it looked viable and I was pleased. I'd be able to get about.

Next to the hotel was a café-bar called the Galerie des Lilas. There was barely room for two small tables and chairs on the pavement outside which meant that passers-by had to step into the road, but no one seemed to mind.

That first afternoon as I sat at one of the café tables I considered whether I was doing myself a disservice by keeping on with the massage and manipulation. There was a risk that Pike would get mobile before Cherrimay's patience ran out. On the other hand, he must be made to understand – they both must – that he was no good without me. If I say he's precious little good with me, that's my business. It's the choice I made thirty years ago, and even knowing what I know now, would make again. Where does that leave me? It leaves me with Pike.

It was hot and I was grateful for the shade and the cool at the bottom of this canyon of a street. I ordered tea which came in two bags hung in the pot like drowned mice.

At the other table were a boy and girl in their late teens. He wore shredded denim shorts, nothing else, and was the colour of teak, his skin glistening with sun-oil, which obviously gave the girl great pleasure. She ran her finger down his cheek to the muscle of his upper arm and back again. She was in pink satin trousers, poured into them, without a hitch or a crinkle. Over the tips of her breasts two rosebuds were held in position by an arrangement of silk straps. I expect a certain style of undress Abroad. Usually it's indecent or it's a positive eyesore. But these two were gloriously innocent, and what they were doing – claiming each other by touching, stroking, kissing eyelashes – was as green as Adam and Eve before the apple. It was what Cherrimay should be doing. Tied to Pike she was missing her greenness. She wouldn't even know she had had it, she'd dry up before her time. I hate to see anything wasted, especially on Pike.

When the waiter came they waved him away. They didn't want anything and he didn't insist. He stood in the doorway, arms folded, watching them. I watched too. It was quite an exhibition, a touching demonstration of tenderness. I have never been on the receiving or the giving end of anything like that. When I met Pike I was a fun-loving girl with a secret streak. I used to pray. Night and morning I knelt down – there was something I wanted and thought I shouldn't want. Daytimes I left my desk in the typists' pool and went to the staff toilet to ask for guidance. I enjoyed a joke if it was clean but I wouldn't hear God's name being taken in vain.

I told myself that Pike was the perfect man for me. He was happy and big, big-built, big-hearted, generous to a fault. Generosity is his fault. It's constitutional. Physically and mentally he's too big to concentrate. He's a roaring empty shell, as I found after we were married. And that's when I stopped praying. It didn't seem reasonable to ask God to undo His handiwork.

It's a pity about me. I have this streak which might be romance, or sex. It won't let me quite give up my expectations. Even now.

This boy at the café table took his girl's hand and nuzzled his way to the crook of her elbow. She stroked his hair. Then he sprang to his feet and brought her to hers with the same movement. Hand in hand they ran into the Hotel du Grand Place.

When I went up to room 32 for the evening massage session it was like an oven, the shutters were closed and Pike was face down on the bed with a hot-water bottle in the small of his back.

Cherrimay declared that he was better, but when I lifted his pyjama jacket the shape of the hot-water bottle was burned on him bright pink. 'You made it too hot,' I said.

Pike said, 'I thought you weren't coming,' and in the next breath, 'We don't need you.'

'You'll need a skin graft if she goes on like this. Don't

blame me if it hurts.' I started the massage.

He yelled into his pillow and Cherrimay rushed at me like a demented housefly. I swatted her with the hot-water bottle.

Pike has a nice back, broad shoulders, flat blades and a well-buttoned spine. He's broad in the beam but it all looks right. Each time I see his back I get a pang.

'I saw the car,' I said, 'and I'd like the keys.'

'What for?'

'To drive it.'

'Where to?'

'I want to call on my brother.'

'What brother?' said Cherrimay.

'Rex Snowdon, the film star.'

She knew that, everyone knows. It's a five-minute wonder. 'You're not!' people say. 'His sister? Never!' The men say, 'Pull the other one', and the women ask for details.

'We're twins,' I said. 'We happened to be born together.'

Certainly we never did anything else together. As children, told to run away and play, we ran in opposite directions. I played with bat and ball and skipping-rope, I liked action. Doug messed about with cigarette cards and beetles in matchboxes, very private. Sneaky, I said then.

Pike turned his face up from his pillow. 'He's in America.'

'He's here, at his villa in the hills.'

Cherrimay said, 'Does he look like you?'

'Hardly. He's the beauty of the family. Girls flock to him like moths to a candle and if they don't get burned they drop in the grease.' My fingers were leaving white weals on Pike's inflamed skin. 'It's easy come, easy go with Doug.' He went through a bad patch in his teens, I was the better-looking one then. He grew too fast, he had boils on his neck and he knocked out his front teeth in a motor-bike accident. 'He has what it takes.' I laid my palms very gently on the weals on Pike's back. I believe if I gave my mind to it I could develop the healing touch.

'He never comes to see you,' said Cherrimay.

'What would a man like him, leading the life he does, do in Sidcup?'

'What life?'

'Mixing with film and TV personalities, directors, oil millionaires, Presidents – he did a film with Ronald Reagan once – he owns a ranch-house and a swimming pool, he runs half a dozen cars and a chauffeur. When he gives parties he hires a firm of caterers and the parties go on for days.'

'He gets in takeaway food,' said Pike.

'Doug makes more from one film than anyone I know makes in five years.'

'And spends it.'

'Why not? He doesn't owe us.' When our parents were alive he sent them a cheque every Christmas. It was too much for them to spend or to talk about and they used to put the cheque away and try to ignore it. When we asked if they'd heard from Doug, my mother would say, 'He always writes,' and show us the typed envelope. All he'd written was his name on the cheque. After they died, we found uncashed cheques to the value of five thousand pounds in a biscuit tin. 'My brother's a free agent, not like some of these show people, married and divorced several times and paying fortunes in alimony.'

'Why isn't he married?'

'Because he's queer,' said Pike. 'He has to be, to do the things he does in front of an audience.'

'What things?'

'A real man wouldn't be able to stop himself.'

That was wonderful, coming from Pike. 'Jealousy is natural,' I said. 'Doug has his pick of the beauties of stage and screen. He may not be real, actors seldom are, but he's man enough.' It used to upset my mother, seeing magazine pictures of him draped round half-naked women. I used to tell her that it was a publicity stunt, deny his promiscuity; it was what people expected of him and of every film star. I remember how she would fold her thumbs under her pinafore and say she supposed so and go on living somewhere else in some other time.

'How do you know he's here?'

I saw that Cherrimay was getting interested. The situation she was in, anything would be interesting. 'I read an article in the paper. It said he's living at his villa in the South of France. Hiding.'

'Why?'

'If anyone knows the film business, when to be available and when to be hard to get, he does.'

'The car's like me,' said Pike. 'Out of action. If you want to see your brother you'll have to take a taxi.'

'What's wrong with the car?'

He rolled over. I know his face like the back of my hand, but he introduces some funny wrinkles sometimes. 'Let's get this understood, Dulcie. We don't need you, we don't want you. You can't turn back the clock. You ought never to have come here. Be sensible and go home.'

'Can she massage your back?'

'She does better than that, she keeps it warm. In bed we're as cosy as a banana and a banana skin.'

I'm not given to visions, but I had one then. Pike disgusts me not for what he is, but for what he isn't. I went to the basin and washed my hands. The last thing I would be able to bear was to take his smell with me to that room downstairs. Those two watched, Pike open-mouthed, having said his say. Each time he opens his mouth he thinks he'll win.

I rolled down my sleeves and buttoned my cuffs. On the dressing table I'd seen the ignition key among Pike's loose change and her back-combings. I picked it up and put it in my handbag. 'I'll take the car to a garage and get it fixed.'

Pike forgot himself so far as to swing his legs off the bed. His feet touched the floor, but then his knees gave way and he fell. I left Cherrimay draped over him – just like a discarded banana skin.

I could find nothing wrong with the car. It was reluctant to start but it often is, and it had been standing idle for days. I ran the engine, engaged gear and inched to and fro. A plastic bottle burst under the back wheel. The gauge showed an almost empty tank. I switched off, locked and walked away.

My clothes were sticking to me and I decided to have my breakfast outside, at the café. The lover-girl sat alone at one of the tables, waiting for the loving to begin. Or continue. This morning she had on a see-through garment, everything could be seen through it. Personally I believe some things should be left to the imagination. As I didn't fancy witnessing love-play so early in the day I sat at the other table with my back to her.

Cherrimay Pugh, the chosen, the chooser, of my husband, looked none too fresh that morning. She appeared in the hotel entrance carrying the flight-bag. I beckoned her over. She frowned, but came nonetheless. 'Are you leaving?' I asked her.

'I'm going to get something for lunch.'

'What did you give him yesterday?'

'Why?'

'There's a connection between what he eats and what he suffers.'

'We had crab sandwiches and apricot tart.'

'Was that wise?' She fiddled with her hair. I don't think she'd washed, her face was smudgy and half rubbed out. I said, 'It's no diet for a man in his situation.'

'What situation?'

'Why, lying in bed all day, taking no exercise. Crab's binding, it's a well-known fact. So is pastry. He has problems with his bowels. He's not all that young, you know, he shouldn't take chances.'

'I'm not a chance, I'm a certainty.'

Cherrimay had sent that back like returning a ball. Obviously she was learning. Her face sharpened and her Muppet eyes, the same as Darlene's when she was young, turned gooseberry-grey.

'Well,' I said cheerfully, 'that being so, you want him on his feet as soon as possible. Proper food will help, improper food will hinder. Get him an underdone steak with chips. A green salad – lettuce, cucumber, watercress – there's iron in watercress – and fresh fruit, apples and oranges. No bananas.' I smiled, but of course she didn't. 'And milk – there's calcium in milk – it's better for him than tinned beer.' Pike hates milk, with luck he'd throw it at her. 'Go to the supermarket and pick out the best stuff.'

'I can't speak French.'

'You don't have to; just help yourself and pay at the cash-out like we do at home.'

'He doesn't like me to be away long.'

'I'll take you in the car.'

She sat down suddenly. 'Is Rex Snowdon really your twin brother?'

Aha, I thought, but not laughing. It had been on her mind, and still was. 'Yes, but we're not identical, he's altogether different from me. A different personality. Of course film people live in another world.' I sighed, playing at being fuddy old Dulcie admiring her glamorous brother. 'He's got a wonderful place up in the hills, sauna, sun lounge, patio, swimming pool.' When I was there he'd had a puddle on the kitchen floor.

'But he's old.'

'He's younger than Pike. I'm younger than Pike.'

She stared past me. It was sinking in, I thought. Then she said sharply, 'That's disgusting!'

'By two years – not thirty.'

'Those two are carrying on as if they're in bed.'

I realized that she was talking about what she could see over my shoulder, the young sweethearts at the next table. 'Oh, I don't know,' I said. 'They're in love.'

'You call that love?'

'They're on their honeymoon.'

'I don't want to watch that sort of thing in the street.'

'But you wouldn't object if you were the girl and he was the only boy in the world.'

'You call him a boy?'

'In years. You can't call Pike a man in anything.'

'What do you mean?'

'You must know by now. If he tells you that what he does in bed is all there is, don't believe him. You're being cheated.'

'What of?'

'Your birthright. Every woman's born with the right

to full and happy sex. You could say she's born out of it.'

'I don't know what you're talking about.'

'I'm talking about what matters to a normal woman.'

'You needn't worry about me then!'

Darlene used to be like that, bold as a balloon one minute and the next tearful and deflated.

The couple from the other table passed us as they went into the hotel. He held her to him with a hand thrust under the waistband of her see-through trousers, his fingers could be seen between her thighs. And he wasn't the one she had been with yesterday. He wasn't a boy, he was paunchy and bald and had a Mafia face.

'She's a common prostitute and I call it disgusting!'

I admit to being disappointed. My sentimental streak leaves me open to it. I said, 'You only have to look at Madame Rosier to know the sort of place she's running.'

'Give me the key of the car.' Cherrimay held out her hand without a please or a would you mind.

'It's our car, mine as much as his. I'm going to Ile-Marie this afternoon. You ought to come with me.'

'Why?'

'It's not every day you get the chance to meet a famous film star. And it's bad for you to be confined to that room all day. I suppose Pike wouldn't let you come.'

She stood up and looked down her nose. 'I do whatever I want and I don't want to come.'

'I'll be leaving at two o'clock.'

I waited till half-past. It was stiflingly hot, but I sat in the car like a chicken in the oven in case she changed her mind. I was hoping she would. I had no plan, I had to play it as it came and every time I peeled her off Pike's back it came my way; a little win for me.

When it was obvious that she wasn't coming, I asked myself, not for the first time, what kept her with him. What keeps a girl, any half way to normal girl in her busty teens, with a non-event like Pike? I knew what she could see in him but surely by now she'd seen that it wasn't there.

How long had it taken *me*? In terms of time, four days.

Our honeymoon was less than half over when my doubts crystallized. I tried again and again, ardent young wife as I was longing to be, to dissolve them. They dribbled slightly, but at the core they remained rock-hard. Petrified. In terms of emotion – faith, hope and charity – it took longer. Viability a human being must have, it's what makes the being human and I'm reluctant to rule it out in anybody. And I was most of all reluctant to rule it out in my husband. That's why I followed him to Nice.

The car had its front wheel jammed against the kerb. I fought with the clutch and accelerator to get it out. Then I crept it along to a garage which I had located nearby, filled up with petrol and had them check the oil, battery and tyre pressure. Finally I rumbled off, the car picking up courage, or resignation, and some speed.

I can't say I like the way they drive Abroad. It's one place where you're sure of being chased, whatever your sex, age, or vehicle. I know my capabilities and I try to suit them to the car. But anything on wheels was on the autoroute that day: cars from A to Z, caravans, tankers, juggernauts, dodgems, Japanese fire-eaters and animals – lions, tigers, elephants and monkeys in cages on a string of trailers. A clown waved from the back of a truck. He was in full circus rig, white face, bottle-nose, ginger wig and check plusfours. The whole lot swept by, that road's a circus anyway. I pulled into the backlash behind the last truck and overtook a French car which was wallowing about in the middle lane.

After the N7 I turned off on a D road, one of those which are yellow and wormy on the map. They go to godforsaken places like Doug's. I had a very general notion where it was, the one and only time I'd been to it was years ago, by taxi from the airport. I was picking up the signposts, climbing high, then dropping, then the road pushed into pine woods. There were glimpses of sea and mountains in the distance and glasshouses winking in the valleys. I passed through a village where they were having a saint's day and had to wait behind an army of little girls dressed as drum majorettes, blowing whistles and beating biscuit tins. I asked some bystanders the way to Ile-Marie. They pointed onward and slapped the back of the car as if it were an obstinate cow.

After that the country got wilder, with gorse bushes and fireweed and rustic berger-bars like in deepest Surrey. The road doubled and re-doubled. I would have missed the turning to Ile-Marie if a goat hadn't run out of it in front of my wheels and scrambled up the bank.

I swung on to a narrow road where bushes and branches reached out and swiped at the car, a place where the natural world was taking back this little macadam strip. I remembered Doug saying something about it being a secondary road, used only by locals. He said it was impassable in the spring, melting snow came down from the hills and made it a raging torrent. It occurred to me that he was showing off because we live in Sidcup.

I passed some isolated villages and a wayside shrine – probably Marie's – and a man breaking stones in a ditch. Then the ground opened out, I left the trees, and what had started as a rock-strewn common became a green meadow, spiked with rushes. We're there, I said to myself, I remember this bit.

I didn't remember the next, however: a wall topped with broken glass and under it pits full of bramble and thistles. A track led into the trees, there was a gate knitted up with barbed wire. A board nailed on a tree said 'Propriété privée, défense d'entrer'. No name, no pack drill, but I got the meaning.

When I think he makes a big living pretending to the world, I have to ask myself who started it. The answer is the aunts and uncles and grandparents and cousins and schoolteachers and, of course, my mother. And my father. Because he let them take Doug over, left him with them when he should have knocked out the kinks and steered him into a proper job. Doug was good at drawing, he could have been a draughtsman. He read encyclopedias, he could have been a teacher. He read the medical dictionary, he could have been a doctor. He's got this knack – I don't call it talent – for making himself out to be what he isn't.

Its finally taken him over. A wall with glass splinters on top and a barbed wire gate are the permanent things he has to show for years of fooling and they're to keep people out, after he's made his money by bringing people in.

I left the car and went to the gate. The padlock was unfastened and hung on its chain. There wasn't a sound, which was remarkable, because if nothing else there are always insects cracking away, rubbing their legs together, I'm told, something British beetles do without fuss. The air smelt like a hot mince pie. I pushed at the gate. Half of it moved a little then stuck on a clump of daisies. The bolt of the other half was jammed in its shaft, I had to kick it to release it. The screech of those hinges set my teeth on edge, I'm sensitive to sounds; being a singer with perfect musical pitch, a noise like that does me an injury. But it's typical of Doug, he's always been able to upset me without trying.

I hadn't seen him since he turned up at father's graveside in a floppy panama with a red and green band, a linen suit and spotted cravat. I caught him trying to sneak away afterwards and asked him where he'd got the hat. He said it was the only one he could find and he'd worn it as a mark of respect. Whereupon I reminded him about black armbands.

I wasn't anticipating seeing that hat again, but suddenly it was there, on the other side of the gate. It took me right back to the day of the funeral, seeing the mud waiting to be shovelled on my father. He was the only one who had time for me. Everyone loved Doug because he was so pretty. Dad used to say, 'He takes after your mother. You and me are a different breed, Dulcie.' He didn't smile when he said it; he was a plain man, plain-spoken. And I didn't mind being like him.

But it wasn't Doug on the other side of the gate, it was a tall old man wearing the floppy panama which had been present at my father's graveside, the same red and green band, the self same pimple on top, a personal affront to the dead. The man had a hook knife in his hand. He had been cutting grass, the blade was stained green and from the look of him it might be stained another colour any moment. I said, 'That hat belongs to my brother.'

477

He lifted the knife and swung it to and fro. I was close enough to feel a breeze. I looked him in the eye, not a pleasing experience because his whites were yellow and the middles like black bullets. 'Let me pass, please.'

He said something, in fact he said a lot and took trouble saying it. I had to suppose he was speaking French but it might have been Arabic. He exploded words at me, I was reasonably sure he was being offensive.

'I'm Rex Snowdon's sister. His soeur. Compris?' I made as if to get by him. He made as if chopping the air, and spat. Some of his personal juice landed on my dress which was a nice one, put on specially for Doug.

I snatched off his hat and threw it away. My mind doesn't desert me at such moments. I act on the spur and follow through, 'I'll have you sacked,' I promised him. But Doug's not loyal. Would you expect him to be, a man who dresses like a gigolo for a solemn family occasion?

The old man cursed. Blasphemy sounds the same in any language. He was torn between shutting the gate on me and going after his hat. It had fallen in front of the car, which gave me an idea. I got in and started the engine. I turned the front wheels on the hat, revved and moved forward. The old man left the gate and ran. I let him snatch the hat from under the wheels and then I drove in. He threw his billhook. That I did run over. If it's cut the tyres, I thought, I'll make Doug pay.

The track was terrible, flints and upended bricks, but I had to drive fast to get away from Father Time. I thought if I don't get a puncture I'll break an axle. Either way, my little brother – nervy, secretive and cold as a fish, hiding himself back of beyond in Shangri-la or Mon Repos or whatever he calls this place – would have to pay.

The track plunged between walls of rock. I scraped my near wing, hitting the mirror and clipping it to the side of the car. I couldn't see if I was being followed. The rocks were like huge cheeses, roundly stacked and chipped to show creamy pink under brown rinds. The car bounced and bucked, any minute I could hit a cheese and I knew it wouldn't be creamy.

Then the track opened out and I was running under olive trees. Beyond, to my left, the ground dropped away, in fact it stopped in midair because there was a lot of shagged blue haze and no solids. The track took a sharp right bend; and luckily so did I. It went uphill and had been roughly cobbled by someone with a thing about cars. I went into heavy-duty gear and roared through the trees. Doug must have heard me coming.

I stopped over a patch of oil stains in the only space between bushes of strapping great flowers like trumpets. As I turned off the engine I seemed to turn on the heat. It threatened to cook me. I'm a big woman, womanly, my flesh melts on occasions: too much sun is one occasion I like least.

The last – and first – time I had seen Doug's house was before he moved in. It was more or less a ruin and I couldn't tell that it was any less now, but you'd have thought he would have smartened the place up. I'd have thought he would have pulled it down and built a nice bungalow if he was so smitten with the situation. Why he should be, though, I'll never know. There was no view; to see the coast he would have had to chop down the olives and everything that was getting beside itself. Distance lends enchantment, so it might have been worth it.

Except for the roof which had been retiled, and a new front door, the house looked much as it did years ago. Not a lick of paint anywhere, the shutters bleached and peeling, and the walls which had been white were grey except round the stack pipes where they were green. The dome – yes, there was a dome to top it all – was smothered with bougainvillea.

I called 'Doug!' But the shutters remained closed. They would be, to keep out the heat, and I longed to have them keeping it from me while I drank a cup of tea. I was going to make sure I didn't get the boiled straw-water he had given me last time, rosemary tea he said it was.

'Doug!' With all this alfresco living I didn't reckon to have to knock on the door. He would be somewhere here, flat on his back, Sleeping Beauty. 'Doug!' I called as I pushed into the jungle: with the sort of spell that was on that place it wouldn't require a hundred years to truss my little brother up like a fly in a spider's web.

I came across one of those luxury swing beds, with canopy and fringe, and sat in it for a breather. 'Doug!' If he was within a mile he must have heard.

So must the old man with the knife. I'm not fanciful, but if overexposed I get the creeps. Nature does that to me; it's so messy. I never liked Sunday-school treats because they were invariably in the country or at the seaside. And here everything was out of proportion, threatening: the butterflies big as birds and the weeds shoulder-high.

I tried the front door, then I went round to the back of the house. There was some still life – a bin overflowing with empty bottles, grapefruit and avocado skins, yellow newspapers, and plenty of movement – swarms of flies and lizards going into cracks in the wall. I tried the back door. It was locked, but the window shutters were open and I looked into the kitchen. I had seen it before Doug moved in: all easy-clean stone, stone walls, floor, sink, and a veined marble dresser which Doug said was for home butchery. It looked like a morgue then, though I've never been in one, and it didn't look cheerful now. There were dishes in the sink and a tap dripping on them making a crater in the grease. I'm hypersensitive to mess.

Obviously the film star wasn't at home. But Father Time was, and probably coming for me with his scythe at this very moment. I had knocked off his hat and I wouldn't put it past him to reciprocate with my head.

I pushed on, meaning to do a circuit of the house before going back to the car. I trod on a yoghurt carton, it went off like a pistol shot and someone laughed. I assumed it was laughter but it was more of a cackle, an old man's cackle and still some way off.

I was hotter than I had any business to be; and the dripping tap made me realize how thirsty I was. A cup of tea would have been nectar. I had come to the end of a path and a kind of cave under the rock. It looked cool and turned out to be quite tidy, not all over itself like the rest of the place. There was a trickle of water coming from a pipe and filling a natural basin on ground level. The ground had once been tiled and recently washed over, revealing what was left of the pattern. In the rock were two niches: in one was propped a mirror, in the other a black and gold flask. I took it down, it was empty, but smelled expensive. One of Doug's whims was to come here for a bath, I supposed. Or was it where Father Time did his toilet and had run out of aftershave?

The water in the basin was amber colour, the coolness reached out to me. I knelt down and put my hand in, then my arm. I didn't disturb so much as a grain of mud, and the water was so soft it didn't feel wet. I put my other arm in, and there I was, enjoying myself, up to my elbows in water that could have come from anywhere. A cup of tea couldn't have been more refreshing. For two pins or less I'd have dipped right into the pool without stopping to take my clothes off. There was something special about it, about the grotto or cave or whatever, and I was so pleased with myself, with being myself and being there, that I leaned down until my face was touching the water. I wanted to get into that cool, amber colour.

I know now that what I saw in the pool was what made it special. At the time it gave me a terrible jolt. One minute I was looking into restful water, the next I was looking at a devil.

I believe in devils, I just hope never to see one – they do well enough without showing up in the flesh. But I saw one then. His reflection was as solid as mine, amber-coloured, and quaking with the movement of the water. No one should look like that, not even a devil. There are limits, the ugliest creature has reason for its ugliness – snouts for snuffing, buck teeth for biting, scabs for putting off other biters, or as marks of war. But to screw up and throw away a face is not reasonable.

It took me a full minute to get myself together and realize that it must be the current distorting reflections, mine included. I scrambled to my feet and swung round. There was nobody in sight, just the grasses shaking.

Madame Rosier had it in her to be a professional snoop,

paid to report other people's business. But she hadn't fully understood that discretion is part of the job. She must have risen at dawn to put on her face. Once I got up to look out of my window – I couldn't sleep in that place – and there she was, down in the yard among the empty bottles. It was barely daylight, but she showed up like a traffic-signal: green eye shadow, red lipstick, orange scorchmarks on her cheekbones.

Whenever I glimpsed her in the passage at the hotel she'd remove herself so fast I'd be left with her colours on my eyeballs, as if I'd been looking at the sun.

There was plenty of snooping potential at the Grand Place: couples coming and going – no luggage: single men with document cases – I asked myself what documents? And girls with prix fixée written all over them. There were older women in pearls and eye-veils and one with a moustache and size nine slingbacks, some sort of specialist I daresay. I never felt easy there, though I kept myself to myself and Madame R. had no opportunity to find anything out about me. Or so I thought. Then when I went up to Pike's room one morning there she was.

I never liked that room. To Pike it was the Garden of Eden. When I saw Madame R. there I felt I'd come face to face with the serpent.

Pike was on his back, smiling his patient smile. Those two women, Cherrimay at his feet, stroking his hammertoes, and Madame R. holding her elbows and showing stop, wait, go, were encouraging him to make the maximum fool of himself. It's a classic situation and I don't like to see it. I'm not a man-hater, men have a certain superiority and I like to see it respected.

I was still getting a jolt every time I saw Pike and Cherrimay together, but I could handle it now. Finding Madame Rosier with them shook me up again. I suppose I was seeing for the first time how it could look to people who weren't involved and didn't know the first thing about us. She was the last one I would want to know, but it struck me forcibly then that the three of them had been having me over.

'What's she doing here?' I said straight out. She

pretends not to understand English and that can work both ways.

'This lady called to ask how I am,' said Pike.

'What did you tell her?'

'That I'm as well as can be expected with a damaged spine.'

He can be bold, can Pike; with support, even cocky. Especially with female support – it was me gave him his faith in the opposite sex. Sensing that I'd have to be careful I said, 'I'll soon have you moving.'

'No – don't touch me.'

It must be some sort of subconscious joke when a man with no backbone chooses to have a bad back as a general excuse.

I rolled up my sleeves and went to the bed. Pike sat up, without a wince or a moan, and put up his fists – the gallant welterweight fighting back from the floor.

I said, 'What's this?'

'You do me no good, in fact you do harm, you manipulate all the wrong things. Rubbing me up the wrong way is what you've always done!'

I turned to Madame Rosier. 'You a qualified masseuse? All part of the job?'

'When I think what he's suffered,' mourned Cherrimay. 'You banging and slapping and grinding his poor bones!'

I said, 'It's like kneading dough, you knock it down to make it rise.'

'I'll never let you hurt him again –'

Madame Rosier murmured something. I said, 'She understands more than you think and I don't intend to discuss my business in front of her.'

'There's nothing to discuss,' said Pike.

Madame Rosier uttered a hiss and snaked across the room. At the door she let go her elbows, inclined her head, and was gone.

'We can't afford to upset her,' said Pike.

'There's such a lot you can't afford.'

'We've got everything we want.'

'We've got something you never had!' cried Cherrimay.

'How would you know what I had?'

'I know what you didn't have. So there!' She really did say it – so there! – and only just didn't stick out her tongue.

'You're easily pleased,' I said. 'Having no standards, you would be. That's one thing you've got in common with him, and it's just as well because you'll have to get used to doing without.'

'We don't need money to be happy!'

I knew then that it was going to be all right, I even felt sorry for Pike.

'Dulcie, I know how you feel –' that's what he used to say in bed when he hadn't the remotest notion how I felt – 'it's come as a shock. I wanted to tell you, I tried to tell you, but I couldn't find the words. There was no way to break it gently.'

No way to get me blinking back the tears, murmuring 'I won't try to hold you', grateful for having had my share of him and ready to stand aside and give someone else a turn. I went to the door, opened it and looked along the passage. 'Does she talk English to you?'

'Who?'

'Madame Rosy.'

'Well we don't talk French,' said Cherrimay, sounding affronted. 'She's very nice, she's going to get us an electro-massager. We can hire it by the hour.'

'It'll release you,' said Pike.

'For what?'

'You needn't feel you've got to stay. I'll be on my feet in no time.'

'You can go home,' said Cherrimay.

'Don't think I'm ungrateful. It's not your fault our marriage didn't work, God knows you tried –'

'Oh, He knows,' I said.

'I did too, morning, noon and night. I tried too hard and stopped my natural reflexes.'

'Especially at night.'

Pike's face lacks any hardening ingredient but it gets thoroughly basic so that you see his ground plan.

'It wasn't dignified, chasing after us,' said Cherrimay. 'My mother would never have done it.'

I gave her a look of mild surprise. 'Wouldn't she have chased after your father?'

Then Pike came up with his thought for the day: 'We're not compatible, you and me, we're chalk and cheese.' It was all I needed.

'I wonder what that makes you?' I said to Cherrimay. I was getting tired of the long slow take, I could see the end, and I wanted to get to it. 'Aren't you sick of being in this room? A young girl like you should be living your own life.'

'I *am* living it.'

'We'll soon be able to get out of here,' said Pike.

'Give us back the key of the car!'

Young people nowadays don't ask, they demand, and not even as if they're doing you a favour, but as if you're doing them a *dis*favour by obliging them to speak to you at all. If she'd said, 'May we have the key?' if she'd said 'Please', I'd have thought about it. I don't know what I'd have decided because of course while I had the key I had them. But as it was her bad manners decided me. 'I'll keep it for now. Doug wants me to go to see him again. And I'd like to. It's another world up there. You can relax, forget your problems, get away from yourself. It's something to do with the isolation, being cut off from the rest of humanity, and of course that's a lot to do with money.' It takes money even to keep that place dropping to bits.

'Why didn't you stay there then?' said Cherrimay.

'I wouldn't like to leave you just yet. Later on, perhaps. I'll need to keep the car, but I promise not to go until you're able to get about by bus.'

'What did I tell you?' cried Cherrimay.

What indeed? I would have been interested to know what Cherrimay Pugh could tell my husband about me. I sighed. 'Nice to be rich, not just comfortably off, but loaded – like Americans.'

'Doug's not American.'

'His money is.'

'It's not your car,' said Cherrimay.

'When we married, Pike endowed me with all his wordly goods till death did us part. Of course I'll drive

you anywhere you want to go. Let me know when you
feel like an outing.'

'This is good enough for us,' said Pike. 'It doesn't
matter where we are so long as we're together.
Cherrimay's the part of me that's been missing all my
life. I didn't even know I ought to have it. You wouldn't
understand, I don't understand it myself, it's the way I
am.'

This was the same Pike, eating his cake and having it.
'It may be the way you are,' I said, 'but what about her?'

'I'm all right! Aren't I?' She ogled Pike: her mother
while she remained unspoken for had rolled her eyes at
everything in trousers. With Darlene it had been more
automatic than promiscuous.

'Well then,' I said, 'as you're so snug and happy you
won't mind me having the car.'

The look that passed between them started out
electric from Cherrimay but got bogged down in Pike's
low wattage. She bounced off the bed. She had the
energy, she was the one who would set the springs a-
twangling. She'd soon find out that there's nothing
much only one can do.

'We paid to bring that car here!'

'Till Friday,' I said, 'or Saturday. I'll keep it till the
weekend. By the way, how long are you planning to
deprive me of it? I'll want it at home.'

Cherrimay started prancing again, flinging out her
arms and dodging in front of me. 'Make her give it
back!' She wasn't learning. Pike lay there on the bed,
white and greasy as if he'd dropped off a spoon. I
recalled how long it had taken *me* to learn. I had to have
the first lesson over and over again, I couldn't accept it. I
was full of trust, and I blamed myself, I thought Fate was
testing me and through me, him. I thought we were
being given a dummyrun of life together.

'You're looking puffy,' I said to her. 'You remind me
of your mother and you shouldn't. Not yet.' She stopped
prancing and turned a deep garden pink. With youth in
her favour she was like a cabbage rose. 'When she was
carrying you, Darlene put on air. We thought she'd float
away. Remember?' I said to Pike. 'Us putting a pound's

worth of coppers in her pocket to weigh her down?'

And he said, Pike the astonisher, Pike the obscure: 'If you're going to see Doug tomorrow why don't you take Cherrimay with you for the ride?'

'I don't want to go!'

'I've been thinking, I'm being selfish.'

'You're not!'

'Keeping you with me all the time is asking for trouble.'

'What trouble?'

'You could get tired of it.'

'I'll never get tired of you.'

It wasn't quite what he had said, but he had to take the shift in meaning: after all, he is forty-eight years old. 'I'm responsible for you, I'd never forgive myself if anything went wrong.'

'What could go wrong?'

'What indeed?' I said. 'At her age everything ticks. You're fussing over her like a father. Is that what she wants?' She looked from me to him and burst out laughing. I said, 'It's well known that girls tend to fall in love with their dads.'

Pike said, 'She'll be glad to go with you.'

Cherrimay stopped laughing and started to cry.

I missed the daily chore of waking Pike. He has to be fetched back to consciousness. It's like a rebirth, I've brought him into the world every morning for thirty years.

I was starting the day at the Hôtel du Grand Place with a sense of loss. It showed me that I needed to know my blessings before I could count them.

I was down in the street next morning while they were hosing the gutters. Our car doesn't like wet underneath. We have trouble on wet days. I've told Pike whoever heard of a car that won't go in the rain? He says it's my imagination, although imagination is one thing I don't cultivate, there's enough going on without me adding to it. Pike puts his hand into the engine and fumbles it, my method is to sit in the driver's seat and pull and push everything. I get results with the right combination of choke, parking lights and Radio Four.

Driving off at last I forgot about keeping to the right of the road and found myself facing a taxi. I shot past and left him climbing all over his cab. What's with these people? There's only a strip of water between us and them, but they're *foreign*. No balance. And Nice isn't real, it's like the old Crystal Palace, all hairy palms and fountains.

Doug could have bought himself some place in England, in Sussex where our father's father came from. Stage and radio stars – Naunton Wayne and the Crazy Gang – built themselves lovely houses on the Kingston Gorse at Ferring-on-Sea. But Doug has to be different. He works at it. I've watched him stop himself doing what comes naturally. He does the opposite, upside down, inside out, bad for good, black for white, tit for tat. He took up acting, because it's against his grain, and he chose to settle in another country, as near as he could to his own, without living in it. But I understand that, as far as I can understand anything about him. People don't change, they just get more like they are.

I stopped at a café. A wind was blowing and the waiter was pegging down the plastic tablecloths. I went inside. The place was empty. The waiter served me and then stood in the doorway tapping his teeth.

They make good coffee in France. Everyone has a gift for something: my father used to say mine was an extra special one, but he wouldn't say what it was. He said if you know you've got a gift you're liable to misuse it.

While I was drinking my coffee, I wondered what I was doing there. It's a question I don't normally ask myself because at any given time I know what I'm doing. Fundamentally I was there to get Pike back: sitting in an empty café listening to a waiter tapping his teeth and the wind flapping the tablecloths was part of it. And I wasn't going to see my brother, because he's one of the half dozen last people I'd go up a mountain for, so much as to be seen going, to give to Pike and Cherrimay Pugh the idea, plus gall, that my glamorous film-star brother wanted to see *me*. This was one of those times when every little counts.

As I left the café the waiter had to stop teeth-tapping and chase a metal menu-holder which a gust of wind sent bowling down the road. Currents of grit were crossing each other, the air was khaki colour, as were the pink geraniums they go in for over there – bowls and showers of them everywhere. No place looks the same without sun and sun is about all they've got that we haven't, on a regular basis, anyway. When it goes in, there's just the smell of Ambre Solaire.

The sky worsened as I drove, clotting up like a bad egg. Every bit of plastic, sunbrellas, awnings, flapped and swelled, a Pris-Unic bag spread itself over my windscreen. Dust came into the car through the places usually reserved for the rain. It came in farther than the rain, it reached down my cleavage and under my tongue.

I remembered the old man in the hat, Doug's hat, Doug's old man. Doug turns himself upside down, inside out, but he's no different from me. He's ordinary, like the rest of us. Ours is an ordinary family. Grandfather kept a sweetshop and father kept pigeons; they were good plain men and you wouldn't need a crowd to pass them in. We were brought up without fuss, we ate our greens and potatoes as soon as we were on solids, and went to the primary school when we could manage the toilet. But Doug has chosen to live in a mess when he could have anything he wanted.

I could handle old Papa Time, but there was going to be the wall and the barbed wire. If the gate was locked I couldn't see myself waiting for it to open. I once queued for a film of Doug's and was so annoyed with myself for queuing that I walked away when I got to the box office. At least if I didn't get in this time there would be no need to mention it to Pike and Cherrimay. It's loyal not to talk about your family failings.

Up there where Doug lives, the only let or hindrance to the wind are trees, the wall, and that gate which was open, dragging its padlock to and fro. I remember Doug telling me about the wind. He said it was known to have flash-cooked a goat and people in concrete tower blocks in the towns had to stay out of doors to avoid being roasted alive. I said why live in such a place. He said there were other advantages and smiled the smile he uses on the screen. It's supposed to melt women.

This same wind was burning my breath and blowing dust into my bosoms and led me to put the same question: what was I doing there? It was the second time of asking and the last answer was stretching it a bit. Going half way up a French alp in a grit storm to get Pike back? Could he be said to have got away? He was having a male menopausal symptom: trust him to have the symptom without the sex, and when it passed, he would have no option but to come back to me. I could be just wasting my time.

I might have gone further: asked if I could be wasting it because what else was there to do with it. But I don't encourage morbid thoughts.

I pushed back the gate and drove into Doug's private mess. The wind was whacking at the alfalfa grass, it had torn down a vine and was turning it like a skipping-rope. Upstairs a shutter had broken loose and was battering to and fro. For all the liveliness of the place there was no sign of life.

I leaned out of the car and shouted: Doug had to be up and about, he was a light sleeper and he'd never sleep through banging shutters. I left the car and walked up to the house.

The last time I saw Doug he was showing our age. It was at the funeral. I saw that he was getting heavy round the jaw, he had bags under his eyes, and some red threads. That's because he drinks too much, eats too much, generally overdoes it. He has women, but I can't pronounce on that, because I wouldn't know how much sex is too much.

Having made up my mind that I was about to see him again I was vexed not to. 'Doug!' My voice bounced back. I shouted 'Rex Snowdon!' Then I started coughing. A grass seed or an insect had slipped down my throat.

I struggled on toward the house. I'm shortwinded, I need all the breath I can get and I wasn't breathing. I thought, I'm choking on a grass seed – one of Doug's. It was one way of dying.

I made it to the kitchen door. The door was locked. I
beat my fists on it and that took the last of my wind. I
could see the dishes still in the sink, the tap still dripping,
and I couldn't get to it. I had to have water to clear my
throat. Then I remembered the grotto, the amber water,
and my legs took me to it, my last breath was in my legs.

Someone was there, with his back to me, a naked
back, a boy's, judging by the big shoulder blades. His
jeans hung from his hipbones. He was busy at the mirror
propped against the rock wall, turning his head this way
and that, sticking up his chin, tucking it down again.
Fancying himself. He took his face in his hands and held
it to the glass, perhaps he was kissing his reflection. I
didn't wait to see. I wasn't interested in him at that
moment in time, though it was coming up fast to the
moment when I would be.

He was between me and the rock pool. I pushed him
aside, scooped up water and drank out of my hand. The
water tasted sweetish. I scooped up another handful. It
may have been that the water washed the grass seed out
of my gullet or it may have been the shock to my system
that shifted it. I think it was mostly shock, because it
stalled a few other bodily functions. My blood froze and
after a big jump so did my nervous impulses. I stopped
coughing.

The fancier had turned round, I was looking him full
in the face. Full, but you couldn't call it whole. He
would be about sixteen years old, but you can't put a
time to something you don't recognize. One side of his
face, the left side, was no age. It was no face. Just a piece
of raw meat like the meat on butchers' hooks, purple
over the bone and dried up, the sort of cut you wouldn't
buy. He had something that passed for an eye, though I
couldn't pass it, and a puckered-up slit like a drawstring
purse. All that was bad enough, but it stopped on a line
from his forehead to his chin; no merging, no blending,
one skin-cell dead and rotten, the next one to it living
and sweating. The right side was all right, eye, nose,
mouth perfectly formed – they used to call that sort of lip
a Cupid's Bow till Cupid went out of fashion – half a
perfect face.

I realized I'd seen the other half yesterday reflected in

the water I had just been drinking. But I wasn't
prepared to see it again, and the two halves together
really shook me. Putting the worst alongside angel's
delight is the sort of thing Nature does all the time. But I
did ask God why He allowed this. The answer came: for
the same reason as devils are allowed in church, to keep
our ends in sight, so we remember where we come from
as well as where we hope to go.

'Hullo,' I said.

His eye was blue, any girl would have envied his blue
eye and his eyelashes. His hair was the sort of Afro
shower the youngsters cultivate, though his was
naturally curly and yellow as a guinea. A guinea would
be that colour, soft and valuable-looking.

'Sorry I shoved you.' His eye was on me, his good eye,
blue and blank as a doll's. 'I had a coughing fit, almost
choked. I had to get a drink of water.' The eye
narrowed, if it saw me it was with suspicion. I said, 'You
must have heard me' – if he hadn't been so busy with the
mirror. 'What were you looking at?' I was needled, and
anyway it was best to treat him as normal. 'Look,' I
moved closer, putting myself into his field of vision, 'I'm
here to see Rex Snowdon. I'm his sister.' Of course he
couldn't understand. And I thought if he's the gardener
it could be why there's no garden.

All at once I was angry, with the wind and the shutter
still banging and with Doug and Pike. And myself. Not
this boy. It struck me that his face was complete because
other people show you a bit, then switch off and show
another bit, never the whole picture.

'You're a proper little Jekyll and Hyde.' Something
moved under a tuck of flesh, something bright.
Something was looking at me, we were having a
conversation. 'What's your name? Jekyll was a better
man than Hyde, but it doesn't matter to me.'

He took a breath and let it out of his Cupid's lip: the
other, the drawstring, tightened. He may have been
sighing.

'You've got an interesting face. You're interested in it,
aren't you?'

He exploded, seemed to break up, burst apart.

Without a sound. I got the impression he was laughing. I got it from his stomach which kept filling and half-emptying the waistband of his trousers. It must have been what they mean by a belly laugh.

'I'm glad you can see the funny side.' I *was* glad, he didn't have much going for him. 'It's been nice talking to you, I'm going to find my brother now.'

I looked for my bag which I had dropped somewhere. He moved faster and got to it first. I held out my hand. He folded his arms. 'Give me my bag, please.'

It bothered me, seeing it against his chest. He had a broad chest, hairless and brown as a nut. His arms were folded over my handbag, squeezing it to his square breasts. It made me breathless.

'Look –' I had yet to see his Jekyll eye look at anything – 'if you're thinking of stealing my money, don't. I'll call my brother, he'll call the police, and if you don't mind me saying so, you won't make a good impression.'

What he had going for him was youth, strength, and no moral tone. I went close, I thought at best he's only a boy and he's not the best of that. In case he hadn't understood, I tried to pull his arms apart. 'Give me my property!'

I wish I could remember what happened next. I've tried to play the whole thing back, I've gone over it again and again. It's clear up to the moment when I touched him. I touched him with anger, that I do know. I was ready to hit him, next minute to hate him. But that minute didn't come, there was a split in time, and I was taken right out of myself. By that I mean what I've made of myself, Dulcie Bysshe as was, Dulcie Pike as now is. I realized what was happening but not that I ought to stop it. That required a mental process and I wasn't having mental processes. I was having a brain and blood storm combined.

I *need* to know how it happened, and in detail. I need the details because I'm living with it, it's personal history and altogether too personal. Anger's not enough, anger should have put me off. I don't want reason, I want a let-out. Because one minute I was defying him, the bag-snatcher, and the next I was where my bag had been, in his arms, against his chest. And I was kissing him on both sides of his mouth. I must have done, I must have put my lips to that cobbled-up slit. It turns my stomach to think of it. I kissed his soft Jekyll cheek and that other, the Hyde side – bone under baked skin. It was what I'd been wanting to do, I took the half a chance to do it, and there was nothing would have stopped me.

I had on my nice dress for Doug. It's very soft silk, this boy spread his hand and moved it up and down my back, getting the feel. His fingertips were rough, they dragged, but nothing would have made me stop him.

I didn't think this is wrong or this is right. I have no thoughts to fall back on now. I have all those feelings which I prefer not to remember. They're mine insofar as I have a system which is capable of them. To that extent I'm responsible. So is the boy. And so, ultimately, is Pike – because Pike's system is not capable.

Nothing could have stopped me. Except the boy. The boy got scared – as well he might – of what he was doing and what he had already done. He suddenly slipped under my arms. He was a gentle mover, anyone else would have thrown me aside, regardless of my state, thinking only of his own. He went, leaving my bag at my feet.

Crying's not common with me. At my father's funeral the cleaning woman cried and I couldn't even get started.

I was ready to drop. I sank down on the edge of the stone basin and blubbered into the water. When I tried to wash away the tears I made a thorough mess of myself. I couldn't face Doug after that. I drove back to Pike.

I remember once asking my mother where children came from. She was rolling pastry at the time and said their mothers made them. I said how, and she said with sugar and spice and all things nice. Even at five years of age that sort of thing infuriated me. I said why had she made two of us at once – it was what I was really after. She finished off her tart and trimmed round the dish with a knife. 'Because I had some bits left over.' Then she scraped up the pastry and made me a doll with currant eyes. I don't think she meant me to draw the obvious conclusion. She wouldn't think I was able to. But when the pastry man came out of the oven I bit his legs off.

Later I collected pictures of the reigning boxing and tennis champions. I put them on the walls of my bedroom. The men were beginning to wear those very short shorts and I wasn't particular where I stuck the pins. Doug tried to make out that meant something, and asked why didn't I like men. I said I'd love a man when I found one.

The only reason I can think of for remembering those days is that I had started to wonder just what bits had been left over. To make me. I've always been pretty sure of myself; I know what to expect, give or take a quirk or two. This episode was more of a bomb than a quirk but I was going to have to take it.

Mummy, I said, my feeling is it's one of your leftovers. You kept it for me. You decided it wasn't for your Dougie, he had to be nice throughout. It'll do for Dulcie, you thought; the chances are she'll never know she's got it. Sugar and spice for Doug, puppy dogs' tails for her.

I was flopped on my bed at the hotel, heavy as lead, empty as a glove. Genuinely exhausted. I kept dozing off, silly ideas came into my head, and sillier dreams. It was an unhealthy way to spend a morning. And that was an unhealthy room, the furniture cheap old stuff hanging on long after it should have been chopped up. Twenty thousand mosquitoes had been swatted on the walls, and whoever puts velvet curtains in a bedroom is making it nice for bugs. But no other way to spend that morning sprang readily to mind. The wind was howling and what I could see of the sky was the colour of ironmould.

I dreamed I was shooting Doug's hat. It was perched on top of a pole, I had a gun and I fired bang into the crown. The hat bled. I woke to hear knocking on my door.

Pike was the last person I was expecting to see in the flesh just then. When I opened the door and saw him there everything came back to normal. Here was Pike

standing before me, the way he always stands, as if he's
been kicked from behind. He stood at the altar like that
the day we were married, sagging at the knees. It was
one of the things I had meant to change.

'So you're up and about,' I said. I was glad to see he
was still the same, Cherrimay Pugh's love hadn't been
able to change him. 'How are you feeling?'

'I think I'll have to wear a corset.'

'I'll lend you mine.'

'I've got an inarticulate spine. That's what the doc
said.'

'The French one?'

'The one I saw before we came away.'

'To check if you'd be up to Cherrimay? That was
thoughtful.'

'God, I must sit down!'

He lumbered into the room and lowered himself on to
my bed. 'I can't stand, I can't walk, I can't hardly sit.
What's to become of me?'

'A vegetable.'

'You've got no feeling.'

'You've got too much. Stop feeling sorry for yourself.'

He blinked. 'In actual matter of fact I'm pleased for
myself.'

People think it's easy dealing with a fool. But a fool
has the advantage of not being bound by commonsense.
The great thing is to keep your temper. It took me a long
time to learn that. I used to wallow in my rage, while
Pike got sillier and sillier. Now I disconnect. I look at his
foolery as I would a bit of junk before throwing it out.
What worries me is that when I'm old and dried up I'll
have a dead seam where hope and charity should have
been. 'Were you thinking of making a life with her?'

'Making a life?' He looked alarmed.

'Living together.'

'Yes.'

'Well then,' I said, 'the difference between living with
her and living with me – and it's the only one so far as
you're concerned – is that I won't let you be a vegetable.'

'Cherrimay and me are meant for each other. To
think I nearly lost her that time when Darlene wanted to
go and live up North –'

'When Cherrimay was still in her pram.' I tried hindsight, seeing them together, Pike and Baby Pugh, him dancing her on his knees, helping her toddle. I remembered him turning away when she grizzled. She was fat, sluggish and leaky. 'Are you telling me you fancied her then?'

'Age does matter,' he said, not giving me a glimmer of a smile. 'It matters a lot. She makes me feel young – so I can have life over again. I know I missed a lot the first time round.'

'Like what?'

'I take pleasure in her pleasure.'

'I don't mean to be unkind –' I think if you do mean to be, it should be in a good cause and not just for spite – 'but what pleasure can she find shut in with you all day?' My cause was to show him the trouble he was laying up for himself. Besides, I needed to know what they made do with, the two of them, in Madame Rosy's grotty back room. I needed it for when I woke at night, and the times when I couldn't bear myself.

I was hoping – how long does hope last? – for a short answer, like 'We hold hands', 'I tickle her feet'. But Pike put his hands over his face and spoke out of his palms, muffled. I think he said he was sorry. It's the sort of thing he would say, late and much better never. I could have killed him. I came close enough to it as to be answerable for the crime: only the action was missing. I could have done it with my bare hands.

'Look,' I said, 'you don't apologize for short-changing when you've been doing it for thirty years.'

'It wasn't all my fault. Nor all yours. We just didn't – we couldn't. Some people, some things, don't mix. Oil and water don't, it's a fact of nature. That's all.' When his brain is working he blinks, his eyelids take the strain. 'There are some substances which are harmless in themselves and poisonous together.'

'Is that what we are? Poisonous?'

'We couldn't know how it would be.'

'I know how it was. Exactly.'

'It's over. For you and me it's all over.'

I'll say this for Pike, you won't come across any streak of native cunning, he's bull-silly all through. But I felt that if I lost my temper I'd end up crying, and in a queer sort of way it would be carrying on from where I left off in the grotto at Doug's. I couldn't have that, so I kept a grip on myself. 'And now you're going to put it all behind you and start a brand new life by starting in on hers. That's handy.'

'We love each other.'

'Does she know what she's letting herself in for?'

'Yes.'

When Pike's definite, he stands on the burning deck, about to go down for the umpteenth time, and ten to one he'll never know it. But this was one time when he would have to know.

'So,' I said briskly, as if it was settled, 'what are you going to do?'

'Get away from here. We only meant to stay overnight. Then my back flared up. It's been expensive. The fact is, we're short of money.'

'You'll have to come home.'

'No.'

On the burning deck, trying not to notice that his feet are getting hot. 'Everything comes down to money. Even love's middle-aged dream.'

'I suppose you told Doug about us.'

'Some things I don't tell to anyone. Do you think I want to broadcast the fact that my husband has left me for a schoolgirl?' Of course Pike's always been jealous of Doug's success with women, he'd want him to know about Cherrimay.

'In some ways she's grown up.'

'What ways would that be?' Shame is not in Pike's nature, when he blushes it's for other reasons. But he makes a thorough job of it, I've seen when he's been stark naked and little pink paddies have rushed all over  him.

'What I mean is, she's not a child.'

'God knows what she is. He made her, so He must know.'

'We can't leave until we've paid the bill.'

'That's usual.'

'We can't pay. The doctor and the massager cost a packet. I'm skint.'

'Even I wouldn't expect you to expect me to lend you the money.' But I could see he was expecting just that.

'Do you think she'd take an IOU?'

'Madame Rosy? Let me know when you ask her, I'd like to be there.'

'Could I get a loan from the bank?'

'You could try the British Consul. They'll be bound to ask what you're doing here.'

'Doing?'

'You needn't say you're here for a grubby weekend. But they'd find out, through official channels. I doubt if they'd help.'

'What am I going to do?'

'Try sneaking away at night when there's no one about.'

'They're about all night long.'

'I've noticed.'

'At home I could get it out of the slot.' I forbore to mention that he would first need to have it in the slot, he can overlook essential detail better than anyone. 'God, what a country!' He sat on my bed cupping his buttock bones, one to each hand. 'I'll never get better here. They call this the sunny South and you could stew an onion in these rooms.'

'They already have, judging by the smell.'

'What the hell am I going to do?'

'Get away, you said when I asked. I certainly think you should.' He groaned, fondling his bones as if they were soft fruit. 'Look,' I began, 'when all's said and done – but don't think it has been yet – you're my husband and I'm the only one who can get you out of this trouble.'

'Yes.'

That was Pike, the everlasting Pike, handing me back my responsibility. 'So I'll settle your bill.'

'Dulcie, I'll pay it back, I swear I will, it'll only be a loan until I'm on my feet again –'

'And I'll drive you home.'

'We're not going home.'

'Not we,' I said, 'you. I'm not driving that girl anywhere.'

'You think I'd go back without her?'

'She can fly. I'll take her as far as the airport.'

'We've got no money for a ticket –'

'I'll telephone Darlene, she can pay the other end.' I didn't know if she could and I didn't care.

Pike started shouting. I don't pay too much attention when he shouts, I let what sense there is blow over me, rhubarb noise. Of course those two would get together again at home, but if I broke them up now the next break would come easier. And sooner.

He got up shouting that he wouldn't part from her. Then he seemed to get an almighty kick from behind and collapsed over the bed.

'Suit yourself,' I said. 'Stay with her or come with me.'

'Christ – I can't move –'

I must say he gets himself into some odd situations: he was doubled over my bed as if waiting to be spanked.

'Help me – do something!'

I looked at his big soft bottom and was tempted. My hairbrush was on the dressing table, it's a heavy one and has strong bristles. I could have given him a new sensation and it might have helped. They say one pain cancels out another.

'Get me a hot towel –'

'Where would I get such a thing?'

'For God's sake, Dulcie, I'm in agony!'

I went into the shower room, turned on the tap and soaked a towel. I took it to him still dripping. 'What's it to be?' I pushed the towel into the small of his back. He swore as the water ran down into his trousers. 'Are you staying here with her or coming with me?'

'She's frightened of flying –'

'Everybody's frightened of flying.'

'Why can't she come in the car?'

'I have a forgiving nature, but I'm not prepared to drive across France with you two billing and cooing in the back.'

His face opened to cry like a baby's. 'What am I going to tell her?'

'Tell her we'll be leaving first thing tomorrow.' I felt it was all coming my way, and I shoved the wet towel down into the seat of his trousers.

\*

She got him by being thirty years younger than me, no virtue, no merit. Losing him isn't the end of the world for her, she'll forget him in a week. For me he's the way of life I've worked at ever since we were married. I'd like to have been a fly on the wall when he told her.

But little girls have no conscience, they want their own way and don't care how they get it. Cherrimay would put on a show – one big burst followed by a steady leak, then she would twist his arm. She would twist anything if it helped.

After he'd gone I looked out of my window at his flannel hooked on their shutter and tried to get a fly's eye view of what was happening up there. Then I gave up and went and rang Darlene.

'It's over,' I told her. 'They're coming home.'

'I'm just going out shopping –'

'Don't worry, you'll be back by the time they arrive. And they won't be together. I'm bringing Pike, she'll have to come on her own.'

'Why?'

'Because I won't play gooseberry.'

'How do you know it's over?'

'They've got no money, they have to come home.'

'What are you going to do? You'll have to divorce him –'

'We can't continue this conversation on the telephone. Your daughter's penniless, send her her fare or buy her a ticket at your end.'

'What?'

'If you want to see Cherrimay again you'll have to pay. She's not my responsibility and it's not in my interest to have her within a hundred miles of Pike. I've told you the situation and I'm going to ring off. This call's costing me money.'

'I don't know what to do!'

'Ring the Citizens' Advice Bureau.' I hung up, feeling pleased with myself. Pike's natural drawbacks include lack of money and I thought it was a neat move to use a risen situation rather than create one.

I stood myself lunch at a place where the waiter pulled out my chair and brought a bottle of wine in a bucket.

501

He made such a ceremony, wiping and displaying the bottle, that I decided to try it. It was sour to my taste, but I drank it down with veal cutlets and a peach tart. When I left, the waiter gave me a red rose. He was being paid for it of course, and for the way he watched me poke it down the front of my dress – as if he would like to have done it himself.

I went to the bank and changed travellers' cheques to pay the bills and buy petrol. I was looking forward to the drive and now that I was leaving I felt charitably inclined towards the place. I walked down to the front for a look round. The sea was on the other side of the fancy palaces and palms and didn't declare itself with that white gap in the sky which advertises our sea at home. I nearly missed it. It was the colour of weak coffee, and a few people were trying to have fun in the dregs. The wind screwed the palm trees and hunted torn paper and empty cartons and geranium heads. Everything looked scraped. I went back to the hotel.

I stood at the window of my room looking up at Pike's flannel with the dried germs on it and was sickened. I'd been that all along. Of course you can't localize a sick feeling, what I felt took in Pike and the girl, but didn't stop with them. At that particular moment I was sick of everything, including myself. And angry that sickness was getting the better of me. To take my mind off it I thought I'd get the car filled up and checked for the journey. I looked for the ignition key. It wasn't on the table or the bed, it wasn't in my purse or my pocket. I looked under the bed and in the bed. The wine I had drunk was making me very aware; I had a clear mental picture of the key and key ring lying where I had tossed it. I even heard the clink, muted, because it had landed somewhere soft. On the bed. When I came back from Doug's I threw everything down, myself included, on the bed. Pike could have picked up the key ring. He had the opportunity while I was fetching the towel.

Pike the opportunist. He wouldn't have registered the key ring until he sat on it; in his case opportunity has to do more than knock. I searched the room, then I went out to where I had left our car. That was gone too.

I blamed myself. I know all about Pike but not so much about Cherrimay Pugh. Coming to me to borrow money could have been a blind, a way of getting into my room and she could have put him up to that. My carelessness had done the rest. Even Pike will look to see what's sticking in his bottom. They could be packed and gone already.

I went back to the hotel and straight up to their room. And there was Madame Rosy in the act of letting herself in. She tried to shut the door in my face. We struggled. I'm bigger than she is, I got my knee in, then my hip. I broke her hold and pushed her in backwards.

One glance was enough. Their things were still scattered all over the place. I went in and sat down. Madame Rosy came after me.

'I have every right to be in this room,' I said.

'Monsieur and Madame Pew –'

'Mister Pike's my husband. She's nothing.'

'Madame, if you please.' She was at the door, signalling stop, ready, go.

'I'm stopping.' I had seen his passport on the bedside table. I picked it up. 'Here's his name – Pike. I am his wife.'

'Madame Brochet?'

'Pike. I keep telling you. I am Mrs Dulcie Pike.'

'This is not your room.'

'You're so right it isn't. I wouldn't leave a dog kennel in this state. I wouldn't stay in your hotel anyway. But for what those two are up to it's very suitable. Know what I mean? Dirty.'

She came on full current then, really lit up. 'I shall speak to Monsieur Pew –'

'He knows what I think.'

'If you do not go I must shut you in.'

'Suit yourself.'

She said something in her language, bit it up and spat the bits at me. Then she marched out and slammed the door. I was suited. I had to wait for them to come back and I was doing them a favour by keeping Madame Rosy out. She had come to snoop.

I didn't bargain – I should have – for Pike's mark. It's

a sort of spoiling: he roughs and generally messes up wherever he goes and whatever he touches. This room had turned into Pike country. Nobody wrecks the bed and strangles clothes and moults over the furniture like he does. Nobody can twist the toothpaste and get shaving cream on the taps like he can.

I picked up her nightdress, one of those Baby Doll efforts. And she had a drawer full of seethrough undies. On top was the pink bow tie he wears because someone once said it makes him look like Frank Muir.

I've said I'm not imaginative, I have to see to believe. What those two do together doesn't worry me, they can't do much. But seeing their things together, side by side, on top of each other, that gave me pain. I'm funny that way.

But not vindictive. At least I wasn't until I found the rabbit. Under the bedclothes. A blue nylon rabbit made in Korea, with red plastic eyes and reinforced ears. It was at least three feet long and smelled of Pike. It had been in their bed, it had her smell on it too, so I picked it up by the ears and threw it out of the window. It fell in the yard among the empties.

I had to wait a long time before they came back. Any time would have been long. It wasn't just the matter of his things mixing with hers: those two had spread themselves and I couldn't separate them from each other or from the room. Pike and Cherrimay Pugh were like jam, over everything, while my pain was low down. Gynaecological they call women's troubles.

Madame Rosy warned him, of course. When he opened the door of their room he was holding up his functions. When he does that, he looks fit to burst.

'Relax,' I said. I worry about his arteries. I worry about them seizing up and not letting his trickle of blood through. 'That was clever, the way you got the key of the car.'

He stared at me, blinking, swallowing, putting two and two together. He reached a decision – I saw it go down his neck to his arm – and pushed the door wide. 'You needn't stay.'

'Where's Cherrimay?'

'In the car.'

'Aren't you the one that needs to stay?' When he moved from the door it slammed, shutting us in. 'There's a little matter of an unpaid bill.' He reached under the bed and dragged out the flight-bag, stuck over with old tour labels. He started taking up things and pushing them into it: dresses of hers were bundled round shoes, black beetle-killers of his. I laughed. 'Packing, are you?' Everything from the dressing table – brushes, make-up, creams, aspirins, hair-combings, powder-spill, cotton-wool buds, dust, and their passports were swept into the bag. 'I could have taken a bet on how you pack.'

'I wish to God I'd never seen this place.'

'God sent you here to show you what a fool you're making of yourself.' Her nightdress was balled up with his dirty underwear – to see Pike packing is to witness an act of gross indecency. I said, 'You've got the car but what will you do for money?'

'I'm taking Cherrimay home.'

'Who's going to pay your bill?' He stood blinking and thinking – still thinking that I would pay. 'Not a penny,' I said. 'Not a Frankie or a Johnny, whatever they call their money. You don't think she'll let you get away without paying, do you?'

'She's pregnant.'

'Who is? Madame Rosy?'

'Cherrimay.'

'She's what?'

'She's going to have a baby.' That was Pike, spelling it out. At last. For me. For himself.

'Well,' I said, 'well,' while everything fell down round me with a sneaky little noise. And yet it was predictable, and totally logical. Cherrimay Pugh would start a baby with less ado than I would make about starting a batter pudding. And she was doing it early. 'You don't suppose it's yours, do you?' (I could see he did.) 'My God –' who else should I call on? Pike is God's mystery, mine not to reason why. Though I do. I'm as I was created, in the human condition, I was given certain thoughts and certain feelings - oh very certain – and given Pike, what am I supposed to do? – 'Nothing's sacred to girls of her age, least of all their own selves.' If you're going to be unkind it ought to be in a good cause. '*You* didn't get her pregnant. Oh, she'll say you did and you'd like to think you did. Any man would.' Pike longs to be any man, he lives in hope. I could say he lives on trust because that's how people take him. Men and women. He looks, sounds, smells and acts like a man in all but one respect. As his wife I'm well placed to know what that respect is. 'Don't worry, I'll get the truth.'

'She's in no condition to talk, to you or anyone. She's shocked and upset, she can't stop crying. I don't know what to do, what to say to her. I don't know how bad it is, what harm's been done.'

'Harm? Is she bothered about losing her virginity?'

'Christ, I don't know anything!'

I admit to being sorry for him. He goes to bits in a crisis, in little fraught moments like when the frying pan goes on fire. And when he's stranded Abroad. 'What's the hurry?'

He was blundering round the room as if he meant to pack the furniture. What had happened to his back? One pain cancels out another.

'I've got to get her home!'

It seemed a good idea. In England Darlene could take over. He zipped up the bag, gave a last look round, as you do when you're all packed and ready to go. But he hadn't looked in the wardrobe or the chest of drawers and I knew for a fact that she had a suitcase with her, a white plastic thing still under the bed. 'Don't forget your flannel.'

There was something else he wanted to say. He blinked hard. I prepared myself for something wide of the mark.

'That man whose mother was frightened by an elephant –'

'What?'

'The elephant man. He was born like it because his mother was attacked by an elephant while he was in the womb.'

506

I got some surprise hearing him use that word. It's a bit technical and Biblical for him, so I supposed he had picked it up from her. After five minutes pregnancy Cherrimay would be into details.

I got some more surprise when he said, 'It really happened, didn't it? He was born a monster, it was an actual matter of fact.'

It was so wide of the mark I could scarcely stop myself from laughing in his face. But I did stop myself because I could see he was seriously frightened. 'Old wives' tales,' I said. 'How could a man look like an elephant? A parrot, maybe, or a monkey. Some people look like that anyway. If Cherrimay has a baby with a big nose it won't be because she's seen an elephant.'

'I blame your brother!'

'Doug? What's he got to do with it?'

'You've been to his place, you must know what goes on.'

'Goes on?'

'You've seen the company he keeps. I know what film people are, but he's got something running loose up there that ought to be in a cage.'

'You mean you've been to see Doug?'

'Yes. But I didn't see him and he lives in a right dump.'

'What did you go for?' I gave myself one guess. 'Money.'

'All I want is to keep her with me.'

'You think my brother would give you money for that?'

Pike still has his own teeth and shows them in his own gums. 'I wasn't going to tell him. I was keeping her out of it. I left her in the car outside the gate. I had a story ready about you needing money and not liking to ask.' I laughed out loud then because that's all Pike knows about Doug and me – after being married to me a lifetime. 'I walked up to the house and while I was gone this freak frightened the life out of her.'

'Freak?'

'She was screaming. When I ran back he had his head in the car window.'

'Freak?' I said again.

'She was hysterical. I chased him away but I couldn't calm her down. She's so highly strung; it's bad in her condition. It's bad to get worked up.'

'Don't worry about her. She's like her mother, dizzy as a gnat. Gnats don't run into big trouble.'

'It turned me up. He only had half a face. Christ knows what the other half was. He was reaching into the car to get his hands on her. I pulled him out by the scruff of his neck. He was foaming at the mouth –'

'Surely not.'

'I tell you he was like a wild animal!'

'He was frightened.'

'He was mad.' Pike blinked. 'He had flowers in his hair.'

I laughed. He picked up the bag and went to the door. I said, 'She doesn't have to have it, you know. She could get rid of it.' That was unkind, he wanted to believe the child was his, but the sooner he faced the truth the better. Everything I do for him is for the best.

He said, 'She's started buying things.'

'What things?'

'For the baby.'

'That rabbit?'

'She wants it and I want it.'

'The rabbit?'

'The baby.'

He didn't say goodbye, or what will you do. He simply went, leaving the wardrobe full of their clothes and her suitcase under the bed and his flannel on the shutter.


And that rabbit in the yard with the empties. If it had been to hand I'd have torn the stuffing out. Toys like that are dangerous for young babies.

I don't bear malice. If Cherrimay gives birth, good luck to her. And to Darlene. Darlene will need luck, she'll be a grandmother once removed. Removed from the father who is not her son-in-law and in all probability a total stranger and in all probability no more than a random guess for Cherrimay. He certainly isn't my husband.

I waited to see if Pike would come back for the rest of their things, but he didn't: Cherrimay, weeping her head off, wouldn't notice that they were short of luggage.

He was right about one thing: I need not stay. I hated the place, I couldn't wait to get away. I packed my bag and took it to the hall. Madame Rosy came out from under the tapestry. She handed me two bills, one for more than twice the other.

'What's this?'

'It is the account of Monsieur and Madame Pew.'

'And?'

'Monsieur Pew has said you will pay.'

'Has he indeed.' I counted out four hundred-franc notes. 'This is for my room, a lot more than it's worth, and all you're getting.'

'There is again a thousand francs, Madame.'

'That's nothing to do with me.'

'You have said he is your husband.'

'My husband's name is Pike.'

For a moment she was all green for go. 'In France we call such a fish "un brochet".'

I screwed up their bill. 'You may keep what they've left in lieu.'

'Madame?'

'I'm not paying.'

'It is the law.'

'I'm not liable for what they owe. Any lawyer, even a French one, will tell you that.'

'It is unfortunate –'

'Not for me.'

'I regret, if you do not pay you cannot leave.'

'Try and stop me.'

I turned. There was a man in the doorway, a big man, black as coal, grinning like a piano.

I had yet to see an expression on Madame Rosy's face; the paint was too thick to let anything through. Though I could make a guess. She was probably looking triumphant. 'I shall report this to the British Consul.'

She smoothed out Pike's bill. Her nails were green like her eyelids, the untreated skin on the backs of her hands bluish and scaly. No wonder, she'd blocked up her pore-holes.

I paid. It was worth it to get out of that place. The negro showed all his white notes when he let me pass.

Pike had shown initiative. He must have been desperate – for Cherrimay Pugh, the mother of his child. I can't respect a fool or his folly, but I had to respect its origin. Pike has the makings of a man but not the mix. I respect his ambition, it's the same as mine for him: I've fostered and tried to further it. Without success. Here was Cherrimay Pugh, with no trouble at all, with probably the greatest pleasure, demonstrating that someone had been a fully paid-up man. And here was my poor Pike, ready and eager to believe he was that man. A father. Cherrimay had him in the palm of her hand. She had me in her palm too.

I sat myself down at the pavement café. The girl in the pink satin trousers and rosebud bra appeared at the entrance to the hotel. She crossed her knees and folded her arms to make a display shelf for her breasts, and leaned her shoulder on the doorjamb, not filling the doorway like the negro, but decorating it. She drew the eye, she drew mine, and I was getting the old gynaecological pain. Two men crossed the street, a French sailor and a hunchback. The hunchback got to her first. She put her arms round his hump and they went into the hotel.

'Madame?' said the waiter.

'Forget it.' I took up my bag and walked away.

I don't like waste. There's only so much in the world and we're getting through it, things are being finished up. Soon there won't be anything left worth having, we shall eat dirt and drink rain. Sometimes I think we're here to get rid of it all, ourselves included. It seems long-winded, but God has plenty of time. And it starts, before they get round to destroying the animals and the forests and polluting the seas, with people wasting their own resources. They do it out of ignorance, like Cherrimay.

Or for money, like that pro in the rosebud bra. At least she appreciates she's dealing in something valuable.

I stood in the street, my bag beside me. There was no sun to go down, just yellow sky and the earth-grabbers floodlit in their glass tower. I had lost track of time. It was getting late, I needed somewhere to stay overnight. I thought why not Doug's place. I hadn't yet managed to see him and it could be five more years before I got another chance.

It came to me as I stood in the grand place – quite a lot was coming to me just then – that I'd benefit from talking. Not to gripe or be comforted; to sort things out. There were things I needed to say and I needed someone to hear them. My brother was handy. He's a success, and it's true to say he's done it by wasting himself. He couldn't have got where he is if he'd tried to make the best of himself. The people he mixes with don't want his best, or anyone else's. There's no money in it.

I don't envy him, he has had to work at it. And I knew it would amuse him to hear I'd lost my husband to Darlene's little daughter, it would bring on a smile, but he's so full of himself that anything I said would go in one ear and out the other. And that's how I wanted it; I didn't want it remembered.

I turned my back on the hotel. Words can mean anything and nothing. Whose joke was it to call it the 'Grand Place'? Only a fly on the wall could have found grandeur in that place.

A taxi was putting down a fare at the corner. I asked the driver to take me to Ile-Marie. He muttered. 'Rex Snowdon,' I said. He opened his mouth and tapped a gold tooth. I got into the cab and we drove off.

When I can't sleep I think about what Pike and the girl might be doing; I run through his repertoire. There isn't much. But a child's another matter, a child is a fact, born or unborn, a fact I have to deal with because Pike thinks it's his.

'Do you take many people up there?' I asked the driver. 'To Rex Snowdon's?' He nodded. 'What sort of people?'

'Onglay, Americain, Yapponay.' He turned in his

seat, pulled his eyes into slits and grinned.

I didn't say any more, but he did. He talked all the way; he seemed to be having a row with himself and a lot of fun. He kept turning round and laughing even though there are places on that road with no more than a tin fender between the car wheels and several thousand feet of air.

He drew up with tyres spitting grit outside Doug's gate and flashed his gold tooth. 'Wulla!'

'Wait here for me.'

He put out his hand. 'Truss aunt.'

'I want you to wait.'

He licked his finger and wrote 300 in the dust on his windscreen.

'It's too much.' But I thought if Doug's not here I'll have to go back to Nice. 'I'll pay later.'

'Madame –'

'Stay!' I pointed to the ground, as if commanding a dog, and it worked. He leaned against his cab and watched me go.

Doug's garden was dead quiet. The wind had dropped. A vine thing had been torn up and lay across the path. Its fleshy flowers had died a fleshy death. The dark in the depths of the undergrowth was Brown Windsor soup colour. Soon it would be Brown Windsor everywhere. I saw no sign of life around the house. All but one of the upstairs shutters were still closed.

I thought this is the third time I've come and it's not lucky; I'm not going to find Doug. I thought there are a lot of things I'm not going to do. Suddenly I was tired, I was tired to death. It had been a long week. Only one week since Pike left home, only five days since I followed him. If there was a button I could have pushed, just switched myself off and been done with, I would have.

I went into the front porch. The bell pull was rusted solid. Something flapped down and skimmed away over my head; a bird, a bat perhaps. There was no letter box, there is a tin nailed on a post at the end of the track for his letters.

My brother was born the same as me. My father was different but Doug and I are the same – my mother's flesh and blood. And she was definitely standard. If Doug's a success – I'm not referring to the films and the money he's made, but what he's got out of his life – if it's more than I've got he may have it, but how much can he take? Can he appreciate? Because it would be like him, it would be him all over, to value only what he hasn't got.

I'm single-minded and single-hearted. I chose Pike because I thought I saw everything in him I wanted. As it turned out, the every thing was missing.

Doug has tried to be different and it's cost him. He's ending up nobody, living in a nowhere place. I used to be happy being like everyone else, and in the expectation of it. That was years ago. I never wanted to be different, but I'm the one that is. I've been forced to be. That's how it's turned out.

I passed the grotto. It was dark in there, not a glimmer from the water in the stone basin where first I'd seen that face. Some things don't improve with thinking. They're unproductive, you end up with a personal minus.

I had Pike to think about, and Cherrimay: those two. Those three, if Pike is to be believed.

That's what I'm up against. He can be trusted to believe, but not to be believed. Cherrimay Pugh needn't be carrying his child, or any child. With him it's the thought that counts. There's a limit, there's nine months. Even Pike knows how long it takes to produce a child. If Cherrimay doesn't produce, he'll have to accept that he's not a father. On the other hand, if she has a child, if she has a miscarriage or even a false pregnancy, he'll be certain he's a father. A *father*.

Darlene cried all the time she was carrying. Cherrimay takes after her mother and Darlene's quite equal to crying while Cherrimay's carrying. Or not carrying. We were in for a wet winter.

At the back of the house I came upon young Jekyll and Hyde emptying the dustbins. He was tipping the rubbish into an oildrum mounted on pram wheels.

He was still wearing those baggy jeans, no shirt, no shoes. And Pike was right, there were flowers in his hair, blue funnel-shaped flowers stuck into the Afro mass. On anyone else it would have looked silly, but that's one thing his face can't look, whatever's added.

When he saw me the Hyde side had a sort of spasm; it was smiling perhaps. He left the bins and came to me. How long and clever his toes looked, he could have peeled a banana with them.

'Well, we meet again.' I felt myself colouring up. Blushing is for girls, I go dark like overdone beef. 'Where's Mr Snowdon? I'm his sister, I told you, didn't I? I'm Miss Snowdon.' Jekyll was wooden but Hyde twitched. 'I'm going home tomorrow. To England. I'm here to see my brother.'

At the same moment I was asking myself what would I do if he appeared. Doug was the last person I wanted to see. I didn't want to see anyone or have anyone see me. At that moment in time it was all then and there.

But you can't get anywhere without lies. So who was I lying to? A lie has to be understood or it's not a lie.

'Let me look at you,' I said. I had to know just what had frightened Cherrimay out of her wits. The thought did cross my mind. Suppose she gave birth to a child with a screwed-up face, what would Pike do then? But God wouldn't stoop to that.

The face was so close I could see in detail all the pinches and tucks. When a *thing* is damaged it means someone has burned or broken a finished object. With flesh and bone the damage can start in the mix. Pastry crumbles and green wood swells. There was no knowing what had happened to this boy, whether he had been dropped or scorched or badly done. His face didn't frighten, it moved and disturbed me. But then I'm older, I don't frighten easily and I'm not pregnant. That's two plusses and a minus. Things were looking up. Ever so slightly.

Jekyll didn't smile, he left that to Hyde. It was Hyde who kissed me. I'd been waiting years, donkeys' years my time – the calendar year is for calendars – and how many girls would bring themselves to be kissed by that stitched-up mouth? We sank to our knees, drew each other down. It was need, not passion.

I ask myself who makes love? Animals don't, nor do people. Love is there or it isn't. We do what we must and

we're not answerable for the way we work any more
than guns are for the killing they do.

We clung to each other, rolling and devouring each
other. With Pike I used to keep my eyes open. I had no
faith and tried to see where I wasn't going. But this boy
knew what Pike had never known. He took me without
by-your-leave or foreplay, he took me with him. Who
said it's better to travel than to arrive – anyone half way
to normal doesn't need me to tell them it's all
marvellous.

His power and mine – that's how the world was made.
And I was one of the last to know it. I had my eyes shut
because I knew where I was going and I knew I'd get
there. I cried aloud things that I'm glad I can't now
remember. If I'm required to rise above myself in future
I shall need help. I was fully conscious that I'd never get
another moment of glory like this one. No need to
remind myself to make the most of it: you don't quantify
at a time like that.

It ended in comic strip. Naturally – some of Pike's
nature has rubbed off on me. And naturally I wasn't
aware what else in the wide world might be happening.
There was no world, just the wide, wide me. When I
looked up into black beady eyes it seemed like snakes
hanging over me.

Then I saw it was a flock of Christmas dinners.
Surrounding us, swaying their big soft bosoms and
snapping with their big hard beaks. Aiming at my face,
trying to peck out my eyes. I rolled away. They came
after me, trod on me with their big hard feet.

They say a swan can break a man's arm. These birds
pulled my hair and nipped my behind. I expected to be
pecked to death and wondered how long it would take
them to do it. One stood on my back and beat its wings
and they all stretched their necks and honked. It
sounded like dirty laughter.

Then they went quiet, as if they'd been called off. The
bird on my back trod through my hair. I heard rustling
and subdued cackling. They were moving away.

The white birds going leisurely through the grass and
him following was the last I saw of the boy. A picture

remembered from a book of fairy stories. And now that there was nothing to smile at or delight in, it was real.

# 3

Bysshe had been looking forward to going home with all strings detached. He might have known he wouldn't get away so easily. A publicity sendoff, war dances on the runway and an elephant parade through the departure lounge would have been enough for Erckmann. A private departure, one man going back to his own place, was too much. Erckmann could die of quiet: it was the death he was fighting off.

Bysshe flew from Brazzaville in the company of Hilda Latouche and Nat Twoomey. Hilda was the journalist, Twoomey the photographer commissioned to do a feature on Rex Snowdon, newly retrieved for Erckmann's classic about the life of Anatole Zwemmer. The casting had been a long throw – Erckmann liked it to be known as his stroke of genius.

Certainly it had taken supersensibility to visualize Rex Snowdon in the part. Erckmann had said more than once that Snowdon was unaware of his potential, didn't know he had it in him. Erckmann had said it before invited and uninvited audiences, cuddling up to Bysshe from his four feet ten inches, the inference being that Snowdon was Erckmann's Pandora's box and what was allowed out was at Erckmann's artistic discretion.

Bysshe's conception of the part had been fundamental. He saw Zwemmer as a man moved by hate and paranormal disgust, for whom the only answer was to

rub his own nose in the world's dirt. It had activated the
actor in Bysshe and he had kept it private. Erckmann
hadn't suspected.

Erckmann had been prodigal of Zwemmer's amorali-
ties. 'This guy's been a baddie all his life, searching for
his real self. That's part of it. He doesn't realize he's got
to *lose* himself, be purified by suffering. Okay, so it's
other people's suffering – that's where he loses himself.
But he's a full man first, a sinner: that's how you get to be
a saint.' When Bysshe suggested that some people were
born good, Erckmann waved a dismissive hand.
'They're no help to the rest of us.'

Bysshe let Erckmann think he was portraying
Zwemmer as a man beset by splendid demons, arcane
horrors and superpowers. It was Erckmann's own
cherished conception – one of the easiest to realize.
Bysshe had played along with it, given a deeply focused
performance of a 'haunted soul, a condemned heart'.
Those were Erckmann's own words, believing, as he did,
that the pure in heart must by definition be heartless.

Erckmann was a romantic and what could be more
romantic than having a latter-day saint played by a
current sinner. Now he was looking for a personal story
to titillate the popular imagination. Something moody
and magnificent, high-class erotica. And all Bysshe
could hope to supply were the usual dreary little
transgressions which no longer shocked anyone. He felt
himself to be in a tight scenario, he who longed for
freedom of action and – preferably – inaction.

He was glad to be leaving Africa: it would never be his
place. The lack of discrimination offended him. The
ants couldn't wait for carcasses, they fed on living flesh:
frogs snapped up the ants and great birds stalked about
spiking up the frogs as if they were wastepaper. The
jungle was a digestive tract, and the spirit of Africa was
appetite. Dissolution and decay consoled him: this
system of eat and be eaten turned his stomach.

He was looking forward to getting home. But not with
Latouche and Twoomey. They were sure to produce
some lucid shots of Ile-Marie and a grainy reputation for
him. No one wanted truth from Hilda. She specialized

in the sort of scurrilo-moral essay that was most sought after and enjoyed. Rumour had it that some people paid her to do a job on them.

She was talking to Twoomey. Seated across the gangway, they had their heads together, Twoomey's still under the bushwhacker's hat which he had worn in Africa. Hilda used her hands when she talked, carrying on a double entendre, unsaying what she was saying as much as implementing it. You could be in several minds with Hilda, none of them hers. When she caught Bysshe's eye she lifted her sunglasses for a steady appraisal – unwarranted because she had had plenty of chance to do that in Africa.

Twoomey also looked at Bysshe, tilting back his hat with a howdy-pardner gesture. Erckmann had brought them out on location to do the story on Zwemmer-Snowdon but they hadn't come up with anything to please him and he had told them: 'Go back to his place, wherever that is, and pull out the plug.' Useless for Bysshe to protest that surely Hilda could write as well in Africa as in France. If not better. Erckmann had turned on him: 'You were the housewives' choice in the days when there were housewives and it's going to take art to update you. I picked you for Zwemmer and people said to me, "Snowdon makes movies?" and I said, "Not that one. This is the Snowdon you saw in *Dreams Are Not Enough,* and *Wuthering Heights.* It's Rex like in Oedipus."' 'I was never in *Wuthering Heights* –' 'Isn't that what I'm saying? Believe you me, nobody will forget you were in *my* picture.' Erckmann, who was as uninhibited as he was small, had climbed on a table which was big and laid for lunch and postured among the vichyssoise. 'It's a classic. Twenty years from now they'll still be talking about Erckmann's Zwemmer.'

Africa, from this height, was a dish of cooked spinach. People down there were cooked too, half-digested and still clinging to a separate existence: the whites soft-boiled, the blacks glossy with gastric juices. There was another extreme, people picked to the bone and rocks bitten into dust.

Would he like a drink, asked the air hostess with rare

percipience. Bysshe ordered a daiquiri. Hilda hauled herself across the gangway. Unfortunately there was a spare seat next to him.

'Prophylactic.' She filled a paper cup from a vodka bottle.

'Against what?'

'Erckmann's phoney pustules. I find them more contagious than the real thing. Why didn't he bring in local talent instead of lot hoppers?'

'Perhaps because the real thing doesn't look real on the screen.'

'Do you ever wonder what sort of business you're in?'

The plane started bucking, and there was a noise from the luggage area as if a pride of lions was breaking out. Bysshe said, 'It's an air current. We experienced turbulence at this altitude when we flew in.'

Hilda drained her cup. 'When you've seen their roads you don't expect them to fill in their air pockets.'

'I expect to die each time we hit a bump.'

'Is that why you hold on to the whiskers?'

'Why should it be why?'

'To cover up your air panic. And then there's the rest.'

'What rest?'

'Broken veins, dewlaps, superannuation. I wish I could get behind something. I'd grow a beard and moustaches like a Norseman.'

'I hadn't thought about it.'

'You're lucky. Women have to put on faces in the morning and take them off at night. It's time-consuming.' Hilda spilled vodka over them both as she refilled her cup. 'How do you see yourself?'

'Much better for getting this part.'

'It gave you the chance to act and you're still at it. You know that? I've watched you keeping up the routines, stroking your beard like it's a nice cat, flexing your nostrils, walking stiff-legged, and last night you did that shot where he empties his whisky into the river all over again.'

'In my case it was beer and there was a fly in it.'

'You know what I think, I think actors never give up a

part. They keep it by and keep trying it for size. I don't trust actors.'

Being herself devious, there was small chance she would write anything acceptable. Acceptability was a question of taste, and on this occasion the taste had to be Erckmann's, Erckmann who was fond of saying that qualitatively speaking, all publicity was good.

When they put down at Nice, Hilda's vodka bottle was tucked into the seat-net while her upturned palms cradled an empty paper cup.

Twoomey said, 'This is the only time she gets rest, when she's travelling.'

'She's out cold.'

'She says she never found any benefit from being unconscious. If she's on the move and she's getting somewhere in time and space she feels vindicated and she can sleep.'

Bysshe took the cup. Empty-handed, she looked pathetic, as if she was asking for alms. 'We'll have to carry her.'

'I've got to carry my cameras.'

'You take her feet.'

'She's a very sensitive lady.'

'Take her torso if you think that would make her feel better.'

'Hilda hates to miss anything. If it's happening, she's got to know, and what she don't know hasn't happened.'

With difficulty they steered her into the gangway. One of her arms dropped between Bysshe's legs and caused him further difficulty. He got Twoomey to support her while he lifted the arm and positioned it across her chest. As soon as they started moving her again the arm slid off her chest. There was inevitability about the way it dropped straight into Bysshe's crotch, partly due to the law of gravity but more especially, he couldn't help feeling, to Hilda herself.

Once off the plane he fetched a luggage trolley and they sat her on it. Twoomey snapped Bysshe trundling her over the tarmac. 'A vignette. Might be useful.'

'As blackmail?'

'Not of Hildy. She'd only pay up if she was whitemailed.'

'Me?'

'I should hope you've got something better to hide.'

Between them they manhandled Hilda into a cab. Twoomey refused to be parted from his cameras and rode with them on his knees. The road to Ile-Marie was steep and every time it looped Hilda toppled out of her corner. She would certainly have dealt herself a straight uppercut on the front seat if Bysshe hadn't pushed her back. She came forward slowly, eyes closed, dreamily smiling, and he had the absurd impression that he was preventing her from some act of tenderness.

Ile-Marie being in the change and decay business, he never knew how far it might have progressed when he returned after absence. During the weeks he had been away something terminal might have happened, like the roof falling in. Then the two kinds of comfort, body's and soul's, would conflict.

As the taxi wallowed along the track a raucous honking followed them.

'What's that?'

'Geese.'

'This a farm?'

'I keep them as watchdogs.'

'Why not have dogs?'

'Geese are less trouble. They keep the weeds down. I give them mashed potato and cereal and a few old greens and they give me eggs.'

'They sound ugly.'

'No, they're pretty placid. The Greeks and Romans used them as sentries.'

'What are you afraid of?'

'Barbarians.'

There were scratches in the dust where Gluvas had switched it with the bunch of gorse he used as a broom. That, and opening the shutters were the sole acknowledgements of Bysshe's homecoming.

'This it?' said Twoomey.

'Welcome to Ile-Marie. I've mislaid my key. Again. Someone said routine makes a home.'

Twoomey got out of the car. He formed a frame with his hands and looked through at the house. 'It's lovely. Gone Without the Wind.'

'I'll go round the back and open up. Try and wake Hilda.'

He was glad to see that the bins had been emptied. And yes, Madame Gluvas had cleaned the kitchen. Her presence was still palpable. She and Gluvas lived on onions and she sweated them. There was a baguette on the table with ants trekking its length. They were few, and seemed to have no actual concern with the bread. Unlike the traveller ants he had seen killing chickens in Africa only days before.

He brushed the insects away and put the loaf on the dresser. In the hall he trod on grit which had blown in under the door. Obviously there had been a mistral.

Twoomey was unloading the luggage while the cabdriver talked to Hilda. 'Tell him to can it,' said Twoomey, 'she can't hear a word.'

The driver slapped Hilda's face. Bysshe said, 'I think he thinks we've drugged her in order to have our evil way with her body.'

'Tell him who you are.'

'He knows who I am.'

'Then tell him who she is.'

They got rid of the driver by opening Hilda's flight-bag and demonstrating her reserve of two bottles of vodka wrapped in her nightdress. He went away tipping his hand to his mouth.

'What's this place called?'

'Ile-Marie. Don't ask why it isn't an island.'

'I guess you don't need water to cut yourself off.'

'Help me get her inside.' Hilda was starting to snore.

'This is your island.'

'It's where I choose to live.'

'In the boondocks.' Twoomey looked bright. 'I'll get hold of shots of those panic scenes from your premieres – when women used to pull your hair out – and line them with a king-size view of here. Caption: "Where he goes to escape the barbarians."'

'Take her feet.' Bysshe propped Hilda's bag on her chest and they carried her with some difficulty up to a room on the first floor. 'I'll put you next door in case she needs anything in the night.'

'I can't supply what she needs in the night.'

They laid her on the bed and Bysshe took her shoes off. As he covered her with a blanket she reached up and hung her arms round his neck.

'Looks like you can,' said Twoomey, walking out.

Hilda pulled Bysshe down and nuzzled his beard. 'Stay with me.'

There followed a struggle to get him on to the bed. He jackknifed, held himself off at arms length, both hands braced on the pillow. He was aware that his back must be arching like a randy tom's.

Hilda was not physically undesirable, but just now he wasn't in the mood to make fond, or unfond, love. And if he were to, he knew that all his private inclinations would be immortalized in print. On the other hand, he had better not seem to be rejecting her.

He allowed himself to be drawn to sitting position on the edge of the bed and then, bringing into play the element of wonder requisite for a first caress, put a strand of hair back from her face. 'You're tired.' He gently broke her hands from his collarbone and brushed each palm with his lips. 'Try and get some rest.'

'Snowdon, you just spoke one of the two corniest bits of dialogue in films. I'll tell you what the other one is tomorrow.' Hilda opened an eye and stared. The effect was of a prolonged wink.

Bysshe told Twoomey he hoped he liked spaghetti. 'I could supplement with eggs.'

'I'd prefer steak and a beer.'

'I can manage the beer, but tinned spaghetti is all I've got in the house.'

Twoomey sighed. 'What's your set-up?'

'As you see, I'm alone.'

'You've had women.'

'None of them home-lovers. I have an old fellow who sees to the garden and his wife cleans up in the house.'

'There's no one else?'

'A boy who takes care of the geese.'

'If I make money, I spend it, and if I don't make money I spend it. You make more in a week than I do in months, so what do you do with it?'

'Bury it. Like the peasants.'

'What a way to live.'

'I've come to it by a process of elimination. I've tried country mansions, penthouse suites, hotel apartments, a hunting-box in Brooklyn, Dracula's castle in Beverley Hills, a houseboat on the Seine and a yacht on the Med. I'm suited here.'

Twoomey flipped his braces and Bysshe, who at times questioned his own contentment, guessed that Twoomey was looking for a reason. Bysshe had one worked out, tracing back to the moment of his conception, when an arbitrary shower of genes and globins had given him blatant good looks and a retiring disposition. Being on permanent display and not having it in his nature to display himself, he had compromised by displaying other people. That was how he made his living. He might say he made one living in order to provide for another, quite different one. But he saw no reason to explain that to Twoomey.

'Hilda will like it.'

'I wouldn't have thought she appreciated the simple life.'

'We thought you'd live in a reconstituted barn with a jacuzzi.'

'She must have been talking to my agent.'

'She doesn't talk to agents.' Twoomey came to the stove to watch the spaghetti being stirred into a pan. 'In Africa I got steak, elephant and antelope. I fly to Europe and get a can of worms.'

'I'm sorry. I haven't had time to fetch supplies. I could make you an omelette.'

'Hilda likes to do her own groundwork.' Hilda, too, would look for a reason. She would come up with dope or gambling or alimony or deviationism. 'Hildy's the artist. I'm the camera. The lens is in my head and the picture's in my mind. Maybe it's one you'll never see, but it's there. I take it with my eyes – the light, focus, composition, texture, I'm one hundred per cent in control, no silicon chip's going to do my job for me.'

'Have you any idea what Erckmann wants?'

'My business is to show the world the inner man. It'll be up to Hilda to make that right with Erckmann.'

'Which means she'll make me a good old-fashioned muckrake.'

'She'll do what's best for all of us. She wanted this job and she went out of her way to get it.'

'I thought it was Erckmann who wanted her.'

'He did, once he knew she was interested. What's that you're putting in?'

'Plonk du Place. To stimulate the tomato sauce. Would you say it's a good or a bad thing, her being interested? For me, I mean, in the final analysis?'

'It's a waste of time speculating. How you come out will depend on factors. Hers.'

Bysshe had been to the village and back before Hilda emerged next morning. She moved as if she was stuck down with Sellotape. But as her drunkenness had seemed more a ploy than a frailty, he was cheered that she actually had a hangover. She looked dewy but unfresh.

She came into the kitchen as he was unpacking the shopping. A rare steak lay bleeding on the table. Hilda took one look and walked out.

Bysshe called 'Sorry!', pushed the meat into the fridge and swabbed the table. Hilda came back. 'Twoomey fancies steak. I had to disappoint him last night, he only got tinned spaghetti.'

'Where is he?'

'I don't know. He went out before I did.'

On Hilda make-up was a concession: without powder, lipstick and the burned-blanket tint she used on her eyelids her face gave no quarter. Bysshe poured coffee, black and strong, expecting she would be glad of it. She took it to the sink and poured it away. 'Is the water potable?' Bysshe nodded. She filled the cup and drank. 'I couldn't find the bathroom.'

'What?'

'In the middle of the night I needed to evacuate. I couldn't find where to do it.'

'From your room it's up one flight of stairs and halfway up another.'

'You left me in ignorance.'

'I left you sound asleep.'

'I ended up on a balcony which was lucky. I managed, but it's not an experience to be enshrined in the memory.'

'I'm sorry.'

'Show me the house.'

'Of course –'

'Not now, for God's sake. Before nightfall is all I ask, before dark. What's with your dark? It's blacker than Africa. When I did finally find a switch and pressed, nothing happened.'

'The bulb must have blown. I'll see to it.'

'What's that smell?'

'You mean this?' He peeled *Nice-Matin* from a sizeable fish. 'It's for supper.'

Hilda lowered herself into a chair, she was plainly at risk up to, but not including, her eyeballs. There was nothing vulnerable about them. 'I don't eat catfish.'

'This isn't catfish. See, it's got quite a big mouth. Perhaps it's a pike.'

He hadn't thought of Dulcie in months. She rarely surfaced and when she did it was usually, as now, at the bidding of his jokey subconscious. He could guess what Hilda would make of Dulcie, and of Pike. Dulcie Bysshe married a fish. It wasn't safe to think about her in Hilda's presence.

'Tell me about the house.'

'I bought it before prices rocketed, the house and several acres of land – garden, orchard, meadow and a stand of Kermes oaks. It had been a family apportionment, passing to the next in line without anyone actually living in it or looking at it. It came on the market when the last of the family died. I saw it from the air.'

'You saw it and fell in love with it.'

'Hardly. It looked like a collar stud on a cabbage leaf.

But I did think, now that would be a secluded spot.'
'Is it?'
'People tend to find their way here.'
'People you don't want?'
'People I could do without.'
'Women?'
'It's ungracious of me.'
'Yes.'

Bysshe, who had been fifty per cent sincere, wondered at the tartness of her tone. He put it down to hangover which, as he knew from experience, is better one minute and infinitely worse the next. 'I shouldn't object to my audience seeking me out. But when they come and stare as if I'm a bad accident –' He observed that Hilda was not staring at him or anything else, she was fighting it out with the daylight. 'Could I get you something? Seltzer? Aspirin?'

'Nothing.'

The fish bothered him. He carried it to the sink. Through the window he saw Twoomey coming across the yard. Twoomey held his hat in the crook of his arm, his camera cradled on it. Bysshe cut off the fish's head. 'Excuse me.' He spoke to Pike rather than the fish. He had always felt sympathy for Pike.

Twoomey sent the door crashing against the wall when he came in.

'Damn you!' cried Hilda.

'Sorry, Hil. You should have been with me. I've been looking round. There are big clouds with plenty of depth and I hate to waste depth. Is there breakfast?' Bysshe poured him a cup of coffee. 'Ham and eggs?'

'Sorry. There are croissants.'

'I asked myself what would Peter Paul Rubens have done with these clouds. If he could have been here with a Polaroid, in his own time, never having seen a jet or a TV show, what sort of picture would he take. The answer was my sort. P. P. Rubens, being a great artist, he'd have had no choice.'

Hilda said, 'A commercial photographer has no business being modest.'

Twoomey dunked a croissant. 'I'd reached that

conclusion when I turned around and saw something
P. P. Rubens never did. Well, to the best of my
knowledge and belief he's left no record of it.' He carried
the croissant, dripping, to his mouth. 'You might have
warned me.'

'You got a surprise?' said Bysshe.

'I would, wouldn't I?'

'He's harmless.'

'Who is?' said Hilda.

'A kid with half a face. Split down the middle. One
side's good-looking, the other's a disaster.'

'A kid?'

'How did he get that way?'

'I don't know,' said Bysshe.

'Someone surely screwed him up.'

Hilda was taking notice. Those fine nostrils of hers
were picking up a scent.

'I know nothing about him. He turned up here a year
or so ago. He comes and goes as it suits him. When he's
here I give him food and a few francs for helping about
the place. He sleeps in Gluvas's fort.'

'Where?'

'A shed in the orchard.'

'What's his name?'

'I don't know. He doesn't talk. He can't, he's almost
completely deaf. To me he's the oieboy.'

'The what?'

'"Oie" is French for goose.'

Hilda closed her eyes. 'If I remember rightly there was
a goose*girl*. In the fairy tale. She was a ninny but she had
a talking horse. What's this gooseboy got?'

'Zilch.'

'He's happy enough,' said Bysshe.

'Enough for him, you mean?' Twoomey mopped into
his coffee cup with another croissant. 'That don't
amount to much.'

'What was he doing?'

'Sitting in a pool with his knees to his chin, splashing.
Seeing all that frizzy hair I thought he was a girl. Venus
observed, I thought, I'm in luck. Then he looked round.'

'There's a pool?' said Hilda.

'It surfaces in a shallow cave in the rock,' said Bysshe. 'A small pool fed by an underground spring. He uses it as a bathroom.'

Hilda stood up. 'Where?'

Bysshe said, 'There's one at the end of the passage.'

Twoomey said, 'Across the yard, left at the prickly pear and down the track. But the kid's gone. He took off when he saw me. Mother-naked. P. P. Rubens would have liked it.'

They watched Hilda cross the yard, perching on her hipbones. 'Trying to break the Sellotape,' said Bysshe.

'Say?'

'The way she's walking. She looks tied up.'

'She's dedicated. Say, that kid of yours –'

'He's a migrant, with his own seasons.'

'I must get some shots of him.'

'Why?'

'Photomontage.'

'He's easily upset.'

'I won't be using a black cloth and touch powder.'

'You want to take close-ups for people to gloat over? He's not a freakshow.'

'Every picture should tell a story. There are messages everywhere and my business is to pick them up.'

'What will this message be?'

'I don't know yet. I make images to show other people. And myself. To educate myself, get into perspective.'

'How do you know you've got the message right?'

Twoomey tipped back his chair and hung his thumbs in his braces so that Bysshe felt the weight of what was coming.

'I'm surrounded by the raw material of consciousness. We all are. And what do we do? We each try to get a lion's share. But we have to relate to it and some of us don't ever get that far. The raw material of consciousness is my subject.' Twoomey tapped his forehead. 'Here's the camera and maybe I'll pick the wrong thing to show or the wrong way to show it or the wrong person to show it to. Or all three. It's still my way. I am what I am. What I'm not, is the angel with the flaming sword. I'm here to make people look.'

Bysshe looked, and glimpsed the fish's golden eye staring up from the sink. He wrapped the head in newspaper and took it outside.

The air was heavy with the smell of thyme, mint, rosemary, terebinth. He had once tracked each smell obsessively, gone about his garden on all fours, sniffing like a dog. Now there was the fish smell. He threw the parcel into a bin, knowing that he might well have bought a lobster for his supper if he had been alone. But the smell of fishy newspaper was evidence that he was not alone. As if he was in need of conviction, as if he was liable to forget there were foreign bodies present, as if his hackles weren't stirring –

Bysshe rammed the lid on the bin and walked across the yard to the garden. Latouche and Twoomey, enemy aliens, posed a limited threat. They would interrupt his way of life, interpret the interruption, and leave. He picked up a carob pod and cracked it. He didn't fancy their chances here, any more than he fancied his own. He was glad about his own, however, and breathed in the sweet smell of decay.

He had a mind to see Gluvas. Gluvas was a creature of the place, had lived here all his life and was openly sceptical of the existence of anything beyond the Estoril. If Ile-Marie wanted a voice, it had to be his – the old devil without a drop of charity in him. Ile-Marie's strength and saving grace was its inhumanity. It was proof that one could be freed of all responsibility – moral, social and personal – and look forward to desiccation, to the ultimate conclusion; a little calcium dust on carbonated beetle wings.

But it was Bysshe who wanted a voice. Somehow he couldn't feel that he had been received back until he had heard Gluvas, he needed to be told he was there. He went down through the orchard to the old man's 'fort', where he kept his onions and his cider. The cider was primal stuff, even Gluvas wasn't equal to more than a quart at a time and frequently slept where he dropped, among his casks.

The boy was there, alone, and motionless, though without tranquillity. He had only just stopped, the air was still spinning round him. When alarmed, he froze on the brink of his next move, whether it was flight, or fight, or his brand of rejoicing.

Bysshe realized that Zwemmer's whiskers would have altered his appearance. He touched the boy on his shoulder, in reassurance and greeting. 'It's me.' The eye did not flicker: the hole in the cheek stretched, painfully.

'How have you been?' Bysshe struck a match to light a cigarillo. The boy uttered a strangled sound as the flame approached Bysshe's beard. Fire was what he feared most. Understandably. 'It's all right. Let's talk.'

Bysshe sat on a cider cask and the boy touched his own chin as if there might be tender stubble somewhere.

'Where's the old man? Sleeping it off with Madame G.? He hasn't done much while I've been away, though I can see the mistral's been busy.' Bysshe shrugged. 'At least I'm keeping the status quo going. Underdevelopment has to be paid for.'

The boy sank to his knees in a movement which a ballet dancer might envy. He sat on his heels, his bad side turned to Bysshe, who had observed that he seemed to experience, to register, on that side.

'Of course the status quo will keep going without me. The polymers and nuclear waste will start something special in due time. I'm doing this for *my* sake, so I can watch it happening. You see, I like the way recycling's done here. Discreetly. I'm just back from Africa where it's shoved under your nose. Messy. Even the trees bleed. But would you believe it – all that real life wasn't real enough for the cameras. They had to fake it.' Bysshe squared his hands and held them in front of his face to peer through them as Twoomey had done. 'And something happened to me.' He flung wide his hands. 'I was shot to pieces. And when the pieces reassembled, they weren't all mine.'

The boy gripped his own forearms. It was a movement expressive of something, and to Bysshe it seemed relevant. 'Some were Zwemmer's pieces. They must have been, how else could I have come by them. That man was a mess. I played him as a psychopath. I did heart-warming scenes when he stuck his needle into sweet old lepers and carried leper babies in his bosom.

When I raised up a dying woman I held her stumps in my hands as if they were ladies' fingers. But it wasn't tenderness, it was disgust. That was the only way I could do it, reacting in a real way to total unreality. They brought a live leper on the set, he was what's called a "burnt-out case", and from him the make-up department contrived dozens of combustibles. Variations on the theme. I ask myself how would I have felt if it was pus I was swabbing and not Vaseline jelly. Suppose they'd been live and dying people, would I have hated them? Did Zwemmer? It doesn't matter about him, he's past and done with, it's not even history, because no one will ever know what he felt. But it matters about me. I could so easily say I was disgusted because it was faked. That would be a good reason, humanly speaking. But was I? Or was I thinking into the part? Thinking myself into the part, reacting as *I* would to real disease? To do a thing for the right reason makes it all right. Are we sure about that? If we do a right thing for the wrong reason does that make it all wrong, or half right? What we're getting to is, it's not what we do that matters, but why we do it.'

One of Gluvas's onions dropped one of its skins. A fragment floated onto the boy's shoulder. He snarled like a puppy and beat it off.

Bysshe said, 'Did you do that because you don't like onions? If that's your reason, it's right. And if you dislike onions so much you shouldn't have to sleep with them. I think Zwemmer so disliked the world he gave his only beloved self in atonement.' Bysshe blew a smoke ring, the boy put a finger through it. 'I think he was bored being a rakehelly and decided to try goodness for a change because it was all that was left for him to try. And he found that even more boring. I tried to put his boredom across by shutting my eyes very slowly and opening them fast. Erckmann thought I was expressing emotion.' Bysshe blew another ring for the boy. 'I think I'm becoming addicted to these weeds. Zwemmer smoked them all the time, many a shower of ash went into the sterile dressings.'

The boy reached up to touch Bysshe's beard. His

fingers stroked it with a gentle, lingering movement. His chest swelled to a sigh. Of relief, or pleasure, or envy.

Bysshe guessed how it must look to Hilda, arriving at the shed door at that particular moment. The boy on his knees, stroking Bysshe's face, was an interesting little cameo which she might make of what she liked. And he knew the sort of thing she liked.

To do her justice, she didn't exclaim when the boy turned his face towards her. She quizzed him as she might any personable male. Her eyebrows went up slowly, she smiled a buttoned-down smile.

The boy clasped his arms across his chest. He leaped up, and flattening himself to avoid touching her, he ran from the shed.

'Strangers alarm him,' said Bysshe.

'Is he yours?' She was looking around, at the dirt floor, the onions, the stretcher-bed trampled like a dog's, cider casks, goose droppings, feathers impaled and lightly stirring on the splintered walls. Bysshe knew what she was doing: she was isolating what she could use for the story.

He said, 'So you noticed the likeness. Mind you, I don't know who the mother was. I surmise it must have been one of the village girls. I was terribly young at the time – just thirty-five – and libidinous. But it could have been any of the starlets who were around then. They used to flock to this place like moths to a candle.'

'What do you mean, you don't know who the mother was?'

'The child was left on my doorstep, in an onion bag. That made me wonder about Madame Gluvas, the gardener's wife. She was around too.'

'What does he do?'

'Comes and goes. Of his own free will.'

'Goes where?'

'I don't know. I don't ask because he can't hear me; and even if he could, he couldn't answer.'

Hilda lowered herself gingerly on to the boy's bed. She still looked groggy. 'Free will exists only in the very first years of life, at a time when we're incapable of doing anything with it. Thereafter the system is formed and the IQ fixed. What's his mental age?'

'As old as the rocks I should think. Do you like herbs?'

'Why?'

'I'm considering how to cook the fish for supper.'

'I'm trying to figure what advantage a retardate of sixteen with a mental age of six would have over the rest of us.'

Bysshe had found comfort from fingering his whiskers at uncertain moments. He would miss them. He thought perhaps he wouldn't shave.

'Bollocks to supper,' said Hilda.

By evening she was taking a stimulant, white wine laced with Greek brandy. Bysshe put out chairs on the terrasse. 'You needn't worry about the bats, they won't fly into your hair.'

'I never thought they would. It's the smell that gets to me. Like supermart scent. Do they spray the grapes with it?'

'There are no grapes.'

'Then it's a herbicide, and from the look of the vegetation it's a killer.'

'Indoors smells different,' Twoomey said. 'Like there are things living in that ought to be out.'

'It's early for the rats,' said Bysshe. 'We're usually free of those until the colder weather. The mice are always with us.'

'Not to mention the bugs.' Hilda said irritably, 'You could provide nets.'

'I keep forgetting. The mosquitoes don't come after me, I've been here too long. They prefer new blood.'

'What's that noise?'

'The frogs down by the cistern. I like to hear them. They're my lullaby.'

'The kid –' said Twoomey – 'what do you call him – Warboy?'

'Pronounced as in "oiseau".'

'What's he do evenings? Go dancing?'

'With the geese.'

'Has he got a girl?'

'I shouldn't think so.'

'Why not? He's got pazazz and he's young. Young beats everything, even a face like his. I'd like to do something for him.'

'Like what?'

'Nat,' said Hilda, 'you're here as a photographer, not a plastic surgeon.'

Twoomey ran his thumb round the rim of his beercan. 'I'll take his picture – make his portrait.'

'No,' said Bysshe.

'Gotta reason?'

'I told you my reason.'

'I told you mine.'

Bysshe smiled. 'I remember. The raw material of consciousness. "I am a camera".'

'It's my work ethic.' There was entrenchment behind Twoomey's grin. 'I read it in a book and if it was good enough for Höpker and Glinn, it's good enough for me. There's no copyright in principles, and the way I look at it, I'm in every portrait I do. Because that's the way I look at it.'

'Every picture an ego trip,' said Hilda.

'I'll photograph the kid as he looks to me, as he *is* to me.'

'And people will see what you saw and make something else of it.' Bysshe knew he was stating a truism which had already been broached, and would bear going into. 'Please, don't make anything of him.'

Twoomey aimed his finger. 'I'm going to make a record of that face.'

'Why?'

'Because I saw it and I've a right to everything I see. I'm a photo-journalist, I make pictures to tell how it is.'

'There's no way to tell how it is with him.'

'There has to be. I started in a chain-portrait studio, taking pictures at ten dollars a time. They had to be the kind of pictures people would want to frame – that was the criterion, and I didn't find it demeaning. I worked on them, and when I'd finished they looked better than life. But I always found a statement to make.'

'I read somewhere that you have a twin sister,' Hilda said to Bysshe. 'What's her name?'

'Dulcie.'

'Dulcie Bysshe. Have you a photograph of her?'

'No.'

'When I do a picture of someone I go for the soft centre where there's usually a leak. But if there's no break in the candy I go for the fancy wrapper and make my statement.'

'Does she look like you?'

'We're not identical.'

'Neither are the two sides of any one face. Did you ever wonder what a face is? Where the original design comes from? The practical considerations aren't all that good. We'd do better with recessed holes and dermal scales. What interests me about this boy's, is which side registers which. Does the left register the same emotion as the right? Or does it come out sweet and sour, like a Chinese takeaway?'

'If looking at the original tells me nothing,' said Bysshe, 'neither will a photograph.'

'That's where you're wrong. I'll show you what's there when you're *not* looking.'

'In glorious Kodachrome?'

'Colour's a liberty I wouldn't take with him. I want him black and white.'

'What will you do with the pictures?'

'What does any professional do with his work? He gets the best price he can for it, taking into account the time and materials he's expended; or he gives it as a gift if there's someone he wants to give to; or he gets a Pulitzer; or he puts it in his portfolio and never shows anybody.'

Hilda said, 'Tomorrow you'll be working with me.'

'Doing what?'

'What we came for.'

'I forget what that is.'

She said to Bysshe, 'Shave off the lace so we can see Rex Snowdon.'

'Aren't I recognizable?'

'As a prairie dog.'

Bysshe had been surprised and charmed by the softness and luxuriance of his facial hair. When he held it, it felt like a bird in the hand. 'I was planning to keep the beard.'

'You were planning to keep Zwemmer.'

Twoomey said, 'If the human face is a piece of plumbing, whiskers are grass in the downspout.'

Bysshe experienced the old sense of annihilation, and rage that it should be happening to him here, in his place. He wanted to tell them to go away and leave him alone. 'I think I'll take a bath. Association of ideas.'

In the bathroom mirror he came face to face with Zwemmer. As portrayed in Erckmann's life of the sinner-saint: Rex Snowdon with whiskers.

He turned the bath taps. The water rushed out like ale, frothing slightly. The bubbles raced the length of the bath and expired in tiny vortices. The water came from a mountain spring, a spell in the hot tank had not subdued it. There were even times, as now, when sundry organisms came through the taps, insects and tiny amphibians.

Try as he might, he could detect neither sin nor sanctity, no signs of inner strength or moderate zanyism in his face. Had he looked the Latin lover playing Zwemmer? If so, where was Erckmann to have allowed it? Had Erckmann even noticed? Or had he approved and fostered the image? That was possible. Erckmann was a gambler who thought God was personally directing his throws. Bysshe pulled down his eye sockets and bared his teeth.

'May we share?' He swung round. Hilda was behind him, her eyebrows hitched to a sweet reasonableness. 'I do have to have one.'

'One what?'

'Bathroom. Nat's using the upstairs as a darkroom. He's blacked out the windows and locked himself in. I've nowhere to pee.'

'This is my bathroom –'

'I don't mind waiting.' She sat herself on the edge of the bath. 'Are you going to get into this soup?'

'I was.'

'Go ahead.'

'I prefer to bath in private.'

'I want to talk.'

'Not now – not here.'

'Here and now. Nat's ears are long and I'd sooner he didn't hear what I have to say. You'd prefer it, too.'

'I want to have my bath.'

'I'll scrub your back.'

He considered what he could do. He could take his bath and ignore her – try to – or he could pull out the plug on the pretence that the water was too mucky.

'I want to talk about my sister-in-law.'

Another option was to push her into the bath. He had an acceptable vision of her rising up with her dyes running.

Hilda said sharply, 'Caresse.'

It sounded like a command and he blinked. 'I beg your pardon?'

'That was her name.'

'Caresse? Caresse Latouche?'

'Latouche is my professional name. Our family name is Nussbaum. Does that mean anything to you?'

'It could mean you changed your nationality.'

'You knew my sister-in-law.'

'I never knew any one called Caresse.'

'Carrie Nussbaum, my brother's wife. She was here with you.'

Bysshe felt he was getting into a minefield. But there could be no risk in looking pleasant. Or foolish. 'Ah. Small world.'

'She's dead.'

The tone alarmed him. The words, the meaning, were not assimilable at once. They were like a blow which he needed to know the provenance of, and the purpose – if there was one – before he could actually feel it. And then she said, smugly, 'She killed herself.'

Playing for time – time out of mind – he said, 'Are you sure?' Hilda nodded, seemed not to take offence. 'When?'

'A couple of months ago.'

'Did she – what – how did she –'

'An overdose. She was never original.'

The blow was delivered, there was now no point in defending himself, but he tried. 'I didn't know. I was in Africa. We missed a lot of the American news.'

'She didn't make news.'

'I had no idea.' But he had it now all right, and didn't know what to do with it. Not in Hilda's presence. 'I can't believe it. She was too – sensible.' Was 'sensible' the word? There could be two interpretations and in this connection, the connection of Carrie Nussbaum, one refuted the other.

'Carrie couldn't start anything. She picked up after other people. But it was her first time for dying.' He wondered where this was leading. Hilda said, 'If her feelings were like everybody else's, it doesn't mean they weren't new to her.'

'Of course not.' He wanted to put it aside until he was alone. 'I didn't know her well.'

'Biblically you did. You were lovers.' It was a confrontation on his own ground, at Ile-Marie. He felt Zwemmer's whiskers stiffen – the old animal reflex was still there. 'She called me long distance. She said, "He doesn't want me the way a woman wants to be wanted, he used me like a kitchamajig."'

'A what?'

'Everything a man uses a woman for.'

'She wouldn't say that.'

But Hilda would. Hilda was showing her teeth in something that was only fractionally a grin. 'She told me about you and about this place. She and I were never close, and calling me up to tell about a love affair that had folded simply wasn't like her. But she'd got to the point where she had to talk to someone. Mind you, she wasn't giving anything away. No names were mentioned, it was "He", uppercase, like in God, and this place was Heaven the way she told it.' Bysshe consoled himself that even coming in by the back door – Hilda's method of entry – she would find nothing new, nothing that hadn't been done already. He too was unoriginal. 'When she'd told me all she intended to, she hung up and fixed herself a barbitone and oxyzine cocktail.' Bysshe went cold, then hot. Then sick. The back door afforded unfair advantages but he had not yet reckoned on what might be done with them in the right hands. 'By the time they got to her it was too late for a stomach pump. I suspected she was going to do something and I called my brother, he's in the wig and hairpiece business. He told me their marriage was finished and he wasn't liable for her. He said he'd been cuckolded. I said did he know the word stems from the French for cuckoo and he slammed down the phone. I called the janitor of her block. He went to her apartment with his master key, but she'd bolted the door. He told me there was nothing he could do, he wasn't allowed to interfere with tenants' private arrangements.' Hilda let out a hoot which was one part laughter. 'Afterwards I put it together: the screen-lover with his love nest on the Côte d'Azur.'

'This is no nest, it's where I live.'

'And the grotto and the garden where you played ball. She told me you played ball.'

'Boules. Everyone plays boules.'

'And there were fireworks at the village carnival which you watched in bed together.'

'There are fireworks and carnivals all over France in the summer.'

'She didn't mention the boy with half a face.'

'She would have, wouldn't she?'

'Are you saying she wasn't here?'

'He's at least as remarkable as a grotto and fireworks.'

'I suppose you were just good friends.'

'We didn't have what it takes for good friendship. We were both rather bad at it.' Bysshe knew now where the blow had come from and it wasn't a clean punch. It was a spreading clout.

'I know now that I love you' she had written, and he had put the letter down the lavatory because surely she would regret sending it. When other letters came he returned them unopened. She had to know what he felt without his telling her in so many words. How many? Thousands, and all wrong. There were no right ones for telling a thing like that. But there must be some which were better chosen than others. He had doubted his ability to choose, and Carrie's to make allowances. She was more easily hurt than anyone he had ever known which had made her tiresome to be with. At times he had felt mentally cramped, trying to avoid thoughts that would damage her. Sad she was, but independently of circumstance. Life had been charitably disposed towards her, and she knew that she had no right to sorrow. She tried to disown it, with laughter and little sallies of her spirits, spontaneous and often irrelevant. In fact it was the first thing he had noticed about her, those obligated joys. He had thought then that she had to be mildly crazy, or perhaps just taking the mickey.

They had encountered each other at the Picasso museum. She was alone, so was Bysshe. She came and stood beside him as he was looking at the cartoons. He waited for her to move away because he couldn't appreciate pictures in company. He needed a private view if he was to see anything for himself.

She said, 'They frighten me.' He nodded. She said, 'I mean – if it's that simple – after all?'

'I find them refreshing.' He had walked away.

A party of German students arrived. They laughed a lot, mocking, miffed at the drawings. They were young and did not need refreshment. Finding a seagod to himself, Bysshe realized that he was looking for fright in the single line of the drawing. Her 'after all' had been a cry more than an exclamation, referring he supposed to life in general rather than a specific hassle.

He glanced sideways to where she still stood, staring over the top of her glasses at the picture. The students approached, surrounded her. She turned, listening or speaking to them. They laughed and moved on, and she was left, a tall woman, gawky, with a misapplied air. She wasn't pointing herself in the right direction. At that moment she was aimed at a picture of a mermaid with astonished breasts rising from a sea of kisses.

Bysshe went back to her. 'I suspect it is.' When she turned to him her eyes drowned under her glasses. Then swam to within millimetres of the surface. He added, smiling, 'I certainly hope so.'

He watched her take the thought and worry about it, worrying because she hadn't had it herself. Then he walked out of the Musée and was aware of her following.

It was an afternoon of occluded light, the dregs of a

dust storm in North Africa blotted out the sun. They stood on the ramparts and she told him that she had travelled from Bakersfield, USA with an arts appreciation group and had seceded for the afternoon because the group had gone to look at cave paintings. 'It frightens me, being underground. In London we took the subway to the Tate Gallery. I went down the escalator, turned around and came straight back up.' Her laugh was reflex, a gasp without vocal backing. Bysshe looked over the parapet, there were things floating on the water which he hoped she could not see. She claimed she had no knowledge of art. 'Picasso' – she said, handing it over, making him a present of her ignorance. Perhaps she thought it was owed to the conversation she hoped they were going to have about the basic simplicity of life.

A ship was slipping out of the bay. He pointed to it, sugar-white, dissolving into and sweetening the haze.

'Yes.' She pushed her glasses into her hair, unseeing.

He was himself attracted to a linear concept of life and would have liked to believe in its comedy. But he was not prepared to proselytize. And much later, when she asked if he really thought everything was simple, he knew that she was seeking guidance, not confirmation, and at that later time he had to say no.

He left her on the ramparts at Antibes with a wave of the hand, and forgot her.

When she did return, briefly, to his mind, it was via Picasso's mermaid. That came first. He had to smile, recalling the sea of kisses, fifteen – he had counted them. Also he remembered one of the students, a butter-blonde with fiery bloom along her jaw. She belonged with the mermaid. Of the woman from Bakersfield he remembered only her eyes going down for the first, or was it the second, time.

When he thought of her now it was with a sense of having forgotten more than he remembered. Because she had been slipping away, dissolving like the ship, though without sweetness. Absenting herself. As they had both agreed.

When the letters started to come he was angry: with

her, for not keeping to their agreement, and with himself because what had meant so much to her meant so much less to him. He had thought they were escaping involvement. He had been careful, even distasteful of her, because of her vulnerability and the dangers of it. He asked nothing of her, nor she, he had hoped, of him. As he saw it, they might lightly purloin anything they needed.

Going had been her move. 'I'll go,' she had said. 'And when I get home I'll forget all this.' He had teased, 'All of it?' and she had laughed her reflex laugh. 'Memories have their place and Bakersfield's not the place.'

The day following their first encounter, a bus had drawn up outside Ile-Marie. To a burst of muzak and a voice-over, the driver got out and examined the padlock on the gate. He shook the gate, kicked it and shouted. Bysshe, in a dirty singlet and ruptured jeans, was dragging a handcart up from the orchard. The driver appealed to him. Bysshe shrugged. Dozens of pairs of sunglasses levelled through the windows of the bus. The voice-over said: 'We are now approaching one of the oldest oil-mills in the area. The olives are gathered and brought for pressing. Here you have a unique opportunity to witness a method which has remained fundamentally unchanged throughout the ages –' The driver climbed into his cab, hauled on the wheel and drove off in a burst of diesel.

Then the bus stopped again and someone else got out, a woman in a chemico-pink dress and a headscarf knotted under her chin. She waved to the bus, it moved off and she walked towards Bysshe.

Carrie Nussbaum had come to Ile-Marie. She had prevailed upon the tour operator to depart from the schedule sufficiently to show her where Rex Snowdon lived. 'I thought you might be, but I wasn't sure,' she said. 'Yesterday in Antibes you looked older.' The shocking pink dress was the colour for candy, but not for her. In it, over-pinked, she was well nigh invisible.

Bysshe pointed out, 'You've lost your bus.'

She said that the tour was going to St Paul and would pick her up on the way back. Then she waited, with an air of having done all she could. He had to ask her up to the house. With any other colour he would have felt less constrained, but the strident pink was such an affront to nature – in particular the nature of Ile-Marie – that he felt he ought not to leave her alone.

He offered her lunch. She said she couldn't put him to trouble, she was being a nuisance. Bysshe said it was no trouble, no nuisance, she was welcome to what there was. She said she always seemed to arrive at wrong moments – people's mealtimes, when they were in the bath, or having a fight, or icing a cake. Bysshe demurred, said mealtime was the right time to arrive and brought out bread, goat cheese, tomatoes and a bottle of red ordinary. She said she wasn't hungry, she would wait outside.

Bysshe went to the sink to wash his hands. When he turned round she was sitting at the table. They ate together. She had a large appetite, despite her earlier protestations. And when they had finished the bread and the cheese, Bysshe fetched a basket of Mirabelles and some cat's tongue biscuits. He made coffee and by then he would have said he knew all there was need to know about her.

It was a natural, if cruel assumption. Even thirty years ago she would not have been to his taste, she would have been blanched but impure. She was a middling, and in middle-age, as might be expected, that was manifest. And he did not question his right to expect it after a mere couple of hours' acquaintance.

She started to talk about films. The group had been told that the cinema was an art form. They had listened to a talk about sound and colour, very technical, and without a single shot of any of the stars.

'Very commendable,' said Bysshe.

'I saw you in a historical film. *The Naked Flame.*'

Bysshe closed up. 'I'll show you the garden.'

People didn't know whether they were meant to admire or commiserate about his garden. Carrie resorted to the acquisition of knowledge. 'What's that long topsy thing?'

'An agave.'

'Will it fall?'

'Eventually.'

'Are those immortelles?'

'Should they be?'

'They look as if they've been here a long time.'

In the grotto she hung over the pool, stirring it with her finger as if she felt she had to do something. She asked if it was a wishing pool.

'If you like. Yes. Anything can be anything you like.'

'I've tried that. It doesn't work.' She gasped with dismayed laughter.

'It does here.'

That seemed to throw, rather than reassure her. She looked about, mistrusting what she might make of things. She saw the piece of mirror on the ledge at the back of the grotto and turned away with a question unasked. Fortunately the oieboy was not around. She would have been mortally distressed by the sight of him and Bysshe would have found that tiresome.

They went through the orchard into the meadow. The geese followed them, cackling. 'Don't run,' said Bysshe, 'they've been encouraged to harass women.'

'They're pecking my legs –'

'Tell them shoo.'

She lifted the skirt of her dress and shook it at the birds. It was a country gesture and made a picture: Carrie shaking her pink dress at the white geese. Bysshe could never afterwards determine why it was significant, or what it signified, but it recurred at incongruous moments.

The geese sidled away, honking uproariously.

'Do you encourage them to harass women?'

'No, my gardener does. It saves him trouble when people turn up whom I haven't invited and don't care to see.' She blinked at him, a weight of water on her eyes. 'Some of the taxis make extra francs telling people I'm on view in my cage and bringing them here to feed me bananas.'

'I wasn't invited.'

'That's different. We'd already met and I'm glad to see you.'

He rarely concerned himself about the colour of his

lies, but at least this one was neutral. He wasn't rejoiced to see her nor was he altogether sorry. Softly, softly, in a way she had, she grew on him.

She said, 'I'd better go.'

Then would have been the time to stop it, if he had had less faith in himself and more in her. It seemed such a passing thing. 'No, you'd better stay.' But her staying did, in fact, turn out to be a whole lot worse.

They spent the afternoon picking plums. They picked too many because Bysshe found it a pleasant occupation and couldn't think what else to do, though he need not have because time, with her, was apt to slip away.

'What will you do with these?' Bysshe shrugged and she offered to make jam. He agreed, thinking it would be something to occupy her.

All he could find to cook the fruit in was a stewpan. They stoned the plums and cracked the stones. It was a messy job, but Carrie said the thing was to boil the kernels with the pulp to enhance the flavour. Bysshe had no jars to pot the stuff when it was done, so she put it into a salt-glazed crock.

'It ought to be hermetically sealed. Otherwise I'm afraid it won't keep.' Bysshe hoped it wouldn't. The burnished green and gold of the fruit had reduced to a khaki porridge. 'It will be lovely with cheese. Or for breakfast on crusty bread.' She sounded wistful.

Evening came, but the tour-bus did not return. Bysshe remarked that he wouldn't have thought there was so much to see in St Paul. He poured drinks and took them to the terrasse. She hesitated on the threshold, waiting, he supposed, to be asked to join him.

'We weren't just going to look, it was to be implemented study, we each had to make a drawing or painting of something to establish creative rapport.'

'Would you say you have colour sense?'

'I like to look at the colours in Nature.'

'Then why wear an unnatural colour?'

He had decided to be honest because kindness could implicate them. It was too soon, by about half a minute, for him to realize that honesty was not going to be the best policy with her.

She stood and drowned, went down for the third time

under the pink dress. 'I'll go.'

'Where?'

'I'll wait in the road.'

'They may not come back for you.'

'I'll get transport from the village.'

'The last bus went at five o'clock.'

'I'll walk. I've stayed too long.'

'Don't be ridiculous. Come and have your drink.' He went and put his hand under her elbow. He had the idea that touching her would bring her to the surface. It was an act of curiosity, not charity. For one who drowned so easily he thought there must also be an easy revival.

The revival wasn't easy, but it was worth watching. She looked at him without fear or favour, without emotion, recognition, or intelligence. Her slowly evolving bubble eyes were covered by a pearliness, a protective membrane, so that she appeared both blind and potent. It was like watching the evolution of a mollusc on speeded-up film. But the film was too fast. He missed the actual moment of repossession, caught a glimmer, then a gleam, then beheld the unresplendent whole of Carrie Nussbaum. Holding her own against the pink.

She offered to make supper for him. He said he would find something to cook. She cried, 'It's the least I can do!' as if she had already figured out a minimum. He was warned, but not seriously, she still seemed riddable.

'You don't have to do anything.'

'I'd like to – before I go – while I'm waiting.'

She made a potato omelette and a plate tart with stewed plum filling. He would have preferred something more substantial but she was good at pastry and it was a nice enough meal.

After they had eaten, she went to the kitchen to wash up. He watched her scraping pots and swilling dishes.

'Do you have a drying-up cloth?'

'I don't dry up. Nor does Madame Gluvas. She doesn't wash up until everything's been used. I average two plates a day and the frypan's perennial. The more you leave in it, the better. Like your plum kernels, it improves the taste.'

'I had to wash the pan before I could cook the omelette. I'm sorry –'

'They haven't come back for you.'

'I expect they forgot.'

'You don't expect to be remembered?'

She looked at him in alarm. 'I asked them to.'

'They're not likely to now. Not tonight.'

'Tomorrow they're going to Florence, then to Venice and Rome. It makes me sick.'

'Art appreciation?'

'No, coach travel. I have to try not to upset the others. So I pretend I have got hay fever and I'm sneezing. But they're beginning to realize I'm throwing up, and nobody likes sitting near me. So I'm going to skip Italy and stay on in Nice until it's time for the flight home.'

He could have driven her to the coast, but was finding in himself a curiously compounded inertia. There was common politeness in it, and caution, and the Christian wish to save her from drowning.

When she was done in the kitchen and had left all clean and tidy, she went and sat in the garden. He found her there, hands spasmodically stirring, like separate animals, in her lap. She herself seemed tranquil, even dreamy. The pink dress put a spat on his umbers and olive greens and lion yellows. He supposed it was her attempt at making a mark, any mark. Certainly it must mean something that she should have chosen chemico-pink to do it in.

He brought her a silk shirt and a pair of jeans. 'Put these on.'

She stood up at once, no question, no surprise, pulled off the dress and let it drop. What more he saw of her did not appeal. She was big-boned and in youth would have been raw-boned. Middle-aged, her flesh looked par-boiled. There was a disharmony about her: breasts, thighs, big soft belly and pubic cup did not make up the figure of a woman, they were just the component parts hung together. And what emerged was the vulnerability which he had identified as danger to be reckoned with. Perhaps the pink, after all, had been a declaration of strength.

She pulled on the shirt and buttoned it. She had trouble with the jeans which were too tight. 'My husband doesn't like women in trousers.'

'You'll be more comfortable. And so shall I.'

Comfort was not the word. She stood clutching the fly zip in classic Venus pose, looking like an unsuccessful drag artist.

Bysshe handed her his belt to secure the jeans. Her eyes, he now saw, were blue, still with that slight opacity as if brushed with milk. He picked up the dress. 'You'll need it to go home in.' Still pink, still crude, he put it into her hands, with the bodice still rounded to the shape of her breasts. She gazed at it as at something thrust upon her and he wondered what it reminded her of. Pretending to sneeze all the way home to Rome? Bakersfield, California? 'Stay as long as you like,' he heard himself say. If it proved to be longer than *he* liked he was confident he could handle it.

She stayed five days and did not intrude on his company or time. She took over the cooking, making the meals substantial to suit his taste. She liked to do the marketing herself and insisted on paying for it as part of her keep. Their wants were few, so he let her have her way.

She spoke no French and he was curious to know how she managed in the village where they did not take kindly to foreigners. She laughed her gasping laugh. 'I give them a hundred franc note.'

'And?'

'I take what I want and they take what they want.'

Some days he did not set eyes on her for hours. He followed his own routine, working in the garden and the orchard, grubbing about, though not so as to inhibit the business of decay. She did not arouse extremes of feeling, there was something off-putting about her. Her own diffidence, probably. All he had for her were reservations, he was halfway everything about her. But he found solace in the presence of another human being without having been aware of any need for solace.

One night she came to his bed. He was watching fireworks. Through his window he could see rockets and chandeliers and the *Nice-Matin* gas balloon. She came into his room without knocking, or if she had knocked he did not hear because of the noise of the fireworks. He looked up to see her beside his bed and his first involuntary response was 'Down, Carrie!'

'What's happening?' she said. 'What's going on?'

'The village fête.'

'I thought it was a gunfight.' She panted with laughter – a big crossbreed, eager, clumsy, chicken-hearted.

'Might it have been – in Bakersfield?'

'I wasn't to know.' She could retrieve a point, like a stick. 'I'm never to know, am I?' and bring it back and drop it at the feet of the thrower. It was a kind of begging.

'Come and watch.' He pulled her down on the bed at his side, put his arm under her neck. It was well meant. She had afforded him some objective comfort, he could do as much for her.

She sighed and snatched up the sigh in a gasp. She couldn't trust anything that came from her.

'Relax, there's nothing to worry about.' He patted her with the hand that was left over from her neck. It wasn't his fault, or design, that he chanced to touch her breast. But right away there was something for him to worry about. She came up like a marble under his fingers. 'It's the village saint's day. A girl called Marie – not *the* Virgin, though I daresay she was required to be one – prayed down a thunderball on the Saracens as they tried to sack the town.'

He withdrew his hand. Good dog, I've nothing for you. The *Nice-Matin* balloon rolled in a current of air.

'I shan't be here long enough to worry.'

So that's what she was getting at. He felt a sudden principled aversion to physical contact. God knew he hadn't been pretending anything, had not put on an act, and was incurious but genuinely sorry about her. One arm under her neck was hardly an embrace.

But it was halfway to one. And he should have given her nothing to build on: a woman, any woman, could make a palace out of a wisp of straw, and Carrie could do it on less. He was afraid for her.

His arm was in the crook of her neck. He began gently to withdraw it. She turned her cheek into his hand. He thought Oh God, knowing he had only himself to blame. It hadn't been enough – was it ever? – to watch his own step. He should have taken note where *she* was going. There were no half measures this time, she had started to shake. Was there anything worse than a woman, or a man, who shook?

'You're cold,' he said. 'Let me get a blanket.'

Let him nothing: she had his hand in both hers and was snuffling into his palm, kissing, he had to suppose. Or it was deprivation, a hunger of the senses for taste and smell and touch.

He could feel himself warming to the idea of a sex-starved woman, though he still felt a proper reluctance to get into an animal lather over Carrie Nussbaum. Not because he disliked or despised her; she neither attracted nor repelled him. It was simply the sum of his reservations. She was not for mauling.

Obviously she didn't feel the same. Those badly-hung thighs of hers had been predisposed, more than ready, from the moment she walked into his room. They were quivering beside him now. Someone said it was bad form for a man to refuse to make love to a woman who desired him.

'Look –' look at the fireworks, look at the stars, but don't look at me, I've got a headache – 'there'll be dancing in the Place. It has to be seen, it's something out of Breughel.' A series of pawnbrokers' balls, red, green and yellow, appeared in the sky. By their light he observed that her knees looked medieval too, big and knobbly, like a martyr's.

Next moment a rocket sheared the air and exploded in a shower of sparks. She turned to him with a violence he would not have believed her capable of. Pressed against him, she openly and shamelessly begged.

He thought Good Christ, this is too much. The erotic and the holy joining up in his bed was bad enough: with concentration he might adjust to it, might even enjoy it. But jazzed up with the spirit of carnival –

'We're going to be sorry,' he said.

Twoomey's hat bothered Bysshe. There had been funny hats before at Ile-Marie: Bysshe himself had sported a bowls' panama with a pimple in the crown and had passed it on to Gluvas. The bushwhacker was incongruous here as it had not been in Africa where everything was ingested.

With his jeans tucked into canvas boots, the hat set back on his ears, Twoomey was a cowpunch strayed on to the wrong set. He was in exultant mood, aiming a heathen kick at the Christ's Thorn as he passed. 'I've got pictures worth a million words.'

'Not a million of mine,' said Hilda.

'I have to thank you,' Twoomey was addressing Bysshe. 'If I hadn't come here I wouldn't have seen the most telling thing I or anyone else ever captured on film.'

Hilda said, 'We get the feeling that this is where we keep coming in.'

'I can create a Dutch still life with a can of beans and a meat loaf. Or I can make those beans fat and sweet and vulgar, so your mouth waters for them. I can do a mail-order shot of plastic bowls so they look like Ming china. That's advertising.'

'What's this about?' said Bysshe.

'Can't you guess?' said Hilda.

'Here's something I don't have to sell. The statement's made, and it's plain enough for a child to understand.'

'What statement?'

'The more you look, the more you see. It goes way back.' Twoomey couldn't keep still, he was doing restricted gallops to and fro. 'This is Bible stuff!'

'What is?'

'If it was man and monkey it would be evolution.' He fired a forefinger into the air. 'But it's man and devil. Each one of us is born with our quota of good and bad. Nobody's pure. We may be any ratio – sixty-forty, twenty-eighty – it doesn't show. But that – what d'you call him? Warboy? – is fifty-fifty and staked out for everyone to see.'

'I asked you not to photograph him.'

'I'm showing him to the world.'

'I forbid it.'

'You can't keep something like that hidden.'

'Something like what? What do you think he is – a monster?'

'You said it, not me. I say he's a prototype of us all and if he doesn't mind being photographed, why should you?'

'He doesn't understand what's going on, and certainly not what it entails.'

Twoomey hung his thumbs in his braces. 'What's it entail?'

Hilda said, 'Are the pictures good?'

'They're terrific. I can talk to him, he did what I said to do: look here, look there, snarl please. It's best when he smiles, because then it's worse. Did you know the human face has an average of eighty muscles? Warboy's is minus half, including the risorial, the one that works the mouth. I turned my hat upside down and fooled about to make him laugh and it was like a horror movie. I got every bit of that boy's war.'

'Would it make a popular science story?'

Bysshe said sharply, 'There is no story.'

Hilda ran a fingernail against her empty glass. 'How's this: he comes from a remote mountain village where they see the sun a couple of days a year, but generally it's fog and ice, so tourists don't visit. The folk are invert and sequestered. The young leave, the oldies stay on, doing what they've always done. They may get washing machines and television, but they retain their old customs. One of which has always been to make a scapegoat carry their sins away. So they can start again with nice clean souls. Is there any drink?' Bysshe brought another bottle. Hilda splashed herself a glassfull. 'If there's anything worse than white wine, it's red.'

'I read that story,' said Twoomey. 'They draw lots and whoever gets the short straw is stoned to death.'

Bysshe realized that anger would put him at a disadvantage. These two would play patball with him. 'That's superstition, not science.'

'It's basic shrink,' Hilda said. 'And popular. What does he do for sex?'

'I haven't the slightest idea.'

'That's where it all starts. I'll think of something.' Hilda grimaced at the wine. 'So he's picked – a virgin child – to absolve the sins of his elders. They set fire to him and chase him away. After that his mind goes blank. Naturally.'

'And he's never spoken since. It figures,' said Twoomey.

'He's all locked up. There's dynamite inside him. One day he'll break out and make mayhem. Have you thought about that?'

Twoomey told Bysshe, 'You'd be responsible.'

'He ought to be restrained. Does anyone know he's here?'

'We could go and get shots of the mountains where he comes from.'

'For God's sake! There are no savage or inaccessible ranges –'

Hilda grinned. 'The range is immaterial.'

'Wait till you see what I've been doing. I'll go fetch it.'

As they watched Twoomey gallop away, Hilda said, 'When I first met Nat he was into the Harvey syndrome, doing pictures of people with rabbit shadows.'

'What must I do to convince you that I won't let that boy be pilloried?'

'You're dramatizing again. Nothing's new, not even a bifacial. There'll be some morbid speculation, perhaps some high-tech interest. But it will be shortlived, and the kid won't be quick enough to catch it.'

'He's made his life here. I don't know why, or where he goes when he goes. One day he won't come back. That will be his choice, he does as he likes.'

'What does he like?'

'Living, breathing, putting flowers in his hair, dancing with the geese.'

'He's blocked. Someone should take him in hand,

show him how to face up to himself.'

'And why he shouldn't be happy. He'd learn that soon enough.'

'Why didn't you answer her letters?' Bysshe had been expecting it. Hilda had repossessed Carrie – for the family, for her own purpose – whatever that was. Carrie now would never come to his mind without Hilda coming too. 'She wrote you and her letters were returned to sender.'

'We'd agreed not to write.'

'When she telephoned, you hung up.'

'We had nothing to say.'

'She had. She said it to me.' Hilda's well-fleshed but illiberal lip curled. 'She said she was in love.'

Bysshe had the use of his damaged smile again, until so recently wasted under Zwemmer's whiskers. 'Let's be sensible. I'm pushing fifty and Carrie was – mature.'

'You telling me the menopause isn't real? She was crazy, point. She was crazy about you, and there's where the full point goes.'

'She didn't kill herself on my account.'

'You don't give a monkey's.'

'I've said I'm sorry. We had no future together and we both knew it.'

'She never had a future with anyone. She was a sad sack.' Hilda probably described her eyes as hazel. Certainly they were hard as nuts. 'I guess you didn't find her empty.'

'You're not going to write about us?'

'Would it bother you? It's good publicity. In the grey fact of American life, sex is the bright spot. Twinned with death it's the definitive statement we're all looking for.'

'Do you remember asking if I wondered what sort of business I'm in?'

'This stuff gives me a headache.' Hilda shoved the wine bottle, it teetered on the edge of the table and Bysshe caught it as it fell. 'We were talking about ulcers and I guess they're real if you have them. But my business is with words and there's more than one way of telling the truth.'

'You must know them all.'

'I couldn't use your way.' Bysshe saw the minefield quite clearly. It had been laid by Carrie in all ignorance. A trained sapper could not have done a better job. He felt that Hilda knew his thoughts. She was smiling, warmed to him, as to her victim. 'Your conventional screen-lover is squashed pie. Erckmann wants something different and that's where Warboy can contribute.'

'Leave him out of it.'

'I can't afford to. He's a gift.'

'To your morbid imagination!'

'My professional faculty. You see, you don't inspire me and he does.'

'He's nothing to do with me. He's a stray who happens to have strayed here –'

'You said he was yours. I make that a love story. It will go like this: ageing amorosos – you said that too – parted by a nubile retard with half a face. Mad with jealousy, the lady amoroso junks herself, leaving the man and the boy to consummate their love in a grotto. How does that grip you?'

'I'll sue anyone who prints it.'

'Surviving ageing amoroso finds that ripeness is not all. The question arises, how long can he hold his pubescent lover?'

Even as ribbing it was poor stuff. But hard-nosed. Hilda would leave out as much as she put in, and like self-service, it would be there for people to help themselves.

'It would be naive to ask what happened to scruples.'

'I'll touch on them. Within the framework of the human dilemma.'

'I meant yours. As a matter of interest, what would you write if you didn't dislike me?'

'Honey, I don't dislike you.' She could switch on a beam like a wall-heater. 'You'd have to get to me for that. Like you got to Carrie, but with her it was you *and* the rest. Her husband had left her, she was full of goofballs and you were nobody to love her.'

He had wondered, though not pressingly, what

Carrie was getting from life. He had spared thought to her prospects as he might to those of a caged budgerigar: they were as limited and as inconceivable, and certainly incapable of being implemented by him.

'It didn't make her special, but I guess she thought it did, and she thought you not being able to love her made her very special.' Hilda raised her brows in enlightenment. 'Actually she was just one of the crowd.'

Bysshe preferred to think Hilda wasn't serious. Consistent, she was dangerous: inconsistent, she would be unbeatable.

Twoomey came out of the house firing his finger. 'Tell that boy if he should break his neck he'll have nowhere to put his face.'

'What have you been doing to him?'

'A kindness.'

'What kindness?'

'I showed him his picture.'

'You call it kind to show him a photograph of himself?'

'Not the ones like he is, but one like he ought to be.'

'Invisible,' said Hilda.

'He wanted that picture, he wanted to take it with him. I said you can't have this, it's my only copy. I'll do you another. He was over the moon, he ran out and jumped the stairs. The whole flight. He hit the ground running.'

'Let's see the picture,' said Hilda.

Twoomey had it in the breast pocket of his jacket. He took it out, flourished it and held it up, panning it closely from Hilda to Bysshe. It was a monochrome, head and shoulders of a virtual stranger. Bysshe could detect a teasing resemblance to someone often seen but not known. It made him realize how little he relied on the good half of the oieboy's face. It had always been so composed, untouched by emotion, blush and sweat. The photograph gave the impression of a stone face, a funerary angel's, without a granule of personality and just enough life to open the eyes but not to blink them.

'Classy,' said Hilda.

'It's all wrong.'

Twoomey bridled. 'How can it be wrong when it's all right?'

'It's not him.'

'That's because you've never seen him. The two halves of any one face don't match exactly. The pigments and pimples and planes, eyes and ear placements are different on one side than the other. In a normal face they harmonize.'

'How did you get this picture?'

Hilda sighed. 'You really want to know?'

Twoomey hung up his thumbs. 'I took Warboy en face, in full sun, though I didn't get both sides as evenly lit as I'd like. I processed the film, then printed the good side with the other side covered. Reversed the negative, and using a red filter on the enlarger arranged the negative to fit the other half, removed the red filter, printed the other half – holding back the side already exposed and then developed the complete print. Now he's got two good sides and no gothic.'

'It's the completeness that makes it completely wrong.'

'I've given him back his face.'

'Didn't you stop to think what harm that might do?'

'Harm?'

'Showing him what he can never be.'

'Giving him ideas,' said Hilda.

'He's an unknown quantity, totally unpredictable. I never know what he's thinking or what he will do when he's upset.'

'Hell, it's only a gimmick.'

'To you. But to him –'

'He wouldn't know himself,' said Hilda.

'He knew, and he loved it.'

Hilda turned to Bysshe. 'Take us to Nice?'

'When?'

'Now.' She took out a lipstick and drew herself lips in tiger orange.

'I can't, not right away. I've got a flat battery.'

'With a puss like his you don't know if he's mad or glad. But a baby tries to eat something it likes, and he tried to eat that picture.'

'Call us a cab.'

'Why do you want to go to Nice?'

'We're leaving.'

Bysshe's heart bounded. He did not have to question it, Twoomey did that.

'Leaving? What about my pictures?'

'We've got all the pictures we need.'

Twoomey aimed his thumb at Bysshe. 'Mug shots of him. I'd like more character.'

'So would I.'

Twoomey grimaced, Hilda went on drawing herself a new mouth, sight unseen.

'What about a flight? You're not booked,' said Bysshe.

'You can get a flight if you pay. Erckmann's paying.'

'He's paying for a story.'

'He'll get it.'

'We haven't discussed it.'

'I never discuss what I write.'

Bysshe could believe it. The wonder was not that she got away with murder, but how she made murder acceptable, enviable. Charismatic. Some people would say he was lucky and that Erckmann had done him a favour by getting Hilda to write about him. But according to Twoomey she had badgered Erckmann for the assignment. Why? She must know that her stories were considered an underwrite. If Hilda Latouche did a piece about you it was a guarantee you would be talked of whatever the world news, and remembered wherever a morbid few were gathered together. It posed the question: if publicity was amoral, but like daylight you had to have it, why should Hilda be doing him a favour? The answer was that she wouldn't. She wasn't.

The matter of Carrie Nussbaum who might, or might not, be related to Hilda by marriage; who might, or might not, be dead by her own hand, was incidental. He couldn't help thinking how like Carrie it was to be immaterial. Absurd to think she could kill herself because of him, and absurdity, too, was beside the point. So was the question of what Hilda chose to believe. The fact somewhere at issue was that Hilda had it in for him.

THE GOOSEBOY

'Erckmann will be happy,' she said.

'I'd like to be happy too.'

She parted her new lips in a lovely smile. She could, on occasion, look enchanting: one had to remember that sorcery was a big pond. 'Are you worried about something?'

'I don't care what you do about me –'

'That's sensible. Your public image is at the stage where it can only be done good to. The problem has been what to do. I never do snow jobs.'

'So far as Carrie's concerned, I have nothing to be ashamed of. Or regret. We were comfortable together, she stayed as long as it suited her and left to rejoin her party when they went home. We both knew that was as far as it went. We were being our age.'

'Hers was a climacteric. If that doesn't worry you, what does?'

'The thought that you're planning to use the boy, make him into a freak show.'

'How would I do that?'

'Simply by writing about him. Making people aware of his existence.'

'He's at least as remarkable as the white rhino. A lot of people will want to remark on him.'

'Conservationists?' suggested Twoomey.

'Psychophysicists, psychobiologists, physiognomists. Anyone who thinks your fate is in your face is going to be interested in his split level.'

'He ought to be seen,' said Twoomey. 'There were faces back from Vietnam getting fixed as good as new. Someone might do as much for him.'

'Is that a nice thought?' said Bysshe.

'It may surprise you to know –' Twoomey aimed between Bysshe's eyes – 'we communicate, Warboy and me. We understand each other. Empathy is what you need in visual art. You learn to get into the skin of the girl or the brick – whatever it is you're photographing. I'll show you three sides of the brick and one of the nude, but I'll show some of her inside as well.'

'How do you get into the skin of a brick?'

'Mind you –' Twoomey was set to roller on – 'it takes

more than practice to get the feel of people –'

'Call the cab and collect your gear, Nat.'

'I promised the kid his picture.'

'There's an afternoon flight we can make.'

Twoomey might fire his fingers, Hilda held the lipstick like a bullet in hers. Muttering, Twoomey went away.

'Must you go?' Bysshe could still arrange his features to look wistful, though he was now aware that crowsfeet and puckering round the mouth lent him a certain wryness.

Nut-eyed, Hilda showed her kernels. 'You've never had a genuine emotion for anyone. That's not a crime, but we were talking about love, and I question how many people know what it is.'

'Do you?'

'Thank Christ I don't make my living pretending I do. You'd like to be that old sweet Zwemmer, all loving and giving. And you looked the part till I made you shave him off.'

So of his hating man, the leper doctor who hated lepers, not a glimpse had come through. Hilda was more than usually perceptive and if she saw no hidden depth in his performance, the average audience certainly wouldn't. He had too well concealed the misanthrope under the beard.

It gave him a jolt before he reflected that Hilda's function – and privilege – was to cut the ground from under his feet. Anyway, his purpose had been served. He had used a ploy to deceive the camera.

What mattered was the result, getting a good one, *any* good one. He had got what would be seen as a simple turncoat case, black turning white, the sinner turning martyr. No rage, no deviousness. It happened all the time, all historical time, anyway, and to the average audience it would be acceptable. Wheels within wheels had no place on the big screen. He had better be satisfied. It was a compliment to be accused by Hilda, especially by Hilda, of living the part. The irony he could reserve to himself.

'Never mind,' she said, 'you're a hairy man, you'll soon grow him back.'

They heard Twoomey come bursting out of the house, effecting an explosion between the door jamb and himself. He shouldered through the rosemary, achieving a burst of sweetness, and stood before them, his breath gathered like a child's ready to scream.

There was nothing childish about his veins, a zigzag red and purple bunch pulsated on his temple.

'Did you call the cab?'

Twoomey's hands seemed to be sticky. He scrubbed them on his chest, leaving stains which were almost certainly blood.

'Have you been messing with fixers?'

'I think he's cut himself,' said Bysshe.

Twoomey fired a bloody finger. 'I hold you responsible!'

'Sorry. I keep meaning to cut back the thorn hedge.'

'For damage to my property while on your premises!'

'Damage? Property?'

'I had the best part of my stuff in your bathroom – lenses, film, filter, fuses, adaptors – my tripod's turned inside out, my changing-bag's ripped up, my enlarger's been stomped on –'

'You don't say,' said Hilda.

'But who would do it?'

'I'm giving you one guess!'

There was a pause. Bysshe said 'Look –' without knowing what he wanted looked at.

Twoomey shouted, '*You* look! He goes to the darkroom and junks everything. It so happens I keep my cameras under my bed or I'd have lost them too –'

'Why would he do that?'

'He's crazy, he's hyped, he's certifiable!'

'He's harmless.'

'How do you know? You said yourself you don't know what he'll do.'

'There would have to be a reason.'

'Maybe he didn't like his picture after all.' Hilda yawned. 'It could be he thinks if you've got his likeness you've got his mana.'

Twoomey exhaled, 'Lord Christ, I'm going to get *him*!' and shot away under his own steam. The rosemary rocked, again there was a burst of sweetness which gave

Bysshe, at this inopportune moment, a pang of pure nostalgia.

'I wonder did he call the cab?' said Hilda.

'Will he do anything violent?'

'I shouldn't think so. His violence is confined to his blood vessels.' Bysshe got to his feet. Hilda said, 'Check on the taxi.'

Bysshe ran down to the orchard. If it was only a question of running, the boy could outdistance Twoomey. But if Twoomey took him unawares – of course he couldn't do that while the geese were about.

But the geese were resting under the trees, a flotilla of white one-masters. They heard Bysshe approaching. They stretched their necks and began the slow gargle which preceded full-throat alarm. Bysshe turned back.

As always, a passage in that dry land was susurration. He paused occasionally to listen. The geese had subsided, the cicadas were part of the vegetation, the barking of a dog far away in the valley enhanced the silence. To Bysshe the silence sounded ominous. He would have called out, but was prevented by indecision about what to call. He had not been on Christian name terms with Twoomey and to shout his surname would be peremptory and might enrage him further.

He took a short cut and was winded climbing the scarp. Twoomey stood at the entrance to the grotto. There was a stillness about him, an arrest. He was watching but he wasn't poised, he wasn't even waiting. Bysshe stopped to draw breath and Twoomey acknowledged his presence by blowing a sharp blast through closed lips.

The boy was inside the grotto with his back to them, facing the mirror propped on the rock ledge. He was positioning and re-positioning Twoomey's hat. He set it squarely over his brows, snatched it off, furled it, punched the crown and lodged it on his ears.

Then he removed it, and holding it in both hands lowered it slowly on to his head. Bysshe was reminded of the scene in *Richard the Third* when Olivier tried on the crown. The boy adjusted the hat, tilting and tipping it ever lower. When he turned to face them, the brim was pulled down over his right side and raked high over the left. His calcined cheek twitched in the spasm which served him for a smile.

Twoomey spoke with awe. 'You know something? He's conceited.'

# 4

I used to think there was a reason for me being as I am, and all I had to do was dig the reason up. I thought we were a single unit, separated for living purposes. I thought that for years. Doug never did. I suppose it was a kink left over from the womb and I was the one who got it.

People talked about us when we were in our pram. They talked above us as if we were animals that couldn't understand. But a baby knows if it's being passed over. I knew, and I let them know I knew. They said, 'She's got a paddy on her, if nothing else.' And Doug would look up with his sweet hurt look – hurt, mind you, though he'd been dealt all the aces. That look is one of the aces.

When we were out of infant school they cut off his curls. I screamed and screamed, trying to make them understand that we were really one person and it was my hair they had cut off. They put me in the meter-cupboard to calm down.

Later on, when I knew about how babies were made, I blamed my mother. She should never have had twins if she couldn't divide us properly.

I haven't been clever and I haven't been lucky. Luck isn't something you're entitled to, and the way things have turned out there's not much to choose between us. Doug's had what I wanted, but he couldn't take it. I could have taken it, but didn't get it. Our plusses and minusses are mixed up.

*

He sent tickets for the première of his new film. Pike said he wasn't going: 'If I saw him I'd knock him down.' He blames Doug for everything.

But we watched the ballyhoo on television. It was wet on the night of the première, and rain either makes things look more expensive than they are, or very, very cheap. The cars arriving at the West End cinema sparkled like diamonds. Even the gutters twinkled. In the foyer the diamonds were smaller and had to contend with platinum blondes and blazing shirt fronts. There was a superior moral tone – a big donation was being made to leprosy research – and Royals were present. We had a back view of Doug bowing over their hands. He has poise. Even when he was at the pimply stage he could charm the pretty girls into getting up to dance with him.

'This sort of thing makes me sick,' said Pike.

It would. But there are so many sicknesses: fear, envy, hunger, rage, disgust, and simple stomachache. And longing: I know about that.

'It's his living,' I said.

Pike doesn't understand finesse. He showed me what he thinks it is, waggled his bottom, smirked and fluttered two fingers in the air. Then switched off the television.

I made him come with me to see the film when it was generally released. He said he didn't want to watch Doug poncing about and I said that was what I wanted. I wanted to see him making his living.

There isn't any poncing in this film. Doug takes the part of a doctor who went to Africa to look after lepers. I hardly recognized him. He was made up with a bushy wig, beard and false eyebrows. He stooped from his shoulders so that his neck stuck out like a tortoise's: he dragged one leg and whipped the other along with a stick. They had emphasized every line on his face and added more. Only his eyes were the same. Only Doug looks at you like that.

Pike sat beside me, giving the screen all his attention, his bones creaking now and then – they do if he's still for more than two minutes at a time. Then they started showing close-ups of sores crawling with maggots, stumps of limbs, children covered with flies. And a face like a rotten apple, eaten to the core.

Pike jumped up and pushed his way out, not giving me or anyone else time to move aside. A woman at the end of the row with a shopping bag in her lap had the contents tipped out into the aisle.

I followed him, stepping over margarine, cracked eggs, crinkle chips and a spilt kilo bag of sugar. We left a first-hand drama going on which must have entertained some people more than the one on the screen.

Pike made straight for the car. He got in and sat behind the wheel, making no attempt to open the passenger door for me. I had to bang on the window to remind him to release the lock.

I said, 'You know you started a cake-mix without a mixing bowl back there?'

He put his hand over his face. 'I can see it now.'

'Let's go before they get our number.'

'I shall never forget it.'

'The memory will fade.'

'It brought it all back.'

'Don't fret, they'll clean the carpet,' I said. 'It must have to take a lot of rough treatment.'

'It finished us – Cherrimay and me.'

To do myself justice, I knew what had started and where it was going. I just didn't want to go with it. Some things shouldn't be remembered in company. Any company is wrong, and Pike's is lethal.

'That face –'

'If you won't drive, I will.' I leaned across and switched on the engine.

'It was because of him she had the abortion. She was afraid she'd have a baby with a face like his.'

'If Cherrimay had an abortion it was because she didn't want to have a baby – any baby.'

'What do you mean "if"? She killed our child because of what she saw at your brother's.'

We'd been through this before, none of it was new. I'd seen Pike weep, he sheds tears like other men sweat. Any delicate sensitivity is liable to get swamped.

Personally I don't believe there was an abortion. I

don't believe Cherrimay Pugh was pregnant, and certainly not by Pike. The whole thing was so convenient – an anticlimax. One day we had the lover-child, carrying within her the future of the race – Pike's race – the guarantee of man- and woman-hood both: the next we had a burnt soul, she'd been through the fire, she was all dignity acquired by suffering. Sinned against.

I wasn't present at the monumental row there must have been. Darlene was. 'He stamped up and down, shouting, I thought he'd have gone through the floor. He was like a man possessed. You know what I mean?'

'I know.'

'He kept shouting "Why? Why?"' – which was taking the word out of Darlene's mouth – but she had countered with, 'What else could we do?'

'Did he tell you?'

'He called us murderers and kicked my sideboard. You want to be careful of him, he's unbalanced, he could do you an injury.'

'I know.'

I daresay Darlene will leak more information in due time. But I've already made up my mind. I don't believe Darlene could organize an abortion, she wouldn't know where to begin. Cherrimay just might. But then she's capable – she's most capable – of organizing the whole nothing.

Pike is a believer, he has to be. I don't grudge him his faith.

'You know what I think?' He knows I know, he has told me often enough. He is going to tell me again. 'Your brother's a pervert. He gets a kick out of this sort of thing.'

'What sort of thing?'

'He didn't have to act the part, he really loved messing with those lepers.' I had seen that he hated it. Doug has to be different from his natural self and it comes over big on the big screen. 'You know what I think – I think that sort of thing turns him on. That's why he keeps the boy.'

'The boy's gone. No one knows where. And Doug's living in Greece.'

Does it matter what Pike thinks? Only to Pike. And his memory is short, he is a survivor.

But I can't help being conscious of what he thinks, even when he isn't thinking it. His thoughts coexist with my moment of glory.

'A kid with half a face!'

But a whole man. Pike doesn't know what I'm thinking.